"Brianna, open the door. I've words I'll have with you!"

The anger in Jesse's tone was enough to alarm Brianna.

"Go away!" she ordered, not thinking of the consequences. "I need my sleep."

"Like hell I will!" Jesse stormed, and the door flew open with a mighty crash, wood splintering as the lock was ripped away. He stood there, terrible in his fury, his big muscular frame filling the doorway.

Instinctively crossing her hands over her breast, Brianna stiffened against his advance. "How *dare* you break into my chamber!"

"I'll tell you how! Because you are my ward—a ward who has insulted one of the most powerful men in this land and destroyed everything I've worked for on this mission. Now you've got to be taught a—"

As Jesse reached for her shoulders, intending to give her a shake, one of the straps of her chemise fell, stopping him short. Suddenly he was aware of the balmy night air and the strong scent of gardenia from the beautiful woman he held. The anger he felt turned into passion and he pulled Brianna to him, punishing her with the urgency of his kisses....

Dear Reader,

Fans of *Romantic Times* Career Achievement Award winner Veronica Sattler will be thrilled to see this month's reissue of her Worldwide Library release, *Jesse's Lady*. This bestselling author has been compared to Kathleen Woodiwiss and Judith McNaught, and praised for her "sensual love scenes" and "superb storytelling." We hope you'll enjoy this exciting story of a young heiress and her handsome guardian who must survive the evil machinations of her bastard brother and a jealous temptress before they can find happiness.

Beloved Outcast by Pat Tracy is a dramatic Western about an Eastern spinster who is hired by a man with a notorious reputation to tutor his adopted daughter. *Affaire de Coeur* recently labeled Pat as "one author definitely worth watching," and we hope you agree. This talented author just keeps getting better and better.

Whether writing atmospheric Medievals or sexy Regencies, Deborah Simmons continues to delight readers. In this month's *Maiden Bride*, the sequel to *The Devil's Lady*, Nicholas de Laci transfers his blood lust to his enemy's niece, Gillian, his future wife by royal decree. And our fourth book is *The Wager* by Sally Cheney, the story of a young Englishwoman who reluctantly falls in love with a man who won her in a game of cards.

We hope you'll keep a lookout for all of our titles wherever Harlequin Historicals are sold.

Sincerely,

Tracy Farrell
Senior Editor

Please address questions and book requests to:
Harlequin Reader Service
U.S.: 3010 Walden Ave., P.O. Box 1325, Buffalo, NY 14269
Canadian: P.O. Box 609, Fort Erie, Ont. L2A 5X3

VERONICA SATTLER

JESSE'S LADY

Harlequin Books

TORONTO • NEW YORK • LONDON
AMSTERDAM • PARIS • SYDNEY • HAMBURG
STOCKHOLM • ATHENS • TOKYO • MILAN
MADRID • WARSAW • BUDAPEST • AUCKLAND

ISBN 0-373-28931-6

JESSE'S LADY

Copyright © 1986 by Worldwide Library.

This edition published by arrangement with Harlequin Books S.A.

Printed in U.S.A.

Books by Veronica Sattler

Harlequin Historicals

The Bargain #191
Jesse's Lady #331

VERONICA SATTLER

was born and raised in New Jersey and now lives in rural Pennsylvania with her daughter and an Irish wolfhound named Brendan. Over the years, Veronica has written several historicals for Worldwide Library and St. Martin's Press, and is currently working on her second contemporary for Harlequin Superromance, to be published in 1997. She admits that she writes romance because she's an incorrigible romantic, and because it's a good antidote for a runaway imagination. She believes that stories about relationships, "about men and women who love, are the very stuff that not only dreams are made on, but the ultimate business of life, as well."

To Peg and Bill with love

Chapter One

~~~~~~~~~~~~~~~~~~~~~~~~~~

Paris, The Summer of 1792

A giggle. A definite giggle.

Again the giggle erupted, then blended with the sounds of a splashing fountain, which was all that broke the silence of the Abbaye de Panthémont's inner courtyard. It was mid-July, and the warm air hung heavy over the well-tended beds of summer flowers, the pride of the Abbess, Madame Mézières. Now it came again, a soft giggle riding on a burst of ill-restrained breath that was clearly feminine.

"Brianna! Shh! We'll be caught this time for sure!"

In reply there rippled a half-muffled peal of laughter from beyond the southern end of the courtyard; had anyone been standing within the convent's interior, facing its southern wall (the very wall that was shared by M. Fourney, owner of a splendid cherry orchard on the other side), he would now have begun to view the source of this merriment.

Over the top of the smooth quarry stone appeared a small brown face with ebony curls—or half a face, for all that showed was from the nose to the crown, including a pair of bright black eyes as its owner peered warily over the brink.

"Aimée, I'm *dying* down here! I swear, you've put on half a stone with those cherries!"

"Shh! Brianna, if you make me laugh again—" Another fit of giggles, and the face disappeared from view.

In its place only moments later popped a second face, this one heavily framed with auburn locks, its large, light green eyes at once intelligent and merry. Two deep dimples worked furiously in a slender jaw which seemed ill-disposed toward the necessary suppression of further laughter.

"I don't see a soul, Aimée. Can you give me a little more boosting? Yes, that's good— *Voilà!* I'm over!"

As Brianna Devereaux hit the ground in a crouch, her bright scarlet school uniform fanned out around her, playing eye-catching counterpoint to the cheery yellow phlox nearby. Instantly she was erect and on her feet, a tall, slender form in the afternoon sunlight.

"The 'line of rescue,' Aimée!" whispered Brianna urgently.

Immediately there came hurling over the wall an outrageous contraption of what seemed to be several gaudily colored lengths of cotton muslin, connected at irregular intervals. The colors soared through the air high above Brianna's head, then floated conspicuously to the ground near her feet. Bending forward to retrieve this phenomenon, Brianna grasped it securely and whirled to face the wall. The bits and strips of muslin in hues of crimson, orange, lavender and vivid green became, upon anyone's closer inspection, several scarves, knotted together to form a makeshift tether or line of sorts, and Brianna now aimed one end of it over the wall, holding firmly onto the green scarf at the opposite end.

"Here she comes, *mon amie*! Grab tightly, and, pray, watch your knees!" This whisper was accompanied by a turn of the auburn head and a furtive glance over one slender shoulder.

Soon the dark-haired girl's face reappeared, followed by neck, shoulders and the remainder of a much shorter-statured figure, also clad in scarlet; this one, too, dropped to the ground, clutching the extravagantly colored scarf-line with both hands as she landed on two knees.

Breathless, Aimée rose to her feet and studied her partner in crime. "You had better repair your curls," she said in rapid French. "You look like a wood nymph!"

"A *cherry* wood nymph?" questioned the taller girl. She also spoke in French, perfectly accented, though not as rapid, as she smoothed at her hair with long, delicate fingers.

Aimée's response exploded in a guffaw, and then, a rapidly building fit of yet more giggles.

"Shh—here, give me those," said Brianna, taking the scarves and stuffing them high under her skirt. Her green eyes twinkled as she worked until she, too, was again breaking into laughter.

"If—if . . ."—more laughter—". . . if you don't do that carefully, *mon amie*, someone is liable to think you are *enceinte*!" chortled Aimée.

"Or simply that I've been availing myself of too much food," said Brianna with a mock frown.

"Like . . . like" —another trill of laughter— "like Monsieur Fourney's cherries?"

"And what else?" demanded Brianna, stamping her foot as she worked a short twig out of a hip-length auburn curl. "It certainly would not be something from the kitchens of the good sisters," she said, wrinkling up her straight little nose in disgust. "I thought you French were supposed to be the masters of *cuisine*!"

"Ah! Do not call me one of them, *s'il vous plaît*!" replied Aimée, wagging a petite brown finger in Brianna's face. "Remember, I am *Gitane*. And everyone knows, a gypsy has other, more . . . um . . . exotic origins, and even being placed on the doorstep of a French convent at birth docs not make one French!"

The taller girl smiled at her little friend. "Well, Aimée Gitane—gypsy, French or whatever, you had better rearrange the folds of your skirt to hide those bulging pockets—quickly—for here comes Sister Marie, all huffing and puffing, with a message from Madame, no doubt." And with this, Brianna worked at disguising her own cherry-laden pockets, simultaneously doing her utmost to arrange her features into a look of studied innocence.

Aimée looked up to see a cherubic little nun scurrying down the walk toward them, her round face all pink from exertion, its plain but benign little features screwed up with impatience.

"Brianna! Aimée! There you are, you naughty girls," chirped Sister Marie, whose main duties at the convent included acting as chief messenger for Madame, the Abbess. "I have been searching everywhere for you! Why is it the two of you are never to be found when you need to be found, eh?" She stopped before the girls as she said this and then drew herself up with a deep breath, as if in a late-remembered attempt at assuming the aura of serenity for which the Sisters of the Abbaye were noted. Then, but not before eyeing suspiciously a conspicuous green leaf clinging to Aimée's collar, she said more quietly. "Madame wishes to see you immediately. You will please follow me." And once again Sister Marie was in motion, pivoting herself about on the path and making a beeline in the direction from which she came, her black skirts flying behind her. With a questioning look at Aimée and a rather Gallic shrug, Brianna fell into step behind the departing habit; Aimée quickly followed suit, but not before flicking away the tell-tale green leaf with a snap of forefinger and thumb.

Several minutes later, as they traveled the darkened halls of the convent's cool interior, Brianna wondered about the nature of the upcoming interview with Madame Mézières, for it was clear they were being escorted to the seldom-glimpsed interior of the Abbess' private apartments, and not to her outer study, the chamber where routine meetings with students took place. Brianna had only been here twice before during her seven years as a student at the Abbaye—there was the time she learned her sister had died, and then last year when Mother— Suddenly Brianna's hands went cold and clammy as she felt her fingers clench, and a tightness spread itself across her chest. *Don't be a silly worry-wart*, she told herself. *It's probably nothing!* But the words, as she thought them, left a hollow feeling that would not go away.

At length they entered a large oval salon through heavy gilded doors held open for them by a panting Sister Marie. A tall, thin woman in a snowy white habit rose from behind an ornate Louis XIV desk at the far end of the salon and smiled softly as she greeted them. "Brianna, my dear, come in, and yes, Aimée, you, too, for what I am about to say includes both of you."

As she bent in curtsey to the Abbess, Brianna let out the breath she had unwittingly been holding and began to relax. Whatever the subject or news, the interview was to be with Aimée also, so it couldn't be akin to those others which had been of such terrible personal import, now could it? No awful family tragedy would involve Aimée as well, she reasoned, so it was with a warm smile she addressed the Abbess as she rose. "You have something for both of us, Madame?"

Madame Mézières' gentle brown eyes fell briefly on Aimée before returning to the taller girl with what seemed to Brianna to be an all-too-familiar hint of sadness. Then they glanced over toward Sister Marie who waited at the still open doors. A brief nod of dismissal was enough to see the little nun gone, the doors softly closed.

"Sit down, my dears," said the Abbess. She gestured at two armless chairs placed facing the desk at either side.

There was a rustle of petticoats and skirts as the girls obeyed, and then it was suddenly silent in the large chamber, although a distant clock chimed the hour of three.

Madame Mézières continued to stand at her desk as she picked up from its surface a large envelope of white vellum and held it before her in a contemplative gesture. With a somber sigh, she looked at Brianna. "There is news from home, Brianna," she said, intoning the words so softly, so carefully, that suddenly Brianna knew, knew with a certainty that even Aimée's presence could not dispel. Something was wrong.

"Papa," said Brianna in a half-croaked whisper. "Something's happened to Papa!"

The Abbess gazed sadly at the stricken look in the green eyes before inclining her head slowly in a nod. "He is very ill, Brianna. Oh, my dear, I wish there were an easier way for you to hear this. This letter comes to me from your family priest, Father Edouard-Gérard—"

"Father Edouard! *Father Edouard* wrote to you? That must mean that Papa himself couldn't even—" Brianna's words broke in a sob as the green eyes filled up with tears.

Aimée rose from her chair and rushed to her friend. "Courage, *mon amie*," she whispered. "He is not gone...at least, not yet," she added; her black eyes held a strangely lighted expression.

Madame Mézières nodded again. "So, it seems our little gypsy 'sees' something again." She gave an impatient shake of her head as if in an attempt to ward off the unholy implications of a fact the entire convent had been aware of for some time now. Aimée, it was well known, sometimes "saw things," and given her generally impish, and perhaps even *impious*, nature, there was great doubt as to whether this Sight was of heavenly origins. The Abbess moved from behind the desk and came to place a gentling hand on Brianna's shoulder. "Aimée is correct, you realize, Brianna. At least, at the time your priest wrote this, your father was alive, though gravely ill. Unfortunately, with all the difficulties in transportation of mail, owing to these uncertain times—the revolution and various declarations of war involving France—"

"You mean Papa *was* alive when this was written!" sobbed Brianna, "but—but when—how long ago? Even now, he could already be gone and—" She cast an appraising glance at Aimée who shook her head in a negative reply but would not look at her.

"Six months ago, I fear," said the Abbess, shaking her own head slowly.

"Six months!" cried Brianna. "Oh, God! Another one dying while I rot away here on foreign soil—in this—this prison!"

Madame Mézières' reaction to this was far from the shock Brianna's tearful anger intended. She had long been aware of her young American charge's pent-up—and often not so pent-up—frustration at being forced into a structured program of education aimed at teaching her obedience, self-composure and gentle ways, while her fiery young nature chafed at the restraints of such confinement. With a weary sigh, Madame bent to take the young woman by both shoulders, letting her feel the strength she willed out to her through her own hands. "Look at me, Brianna," she said.

As if suddenly shameful of her outburst, Brianna complied.

"Oh, seventeen is so *young*," said the Abbess. "And yet, for all your tender years, you have had more than your share of grief and loss. Remember, it was I who broke the news to you, and prayed with you at your sister's passing?"

"Yes!" snapped Brianna, angry again. "And I was not even allowed to go home when that occurred. They made me remain here—" She rose and broke the Abbess' hold, forcing her to step backward a pace. "First, they sent me away, treating me like—like some kind of a stepchild—"

"My dear—"

"No! It's true. They never sent Deirdre away to school, as they did *me*! I pleaded with them—*begged* them to allow me a

tutor at home, as Deirdre had had, but they would not listen!
They—'' Suddenly stricken with what her words might imply,
Brianna stopped and looked at the Abbess, remorse in her eyes.
"Oh, forgive me, Madame," she said softly. "You know that
in many ways I have been happy here. And there could be no
one kinder or more understanding than you, but—but—"

"But yours is a spirit which suffers much in narrow confines, is that not so, my child?" questioned Madame softly.

Mutely, Brianna nodded as two tears traced a twin path down
her cheeks, and the Abbess moved forward and placed an arm
gently about her shoulders.

"Yet, you must realize, my dear, that in sending you away to
school, your loving parents—and they *were* truly loving—their
letters clearly indicated as much—your parents were concerned only for your welfare. When you first arrived here, you
were truly—forgive me—a . . . a *hellion*!" The Abbess smiled.
"Far, far too unruly to be governed at home by a mother and
father who *tried* to be stern, yet continually found themselves
operating from hearts that were *doting*. Yes, do not look so
surprised. It is true. They loved *both* you and your sister *very*
much, but, as your mother pointed out in the letter which preceded your arrival here, with Deirdre, this doting caused a
docile child to blossom into a lovely young woman, mild-
mannered and gentle, whereas with you, their beloved younger
daughter, it seemed this very same doting only succeeded in
fostering a rampant wildness, a rebellious, undisciplined—"

"Please, Madame, spare me!" retorted Brianna, angry once
again. "Forgive me—it seems I'm always asking your forgiveness, doesn't it?" Brianna's tone was bitter. "But we have been
over this ground before. When Deirdre succumbed to the
smallpox—" Here Brianna winced as if struck by a blow. "Oh,
Heavenly Father, the *pain*—at not even having been allowed to
go home to be *with* Mother and Papa, let alone at losing Deirdre herself or—or missing the funeral." Angry tears were
streaming down Brianna's face now.

"But my child," began the Abbess, her tone denoting patient kindness, "surely you could not have expected your parents to think of exposing you to the same disease that killed
their other offspring! There was an epidemic, as *well* you recall. Don't you think they would not have *wished* to have you

by their side during their grief? Do you still refuse to see their act of keeping you in France as one of total unselfishness on their part? Believe me, my child, it was an act born totally out of concern for only one thing—*your safety*!''

Wiping away at her tears impatiently with the back of her hand, Brianna remained silent for a moment as she considered the Abbess' words, and the Abbess seized the opportunity to gently drive her point home.

''And if you need proof of the truth of this, consider how your father *did* send for you last year, when your mother passed away so suddenly—''

''And I was again—*still* half a world away?'' challenged Brianna, but the angry light was gone from her eyes, and her voice a great deal softer than before.

The Abbess nodded sadly. ''You have, as I have already stated, borne more than your share, Brianna. And I know it sounds like a weary platitude, but, dear child, you *must* look on the brighter side. Just think of what a comfort you were to your poor father for the fortnight you remained with him. And before you go off into another spin of anger at his sending you back to us, please, my dear, allow this wise old head to give counsel?''

At this the Abbess smiled and raised a tentative eyebrow, and Brianna weakly returned the smile and nodded.

''You cannot guess at your father's pain in deciding to send you back to complete your schooling. I know. He wrote to me often about it. You see, you were all he had left.''

''There was Honoré!'' spat Brianna in one final, though weakened, burst of anger.

''We will leave Honoré out of this,'' said the Abbess firmly, yet not unkindly. ''They have never been close. No, as far as Etienne Devereaux is concerned, you are all he has left in this world, and it has been solely with an eye to your future, to preparing you for the place you must take in that world, that he has continued to keep you here, even when his breaking heart has yearned to have you at his side.''

Seeing that she had Brianna's full attention and that the girl's emotions were under better control now, Madame Mézières began to move back toward her desk, continuing to speak as she did so. ''Your time here with us has not been without its rewards—for both you and your Papa, Brianna. True, yours has been a rebellious spirit, too much given to anger and incautious outbursts, let us say. You have found the lessons of obedience and patience difficult ones to learn, and, I daresay, given your intrinsic spirited nature and love of freedom, perhaps there are areas of self-discipline you will never really master—and perhaps were not *meant* to master.''

Having reached the ornately carved chair behind her desk, the Abbess seated herself before continuing, but the steady brown eyes remained on Brianna's face. ''But you have other qualities, Brianna, which I cannot help feeling the years you have spent at the Abbaye have served to bring out in the most positive ways.''

A smile lighted the older woman's face, making it seem to Brianna truly beautiful. Back in her chair, Aimée squirmed restlessly as she surreptitiously rubbed at some cherry stains on her fingers. The Abbess resumed, her warm voice richly resonant in the still chamber.

''You have a good—a wonderfully good—heart, Brianna Devereaux. I have seen you with little ones—the orphans you and some of the other girls chose to make gifts for at Christmastide.'' Here the Abbess smiled again, this time nodding in kindly fashion at Aimée. ''And who can forget your all-night vigil with Sister Celeste when she took ill last Michaelmas with an ague, or, for that matter, how you lost numerous nights' sleep nursing countless sick and injured animals back to health over the years? Why, the old halls of this place fairly ring with remembered sounds of young robins flapping newly mended wings, kittens pouncing upon balls of yarn with once-again healthy limbs, old Boulanger, the groundskeeper, laughing with tears of joy at his faithful old dog's new lease on life—all of these, thanks to you and your tender ministrations and heart.''

Brianna shook her head at these words, but her smile at the memories they evoked was warm and wistful. ''I only did what had to be done, what anyone—''

''No, my dear child, not anyone, for that is the sad fact which those of us who are dedicated to promoting Christian charity quickly come to realize. Those of us who were blessed with the seeds of His mercy would like to *think* they were sown in all of mankind, but the simple fact is, compassion is all too rarely

seen a quality among men. Therefore, when it does exist, when
its presence is found—especially in one as young as you—it
must be nurtured and watched over, like a holy thing. Yours is
a great gift, Brianna. Honor it and bear it well. The world has
untold need of compassion and humanity. Use your capacities
in this regard where they are sorely needed."

Suddenly the Abbess laughed. "Forgive me, my dears, for I
did not mean to take this occasion to make speeches or moral-
ize. You have had enough of preaching at the Abbaye de Panthémont, I think, and the time of your instruction is at an end."
The Abbess rose and faced Aimée. "Mademoiselle Gitane, you
are likely wondering why I summoned you here along with
Brianna."

Aimée nodded solemnly, her black eyes darting across to
Brianna and then back to the Abbess.

Madame Mézières gestured with the white envelope she still
held in her hand. "It is Etienne Devereaux' wish that you accompany Brianna to America." She paused as both girls' eyes
grew wide with surprise. "You have, after all, no known family and, *clearly*," emphasized Madame, "no vocation for the
veil." Here the Abbess' gaze fell upon Aimée's fingers with
their tell-tale red stains.

Aimée squirmed and quickly thrust her hands into her
pockets as Madame continued.

"Therefore, since you are eighteen years of age and no longer
a child to be cared for within the Abbaye's rules of protection
for orphans, Monsieur Devereaux has been prevailed upon to
offer you a position within his household as companion and
ladies' maid to his beloved daughter, Brianna."

There was a simultaneous cry of joy from both girls as they
rose to approach the Abbess who had again moved from behind the desk. Tall and stately, yet curiously bright in the eyes,
the older woman reached out long, white-garbed arms and en-
folded the two in a warm embrace.

"Oh, Madame," cried Brianna, "how can I thank you? Aimée and I—"

"We are like sisters!" chirped Aimée, her brown face alight
with joy. "And Madame is the kindest, most understanding,
most—"

"Yes, yes," said the Abbess, her voice a bit unsteady. "Well, enough of this business, eh?" Madame's voice resumed the matter-of-fact Gallic qualities of the Frenchwoman she was. "We have much to do to see the two of you ready to board the coach that leaves for Le Havre at nine in the morning! Off with you, now. I shall see you at Vespers."

Bending to curtsey in turn, each girl kissed the Abbess' ring before murmuring some final thank-yous and turning to leave, but as they reached the double doors, the Abbess' steady voice rang out with a final admonition.

"Oh, Aimée?"

"*Oui*, Madame?"

"You will find that lemon juice is an excellent remedy for stains on fingers, stains left by Monsieur Fourney's cherries!" And with a final nod in their direction, she saw the girls dismissed.

Chapter Two

Charleston, South Carolina, Later in the Summer of 1792

Jesse Randall yawned and stretched lazily, the huge bulk of his lean, muscular six and a half feet nearly filling the battered, old red campaign bed. His vivid blue eyes, usually the focal point of an arrestingly handsome face, gazed, half hidden in heavy-lidded sensuality, at the buxom strawberry blond at his side.

"You are thoughtful this morning, Kathie," he drawled. "Would there be something on your mind?"

Kathie Carver gave a start as she looked up at her splendid bedmate. *Oh, but 'e's a manly one,* she thought, and a shiver went through her as she recalled the night they had just shared. *'Tis lucky I be ter be sharin' me sheets wi' th' likes of 'im! An' 'e's a true gen'lmun too, not like that other—* Suddenly Kathie frowned and looked away.

"Come, lass," said Jesse gently. "There *is* something that troubles you, isn't there?" He raised himself up on one elbow and the sapphire blue gaze became intense.

"'Tis—'tis just as ye said, sir," Kathie answered. "Somethin' on me mind— But—oh, sir, 'tis nothin' fer me ter be troublin' *ye* with!"

Strong bronzed fingers reached out to straighten a lock of hair which had fallen across one of Kathie's ample breasts; as they brushed the swollen coral nipple, another shiver rippled through the young woman's body. Kathie took a deep breath and fought the urge to run her own fingers through the jet-black curls that covered Jesse's beautifully molded head; one lock had just fallen negligently over his forehead, giving him a near-boyish expression that was in stark contrast to the otherwise overwhelming masculinity of the man.

"Kathie, we've known each other for over two years, and if it's something I can help with—"

"Oh, but 'tis too late fer that!" exclaimed Kathie. "I—I mean, 'tis too late fer *anyone's* 'elp, Mister Jesse." Suddenly the girl's wide, gray eyes filled up with tears and a sob caught in her throat. "An'—an', anyway, 'tis fer that bounder, Jack McNulty, ter make it right, an . . ." Kathie's voice broke, and Jesse waited patiently for her to continue. At length she took a long, watery breath and went on. "'E's not *goin'* ter make it right!" she wailed. "'E *promised*—promised ter *marry* me, an' now 'e's *gone!*" The wail gave way to more sobs.

Jesse gazed pensively at Kathie's tear-streaked face, then at her slightly enlarged nipples, and again at her woebegone features. He nodded slowly in understanding. "You are with child, then?" he queried softly.

"Aye, sir."

"And you know it to be McNulty's child? You're sure?"

Downstairs, in the common room of the Black Swan Inn, the tall case clock chimed the hour of six, and Jesse reached for his breeches as he awaited her answer.

"I'm dead sure, sir," replied the girl, pausing to blow her nose with the soft lawn handkerchief Jesse had suddenly produced. "Ye see, 'tis—'tis not jest anyone I be free wi' me favors fer, sir. I—I mean, well, 'ceptin' fer ye, Jack's the only man I—I been keepin' comp'ny wi' these past few months, an'—an' ye an' meself, we ain't been t'gether like this since, well, it's been at least since plantin' time," sniffed the girl as she cast about for her own apparel. Finding her worn cotton shift on the floor beside the bed, she sat up and began to don it, adding, "Besides, I—I ain't never known ye t' bed me wi'out takin'—takin'—"

"Precautions?" smiled Jesse, on his feet beside the bed now as he bent to retrieve a pair of shiny black riding boots.

"Aye, sir," nodded Kathie. She too had risen and was doing her best to comb some order into the wavy mass of strawberry curls at a small cracked mirror that hung over a rickety washstand; this was the only other piece of furniture, besides the bed, in her tiny attic bedchamber.

Jesse smiled to himself as he watched her. Kathie Carver was unusual as serving wenches went, and not only because she was inordinately pretty. For one thing, she was clean, always presenting a sweet smelling body and freshly laundered clothes and bed linens the half dozen or so times he'd bedded her the past couple of years. And then, there was her honest demeanor, coupled with an admirable sense of pride and independence, especially considering she was a lower-class white without family, in an occupation where many of similar status plied their favors far and wide for extra cash. Not only was Kathie highly selective about those she shared her body with, she always insisted on using her own humble chamber when doing so; she never hopped from one gentleman's guestroom to the next, as did Abigail, the barmaid, for instance, or Janie, the scullery, who doubled as chambermaid and thus gained access to the chambers of paying guests. And, as far as he was aware, Kathie was monogamous, sleeping with only one man at a stretch. Yes, he could believe she knew who the father was. Sadly, Jesse shook his head. Kathie wouldn't have been the first poor lass who had succumbed to Dandy Jack McNulty's lies. He knew the man, or had encountered him in taverns several times. A good-looking, sweet-talking Irishman, if there ever was one, and the blarney he spouted didn't stop with unsuspecting innocents like Kathie, either. The last he'd heard, the man was swiftly pursuing a one-way trip westward, a bevy of angry creditors making any question of his return highly unlikely. Well, there was no chance he could procure a reluctant bridegroom for Kathie; nor did he feel, even had that been possible, that Jack McNulty should occupy such a position. Kathie Carver deserved better in life.

"Kathie?" Jesse questioned quietly.

The girl turned from the mirror to face him, her eyes swollen and red, but the tears were gone now. "Aye, Mister Jesse?"

"Do you have any idea what you'll do now?" The blue eyes spoke compassion.

Dumbly, Kathie shook her head, and immediately the tears reappeared. "Oh, sir," she sobbed, "I don't know what's ter become o' me!"

Jesse was now fully dressed except for a dark blue riding coat he held slung casually over one shoulder, and he came forward to put a lean, well-muscled arm around the girl's heaving shoulders. Tentatively, knowing the wench's pride was at stake, he set forth his question. "Will you accept some aid from a friend?" he asked gently.

Kathie raised her head to look at him, for he towered over her by more than a foot. "From—from *ye*, sir?"

"From me."

"Oh, but—"

"Now, I think I know what you're about to say, but listen to me, sweetheart. Hear me out, won't you?"

Silently Kathie nodded.

"I think I know you well enough to realize you're not one to accept charity, but you must remember, it is not only yourself you've got to think of now. There's the babe." He watched Kathie's hand go to her abdomen. "Also, what I am about to propose is not charity. Rather, you will be doing someone else a favor in return for the same."

Outside, on Meeting Street, a carriage rumbled by, and downstairs in the common room, Timothy Barnes, the innkeeper, was bellowing for firewood as the sounds of early morning came alive, and Jesse helped Kathie hurry into her plain homespun serving dress as he continued.

"I know of a family a few miles upriver from Riverview—my plantation—that is in need of a female servant, now that the wife is expecting her second set of twins. The work would chiefly involve child care, as the first pair are yet toddlers. It would not be heavy labor, something a woman in your condition should likely avoid, but it would require someone industrious and quick, which I know you to be. I'm sure, if I spoke to Melanie and her husband, Jonathan, you could have the position, with adequate time off for your lying-in. Then, once your child is born—well, it would not be unusual for a servant to be allowed to raise her own, along with the master's children, on a plantation. As a matter of fact, knowing Melanie and Jonathan, I'm sure they would welcome someone as bright and energetic as you to provide cheerful companionship to Melanie as the two of you await your—uh—arrivals together. Well, what say you, lass?"

Kathie's gray eyes had grown wide and thoughtful as she took in Jesse's words. She stood before him in quiet contemplation and considered his proposal. At length, she cocked her head to one side and offered him a shy half-smile. "Ye're *sure* they be truly needin' the 'elp?"

"I'm sure," said Jesse, his own smile white and dazzling in the early light.

Kathie's heart did a quick little skip as she took in the sheer male beauty of him. *Oh, but 'tis a shame yer 'eart's not up fer th' takin', Jesse Randall,* she thought. *Ye'd make a magnificent lover—not that ye ain't already—but somethin' extra-fine 'n wondrous ter be'old, should ye ever lose it in love.* Sighing, Kathie nodded her head. "Well, sir, since I must be thinkin' o' th' wee one, I'll do it," she said, "but I still think it makes me be'oldin' ter ye—"

"And you don't care for that aspect of it, right?" questioned Jesse, running his fingers over the fine stubble that covered his chin; he made a mental note to call for a bath as well as a shave when he reached his own chamber. Seeing the girl's troubled look, he ventured the next statement carefully. "Then you will hardly care for what I'm about to do as well, Kathie, but, again, hear me out." Jesse reached into his jacket pocket and produced a brown leather pouch, obviously laden with coins, for they jingled as he tested its heft. Seeing a protest forming on Kathie's lips, he reached out a finger to still them as he added, "This is a loan. It comes interest free, with the stipulation that you pay me back only after you've earned a year's wages. If you don't accept, the rest of my offer is null and void—uh, that means I withdraw it." He saw the girl frown. "Kathie, you *must* let me help. For the child's sake?"

"Ye mean, 'tis all 'r nothin'?"

"Aye," grinned Jesse, for he knew he had her now. "You see, I can be stubborn too!"

"'Tis an 'ard bargain ye drive, sir," sighed Kathie, holding out her hand for the pouch. "I'll be repayin' every cent, ye may *count* on it," she added, raising her chin a notch.

Jesse was about to comment when a knock sounded at the door.

"Psst, Kathie, 'tis me, Janie," said a female voice. "Old Barnes be barkin' 'is lungs out fer ye! 'E needs ye downstairs. Make 'aste!"

Hurriedly Kathie donned a heavily patched apron and reached up to Jesse for a quick hug. "'Tis a fine gen'lmun, ye be, Jesse Randall, an' I thank ye." Then she turned and reached for the door latch.

Smiling, Jesse gave her a parting pat on the backside and watched her run off in the direction of the stairs.

"Just take good care of that babe," he called softly, "and of yourself," he added before turning to close Kathie's door behind him.

"So that little twit's gone 'n got 'erself wi' a babe in 'er belly!" sneered a familiar female voice.

Jesse turned in the direction of it, discovering Janie Simms lounging desultorily against the doorway of her own chamber, in the darkened hallway, a few yards down from Kathie's. There was a knowing smirk on her face.

"Never knew ye ter be one fer gettin' a lass wi' child, Mister Jesse," she said slyly. "O' course, that Kathie Carver's a stupid one. She—"

"That's enough, Janie," said Jesse, his tone curt with annoyance.

"My, my, touchy, ain't we?" retorted the girl. Taking a hand and snatching her floppy white mobcap off a head that sprang alive with bright red curls, she sauntered closer to Jesse, her full hips swaying suggestively.

Jesse eyed the display with a contemptuous raising of one eyebrow. He met the girl's bold gaze with his own, which had gone steely blue and hard. "It seems that eavesdropping joins your other questionable pastimes, Janie. I wonder, does it pay as well as some? Ah, well, no matter, I suppose. At least the plying of such a trade won't render you eventually useless—addled with the pox."

Janie gasped and took a backward step, and Jesse's face assumed a satisfied expression. He knew his words had found their mark, and he seized the advantage. "Now, you hear me, Janie Simms, and hear me well. Nothing that you overheard concerning Kathie Carver is to escape your lips, do you hear? Nothing!" He watched the redhead nod, her brown eyes fearful. "Kathie Carver is a decent young woman, worth twenty of your kind any day of the week, and I won't have her name muddied about. For the record, I am not the father of the child you so cheaply learned of, but that is of no import, because if I ever catch you carrying one tale of it on your nasty little tongue, I will behave as if I were, and you will answer to me!" The blue eyes were like flint now. "Is that understood?"

Janie shook her head rapidly in the affirmative, then whined, "I ain't sayin' a word, Mister Jesse, I swear it. Why, I meant nary no 'arm. An'—an' I ain't been eavesdroppin', neither. I— I was jest waitin' out 'ere fer *ye*, sir, ter—ter give ye this!" She held out an ivory envelope to Jesse. "It come fer ye downstairs, not a quarter hour ago."

Jesse took the envelope from her, recognizing the familiar seal in red wax.

"So you just thought to hang around Kathie's door for a while before deciding to deliver this, is that right?" Jesse's words were still hard, but they had lost their threatening tone.

"Oh, sir," sniveled Janie, "I jest didn't wish ter disturb ye, is all."

"Well, see to it that you hold your tongue, as I've instructed, or you'll be seeing me disturbed in ways you'll truly regret," Jesse admonished. "Now, don't you have duties belowstairs?"

The words were a statement, not a question, and Janie knew she'd been dismissed. Hastily drawing her mobcap back over the wiry red locks, she dropped a quick curtsey and ran for the stairs.

Jesse stared at her retreating form for a moment, a last, brief frown of annoyance on his handsome features. Then he broke the seal of the envelope in his hand and read:

Jesse—
I will meet you at the Black Swan at two, as planned. The letter from Columbia I spoke of, has been followed by a second, and I look forward to our meeting, where I hope we shall draught a favorable reply.

Carlisle

Jesse smiled. James Carlisle was one of his oldest friends, indeed, had been his father's friend years ago, as well as the trusted family solicitor, and he knew the old gentleman well enough to suspect he'd better have his wits about him, his questions well prepared, if he wasn't going to be led into a scheme he had no business involving himself in. He knew where Carlisle stood politically in the matter, and the old fellow wasn't above playing upon an old friendship to ensure that certain ends were gained. So, tucking Carlisle's letter into a waistcoat pocket, Jesse made his way briskly toward his chamber.

Chapter Three

"I am so delight to make ze acquaintance."

"No, no, Aimée, 'delight*ed*'—'I am so delight*ed*,' and it's 'to make *your* acquaintance,' not '*the* acquaintance'! Now try it again, *mon amie*."

A resigned sigh escaped Aimée's lips, but she set them in a determined line, took a deep breath, and repeated slowly, "I am so delight*ed* to make . . . *your* acquaintance." Then, seeing a look of approval on Brianna's face, her gamin's features broke out in an ear-to-ear grin. *"Très bon, n'est-ce pas?"*

"Oui—I mean, yes, Aimée, very good." Brianna smiled. "Now let's try—"

"Please, Brianna," begged the smaller girl, lapsing back into her native tongue, "we have been at this all morning, and I fear this head is about to burst if I try to cram one more English syllable into it. Can we not take a small rest now? Besides, it is nearly time for the mid-day meal, and I, my friend, am starving!"

Brianna looked at the onyx-bright eyes that implored her so hopefully and relented. "Very well, Aimée, I'm tired of concentrating, too. And you may not think so, but we've made tremendous progress since we began, all those weeks ago at sea."

Aimée made a face.

"No, really. I assure you, but I would like to make a suggestion about how we handle your English lessons, now that we're almost home."

Aimée's look was wary. "What kind of a suggestion?"

"Well," replied Brianna, slipping off the large Hepplewhite tester bed where she had been sitting. She walked to a small lowboy on the other side of the room they had taken at the Black Swan Inn while awaiting an escort from her father's estate to see them home. "I think, from now on, I ought to speak to you only in English; you may reply in French, except during our actual lessons, and, of course, the rest of the time you feel inclined to use your new language." She picked up an ornate silver repoussé hairbrush from the lowboy and began wielding it in long, steady strokes at her heavy auburn mane. "Well, what do you say?"

Aimée, who was sitting in a small alcove, on a built-in seat under the window, pulled her legs up in front of her in a tailor's position and gave Brianna a pleading look. "But French is so much *easier*, and as long as we're alone—"

"Ah, but we're not *going* to be alone all the time as we have been, my friend. That's just the point!" exclaimed Brianna in English. "In just a short time, you'll be hearing almost nothing but English anyway, Aimée, so why not get used to it?" Brianna began to shrug out of the apple green baize dressing gown she had been wearing; the August mornings at sea had been cool, but the temperatures on land were much warmer, and as she stood, clad only in a light cotton shift, she made a mental note to adjust her wardrobe selections accordingly.

Aimée gave a nod of acquiescence as she accepted the inevitable and slid off her perch by the window. "You are right, of course, Mademoiselle—er—*Mees* Devereaux," she smiled. "And now I think I had better begin applying my studies as ladies' maid," she said, taking the hairbrush from Brianna. "How shall we dress these tresses today?" She began brushing the shining auburn mass.

"Oh, in anything you like, Aimée. It's not as if I'll be seen going about, you know." She made a brief grimace of displeasure. "Sweet Mary, I wonder how long we'll be shut up here before Papa's escort comes—you did post the message of our arrival the moment we landed yesterday, did you not?"

"Even before I unpacked," assured Aimée. She began working Brianna's yard-long curls upward from the nape of her neck, toward her crown.

"*Très bon.*" The taller girl smiled. She had taken a seat on a small stool to allow Aimée to reach her hair. "And, do you know something, Aimée? Even after all those weeks aboard ship, I still don't know if—if I'm ready to—to face...oh, I don't know, exactly... the future, I guess is what I mean."

Aimée nodded. "I understand perfectly." She had begun fastening the heavy locks securely at Brianna's crown with a series of hairpins she carried in a pocket of the plain gray muslin dress the sisters had provided before they left. "The future is, at the least, a thing to respect, if not hold in awe." She gave a familiar, knowing look that was caught by Brianna in a silver repoussé hand glass she held. "And, my friend, given your particular set of circumstances, I would say you have more to be respectful of than most." She secured a final pin beneath a particularly wayward tress and reached again for the hairbrush.

"Aimée, what do you mean, 'more than most'?" questioned Brianna suspiciously. "Is—is there something you—you've *seen*—something you aren't telling—"

"Not at all," replied Aimée, a bit too quickly, Brianna thought. "It... it is just that your known circumstances are so... unsettled. First, you have left your sequestered life at the Abbaye forever. In effect, childhood is behind you." She gave a small nod of satisfaction at that assessment, pleased with herself at her ability to summarize analytically. Having brushed the long overhang of Brianna's hair that fell from where it was secured atop her crown and divided it into several sections, Aimée began to plait these into a pair of intricate braids, continuing, in French, as she worked.

"Also, you are returning to a home you have been absent from, for seven years—I do not count your fortnight of shared mourning last year," she said to the face in the mirror. "One hardly learns much about one's surroundings when most of one's waking hours are spent in church or at a grieving father's side." She gave Brianna's reflection a meaningful look. "And then there is the— Brianna, are you listening to me?"

Brianna's eyes had suddenly assumed a far-away look, their expression sadly dreamy. "Hmm? Oh, beg pardon, Aimée. I was just thinking. Remembering how Le Beau Château had looked when last I saw it. It was late spring, and there had been plenty of rain, almost as if... Papa said it had rained for weeks after Deirdre died, too. And for Mother's funeral, he said the coach wheels were almost up to their axles in mud, it had poured so.'' Suddenly she gave an impatient gesture with her fingers and tossed her head, almost pulling the final plait out of Aimée's deftly moving fingers. ''I'm sorry, but enough of this maudlin reflection,'' she said, changing her tone. ''What I had started to recollect was the way the sun had shone, finally, after days and days of downpour, on the morning I left, and—oh, God, Aimée, it was beautiful! All that lush green!''

As she spoke Aimée noted the excitement in her eyes, the vivid animation lighting her features as she described the vast estate which would soon be home again.

Aimée had just fashioned the plaits she had woven into a coronet at the crown of Brianna's delicately shaped head and was reaching into her pocket for more hairpins. ''This Le Beau Château—you love it very much, do you not?''

Brianna nodded, carefully, so as not to dislodge her friend's handiwork. ''Oh, Aimée, it is a *wonderful* place! I never realized how much I had missed it, until I returned last year. And then, to be forced to leave once again—'' Abruptly, she fell silent; this type of negative thinking would never do, if she was going to work at the kind of self-discipline Madame had spoken of. Indeed, the final conversation between her and the Abbess, the morning she had left, had again been about such matters, and Brianna had voluntarily given her word that she would work at dissipating old regrets and try to curb her fiery temper and walk a milder path toward maturity. Now she gave a small sigh of satisfaction and congratulated herself on this tiny victory over her poorer self. She turned and gazed up at Aimée, who was critically eyeing the coronet, but a quick glance from the little gypsy told her she had been avidly taking in Brianna's every word—and probably her thoughts as well.

''It was a good place to be carefree—a good place to be a child,'' said the foundling, surprising Brianna with the perfection of the sentence in English.

''Yes, truly,'' said Brianna. ''Acres upon acres of wild Up-country freedom. You'll begin to appreciate what I mean after we leave Charleston. You'll see the vast, flat, rice-growing tidewater plantations give way to more mountainous terrain as

we head toward Columbia. That's our capital now, as of a
couple of years ago. Oh, Papa said there was a lot of grum-
bling among the aristocratic Charlestonian gentry at having to
relocate to the barbaric northwestern part of the state, at least
for part of each year. They regard it as all too primitive, and
perhaps they're right. Le Beau Château is the only cultivated
estate of any size in the area." Here Brianna gave a wistful
smile. "People said Papa was crazy to settle there and make any
attempt at a civilized lifestyle, but Papa was a Frenchman—and
not just any Frenchman, but one who valued his freedom too
much to remain in France under the old king, and who valued
other men's freedom too much to settle in an area where all of
the profit is made by the sweat of an enslaved people."

Aimée gave her a thoughtful look as she pulled loose a few
wisps of hair at Brianna's temples and in front of her ears.
"Then I take it that this—'Upcountry' is not a big slave-holding
area?"

"You take it correctly, my quick little friend. No, the mountain uplands were settled by a fierce, freedom-loving group of
men who value hard work and independence more than grand
estates and aristocratic yearnings."

"And yet they accept your Papa?"

"Accept him and respect him. Oh, Mother told me once it
wasn't always that way. When Papa and she first arrived—from
Ireland, by the way, where Mother was born, and where they
met while Papa was there on business—when they first came to
South Carolina and purchased hundreds of wilderness acres
upstate, many of the rough-hewn natives of the area were prepared to do battle. They were automatically suspicious of the
son of a French count—even a second son—and the daughter
of an Irish horse breeder who had lost his lands to the English.
What an odd pair, they thought! And, then, if that wasn't
enough, they were Catholics! You see, there are Frenchmen
aplenty among the early settlers in South Carolina, but the
majority, by far, were Huguenots, fleeing from injustice. Of
course, as time went by, they learned that my father's Catholic
forebears had secretly aided a great many unfortunate Huguenots, helping many to escape persecution in France, although
never wavering from—or even *thinking* of giving up their own
faith."

"But committed to some kind of an ideal of human freedom, no matter what the religion or background?" asked Aimée, extremely interested now.

"Exactly," replied Brianna. "And in my mother, Aileen, the liberty-loving Devereaux line found its perfect joining. Not that Mother was ever one of those intellectualizing, pamphleteering bluestockings, as the English call them. No, Mother was a feminine, gently reared lady, but she grew up on a large enough piece of property in Ireland to know the value of land—and to know the pain that comes with losing it."

"And she left her love of the land for her daughter to carry on, eh?" questioned Aimée. She had stepped back to view her handiwork now, darting bright eyes swiftly over the charming coiffure that framed Brianna's face, but her attention was clearly riveted on their conversation.

"True," answered Brianna. With a final peek at herself in the hand glass and a smile in Aimée's direction, she rose from the stool and ambled toward a tall armoire that faced the bed. Here she stopped and turned to her friend. "Oh, Aimée, I wish you could have known my parents as I remember them from my childhood! I swear, Deirdre and I thought Mother the most beautiful woman alive, and Papa! So handsome, so charming, and yet always the rugged individualist. Both of them were, and they instilled within us girls all of the fervent ideals and principles they believed in."

Aimée now took a seat on the stool Brianna had vacated. She wore an expression of studied thought as she smoothed out some folds in the gray expanse of her skirts. "Your parents—they never held any slaves, then?" she queried.

"Never!" Brianna's tone held a proud ring. Then, noticing Aimée's pensive features, she questioned, "Why do you ask?"

Aimée looked up with a start. "Oh, I was just wondering." She was quiet a moment when, almost as if she had made up her mind to something, she gave Brianna an assessing look. "How much do you know about my own background, my friend?" she questioned in English.

Brianna was poking into the armoire she had just opened. Pulling a lively, violet sprigged muslin gown from its contents, she straightened and turned to face Aimée. "Why, only what we were all told at the convent," she said. "That you were left at the Abbaye when you couldn't have been more than a few days old, in a basket, with a note in ungrammatical French, sprinkled with a few phrases in—Romany, was it?—saying your mother deeply loved you but couldn't keep you, for you were born of—of—"

"Shame, I believe, was the word they had Sister Rosalinde translate from the Romany," supplied Aimée.

"Well, yes," Brianna acknowledged. "But even if you were born out of—uh—what that word implies, there's no fault adhering to *you* in that! Everyone always said so." Here she gave Aimée a look that was part compassion, part embarrassment. "Well, there always will be a few nasty little snobs who attach importance to such things, but—"

"More than a few, *mon amie*," Aimée broke in. Her small face suddenly wore a wide grin, the look of mischief in the black eyes unmistakable. "Of course, the likes of Nicole de la Chambourtin and Annette Ravelle found their comeuppances for their little snobberies, eh?"

Both girls giggled as they recalled shortened bedsheets causing screams and not-so-ladylike curses after lights went out, rougepots spiced with the hottest of pepper powders, bringing stinging tears to outraged features, and not a few other well-planned escapades designed to lower the proud and cruel to their silly little knees.

But soon Aimée's face grew serious again, and she posed her question thoughtfully, pronouncing the English syllables with care. "But tell me, Brianna, did you not ever"—Aimée's pronunciation of the English word was closer to "evair"—"hear some of the—er—*darker* rumors which circulated about me—or I should say, my *mother's* background?" Seeing the puzzled look on her companion's face, she shrugged. "No? Well, it is possible, I suppose, since everyone knew how close we were. Nevertheless," Aimée gestured with a brown forefinger, "they did circulate."

Brianna grew more attentive. "What kind of rumors, Aimée?" She had stepped into the sprigged muslin gown and Aimée rose to help her with it, giving a quick sidestep to keep her balance as legs which had grown accustomed to shipboard rolling refused to remember they were now on land.

Aimée uttered a small sigh. "Over the years," she began, once more in French, "some of the girls had traffic here and there with gypsies who came to Paris—oh, to peddle, to sell wares or services of one sort or another. And some of them, the bolder ones, engaged them in conversation, seeking... seeking—"

"Gossip?"

"*Oui*. Seeking gossip, about me—or my unfortunate mother." Aimée reached up to begin closing the long row of tiny buttons that traced a line down the back of Brianna's gown.

"And, surprisingly enough, they found something." Here she paused a moment, as if hesitant to continue. "The stories they gleaned told of a proud gypsy princess, daughter of a Romany gypsy king, who refused to marry the one her parents had chosen. It was said she disappeared from their camp one night and could not be found when it was time to move on. Well, move on, they did, but friends of the girl were heard to say they had seen her early on the day she vanished—and also for several days previous—at a country fair outside of Paris in the company of a proud man—a man who was quite unmistakable in his appearance." Here Aimée's voice grew very soft, and Brianna strained to hear it. "You see, he was a black man—an Ethiope—with skin as dark as the earth, where it's fertile." She bent forward, around Brianna's still shoulders and caught her eye. "An Ethiopian prince, if the rumors are to be believed, although with rumors—" She stepped to the side and gave a shrug. "Who knows how much is accurate?" Her laugh was light, but not completely mirthful.

"So you think—or the rumormongers thought—"

"Have you not ever wondered about the color of my skin, *mon amie*? A shade too dusky for olive, don't you agree?" Aimée resumed her place at the row of buttons, and the room fell silent.

Finally, Brianna took a deep breath and spun around to face her little friend, nearly tearing a button out of its cloth. "Aimée, why have you not told me anything of this before? I thought we were friends, but, really, more than friends—intimates, 'like sisters,' you told Madame." Seeing her companion's abashed look, she hastened to continue. "Not that it means a damned thing, I want you to know!'' Here Brianna lapsed into French herself, deliberately breaking her own rule, for she wanted no misunderstandings between them. ''Who cares what color you are—certainly *not I*! And besides, if the rumors are true, it is *you* who have royal blood in your veins, something none of those little snoots can lay claim to! And furthermore, rumors, it must be remembered, are only rumors, and they grow grand with the telling.'' Here Brianna's volume rose slightly, and she raised her chin a notch with it, confident in the rightness of what she was saying. ''You are no less nor are you more to me, for what you have just told me. But I know what you are—you are Aimée Gitane, my dearest friend, and I rejoice in it!''

There was a soft smile on Aimée's face as she looked at Brianna, and then a quiet nod of the head. ''It is, of course, what I expected you to say, *chérie*. Forgive me for not sharing any of this with you until now. Given our closeness, it was unforgivable.''

A protest formed on Brianna's lips, but Aimée forestalled it with a negative headshake. ''No, it is true. I should have confided in you, if only to explain to my 'partner in battle' the full extent of those wicked little snobs' cruelties. But you see, I suppose I made the mistake of assuming you already knew, and were too gracious to bring it up.'' Aimée grinned. ''You certainly aided and abetted me with the kind of—of fervor which would have come of knowing!''

''I merely detest snobbery and its cruelties in any form!'' exclaimed Brianna. ''I thought it was just your gypsy background and foundling status they were being catty about. Cause enough to make me angry—''

''Mon Dieu!'' chortled Aimée. ''And *such* anger! You were a veritable *enfant terrible* with them, *chérie*! Tell me, if your *maman* was so much the gentle lady, who is it you have this temper from? Your papa?''

''Ah, I daresay, Mother could 'raise her Irish' when she felt the need, Aimée, but it was always controlled, and we girls never once saw her raise it toward us, or with Papa—but you've guessed right about the true source of my 'inheritance.' Papa was something fierce to behold when angered. He—'' Suddenly Brianna winced. ''Oh, merciful Jesus—please—I cannot *bear* to lose him, too! Aimée, tell me, for you hinted at it back at the Abbaye, but I haven't—I've not dared to raise the question again—but now—is he—do you *know* something—*see* something?'' She cast an imploring look at her companion, who had moved back to her window seat and now regarded her with sadly knowing eyes.

Slowly, Aimée nodded. ''*Oui, mon amie.* There is something . . . I have *felt*, let us say. And I will share this with you.'' Aimée rose and crossed to join Brianna, who had taken a seat on the bed. Sitting carefully beside her, the smaller girl reached to take one of the slim white hands which had been lying, clenched, in the sprigged muslin lap.

''He is not gone yet, *chérie.* This, I feel very strongly. But...'' Here she threw Brianna a look of compassion. ''But you must not hope too much, either.'' She shook her head sadly. ''Forgive me, *mon amie*, but I do not think he has much time left.''

Brianna sat very still, digesting the words without surprise. Rather, a look of resignation settled across her features, for she accepted Aimée's pronouncement as a confirmation of what she already knew. Slowly, she nodded, her voice, when she spoke, barely audible. ''Just let me be in time,'' she whispered.

Aimée nodded her understanding. ''There is much you wish to tell him, *non*?''

Brianna sighed. ''A great deal. But mostly—mostly I guess I just want to tell him how awfully much I love him, and how all his and Mother's efforts on my behalf have not been in vain.''

''He already knows this,'' Aimée stated flatly.

Brianna looked at her and gave a nod of acknowledgment, then hastened onward. ''But I also want him to know I will be trying hard—*very* hard, to become the self-possessed young lady I know Deirdre was, and—''

''You are *not* Deirdre, my friend!'' Aimée's words, in English, were vehement.

''Yes, but...oh, Aimée, how can I explain it? When we were growing up, it was always I who was a trial to them. Forever getting into difficulties, questioning their authority—and not only theirs! There was poor Mistress Delaney, sweet old thing! Do you know she came all the way from County Cork with my mother, out of sheer loyalty and—and love? She *adored* Mother, and Deirdre, too...but—but with me...well, I know she gave up on me!''

"Not entirely," Aimée commented with the air of one who knows the complete truth of what she is saying.

Brianna sensed this and threw her an exasperated look. "Very well. You 'know' these things, somehow. But tell me this. What about yet a fourth person I disappointed, my—"

"Your priest, Father—" Here Aimée hesitated. "He is a large, round man, his girth given to stoutness, rather than—er—flabbiness, I think, for he does not disdain physical labor and exercise. It is merely—" Aimée laughed gaily. "It is just that he loves the good food and drink too much, *non*?"

Brianna's mouth fell agape and she stared in wonder at her friend. "What color hair does he have?" she asked quietly, when she could finally phrase the question.

Aimée's face grew merry with impishness. "Oh, red, I think," she grinned, "thick, but with a slightly balding pate...of rosy hue, as of one who spends much time out of doors, in the sun. But do not worry about him, *chérie. Le bon père*, he has not given up on you. He loves you—has always loved you the best in the *famille*, I think."

"Oh, stop!" cried Brianna, pushing herself up from the bed. She whirled to face Aimée, arms akimbo, skirts swishing. "And it's 'family,' not *famille*! So you truly do have it, don't you, Aimée Gitane?"

Aimée continued to grin at her.

"Well, then, just tell me one more thing, won't you? Just what does the future hold in store for me? Can you give me an inkling of what I may expect, once we go home?"

Aimée's face suddenly grew enigmatic. "It is not wise to look too deeply," she murmured.

"Too deeply!" Brianna gasped, her face incredulous. "For heaven's sake, Aimée, here we stand, on the threshold of—God knows what, and you say—"

"I say what I know—what I have learned, the hard way, my friend." Her English was better than Brianna had ever heard it. "Sometimes it is better not to know too much."

"Aimée! *Will* you tell me *nothing*?" The vexation in her tone grew, and Aimée watched the green eyes flash and deepen in color.

Aimée smiled, for she knew Brianna's temper well, and with this also came the knowledge that her firebreathing was never really hurled at a friend in earnest. "Enough! Mercy!" she begged in mock solicitousness. "I relent." Suddenly she assumed a merry look. "I predict," she intoned in a voice not her own, and then Brianna recognized the pontificating, finger-pointing stance of Sister Cecile, their pompous old Latin teacher, who was always giving unwanted advice.

"Ye-e-s?" giggled Brianna, having fun now.

"I predict," continued Aimée, "that there will be many surprises waiting for you at Le Beau Château." She walked toward the stool near the lowboy they had used earlier and raised one leg and placed it there; then, with a bouncing movement, she was standing atop the stool, her finger pointing skyward. "Some of these may not be to your liking, Mademoiselle Devereaux!" Brianna pulled a face and "Sister Cecile" grew increasingly ominous. "But I do think—"

Suddenly the stool tipped, sending a startled Aimée hurling on top of Brianna; both girls landed on the floor, their voluminous skirts and petticoats breaking their fall. Unhurt, but breathless, they broke into laughter. When at last this had died down, Aimée pushed herself to her knees and looked at her friend.

"A moment of seriousness, please!" she intoned, still Sister Cecile.

Brianna's face struggled to look properly somber. *"Oui, Madame!"*

"You will—" suddenly the gamin's voice was her own again, and she continued in English "—find whatever it is you have been searching for, for many years, now, Brianna." Her tone was serious, but then, almost as if she were saying seriousness was not to be endured for too long, her impishness returned and the black eyes signalled pure humor. "But only after much *travail* and *travel*!" She laughed at her own French-accented pun, in English, and Brianna laughed, too.

"Oh, Aimée!" she chuckled. "You are such priceless fun! Promise me—"

Just then, a loud rumble from Aimée's abdominal area interrupted their camaraderie. The look on Aimée's face was one of total disgust. "Enough of the far-off future, and more of the immediate future," she snorted. "I must go downstairs and acquire us some food—now—or I shall *starve!*"

Brianna laughed. "Oh, Aimée, you are the most delightful person—I swear, if anyone else thought about, and ate, food as diligently as you, she'd weigh ten stone! 'I shall starve!' You and Father Edouard should get along famously! You have the same—er—concern for your stomachs!"

"Concern! Bah! Respect, you mean!" asserted her friend, rising, at last, from the floor. She gave Brianna a hand up.

"Well, La Gitane," said Brianna, "if I promise to send you below for a dinner tray, *tout de suite*, will you do something for me?"

"At your service," said Aimée, her hand moving to her stomach.

"Never stop being my friend," said Brianna, taking her turn at seriousness.

"You take me for an idiot maybe?" She reached up and embraced the taller girl, Brianna hugging her in return. Then Aimée headed for the door, visions of juicy victuals watering her mouth.

When she had gone, Brianna settled down in the alcove at the window with a book the Abbess had given her as a parting gift, but she had no sooner opened it when the door flew ajar and a breathless Aimée reentered, skirts aswish.

"Mon Dieu!" exclaimed Aimée, slamming the door behind her. "I think I have just seen a god!"

Brianna raised her head from the book and regarded her with frank curiosity. "A god? For heaven's sake, Aimée, what are you talking about? I've never seen you so excited."

Aimée stood with her back flattened against the door, rolling her eyes as she gestured toward the hallway beyond.

"Well, perhaps not a god exactly, for his smile was human enough," she grinned. *"Sacré bleu!* But he was *magnifique*."

"Who?" At this point Brianna's curiosity had gotten the better of her and she closed her book in anticipation of an interesting answer. Aimée's features sported the widest of grins. "The man I just saw, out there, in the hallway." She gestured again toward the closed door. "I tell you, had anyone told me American men were at once so-o-o beautiful and so-o-o male, I assure you, I would have found a way to make our journey much, much sooner!"

Intrigued, Brianna rose from her seat near the window and stood, arms akimbo, and stared at her friend. "Aimée Gitane! Now I do believe I've seen everything! After years of listening to you nonchalantly dismiss the appearance of anything wearing breeches, from the most comely of lads in the marketplace to the king himself, do you mean to tell me I must now hear you extolling the virtues of one American gentleman to such an extent that you have even forgotten to fetch the *food* you were going for?" She cast a mock scowl at Aimée's dreamy expression. "You *do* remember you were on your way to secure our dinner, do you not?"

"Ah, but you should have *seen* him, *mon amie*," sighed Aimée. "*This* one was worth exclaiming over."

"And worth missing *dinner* over?" Brianna's tone waxed incredulous.

Quickly brought back to basics, Aimée massaged her rumbling abdomen and threw Brianna a sheepish smile. "No, no, of course not, *mon amie*. I shall return at once." Her eyes danced merrily as she turned toward the door, adding, "But you truly should have seen him, Brianna!"

"Well, I just wish it *had* been I who was venturing downstairs by myself, Aimée. I swear, I'll not be able to stand much more of this—this incarceration: First, it's seven years in a convent, then it's weeks and weeks at sea, and now, God knows how many days stuck up here in this miserable little chamber as I await Papa's escort! At least *you* have the freedom to move about a bit, while I—I must play the lady—" Here a brief sneer flitted across Brianna's delicate features. "—too *proper* to move about even a respectable inn without a *proper* escort!"

Aimée stopped at the half-opened door, suddenly shutting it as she turned to face her companion. There was a look of crafty inspiration in the black eyes as she gazed at Brianna for a silent moment. "Tell me, Brianna," she said, "do you really wish you were in my place for the freedom I enjoy?"

Brianna's green eyes sparkled. "Aimée, you know I do! Heaven knows how long it will take the news of our arrival to reach Le Beau Château, and I'm about to go mad sitting here, waiting for—'' Brianna caught the look in Aimée's eyes, and the corners of her mouth turned up while she lapsed into a momentary silence. ''Do I really wish I were in your pl—'' The dimples in her cheeks deepened. ''That's it! We exchange places!''

''It shouldn't be difficult,'' Aimée grinned.

''And we won't overdo it.''

''Just an hour or two, at the most.''

''We're almost the same size in the waist.''

''And that floppy mobcap can—''

''—conceal much ... just in case—''

''—there's someone downstairs who might recognize me from a year ago.''

Suddenly the sedate chamber was a beehive of activity as the two young women began removing clothing, rummaging through drawers, running to the armoire and donning unfamiliar apparel. All the while they maintained a constant stream of excited chatter.

''You are much fuller in the bust, Brianna...perhaps a fichu to cover ... ?''

''Oh, piffle! Servant wenches are in far less constraints to be modest! But what of my height? Do these skirts reveal too much ankle to be graceful?''

''With ankles like yours? *Nevair*!''

''Ah! An accent! I'll use ze Fransh accent. Eet weel complete ze disguise, *oui*?''

''*Oui, et voilà!*'' chortled Aimée, striking a pose before the full-length mirror they'd discovered inside one of the armoire's doors. ''How do I look?''

She was wearing a bright yellow gown of the finest silk voile. It was cut in the latest Parisian mode, having been purchased by Brianna that spring for one of those rare occasions when the detested scarlet school uniform would not suffice, a garden party at which the Queen herself had been present and to which several of the older girls at the Abbaye had been invited to accompany the Abbess.

Brianna had to chuckle, however, as she beheld the overlong sleeves that caused lace to dangle far beyond Aimée's tiny hands, the gaping bodice which had been only partially remedied by a stuffing of silk scarves, and the half-dozen inches of hemline that puddled around her friend's tiny feet even as she stood on tiptoe.

"The sleeves, Aimée, push up the sleeves. And what about that pair of high-heeled mules I bought you on your saint's day?"

"Yes, yes, I can make some adjustments," giggled Aimée as she held a yellow hair ribbon against her dark hair. "But it isn't as if I'm *going* anywhere in this. *I* am now the *lady* and—ugh!—must remain in *ma chambre*. It is *you* we must ready for the real masquerade!"

She cast an appraising eye down Brianna's tall, slender figure. "Those kid slippers are much too fine for a servant's feet, but you'll never fit into mine, and at least they are flat. Another inch at the ankles, and even you wouldn't dare go out in that dress! Perhaps if we smudge them with this soot from the fireplace."

"No, no, Aimée. Let me do it. A lady in a silk gown never soils her hands! Now, where's that mobcap?"

Aimée handed her a floppy piece of shapeless white cotton and Brianna turned toward the mirror and carefully pulled it over her coiffure, making sure each auburn tendril was tucked out of sight before tightening and securing the drawstring that held it in place. As she peered at herself in the glass, she patted the three-inch extension of cotton that formed a ruffle beyond the drawstring, all around her head. A smile curved the corners of her mouth upward.

"The *citoyens* of Paris knew what they were doing when they invented these, Aimée. Any female who didn't want to be recognized storming the Bastille, or whatever, could rely on one of these to hide her face."

Aimée nodded. "It will suffice—a perfect disguise," she grinned.

Brianna took a couple of steps back from the mirror and appraised the reflection there. It was a transformation, from head to sole. From the concealing mobcap her eyes moved downward to the plain gray dress which, on Aimée, had had a modest enough scoop of neckline, but which, on her, formed a daring *décolletage*. Generous breasts had to find somewhere to go, and hers pushed saucily above the neckline's narrow gray piping like the halves of twin melons; the waist, not a problem, nipped in severely below, the material hugging it snugly before billowing outward over softly rounded hips and derriere. Below the radically high hemline, soft white hose in no way concealed her lower calves and the ankles that had already been the subject of so much discussion. She bent to work a final smudging of soot across the toe of one of the delicate kid slippers as a gasp from Aimée claimed her attention.

"Brianna! *You* may feel you can forego a fichu to conceal that *décolletage*, but, *chérie*, I must insist, *only* if you remember to keep from bending over that way!"

Brianna, who had not yet straightened, cast a glance at the mirror and went beet red. Quickly she resumed an upright stance, her hands coming instantly to the breasts that a moment before had threatened to leave their enclosure. Carefully, she pushed, until the rosy pink nipples again disappeared from view.

"You have a point, Aimée," she replied, not without some embarrassment.

"And you have *two*! Which you are in danger of exhibiting to Charleston society," Aimée chortled.

Again, Brianna felt heat go to her face, even as she laughed at Aimée's bawdy riposte.

"Well," she chirped, casting a final glance at the mirror, "I'd better get going before my courage melts away—*and* before your American *god* melts away for that matter!" She headed for the door.

"Ah, so you are intrigued after all!"

"I nevair said I wasn't," Brianna grinned; she disappeared into the hallway with a confident wink at her friend.

But once on her way to the staircase leading below, Brianna felt the confidence she had exhibited quickly evaporate. As taproom noises rose to greet her, she slowed her steps, thinking, what if the mobcap is not enough? What if one of Papa's friends happens to be taking a meal and recognizes me from the funeral last year? What if the innkeeper remembers my maidservant was a much smaller girl? What if, what if—? But then, suddenly, she stopped herself, chiding, *you silly ninnyhammer! Is that all a breath of freedom means to you, that you would recoil from it at the slightest chance something might go amiss? The price of freedom*, she reminded herself, *has ever been dear!* And with a sudden bounce to her step, she ran for the stairs and into the breach.

The commonroom, as she entered it, buzzed with sound and movement everywhere. It was a large room, running the full length of the lower story and more than half its width. Heavy wooden beams crisscrossed the smoky ceiling, and a dark wooden chair rail ran the room's periphery, above dark red painted wainscotting. Numerous heavy oak tables occupied the bulk of the space she encountered, although her eyes, as they grew accustomed to the smoky air, were soon drawn to the room's most imposing feature, a red brick fireplace that took up the entire far wall. The majority, by far, of the room's crowded inhabitants were male, although, here and there, a skirted figure was seen flitting and bending, attendant to customer needs.

"Yes, mistress, what can I do for you?" The innkeeper himself, judging from his proprietary air, had quickly noticed her, but his businesslike tone belied the examining glance he gave her *décolletage.*

Reaching up to make sure the mobcap was still in place and doing its job, Brianna took a quick gulp of air and responded in her best French accent, *"Mais oui, monsieur*, ah—my meestress wood like to 'ave ze dinnair, up ze stairs, een ze *chambre, non?"* She threw him her sweetest smile as her soft voice worked its sultry magic.

Timothy Barnes reddened, for while her head apparatus got in the way of his seeing her entire face, it was clear, from the soft pink lips, the charming dimples, and the curves she presented—here the red spread to his ears—this was a French beauty, even if she *was* a servant wench. "Er—right away, *mademoiselle*," he replied with a grin and another quick glance at her neckline. "Janie!" he bellowed to the far end of the room. "Come and bring a tray for the lady here."

Brianna cringed as most of the occupants of the room turned heads in their direction. Soon the barmaid he'd summoned was sauntering up to them, a frank, curious look on her saucy features.

"Janie here will fill a tray for you from the kitchen, miss— er *mademoiselle*. You just have yourself a seat out here..."

Barnes began casting about for an empty seat, but as his eyes
scanned the room, a smooth male voice drawled from a place
immediately behind Brianna, "I'd be pleased to offer the va-
cant seat at my table, miss. My companion hasn't arrived as
yet, and you're welcome to it."

Brianna whirled quickly toward the sound of the voice and
when she beheld its source, her breath caught in her throat—
Aimée's American god! It had to be, for gazing down at her
from a lofty height well above her head was the bluest pair of
dark-lashed eyes she'd ever seen. Why, the sheer length of those
lashes was positively *indecent* on a man, she thought. And then
there was the *rest* of him! From its straight, carefully chiseled
nose, to its strong, square jaw, the face was a study in perfect
proportions. The firm, broad mouth that smiled at her now
showed even white teeth that flashed against well-tanned skin,
and the shock of curling black hair he wore fell unclubbed to
his collar. Then, framing the smile, making her knees turn to
jelly, was a pair of deeply grooved male dimples. They worked
below high, angular cheekbones in the handsome face now as
if at hiding some secret amusement as he fixed those sapphire
eyes on her in a steady, unwavering gaze. This succeeded in
forcing Brianna to lower her own eyes as she felt the heat creep
up her neck to her cheeks, but then she was forced to contemplate the body of the god, and a god's body it was! Wide,
muscular shoulders, apparent even beneath the carefully tailored blue riding jacket; broad, well-muscled chest, tapering to
a trim male waist; lean hips, giving way to long, muscular
thighs encased in tight-fitting... *Oh, mon Dieu!* thought
Brianna, *what am I staring at! If he doesn't move or say something else soon, I'll be in a fine pickle. My tongue feels as if it's
been tied to my teeth!*

But just then the god did speak, giving her the gracious rescue she required.

"Ah, how remiss of me—um—*mademoiselle*? Allow me to
introduce myself, for, of course, a lady cannot join a gentleman's table without an introduction. Jesse Randall at your
service." And with this, the god's huge frame belied its size by
performing a bow so graceful, it would have put any of Louis'
courtiers to shame. "Will you permit me to offer this seat,
then?" The drawl was lazy and sensual, and Brianna felt her-

self nod and sink into the proffered chair gratefully, her treacherous knees threatening not to support her another second.

Finally, after he had taken his own seat, and with a nod to the innkeeper, who smiled and departed, Brianna found her tongue.

"*Merci, monsieur*—er—Meester Randall," she breathed. Mentally, she applauded herself for the idea of using a French accent, for it forced her to concentrate on something other than the devastating male presence across from her, thus allowing her to regain some poise. "I am called Bri—Brielle, Brielle . . . Gitane, and I am most grateful for ze accommodation."

When Jesse beheld the dimpled smile she threw him, he cursed the fashion in headgear that prevented him from seeing enough of what, he was now sure, was a beautiful and charming visage. He could see a pert, straight little nose and perfect white teeth, not to mention lips that beckoned to a man. *Damn!* And was that a flash of green from the eyes that regarded him beneath the shadows of those damned ruffles?

"Gitane," he murmured. "It's funny, *mademoiselle*, but you somehow don't look like a gypsy. Your skin—" *your flawless skin*, he noted to himself "—is very fair, and you would seem to be much taller than those I've seen of that race," he smiled.

Again, those dimples! Like twin slits hewn by his godmaker into that perfect masculine face! *Oh-oh, better concentrate on my accent*, Brianna scolded. She stammered only slightly, then. "Eet—eet ees a surname we—my *famille* and I—were forced to take because of ze revolution," she fabricated. "Our true name was too well known, *monsieur*, as zat of a—a long line of servants deeply loyal to ze Royalists."

Jesse nodded thoughtfully. "Yes, we've heard something of what's been happening over there in your homeland of late. You and your—mistress, was it?—are fleeing the Revolution, then?"

"Ah, *mais non, monsieur*, not my meestress, only I. She ees an *Americaine*, but *oui*, I 'ave taken zees position weez 'er *Americaine famille* as a form of refuge, one might say."

Brianna was beginning to wonder at the ease with which she concocted this tale, the enormity of the lies she was spinning, when suddenly the blue gaze focused intently on her mouth.

"Do you know you have very sensual lips?" he said, as boldly as if he were commenting on the weather.

Instantly, Brianna's composure slipped, and she folded her arms under her breasts to keep from squirming. But this was exactly the wrong thing to do, for it succeeded in pushing forward and upward the already daring display of charms she presented, drawing Jesse's gaze downward in their direction. He leaned lazily back in his chair and grinned. "Charming." The blue eyes danced with amusement as he watched her quickly unfold her arms and flush.

Just then, Janie approached their table with a tray heavily laden with food, and Brianna let out an audible sigh of relief as she saw her chance to escape. *Escape! But this is what you wanted!* she chided. *This was to have been your escape!* But now, all she wanted was to return to the safe haven of her chamber, away from that piercing blue gaze. What was it about this man, to unnerve her so? Surely not the good looks, even if they were god-like—she'd seen handsome men before, albeit always with a proper escort. *Ah, that must be it,* she thought. *It's just being alone in conversation with one so handsome that must be causing these reactions.* But as she turned toward the oncoming barmaid, something in the back of her mind niggled at her, suggesting such an answer was perhaps a little too simple.

Jesse stood as Janie reached them; he came quickly around the table with what seemed to Brianna an effortless grace as he helped her to her feet.

"'Ere's yer tray, Frenchie," said Janie snidely as she looked Brianna up and down in flagrant fashion.

"I'll take that, Janie." Jesse's tone was curt as he took the tray, his words clipped in obvious suppression of anger, Brianna realized. The embarrassed barmaid saw herself reprimanded and dismissed by the action, and she quickly dipped a curtsey in their direction and fled, red-faced.

"Allow me to carry this up for you, mademoiselle," Jesse offered. "It's clearly too heavy for one so slender," he added, taking the opportunity to peruse her entire figure.

As his eyes lingered over the area about her ankles, Brianna found herself regretting her boldness in disregarding Aimée's admonitions. "You and your breath of freedom," she muttered to herself.

"Mademoiselle?"

"Ah—um—nothing, *monsieur*—er—Meester Randall," she replied, renewed concentration strengthening her resolve. "But, sir, you must not do zees," she protested. "A gentleman does not do servants' work!"

"Nonsense." Jesse inclined his head toward her. "Please lead the way, Mademoiselle Brielle."

Brianna knew a made-up mind when she heard one, and shrugging at him in Gallic fashion, she smiled and headed for the stairs she had descended—was it only a short while ago? As she trod the solid oak staircase, however, she found some of her pent-up energies dissipating and a curiously new mood taking over. *You silly ninny! This was what you wanted, wasn't it? Now the escapade is almost over, and have you allowed yourself to enjoy it? No! And why not, for heaven's sake? He's so-o-o handsome, and so-o-o cooperative, and he'll be gone in a minute, never to be seen again, so why not make the most of it? This is your only chance!*

So it was that, as they drew to a halt before her door, she turned to him and flashed a disarming grin. "You are too kind, *monsieur*. 'Ow can I evair repay you?" As she spoke, she ran a slender finger lightly up one of the muscular forearms which supported the dinner tray.

Jesse's grin exploded across his surprised features. *Why, the little chit,* he thought. *So she's suddenly not all that demure and innocent now that we're alone.* Quickly, he set the tray down on a stand that flanked the wall a few feet from the door.

"Like this, Mademoiselle Brielle," he murmured, taking the hand she had just touched him with and raising it to his lips. But just as he did so, he turned it, palm upward, and as his lips reached her damp flesh, Brianna felt his silken tongue caress her palm, sending a shower of tingling sparks through her body.

"And like this," added Jesse, raising his head and looking intently into her mesmerized face. The fingers of his right hand curled and came up under her chin, gently forcing her face upward as his left arm drew her close. Brianna had barely time to draw in a breath before the dark head descended and the beautiful male mouth closed over hers. His lips were warm and astonishingly soft as they found her own, and when the right arm joined his left in drawing her closer than she'd ever been to any man—even Papa, she realized dizzily—Brianna felt that shower of sparks break into open flames that threatened to ignite her entire body. But then she felt his tongue again, this time gently touching between her lips, seeking and gaining entrance. Then it lightly grazed her teeth—across, then back again, and as her mouth opened in accepting wonder, it lightly touched her own tongue.

Now the flame in Brianna's body began to find a more specific location, for she felt a curious sensation rush to her lower limbs, but she only had seconds to contemplate this, when his mouth released hers, hovering only a couple of inches away.

"Magnificent," he breathed. Suddenly Brianna felt his hand move from the small of her back and slide sensuously around, under her arm, until it found her breast. She opened her mouth in alarm, but again his lips closed over hers, and as his tongue once again teased her open mouth, from lips to teeth, to the very roof of it, she felt his warm palm cup her bared breast.

Brianna knew she should be protesting, but as his strong brown fingers found the taut pink nipple, an overwhelming sensation shot from the peaking crest directly to the place between her thighs, and she felt a rush of something warm and wet at her core. Softly, almost as if it wasn't her own voice, she heard herself moan.

Again Jesse raised his head, still keeping it only inches from hers. Deftly, he brushed his thumb across the throbbing nipple and back again as his eyes searched her upturned face in the darkened hallway. Once more the thumb worked its magic.

"You are delectable, *chérie*," he breathed, and Brianna noticed his voice had become hoarse and low in his throat. "When," he added, "can I see you again? This evening, perhaps?"

Hearing his words, Brianna found her giddy senses making a brief try at returning, and with an effort she didn't know herself capable of, she pulled herself away, winding up still in the circle of his arms, but this time at least a foot from that mouth, for he held her loosely now.

"You...you take liberties, *monsieur*," she breathed, watching him covertly from lowered lashes, her heart hammering away in her chest. Her answer was a broad grin as Jesse proceeded to tuck her exposed breast carefully back inside her bodice.

"I—I fear I cannot be sure of tonight, *monsieur*," she continued. "I must see what my meestress will allow. Eef—eef I can, per'aps I weel return for ze tray for ze evening meal, *oui*?" Brianna smiled at him weakly with the lie.

Jesse acknowledged her reply with a mocking grin as he released her, stepping toward the forgotten dinner tray. As he handed it to her, Brianna knew that somehow *he knew* she had no intention of meeting him later, but the blue eyes, for all their mockery, held no anger.

Ah, but she was something he'd like to pursue, he thought as he landed a sharp rap on the door for her while she held the tray. *But you haven't got time to dally right now, old man,* he reminded himself, and with a courtly bow in her flustered direction, he turned and headed back downstairs.

Seconds later Aimée opened the door to behold a rapt and shaken Brianna.

"Aimée," she said, "I've just met your American 'god'!"

Chapter Four

"I tell you, Jesse, Jefferson and Hamilton are at each other's throats! Something must be done, and done soon, or the President will receive Jefferson's resignation, forthwith, and then where will we be?"

James Carlisle tamped down the tobacco he had stuffed into a long clay pipe, his thick fingers moving steadily, as if to punctuate the rhythm of his speech. He was a stocky man of medium height, with alert, hazel eyes, a mildly florid complexion, and a mouthful of even teeth, all intact, despite his sixty-one years. A well-powdered white periwig rested atop the head he now inclined in the direction of his table companion; his voice lowered to a whisper. "Pinckney means to have an answer by way of this afternoon's post."

"And I mean to send him one," replied the younger man, "but if I'm pressured into a hasty decision, it may not be the one our good Governor wants."

Carlisle sighed. He had known Jesse Randall since the day he was born, had stood up as his godfather over thirty-two years ago, and owing to the tragic deaths of his parents when the boy was but nine, had, indeed, in many ways functioned as a parent to him and his older brother all these years. So it was with this intimate knowledge of the man's character, a knowledge beyond that of solicitor-to-client, that he had girded himself for this meeting. He was well aware of the intellectual thoroughness Jesse brought to bear on matters requiring his commitment and should have realized he wouldn't be able to rush him when he didn't want to be rushed. Such action would only succeed in prompting a stubbornness and inability to be moved that was past all description. But—dammit—the matter *required* haste! A second sigh broke from Carlisle's lips before he leaned back in his chair and took a slow draught on his pipe, deciding to wield a different approach. "Very well, my young friend, let us put Pinckney and the South Carolina Assembly aside for the moment." The hazel eyes regarded Jesse's blue ones with shrewd intelligence. "What is your private understanding of the clash between Federalist and Republican forces?"

Jesse smiled and leaned back in the Windsor armchair he fairly dwarfed with his massive frame. He understood the switch in tactics and nodded, giving Carlisle his due. Then, as if to underscore his wish not to be hurried, he slowly extracted a cheroot from inside his waistcoat pocket and took his time lighting it. Finally, as the blue smoke curled lazily over his head, he spoke. "Why, James, any freshman at my alma mater, William and Mary, could answer that. The Federalists, led by Hamilton and his coterie of bankers and monied interests, desire a strong, centralized government, one where they can keep their fingers on the pulse of everything, through controls on pursestrings. Jefferson's Republicans, however, fear such centralized control as undemocratic, to say the least. They avow the welfare of the common man and the social and material promise of frontier America, with a chance for every ragtag plowboy of sense and energy to make a way for himself through free enterprise and—"

"Dammit, Jesse, that's not what I wanted, and you know it!" exploded Carlisle. He sat forward in his chair again; his complexion had grown more florid, and he was about to add something when he caught the amused twinkle in the blue eyes. "You young whelp! You had me going there for a moment." Carlisle leaned back into his chair again. "Now look, son, I am sorry, truly sorry, for this uncharacteristic pressure I seem to be putting on you, but God almighty, man, it's the Governor—"

"Exactly right," Jesse broke in. "The Governor. And that, Carlisle, is where I have my first problem. Charles Pinckney has always voted as a Federalist. In '88 he was at the fore of those who espoused centralism. In fact, I'd say he saw eye-to-eye with every Yankee factory and shipowner, leading the large-scale planters among us who produce for a world market and who know a strong central government is essential to overseas trade. Why I'd say Hamilton couldn't have had a better friend in the South. So tell me," —here Jesse leaned slightly toward his companion, his blue eyes canny and intense—"why is our good Governor suddenly so attracted to Jefferson and his Republicans?"

The older man shifted uncomfortably in his chair before looking his companion in the eye with his answer. "There— there's been some talk of a—a change of affection that has more to do with—now, Jesse, you understand, this is in total confidence—"

Jesse gave an impatient hand gesture to indicate this went without saying, and Carlisle continued. "Well, the scuttlebutt has it that Pinckney's had a tremendous row with his cousin Thomas. A big one, and you know how these proud old aristocratic families are. Well, dammit, man, don't give me that look! All right, I should have known you'd be perceptive to the core—as usual—in smelling out something fishy. But look, what difference does it make? I'm not about to rationalize or justify Pinckney's politics. The point is, he's switched to the right side, and I'm for taking advantage of it. Can't you see that? Good God, man, Jefferson's the only hope this country has against that little bastard Hamilton and his money-grubbing lovers of English-style aristocracy!"

Jesse smiled as he watched a smoke ring rise over his head. He studied for a moment the cheroot he held casually between strong, tanned fingers. "I had forgotten one of the reasons we've stayed such friends over the years, James. For my part, I've never found you dull. Take your strange combination of reasons in this matter, for instance. On the one hand, you're the complete pragmatist: as long as Pinckney's switched, use it to an advantage; on the other hand, you're ever the idealizing humanist: you know that Hamilton despises human nature and believes in the necessity of a privileged class with all but the titles of English aristocracy to arm it against the common masses, and so you support the Secretary of State, a man who thinks well of human nature and believes firmly in the capacity of the people to govern—"

"Providing they are educated, and as long as a majority of them live by farming," added Carlisle with a wag of his finger.

"And unless I've been your complete dupe over the years, I'll wager every penny I have that your political sympathies are the same as mine and Jefferson's!"

"You're no dupe and we both know it," Jesse smiled. He paused to watch Abigail the barmaid lean over their table to set two brimming tankards of ale in front of them. The wench cast a lingering eye over Jesse, her grin saucy and bold as she displayed a generous amount of cleavage. Jesse nodded politely in acceptance of the ale, but his look told her the added sideshow of charms would go unappreciated here. Clearly disappointed, the girl departed, her eye darting over the commonroom for easier prey.

Jesse reached for his ale and raised the tankard in a toast. "To humanism—and a Republican democracy," he offered.

Carlisle raised his own tankard, adding, "And the success of Jefferson and his belief in the virtue of the common man."

Jesse nodded and there was a pause as they drank, their silence counterbalanced by the background hum of tavern noises. The commonroom was still filled with customers, both those who were guests lodging at the inn and those who had stopped to take the mid-day meal; the shirt-sleeved figure of portly Timothy Barnes could be seen moving among them, making small talk and overseeing their comforts. At the far end, near the hearth, Abigail danced flirtatious attendance on a pair of young dandies in peacock-colored frockcoats and high heels.

"So, am I to assume," queried Carlisle as he set his empty tankard on the heavy oak table, "that you will allow me to answer Pinckney in the affirmative? Will you at least go to Columbia to hear him out on the matter?"

Jesse gave him a long look. "On one condition," he replied.

"Name it." Carlisle's look was hopeful.

"That you make it clear to him that I have in no way committed myself in the matter." Jesse gave his friend's face a careful scrutiny. "James, I have no doubt that you have done your share to sing my praises to Pinckney, and, no doubt, others up there in high office, but, frankly, I'm still rather curious as to why these men seem to want *me*. After all, I have no formal diplomatic training."

"No, nothing formal," said Carlisle, signaling to Barnes for their bill as he reached for his purse. "But all of Charleston, and I daresay, Columbia too, knows of your usefulness to certain people hereabouts, last year, when you performed several liaison duties during President Washington's tour of the state."

Jesse chuckled. "You mean I impressed them with my chief 'connection,' the fact that my father and Washington had studied together and knew each other well." He rose with a nod of appreciation of Carlisle's payment for the meal, even though it was unnecessary. They had long ago decided to alternate taking care of expenses when dining out; it saved arguing over who would assume the privilege, and today it was Carlisle's turn.

Carlisle rose. "I have some business on Meeting Street. Care to saddle up and join me for the ride?" At Jesse's nod, he continued. "Now, Jesse, about the Washington tour. You know damned well you're being modest!" At Jesse's wry grin, he amended, "And cynical!"

The hoot of laughter that greeted this made Carlisle glad they had moved outside.

"Dammit, Jess, I mean it! Whether you like it or not, your diplomatic abilities have become well known among those who count in the state, and it's about time you recognized your worth in these matters!"

More laughter, bordering on the derisive, James thought.

Finally Jesse quieted and stopped on the path leading toward the stables to give his friend a steady look. "James, if you want to call it 'diplomacy' and 'abilities,' that's fine with me, but just so you'll understand where I stand, listen to me a moment. I have no illusions about the grand art of politics in this or any other state, or in the world, for that matter. Some of the time it's a noble business but more often it's a dirty business, although sometimes a necessary one. Maybe that's why the men who met in Philadelphia in '87, to draught the Constitution, made no provision in it for political parties. But the factions within our political structure have already sprung up, haven't they?" Jesse smiled ruefully. "It cannot be helped, as an old pragmatist like you—and a sometime one like me—has to admit." He watched Carlisle's smile meet his own as they continued along the path. "Well, I'll go to Columbia, and I'll talk to our blue-blood governor who isn't looking a mite too impractical himself right now, but when I ask my questions, he'd better have the right answers if he expects any help from me."

At that moment a shrill whinny broke into the soft sounds of the summer air and both men turned their heads toward the inn's stables, now visible some fifty or so yards ahead.

"That would be your mare, Gypsy, if I don't miss a guess," Carlisle smiled.

"Never misses a greeting when she hears me coming," said Jesse. "Of course, it's a good thing I remembered a little something I have right here for her," he added, patting his waistcoat pocket, "or she'd be sure to let me know it soon enough."

Jesse paused for a moment, as if to collect his thoughts before continuing. "You know, James, although we Randalls have been major landowners—horsebreeders and planters—for decades now, my family—Garrett and I, and Father before us, are in a hell of enough trouble with a lot of people in the state for our refusal to use or own slaves—"

Suddenly Jesse's eyes darted toward the older man, and finding the hazel ones, held them fast. Silently the seconds passed.

"Ahh, comes the dawn!" he murmured, his face alight with comprehension.

"What?"

"That's it, isn't it? *That's* the reason they've decided to use my so-called diplomatic skills and, more to the point, my family connections. I hold no political threat to them! Isn't that so, James?"

Carlisle sighed. "If you mean that your refusal to own slaves—"

"That's *just* what I meant!" retorted Jesse, a gleam of satisfaction in the blue eyes. "Ten slaves, if you want to run for the House, twenty for the Senate, plus owning the necessary thousands of acres of land, of course, and in the latter the Randalls stand more than qualified, but as long as we refuse to own slaves, we can forget about running for any seat in the Legislature of South Carolina, right?"

Carlisle stood still, regarding his young friend quietly. "You always were able to see through to the facts, Jesse."

"Oh, it sometimes takes me a little while, but I usually get around to fitting in the missing pieces when I feel there are holes in a puzzle," said Jesse. "So they think I'm safe, do they?"

The smile on Jesse's face struck Carlisle oddly, and he found himself remembering a black-haired, blue-eyed youngster's identical smile once, just as a carefully aimed slingshot had found its mark some twenty or so years ago when that youngster had gotten the best of a town bully.

"Now, Jess," he soothed, "you wouldn't expect Pinckney to make any moves that weren't politically cautious, would you?"

"No, of course not." They had resumed walking, and Jesse ducked as he moved under a low-hanging branch of a mimosa tree as the path veered sharply to their right. The branch posed no problems to his shorter companion. "But let's just say I do find it amusing that the one thing that's kept half this state wary of us Randalls over the years now presents itself as an enticement for her men of power to seek Randall aid. You know, it's only been through the goodwill we've built up as generally upstanding citizens—bought out of firm principles, rooted in honor and integrity, in all of our business and personal dealings—that we've managed to establish and retain what we have in South Carolina. Now, mark me, James, I have no wish to be caught up in the selfish schemes of any man or group of men, or to be used by them for ill-begotten aims, seeing all we've worked so hard for, jeopardized. So, as I said before, I'll go to Columbia, but before I commit myself and the Randall name to anything, I'll have some right answers to my questions. Agreed?"

Carlisle smiled, looking relieved. "Agreed," he said.

They had reached the stables and a familiar nicker greeted Jesse as his mare, Gypsy, arched her sleek neck in their direction. Jesse moved to stroke the velvet nose while with his other hand he fished in his pocket for the lump of sugar he hadn't forgotten.

"How goes it, Gypsy girl? Ready for some exercise?" He watched the mare's ears prick forward as she appeared to understand each word.

"I've yet to see anything like the thing that passes between you Randalls and your horses," said Carlisle as he led his own mount from its stall. "Not only are yours the finest pieces of horseflesh anyone's ever seen, but the ones you and the family keep for personal use seem sometimes close to human. Now where's a stableboy when you want one?"

"Never mind, James, I'm used to saddling her myself—I don't usually trust outside help with her, anyway."

Since Carlisle's gelding was already saddled, he merely tightened the girth and mounted while he waited for Jesse to get his tack and do the same. Finally, they were off in the direction of the market district of Charleston. As they rode, there was further talk of the details Carlisle would set forth in his reply to Governor Pinckney, as well as exchanges of information about their families and various acquaintances. They had gone along like this for about twenty minutes or so, when they noticed the usual Friday afternoon traffic along the thoroughfare begin to thicken. Just then, a shiny black landau with the top folded back pulled alongside them. A mass of shiny black curls bobbed energetically under a chip straw bonnet in the latest mode and signalled their owner was trying to catch their attention, for the elegantly attired woman who wore them had turned her head sharply in their direction.

"Why, Jesse Randall! How you *do* disappear and reappear from time to time!" The greeting belonged to a petite, ivory-skinned woman in her early twenties, her deep, almost violet-blue eyes coyly assessing Gypsy's rider.

"Mary," Jesse nodded, his smile faintly acknowledging familiarity as it fell on the pretty brunette. "You know my friend James Carlisle?"

As Carlisle tipped his tricorn, Mary Lucas gave him the briefest acknowledging smile before returning her full attention to his companion. "La! But you *are* the *naughtiest* man," she simpered. "Isn't he, Kathryn?" She turned momentarily toward her carriage companion, a dour-faced woman of about forty whom Jesse and Carlisle recognized as her late husband's sister. "Shame on you, sir, for sending those regrets to our St. Cecelia's Day musicale last year! You must have known how we were counting on your company!"

Jesse's smile was dazzling in the August afternoon sunshine as he recalled the invitation he had managed to evade. *Invitation!* It had been more like a summons! The comely widow had been bent on pursuing their intimate relationship along more binding lines, and he, who had never made any commitments, had sensed her attempts at fashioning an invisible snare, and had smoothly—and quite finally—put an end to their involvement. Indeed, on the very afternoon before the evening he had penned his regrets, he had made a point of introducing Mary to a handsome business acquaintance, a horsebreeder from Richmond, whom she had promptly invited to her musicale as well. Later he'd heard how the widow had wasted little time in becoming well acquainted with the Richmond bachelor.

"I trust Jeffrey Burgess further conveyed my regrets at not being able to attend?" he grinned.

Mary Lucas hadn't blushed in years, but the pink crept up her neck and infused her cheeks at the reference. Nevertheless, she returned a smile as she rushed to cover her discomfort. "You're just a devil, you are, but it was certainly thoughtful of you to think of those you left behind as you retreated to that old plantation of yours. Well, what *is* it Kathryn?"

The older woman had been tapping at Mary's sleeve with her fan and now whispered something in the young widow's ear.

"Oh, yes, of course. My sister-in-law—er, do you gentlemen know Kathryn?" As both men nodded in the proper direction, Mary continued. "Well, Kathryn here reminds me we must be hurrying along. There's a major auction today, and we just have to have a couple of new maids, and, well, I heard that there's a good group of well-trained Nigras in this batch—oh, not that we'll attend, you understand." She smiled in deprecating fashion. "No well-bred woman attends a slave auction! But my brother George has gone to bid for us, and we'll be waiting at Louisa Tuttle's house, just up the street, so he can confer with us after he's looked them over, you see. Oh, very *well*, Kathryn!" She gave Jesse a long, sidelong glance as she signalled their driver to start up the matched bays that had been standing patiently before the landau. "Don't make yourself entirely scarce, Jesse. We *do* miss your stimulating company!" And with a flash of the violet-blue eyes, she leaned back on the carriage's seat and the vehicle moved briskly off into the ever-thickening crowd.

Carlisle cleared his throat conspicuously as they watched the landau depart. Then he chuckled. "I've got to hand it to you,

Jesse. You do have a way with the ladies. Both you Randall men, you and your brother, before he married, have had a reputation for winning ways, shall we say, with the fair sex?" At Jesse's responding grin, Carlisle continued. "But there's a big difference between you two in that respect."

They were cutting their way through the crowd that was moving slowly but steadily toward the square where Charleston's slave block stood.

"Do elucidate," Jesse grinned.

"Well, take that little encounter just now. Everyone knows she was your mistress for over a year—although hardly exclusively so. And all of Charleston is equally aware of how you...uh—"

"Uh, set her aside?" supplied Jesse.

Again, Carlisle cleared his throat. "Precisely. And yet, here she is, all smiles and coy looks for you. And yet—" here Carlisle lowered his voice to a level of greater intimacy "—word has it that when that female first found out you'd left town for obvious reasons, she had a purple tirade over it. Her brother George said she wasn't fit to *be* with for *two days*! And now, this! That's what's different about you. You've had 'em by the dozen, just like Garrett used to, but the thing is, when you're done with a woman, it's always as the complete gentleman. You never let them down harshly. Now, Garrett, he was something else. A total rake, to some people's way of thinking. Why, before he settled down with that sweet Christie of his, his reputation as a rogue was legendary. Yessir! Left a trail of broken hearts and outraged female sensibilities from one end of the country to the other. But you—you always manage to stay courteous and friendly with the women you've loved and left. I've never seen the likes of it before."

As Jesse listened, a subtle upturn of one corner of his mouth betrayed his amusement. "Garrett was never intentionally a rogue, James. He just never gave much of a damn about most people in those days, whereas—"

A shout cut loudly through the crowd and street noises, and the unusual quality of the sound turned all heads in its direction. It had come from the area of the auction block. Then there were several more shouts and the sounds of a scuffle, followed by noisy and threatening echoes from several people in the all-male assemblage. Jesse edged Gypsy into an opening to his left, with Carlisle following, and from their vantage point on horseback they were quickly able to view the source of the commotion.

An auctioneer stood on a large dais, approximately eight feet square. He was a small man, dark hair neatly queued, his clothing, the business attire of the day: dark blue frockcoat, pale gray vest, darker gray breeches, meeting neatly fitting hose and pewter-buckled shoes that were mildly dusty. His narrow black eyes were focusing nervously on a pair to his left; one was a large, burly man dressed informally in an open-front shirt with rolled-up sleeves, dirty leather vest, worn brown breeches and dark brown boots that had also seen much wear. Before him he prodded the hugest black man Jesse had ever seen. He was young—about twenty-five—and looked to be near Jesse's height, but he had to outweigh him by four stone, and the muscles that rippled in gigantic biceps as he strained against the wrist shackles he held before him suggested a body well conditioned by heavy labor. He was sparsely dressed in a ragged muslin shirt that had had the sleeves torn off and threadbare knee-length britches, and he was barefooted and hatless. Jesse was just trying to put together something else about him, something that seemed odd, when another sharp prod at his back from the burly auctioneer's assistant, brought an outraged bellow of rage from the shadows behind them.

It was then that Jesse took in what had prompted this scene. To the rear of the dais there stood some eighteen to twenty blacks of both sexes in varying shapes and sizes, and there was little that spoke the unusual in this array for anyone who had witnessed a slave auction before. But what held Jesse's eyes, and, indeed, held the attention now of everyone there, was the figure that stood to the far right of this line of slaves, a figure that now emerged from the shadows that had been partially concealing him and his companions. It was another black, just as huge and muscular, and *identical* in form to the one being led to the dais! *Twins!* In every respect, except for the details of their clothing, physically the mirror images of each other. But there their resemblance ended, for where the one about to go on the block seemed docile—reluctant, to be sure—but nevertheless gentle and meek, even to the large tears that rolled heavily down his cheeks, the other was a study in outraged defiance. Where his brother's head was bent in submissive defeat, his was held high and proud, the look of mayhem in the large, dark eyes, unmistakable. He, too, had been shackled, hand *and* foot, but this seemed immaterial to him as he worked massive chest and shoulder muscles in gargantuan efforts to free himself of these restraints, as well as from the grips of two additional assistants who sought to subdue him. At the cruel yank the burly assistant now gave to his brother's chains, there issued from this one's throat a sound that was barely human in its agony. In it there were the sounds of all the human misery of the ages—anguish, rage, grief and pain—untold pain.

At the sound, the docile brother raised his head but did not turn it; then it became clear to Jesse what there was about him that had been puzzling. The eyes that should have mirrored the color and shape of the defiant twin were closed, the head held in a way reminiscent of deer as they stood in the forest listening, depending on their hearing. This brother, Jesse realized, was *blind*, and as if to punctuate this discovery the sightless one stumbled as his foot hit the base of the dais steps, sending him helplessly sprawling over them.

Another scream of rage tore from the sighted twin's throat, and then a more intelligible sound—"Festus!" screamed the giant. "Festus, *no*! Dey ain' gonna do it, man! We goes t'gethah o' we *dies*!"

"Shut up!" shouted one of the men who were trying to restrain the obstreperous twin. "Shut up, or ye'll git this!" He brandished a horsewhip threateningly.

"Now, now, gentlemen," soothed the auctioneer, finally finding his tongue. Nervously he clutched a paper in one hand as he signalled with the other for the crowd's attention. "We don't want too much of the wrong kind of excitement, do we, gentlemen?" His eyes darted tentatively over the crowd, back toward the potential source of trouble, and then to the assistant who was doing his best to help the fallen black to his feet and up the steps.

"Come on, James," whispered Jesse tightly. "I've seen about all I can take." He urged Gypsy forward a couple of yards.

"Hold on a second, Jesse." Carlisle drew his gelding alongside the mare and was placing a restraining hand on Jesse's
shoulder. "Just what do you think you can accomplish, son?"

"Think! Not *think*, man, I *know*! You heard what's going
on! They're selling those two individually—separating them!
Damn it to hell! It's inhuman! And I haven't seen treatment like
that at an auctioneer's block since I was a boy, before they
ended the slave import trade here. Somebody's got to teach
those bastards—"

"And you think Jesse Randall, of the famous slavery-hating
Randalls, is going to have an influence here?" Carlisle's voice
was calm, but there was an underlying tinge of urgency to it. A
few nearby heads turned in curiosity, despite the muffled quality of their conversation, and Carlisle hastened to make his
point in even lower tones. "Son, there's not a damned thing
you can do about the immediate situation here, short of starting a bloody riot in which you're sure to come up short."

"Do you expect me to just stand by and watch this sickening display of—"

"Hell, no!" exclaimed James. Then the hazel eyes narrowed. "But there's more than one way to skin a rabbit."

Jesse looked at him carefully, a respectful gleam growing in
the blue eyes, and slowly he nodded. "Go on."

Carlisle signalled with his head for them to pull aside of the
crowd as the auctioneer's stentorian tones could be heard
summarizing the attributes and vital statistics of the brother the
other had called "Festus."

" . . . trained as a blacksmith's assistant, sound of body and
mind, except for his blindness, obedient . . ."

"All right, James, and it had better be good," Jesse whispered, his eyes fastened firmly on the rebellious brother who,
by now, had been gagged, and bound with heavy rope about the
chest and shoulders as well. But the proud head was still high,
the fury in the dark eyes, noble and chilling.

"What," asked Carlisle, "short of starting a brawl, do you
figure is the best you can do to help those two poor devils?"

Jesse's answer took only seconds. "Buy them both," he answered.

Carlisle looked relieved. "At least you're thinking rationally, like the Jesse I know," he said. "For a minute there, I

thought that Randall temper was going to win. Very well, and then what? Set them free?''

"Of course. No Randall's owned a slave since that day my father took us on that slaver to see the reality behind the institution. You know that, James.''

"Yes, yes, but then what? Will you offer them jobs at Riverview? Seems they're trained in blacksmithing, from what we've been hearing.''

"Yes, I can use such skills," said Jesse as his eyes moved to the dais. The auctioneer was winding up his speech, and Jesse knew the bidding would begin soon.

"Well, I'd like to know how you're going to pull it off in a town where you're known for your anti-slavery attitudes.'' Carlisle looked out over the crowd. "There are several men here we both recognize who would immediately grow suspicious, and at the very least, they'll force the bidding up to ridiculous heights, just to out-do you and your sympathies. At the worst, they might not leave it at that. Then what happens to all the goodwill you and your family have so carefully established?''

"Your point, Carlisle," said Jesse urgently. The auctioneer was asking for a starting bid.

"Let *me* bid and buy them for you. If I move away from you now, chances are, nobody will make the connection. Once I have the blind one at a fair price, the other shouldn't be a problem. At this point, I wonder if he'll even get an opening bid on that devil. No one wants a troublemaker, so the price will be low, despite the size and strength of him. You can repay me when we meet back at my office, where I can draw up freedmen's papers for the pair of them. Is that acceptable?'' The florid face had grown rosier in mounting excitement and satisfaction with this plan.

Jesse gave him an admiring look and raised his arm in a brief salute. "There's another reason I'm your friend, James. I've ever admired quick and rational thinking in a tight situation. See you at your office.'' He threw Carlisle a quick smile, turned Gypsy's head and cantered away.

"Another cup of coffee, Jesse?'' Johanna Carlisle's soft gray eyes regarded Jesse affectionately as she appeared in the doorway of the cozy sitting room that was adjacent to her husband's office in their townhouse on Oak Street. "I've just had Delia brew a fresh pot from a new blend of Jamaican beans she purchased down on Dock Street on Tuesday." The small woman's soft gray curls were tucked under a frilly white mobcap, and she cocked her head slightly to one side as she added with a shy smile, "I know it's one of your favorite brews."

Jesse returned the smile. "Since you've gone to all that trouble, Johanna, yes, thanks, I'd love another cup." Jesse grinned at the little retreating figure before settling back in the flame-stitched Chippendale wing chair by the door. How many times during the past twenty years or so had he sat in this room accepting this dear lady's hospitality? She was a shy, quiet soul, rarely given to more than a couple of sentences of conversation at a stretch, but he always felt comfortable in her society—welcome in the Carlisle home. Perhaps it was because she and James had known his parents well, perhaps it was just because they were warm, kind people, but Jesse had always felt a closeness to the childless couple over the years. He remembered coming here as a boy with Garrett in those first years after the massacre that had claimed the lives of Marianne and Jeremy Randall— Good God! Was it almost two dozen years ago? That had been a dark period in the lives of the two brothers who had escaped their parents' fate that bleak November day, merely by virtue of the fact that they had been away from Riverlea, the original Randall plantation, on a hunting trip with some Cherokee friends. Leaning his head back, Jesse closed his eyes for a moment as he tried to recall the faces of the parents he had deeply loved and lost so early. The memory was dim with time. There had been a pair of miniatures miraculously entrusted to the care of Johanna Carlisle who had offered to take them to be properly framed as a favor to her friend Marianne, thus allowing them escape from the fire. He wasn't sure, if they hadn't survived, if he'd still be able to put together his parents' features accurately. And it had been bits and pieces of recollections from Johanna and James, he was sure, that had enabled him to keep alive his other memories of those two magnificent people—Marianne's habit of humming to herself softly as she went about the house, or of snapping her fingers several times, quickly, as she searched for the precise word or phrase; Jeremy's habit of gesturing with the pipe that never seemed to be out of his hand, unless he was on horseback; his father's tall frame as it bent over a small boy's model fort, examining the handiwork, dark head nodding with approval at the details of the stockade fence.

The front door latch clicked loudly in the stillness of the late afternoon as James' voice broke through Jesse's reverie. "Damned Middletons! You'd have thought they'd have had enough sense to know I wouldn't quit that easily. Er, sorry, Johanna, m'dear. Know how you'd have me mind my tongue more, once I'm within your hearing. Where's Jesse?"

Jesse rose as Carlisle came through the door. "I take it the bidding went higher than you anticipated?" he queried.

James' face was as flushed as he'd ever seen it. "That's putting it mildly, Jesse, and on the second one, not Festus," he added with a growl. "Seems Middleton Place lost its best blacksmith to the fever last winter."

Suddenly James stopped in his tracks, and, looking as if he'd misplaced something, turned back toward the door. "Well, come on, don't just stand there! Come in, come in! I told you we don't stand on formalities around here. We haven't used a separate servants' entrance in years!"

In a moment a massive dark figure emerged through the front door, his wooly head just clearing the aperture. It was the sighted twin, and in step right behind him, the blind one called Festus. As they entered the room where Carlisle and Jesse stood, the first brother regarded the two white men warily.

"Dis be de new massah, suh?"

Carlisle chuckled. "He's the one who's paying for you, the one I told you about, yes. But I'm afraid he'll be your *master* for only a few more minutes." With this, James went quickly to a cluttered desk nearby and reached for a pair of spectacles as he sat down.

The sighted black threw Jesse a suspicious glance. "You means t' sell us agin...suh?" The "suh" was obviously a carefully debated addition.

"Oh, Jesse," said Carlisle, over his shoulder, "I haven't told them about the arrangement. Thought you'd like to have the pleasure. You certainly have the right."

Jesse's forehead creased in concern. "I'd have spared them even these few additional minutes of not knowing, James, but, all right, since it's already done." He faced the two black men, looking the nearer twin in the eye. "My name is Jesse Randall, and I don't hold with owning slaves. That man over there is my solicitor, James Carlisle, and what he's doing at that desk is drawing up freedmen's papers for the two of you. In a few minutes you'll be free men."

The blind twin's head, which had been lowered until now, flew up at the words, the expression on his face, incredulous. The other one took a step backward, almost slamming into his brother's chest. "Dis—dis some kind 'o crazy—*mean* 'n crazy *joke*?" he shouted. "You playin' wid us, mistah?"

Jesse shook his head, the expression in his eyes bordering on sadness. "It's not a joke," he said quietly. "I don't believe in slavery, and I'm setting you free, although I hope you'll both come and work for me, for fair wages, on my plantation. And I'm sorry you would have to think this might be some kind of cruel joke, but I can understand why you would, and...I'm just sorry, that's all."

"Vulcan!" shouted the blind twin. "He *means* it! Ain' no man whut sounds sincere lahk dat, gonna flim-flam us! Ah *knows* voices, and Ah tells yo, dis one, we kin *trust*!"

The one newly identified as Vulcan turned and placed mammoth black hands on his brother's shoulders. "Festus, oh Festus, Ah heahd 'im, but—but Ah kin hahdly—oh, Festus, we ain' nevah gonna have t' worry about losin' each othah agin—*nevah*!"

He turned slowly back toward Jesse then, the tears streaming freely down his cheeks, and stuck out a trembling hand. "Name's Vulcan, Mistah Randall, an' Ah sweahs, Ah'll give y'all a honest day's wuk fo' a honest day's wages, an' so will mah brothah, Hephaestus, heah. An' God bless yo', suh."

"The name's Jesse, and I believe you will." Jesse took the proffered hand and clasped it and then did the same with the outstretched hand of the blind man, whose face also ran wet with unashamed tears.

"Hephaestus!" exclaimed Carlisle, who had been watching the proceedings from his place at the desk, and whose eyes also looked suspiciously moist. "That would be the Greek god of fire and metalworking. I'd better look up the spelling in this old

Greek primer here." He turned toward a bookcase at his right side. "An appropriate epithet, young man."

"And 'Vulcan' was the Roman version," offered Jesse. "Come and sit down, Vulcan and Hephaestus. We have a lot to talk about."

"Jus' 'Festus,' is all, suh. Jus' call me Festus," grinned the black as his brother led him to a chair.

And as Jesse and Vulcan joined him, Johanna Carlisle appeared with a pot of tea and biscuits on a tray, looking for all the world as if the appearance of two huge blacks in the parlor was an everyday occurrence. Then four male voices merged quickly in a steady conversation that was to last far into the evening.

Chapter Five

⚜

J esse gazed with satisfaction at the long sweep of green lawn that sloped gently downward from the new foundations of his nearly completed home; his eyes followed its descent toward the river which could be seen in the near distance, and which had given it its name: Riverview. It was a good enough name, he felt, although hardly very original or creative as names go, but appropriate. This, his own plantation, had been carved out of the thousands of tidewater acres that had formed the original estate of his parents, an estate he had co-inherited with his brother Garrett years ago, and that property was called River-*lea*. It had been shared equally by the brothers during all the time they had remained single, but a little less than three years ago Garrett had at last married, and according to an agreement they had made years earlier, as the first to wed, had retained the Big House they had always shared, for himself and his bride, while unmarried Jesse had taken his half of the land and built himself this new Big House on one of its choicest spots.

And not only a Big House had been built in the incredible space of about two years, thought Jesse as he sat perched high atop the roof of the new dwelling, where master mason Josiah Purdy had called him to approve his final work on the east chimney a few minutes ago. Jesse's eyes glanced from left to right over the landscape, resting briefly here and there on the numerous outbuildings that dotted the scenery; barns, stables, granaries and the like stood new and complete in the summer sunshine, and Jesse again felt a surge of satisfaction. He had acted as his own planner-architect and sometime builder in this new assemblage, frequently spending time on the site of each piece of construction, as he was now, sitting high above the ground, looking for all the world like one of the many master craftsmen he had hired and not at all like the wealthy master of the place.

"It looks just fine, Josiah. Of course, I knew it would. There's nothing that can be worked with trowel, brick and mortar that you can't turn into a masterpiece. It's been a privilege to have had you on the site all these months." Jesse extended a handshake to the middle-aged craftsman who, like him, straddled the crest of the main roof, and the man's sun-wizened features broke into a toothy grin.

"Pleasure to have worked for ye, Mistah Jesse ... and *with* ye," he added. "Ain't too many men of yer station whut'll roll up their shirtsleeves 'n join in. A real pleasure, suh."

Jesse touched his fingers to his hatless head in acknowledgment of the compliment, swung a long, well-muscled leg over the roof's crest to join the other one in preparation to slide downward, and then stopped as he spotted a large figure emerging from the summer kitchen below on his far left. "Vulcan!" he shouted. "How's that flue working now?"

The black man raised his head, drawing a hand over his eyes to shield them from the sun as they squinted in Jesse's direction. "Smooth as buttah, Mistah Jesse. Ol' Zeke jes' hadda git tol' how t' wuk it, dass all," he grinned.

Jesse nodded and grinned back. He hadn't regretted for an instant making Vulcan his new overseer. No, not even when two of his white staff had quit at the news, refusing to take orders from a black, freedman or not. Intelligence like his must not be wasted, thought Jesse, as he lowered himself onto the scaffolding on the house's east façade. Actually, he had found both brothers extremely quick and eager to learn, but of course, Festus, with his handicap, had his limitations, although Jesse marveled at the manner in which the man functioned as a blacksmith without benefit of sight. But he used his brother's eyes as they both plied that trade, for Vulcan had made it clear that he would accept the overseer's position only if he were allowed to continue to work with Festus at the forge. Jesse had readily agreed and now had to admire the pluck of those two,

Vulcan's industriousness never waning as he managed two jobs at once, Festus' skills as worthy as any sighted man in his trade.

Suddenly the echo of horses' hooves broke in on his thoughts, the sound coming from just beyond the bend of the main drive as it curved around a copse of trees a couple of hundred yards away. Then a pair of riders appeared in the distance, and even if he had not had his vantage point from the scaffold, Jesse knew he would have recognized them from their mounts. Grinning, he watched the two powerful stallions, one black, the other gray, canter up the drive.

He hadn't seen Garrett and Christie in the week since he'd come back from Charleston, having been eager to head straight for home with Vulcan and Festus and settle them as quickly as possible in their new life. Now, as he hurriedly reached for the rope ladder that swung from the scaffold's base, he realized he'd missed their company.

"Vulcan," he called, "go and fetch Festus, would you? There are some people I'd like the two of you to meet."

"Sho thing, suh!" replied the black man before breaking into a loping gait as he headed for the group of buildings that contained the forge.

As Jesse's feet met the ground, he hailed the oncoming riders with a wave of his arm. "Hurry up, you two! It's about time you showed your fancy faces!"

Slowing their magnificent mounts to a walk, the new arrivals neared the white-columned portico that ran across the entire front of the Big House. The man, who was large and raven haired, closely resembled Jesse, except for eyes that were a deep green, instead of blue; the woman, much younger than either of them, was fair haired and exquisitely beautiful.

"Listen to him, Christie. You'd think we were the ones who'd cut right past Riverlea after a fortnight in Charleston, never stopping to say hello."

"Now, Garrett, darling, I'm sure our favorite neighbor had his reasons." Christie Randall smiled as Jesse extended his arms and helped her dismount, and her smile reaffirmed her in his mind as the loveliest woman he knew, both inside and out. Her eyes, the color of deep, sea-foam turquoise, twinkled in good humor as they met his, and her clear, melodious voice hinted at laughter as she added, "Of course, I've learned never to pry too deeply into whatever it is that keeps my handsome brother-in-law in the city, but I do wonder what's been so all-consuming at Riverview in the week since we heard he'd returned. How are you, Jess?''

"I couldn't be better, little one," smiled Jesse as he took charge of the big gray stallion she'd ridden. "Here, let's tether these big boys over here, out of the sun.'' He gestured toward the black stallion from which his brother was dismounting as he began to lead Christie's gray. "These two been behaving themselves together lately, or do we tether them a mile or two apart?'' Jesse's eyebrows cocked an inquiring expression in the direction of his two guests.

Garrett's eyes met his wife's and they broke into simultaneous laughter at the question.

"Better separate them just a wee bit, little brother," chuckled Garrett. "Thunder's never been a problem at Riverlea, as you know, but my Jet—well, just last Sunday Christie and I were discussing how well the two of them had been getting along together and how maybe Jet had finally accepted Thunder, when, on the way home from church, mind you, that black son of Satan got a whiff of a new mare one of the Beatty boys had just brought over from Ireland, and although Thunder wasn't with us at the time—Christie rides to services in the barouche—as soon as Jet got back home and was being led to his stall—and past Thunder's stall—why, damned if he didn't reach out and nip his unwanted stablemate right on the neck!''

"Poor Thunder," laughed Christie. "There he stood, peacefully munching his oats one minute, and finding himself the victim of a jealous would-be Romeo the next. Oh, but if you could only have seen the look of outraged indignation he wore!''

"Wore!" exclaimed Garrett. "He's been going about with an expression of righteous disdain all week! Take a look at him now!''

And as if on cue, as the three of them watched, Thunder, who'd been tethered loose-reined at a hitching post a good distance away from the black, proceeded to turn his powerful head, in dramatic fashion, into the distance and away from the other stallion. Then, as if to punctuate the action, he gave a mighty snort and twitched his long tail in Jet's direction.

This time Jesse joined his guests in the laughter as he ushered them up the great steps onto the veranda.

"Sorry I can't offer you two any chairs. Will these do?" he asked, gesturing at a group of overturned wooden kegs.

"Oh, hasn't any of your furniture arrived yet?" questioned Christie as she took her seat amid a graceful swirl of deep blue riding skirt. "I would have guessed the pieces from Newport and Philadelphia, at least, might have begun to arrive, even if the European—"

Seeing her brother-in-law's eyes suddenly focus on a point behind her and past her left shoulder, Christie broke off and turned to see what had claimed his attention. Walking up the path toward them were two of the largest human beings she'd ever seen. The black men were neatly dressed in well-made garments that were suitable for working about a plantation. Both wore full-sleeved casual shirts of white homespun. The man on the left, who now stood looking at them with an expression of open expectation on his face, wore tan knee breeches over plain white cotton hose and new-looking brown leather shoes with pewter buckles. His identical companion wore black breeches with sturdy black work boots that were covered with a fine layer of soot and ash. Over all this he wore a leather blacksmith's apron. She saw that his eyes were closed as he stood quietly beside his twin with an expectant smile on his face.

"Vulcan! Festus! Join us up here, will you?" Jesse rose as he gestured a welcome. "Christie, Garrett, I'd like you to meet two new friends who also happen to work here—Festus and Vulcan—" Here Jesse smiled as he placed an arm about each gigantic shoulder—"This will will be the first time I'm using the new surname you've chosen for yourselves, gentlemen," he smiled "—Festus and Vulcan Noslave."

Garrett Randall held out his hand to Vulcan, who was the nearer of the two, while Christie, who by now had deduced Festus was blind, rose and reached out her slender gloved hand and touched the aproned man on the arm. "A pleasure to meet you both," she intoned warmly.

Festus felt the gesture and found her small hand with his own, the enormous size of it totally engulfing hers. "Mah pleasuh, Miz Randall," he smiled.

"And mine," added Vulcan as he nodded in Christie's direction.

Then Garrett found the hand of the blind man and introductions were completed. "I knew little brother had something, or some*one*, special he was hiding over here all week," said Garrett as they all found seats on the kegs. "And now that I've met you gentlemen, I can begin to guess why."

"Little!" exclaimed Vulcan. He turned toward Festus. "Dis *little* brothah heah, ain' but two o' three inches *biggah* dan his brothah we bin hearin' 'bout, Festus," he grinned. "Guess it mus' be all 'bout Mistah Jesse bein' de *youngah*. Now, does yo' spose Ah kin git t' call yo' *little brothah*, bein' as how Ah is 'leben minutes oldah dan yo' is?"

Festus grinned. "Funny how dese *oldah* brothahs kin git uppity 'bout whut don' 'mount t' nuthin', ain' it, Mistah Jesse?" And with this he purposefully opened both sightless eyes so he could cast an exaggerated wink in Jesse's direction.

"Oh, no!" groaned Christie. "Not another pair of brothers I have to keep an eye on when I'm around, just so they don't run out of breath making quips about each other! Now all four of you gentlemen behave yourselves and settle down so I can hear the Noslave brothers' story," she admonished, brandishing a wagging finger in their faces. "I'm just dying of curiosity, you see."

So with sheepish smiles in her direction, Jesse and the two black men began to fill Garrett and Christie in on the specifics of the brothers' appearance in Jesse's life.

Later, as this explanation drew to an end, Christie went over to Thunder to get a picnic basket she had brought along, spreading a welcome repast out over a blanket on the veranda floor. As they partook of the various morsels that ranged from tenderly succulent baked grouse and candied yams to loaves of freshly baked, crusty bread, pickled watermelon rind, creamy golden cheese and deep-fried chicken, the conversation turned to talk of the work being done on the plantation as it neared its completion. Christie was just watching with satisfaction as Festus plopped an entire large, juicy peach into his mouth, when she remembered one of the reasons for the visit.

"Oh, Garrett! The mail! Did we forget it? I didn't see it in Thunder's pack and—"

"No, love, I've been carrying it right here," said her husband as he extricated a long white vellum envelope from a pocket inside his waistcoat. "Almost forgot about it in the course of meeting these two, though." He handed the letter to Jesse. "This came yesterday, addressed to you at Riverlea."

Mildly curious as to who would still be writing to him at the old address—he'd been receiving all his mail at Riverview for a couple of months now—Jesse examined the envelope.

"Mind if I open it right now?" he asked.

"Christie would start imitating Thunder's air of indignant injury if you didn't," said Garrett. "She's been curious as a puppy just let out of the litter box ever since it arrived."

"Garrett Randall, that's a disgusting exaggeration!" Christie's eyes sparked turquoise fire. "Puppy, indeed!"

Grinning, Garrett reached for his wife's waist and drew her firmly to him as he planted a kiss atop her delicate little nose. "Well, you've a point there, love. Your nose certainly isn't cold and wet."

"Ooh!" seethed Christie, hardly mollified by the gesture, and certainly not by his words. "I was merely curious about a letter that was hand delivered by a courier who came all the way from Columbia, that's all." She wrinkled her nose at her husband. "Just say you weren't curious yourself, Garrett. I *dare* you!"

Laughing, her husband caught up her delicate, heart-shaped face between both of his massive brown hands and, looking lovingly into her turquoise eyes, said, "Probably twice as curious as you, pet." And he kissed her lightly on the lips.

Instantly Christie melted as she returned her husband's gaze. "Ohh . . . but why—"

"Because sometimes I can't resist the teasing that brings those blue-green sparks to these eyes," replied Garrett with a soft smile.

At this juncture there was a loud and conspicuous clearing of throats as both black men rose awkwardly to their feet.

"Hah!" exclaimed Jesse. "Two more embarrassed victims of you lovebirds! Now, cease and desist, you two! Can't you see Vulcan and Festus aren't used to your open displays? It's bad enough I have to put up with the two of you mushing around all the time." He turned to the twins. "My brother and his wife are the scandal of the tidewater belt, gentlemen. A man and wife in love with each other, and nearly three years married, too!''

The two black men found their composure at this and grinned delightedly at the still-embracing couple.

"Festus," chuckled Vulcan, "dese white folk 'mos aks lahk black folk, don' dey?"

"Sho do seem so, brothah," Festus grinned. He accepted his brother's arm as they made their way toward the steps. "Really has been a pleasuh meetin' bof o' yo' Mistah 'n Miz Randall, an' thank y'all fo' dat delicious meal," he added.

"Call us Christie and Garrett please, or just as soon as you feel comfortable doing it," smiled Garrett. "And the pleasure—and honor—has been ours."

A moment of common understanding passed among them and the twins took their leave. Then husband and wife turned back toward Jesse, finding him deeply engrossed in the letter from Columbia; he looked disturbed.

Garrett glanced at his wife, who returned his glance with a questioning frown. Garrett shrugged and quietly began to pack up the remains of their picnic luncheon indicating she should join him. Presently the clink and clatter of china plates and dishes met with Jesse's mildly reproving voice.

"Sit down, you two. I'll help you clean up in a minute, and I know you're both wondering what's in this letter. Moreover, I'm in need of sharing it, so—" he smiled at them now, adding more softly, "please . . ."

Nodding, Christie and Garrett took their seats.

"It's from Etienne Devercaux," said Jesse, his voice heavy. "He's Deirdre's father," he added, and Christie thought she saw a look of pain in the blue eyes before they quickly shuttered and bent on the page he held in his hand.

"My Dear Jesse,
"I thought long and hard before sending you this letter. You have not heard from me for some many months, now, for I have been ill and bedridden for the better part of a year. Even now, this missive is being penned for me by my good friend and family priest, Père Edouard-Gérard, for I am too weak to ply quill and ink.

"For reasons I hope to afford you in person, I am requesting your presence here at Le Beau Château. Please, I beg of you, come quickly, for I fear I have little time left in this world, and I am in great need of your help.

> Yours in friendship,
> Etienne Devereaux"

There was a long silence as Jesse continued to stare at the paper in his hand. In the near distance the steady clanging of hammer on metal indicated the twins were back at the forge. Garrett and Christie bore looks of patient expectation as they waited for Jesse to speak. At last Jesse raised his head and looked at Christie.

"Garrett knows who Etienne Devereaux is and who his daughter—who Deirdre was," he said, "but do you recall ever hearing their names?" At Christie's negative shake of the head, Jesse continued. "But you do recall my telling you of a girl...of a young woman, once, a woman I was to have married?"

Christie's recollection was immediate, and the look on her face told him as much. Compassion flooded her features, as she nodded gravely at him. "She died before you could wed, didn't she?" Christie whispered.

"Of the smallpox, on a summer night some seven years ago," said Jesse softly. "She was only sixteen, too young to wed, her parents said, and although I felt otherwise, I agreed to a year's wait—and separation—as a parental means of testing our love, I suspect." Here Jesse looked away from both of them and off toward the distant horizon before continuing. "Her mother died only a year or so ago, but before that I kept in close touch with both parents over the years, by letter and through occasional visits. One of the things they made a point of letting me know during this time was how deeply they regretted having made us wait, and I—" Here Jesse sighed deeply before turning his attention back to them. "I, having no wish to see their grief and loss compounded by guilt—"

"—made it your business to comfort them and do your best to assuage that guilt," Garrett finished for him.

"You could put it that way," said Jesse, rising at last from his makeshift stool. "Well, let me help you pack up the remains of this much appreciated meal," he added, "and then, if you both will excuse me, I must prepare for a journey to Columbia."

Waving him away, Christie resumed the clean-up herself, saying, "For heaven's sake, Jesse, go and pack. We can handle this, and from the urgent tone of that letter, I'd say you'll need all the time you can spare to make it to that poor man in time."

Jesse smiled and kissed her lightly on the cheek in thanks, then turned toward his brother. "Garrett, I'm leaving Vulcan in charge here, but if anything should come up that he can't handle, would you—"

"Consider it done, Jess. I'll ride over every day just to be sure, though I have a feeling that's all I'll be doing. Those brothers have a capable look about them. Now, if you don't mind my acting too much like an older brother, will you get the hell out of here and be on your way?"

When Jesse had disappeared within the house, Garrett rose from the veranda floor and gave Christie a careful look.

"You're concerned about this letter," said Christie as she carefully thrust the last empty bowl into her saddlepack. "Or, more specifically, about Jesse," she added as her husband helped her to a standing position.

"Let's just say I was wondering," mused Garrett.

"About—?"

Garrett smiled at her. "Curious chit, aren't you, little one?" But at his wife's look of quick annoyance, he softened. "Very well, love," he laughed, and then grew serious. "Yes, I am concerned about Jess. You know, until he mentioned it just now, I hadn't realized it's been seven years since . . . Deirdre. Seven years . . . that's a long time."

"For what?" questioned Christie, ever eager to get to the bottom of her curiosity.

"Oh, a long time to be without a woman, I was thinking, though that's not exactly as it sounds." He smiled at his wife. "What I mean is, that although Jess is never at a loss for—um—female companions, they're never of the—er—more serious kind."

"You mean he has mistresses by the score, but he never seems to have any wifely prospects, right?" asked Christie, a knowing gleam in her eye.

Garrett grinned down at her. "My sweet young wife seems to have come by a great deal of worldliness since that state of innocence I found her in a little less than three years ago."

"Well, I am married to *you*, Garrett Randall," Christie teased, "so how could you expect otherwise?" Christie's grin was as wide as her husband's now. "But, seriously, darling, do you think Jesse's been avoiding marriage, then? I mean, his tragic affair with this Deirdre—"

"Be careful how you characterize it, love," said Garrett as he relieved her of her saddlepack and began to escort her toward the horses. "This was no casual affair. The lady may have been young, and their involvement, brief, but from what I've been able to glean from Jess over the years, it was deep and serious, and I'm afraid *tragic* is right. Make no mistake, Jess was hurt by that loss, perhaps more than any of us have realized."

"But, Garrett," said Christie, "lots of men lose sweethearts—even wives—and get over it to love again. I can't believe that Jesse's any different. Prudent, maybe, and more willing to take his time than most, but surely he's not the sort who would spend his life mourning a dead woman! I know him fairly well after nearly three years, although not as well as you, but I just feel your brother is far too full of life to do such a thing, wouldn't you say?"

Garrett gave her a hand in mounting Thunder before responding. "Christielove, there are all kinds of reasons a man might want to avoid the altar. Take me, for example." He paused to check the girths of Thunder's and Jet's saddles and then mounted, a wry smile on his face as he looked at her. "Before you came into my life, love, I was too angry with the world and almost everyone in it to ever make room inside me for loving a woman. I think we Randalls are like that. When we love, we love deeply, putting our hearts and our very souls into it." Here he gave her a warm smile. "My father loved my mother with a depth and sureness that was so abiding and so apparent to all who knew them, none could mistake it, even after being in their presence but a few moments, and she, him. The only thing that softened the tragedy of their deaths for me was the fact that they died together. Even at the age of sixteen I knew that if either had been left behind by the other's death—"

"—the other would not have wanted to go on," Christie finished for him softly. "Yes, my darling, I can—do—understand that kind of love."

"*We* understand it, love," whispered her husband, his green eyes meeting hers.

They had turned their stallions' heads toward home by now, and were moving at a slow pace.

"But, still," added Christie, "with Jesse I can't see the signs of there having been such an involvement. Why, he acts very much like a handsome, carefree man of the world—and about town, as the saying goes, I daresay—and there's been no indication of brooding, or—or a heart stopped up with grief, has there?"

Her husband turned in his saddle to give her a quiet look before answering. "I wonder..." he mused. "You know, once, when Jess was five or six years old, he had a dog. He was a big black, shaggy thing, named Bear. Lord, did that boy love that dog! And Bear, him, of course. The two of them were inseparable. Our mother was pretty strict about animals being allowed in the house, but Bear bedded down on a rug on the floor near Jesse's bed because she knew—well, to make the story short, one awful day, Bear was accidentally shot and killed by a poacher on our land. Probably took him for a real bear—he was that big. We were all greatly upset, I remember, but Jesse . . ." Garrett shook his head to himself.

"Yes, what did Jesse do?" prompted Christie. "Did he cry, scream, go wild in grief? What?"

"That's just it," said Garrett. "We never saw him do any of those things. He just went quiet. Stopped talking, for the most part, except for necessary things, you know, like 'Pass the salt,' or such. And it lasted for weeks!"

"Well, what did you do—or your parents—what did they do? What happened?"

"Well, I guess a couple of months must have passed, because the seasons changed, and it grew to spring, and then summer. Yes, it was summer, because I remember it was warm when one day Father came home with a lump under his shirt— a squirming lump that, because the shirt was thin muslin, it became apparent to all, was a puppy, a sweet, new, black, shaggy puppy, looking for all the world like Bear looked when he was a whelp. Well, we all made a fuss over it, and the new-comer quickly found a loving home with us, but Jesse . . . Jesse never treated him any differently from any of the other animals about the place. There was the occasional pat on the head and a warm word or two, but Shaggy, as we called him, never found a place near Jesse's bed, as Bear had. No, Jess was content to let him sleep out in the barn with the hunters and barn cats and livestock. In fact, he made it quite clear, even at that young age, that this pup was not to replace Bear in his heart.'' Garrett stopped his horse a moment then to look at his wife. ''But that's not all,'' he added. ''To this day, Jesse's never allowed himself to become attached to an animal in the same way again. Oh, I know, he's awfully fond of his mare, Gypsy, but she's his personal saddlehorse, and after all, we Randalls breed horses. They're our business, and it would be pretty strange if we didn't have a fondness for our own horses. But it's not the same as it was between Jess and Bear,'' he said, looking off into the woods up ahead of them. ''No, not the same at all.''

Then, after a moment's silence that allowed his words to sink in, Garrett urged his stallion forward as he called to his wife. ''Come on, I'll race you to those trees!''

Chapter Six

Jesse's first impression of Le Beau Château was that it hadn't changed much in the two years since he'd seen it. High atop a hill in the Upcountry wilderness, the mansion itself looked for all the world like a French château of the sort he'd seen when on his Grand Tour a dozen or so years ago. He remembered stopping once in the Southwest of France, not far from Bordeaux, in the ancient feudal domain of Perigord, and taking lodging for the night in such a château. Indeed, upon first arriving here some seven and a half years ago to purchase some horses from Etienne Devereaux, he had remarked to him that the huge iron entrance gates leading to a white crushed stone allée, edged with clipped laurel as it was, was totally reminiscent of the château in which he had spent that night in his youth; then he was astonished to learn that Devereaux himself hailed from Perigord and had designed Le Beau Château after his family's estate there. Now, as he approached those gates, Jesse winced as he forced away another recollection—the memory of a shyly smiling, sun-kissed face peering at him from behind a potted fruit tree that stood beside one of a pair of stone lions at the main entrance, beneath the black-roofed façade. Deirdre. Even now, he couldn't approach this place without remembering that first enchanting glimpse of her. He shrugged off the moment of indulgent nostalgia as two liveried footmen approached, and he had just enough time to note that the fruit trees were still there, but grown older and several feet taller over the years.

As an unfamiliar groom appeared to take Gypsy, Jesse asked him, "Where is old Serge? He never missed coming to take my mare personally. He acquired a certain fondness for her over the years."

"Alas, sir. Abed with the gout, I fear," answered the groom. "However, you are expected, Monsieur Randall, and I have been given personal instructions by the old one himself as to the special care I am to give your mare. Rest assured, sir, Gypsy will receive only the best from me here at Le Beau Château."

"What is your name?" queried Jesse.

"André, sir."

"Well, André, I see you are French, after all, despite your perfect American English. I thank you for your assurances and, as you come recommended by Serge, I will trust Gypsy to your care completely. But give old Serge a message for me, will you? Tell him I'll be by his quarters to look in on him later, and that I won't hesitate for a moment to scold him for dining too richly on old Mathilde's cooking, for it is surely that I suspect as the culprit in his attack of gout."

Grinning, the groom swiftly nodded. "That I will, sir, but I'm afraid such chastisement will do little good. As you know, we Frenchmen love to eat well, and in that, no one is more French than Serge Montelle." Then, with a soft word to Gypsy, André was off toward the stables and Jesse found himself being ushered by the footmen inside the double-doored entrance to the château.

Once inside the main entrance hall, he immediately appreciated the coolness created by the château's heavy white limestone walls, for it was late summer, and the three-day journey on horseback had been accomplished at the height of the hot and humid season. Seeing no one about, but noting the quick departure of the footmen toward the doors near the end of the hall, he decided to curb his impatient impulse to dash upstairs in search of Etienne and forced himself to peruse his immediate surroundings. The foyer's walls consisted of a beautiful seventeenth-century boiserie, or heavily carved paneling, painted a creamy white that contrasted smartly with the waxed, red brick flooring beneath his boots, and he noted with annoyance the heavy layer of trail dust gracing his normally well-polished footwear as he glanced downward.

Just then there was a soft rustle of petticoats as the housekeeper, Mistress Delaney, appeared at the doors through which

he'd seen the footmen pass. He smiled as he observed her wad-
dling toward him looking a bit distraught as she pushed an errant gray curl beneath her snowy white mobcap.

"Ah, Mister Jesse, lad, 'tis right sorry I am, not t've been
here t' greet ye," she called in an out-of-breath voice that had
lost none of the Irish brogue she'd brought with her to American shores nearly twenty-five years earlier when she'd accompanied her mistress, Aileen Devereaux, to her new home. The
plump little figure slowed down as she approached him and
now Jesse noted the worried frown she wore and the normally
pleasant features of her face that were etched with lines of strain
and sadness. "'Tis expected ye be," she whispered, glancing
with concern toward the side doors behind which Jesse knew
lay the stairs that led to the château's upper stories, and the
family's bedchambers. "We've nary a moment t' waste, sir,"
she added, "so if ye'll follow me, I'll be takin' ye t' *his* chamber."

Nodding, Jesse followed her lead as she proceeded to whirl
about as quickly as her aging bones would allow and waddle in
haste toward the staircase.

As they ascended the stairs, Jesse noted with familiarity the
dozen or so ancestral portraits that were still in place along its
wall and shook his head at the turn his thoughts were taking
when he found himself grimly noting that soon there would be
another portrait here, taking its place next to those of Aileen
and Deirdre at the crest of the stairs.

They were soon entering a large bedchamber furnished in
typical château style, with Louis XIII armchairs scattered
about, a large Louis XIV armoire on one long wall, and the
room's focal point, a massive canopied Louis XIII bed at its
center. The bed's heavy, embroidered canopies were partially
drawn, and as Jesse approached, a black-robed figure stepped
away from one side of it, and Jesse recognized Père Edouard,
the family priest.

The cleric's usually cheery, cherubic face appeared drawn as
he raised his head from his beads and regarded the newcomer,
but a second later it resumed its characteristic charm as Père
Edouard smiled warmly at him.

"Come, come, my son," he whispered gently. "Etienne,
there is someone here you wished to see," added the priest in
the direction of the bed hangings. Then, to Jesse, "Make haste,

my boy, make haste," and backing away, he retired to a corner near the fireplace.

Softly, Jesse approached the bed, his heavy riding boots silent on the thick Aubusson carpet. He was not prepared for the thin, weak voice which emanated from the bedclothes.

"Brianna, is it you already, *enfante*?" But if Jesse was unprepared for the frailty of Etienne's normally rich, strong baritone, he was even less ready for the shadow of a man that peered out at him from the pillows as Jesse answered, "No, my friend, it is Jesse Randall."

Smiling wanly, the heretofore robust visage appeared gladdened by the news. "Ah-h, it is just as well—no, *better* that you have arrived before her, *mon ami*." A thin, bony finger beckoned as he added, "Come closer, *mon fils*, for what I have to say—" Here a fit of coughing overtook him, and Jesse bent forward in concern before casting about the room for someone to help. Mistress Delaney stepped forward from the post she had assumed near the door and, pouring some water into a goblet from a bedside urn, gently came and held it to her master's trembling lips as Jesse stepped aside and watched with troubled blue eyes.

At last Devereaux waved the goblet aside, rasping, "Enough, enough! Jesse, come forward, *s'il vous plaît*, for what I have to say to you cannot wait. There is so little time..."

At Jesse's would-be protest, Etienne sadly shook his head, saying, "No, *mon fils*, do not play games with me. We have ever been honest with each other, eh?" With this the thin smile reappeared. "It is true. I am dying, but for me, do not grieve. Just listen." Here he paused a moment, clearly trying to gather strength, for it was obvious the exertion of speech cost him greatly.

At length he took a deep breath and continued, the intelligent, dark eyes never leaving Jesse's face. "You know I would have given anything, had you been able to become my son—I say son—*fils*—because it is closer to the truth than this term, 'son-in-law.' You see, my Aileen and I, when we lost Deirdre, we were doubly bereft, for in losing her, we knew we had lost you as well."

Nodding, Jesse acknowledged the truth of Etienne's words. He had long been aware of Deirdre's parents' feelings for him, and he'd felt strangely close to them as well.

"But perhaps—" Another spasm of coughing seized Etienne as he endeavored to resume speaking, but this time he waved away the hovering Mistress Delaney and forced himself to continue. "Perhaps," he smiled—almost secretly, thought Jesse—"perhaps there is still a way to bind you to us, though I will not be here to see this come to pass."

In the background Jesse heard Père Edouard intoning the Latin words of the last rites: *"Ed cum spirit tu tuo . . ."*

"Take care of her, my son. Take good, kind and loving care," gasped Etienne, and then, a look that could only be described as hopeful on his face, he closed his eyes, slumped back into the pillows, and was silent.

"Etienne?" whispered Jesse, already knowing he would receive no answer. He was just stepping back from the bedside, a puzzled look on his face as he pondered Etienne's last words, when the room came alive with movement—movement from everywhere, that is, save the interior of the massive bed. Mistress Delaney rushed forward from the open doorway, a man who had the look of a physician at her heels; Père Edouard reached the side of the bed a few steps ahead of them, just as Jesse was withdrawing; in the hallway a mobcapped chambermaid could be heard sobbing loudly, and behind her appeared a somber-faced gentleman Jesse knew to be Simpson, the Devereaux family's solicitor.

Jesse retreated to a heavily draped window as he saw the physician shake his head at Père Edouard, and then he watched the priest make the sign of the Cross over the still figure on the bed as the Latin words droned on.

Suddenly there was a commotion from below, the sound of at least one sharply raised voice apparently coming from the region of the lower stairway. All heads turned in the direction of the open doorway as the disturbance grew louder, its source, closer; rapid, light, footsteps were heard ascending the stairs, and then a long, piercing wail met their ears.

"*No-o-o-o!* Let me *through!* He *cannot* be gone yet! He *must* not!"

Suddenly, a slender, cloaked figure in dark green burst into the room, a smell of dampness accompanying it, for outside, it had begun to rain. Brianna Devereaux was home!

Dashing wildly toward the bed, she was headed off by Père Edouard. Dumbly, she stared into the priest's face as the man slowly shook his head at her.

Then the still chamber seemed to split in two as Brianna's high-pitched scream reverberated from every corner. *"No-o-o! Papa! Papa!"* she cried, struggling past the priest's arms as they tried to hold her. Lunging madly, she threw herself at the still form in the bed. "No—no, Papa," she sobbed. "You *cannot* yet be *gone!*" Then, after a brief pause, a note of defeat in her voice; "I was so near...so very, very...near..." The slender form became a heap of crumpled green as great, choking sobs emanated from its core.

Gently, Père Edouard bent over the grief-stricken girl he had known since her birth and lifted her away from the bed. Mistress Delaney came forward, her kind face a study in sympathy, and the priest delivered her into the maternal arms that, like his, had comforted Brianna early in her life when comfort was needed.

"There, there," soothed the older woman as she guided her charge out of the room. "Hush yer weepin', now, darlin'. 'Tis time t' be turnin' t' God and the sweet saints..." The comforting words faded down the hallway, and once again, in the dead man's room, the age-old rhythms of the Latin banished the threatening silence, as Père Edouard took his place near the bed.

Chapter Seven

The staccato ticking of the Louis XIV tall-case clock in one corner of the third floor library played heavy counterpoint to the steady rhythm of the rain outside. In the curved alcove caused by one of the château's twin turrets, Jesse stood by a window, his back to the room. Simpson, the family solicitor, had directed him here after the dramatic scene at the deathbed and was expected to join him shortly. He gazed solemnly at the gray weather outside, glad for these few moments alone, for time in which to ponder what he'd just seen and heard.

She was taller, he thought, and her eyes were green, not sherry-brown, but she looked *so much* like.... Jesse winced, closing off the avenue his thoughts were taking. Surprised to find there was still such a residue of pain after all these seven years, he willed his mind in another direction. His friend Etienne—the loss there was also one he felt keenly, but this was something he could at least deal with now. And more than that, there were the things the man had said to him before the end... What had he meant—"Perhaps there is still a way to bind you to us"? And just who in hell was it he was supposed to "take care of"?

"Ah, there you are, Mister Randall! So sorry to have kept you waiting." George Simpson extended his hand as he walked toward him, his thin, narrow frame held perfectly erect under a carefully groomed, white-periwigged head, his pale blue eyes serious. Jesse nodded politely as they shook hands, remembering him from intermittent times, over the years, when the solicitor's presence had been required for the signing of certain horse-trading documents that had passed between Etienne and himself.

"I've asked that a fire be lit to dispel some of the dampness," said Simpson as a footman entered the room and headed for its Carrara marble fireplace. "I would to God it would dispel some of the gloom as well, but perhaps it will make waiting for Father Edouard a bit pleasanter." He indicated they should sit in a pair of dark green leather upholstered chairs near where the servant was now working diligently to build the requested fire.

"Father Edouard will be joining us?" questioned Jesse as he sat and stretched his long, muscular legs out in front of him. He noted again, with brief annoyance, the trail dust on his boots before bending his full attention on the solicitor.

"Ah, yes—or Père Edouard, if you wish. It makes no difference to the good priest which term one uses, but I'm so damnably Anglican in my background, I tend to use the English one exclusively. Ahem—well, er—at any rate, yes, to answer your query, the priest will most certainly be joining us, just as soon as he's finished administering the last rites and comforted the—er—bereft, I should think."

"Bereft," mused Jesse. "That young woman would be the younger daughter, the one who's been in France for some time?"

"Brianna Devereaux, precisely," smiled Simpson. "I'm afraid she's taken it very hard. I understand you've not met her before."

"Afraid not," answered Jesse. "You'll remember I was out of the country at the time of Aileen's death and her funeral, though I understand the younger girl—Brianna—was in the States for a while following her mother's passing. Convent-educated, isn't she?"

Simpson nodded. "A bit of a hellion in her early years, I'm afraid. Sent abroad to the good sisters of an abbey for civilizing, so to speak. A different side of the coin from the older daughter, I can assure you."

Eager to change the subject, Jesse withdrew a pair of cheroots from his waistcoat pocket and offered one to Simpson. As the older man accepted it with an appreciative nod, Jesse caught his eyes. "George, what in hell goes on here?" He watched Simpson quickly shift his gaze and bend forward with his cheroot over a taper that had been left burning in a brass candlestick atop a nearby satinwood drum table. "First, I'm delivered a beseeching letter by special courier to come to Etienne's sickbed—deathbed—then, when I arrive, just barely in time, my old friend whispers a couple of curiously puzzling statements to me—"

"In good time, sir, all in good time," said Simpson. "Just as soon as Father Edouard arrives, actually, all of your questions may be answered. Until then, I fear, I'm not at liberty to reveal very much."

"Not reveal—?"

"No, sir," offered Simpson with an apologetic smile. "It seems he and I are co-executors, you see."

"But that has to do with matters of Etienne's estate! What have I to do with that?"

"Ahem—er—ah—quite a bit, sir, but—now, then, I've already said too much. I'm afraid all explanations will just have to wait until Father—"

"Yes, I know, until Father Edouard arrives. Well, you'll forgive my impatience, George, but there begins to be a few too many bloody questions pending, and, I must confess, I've coupled this matter with some business I must attend to in Columbia and—"

The library door swung open and the bulky, black-clad figure of Père Edouard burst into the room, his skirts flying, his broad-brimmed black hat slightly askew.

"Gentlemen, forgive the delay," he smiled, "but the little one, she needed much consoling. Please, remain seated. I will simply pull over this chair and join you."

The piece of furniture he spoke of was a heavy wing chair with ball-and-claw feet, and yet, Jesse noted with a smile, for all his chubby girth, the cleric lifted it as if it were a matchstick, his obvious strength belied by his appearance. When the chair had been set in place before the now brightly burning fire, the newcomer removed his hat and set it on the drum table, revealing the crisply curling head of bright red hair Jesse well remembered. When his broad girth was well settled, Père Edouard peered briefly at Simpson, then focused on Jesse, with steady, warm brown eyes that held their sparkle, despite the solemnity of the day.

"It is good to see you again, my young friend, even if the occasion is such a sad one. Welcome once again to Le Beau Château. You were missed, perhaps more than you realize," said the priest, a guarded, knowing look on his red-bearded face.

Seeing his expression, Jesse leaned forward in his chair and fixed the priest with steady blue eyes. "Père Edouard, there's something strange afoot, and Simpson here tells me you can now clear up a few puzzles I—"

"Oh?" queried the priest. His bushy red eyebrows shot up with the word as he looked at the solicitor. "George, perhaps you misunderstood. I'm afraid you and I, according to what Etienne told me, are prevented from giving forth with any details until the reading of the will, and since the funeral will not be held until the day after tomorrow—"

"Day after tomorrow!" exclaimed Simpson. "But the body—the heat of August—"

Calmly the priest brushed his concerns aside with a hand gesture. "Taken care of, George, with—er—ice stored deep beneath the springhouse. It seems there are distant relatives a good day's ride from here. A messenger's been sent, and since they've been aware of Etienne's state of poor health, they will leave immediately, but Etienne left explicit instructions..." He made a helpless gesture and gave an apologetic shrug. "Etienne was well prepared, my friends."

Nodding, Jesse gave the priest an assessing look. "Very well, *bon père*, but will you at least tell me what I have to do with the distribution of Etienne's earthly possessions—with this will? I must tell you, I neither require nor want any of the good man's wealth and if that's—"

"To be sure, my dear Jesse," the priest broke in. "I would have guessed your reaction to be such. Well, my friend, I can tell you this much. Yes, you *are* most definitely cited in Etienne's will and will therefore be asked to be present when it is read after the funeral, and, no, it is not in the matter of bequeathing you his earthly wealth—" Père Edouard stopped for a moment, reflecting on what he was saying. "Er—let us say not in the matter of gold, or land and the like, at any rate."

"Then why—?"

"Time, my young friend, time will reveal all to you," countered the cleric. The brown eyes sparkled with a merry light Jesse remembered well. "Be patient, I beg of you. Two days. Such a little bit of time to wait. Surely you can spare it?"

Sighing, Jesse nodded, for he knew the priest well enough from past visits to realize he had a determined side to his genial nature and that, coupled with a well-tended devotion to duty, as well as to the Devereaux family, would prevent him from revealing anything he wasn't supposed to, until the stipulated time. "Very well, sir," he smiled. "It seems I have little choice. And it is not as if the time will be wasted. As I was informing George here before you came in, I have had to combine personal with business duties on this trip to the Upcountry and was planning to meet with Governor Pinckney before I left, so I'll take tomorrow to accomplish that. I trust you don't have any problems with my going into Columbia in the morning?"

For a moment, he thought he saw a look of disappointment cross the priest's face, but if it had existed, the broad smile that now graced the robust features said otherwise. "No, no, of course I have no problems with that. Business with Pinckney, eh? And last year it was, we heard, President Washington you were rubbing elbows with." Père Edouard rubbed his red beard thoughtfully. "For a young man who never struck me as being overly ambitious in the political arena, it seems you're keeping some mighty high company these days. Could it be that breeding those wonderful horses and managing a large estate are no longer enough of a challenge for a man of your abilities?"

Jesse smiled. He'd hardly let any cats out of the bag by mentioning his visit to Pinckney. That would be common knowledge by the time it was finished, but he also knew it would be imprudent to go into the details of why the Governor might be wanting to see him. "Let's just say that anyone in my position, who's interested in taking his personal business dealings seriously, cannot—at least in this state, where major landholders have so much to do with how the state is run—cannot avoid an occasional rubbing of elbows with those who do the running. And believe me, sir, if you could see the work that's being completed at Riverview these days, you'd have little doubt, I think, that the managing of the lands and stock my brother and I inherited from our father could fail to hold my interest.''

The priest returned his smile. "Ah, yes, your Riverview. Etienne had told us how excited you were, in your letters, about creating your own plantation after your brother's marriage. So it's been coming along, well, eh? Do I detect, perhaps, another interest underlying all this domestic planning and building? Is there perhaps at last an urge to settle down as your brother has?'' Here the brown eyes grew curiously less humorous and more intent as they focused on Jesse's face, and the voice lowered. "There wouldn't be a particular young woman waiting somewhere, would there?''

Laughing, Jesse shook his head. "No, but I can't say all the young eligible ladies and their mamas haven't done their best to make it otherwise.'' Then, as if he'd had enough of the bend the conversation was taking, Jesse rose from his chair, saying, "Well, gentlemen, it's been a long and tiring day. I spent close to eight hours in the saddle before arriving, and—''

"Of course, of course,'' said Père Edouard. "How remiss of us, not to have seen to your accommodations by now. Though I think you'd have no trouble finding the guest bedroom the family usually reserved for you, the blue room in the southwest corner, I'll have someone to see you there nevertheless.'' And with an easy expenditure of energy, the priest rose from his own chair and began to usher Jesse out of the room. They were just nearing the door when it opened, revealing a tall, dark-haired man Jesse had not seen before. Immaculately groomed, and dressed like a gentleman, the man bowed as he encountered the two at the door.

"Honoré.'' Père nodded his head solemnly. "I was wondering when you would appear.'' He turned toward Jesse. "Jesse Randall, allow me to introduce—''

"I am Honoré Dumaine, sir,'' the stranger said to Jesse, "and I have the dubious distinction of being Etienne Devereaux' only—and bastard—son.'' The smirk that met Jesse's eyes with this pronouncement was laced with hostility.

"Dumaine,'' said Jesse, giving the man a careful nod as he offered his hand. Then, turning toward Père Edouard, he asked, "Is there anything you need me for now, or shall I find my own way to my room?'' As he spoke he watched Honoré brush past them and head for Simpson who was standing near the fire.

With an annoyed glance over his shoulder, the priest followed his movements for a second before turning back to Jesse. "No need, my friend, for, see, here comes a young woman who, I'm sure, can find a means to light your way to your chamber."

The young woman he spoke of was Aimée, who, indeed, had been sent by Mistress Delaney, after helping to put Brianna to bed with an herbal sedative prescribed by the doctor. She'd been asked, since most of the household servants had their hands full with preparations for the funeral and the guests that would be arriving, if she would lend a hand by escorting one of the early guests to his chamber and, her head full of directions to the library and the blue room, had arrived here to do exactly that. Now, as she beheld that guest and recognized him from their brief encounter at the inn, Aimée's jaw dropped and she stared, her mouth agape. *Mon Dieu! It is the American, the one at the inn! And here I stand, wearing the very dress Brianna borrowed for her escapade!* Awkwardly, she lowered her eyes and made a quick curtsey.

Noting her discomfort, Jesse registered a perplexed look as it struck him that the wench had a familiar look about her, but before he had a moment to examine this notion, Père Edouard broke in.

"Mademoiselle Aimée, is it not?" Glancing at Jesse, he added, "We met briefly in Brianna's chamber. Accompanied your mistress all the way from Paris, *non*? Ah, but it is more than generous of you to help out the staff here during this difficult time, Mademoiselle! You can find your way to Monsieur Randall's chamber?"

"*Oui, Père*," answered Aimée in a voice that she forced to show more confidence than she felt at the moment. *After all,* she thought to herself with typical Gallic practicality, *either he makes the connection and recognizes me, or he doesn't, so I might as well bet on the fact that he doesn't and carry on as if all is normal.* "*Bon soir*, Monsieur Randall," she added, brazening out the situation by facing Jesse squarely and focusing her dark eyes directly on his face. "Permit me to lead ze way to

ze *bleu*—er—blue room.'' She finished with a dazzling smile
thrown directly at Jesse in a bold act of sheer bravado.

Then, at a benevolent nod from the priest, Aimée carefully
raised the candle she held in a pewter candlestick in her left
hand, pivoted on her heel, and with a flourish of swishing petticoats, proceeded to lead the way toward the stairs at the end
of the hall. Both men missed the triumphant grin as she heard
Jesse bid the priest good evening and follow her down the hall.

A short time later Jesse found himself comfortably settled in
the blue room. As he awaited the bath the French girl had offered to have prepared for him, he stretched himself before the
fire that had been thoughtfully set in the fireplace, his bootless
feet propped upon a small, dark blue velvet, upholstered foot-
stool that had been left there for that purpose. Outside, in the
dark, it was still raining. Glancing around, he noted with satisfaction that the room was much as it had been during his last
stay here. It was a decidedly masculine bedchamber, with heavy,
dark blue velvet draperies at the windows and matching bedhangings on the heavy Chippendale tester bed which dominated its space. Even though it was summer, the bedhangings
had not been removed, as they might have been elsewhere, for
inasmuch as the room was on the southwest corner, these furnishings were used to help block off the hot Carolina sun in the
afternoon. There were, however, gold rope ties in place at each
of the bed's four massive posts, should the need arise for pulling the bedhangings out of the way to catch cooling breezes
from the room's four windows, two on each outside wall. And
of course there was mosquito netting in place, but Jesse knew
the mosquitoes were never as much a problem here in the Upcountry, as they were in the tidewater areas on the coast.

Lazily Jesse sipped at a snifter of brandy that had been
poured for him and left on a snake-footed candlestand near his
fireside wing chair. The fingers of his left hand drummed
soundlessly on the dark blue and gold brocade of the chair's
arm as he stared for a moment at the fire's merrily leaping
flames.

Well, old man, he thought to himself, this promises to be an
interesting trip, to say the least. He began to tick off mentally

the elements he'd thus far encountered that made that promise. First, there was the will that was to be read—with *his* more or less *mandated* presence! What could *that* mean? How was *he* involved in something that, by ordinary rights, should be the family's business? And why all this apparent secrecy with regard to it?

Next, there was that—well, he had to say it—ominous looking character, Dumaine. What did *his* appearance signify? Etienne had never, he was sure, even mentioned having a son. Of course, the fact that this Honoré had been born on the wrong side of the blanket could easily account for that. The Devereaux family wouldn't be the first socially prominent one to endeavor to hide a by-blow child. Still, he'd thought his and Etienne's friendship had been one to transcend such insignificant things, as he regarded them. Even the mood of the country at large was beneficent and expansive in such matters. Look at the position that Alexander Hamilton had attained! Here Jesse chuckled to himself as he recalled Carlisle's calling the Secretary of the Treasury "that little bastard Hamilton"; he hardly thought James had meant the *literal* use of the term when he'd used it!

He took another sip of the brandy, noting its smoothness as he swallowed. Fine French brandy—perhaps. He took another sip, rolling the liquid velvet around on his tongue. Then, again, maybe not. He smiled as he recalled that the French priest— *half* French and half Irish, he amended, just like Etienne's daughters—Père Edouard had a wonderful talent: as a pastime the man made some of the finest liqueurs and brandies this side of the Atlantic. This could well be some of his stock, he mused.

As the brandy began to have a relaxing effect, Jesse found it at last possible to hold up the final piece of his fragmented puzzle for examination. The girl, Brianna. How did she figure in all this? Slowly, carefully, he called upon his recollection of her face during the brief moments in which he'd glimpsed it. Even marred as it was by grief and tears, it had been a stunningly beautiful face. Now that he could at last confront his image of her, he was sure of that. And even more than the harrowing likeness it bore to Deirdre's visage, there had been those startling green eyes—eyes not easily dismissed or forgotten. But already he knew that, beyond the difference in eye color, this young woman was different from her sister—the *passion* that had emanated from that slender form! It had been a thing to behold—and in one so young! Jesse shook his head as if to clear it of his vision and smiled. He'd bet those poor nuns over in France had had a time of it with that one!

Finally his thoughts drifted toward his meeting with Pinckney and what tomorrow would reveal. Damn, if it had been anyone but Carlisle asking, he'd have told him to go to hell! The last thing on earth he needed right now was to offer himself as a pawn in the oily machinations of political intrigue. He could well speculate on the nature of such with men like Pinckney and his ilk. And there was Riverview, just beginning to take real shape and bear the fruits of those many months—years—of work and planning. *There* was where he was needed!

Of course, he conceded, as his thoughts grew steadily more languid with yet another sip from the snifter, his own involvement in this young country's affairs wasn't totally without persuasions or opinions. He truly did espouse the Jeffersonian viewpoint. If Hamilton and his band were allowed to go unchecked, there was a good chance these new United States of America would begin to resemble the very country they broke away from—Mother England, with its rigid class system and all the ills attendant thereupon. Of course, he had a sneaky suspicion that the real hope for the country resided in the fact that the Hamiltonians had their place in the scheme of things as well, and that the secret, the key to the future, lay in the country's ability to balance both perspectives, taking the best from each. Indeed, it seemed to be the President's means of steering his young ship of state through these difficult times as a fledgling nation, and if that were true, then Washington was to be credited with a brilliance of leadership he had heretofore failed to recognize. Instantly sobering at the thought, Jesse sat forward in his chair, his blue eyes intense in their forward focus now. Well, maybe it wouldn't be such a damned waste of time to follow through on this mission, if such high matters were at stake. But Pinckney and his—

A soft knock at the door interrupted his thoughts.

"Yes?"

"Your bath, sir," said a French-accented voice.

Rising, and feeling better about this trip than he had since its outset, Jesse smiled as he answered, *"Entréz."*

Chapter Eight

J esse squinted against the late morning sun as he turned Gypsy's head in the direction of the newly constructed South Carolina statehouse. A frame structure of less than stately proportions, the edifice had been hastily constructed when, in 1786, Columbia was designated as the new capital site, replacing Charleston in an effort by the legislature to strengthen the principles of Republicanism; it gave a major symbolic nod to the less-than-aristocratic frontiersmanlike faction which had exerted a minor but vocal, presence within the government. Including men like Patrick Calhoun, Wade Hampton and General Thomas Sumter in its midst, this Upcountry group of rough-and-tumble Republicans with heavily democratic attitudes had convinced the blue-bloods of South Carolina, men like the Pinckneys, John Rutledge and Pierce Butler, that some compromises between the two factions were necessary to avoid splitting the state asunder.

Of course, thought Jesse, as he allowed Gypsy to choose her own slow and careful footing in the foot-deep mud that lined the main thoroughfare after yesterday's rain, it was only two years later that those factions were destined to clash again. In the spring of 1788, many South Carolina delegates met here to debate the Federal Constitution's ratification, which the Upcountry well-to-do felt, favored the aristocratic point of view. Feeling the Constitution that was to be adopted in Philadelphia was essentially a document favoring the propertied, these men voted unsuccessfully to block ratification, though ultimately the South Carolina delegates submitted a draught containing about half the provisions actually adopted in

Philadelphia. And then, thought Jesse, as if things weren't going poorly enough for the Upcountry forces, in 1790, just a couple of years ago last May, a *South Carolina* Constitutional Convention, motivated by aristocratic cries of outrage that they and their families should be forced to spend all their time in this crude, backwater place, had voted to grant Charleston an equal claim on the chief state officers, decreeing that the Governor and other officers need remain in rude Columbia for legislative terms only. Moreover—and it was here Jesse gave a sigh as he guided Gypsy toward the wooden hitching post in front of the statehouse's main entrance—to make matters worse, it was at that convention in Columbia in 1790 that the insufferable hierarchy of the propertied had come about: ownership of five hundred acres and ten Negro slaves if one were to be admitted to the Lower House; one thousand acres and twenty slaves for admission to the Senate. Of course, he smiled, if a bit ruefully, there had been a major compromise involved; in order to strengthen Republican principles, the delegates had also passed laws for the abolition of the rights of primogeniture, those rights which in England, as well as elsewhere in Europe, guaranteed the inheritance of real estate would pass to firstborn children only, thus preserving in the hands of a chosen few, the power that accrued to great landowners, and landowners only. Thank God for that, thought Jesse as he dismounted and proceeded to tie Gypsy's reins to the post. And none too soon in coming, he added to himself. Why Virginia had been years ahead of them, voting similar legislation into being at the first session of *its* legislature after the signing of the Declaration of Independence! Finally, as he mounted the statehouse steps, Jesse remembered with satisfaction that it had been Thomas Jefferson himself who had drawn up that law. Not a bad fellow to rub philosophical elbows with, he mused.

It was barely five minutes later that Jesse, having shown Carlisle's letter of introduction to the Governor's secretary, found himself sitting across a large George III mahogany desk from Governor Pinckney himself.

"Mister Randall, I truly do appreciate your taking the time and trouble to come all the way up here to meet with me. I trust your journey was a safe one?"

"As safe as the horse I rode, Governor, and she's the best," replied Jesse, thinking how initial small talk was the only way to begin a conversation of this kind. *That's right, Governor, keep it light. We both need time to size each other up.*

"Ah, yes!" said Pinckney. "The famed Randall horses. You and your family have gained a horsebreeding reputation that is more than statewide, sir. It may even have become national! Widely known for their excellence, your horses are, sir. I ought to know, I own a couple of them myself." Here the Governor flashed Jesse a wide smile, showing white, slightly uneven teeth against a complexion that showed more freckles than tan, but indicated he was probably something of an outdoorsman, despite the need to cloister himself in stale government offices much of the time.

Jesse returned the smile. "Really, sir? How did you come by them, if I may ask?" *Good, very good, Governor. Flatter your man by showing personal approval of the things he does best, or which lie closest to his heart. And with a Randall, owning Randall horseflesh is about the best bet you could make.*

"Purchased them last spring at that three-day auction on Oxfort Street in Charleston. I believe it was your brother Garrett who had brought them to the sale. I paid a pretty penny for them, too, I don't mind admitting. Damned Middletons also had their eye out for a fine pair of blooded bays like those."

Jesse smiled, but mostly to himself this time, recalling how it was Middleton money—and interest—that had cost him so much to free Festus and Vulcan. "That would make them a pair of three-year-olds by Proud Dealer, out of Misty Morning, the English broodmare we imported in '87," he said. "Guess you have a pretty fair eye for fine horseflesh yourself, Governor."

Pinckney gave a slight nod at the compliment, his white periwig shifting just a fraction of an inch on his head as he did so; the slight flush to his features told Jesse the man was not above being susceptible to flattery himself.

Feeling more comfortable with the situation as he began to know his man, Jesse met Pinckney's canny dark eyes as they assessed him across the width of the desk and decided to take the offensive by bringing up the reason he was here. "Well, Governor, since we both know I'm not in Columbia to deal in horses, can you tell me what you have in mind, sir?" He knew he'd made the impression he was after when Pinckney's eye-brows shot upward ever so briefly at the unexpected directness of his shift in the conversation, but like the wily old patrician he was, the Governor refused to allow anything more than that to betray his surprise, for his immediate response was delivered in a voice as calm and casual as the one he might have used to ask for a second cup of tea.

"I—we, the governing, and thinking, men of this state, desire your help, sir. We want you to be an emissary for us and go to Virginia, sir, to Monticello and persuade Thomas Jefferson not to resign his post as Secretary of State." The dark eyes were level as they waited for Jesse's response.

This time it was Jesse's turn to be impressed. Pinckney didn't beat around the bush either! Coolly, he returned Pinckney's stare. "What makes you think his resignation is imminent?"

"Trust me on this, sir. We have it on excellent authority that the Secretary is so troubled over his differences with Mister Hamilton, he has been practicing penning his letter of resignation to the President."

Pinckney reached down and opened a drawer to his right and withdrew a pair of well creased and crumpled pieces of paper; he thrust them onto the desk in Jesse's direction. Nodding for Jesse to pick them up, he added, "These were found, several weeks apart—note the dates—in Mister Jefferson's—er—waste receptacles. Look at them, sir. They are partially completed letters of resignation, each addressed to Washington, begun, and then discarded! Do you require more proof than this?"

His eyes quickly scanning the papers in question, Jesse had no trouble recognizing the boldly handsome script of the man who had helped pen the Declaration of Independence, a document he had personally seen while still a student at William and Mary and had at one time nearly committed to memory, so in awe of its contents had he been. Shaking his head slowly in the negative, he raised it and fixed his eyes on the Governor. So it was not above the man to use spies, probably through infiltration of Jefferson's household, in this case, to gain necessary information. How else would he have come by the discarded refuse of Jefferson's private chambers? Carefully he regarded the man across from him. That Pinckney was heavily committed to his cause in some way, he now had no doubt. The problem still lay in determining the man's motives.

"How do you expect me to approach this mission, Governor, should I undertake to accept it? And if I do, just what makes you think I possess the persuasive strengths necessary to sway a Jefferson?"

The Governor smiled. He had been expecting these questions. "As you must realize, sir, if the Republican cause is to succeed against the strength of the Secretary of the Treasury and his allies, this resignation must not occur. Those of us here in the South who support the Secretary of State feel that perhaps he is without knowledge of exactly how great and far-reaching that support is. Now—" Here a careful smile as Pinckney's eyes focused assessingly on Jesse's—"suppose someone were to go to Mister Jefferson, armed with numerous letters, letters written by the rich and powerful in this area, all carrying messages of support for the Secretary. Might that not convey a great deal of persuasive power for the cause in question?"

"Go on," nodded Jesse, the blue eyes as assessing as the Governor's.

"Word has it, too, that you're a pretty persuasive gentleman in your own right. Take a little story Pat Calhoun passed on to me just the other day. Seems there's a new device being advertised hereabouts, something called a cotton gin, I believe, invented by some fellow named, er—Whitney, I think. Calhoun's family had been looking about for some kind of a new crop, having gotten out of indigo after the failure in that market a while back. Seems they'd thought about cotton, but dismissed it because of the problem with those damned seeds. I speak of the upland short-staple cotton that has the difficult-to-separate green seeds, not the long-staple sea island cotton whose black seeds are easily separated and which has long been a staple of our commerce." He watched Jesse closely as he spoke and was rewarded by a slow smile he saw spreading across the face of the man he faced. "Well, sir, it's all over town how a trial crop of short-staple cotton produced on the Calhoun plantation has been easily cleaned of its seeds by that very machine, and it's all over town, too, just who it was who had knowledge of Mister Whitney's cotton gin and persuaded Calhoun to take a try with it." The dark eyes fixed Jesse with a knowing look as the Governor smiled.

Jesse reached in his vest pocket for his cheroots before responding, his smile still evident. "I have as an acquaintance a lady who lives on a Georgia plantation, a lady I had occasion to visit a little over a year ago on some business near the Savannah River." He offered a cheroot to Pinckney, who declined, taking up instead his own clay pipe. "Her name is Katherine Greene; she's the widow of General Nathaniel Greene whom my brother had met during the war. While I was at Mulberry Hill, Mistress Greene introduced me to a house guest whom she'd met aboard ship while he was en route to the Carolinas for a tutoring position." Here Jesse extricated a portable flint and rush tool and worked briefly at creating a spark from which to light his cheroot. Succeeding, he passed the lighted rush to Pinckney. Then, leaning back in his chair, the blue smoke spiraling hazily overhead. "After that, things moved along quickly. Mistress Greene was so excited over Whitney's invention, she was sponsoring him, and the two of them didn't take long to convince me it would work. Any man of sense and an agricultural background would have responded in the same way."

"Yes," agreed Pinckney, "but only a man of considerable persuasive powers would have been able to get the Calhouns to act on this information so quickly. And you are that man, Jesse Randall."

Jesse gave him a brief nod. "Perhaps. Calhoun's a pretty tough old nut, but—"

"And that's not all," Pinckney cut in, his own persuasive enthusiasm gathering steam now. "Randy Tuttle tells me of an investment in something called pearl-ash as an export to Britain earlier this year, an investment that made him a ton of money, he assures me. Seems this pearl-ash is revolutionizing the baking industry by the way it causes bread to rise, or some such thing." Here Pinckney paused to suck in deeply on the clay pipe. "Now, anybody around here can tell you what a conservative old fool Tuttle is, especially when it comes to parting with a penny, but he's a rich old fool today, thanks to *your* advice! Don't tell me that didn't take some powerful persuading!"

Again, Jesse smiled, but the smile was a wry one. He didn't fancy Tuttle a fool, just a mild old gentleman whose kindness and quiet friendship had been valued by his father, Jeremy. And if an old friend of Jeremy Randall could be aided by some knowledge Jesse had had of the United States' production of potassium carbonate, or pearl-ash, Jesse had been only too glad to help. But Jesse took annoyed notice of Pinckney's characterization of Tuttle, and out of this annoyance, found himself parrying with the question he'd been eager to ask from the start. "Governor, just why is it you're suddenly so set on Republican views when for years you've always voted as a Federalist?"

It was clear Pinckney hadn't been prepared for such a frontal attack, and he rushed to cover his nonplussed state with a half-minute's fiddling with pipe and tobacco. At length he raised his head and faced Jesse squarely. "Randall, you're being baldly direct with me, and like it or not, I'll be damned if I don't admire your style." Here Pinckney rested both forearms on the desk and leaned forward toward Jesse, the clay pipe cupped firmly in one hand. "So I'm going to do something I almost never do. I'm going to let you, someone I need politically, in on something that has to do with my personal—my private affairs."

With that, he again leaned back in his chair, taking a slow draught on the pipe before continuing, his eyes never leaving Jesse's face. "Yes, it's true that I've always voted as a Federalist up until lately. Why shouldn't I have? As a member of a major landowning family in the South, with shipping interests extending our affairs overseas, it was only to my advantage to espouse interest in a strong, centralized Federal government.

"But a little less than a year ago my cousin Thomas and I had occasion to take a trip up North, to Philadelphia and New York. We talked to a lot of people from both parts of the country, including some pretty important ones—men like Alexander Hamilton, Aaron Burr, the President himself and, yes, Thomas Jefferson. We toured the cities and their outlying regions and we talked to farmers as well as manufacturing men, men from New England with shipping interests as great as our own." He paused for a moment to study Jesse's face, wanting to be sure his words were being taken in. Satisfied that they were, he went on.

"Then, late in our travels one evening, Thomas and I were having dinner together—it was at Fraunce's Tavern in New York, I believe, when I said to him, 'You know, Thomas, something's beginning to become clear to me, that I never suspected before. Having toured certain key areas of the North, now, I've begun to see the germ of some very major differences that it may well take another fifty or so years to become apparent.'

"'Indeed?' said my cousin. 'How so?'

"'Well,' I answered, 'we pretty much depend upon agriculture in both societies, as a mainstay of economic growth, but here in the North, they seem to be pushing more toward commerce and industrialization. You mark my words, Thomas,' I said, 'there will come a day when the North will stand for these things while we in the South will continue to be more agriculturally oriented. And if and when that day comes, I'm willing to bet it will be this industrialized North that's best served by the centralized Federalist government Hamilton and his bankers are pushing for. Not the South. The South would do far better for its individualized agricultural areas if the national controls were looser, allowing individual states their own—stronger—self-government.'"

Again Pinckney paused, as if to allow time for his words to sink in. Jesse continued to give him his complete attention and kept his eyes on the Governor's face.

"Well, what do you think my cousin did?" asked Pinckney rhetorically. "He *laughed* at me! Said I was being 'mystical,' reading too much into the future. Said Hamilton and his boys were the best hope for any of us with commercial ties, differences between North and South be damned!"

"'Oh?' said I. 'And how then, my dear cousin, do you account for Thomas Jefferson, a Virginia gentleman and planter, through and through, being so extremely opposed to all this centralism? Tell me how the brilliant mind that formulated our very Declaration of Independence, the document that laid the groundwork for separation from that other, older form of *centralized control*, Mother England, could be so wrong in warning us against the dangers of the *same thing* evolving within the borders of this, our own fledgling nation!'"

Pinckney glanced down at his pipe and, seeing it had gone cold, began to tap its contents out into a Staffordshire dish that lay on one side of his desk.

"Well, sir," he continued, "we went on into the night on this issue, Thomas and I—or around and around, I should say, neither of us able to sway the other to his point of view. But, Mister Randall, I have to tell you, the further I went with my arguments, endeavoring to convince my stubborn cousin, the more I myself became convinced of my own—changed—point of view. I have come to this conclusion, sir: I may be a businessman, an exporter and member of a family with major shipping interests—as are you and your family, to some extent, I'm told—but I am also the Governor of a great Southern state, and as such I have a duty to uphold; that duty, as I see it, is to do all I can to strengthen the Republican political point of view so it can continue to check the growing tide of Federalism that, if allowed to grow unchecked, will one day *choke* the South. Thomas Jefferson, sir, he is our only hope in this regard. Will you help us keep him?"

The room suddenly grew very quiet after this speech, and Jesse struggled to keep himself from smiling. He had just been delivered a piece of rhetorical bombast that would have been worthy of those in the House of Lords he had once visited, and he saw in this at least one of the reasons Pinckney had come to political power in the state. Privately he wondered just how much of the man's fervor was inspired by the political visions of the future he had just cited—by lofty convictions—and how much was the result of an ego sorely pricked by his cousin Thomas. He suspected the latter, but moved by his own convictions and a sudden recollection of James Carlisle's inclination to be practical: as long as the man's switched to the right side, use it—he decided to give the Governor the answer he was seeking. Besides, he added to himself, he was more than just a little curious to meet the man at the root of all this fuss—Thomas Jefferson.

"Very well, sir," said Jesse. "I'll go to Monticello."

Pinckney looked relieved as his face broke into a broad smile, and the two continued to talk about some of the details of

Jesse's mission when they were disturbed by a knock at the door.

"Come in," said Pinckney, looking mildly annoyed at the interruption.

The door opened, and in walked Honoré Dumaine.

"Ah, Dumaine," said Pinckney, rising from his desk. "I'd like you to meet the man I told you about, Mister Jesse Randall." He glanced at Jesse, who remained seated, taking in Dumaine's full measure. Honoré was taller than average, perhaps a fraction of an inch or so under six feet. He was slender of build, but not underweight. He had a long, narrow face with a complexion that tended toward the swarthy, dark hair that he wore queued and unpowdered, and dark, brooding eyes that continued to signal hostility. Not an unhandsome man, if it weren't for those eyes, he somehow missed the mark of being truly good looking because of the menacing air he generated.

Dumaine's words were clipped as he responded. "We've met."

Appearing surprised by this news, Pinckney looked at Jesse.

"It seems I find myself a houseguest at the home of someone Mister Dumaine is—was close to—the late Etienne Devereaux," Jesse offered.

"Devereaux. Ah, yes, heard the news just this morning," said Pinckney, shaking his head sadly. "Tragic, just tragic. He wasn't that old, if I remember."

Impatience in his voice, Honoré broke in with, "Your secretary said you wanted to see me, Governor?"

"Well, yes," said Pinckney, frowning at the note in Dumaine's voice. "I wanted you to meet Mister Randall so that you two would not be strangers when you embarked on your journey." He turned toward Jesse. "Mister Dumaine is one of my aides, and as such he will be accompanying you on your trip to Virginia, er—now that you have agreed to go," he added. "Of course, now that I find you two have already met ... Dumaine, I'll see you after you've taken care of that Richardson matter. It shouldn't take you too long. In an hour, shall we say?"

The note of dismissal evident in the Governor's voice, Honoré bowed briefly in each man's direction and withdrew from the room.

"Odd sort of fellow," commented Pinckney once he and Jesse were alone again. "How well do you know him?"

"I've been in his company now about a total of two minutes," replied Jesse as he rose from his chair. "And I honestly cannot remember Etienne even mentioning him over the years we knew each other."

"Hmph!" exclaimed Pinckney, moving to escort Jesse to the door. "Small wonder. Rumor has it—but the rumor's been a persistent one—that he's Devereaux' illegitimate son by a distant cousin who, it is said, killed herself when Honoré was born and it was clear Devereaux would not be marrying her because he had already married someone else—a love match, whereas the family had arranged for the cousin.... Well, you know how these rumors go. At any length, if there ever was a man with a chip on his shoulder, it's Dumaine. Can hardly stand having him around sometimes, but he came highly recommended and his work is top drawer, so now I find myself without an excuse for getting rid of him."

"Except to send him on duties that will take him far afoot—like trips to Virginia," smiled Jesse, the wryness not missed by the Governor.

"Hmm, yes, well, better you than I," laughed Pinckney. "Besides, as a liaison between us and Jefferson, I think you may find him valuable," he added.

Finally the men parted with Jesse's promise to return to Columbia in a few days' time for final instructions and a departure date. Then Pinckney, alone in his office chamber, walked slowly back to his desk, his thoughts on the man whose aid he had just enlisted.

Yes, if anyone were qualified for the job, it was this young Randall. Pinckney smiled to himself as he remembered the man's father whom he had known in Charleston years earlier. If he were anything like that one—and he was, he knew it—he'd do just fine. Thomas Jefferson was a man to be greatly influenced by the positive traits these Randalls possessed: high moral fiber, great strength of purpose—sometimes even in the face of indefatigable odds—honesty, and an unflagging will to stand behind their word. Yes, all these; they were in the father, and now they were in the son. And he had seen in just this short interview with Jesse Randall a keen native intelligence, to be sure, and if his spies told him correctly, this intelligence was well enhanced by a solid and widely plied education of the kind that Jefferson respects foremost: the reading of great and important books. "Yes, young Mister Randall," Pinckney suddenly found himself saying out loud, "you'll do."

Chapter Nine

It was nearing dusk as Jesse left the road from Columbia and turned Gypsy's head up the long drive leading to Le Beau Château. For the dozenth or so time since he'd left the capital, he mulled over the events and revelations of the past two days.

Pinckney. He was still not completely sure of the man's motives, but by this time his own natural curiosity in the matter had convinced him to become involved. He still wasn't sure he had what it might take to persuade a man like Jefferson, but he was by this time itching to find out and convinced there would be no harm in trying.

Then there was Dumaine. Why did he have the intense feeling the man was not to be trusted—and trusted for what? And why, in seven years, had no mention of him ever come about, not only through Etienne, whose reluctance was perhaps understandable, but through any of the others who were intimately connected with the Devereaux family? Neither Père Edouard, nor Simpson, nor any of the servants or retainers had ever breathed a word that a son existed—and yet the man *lived in the area*! Strange, to say the least.

And finally, there was the girl Brianna. Yes, of course he had been aware, when he had courted Deirdre, of a younger sister, but at the time she had already been sent abroad, and so he had never actually given her much thought, and now, to have her show up and turn out to so resemble . . . and why *was* he asked to come to the bedside?

Hastening his pace as he spied the Devereaux buildings in the distance, he made himself a promise to waste little time in straightening out these puzzles.

* * *

It was almost dark as Brianna guided her father's stallion, Le Duc, toward his stall. Silently she waved away the two grooms who had come forward to help. She wanted to do this herself. Le Duc had been Etienne's personal mount, and she had ridden him, much as she would now care for him and bed him down for the night, as a kind of ritual of absolution, a desperate means of attempting some last physical contact with her father through close touch with a physical thing he had cared for and loved. Softly, as she rubbed the big chestnut down with a coarse cloth, she sang to him, choosing automatically one of the soothing little French lullabyes she used to croon to the wild creatures she had nursed to health back at the Abbaye.

Perhaps she shouldn't have ridden him quite so hard, she thought guiltily, and then quickly changed her mind. No, it was probably good that she had. She doubted he'd gotten any real workouts since her father—*since Papa took ill*, she thought, forcing herself past the painful moment any recollection of her father brought. Le Duc certainly took some heavy controlling when they had started out.

She allowed her thoughts to drift over the details of the early evening ride. Dear God, but it had been good to ride over Devereaux lands again! The meadows and woods had been so fresh and lovely after yesterday's rain. Rain. Her thoughts took a darker turn. Why had it always had to *rain* when—stoically, she forced the maudlin moment from her and resumed her melody, methodically matching the strokes of her currying to the rhythm of the tune. She smiled as she watched Le Duc's ears prick forward on the high notes while he calmly munched the oats she had doled out to him.

At last satisfied that the stallion was well set for the night, she gave him an affectionate pat on the withers and quietly left the stall. As she neared the open outer doors of the stable, she heard, rather than saw, the approaching rider, for it was close to dark now. Then her eyes caught sight of a midnight-black, unusually large and big-boned mare with an undeniably masculine figure astride. And as the pair came closer and the man began to dismount, a sense of the familiar overtook Brianna, for she could at last make out the man's features. My God! she thought frantically. It's the American "god" from the inn!

What is *he* doing *here*? For a foolish moment she looked about, as if searching for a place to hide, then decided she had no choice but to brave it out. There was always the chance he wouldn't recognize her, and if he did, she could pretend it was a case of mistaken identities, of look-alikes, or some such.

Jesse stopped after dismounting, sensing someone's presence near the stable's entryway. "Hello," he called. "André? Who's there?"

Noiselessly a slender shadow moved into the circle of light afforded by a high hanging lantern someone had thought to light, and the ray of one of its beams fell on hair that looked like burnished copper as it fell in lush waves over the delicate shoulders he recognized as belonging to Brianna Devereaux.

"I'm sorry," she said softly, "but I'm afraid I've sent the grooms away. If you like, I can call someone back for you."

For a moment Jesse stood silent, taking in the full aspect of the young woman before him. After the glorious hair, which she wore loose and which had become seductively tousled from her ride, he noted her green, green eyes, immediately the focal point in a face that was breathtakingly beautiful. Quickly his eyes traveled downward, taking in the slender form which nevertheless was possessed of undeniably alluring curves, clearly evident despite the modest neckline of her—here Jesse found himself grinning despite himself, for what now came to his attention was indeed a surprise. The wench had donned boy's breeches! Attempting to hide the grin behind a pretended cough, he forced his eyes away from the lithe and shapely, long, long legs he'd glimpsed and returned them to her face. The unbelievable, stunning face. Here he puzzled a moment—she was somehow so familiar. Was it her resemblance to—he broke off, conscious now that she'd become aware he was staring at her. "No," he answered at last. "That won't be necessary, Mademoiselle Devereaux. I frequently tend to my own horse."

Breathing out with relief—at least he didn't recognize her from the inn—Brianna frowned as she tried to recollect how he *did* recognize her.

"Sir, have we met?" she queried softly.

"In a manner of speaking," smiled Jesse as he moved closer. "But I don't blame you if you can't recall. I'm afraid it was a rather bad moment for you." He stood just a couple of feet away from her now, and at this close range, her beauty in the lantern light nearly took his breath away. "It was yesterday, in your father's room," he said quietly. "Please allow me to introduce myself properly. My name's Jesse Randall, and I was a friend of your parents—and once, of your sister's." As he spoke, Jesse found himself staring at her mouth. It was without doubt the most sensual, delightfully mobile version of that feature he'd ever seen on a woman, and it was distinctly different, he was sure now, from Deirdre's, yet he had the unmistakable impression he'd seen that mouth, known it before.

As he spoke, his dark, handsome head looming several inches above hers, Brianna felt herself go suddenly—inexplicably—weak at the knees. Was it the kiss at the inn she was remembering? As she gazed upward, the blue eyes captured hers and held her mesmerized. Hotly, her body flooded with recollections of the liberties he'd also taken at the inn—at the memory of his hands on her, his touch. A warning buzzed weakly in her brain, but she was helpless to heed it as she continued to stare into those heavily lashed, vivid blue eyes. Was she supposed to say something? Had he spoken, asked her a question? She didn't know any longer. All she could focus on was the heat emanating from the core of her, the moisture gathering in that secret place between her thighs. Bewildered, she continued to stare dumbly up at him, her lips parted.

Jesse found himself drawn in by the spell of the tension between them, a tension he, for all his experience with women, could not explain, and then suddenly he found himself resisting its pull. Without warning, Deirdre's face swam before his eyes, replacing Brianna's, and Jesse found an overwhelming sense of anger washing over him—anger, and resentment that now, after all these years, this girl should be reminding him—

Then he did something he was to curse himself for, for days afterward, for it was an act totally unlike him, and without any apparent reason. He suddenly lowered his head, his mouth swiftly covering Brianna's at the same moment that his arms captured hers in a fierce embrace. That his movements were fed by his sudden, inexplicable anger he would only much later begin to puzzle out. He only knew—felt—now, that somehow he wanted to punish this bewitching creature, hurt her before she— Cruelly, his lips bore down all the harder, forcing hers apart while they crushed and bruised them, and his arms tightened to a grip that was viselike.

Brianna's head spun as she succumbed to all this. In a lightning series of flashes her mood went from its initial dreamy bewilderment, to surprise, to anger, to outrage, all in a matter of seconds. Frantically, she began to struggle against the overwhelmingly masculine trap she found herself in, and when her efforts came to naught, she began to feel fear as well. *Mon Dieu!* her mind cried out, *am I to be forced—raped, here on the ground in front of my father's own stables?* The thought sent a fresh stab of fear through her, giving her a renewed burst of strength, but just as she would have torn her lips away by dint of this added energy, she found herself released from his hold. Gasping, she fell backward a couple of steps, her legs unsteady beneath her trembling frame.

The shocked silence between them stood like a wall, a palpable thing, and it was Jesse who finally broke it, his anger far from gone but at last under some control.

"My deepest apologies, Mademoiselle Devereaux," he bit out slowly, as if groping for words that could explain what he himself could not understand. "It seems I have acted impulsively." A mocking smile suddenly worked its way across his features then. "Suffice it to say, however, that perhaps a gently reared young lady—as I have no doubt you are—should not be walking about wearing..." His eyes traveled slowly, insultingly, Brianna thought, over her hips and legs and the form-fitting breeches that covered them.

At last finding her voice, but at a loss for words, Brianna stood with her arms rigid at her sides and let out a piercing scream, her eyes shooting green fire at his. Then, finally finding her tongue, she lashed out at him with all the vituperative force she could muster. "You—you—you *beast*! Blackguard! *B-b-b-bâtard!*" she added in French. "You seducer of young women! How *dare* you! Is this your idea of comforting the bereaved?" Then, as if this last thought all of a sudden proved too much for her, reminding her of her grief—or the grief she now—guiltily—felt she *should* be feeling, instead of this utter sense of outrage at his advances, Brianna felt the hot sting of tears prick her eyes, and with a moan of anguish, she choked on a sob, turned and ran blindly for the house.

Silently, Jesse watched her go, his own emotions at last under control. At length he swore an oath, followed by a ragged sigh, and, running a hand through his hair, muttered, "What the hell have I done?"

Back at the château Brianna found her room, having succeeded in reaching the safety of its walls without anyone seeing her. Still badly shaken, she walked to the French doors that were opened to the little balcony beyond and stopped before them to take a deep breath of the warm evening air. Night scents of hibiscus and honeysuckle drifted over to her, perfuming her senses and acting as a balm on her shredded nerves. It was completely dark now, the new moon that had just risen on the horizon providing the only break in the blackness she found herself gazing at. Off in the distance she heard a dog barking, but then that stopped, and it grew very quiet, without even the usual busy evening sounds of the château reaching her ears.

Everyone was walking about hushed and on tiptoe, Brianna thought sadly, because of *Papa*. She stopped. No, she wouldn't think about that now; it was enough that the funeral was tomorrow, and she would gird herself for that later. Later, but not now....

Soon she found herself calm enough to consider what was more immediately before her—Jesse Randall. *That*—or *he*—was something she *could* focus on! Just who *was* he, anyway? Slowly, she let her mind drift back to that day at the inn, but soon the heat of a blush on her cheeks forced her to set aside the recollection and pull out in its stead a mental picture of their encounter a few moments ago.

Actually, she thought to herself as she slowly began to unbutton the white cambric shirt she was wearing, Mister Randall is *two* people. He's Aimée's American "god"—and *mine*, she amended with an additional blush—a complete stranger. But then he's also a guest in my home, a friend of Mother's and Papa's. She paused for a moment, her fingers resting on the last button of her shirt as she tried better to recall exactly what else he had told her out there before he— Again, she found the heat rising to her face, but this time as much from anger as from embarrassment. Frowning, she slowly undid the shirt's final

button and with a shrug removed the garment that, along with
the breeches, she had wheedled out of one of the stableboys.
What had Randall also said about his connection with her
family? Something about Deirdre. Oh, dear God! she breathed.
He was the man Deirdre was to have *married*! Now it all came
back to her. She remembered the afternoon at the Abbaye when
two letters had arrived by the same post, one from Mother, full
of the good news of an engagement, the other from Deirdre
herself, telling of this wonderful young man she had met and
was to wed. Sadly, Brianna turned and walked back into her
room. Draping the shirt over an arm of a Louis XIII upholstered chair near her bed, she slowly began to undo the ties of
the borrowed breeches. Deirdre had sounded happier than she
could ever remember her being in that letter. "You should only
see him, *ma soeur*," she had written. "He is the kindest, gen-
tlest man alive, and yet strong—and so handsome! I grow to
love him more each day, as I know you will too—as a sister, of
course—when you meet him."

Ha! thought Brianna then, the softness of her mood vanish-
ing under the irony the present circumstances placed upon her
sister's words. *Kind? Gentle? That dissolute lecher!?* Handsome, yes, she'd give him that, but— She took a deep breath to
calm herself and plopped down on the chair before proceeding
to finish removing her breeches. When they were off, she held
them in her lap and stared at them, unable to resist the smile
that tugged across her lips. Of course, her attire *had* been rather
scandalous, as had her masquerade at the inn, for that matter.
Sighing, she propped her elbow on an arm of the chair and her
chin in her hand as she at last examined her own behavior where
Mister Jesse Randall was concerned. At last she drew another
sigh from the still air as she silently admitted to herself that
perhaps her own escapades had been partially to blame.

"But why did he seem so *angry*?" she said aloud as she
found herself contrasting the two separate meetings she'd had
with the man, or, more specifically, the two *embraces* those
meetings had brought about. In Charleston, at least, he had
been kind and gentle with the serving maid he supposed her to
be, whereas tonight— Once again, she found herself recalling
Deirdre's letter. Surely her sister, and her parents as well, she
reflected, couldn't have been all wrong about the man.

Suddenly a stab of acute pain shot through her as she allowed herself to think of things forgotten. Resentment, long buried by guilt and grief, rose to the surface as she remembered the anguish she'd suffered as a child at learning she was being sent away while Deirdre was to be allowed to remain here at home. It wasn't that she hadn't loved her older sister; indeed, she had adored and idolized her, forever wishing she herself could be as good and dutiful a daughter to the beloved parents they shared. But somehow, she recalled, Deirdre and she had been compared as children with Brianna always coming up short! *Ah, Mother! Papa!* her mind cried out. *Why couldn't you have allowed me to remain here, so I could prove myself to you? To all three of you? And now—now, you're all gone, the best of all I ever loved in the world, and here am I, never having had the chance to—*

Great choking sobs came from her now, as she bent her head over her lap and began to give in to her grief—the real grief she felt which came as a result of a sense of her own failures, as well as from her loss. And it was well over an hour later that Aimée came in and found her there in the darkened room, asleep in the chair, her bleak face streaked with dried tears.

Chapter Ten

~~~~~~~~~~~~~~

The air in the library was warm and close, despite the fact that several windows had been left open in an attempt at dispelling the August heat, and as Brianna's eyes traveled across the room's generous proportions, she thought to herself, Small wonder! There must be at least thirty people in here! Murmurs of quiet conversation met her ears from the various groups assembled for this, the final act in the drama of laying her father to rest. Carefully she forced herself to put behind her the events of the funeral they had just participated in, willing her grief away to the quieter recesses of her heart.

Just then the hum of noise abated as George Simpson entered the room, a sheaf of official looking papers under his arm. The group near the end of the room farthest from the door shuffled and became completely silent, composed chiefly as it was of the château's servants. In a corner across from the one in which Brianna stood, a swarthy, somber-faced man folded his arms across his chest and stared in brooding silence at the advancing solicitor. Several of Brianna's distant cousins who were gathered near the fireplace reduced their voices to hushed whispers as they made surreptitious gestures in Simpson's direction, one or two of them glancing over at Brianna at the same time.

Then, in the alcove near an open window, Brianna spotted Jesse Randall's huge yet graceful form as he lounged languidly against the wall there; he wore black, as they all did, but somehow, on him, with his wide, masculine shoulders, trim waist and lean, athletic legs, the color looked less funereal than . . . attractive, yes she had to admit it. He was devastatingly handsome to begin with, but clad in the immaculately tailored, form-fitting black jacket, jet-black breeches that hugged his loins like a second skin, the shiny ebony riding boots, he gave off, in addition, an aura of mysterious excitement that brimmed over with a hint of delicious danger. *Dear God!* she suddenly thought as she caught her mind moving along these lines. *What's the matter with me? Surely I ought only to be thinking about how I detest the man?*

Just then, Jesse's eyes caught hers, and she blushed and turned quickly away, for she saw him begin to smile at her open perusal of him. Quickly she sought out Father Edouard, whom she spied standing beside Etienne's desk, and with a deliberate attempt at letting Mister Randall know she was putting him out of her mind, she raised her chin a notch and found her way to the priest's side.

"Brianna, *ma chère*," smiled the cleric. "I was about to go to you. How are you feeling, *enfante*? Your face looked so troubled a moment ago. Tell me, is there anything I can do to make this difficult day any easier for you?" He placed a comforting arm about her shoulders as he bent solicitously over her, and Brianna found herself much comforted already. Father Edouard! He had indeed been like a father to her when she had been a little girl. How could she have forgotten? Perhaps, besides her parents and Deirdre, this kind, good man had been the one from her childhood who had loved her best of all.

Smiling softly up at him, Brianna shook her head. "No, Father. You have done more than enough already. Your presence through all of this has been like a rock for me to lean on, and I shall always remember the beautiful words of the eulogy you incorporated into the mass today." She lowered her eyes for a moment before looking up at him again from under her thick, dark mahogany lashes. "I would appreciate one thing, though," she murmured. At the look of smiling inquiry on his face she asked, "Please, will you remain here beside me until this—" she gestured at Simpson who was laying his papers out in front of him as he sat at her father's desk "—until this is all over?"

Gently Father Edouard patted her hand as he held it between his own two large ones. "They could not tear me away, *ma petite*," he smiled, adding, "Courage, Brianna. Just a little more of the great Devereaux courage you have already shown today, and it will all be over."

Then George Simpson rose from his seat at the desk and, clearing his throat, succeeded in gaining the attention of everyone in the room whose focus had not already been on him. It was suddenly so quiet you could hear the ticking of the tall-case clock in the corner.

"We are gathered here, as you all know, for the reading of the last will and testament of Etienne Alexandre Dumaine Devereaux, whose body and soul we have laid to rest today. I shall read from the will, exactly as it was dictated to me, in Etienne Devereaux' own words, neither deleting from, adding to, nor commenting on its contents in any way until I have finished all of it, beginning to end. At that time, if there are any questions or comments, I shall be glad to entertain them to the best of my abilities." Simpson lowered the spectacles he had placed on the bridge of his nose prior to this speech. "Is that clear?" he inquired, peering over them at the room's inhabitants. Receiving utter silence as his response, the thin little man once again raised the wire-rimmed eye gear into place and, focusing on the first of several pages before him, began to read.

The early paragraphs of the will were devoted to a description of the servants' portions, and Brianna listened patiently to the solicitor's near-monotone as it droned on over the details. "'To Mistress Delaney, a cottage, rent-free, the one down the path from the east wing, with a garden of her own until she dies, and 150 American dollars per year, plus a fifty percent increase in present salary, for as long as she is able to continue working!'" There was an audible murmur from the area of the room where the staff stood. "'To Prenshaw, my flawless English butler...'"

Brianna's gaze wandered over the staff at the far end of the room, trying to find each servant as his or her name came up. Prenshaw, she realized, she had never met, he being someone her parents had hired while she was abroad. And she had yet to find out what he looked like, for she'd been told he was away visiting a direly ill sister in Boston. Funny, she found herself thinking, it seemed so odd that her father should hire an Englishman as his butler when all of their servants had been either French or Irish...

"'To Villiers, my industrious, tireless gardener, 3,000 American dollars....'" As Simpson droned on, Brianna became restless and continued to let her gaze wander. Momentarily it fell on the swarthy—yes, that was *he*! Honoré, her half-brother! How could she have forgotten those awful dark eyes? Reluctantly, she pulled out her memories of the few times she had been allowed in his company, for he was raised by cousins of Papa's who lived a bit of a distance away, and she and Deirdre had always been aware that Honoré's existence was the one thing their father was reluctant to discuss with them.

She smiled to herself as she remembered with fondness that it had been Aileen, their mother, who had carefully explained their half-brother's relationship to them, once each had reached an age wherein she might comprehend. But Honoré himself, and not the fact that he was an illegitimate sibling, had always been the cause of her childhood fears of him. On the occasions when it had been impossible to avoid his presence, at weddings and other such family gatherings—like funerals, she mused grimly—Honoré had always seemed to go out of his way to make himself hateful to her—and to Deirdre as well, she recalled. Like the time, at her First Holy Communion celebration, when he had stolen away on her beloved pony, Mignon, and ridden her half to death under a whip! Brianna's jaw clenched and she gritted her teeth together in fury, even now, as she remembered the incident. Forcing herself into some semblance of calm then, she renewed her perusal of her half-brother's face. He seemed to be attending carefully to the words of the will as they were uttered by Simpson. More than that, he appeared to be anxious—and unctuous—Brianna thought glumly.

Restively, she moved her glance away from Honoré until it found Jesse Randall again; she was surprised to see that he was also gazing at Honoré, his look thoughtful, if not speculative. But then, as if somehow he always knew when she was watching him, Jesse looked up and caught her eyes, and once more that maddening half-smile crossed his handsome features; blushing in spite of herself, Brianna quickly looked away.

Off to the side, against one wall, she spied Aimée, who threw her a ridiculous grin. Aimée had obviously seen the brief look exchanged between Jesse and her, and, since late last night she had made her friend privy to what had happened out by the stables, Brianna felt herself annoyed that Aimée should find anything pleasant or worth smiling about where *Monsieur* Randall was concerned. She was just about to mime a face at Aimée to let her know as much when she had cause to focus again on what Simpson was reading.

"'. . . my beloved daughter Brianna,'" she heard, and then all at once she realized the room was being quietly cleared of most of the staff and distant relatives. Simpson himself paused as Father Edouard, with Mistress Delaney's help, quietly ushered out everyone in the room, save Brianna, Honoré, Jesse Randall and Simpson himself. When the room had been cleared except for these, Father Edouard reentered, softly closed the door behind him, and resumed his place at her side; he took her arm ever so gently and indicated they might sit. Nodding, Brianna found herself being assisted into one of a pair of nearby stuffed chairs, the priest's hand never leaving her arm as he filled the seat of the other.

Having seen them settled, Simpson readjusted his spectacles and continued. "'To my beloved daughter, Brianna Liscarroll Devereaux, I leave the entire remainder of my estate, which includes over 120,000 acres of useful land, some in timber and including two lumber mills thereon, the rest, arable; my entire stable of blooded thoroughbreds; my three carriages; Le Beau Château itself and all its contents and furnishings, plus all existing barns and outbuildings, my cattle and chattel, plus something in excess of one-half million English pounds, currently on deposit with the Bank of England. She, and she alone, will inherit this, the bulk of my estate...'" Here Simpson raised his head and peered over his spectacles, directly at Brianna, saying, "'on the following provisions:'" There was a pause as the solicitor let the words sink in. Brianna's eyes widened as she digested their import, and she glanced across at Father Edouard who seemed to be watching her intently, although his face retained its kind demeanor. To her right she heard a chair creak and realized that Honoré had leaned forward in the seat he had taken, his face darkly ominous. She took a second to cast a furtive glance at Jesse, too, finding him still in the alcove, which placed him physically quite apart from the rest of them; he was looking at Simpson, his face unreadable.

Then Simpson's voice continued as he repeated, "*'On the following provisions*: First, that she *marry*, by year's end, December 31, 1792, and that, in the time remaining before then, she engage in *useful instruction* in the arts of *domestic husbandry*, so that she may become fit to manage the duties adhering to mistress of a large estate; moreover, she is, until she marries, to become the *ward* of Jesse Randall, onetime *fiancé* of her dear departed sister, and when she marries, it is to be only with the approval of Mister Randall and Père Edouard-Gérard.'"

By this time there was a crackling aura of shock and confusion in the chamber. Brianna was conscious of her hands gripping the arms of her chair, their knuckles gone white, of Father Edouard's hand on her shoulder, of Honoré's audible gasp, of Jesse's catlike grace as he suddenly moved closer to the desk where they were gathered, but Simpson droned on.

"'Furthermore, in the matter of her domestic training she is to rely entirely upon the strictures of my solicitor, George Simpson.

"'Furthermore, if she should fail to meet any of these provisions, she will *forfeit* all of the above, save Le Beau Château itself, plus one acre of the land it stands on, along with a stipend of 500 American dollars per year, to be administered through a trust set up for her by George Simpson, and in no way may she touch the principal of that account, for upon her death it will accrue to her heirs, if there be any, to the state, if there be none.

"'Finally, in the unfortunate event of her forfeiture, all that remains of my estate falls to Honoré Dumaine, my acknowledged son of an unlawful union, who has otherwise already received his share from me, in the form of a 100,000 dollar gift on Christmas last!'"

There were a few remaining words of legal drone, but Brianna failed to hear them as she sat in stony shock in her chair. Mutely, she stared straight ahead, but with eyes unfocused, as she felt herself groping for something, some way to put meaning and sense into what she had just heard. At length she became dimly aware that someone was shouting in a voice that was angry beyond measure. She looked up then and saw Honoré, his visage scarlet with rage, making for the door.

"I am his *son*!" he was saying. "Not something to be swept aside or bought off for *pennies*! For my mother's sake, *he owed me*!" Upon reaching the door, he pointed a warning finger at Brianna, saying in a voice suddenly grown much calmer—*ominously calmer*—"Look to your proscriptions, Mistress! You have not seen the last of me yet!" And with twisted lips and eyes burning with fury, he left.

The room again fell silent following Honoré's departure until Brianna, once more conscious of Father Edouard's hand on her shoulder, turned her face to the priest and asked in a broken whisper, "Why?"

"My child," Father Edouard intoned quietly, his brown eyes filled with compassion, "your father loved you very much. You must never believe otherwise. But when he realized he was dying and that you would be left alone, and after years of protected isolation from the world—"

"A condition that was *not of my choosing*!" Brianna spat at him angrily, her eyes shooting green sparks. "You say he loved me. Tell me, Father, Mister Simpson, all of you," she added, looking from the priest, to the solicitor, and then to Jesse, "what kind of love is it that a parent bears a child when he sends her away from him and all she loves and holds dear, to be raised by strangers amid . . . amid . . ." Here the hot tears began to flow, and Brianna swiped at them with an angry, unsteady hand. "Amid foreign corn," she added in a quavering voice, remembering the story of the Book of Ruth she had so frequently read to herself as a child in France. She was standing now, her trembling chin making speech difficult, her legs barely able to support her. "I ask you, Father, was it love when a child was kept on foreign soil and had to watch, at a great distance, while her entire family, one by one, slipped away from her? Oh, sweet Jesus, how I *wanted* to come *home*—to stay—after . . . after each . . ."

"I know, Brianna, believe me, I know," said Father Edouard softly, "for I was with them, here, when your letters came. I held both your weeping parents in my arms after Deirdre's passing, prayed with them as your mother clutched your tear-stained letter in her—"

"Then *why*?" Brianna choked through her sobs.

"I—"

"No! You needn't say it, for I've had all the wise, careful answers already, Father." Brianna was moving away from them now, her face a study in pain as she took a few steps backward, her eyes again traveling over the faces of the three men. "And you will all tell me the same. Say that they loved me too much to neglect my future, that by foregoing their own selfish desires to keep me with them, they were being more loving. Well, let me tell you all something. If ever I have a child who loves me and wishes to be with me, I swear to you, I will move heaven and earth—yes, and hell, too, if need be, to see that it has that place beside me, the place where a child *belongs*—beside those who *love* it!"

Suddenly the room grew still as Brianna stopped her verbal outpouring and looked this time at Jesse, who continued to stand near the desk, his features revealing— Was it compassion she read in them? *No!* The last thing she felt she needed or wanted from this man right now was that he should feel sorry for her. It would be intolerable.

She took a deep breath and forced herself to address the other two men. "Can you gentlemen please explain something to me?" she asked in a voice far calmer than she was feeling. At their assenting nods, she pressed on. "Why only three months to—to marry?"

Clearing his throat, George Simpson gave her a sheepish look before he began. "My dear, I know it is difficult for you, but try to understand. This version—the final version—of your father's will was dictated to us in February when Etienne had been ill for some weeks and suddenly took a turn for the worse. Try to understand, child. We—we thought—"

"We thought God might take him at any moment," the priest broke in, making a movement toward Brianna, but seeing her take a further step backward, he stopped and remained where he was as he continued. "There was then some recovery from the illness, and he lingered all spring and summer, but he was never well enough to change the timing on this provision of the will, despite our efforts to accomplish this, and—"

"But—but I don't even *know* anyone here," stammered Brianna, the tears beginning to surface again. "I am only now newly arrived from the convent, from *years* spent abroad in unworldly seclusion."

"Exactly," said Simpson quietly. "That is why there is the provision for training to assume your place as mistress of a large household, and on this I—that is, we—wish, at—at dinner, perhaps, if you will allow us, to elaborate further."

"Dinner!" stormed Brianna, the anger back and threatening to break beyond control. "Who can eat *dinner*—how can you even speak of—of *food* when—" Suddenly she spun on her heel and raced for the door. When she reached it, she turned back to the three men, tears streaming down her cheeks. "And, I tell you, *I'm too young to marry!*" Then sobbing, she pushed through the door and was gone.

When the door had closed behind her, Father Edouard heaved a sigh and shook his head. "I was afraid she'd take this badly. As a child she was ever open with her feelings, good or bad, but when they were bad, or negative . . ." The leonine red head again shook sadly.

"Did she have to be told this way?" Jesse's voice spoke the words softly, but Father Edouard did not miss the underlying anger implicit in them; he turned and met a pair of icy blue eyes that belied their calmness.

"Yes and no," responded the priest sadly. "I'm afraid I've managed things rather poorly. You see, Etienne was very explicit in his instructions to us, the executors." He included Simpson with a gesture. "The contents of the will were not to be divulged beforehand. His reasons, I am not sure of, and go with him to his grave, I fear, for try as we might—and did— George and I could not dissuade him from this. One might suppose he was afraid of someone laying plans to tamper with the—er—more difficult strictures, should they have been known in advance." He gave a helpless shrug of his heavy shoulders. "Who is to say? Etienne also had a certain—shall we say, flair, for the dramatic? There was the time he hired a troupe of traveling players to present a play he himself had written, advertising the birth of Brianna. In it, he made sure there were lines that indicated he and his wife were proud to have had a *second* daughter, for he was concerned that people might take pity that the child was not a male heir when in fact, that would have been an error, for he and Aileen did, indeed, delight in their offspring of the softer sex. Well, that group of actors played those lines at every farm and estate for miles around, not to mention various establishments in Columbia. Pretty dramatic, wouldn't you say? And then there was the time when, for Aileen's birthday—well, I do ramble on.''

He cocked a steady eye in Jesse's direction. "Suffice it to say, sir, that although Etienne Devereaux had his private reasons for this dramatic presentation, and took steps to ensure its coming about, I, as the one who is close to the family, and therefore the girl, should have done something to at least soften the blow. There might have been ways...hints that could have—but, you see, there was so little time. Somehow the events that evolved between Etienne's death and this moment never seemed to allow me any private time with the child. You don't know her yet, but you'll soon learn she's forever riding off on one of those horses she loves so much, disappearing, then reappearing, only to disappear again like a wraith you're left wondering if you've really seen at all.''

Jesse found himself breaking into a smile as he watched the priest's troubled face go wistful in recollection of the young girl he was describing. He himself could half imagine the child she had been, running off in this direction or that, mercurial in her comings and goings as she tried her freedom in a world that perhaps had always closed in on her too soon. And when he remembered how he himself had come upon her last evening, on what had perhaps been one of those very dashes for freedom they were now discussing....

"Forgive me for implying your thoughtlessness in this, Father,'' Jesse said. "I begin to see, as is often the case, that things are not as simple as they seem.''

"No, no, my friend. You were only too right in questioning the manner in which this was handled,'' said the priest. "I myself have just witnessed enough to realize that.'' Father Edouard's face then grew thoughtful and his assessing eyes found Jesse's for a few moments in the ensuing silence. "And what of you, my friend?'' he asked at last. "Brianna's reaction to the contents of the will is one thing, but what of your own?'' His red-bearded face bore a sheepish look as he awaited the reply.

Jesse was silent for a moment as he contemplated this, his blue eyes searching out the faces of the two men before him. They were standing in a triangle before Etienne's desk which was still covered with pages from the will, and as Jesse's eyes fell on these, his mouth drew into a wry smile. *Just a few sheets of white paper. And now the world is such a different place for more than one of us, perhaps for all of us.* At length he turned his attention back to the men. "I take it, the two of you were privy to all of this—" he gestured toward the desk "—well beforehand?"

"Yes, but the—ah—restrictions...." Simpson's voice trailed off into apologetic silence.

"I know," said Jesse, the wry smile still apparent. "Well, gentlemen, it seems I have an added responsibility in my life. A ward." *A very lovely, fire-spitting hellcat of a ward,* he added to himself. "I can't say the news didn't surprise me, but Etienne Devereaux was my friend, and I see no reason why I should withhold honorable behavior with regard to that relationship just because the man is dead. The reasons for his final request of me I may find elusive—at least at present—but I can assure both of you that I will honor that request without question."

The two men across from him threw him broad smiles that fairly shouted their relief.

"There's a fellow," said Simpson. "Somehow I knew any man Etienne Devereaux was placing so much faith in wasn't just an ordinary sort. Knew, somehow, we could count on you, sir." He gestured toward a group of chairs, indicating they might sit as they continued their discussion, but Jesse shook his head and began to move toward the door.

"I realize we need to discuss this in more detail," said Jesse, "but for now, I've promised old Serge I'd look in on him and the gout that ails him. Perhaps at dinner, as you suggested?"

"Yes, yes, of course," said Father Edouard, moving to accompany him to the door. "We all need time to think, eh?"

But then Jesse stopped as a thought struck him. "In the interim, chew on this, would you? I have an idea that perhaps the best thing for Mistress Devereaux right now might be to get away from here for a while. It may be her home, but it's also the scene of much recent shock and unhappiness. I have a business commitment that will take me to Virginia—to Thomas Jefferson's home, Monticello—for a few weeks. I propose that I take the girl with me for a social visit. I'm not certain, but I think I might be able to arrange an invitation to my ward—

along with a properly devised entourage to chaperone, of course," he smiled. "Think on it, gentlemen. The lady will be needing some social exposure if she's to catch a husband."

And before either had a chance to comment or reply, Jesse gave them a brief nod and left.

"Well, what do you think?" Simpson asked.

The priest was sporting a wide grin. "Why, I think he will do very well, George. Very well, indeed."

Chapter Eleven

"And then, while all this was going on, Aimée, he never said a word! Can you believe it? He had the nerve to just stand there with one of those—those *looks* of his and say *nothing*!" Brianna whirled from the mirror she had been consulting about the damage her recent weeping had done, and reached in great agitation for the cold compress Aimée patiently held out to her.

"If I know you, *chérie*," said her friend, "you banished any silence with enough words to make all others' speech quite impossible, *n'est-ce pas*?"

"But I am to be—already *am*—his *ward*! Shouldn't the sudden discovery of that fact have provoked some comment from the man?" Brianna stepped lightly onto the delicate stepping stool beside her high tester bed and flounced dramatically upon the mattress. "Oh, Aimée!" she wailed, "What am I to do?"

Aimée shook a scolding finger at her. "For now, you are going to keep applying these compresses to lower the swelling around your eyes and then let me help you select something to wear for dinner," she said practically. "As for Monsieur Randall, who knows?" She shrugged. "Perhaps he is the strong and silent type. And besides, he is so-o-o *handsome*!" She finished with a grin in Brianna's direction.

Peering out from behind the wet towel she held over her eyes, Brianna couldn't help returning the grin. "Honestly, Aimée, is that all you ever think about where Jesse Randall is concerned?"

"It is all I can *help* thinking about where Monsieur Randall is concerned. Brianna, you lucky goose! Why don't you make up your mind to sit back and enjoy it?"

Brianna sat bolt upright from the reclining position she had just assumed. "Aimée! Have you forgotten I am to be married in three short months? And that no one, least of all I, has any idea who the groom is to be?" With an exasperated sigh, she flopped back onto her pillows and readjusted the towel over her eyes.

Aimée was quiet for a moment. "No," she said finally, "but if I were you, Brianna, I would not worry too much about such details." Suddenly her voice grew strangely mysterious. "Some things have a way of turning out all right, but don't bear too close examination in the meantime."

Again Brianna pushed herself into a sitting position, the compress falling carelessly aside. She assessed her friend with wide green eyes. "Aimée Gitane, I've heard that tone from you before! You *know* something, don't you?"

"Er—um—I think your face is looking much restored, Brianna. Hadn't we better select a dinner gown for you? It's a shame you may only choose from the three black ones, but at least you can't say black isn't a good color on you." Aimée chattered in rapid French now, the first time she had spoken in her native tongue all day, and she moved quickly over to the wardrobe that stood across from the bed, evasion evident in her speed.

But Brianna was right behind her. "Oh, no you don't, Aimée! You cannot have forgotten that you have shared the knowledge of your gift with me, or pretend you haven't, so out with it!" Suddenly her voice lowered and a gentler look came to the green eyes. "Oh, *please, mon amie!* After all that has befallen me lately, I could use some—some guidance from you. Won't you tell me *something*?" she pleaded.

At once softened and chastened by her tone, Aimée looked at Brianna and smiled. "If I do, will you promise to stop trying to hinder me from helping you dress for this dinner tonight?"

"Oh, yes! Anything! Just tell me—"

"And will you, *please*, Brianna, try to conduct yourself *well*, in a fashion—oh, listen to me! I sound like one of the sisters at the Abbaye! Well, you know what I mean. Because you are my friend, I truly wish only the best for you, and I have a feeling it may be important—how you present yourself at dinner to-night.''

"You wish me to be gentle and docile toward my *keepers*, is that it?''

"Now, you see? That is precisely what I am talking about! If you go down there with all guns loaded for—''

"Oh, very well, Aimée!'' Brianna chuckled. "I just couldn't resist one safe little barb here in the privacy of my own chamber. Now, please, *mon amie*, tell me what you've *seen* in this matter?''

Aimée's face grew serious. "Well, there are no details, mind you—at least, not yet.'' Her voice fell to a lower pitch and her black eyes seemed to glow strangely as she looked at Brianna, but she appeared to be looking right through her when she resumed speaking, her voice barely a whisper. "Ever since we left France, from the time we were on the *Liberté* until just now, I have had a recurring vision. Much of it has been cloudy, but each time it has come, it has been the same, and always, you have been at the center of it.''

Brianna held her breath as she waited for Aimée to continue, her nerves as taut as a bowstring. Her companion's eyes seemed focused on something far away now, and she was breathing shallowly, as if a great weight or force of some kind were bearing down upon her.

At length she resumed speaking. "Today, as I looked at Monsieur Randall in the library, one of the puzzling images became clear to me,'' she whispered. "In it you are in a dark place, a small, crowded place, and there is danger. But before the danger can touch you, two pairs of hands reach out to you and lift you away from it. One of these pairs of hands is black, but strong and huge, and in no way menacing. The other pair is also very strong, also a man's hands, but at the last moment, before the image fades, they become the talons of an *eagle*—''

Aimée's eyes closed for a moment, and then snapped open, bright and alert as ever. She smiled at Brianna and said in her normal voice, "Take a close look at Monsieur Randall's *hands* tonight at dinner, *chérie*—no, do not question me further now, and I will tell you one more thing. Do not ask yet how I know it, for I am unsure myself, but I swear to you, on my soul, that these visions are true." She finished with a look that dared Brianna to question her further. "Now, *mon amie*," she added, "which gown will it be? The silk with the flounced sleeves, or the more conservative taffeta with the panniers?"

Brianna laughed, at last giving in to Aimée's mood. "Neither," she stated emphatically. "I'll wear the new mode tonight. The high-waisted silk sheath with the narrow sleeves."

"And the daringly cut bodice!" chuckled Aimée.

"Exactly! If there's one thing I need to make clear tonight, especially to Jesse Randall, it's that his new ward is not a child to be led about by the nose. And, beginning with this gown, everything I do tonight will be designed to make that fact utterly clear. Do you agree?" she asked with a sidelong glance at her friend and a pair of merry dimples.

Aimée's grin was ear-to-ear. "I agree!" And they broke into a tide of gay laughter.

Jesse relaxed in a large comb-back Windsor armchair near an open window in the head groom's cottage behind the stables. Across from him, one leg elevated on a stool that was topped by several pillows, sat Serge, his crusty old features split by a lopsided grin.

"So, you are now in charge of breaking in the little one, eh?" asked Serge.

Jesse winced at his companion's choice of language, even though he realized that by now he ought to be used to the fact that the old man spoke of everything in terms related to horses. "Serge," he said, "I doubt the young lady would appreciate being told she was being *broken in*."

A raucous howl of laughter met his ears while the old man slapped the thigh of his good leg. "*Non, mon ami*, that she would not, nor do I think our little one will ever truly *be* broken in! But mark my words," he added, pointing a gnarled brown finger at Jesse, "she is every bit akin to a half-broken filly who is in need of careful handling by the right trainer. You would do well to remember that, *Monsieur*. Ah, yes, the littlest Devereaux. How well I remember her childhood comings and goings. And pranks! Pranks, *Monsieur*, and the devil's own mischief, I vow! She led us all a merry chase in those years, I can tell you!"

He leaned closer to his companion, grunting with the discomfort this gave his gout-ridden foot. "Did I ever tell you about the time—oh, she couldn't have been older than seven or eight—that she had her nose out of joint at not being allowed to stay up for a dinner party and, sneaking out of her room after all the guests were inside, she painted all their horses black and turned them loose in the east pasture?" He leaned back in his chair and savored Jesse's incredulous look. "That is correct, *Monsieur*. She *painted* them! Well, actually, *inked* them would be more accurate. Later we learned she had come by gallons of black ink that her father had been storing for his friend who prints the newspaper in Columbia, for the printer had had a fire in his storage shed and had asked the *Monsieur* to keep his new supplies for him until the facility could be rebuilt—"

Jesse began to laugh. "And so little Brianna helped herself to—how many horses were there?"

Joining in his laughter, Serge managed to get out, "Twelve, not counting the three who were already black! And, *Monsieur*, if you think it is difficult rounding up fifteen horses who have been turned loose in a strange pasture—"

"—try doing it when they're all coal black, in the middle of the night!" Jesse finished for him, his own laughter still unabated.

"So, you see," Serge said when they had quieted a bit, "you are going to have a time of it with that one, I fear."

Jesse grew serious, saying, "But Serge, the young lady has been in a convent for a number of years. Surely you cannot mean she might still—"

"A spirited filly is a spirited filly, *mon ami*. I know all about the work of the good sisters of such places and how they turn gentle young ladies out of their holy stalls when they are finished, but I have seen and spoken with *Mademoiselle* Brianna since her return. She came to me early this morning, before her own papa's funeral, with some poultices she had devised for my poor begouted foot—" Serge shook his grizzled head in wonder. "She has always had the compassion, the little one. Yes, a good and tender heart beneath it all . . ."

"Hah!" he added, and the grizzled head shot up as he looked at Jesse. "But I did not fail to see the green sparkle that still shines in those big eyes of hers, *Monsieur*. No, I would bet a year's pay on it. Everyone may think she wears the bridle now, but if I were you, I would look for a bit in the teeth!'' And again the old man was consumed by laughter.

"Well, she's clearly been a favorite of yours," said Jesse, rising, "and I have only to remember the horses you've always favored to realize why. But, good God, man, wish me some success in this, will you? I've got to find her a husband by year's end, and—''

"A husband! *No!*"

"You haven't heard—of all the terms of her father's will?"

"Terms? Bah! All I hear is the gossip, shut up here as I am with this damnable gout. Although I cannot imagine how old Mathilde left that out. A husband, you say?'' All at once Serge was off on another crest of loud and boisterous laughter.

Jesse moved toward the door, turning there for a parting gesture as the old man's laughter continued to reverberate off the cottage walls. "I'll be by again tomorrow," he said. "Thanks for an interesting hour of conversation, and, for God's sake, stay away from those pastries!''

Serge nodded at him through tears of laughter. "Ah, *mon ami*, I cannot tell you when I have had a better time! A husband! In three months!'' And he was off laughing again, barely managing to wave as Jesse closed the door behind him.

Serge's laughter still ringing in his ears, Jesse made his way along the gravel path that led from the cottage to the château. Carefully he turned over in his mind the events this day had thus far unfolded, and for the first time in his life he was hard put not to curse the strong sense of honor he had been raised with and always lived by. His honor, yes it was that, and that alone, that kept him here, ready to abide by the terms of that damnable will of Etienne's when every instinct in him told him to leave at once and not look back.

He halted for a moment on the path as it curved up a small incline near the stables; he thought he could still hear the faint sound of old Serge's laughter, but then shook his head and smiled. His ears were playing tricks on him, he was sure, but the notion had a sobering effect, for the cause of Serge's humor was real enough, and that gave him pause for considerable thought. She might resemble the other a great deal, but now he was certain that was where all similarity ended. Brianna Devereaux was a hellcat! He, too, had seen the defiance in those green eyes during the episode in the library, not to mention the evening before. There was no mistaking. . . .

Jesse caught himself and made a quick gesture of self-annoyance as he realized what he had been doing. Judging and convicting her in one breath, that's what! Hell, he thought, who wouldn't have reacted severely, faced with the things she'd been forced to confront on those occasions? Bitterly, he castigated his own behavior of the evening before, in front of the very stables he now faced. How had he allowed his own emotions to go out of control? Hadn't her father entrusted him with his surviving daughter's care because he'd felt he *could* be trusted with such a responsibility?

With a surge of disgust at himself for coming close to bungling the whole affair before it had even begun, Jesse resumed walking toward the château. Well, it wasn't too late, thank God, to correct his course. Beginning right now, this very night, he would proceed to set aright the mess he'd almost made and begin acting as a responsible guardian for the child. And, after all, that was what she was—a child. One who had been dealt a few too many punishing blows in her young life already, and for whom he was not about to make things any more punishing. He smiled to himself as he laid plans for conducting his new guardianship. He would handle her precisely like the half-broken filly Serge had spoken of, gently and kindly, but with a firm, steady hand beneath it all. It would work, of course. Hadn't he had years of experience breaking in high-strung horses without breaking their spirits? And he'd never had a failure. Patience, that's all it took, and a sensitivity as to when to bend and when not to.

A tiny doubt niggled at the back of his mind, reminding him that Brianna Devereaux was a human being, a very beautiful female of that species, and not a horse, and that perhaps the two were not that similar after all—but he dismissed the notion as quickly as it came, such doubting being alien to his nature. By damn, he would *make* it work! He owed as much to Etienne.

Having settled these things in his mind, he quickly turned to practical matters. He would need the correct entourage assembled for the trip to Monticello, for one thing. And then there was the matter of putting his own affairs in order back at Riverview before making the trip to Virginia. He stopped and took out the gold pocket watch he carried in his waistcoat pocket and checked the time. It was a few minutes before seven. Dinner was to be at eight. If he hurried, he would have enough time to pen a letter to Isaac, his—what was Isaac, anyway?—valet, for want of a better term. Butler-in-training, perhaps, but, then again, secretary, too, for the man was literate, something one rarely found in servants, and Jesse had already used Isaac's abilities with the pen on occasions when he'd been too busy to write himself.

Yes, well, he'd write Isaac with some instructions for Vulcan, along with the news of his extended absence, and then— carefully he considered an idea which had just come to him— yes, it would be good to have one of the twins on the road with him. He'd prefer having both, for their huge size alone would be a deterrent to any highwaymen or others of that ilk they might encounter on such a journey, much of it over rough country. He wanted to take no chances with Brianna's safety. Yet he knew Riverview couldn't spare both himself and Vulcan right now, so it would have to be Festus. Yes, most of the heaviest work at the forge had been done, or as much as was required at present, so, if Isaac were to bring him, Festus could be summoned up here for the trip. He smiled as he recalled his first vision of the blind man riding a horse. If he hadn't known otherwise, he'd have sworn the man was sighted! And Festus had casually explained that a man couldn't spend years shoeing horses without learning how to ride one, so Vulcan had taught himself first and then assisted his brother in learning.

Jesse found himself shaking his head as he considered the extraordinary pair those two made. And if fate hadn't accidentally led him to that auction block that day—with a vehement oath against the evils of slavery, Jesse reached the front door of the château, just as a clock from the interior began to chime seven. As he lifted the huge brass knocker in the shape of a *fleur de lis*, a stale odor of horses met his nostrils. Damn Serge and his horse-permeated quarters! He'd have to hurry far more than he preferred if he was to bathe and change in time for dinner when he had those letters to write, and he found himself wishing Isaac were already here with his civilized assistance.

Freshly bathed and shaven, and immaculately dressed in a jacket of deep midnight blue, close fitting dove gray breeches and high black boots with a mirror shine, Jesse allowed a footman to show him to the *grande salon* where he'd been told the guests were assembling before dinner. On the marble mantel a Louis XIV ormolu clock chimed the hour of eight.

As he entered he saw Father Edouard and George Simpson standing near the fireplace, their heads bent over a large book the priest was holding; both heads shot up when they spied Jesse.

"Right on time, as usual," smiled Father Edouard. "Really, my dear Jesse, sometimes I wonder if you have any bad habits at all. Not that I'm complaining, mind you. I mean, take your habit of punctuality, for instance. I only wish half my parishioners had this virtue. It would shorten my day considerably, I can assure you."

Jesse smiled as he thought of the cold bath he'd taken to ensure that promptness, there having been inadequate time for a hot one after he'd sent off his letter. He wondered what the good priest's feelings would have been, had he heard the accompanying stream of oaths he'd sworn as he endured those icy temperatures, for the well water here was spring fed. But to Father Edouard he merely said, "I've never seen any reason to make the world's affairs more difficult than they already are by failing to observe the common courtesies. It's really where civilization begins, I think."

"Just so, just so," smiled the priest, "but look here, my friend, Simpson and I have just come across something we think you should see." He held out to Jesse the book he'd been holding which turned out to be a Bible, and, inserted between its opened pages was a creamy envelope with the inscription, "Brianna" on it.

"This was Etienne's," said Father Edouard, and he left it with Prenshaw, the butler, with instruction it be given to Brianna upon the moment of his death. It seems he had intended I should hold it for her, but at the time he wrote it, I was out of the area, hence...." The cleric shrugged. "At any rate, the poor man's been away visiting a sick relative and only returned an hour ago from his trip, whereupon he immediately found me and asked that I see Brianna get it.''

''See that I get what?'' queried a soft, feminine voice from the doorway.

The three male heads turned in that direction, and what their eyes beheld proclaimed astonished silence.

Framed by the ornately carved and gilded woodwork of the *salon's* double-doored entryway, Brianna Devereaux stood very still, her unconscious pose reminding Jesse of statues he'd seen, carved by Greeks as silent hymns to pagan beauty. The deep auburn mane was drawn back from her face and caught by a gold and jet clasp at the crown of her head before falling heavily halfway down her back in shining splendor. This drew immediate attention to the beautifully sculpted face with its high cheekbones and large, widely spaced green eyes. The gown she wore, fashioned in the mode inspired by the French Revolution with its freer, more fluid lines, was unhampered by hoops or panniers and clung to her slender, long-limbed form with understated elegance. Delicate sleeves lightly hugged her graceful arms and imparted an air of young innocence, but this was immediately belied by a deeply curved neckline that displayed more than a little of the lush ripeness beneath; the soft folds of the sheathlike skirt fell in easy lines to her toes and told of the presence of a woman's body beneath the silk. Clad in black as she was, with no adorning jewelry, aside from the clasp that held her hair, she made a statement in the direction of being dressed for mourning, but it was barely that, no more, for the high coloring with which she'd been naturally endowed, in every way cried out against the somberness of the black. Rather, the heady combination of the rich hair with its fiery highlights, the green eyes that beckoned like twin jewels in the ethereal face, the creamy, apricot-tinted skin as it played counterpoint to the midnight depths of the gown and the gold of the door frame suggested an exotic pagan quality reminiscent of the Celtic priestesses of her maternal heritage, at once forbidden and remote, yet all too warmly real. And the final statement she made as she stood there, her head held proudly erect above a slender, graceful neck, was the one Brianna had intended: this was a creature who was no longer a child, and

Jesse's head swam with stunned awe at the undeniable truth of it.

"Er—ah, Brianna, my dear," Father Edouard said, at last breaking the silence. "Come in, come in," and he stepped forward in greeting, Etienne's Bible still spread open on his palms. "Look, *ma petite*, here is something for you—from your papa."

Quickly Father Edouard began to explain the appearance of what he held in his hands, carefully watching Brianna's face as she came and took from him the proffered Bible and its inserted missive. When he had finished, Brianna stood before him and quietly regarded the items in her hands. Then, with trembling fingers, she carefully removed the envelope and closed the Bible before laying it down gently on a nearby table.

"Gentlemen, would you—?"

"Of course," Jesse broke in, already moving toward the doorway. "We'll go on to the dining hall and wait for you there."

"Certainly, my dear," muttered Simpson, not yet fully recovered from the alluring impression she'd made with her entrance.

Nodding, Father Edouard murmured, "Take all the time you need, Brianna. We'll have Prenshaw hold dinner for you." He quickly joined the departing figures of Jesse and Simpson.

Left alone with her father's letter, Brianna hesitated before opening it. *Oh, Papa, haven't you done with me yet? What more news have you planned for me to—*

Suddenly aware of the negative direction her thoughts were taking and more than a little surprised at herself for the anger she bore her father, Brianna took a deep breath and forced herself to stop. Such thinking would never do if she was to assume the air of maturity she'd set out to present this evening, she thought, and with a smile at the notion that Madame Mézières would be proud of her self-control at this moment, she tore open the envelope in her hands and began to read:

My Dearest Daughter,
When this letter finds you, I will be gone, but I beg of you, my darling, do not weep or mourn for me, for I truly believe that I go to join my beloved Aileen and your sister in

heaven. Therefore, since death is something I in many ways have longed for, no tears, please, and to indicate how strongly I feel about this, I am explicitly requesting that you put off all mourning for me after today. I am serious about this *ma petite*, and would ask that you have Père Edouard formally make it known throughout the parish that, as my last living wish, I have forbidden you to wear the black of mourning beyond the day of my funeral. If people hear this, I know they will understand and no one will criticize you for being an undutiful daughter because of it. You were always such a vibrant, lively child, my Brianna, so full of the *joie de vivre*, that I could not bear it if I went to my grave knowing you were going about swathed in the color of death.

Next, I have some words for you regarding the contents of my will, which you will be hearing very soon. My only regret in dying at this time, my dear, is in my not having had sufficient time to see you settled in life, and so I have done what I could to try to insure that there will be others who will carry on with this function in my place. Père Edouard, of course, will be here to help you wherever he can, and you should avail yourself of his help. He is a good man as well as a godly one, Brianna. Look to him for guidance when you need it. And, of course, in legal matters, Simpson is without rival; use his help, too, when you must. But there is another upon whom I am relying in this matter, someone you've never met, and I am hoping—no, praying—that you will understand my motives in selecting him to be your guardian until the time you marry and have the protection of a husband. Jesse Randall was the man your sister Deirdre was to have married, but he is also one of the finest men I have ever known. He is my choice to be your guardian and I am begging you to accept this, not only as my dying wish, but as the wisest choice I could make for your protection in a world you cannot protect yourself from, owing to your secluded education and rearing. Trust me in this, Brianna, for it was a decision I made only after much forethought. Not only has Monsieur Randall been a close friend to me; he has been, in many ways, like a son. Never have I met a man at once so strong and yet sensitive and even vulnerable where it is important to have these qualities. He is also possessed of a quick intelligence, as well as a wisdom far beyond his years. And his honor and courage are without question. Did I tell you that he saved my life on two separate occasions, and your mother's as well, on the latter? Suffice it to say, since this is true—and I have neither the breath nor the time to explain the details of those occasions here—but I have told you the truth in this, so if I could trust the man with my own life, what better choice is there for one with whom I entrust my child's? And, believe me, my spirited little darling, I love you more than my own life and would not have undertaken this choice of guardianship lightly. Get to know Monsieur Randall, Brianna. Make it your business to do so, and I am sure you will come to trust and love him as the friend he is, and always has been, to us Devereauxes.

Also, I would ask you to forgive me for that instruction in my will that urges you to marry in less than a year's time. That may seem somewhat highhanded on my part, and perhaps it is, but I am an Old World father who cannot help feeling that a woman isn't safely settled in life until she is married, and in your case, without father or mother to guide you, the sooner, the better. I only hope I am not wrong in this, Brianna, for it is the one provision I have made for you that I have had some doubts about. I kept having the feeling that, if Aileen had been here, she might have advised me otherwise. But, since I have not had your beloved mother's guidance on this provision for a female child, I can only pray it has been wisely made; may God—and you—forgive me if I am wrong.

Finally, my dearest, a word of caution: *Do not trust Honoré.* He is a man driven by selfishness, ambition, greed and bitterness, a bitterness for which I feel I am only partially responsible. As you know, I have legally recognized Honoré as my illegitimate son, though the truth, since it must be told—oh, how it grieves me to have to speak of this to an innocent like you—the truth is, that he may—or may not—be mine. His poor mother, my cousin Suzanne Dumaine, was never a very stable person, mentally, but she was young and pretty, and very much bent upon pursuing me in our youth. Alas, I did not return her feelings and did my best to thwart her efforts to pursue me. But she was set on having me and one night, at a party at her parents' home—yes, I must say it—deliberately set about to seduce me. What can I tell you? I was young and, shall I say, unworldly at the time, and Suzanne, being a few years older, was far more experienced, having spent some time in Paris and Versailles at Louis' court. So she succeeded in forcing an intimacy between us. Oh, I am not trying to excuse myself; it was a moment of great weakness on my part. But I was wise enough in the ways of the world to know one thing: I was not her first lover.

Very soon after that, I met and fell deeply in love with your mother, and she with me, so we married in very short time, owing to my plans to leave Europe and settle here.

It was only after settling on these shores that I learned that, in the interim, Suzanne had borne a son and followed me here, claiming Honoré to be mine, and hoping to force a marriage, for she had not learned of my marriage to your mother in Ireland. Alas, upon the news of my wedded state, Suzanne took her own life, and, I was told, only through the quick intervention of a servant, was narrowly prevented from taking the child's as well. Needless to say, the news left me stricken and guilt-ridden, and I immediately took what steps I could to provide for the son Suzanne swore was mine. My guilt kept me from questioning the circumstances further. I had, after all, behaved dishonorably in the matter, and so only honor could hope to make any amends—if any could be made. Therefore, Honoré became my acknowledged illegitimate son— your mother stood by me completely in this, for I had told her everything—and I provided fully for his support, although it was our cousins, on the Dumaine side, who fostered him; perhaps that is where I made a mistake, for in providing for his financial sustenance, but not his emotional nurturing, I succeeded in maintaining a gulf between the two of us over the years, a gulf that has never been bridged. The results of any personal contact I ever had with Honoré as he was growing up were always horrible. He resented me from the beginning, owing to the fact, I was to learn years later, that his mother's family had believed Suzanne's tale in its entirety, including the fact that *she swore I had refused to marry her after learning she was pregnant*—a lie—and Honoré had been told this at an early age. When I learned of the lie the boy had been raised with, I went to him and tried to tell him the truth, but he would not listen. Bitterness had already done its work. So, listen carefully to me, Brianna, when I tell you again, do not trust Honoré Dumaine!

And now it is time for me to bid you farewell, *ma chère*. Remember, whatever happens, that I have loved you more than I could ever tell you, for words are never enough. Keep that *joie de vivre* that is your greatest inheritance, *ma fille*, and be happy. It is my last and best wish for you. *Adieu*.

Your loving Papa, ED

When she had finished reading the letter, Brianna stood silently staring at it, her green eyes brimming with tears. Strangely enough, she felt only sadness and none of the anger she'd felt at other moments during the day, ever since the reading of the will. So her father hadn't intended the will be read in the manner in which it had, so brutally shocking because of the lack of preparation on her part. He had intended that she see this letter first, as a means of softening what was to follow, and it had been one of those unfortunate quirks of fate that had prevented her from receiving it in time. Smiling, she dashed away now at the tears that came gliding down her cheeks, gently encouraged by what she had read.

He loved me, truly he did, she thought to herself happily. *And Mother, too, I'm sure of it. Oh, I still may not agree with their decisions on my behalf over the years, but at least now, somehow, after reading this, I have the unshakable feeling that, whatever their course of action, my parents worried about me and cared for me, and took great pains to see that care could continue, even from beyond the grave.*

"Well, Papa," Brianna suddenly found herself saying aloud, "the least I can do is try not to disappoint you," and placing her father's letter carefully back in the Bible on the table, she headed for the dining hall, adding, "Jesse Randall, it's time we got to know each other!"

She was met at the door by a formally garbed man of such tall, thin proportions, she nearly smiled. This could only be Prenshaw, the English butler. Everything about the man was long and narrow. In addition to his build, he had a long, thin face, upon which was drawn the longest and narrowest of noses. Long, thin fingers held open the door for her as a voice she could only think of as long and narrow-sounding, said, "Dinner is about to be served, Mistress. And may I take this opportunity to offer my sincerest condolences upon the loss of your father?"

Brianna allowed herself a small smile. "You are Prenshaw?"

"I am, Mistress," said the unsmiling face. "And may I add, it is my pleasure to serve you, as it was, your father."

"Thank you, Prenshaw," said Brianna, taking care not to smile more broadly. Prenshaw obviously took himself very seriously, and she was resisting the temptation of falling into her childhood habit of nicknaming the servants. Prenshaw, however, had already become "Sir Broomstick" in her mind.

As she entered the dining hall, she immediately wished someone had chosen more intimate dining quarters for tonight's dinner. Seated at the far end of a banquet table that in Louis XIII's time had been built to seat a hundred guests, were the three men she had just met in the *salon*, and the huge room with its bejeweled chandeliers and rows of gilt-framed mirrors was so vast and formal that Brianna suddenly felt very small and insignificant as she made her way toward them. All three rose in greeting as she came forward, and as she reached the place which had been set for her, Jesse, whose seat was on her right, held out her chair. She smiled in acknowledgment of the courtesy as she sat down, but all at once her confidence vanished as she felt his presence at such close hand.

Carefully she looked up at him from beneath lowered lashes, trying vainly to assess this effect he always seemed to be having on her. There was no denying the handsome and dashing figure he cut as he loomed above her, the advantage of his height and those wide, masculine shoulders doing nothing to allay her sudden apprehensions. And when he smiled, as now, with those deeply grooved masculine dimples, Brianna began to wish she were anywhere but here, for the weakness of her knees was not in her imagination.

"You are looking quite, quite lovely tonight, Brianna," Jesse said softly, not loud enough for the others to hear. But Brianna silently cursed the heat she felt creeping into her cheeks, for she had seen his eyes linger just a trifle too long on her *décolletage*, and she was sure that a mature woman, the kind of woman she wished to impress him as being, did not blush like a schoolgirl. Moreover, to make matters worse, Jesse had noticed the blush, as that maddening smile and look of his now told her.

"I take it you were—ah—comforted by the words your father had for you, *ma chère*?" queried Father Edouard.

Grateful for the diversion, Brianna answered eagerly, "*Mais, oui, mon père*—I mean, yes, Father." She threw Jesse and Simpson an apologetic look. "Excuse me, gentlemen, but after so long a time in France, sometimes French comes to me as automatically as my native tongue."

"No problem, my dear," smiled Simpson, "but if I recall correctly, I'm the only one here who wouldn't understand you. I know Mister Randall here speaks French. Often heard him using it in conversation with your father."

Brianna's delicate, winged eyebrows rose in surprise. Then she again felt the heat rise to her face, causing it to flame with embarrassment, for she immediately recalled the scene in front of the stables when she had let loose with that series of epithets, the worst one in most unladylike French! Swallowing hard and trying to will her cheeks to cool, she said, "Really? *Parlez-vous français*, Monsieur Randall?"

"*Oui*," replied Jesse with a grin that indicated he'd guessed the source of her discomfort, "but please don't be so formal," he added in English. "Since we're going to be spending a great deal of time in each other's company in the coming months, I think it might be easier if you called me Jesse."

Again Brianna watched those devastating dimples crease the handsome face, and with an effort she replied in a small voice, "Yes, of course . . . Jesse." She was saved from further discussion then as a pair of footmen entered with the first course of their meal, a lovely *potage crème de cresson*, or cream of watercress soup, from the looks of it, and Brianna found her mouth watering, for the château still retained the services of old Henri, a master chef Etienne had lured away from the royal kitchens of King Louis himself, years before the Revolution.

"Ah-h-h!" exclaimed Father Edouard upon tasting his first spoonful. "Perfection itself. I've never had a meal here that didn't rival or surpass the best cuisines this world has to offer, and believe me," he said, patting his generous stomach, "I've sampled many!"

"I dreamt of Henri's cooking for years at the Abbaye," Brianna said smiling, "not to mention the pastries of dear old Mathilde."

"Was the food at the convent not so good?" inquired the priest with a smile of sympathy.

"Well," answered Brianna after a moment of thought, "let us say the good sisters were more interested in feeding our souls than our bellies."

"Well put," chuckled Father Edouard as he ladled another spoonful toward his red-bearded mouth. "And may I say, *ma chère*, that your tongue, under the tutelage and guidance of Madame Mézières, has grown considerably more—ah—diplomatic, than of old. Why, I can remember a time when, if asked to describe cooking that was less than the best, which, of course, you were used to at home, you would have wrinkled up that little nose of yours and—"

"Yes, well, that was a long time ago, Father," interrupted Brianna, "and I hope I have matured enough by now—"

"But of course you have, my dear!" It was Simpson's turn to interrupt. "And since no one has yet taken the opportunity to express what we all knew for certain the moment you arrived this evening, allow me to say what a lovely young woman you've become, my dear. Really blossomed, you have, and all quite grown up."

This was a compliment Brianna could handle, and she nodded graciously at Simpson with a murmur of thanks and a dimple. Then, pleased that things were going in the direction she'd hoped, she turned toward her new guardian and asked, "Have you gentlemen something specific in mind to discuss with me this evening? After all, although I'm sure it's quite pleasant to gather here for the delicious food our kitchens have become quite famous for, we did seem to have been given a few 'loose ends' to try to tie up, didn't we?''

This last was said with a decidedly ironic tone, and Jesse didn't fail to notice a brief flash of anger spark from the green eyes. *She's trying very hard to be the mature young woman tonight,* he thought. *Bravo, Brianna! It's a valiant effort.* But then something in him—he wasn't sure what—made him decide to test that effort. *Let's see just how deep this new veneer of maturity goes,* he added to himself before commenting, "Yes, among other things, we've got to decide on how to catch you a husband."

Now, Brianna had been aware that, if she was to carry off her plan of having them accept her as an adult and therefore capable of having a hand in the decision-making where her future was concerned, she'd have to master her emotions as some of the less agreeable aspects of her father's will came up for discussion this evening, but what she had not been prepared for, was that the discussion should *begin* with the singularly *most disagreeable* item in that document, the business of marrying her off like some kind of package of marketable goods! It caught her quite off-guard and she flared in heated agitation with her response.

"Catch! *Catch* me a husband, sir?"

"It's Jesse, remember?"

Ignoring his interruption, Brianna hastened on. "Do I resemble some kind of fisherman or—or huntsman? Or perhaps it's the other way around," she added, sarcasm fairly dripping off her tongue. "Perhaps I am to be the dainty piece of *bait*! And then, I'm sure all the gentlemen from miles around—"

"Now, now, Brianna," soothed Father Edouard. "I'm sure Jesse didn't mean any such—"

"I'm afraid I meant every word of it," said Jesse, looking directly at his ward now. "You see, Brianna—I may call you by your given name, may I not?"—Without waiting for a reply, he went on. "The simple truth of the matter, Brianna, is that we have been given a rather narrow set of constraints within which to work, the chief and narrowest among them, the problem of finding—or *catching*, call it whatever you like—you a husband, and in just three months! Now, like it or not,

Brianna, you've got to face that, that is, unless you're willing to see the bulk of your inheritance go to Honoré Dumaine?''

Jesse watched her face carefully as he said all this, aware of each little nuance of expression that passed across it as he gauged her reaction. He was at the same time wondering at the tone his own remarks had taken. He hadn't really meant to be this blunt, had, in fact, intended to be fully courteous toward her as he helped her face the harsher realities of her situation, but, once again, he was at a loss to explain his behavior toward this young woman, had been, in fact, from the beginning. And now, as he watched her lovely face show signs of anger and outrage, then chagrin and, finally, confused hurt, he heaved a sigh and tried to soften what he'd begun with such an uncharacteristically heavy hand.

"Brianna, listen to me. I'm sorry if I seem to have put things crudely or hurtfully. Such wasn't the intent.'' He smiled as he spoke to her now, his eyes never leaving hers as he assessed her mood in the face of what he was saying. "It seems we're—all of us—caught up in a difficult situation that was not of our making. It was my purpose to confront, head-on, the problems involved. To help you to confront them, too. Then, once we know what we have to do, we can far more easily go about solving them than we might if we were to pretend they weren't there, or that things were rosier than they truly are.''

Brianna's lips remained compressed into a tight, straight line for several moments before she at last opened them to respond. "Very well, *Monsieur* . . . Jesse. Since you seem to favor the direct approach, what exactly, do you have in mind?''

Jesse noted the green sparks were gone from her eyes now, and her voice, beyond an exactness that was a shade too deliberate, denoted careful control over the emotion that had been present just moments before. *Good girl, Brianna. That's much better. We're making some progress now.* To her he said, "I was explaining to the gentlemen here before you arrived that I have some urgent business that takes me to the home of the Secretary of State, in Virginia. How would you like to accompany me and meet one of the greatest men of our time, Thomas Jefferson?''

Brianna looked dumbfounded. "You mean *the* Thomas Jefferson, the very one who was recently in France? Why, I—I

knew his daughters! They attended the Abbaye de Panthémont!'' Her voice bubbled with girlish enthusiasm now as she
forgot all plans to appear reserved in her growing excitement.
''Well, I'd love to go! Mister Jefferson wrote our Declaration
of Independence, you know, and while at the Abbaye, I'd always hoped to meet him, but somehow it never came about.''
Suddenly her face sobered a bit as she asked, ''But are you
sure? That is, this business you are about, does it leave room for
the added company of a female guest? And what about my being welcome? Surely you haven't had time to secure me an invitation, too, and—''

''Hold on! Slow down,'' chuckled Jesse, himself caught up
in her enthusiasm, which was far greater than he had anticipated and, he found, delightful to encounter. *What a rare
creature of moods she is!* he found himself thinking. *It's going
to be a while before you have this one wholly figured out, old
man.*

He then added, ''I won't know for sure for several days yet,
but I've already taken the liberty of setting things in motion for
such a visit. And since I believe at least Martha, the older Jefferson daughter, is in residence at Monticello with her father,
or will be, by the time we arrive, and since you say you've met,
I'm sure all the details can be taken care of. Leave it to me,
won't you?'' This last was accompanied by a warm smile as the
blue eyes looked directly into Brianna's.

The footmen were clearing away the soup bowls and preparing to serve the next course, and Brianna was grateful for the
interruption for, once again, Jesse's smile, when it was the
warm one he gave her now, was causing all kinds of turmoil
inside her, and she was devoting her energies toward masking
the confusing set of emotions that threatened to rise to the
surface.

''You will, of course, my dear, be requiring a set of new
mourning garments to make such a visit possible,'' said Simpson, ''and in that I can assure you that ample funds have been
set aside to—''

''Oh, but no! That won't be necessary,'' Brianna said
brightly. ''I almost forgot to tell you, I am constrained in some
positive ways, too.'' And she proceeded to tell them of the part
of Etienne's letter that enjoined her not to wear mourning,

finishing with the request that Father Edouard do his part to spread the word, as Etienne had asked.

"But of course," agreed the cleric between bites of deliciously poached, stuffed salmon.

"How fortuitous!" exclaimed Simpson. "Or, then again, perhaps your father knew exactly what he was about when he gave you this last instruction." At Brianna's blank look, the solicitor clarified for her. "Why, I refer to your not having to wear black for courting, my dear. Even though, I must say, you wear the color quite well, it certainly couldn't help matters for a young lady of your position to be confined to wearing black, and black only, as you went about socially—to parties and teas and balls, that is, where all the young folk gather."

"Don't you mean, 'where all the young *men* gather, to inspect the goods'?" amended Brianna between clenched teeth; the reminder of her having to marry was painful, that part of her father's plans for her continuing to be the thing she could least accept, the one constraint she kept trying to push out of her mind, so impossible did she find it to even contemplate. *Oh, Papa, was three short months all the freedom you could spare me?—Or do I even have that much?* Speculatively, she eyed Jesse. He seemed, at the moment, to be oblivious to her as he accepted a refilling of his wine goblet from a hovering servant. *Just how much does he—will he—expect of me in the coming weeks? Are you the Devereaux' friend Papa wrote of, Jesse Randall, or are you just one more jailer?*

Just then, almost as if he sensed her thoughts were on him, Jesse turned and met her eyes, and what he saw there moved him in ways he had not been prepared for. He'd seen a similar expression in the eyes of a trapped fawn, once, before he'd freed it from a hunter's snare intended for larger game. Suddenly, he found himself angry, angry at Etienne for setting up the entire, dubious scheme they were all now caught up in; angry with a society that required females of marriageable age to marry, whether they wished it, or were ready for it, or not; angry with the beautiful creature—half child, half woman—who sat beside him stirring all kinds of emotions he'd long regarded as dead and buried; and, finally, angry with himself for succumbing to a sort of inexplicable force, a compelling aura of some kind about the girl, a thing he could not ignore.

"George, Father," he said, turning to first one, and then the other of two men across the table from him, "this marriage by the end of the year business, how definite is it? That is, given the unintended haste this puts upon us, upon Brianna in particular—" Jesse's arm reached out and he laid a hand gently on her forearm "—isn't there some way of breaking—"

"Not a chance, *mon ami*," Father Edouard answered with a sad shake of the russet head.

Simpson joined him in the negation. "It's ironclad, son," he added. "I myself saw to it, for it was Etienne Devereaux' first instruction to me. 'Design a will that cannot be questioned or broken, George,' he said." His gaze moved sheepishly from Jesse to Brianna, a nervous adjustment of his lips indicating he half expected some renewed outburst on the volatile young woman's part.

But Brianna wasn't looking at George Simpson just then. Nor was she looking at Father Edouard's sympathetic face, or Jesse's, for that matter. What held all her attention at the moment was Jesse's hand as it rested on her forearm, a hand whose third finger wore a silver ring. The sole ornamentation on the ring had been wrought into the shape of an *eagle*!

"Where—what an unusual ring!" Brianna stammered as she continued to stare at the eagle with its wings and talons spread. "Where—where does it come from?" She quickly raised her head and met Jesse's eyes. "I—that is—I hope you don't mind my asking."

Under the wide-eyed look she now gave him, Jesse sensed an urgency to her question that he could not somehow ascribe a cause to, or identify, and he made a mental note not to underestimate the complexities he was now sure existed within her. For the moment, he decided to answer her question simply. "It was made by a Cherokee Indian chief named Long Arrow and given to me when I became a blood brother to his son, and, you might say, an honorary member of their tribe."

"Oh," Brianna's voice sounded barely above a whisper as she focused once more on the silver bird. "Why an eagle? Is—is it significant in some way?" she asked falteringly.

"You might say so," Jesse answered with a smile. "The figure represents their Indian name for me."

"Which is—?" prodded Brianna softly.

"Soaring Eagle, if I remember correctly," Father Edouard answered for Jesse. "How is Laughing Bear anyway? I can still taste the trout we caught on that fishing trip last year."

"Faring very well, Father, especially these days. His personal life is a happy one, I think."

"You mean, since his marriage to the black freedwoman— the servant of your brother's, I believe?"

"That, and the birth of their son," Jesse smiled.

Brianna's head was spinning. All this talk of Indians! And the ring, with the very eagle of Aimée's vision! What did it all mean? Suddenly she felt very closed in and badly in need of a breath of air. One look at the *Boeuf à la Devereaux* that was being served as their next course told her she was no longer hungry, that, indeed, if she had to eat one more bite, she would be ill.

"Gentlemen," she said as she pushed her chair away from the table, "if you don't mind, I think I could use a rest. Perhaps all that has happened today has finally proved too much for me. At any rate I find I am no longer hungry."

The three men rose from their seats as she did, Jesse's arm assisting her retreat from the table. "Are you all right?" he questioned.

"Just fine," said Brianna unconvincingly, but she shrugged off his further attempt at assisting her from the room. "Or I will be, as soon as I get some rest. Prenshaw," she said to the tall figure standing near the door, "please ask *Mademoiselle* Gitane to stop by here and then come to my room." She turned to the three men she had just left standing near the dining table. "I'm sorry to have to leave before you've all finished with your—your plans for me. My companion, *Mademoiselle* Aimée, will be stopping by here in a short while, en route to my chamber. I would ask that you please give her any additional details of how my life is to be run in the coming weeks." Brianna's breath was coming in short gasps, now, as anger once again took hold. "I assure you, she will carry out the task admirably. For a mere woman, she has an excellent memory." And with the sarcasm thick in the air behind her, and a swish of black silk, she whirled about and disappeared through the double doors.

Behind, in the dining hall, Simpson was muttering, "But—but things seemed to be going so well! What do you suppose led to all that anger at the end there, or am I just imagining it?"

"You weren't imagining it, George," chuckled Father Edouard. "And do forgive my humor in the face of the situation, gentlemen, but you see, I am, I'm afraid, just delighted that our *enfante* survived the years in France . . . basically unchanged. Brianna Devereaux is still what I had feared might be lost—*herself*!"

Chapter Twelve

Brianna stepped quietly into the hallway outside her chamber and cast a quick, furtive glance about before closing the door behind her. It was early, about an hour after daybreak, but she knew that already, somewhere belowstairs, there were servants busily starting their morning tasks, and the last thing she wanted right now was to be seen dressed in her stableboy's cast-offs.

Stealthily, boots in hand, she made her way toward the stairs on tiptoe. With a twinge of regret, she remembered things had been easier in former years whenever she'd wished to escape her chamber unseen, but after the pre-dawn horserace incident when she was ten, Papa had had that convenient magnolia branch outside her chamber window removed, and her favorite exit had ceased to exist.

She suppressed a giggle as she moved silently down the huge staircase, recalling the race that had cost her that convenience. Etienne had just acquired Le Duc as a half-green two-year-old, and Ranier had bet her his best pair of riding breeches that she couldn't remain on the colt for more than five minutes. Ranier was Serge's son, and, owing to his small size (he'd matched her ten-year-old frame, pound for pound, although he was sixteen at the time), he was also her father's favorite choice for a jockey whenever there was a betting race among the Upcountry gentry. She'd taken Ranier's bet, wagering her new bottle of an expensive scent from France, an item highly tempting to Ranier, for he had been courting a local milkmaid named Marie who encouraged giftgiving from her suitors. But Brianna had also enlarged the wager, boasting that she could not only re-

main astride Le Duc, but outrace any horse of Ranier's choosing on him, provided the course were not more than a quarter
mile. Of course, she had demanded, if she won, she would have
Ranier's new lawn shirt as well.

Finding herself outside the château, undiscovered now,
Brianna allowed herself a merry chuckle as she recalled Ranier's eager face when he'd accepted the bet. Poor Ranier! she
thought. He ought to have remembered that she had access to
all of her father's horsebreeding and racing records and even
helped keep some of the books at that time. She'd seen the
notes Etienne had made on Le Duc before purchasing him and
knew he was good for short-distance speed, lacking as yet the
stamina for longer distances, stamina he might acquire as he got
older. And, as for his being incompletely trained, well, she had
had confidence in her ability to handle the colt, and, besides,
she'd *needed* those boy's clothes!

The thought caused Brianna to stop for a moment on the
path leading to the stables and peruse her present garb. For as
long as she could remember, she'd begged for, wheedled and
borrowed some variety of male attire to do her serious riding.
And how often that had been necessary! She'd so frequently
been caught and the frowned-upon garb confiscated by a disappointed, scolding Aileen, Etienne or, yes, even Madame
Mézières. Of course, she thought with a smile, sometimes she
got lucky. When she'd won the race against Ranier, it was only
her too-tight set of old clothes that had been taken and burned
after the two were caught at the finish line by an angry Etienne
and a near apoplectic Serge. Suddenly Brianna's face fell and
grew somber. *Or perhaps not so lucky. How could I have forgotten that that was the incident that caused Papa to write to
his cousin in France, Madame Mézières!* She plopped down on
the sun-warmed stones of the path and slowly began to draw on
the riding boots she'd been carrying, her thoughts still far away.
Stupid ninny! she scolded her ten-year-old self. *Trading a moment's freedom for years of incarceration! "Sacré bleu!"*
found its way to her tongue as a particularly stubborn left boot
presented difficulties that coincided with her remembrance of
childhood folly.

"*Quel domage, Mademoiselle* Brianna," a softly chastising male voice proclaimed behind her. "Such oaths from a young lady!"

Whirling around as fast as her awkward sitting posture would allow, Brianna's eyes met a pair of highly polished riding boots and, traveling quickly upward, fawn-colored riding breeches encasing powerful thighs and lean masculine hips, and then a full-sleeved white shirt, half open in the front, exposing the tanned chest and neck and, finally, the bronzed face of Jesse Randall. He stood looking down at her, an amused expression on his handsome features.

"Oh, no!" groaned Brianna, "Not *you*!" She began tugging on the left boot that had been giving her trouble, in an effort to cover her discomfort at being found by him this way.

Jesse bent down near her. "Here, allow me," he said from behind her left shoulder, and Brianna felt him gently push her fumbling fingers aside after his arms had encircled her from behind; swiftly he tugged the boot into place with expert hands. "There, that ought to feel right," he said quietly from a distance of an inch or two behind her left ear. Then he was rising and on his feet again and extending a strong, bronzed hand to help her up.

Brianna accepted the help in awkward silence, her thoughts ajumble, her head faintly giddy from the physical closeness she'd just been subjected to. Once, twice, she swallowed before raising her eyes to his face. "I—I didn't expect—that is—how early are you usually up and about?"

"Well, that depends on where I am and what I've scheduled for my day," Jesse drawled.

He was standing very close to her yet, and Brianna had to look upward to meet his gaze, something she didn't need to do with people very often, owing to her own height. This added nothing to her already shaky composure, and she felt her mouth going dry, her teeth clenching as she waited to see what else he would say, especially now that she saw his eyes traveling slowly over her, taking in her appearance, inch by inch.

"*Quel domage, Mademoiselle* Brianna," he said, shaking his head as he repeated the French phrase he'd used earlier. "Such apparel on a young lady!" This time his words were even more heavily inflected with irony, and Brianna, who had begun to pinken under his careful scrutiny of a moment ago, now felt her face go scarlet.

"I—I loathe sidesaddles," she managed to get out before throwing him a defiant look and then glancing away. Then, hoping to change the subject, she asked him, "Where are you going?"

"I might ask you the same thing," he answered.

"Isn't it obvious?"

"Since I'm unaware of any masquerade balls being given hereabouts at this hour, no."

"That's odd," Brianna countered. "I could have sworn *you* were masquerading—as a *gentleman*!"

"Sorry, that would only be necessary in the presence of a *lady*," came the coolly amused retort.

Brianna shot him a look of cold disdain. "Very funny," she sneered. "But now, if you'll excuse me, I'm afraid I must be on my way." She moved toward the path on his right, adding, "I have some serious riding to do."

Jesse sidestepped to remain between her and the path. "Then I suggest you hasten to your chamber and don a proper riding habit," he said a little too softly.

Brianna stiffened, her lower lip thrust forward, ready for battle. She'd been expecting this. "I intend to ride Le Duc, my father's horse, for he badly needs the exercise. He—he has never worn a sidesaddle and might not take well to one, and since I'm quite proficient at riding astride—"

"So I noticed the other evening," said Jesse, his thorough perusal of her body leaving no doubt he was reminding her of the incident wherein he'd accused her of provoking his ungentlemanly attentions with her dress.

He succeeded only too well, for Brianna felt the heat rise to her cheeks with the recollection, and to make matters worse, she saw the gleam of satisfaction in the blue eyes, telling her he knew he'd hit the mark. "You—you blackguard!" she spat. "Just keep your eyes where they belong and there will be no problems!" She moved to step around him again, but Jesse moved with her, continuing to block her escape.

"And having bidden me to keep my eyes away, what will you do with all the others about?" he questioned. "What of the stableboys, the grooms, the trainers and footmen? Will you also tell them to keep their eyes heavenward while m'lady goes riding in breeches so clinging, they leave nothing to a man's imagination?" He was standing very close to her now, the blue eyes glittering and holding hers as he hammered home his anger with each syllable. "Or perhaps you would have us look, but not touch?" At Brianna's look of dismay he pressed on. "I didn't think so." Then, in a gentler tone, "Brianna, be reasonable. It was one thing to dress this way as a child. You had a child's body then, but now such—" his look told her his meaning all too clearly here, and Brianna blushed anew as he drove his point home " —such is no longer the case, my beautiful little ward. And so, for your own protection, I find myself playing the villain. I order you to go to your chamber and change—*now, please.*"

Brianna stood very still, her face several inches below his, her eyes focused on a point beyond his right shoulder. Finally she turned her face upward, a glint of defiance in the green eyes. "If I refuse?"

"You mean, if you persist in acting like a spoiled child?" There was a warning gleam in the blue eyes.

Brianna's chin raised a defiant notch. She would call his bluff. How dare he call her a child!

Jesse took a step away from her and stood with his legs spread, his arms folded across his chest. "My dear ward," he said softly. "I am, in one minute, going to walk away from you to the stables where I will saddle both your father's stallion and my mare, Gypsy, the latter with a sidesaddle she will have no problem wearing and carrying you on it, her training being complete. I will then mount Le Duc and wait exactly fifteen additional minutes—no longer—for you to appear in the prescribed garb. If you do not, or if, at any other time during the duration of my guardianship, I find you accoutered in your present state of dress, I'll turn you across my knees and spank that sweet little bottom you seem so bent on parading about, until it turns bright pink. Now," he said, reaching forward to raise her chin with his fingers, forcing her to look at him, "do I make myself clear?"

The green eyes that met his were bright with unshed, angry tears now, but Brianna knew when the game was lost. "Quite clear, *Monsieur*," she said crisply. She would have jerked her head away and made her retreat, but the strong fingers held her fast.

"I know it sounds like a weary platitude, Brianna, but I do this for your own good. I'd be a very poor guardian if I didn't protect the virtue you need—*must* have—" he amended, "to bring to your husband."

It was insult added to threatened injury, to be reminded of the hateful wedding that must take place, and Brianna exploded. "You bastard!" she hissed. She pushed at him with both hands and tore her chin out of his grasp. "I don't give a damn what I bring to my—to any man you force me to marry! Oh-h, *I hate you!*" And with an angry sob, she pivoted and ran down the path toward the château.

The following morning Brianna sat in the breakfast room by herself, moodily pushing a biscuit about on her plate. She was glad no one was with her, for, given her disposition at the moment, she felt she would be poor company. The cause of her glumness was, of course, the person who was proving to be her worst nemesis of late, her guardian. Or, to be more specific, she thought morosely, it was the man's most recent act that was causing her present state of irritation, his stricture against her riding astride and the attire it required. Who did Jesse Randall think he was, anyway? she asked herself as she chewed on the end of her green hair ribbon. God? For no one lesser had ever had success in keeping her from her favorite pastime dressed as she saw fit, and she was not about to allow Randall to be the first. There had to be a way to foil him—there just had to!

Suddenly, there were booted footsteps in the hallway, and Jesse Randall burst into the room just as Brianna was about to give her abused biscuit its fourth turn about the plate.

"Oh, excuse me, Brianna," he said casually. "I didn't expect to find anyone in here so early. I'm looking for Prenshaw. Have you seen him?"

Brianna did her best to cover her annoyance at having her thoughts interrupted by the very man who had caused them. Glancing at her tormentor with studied nonchalance, she quickly took in his appearance, which, to her total disgust, proved to be handsome as ever, from the top of his clean, shiny black hair to the toes of his perfectly polished, gleaming ebony riding boots.

"Prenshaw's in the summer kitchen with Mathilde, I think," she said to him. "He said he'd be back shortly—in case I needed to order some more breakfast, I suppose."

"Tell him I'll be waiting for him in the wine cellars." Jesse issued the instruction with the ease of someone accustomed to giving orders and having them obeyed. "He's to help me select some wines that Simpson suggested we take as gifts to our host at Monticello." This last was thrown at her over one broad shoulder as he turned and left the room.

"Hmph!" Brianna steamed. "*Tell* him this! *Do* that! *Don't* do the other! Oh, for tuppence I'd—"

Suddenly, Brianna had a notion; in seconds the notion became an idea, and the idea, a plan. She knew well, the wine cellars of Le Beau Château. She had gone there often as a child, sometimes with an adult, sometimes alone and without anyone's knowledge after "borrowing" the key from Mistress Delaney's ring. She'd spent many a happy hour hiding about the cavern-like rooms, peering around huge wooden casks, pretending she was a lady pirate inspecting her hidden booty. And when she had, there was one thing she had always been careful of; she had never allowed the door to close behind her, had always taken care to place some small object as a wedge between it and the jamb, because the door locked automatically when slammed *and could not be opened from the inside*!

Giggling to herself, she thrust the uneaten biscuit in her pocket for Le Duc's later consumption and left the table. If she timed it right, Jesse would be well out of sight in the wine chamber, for the room nearest the door held only aging brandies. Because of a draught that always existed near the door— someone had once told her it had to do with air that rushes from a warm place to a cold, or some such thing—it would be assumed that the door had been blown shut—she hoped. The one catch to this plan would be if Jesse had had the foresight to place his own wedge...but she thought it unlikely as he was unfamiliar with the cellars and, besides, he was expecting Prenshaw to follow shortly. Ah! She could almost taste her freedom, the wind blowing through her hair as she sat on Le Duc's back—*astride*, with no guardian to say her nay!

As she stepped carefully off the bottom step of the stone stairs leading to the wine cellars, Brianna's anticipation had almost grown to beyond where she could stand it. This would fix Jesse Randall and his highhanded ways! With an elated grin, she saw she was in luck. The heavy oak door had been swung wide open, its face against the adjoining wall. She had a brief moment of doubt about the plausibility of the draught she now felt ruffling her hair and its ability to close the door in its present position, but she shrugged it off. The childhood warnings had said one was never to trust it, hadn't they? With a few noiseless footsteps, she reached the door, swung it on its well-oiled hinges, and saw it shut.

"Goodbye, for a while, Mister Randall," she crooned with a satisfied grin, and then she was off, heading as fast as she could for her chamber and its cache of boy's togs.

She saw no one on her way, it still being early, though she took special care when tiptoeing by Aimée's chamber. She'd never question the little gypsy's loyalty, should she discover Brianna's mischief, but there was no sense in involving her unnecessarily.

Once in her room, she lost little time in changing her clothes, but then, just to be on the safe side, she donned an old blue day gown over the entire ensemble to hide it. Without shift, petticoats and corsets underneath, there was just enough room to close the buttons when she sucked in her breath, though she cursed mightily at having to do the difficult task without Aimée's help.

At last she was ready and took a quick look in her cheval mirror to check her appearance. The old gown, chosen for its high, demure neckline, completely concealed the white muslin shirt and brown broadcloth breeches she wore, although a tightness across the bodice reminded her that it had been purchased in the days before her breasts had finished developing. Quickly snatching a brown velvet ribbon from her armoire—the green had fallen off somewhere—she tied her long hair at the nape of her neck. Then she grabbed the biscuit for Le Duc, peeked to make sure her skirt covered enough of her riding boots, and was off, humming to herself, for the stables.

Her luck held as she ran down the path, for she encountered not a soul on the way, although she suspected she might not be so lucky at the stables. The stable help had a penchant for being about early, thanks to Serge's exacting discipline where care of the horses was concerned, but she had little doubt she could get by them. It might seem odd to see the lady of the château choose to do her riding in a day gown, but she would casually explain that her riding habits were too warm for this weather, mount Le Duc on a sidesaddle—to be discarded in that stand of trees beyond the south pasture—and enjoy her ride *bareback!* The added naughtiness of this latest ploy caused her to chortle with glee as she opened the stable's doors, and she was so involved in her mirth that she failed to notice anything until she was inside, where a destestably familiar male voice greeted her.

"Visiting the horses, lady?" Jesse Randall's tone carried an ominous smoothness as he stood facing her, hands on hips, legs spread, the expression on his face, threatening.

"You!" Brianna blanched. "You were supposed to be—that is, I—"

"Yes? Do continue," he purred. "Just where were you so sure I was supposed to be?" He took a menacing step toward her, and Brianna automatically backed toward the door. "It wouldn't by any chance be the wine cellars, would it, sweet ward?"

Suddenly Brianna straightened and looked him defiantly in the eye. Something had gone amiss and Jesse was obviously not trapped in those caverns, but he had no cause to blame anything on her. There was still no way he could connect *her* with the aborted mischief, she reasoned. For all appearances, she was just taking a stroll through the stables, bringing Le Duc a biscuit treat.

Haughtily, she thrust her chin forward. "What have the wine cellars to do with me?"

"Oh, quite a bit, I think—or perhaps I should say it's what *you* had to do with *them*." He took his hand and slid it inside his half-open shirt and slowly extracted Brianna's green hair ribbon. "Would you care to guess where I found this, sweet? I'll save you the time. It was at the base of the steps to the wine cellars, the very wine cellars where you unwittingly incarcerated poor Prenshaw, thinking, I believe, it was I!"

He advanced toward her another step. "Now the only problem I've yet to solve is why—why did you wish to see me put away for a few hours, hmm?"

Brianna's eyes grew wide as he came toward her, the closed door at her back allowing no more room to retreat. *Damn!* To think that she'd been so confident and caught up in her plotting, she'd missed losing the hair ribbon to that wretched draft!

But she had no time to think further, for Jesse was upon her, his hand fastening upon one slender shoulder while with the other he raised her skirt a few inches.

"Riding boots, my dear? And what else might be hidden beneath this ill-fitting frock?"

Brianna wildly tried to push his hand away from her skirt, saying, "Stop! You are being indecent!"

But Jesse, sure his guess was correct now, only raised her hemline higher, bringing a shapely pair of brown-clad legs into view.

By this time Brianna was frantic at being caught and more frantic to get away; she twisted from his shoulder hold, only to hear a ripping sound as half her skirt gave at the waistline, the faded blue material hanging loosely from Jesse's fist. She opened her mouth to scream her outrage, if not her fear, but Jesse's hand shot out to cover it.

"Young lady, I warn you, unless you wish the staff of the entire château to witness what's about to happen, you will avoid any screams." This said, and seeing the look of comprehension in her eyes, he released her mouth, just as Brianna delivered a swift kick to his leg with the toe of her riding boot. She felt she was fighting, if not for her life—although it almost felt that way—then for her pride right now, and she'd made up her mind not to give in to him without a battle.

"Oh, I wouldn't have done that if I were you," said Jesse; with a swift movement, he dipped and hoisted her over his shoulder like a sack of just so many potatoes.

"You can't do this!" shrieked Brianna, but then, thinking better of the situation and his warning of the noise and the attention it might draw, she shut her mouth and began hammering on his back with her fists.

Seemingly oblivious to her thrashings, Jesse opened the stable doors and began carrying her up the path.

"Where are you taking me?" Brianna demanded.

"Why, to the scene of your crime, sweet," came the reply.

"Crime! What crime? I only wanted— Oh, put me down, you tyrant!"

"Oh, I'll put you down, soon enough, you'll see." Jesse continued down the path, and soon he was pushing open the side door she'd left through, not half an hour earlier; then they proceeded along the route to the wine cellars.

Truly fearful now of his carefully leashed anger, Brianna made one last, desperate effort at gaining release. Stretching her head as it hung over his back, she reached for that well-muscled expanse and bit him—hard.

With a yelp, Jesse twisted to release her hold and set her down on the floor. She saw they were before the door that opened to the wine cellar steps.

"You undisciplined brat!" he ground out between clenched teeth. He reached to massage his injured back.

"*Brat!* You jackanapes! How dare you handle me this way!" Brianna made a dive to his right in an attempt at taking advantage of his unguarded side, but Jesse was quicker. Snaking an arm about her waist from behind, he wrenched her hard against his hip, tore open the door and dragged her wildly protesting body down the steep stone steps. Behind them the door swung shut, cutting off their greatest source of light, though someone had left candles burning in tin sconces at the base of the stairwell. Taking this all in, in a matter of seconds, Brianna began to feel naked panic at the sense of being isolated— trapped down here, away from any possible source of help, with this madman. Gone was her concern that anyone should hear her; indeed, her prime objective now became that someone *should* hear her, and she began to scream and shout at him at the top of her lungs.

"Take your miserable paws off me, you wretch!" she cried as Jesse hauled her through the door to the wine cellar itself.

"Louder—they can't possibly hear you," Jesse taunted. He set her down rudely before him, and, her legs catching in the hanging folds of her torn skirt, she thrust out her arms to keep her balance.

"Whoreson bastard!" she hissed as she picked up her skirt and sought to lunge past him toward the open door.

"My, my, what a convent education does produce these days," Jesse sneered as he caught her easily around the waist. "Or perhaps it's merely that your education with the good sisters lacked the one thing I'm about to provide." He cast about as if searching for something, and, apparently finding it, dragged her toward a stout brandy cask; there he promptly seated himself on it and threw her, face down, across his lap. "You've had this coming for a long time," he articulated in angry syllables. And without wasting another moment, he raised his arm and delivered to her well-positioned backside a resounding *thwack!*

Shrieking in disbelief, Brianna began to kick and tried to twist out of the way, but the punishing palm lifted and descended again to find its mark in unerring fashion.

"This," said Jesse, "is for Prenshaw, who had the misfortune to be directed here by me after I had run into you." The flat of his palm descended: *Thwack!*

"And this," he said next, "is for your plotting." Again, the open palm: *Thwack!*

"And for your unladylike language, this—": *Thwack!*

"Ow! No! Don't!" cried Brianna, tears coming hard and fast now, but more from the anger and humiliation she felt than from the pain to her buttocks.

"Oh, but I shall," replied Jesse as he raised his palm again. "For what's the use of a spanking except that it serve to keep the offender from repeating her errors? And to do that, my dear, you must be reminded of what those errors were. For daring to disobey, this one!" Again, the punishing hand came down: *Thwack!*

"Stop! Ow-w-w!" cried Brianna. "You *bastard*! Oh, I *hate* you!"

"Still no improvement in your language, my dear? It seems you haven't been listening well—or *feeling* well!" added Jesse as, with a quick, wrenching movement, he tore the remainder of her tattered skirt from its waistline, exposing her masculine-clad buttocks in their tight brown broadcloth. "For failing to learn your lesson, even now!" *Thwack!*

This time there was no mistaking the sharp, stinging pain as his palm made contact, and Brianna's cry acknowledged it loudly.

"Thinking it over, my dear?" Jesse bent forward to catch her eye as she stared murderously at him over her shoulder. She saw his palm was again poised for action. "I'll give you five seconds to apologize and it will be over. Otherwise.... One..." he began.

Brianna saw the resolution in his face and knew he meant it.

"Two..." came the count.

He was a brute, but there was no way out.

"Three..."

Oh, but apologies were so *hard* when one didn't *feel* them!

"Four..."

But the stinging, throbbing sensation in her buttocks left no room for argument. "Stop!" she cried. "I—apologize." The final word came out in a watery murmur.

"So be it," said Jesse, and with a quick movement, he was setting her on her feet and rising, himself, to tower over her.

Brianna didn't know where to look, her humiliation was so complete. Casting her eyes downward to avoid looking at him, she began to move toward the door.

"Not so fast, young lady," said her guardian. He strode quickly past her, making for the door himself. Once there, he turned and gave her an appraising look. "You can hardly move about the house dressed as you are. I suggest you remain here for a while to contemplate your—ah—repentance while I fetch Mistress Delaney to bring you a needle and thread—to repair your gown, my dear. After that, when she's released you, you will search out Prenshaw and apologize to him as you have already done to me. Only then, will you be completely off the hook—or should I say, 'off the cask'?" he added with an amused glance at the seat of her recent punishment. Then, without waiting for her comment, he turned and shut the door behind him.

It was over four hours later when a greatly agitated Mistress Delaney opened the wine cellar door with her key.

"Ah, me poor, poor lass. What came over ye, t' be lockin' yerself in th' wine cellar this way?"

Brianna's reply was silence, her look, mutinous as she waited to hear what further explanation her guardian might have concocted to explain her incarceration. Locked herself in, indeed!

The housekeeper continued. "Why, if it hadn't been fer Mister Jesse sayin' he wanted me t' fetch a bottle o' that '79 Bordeaux he's so fond o' fer dinner, ye might've spent half the afternoon in here—or more! Lord, lass, what happened t' yer frock? And why are ye wearin'—"

"I tore it trying to break out of here, Mistress Delaney," Brianna lied. She had no intention of letting *anyone* know of the humiliation she'd just suffered. "And the reason I'm wearing breeches is—is that this is one of the places where I'd hidden a pair for myself, and so I found them in the dark and put them on. You—ah—wouldn't happen to have a needle and thread on you, would you?"

"Why, fancy, but I do!" exclaimed the Irishwoman. "Ye see, Mister Jesse asked me t' fetch one just before he thought t' ask fer th' wine. Said he had a shirt wanted mendin', he did."

"Of course," muttered Brianna as she grabbed the proffered spool and needle. When she proceeded to sew the tattered remains of her skirt to her bodice where she stood, Mistress Delaney protested that she should do her sewing sitting down, but a venomous sounding curse in scathing French and a murderous glance from the green eyes soon silenced the poor woman.

Twenty or so minutes later, her abused garment hastily stitched together, Brianna was on her way to her chamber, her temper barely in check. On the way she ran into Prenshaw to whom she delivered a brief explanation of his incarceration, to the effect that she'd thought the wine cellar empty, the door left open in error, hence her own error in shutting it, followed by a clipped apology uttered in tones so abrupt that they left the poor man apologizing for having gotten in the way of her mistake. This done, she sailed toward her chamber with as much dignity as her rumpled, hastily mended garment would allow, locked her door and remained there for the rest of the day and night.

That evening, Jesse took the bottle of '79 Bordeaux and went to dine with Serge in his cottage.

"And so, tell me, *mon ami*," said the old man as they were finishing the *Cotes de veau* Mathilde had sent over, "how are you and your young *pupille* getting on, eh?" Serge scratched his gray moustache as he added with an afterthought, "You know, she had promised to come by to look in on me this afternoon, but later sent word by her little companion that she was not feeling up to it and would come another time. I hope she is not ill, the little one, for it is not like her to take to her chamber that way—not like her at all.''

In the flickering candlelight they dined by, he missed the glint of amusement in the blue eyes as Jesse took another sip of the excellent Bordeaux.

Chapter Thirteen

The days that passed found Jesse and his ward avoiding each other as much as possible as each prepared for the upcoming trip to Virginia. True to his word, Simpson made available a seemingly unlimited amount of funds for a new wardrobe for the Devereaux heiress, and a seamstress appeared one day when Brianna returned from an unavoidable ride with Jesse who had ordered her to accompany him. As for the ride, she suffered it in a steaming silence that spoke more than words, dutifully attired in a riding habit of hunter green. And while she fumed, Jesse endured her mood with amused silence, breaking it only to sing occasionally, in a maddeningly melodic baritone, to Le Duc, whom he rode in flawless fashion, and then, at the end of the ordeal, to compliment her on her riding prowess—*à la* sidesaddle—on the mare, Gypsy. Afterward, both Aimée and the French émigrée seamstress caught an earful of unladylike French as Brianna vented her ire during the selection of fabrics in the château's sewing room, a nervous and mercifully uncomprehending Mistress Delaney casting a doubtful eye over Brianna from nearby.

Jesse spent the time meeting with Pinckney as the latter briefed him and Honoré Dumaine with the details necessary to their meeting—or mission, as Jesse began to regard it—at Monticello. During these sessions he continued to regard Honoré's presence as something he preferred to do without, but there was no denying the man's competence as an attaché, for Pinckney seemed to favor him over others Jesse met who might have functioned in his place, and had trained him well, making it clear he had come to rely greatly on him in these matters in the past. Remembering his discovery that the Governor was not above using spies to secure information, Jesse ventured a suspicion that it might be in that capacity that Dumaine was in his proper element and made a mental note not to drop his guard around him at any time, now, or during the trip to Virginia. Moreover, it bothered him that Honoré had implied a threat where Brianna and her inheritance were concerned, and with that in mind, he doubled his resolve to keep a careful eye on the man. Only when a note arrived from Isaac, telling him he and Festus were on their way, did Jesse begin to relax over the situation.

One afternoon, a week after Etienne's funeral, Brianna found herself with time on her hands; she voiced her boredom over a cup of tea as she sat in the kitchen with Mistress Delaney, much as she had years ago, the cozy warmth of the kitchen appealing to her sense of noncomformity; it was a place where one could let one's manners relax somewhat. When the housekeeper suggested taking a turn at the harpsichord or plying her needlework to occupy the time until dinner, Brianna's answer was couched in a torrent of expletives she prudently delivered in French.

"I'm sorry, Mistress Delaney," she apologized when the tirade was over, "but I guess I never did enjoy those utterly ladylike pastimes. Oh, I learned to wield a needle and finger a keyboard well enough. The sisters saw to that," she added with a wrinkling of her nose. "But they're not something I would choose over—over riding a horse or—or berrypicking, for instance." She mentioned the latter activity with a meaningful look, having just learned that Father Edouard had come by and invited her and Aimée out to help him pick wild berries that he would later use to concoct a delicious berry brandy, but Brianna had not been given the message to join them because she had been scheduled for yet another fitting with the seamstress.

"Miss Brianna," admonished the older woman as she wagged a finger in her direction, "'Tis foolish ye be, t' be clingin' t' the ways o' yer youth so. 'Tis high time ye be learnin' the ways o' the lady ye were raised fer, a fine lady, like yer poor dead Ma. Why, 'twas just t' other day, it was, I heard Mister Simpson sayin' he was writin' t' a lady he knows, askin' her t' come t' the château 'n' school ye in the arts o' runnin' this place. Ye'd do well t' remember ye've a duty t' maintain if ye be wantin' t' hold on t' yer inheritance!''

Brianna was taken aback momentarily by the housekeeper's words. She'd forgotten about that provision of the will. Oh, she thought, was there no end to the restraints she found herself facing? Suddenly the need to escape the walls around her became overwhelming, and she knew she had to be out of doors somewhere—anywhere but here, taking a genteel cup of tea with her housekeeper.

"Excuse me, Mistress Delaney," she said as she set her teacup down with a clatter. "I'm going out for a breath of air."

"Ye're not thinkin' o' puttin' on that disgraceful clothin' again, are ye?" the housekeeper asked in alarm. She called after the fleeing figure who'd just reached the outside door. "Ye know Mister Jesse gave out the order, don't ye? Told us all t' keep an eye on ye, said we—"

"Oh, a pox on Mister Jesse!" Brianna shouted over her shoulder but then, seeing the old woman's look of chagrin, softened her response, saying, "Oh, Mistress Delaney, don't worry. I'm not going riding. I'm just going down to the stables to have a look at those new kittens Aimée said one of the barn cats had. See you later!"

As she raced toward the stables with all the speed of pent-up energy, suddenly released, Brianna's spirits lifted. She became so eager, she almost tripped over her skirt, the sheer yellow cotton of her day gown catching on a shoe buckle as she failed to raise it high enough to clear her sprinting steps.

It had been warm in the sun, and she felt herself welcoming the cool interior of the brick-floored stables when she entered, stopping a moment once inside to allow her eyes to adjust to the lower level of light. Warm, equine smells met her nostrils, but they were clean smells, coming from a well-tended stable, and she fairly drank them in, reveling in them as she always had. From the loft overhead came the scent of freshly mown hay, and as Brianna glanced upward, she spied three tiny balls of fur peering curiously down at her.

"Ah, there you are," she called to the kittens, "but you're more than just a day or two old! Where's your mama been hiding you, hmm?"

Brianna moved toward the ladder that would take her up to join them when a noisy quacking sounded from the nearby tackroom. "Oh, hello, Dependable," she said cheerfully. Dependable was a mallard duck who had attached himself to the Le Beau Château stables as a useful kind of mascot, she had found out from Serge. His presence had, on more than a few occasions, served to calm down a new horse when it was brought in with a case of jitters because of its new surroundings. Something about the little fellow always seemed to soothe these horses, hence the name, "Dependable." But Dependable's home stall was Le Duc's, and, having greeted Brianna, he was headed in his direction now, quacking contentedly to himself as he waddled along.

"Take care, Dependable," Brianna laughed. "Tell Le Duc I'll be by to see him later, after I've dug up a carrot from old Serge's carrot garden." She smiled to herself as she ascended the ladder to the hay loft, thinking how lucky her family had been to have people like Serge working for them. How many head grooms were so devoted to their charges that they kept a garden of nothing but carrots to be used as treats for the horses?

When she reached the top of the ladder, the kittens were nowhere in sight. Since it was not a large loft, like the one in the hay barn out back, but merely an adjunct to the stables, built as a convenience that would assure a small supply of hay always within easy reach, Brianna knew it wouldn't take her long to find the kittens, and she began to make a game out of it.

"Very well, you little rascals," she called, "let's see you resist this!" Out of her pocket she withdrew a pincushion she had inadvertently placed there during her fitting session with the seamstress. Extracting the lone needle it held, she tossed the brightly striped, ball-shaped object toward a bale of hay a few yards away. Sure enough, a second after it landed, two orange puffs appeared to investigate, and a moment later, a black and white one followed from behind the hay bale. Then, before Brianna could make another move, a rustling noise to her left caught her attention, and there, emerging from yet another bale of hay, was the most beautiful adult calico she'd ever seen, and gently held in its mouth, a fourth kitten, coal black.

"Why, hello, Calico Cat," said Brianna. "Where did they get you? You're much too fat and pretty to be a barn cat, you know."

The mother cat stood very still, her black offspring still in her mouth as she stared at the human intruder. Brianna sat very quietly on the loft floor, unwilling to move, lest she frighten her. Out of the corner of her eye she saw the other three kittens stalking the pincushion in serious fashion. A good minute passed before their black sibling made a tiny mewing sound from where it hung, still delicately suspended from its mother's jaws. The calico gave Brianna another second of unblinking perusal and then proceeded to advance toward her. When she reached the fringes of the petticoat that fanned in an arc in front of her, she very carefully, ceremoniously, almost, deposited her small black cargo on the loft floor, gave it two thorough licks, and retreated a couple of feet. There she sat down and watched.

The tiny black kitten took a couple of tottering steps toward Brianna before it stopped and began to mew again, this time sounding quite helpless. Very slowly, Brianna reached a tentative hand out toward the tiny creature, keeping a careful eye on the cat she'd already dubbed "Calico Cat." The adult animal gave what sounded like an encouraging "meow," and the dark kitten immediately turned in her direction but misjudged its footing in the loose hay on the floor and tumbled over sideways.

All of a sudden, Brianna realized something was wrong. She didn't give it much thought at the moment, but later she was to attribute it to a kind of sixth, or refined, sense she had with animals, owing to her years of doctoring and caring for them as a child at the Abbaye, and even earlier. All she knew now was that something wasn't right about this kitten, and she had the unalterable sense that Calico Cat was asking for her help.

Slowly, taking great care, she reached out and picked the tiny thing up. Several yards away its three littermates were happily entangled in one another's legs, the gaily colored pincushion in their midst. Calico Cat remained where she was.

Tenderly, ever so gently, Brianna lifted the kitten, at last cuddling it to her breast. When she had held it there for a short while, finally feeling it relax and then begin to purr, she bent to examine it. As she moved it slightly in her arms, its tiny head came up with a start, and it was then Brianna knew what was wrong. What should have been two bright, alert feline eyes were instead clouded over with a nearly milk-white film. The kitten was blind.

"Oh, sweet little bits," crooned Brianna sadly. "Alas, I cannot help you. This is no broken leg or torn flesh that will mend, but an affliction beyond cure." Again she cradled the creature softly in her arms, gently stroking its warm fur as she regarded the mother cat. "Calico Cat, you've brought your babe to me and somehow trusted me with it, and I promise you, I'll take care of it for you," she said softly. "We'll have to make a house cat of her—or is it a he? Will you mind?"

The mother cat gave out with a single "meow" as she continued to watch Brianna holding her kitten. Then, as if she'd made up her mind about something, she rose and ambled over to her other three offspring and lay down beside them. Eagerly the three began to suckle.

So, they weren't weaned yet, Brianna realized, but she guessed they might be—or Little Bits, as she now dubbed the sightless one, might be, if she handled it right. And so she made her decision. Leaving the kitten here might spell its end, and she wondered briefly how it had survived thus far. Animals were often known to destroy their own young when they were born sick or less than whole. Quickly, the black ball of fluff firmly in hand, she made for the ladder and began to descend. Her last glimpse of the loft took in a serene maternal feline with her back to the ladder. Calico Cat had made her decision too.

Brianna made her way down the center aisle of the main wing of the stables—she wouldn't forget her promise to visit Le Duc whose stall was the large boxed one at the end—when she heard several men's voices in what sounded like hearty words of greeting. Curious, she hastened toward the door, stopping only a moment to pat Le Duc's velvety nose and whisper a promise of *two* carrots—later.

"Isaac, so help me, if I ever again travel further than thirty miles from Riverview without your civilized presence, they can hang me with my own cravat!" Jesse's voice rang out clearly above the others, sounding relaxed and cheerful.

Curious now, as to the identities of the other men, Brianna stepped quickly through the stable doorway, squinting against the sudden onslaught of bright September sunshine before shielding her eyes with one hand while she clutched Little Bits safely to her with the other. In the center of the stable's brick-floored entry-courtyard were Jesse and two men on horse-back. The latter just then proceeded to dismount, and Brianna grinned at the strange picture they made. Standing side by side, the two newcomers couldn't have been in greater contrast; the one nearest Jesse was a short, dapper fellow impeccably dressed in a riding jacket and pantaloons of English cut, by the look of them; fine boned and utterly correct of posture, he appeared to be in his mid-forties, with pale, neatly clubbed hair and fair skin; to his left, a couple of feet behind him, stood an enormous black man who was dressed in riding clothes of a more casual, or informal, design. A new-looking tricorn protected his head from the sun and prevented Brianna from seeing much of his face, but the wide, even-toothed grin he wore was unmistakable as Jesse shook his outstretched hand.

"Festus," Jesse said to him with a warm smile, "they say a man's done all his growing long before he reaches the age of twenty-five—or is it twenty-six now?—but I could swear you've grown bigger since I last saw you!"

The black man laughed. "Now, Mistah Jesse, y'all knows we's 'bout de same in de *tall* depahtment, but Ah 'spec' Ah coulda put on sumpfin' in de *wide* depahtment, whut wid dat Miz Christie feedin' us de way she bin doin'. She done sent Mistah Garrett ovah wid a picnic basket *every day!*"

Jesse laughed as he reached for the reins of the big man's horse, turning as he did so and thus catching sight of Brianna leaning lightly against the stable entryway. Pausing a moment, he drank in the sight of her. Never had he seen her more beautiful. She stood, graceful and willowy in the sunlight which played upon the rich color of her hair, turning it to shining swirls of copper and gold as it curled freely about her slender shoulders and beyond, reaching nearly to her lithe hips. Her buttercup yellow daygown was of traditional design, with close-fitting sleeves that reached her elbows, where they finished with a feminine flounce of white lace. The bodice had a square neckline that dipped low enough to reveal two tempting mounds of flesh when she folded her arms before her, as she did now, and the artlessly seductive effect was not lost on Jesse in the brief seconds he required to take this all in. "Brianna," he called, "come and meet these gentlemen."

As Brianna began to walk toward them, he added, "I'm sure you'll be wanting to become acquainted—they'll be accompanying us on our trip to Virginia." Then he made a gesture toward the little man, saying, "Mistress Brianna Devereaux, allow me to present Isaac Sommers, the best gentleman's gentleman this side of the Thames—or the other, for that matter."

"Mistress," said Isaac in crisp British syllables as he bowed properly before her.

"How do you do?" Brianna smiled. Then she shifted Little Bits from right arm to left so she might extend a right hand in greeting. "Welcome to Le Beau Château, Mister Sommers."

"Just Isaac will be adequate, Mistress," returned the small man as he took her proffered hand. "I see you've a fondness for kittens," he added as he saw her shift her small burden.

"Yes, well, for all animals," said Brianna, "but this one presents a special problem."

"Oh?" queried Jesse as he brought Festus forward with an arm about the black man's massive shoulders.

"Yes," Brianna said as she glanced compassionately down at Little Bits. "I've just discovered this kitten is blind."

Festus stopped dead in his tracks and raised his head. "Blind? Ma'am, is yo' sho'?"

Wearing a curious expression on his face, Jesse quickly introduced Festus to Brianna, adding quietly at the end, "Festus is a highly competent blacksmith, and he also happens to be blind."

Brianna's lips formed a silent O as she looked at Jesse before turning her attention to the black giant in front of her. She extended the same hand she had given Isaac but was careful to brush the cuff of Festus's shirt as she said, "I'm pleased to meet you, Mister Festus."

Grinning down at her, Festus took the hand she offered, saying, "Jes' Festus, Ma'am."

"Only if you and Isaac both make it 'just Brianna,'" came the reply.

"Dass a mighty levelin' way o' dealin' wid each othah," Festus replied, looking slightly uncomfortable. "Ah don' know if—"

"The world is changing, *Messieurs*," came a bright, feminine voice from across the courtyard. "In France these days we would all be addressing one another as '*Citoyen*,' or 'Citizen So-and-So'!"

Several heads turned to find Aimée entering the courtyard, a smile on her face as she approached the group with bouncy steps.

"Aimée!" Brianna called. "Come, you must meet everyone." She proceeded to make introductions all around while Aimée stood in their midst, her petite figure the center of attention as she bobbed her head at each. Brianna was glad to see she was wearing the new red-and-white striped frock she'd persuaded the seamstress to make for her friend, for it complemented Aimée's dark coloring and enhanced her prettiness, despite the silly mobcap she wore with several unruly curls thrusting their way outside it.

Just then, a series of meows interrupted them as Little Bits decided to make his presence known again.

All went silent for a moment, except for the meowing, until Festus reached out a cupped palm. "Please. Kin Ah hold 'im?" he asked softly.

Brianna took the tiny creature with both her hands and carefully placed it in the big man's huge palm. Then, ever so gently, Festus drew it in to his chest, softly cradling the kitten there as, with a pair of fingers from his other hand, he delicately stroked the downy fur. The small ball of dark fluff settled in and the meowing ceased.

"You appear to have the way—*a* way—with animals, *Monsieur* Festus," chirped Aimée, "or at least with this one. Why don't you keep him?"

There was a second or two of awkward silence before Brianna broke in with a hasty explanation that both Festus and Little Bits were blind, but then, as she looked at the big giant of a man tenderly caressing the helpless mite in his massive hands, she broke off in mid-sentence, saying, "Yes, Festus, why don't you keep him?"

Festus raised his huge head in the direction from which her voice had come. "Oh, Miz Brianna, Ah sho' would lahk dis kitten, but—"

"Then take him!" Aimée chimed in. "You are a man who doesn't let a little blindness stand in his way."

All eyes, save those of Festus and Little Bits, focused on Aimée.

"How did you know that?" Jesse queried softly.

Aimée's face flushed, but she covered it with a Gallic shrug, saying, "I am a good judge of character, *Monsieur*." Then, turning back to Festus, "Well, will you take this kitten or not?"

"Well . . ." murmured Festus as he continued to stroke Little Bits.

"I tell you what!" exclaimed Aimée. "Suppose I offer to help you with him at first, until you developing—*develop*—a routine for his care?"

Festus grinned. "Dis lady don' make it easy t' say no," he said, then was silent a moment. Finally, he asked, "Whut col- oh he be?"

"Black," came a quartet of voices.

Now the black man's grin split his face from ear to ear. "Dat settle it!" he asserted with a decisive nod. "Dis kitten *mine*!"

There was a chorus of laughter, not the least of which was Aimée's delighted chortle. *"Très bon,"* she added, "And now I must deliver the message I was sent with when I came out here." She waited a moment as two stableboys came to take the newcomers' mounts. Then she turned to Brianna and Jesse. *"Monsieur* Dumaine was here. I run—*ran*—into him just as I returned from berrypicking. When I told him neither of you was at the château, he would not wait, but asked that you be given this message: 'We leave on Wednesday, two days earlier than planned.' That is all he have—*had*—to say. Then he rode off." Aimée gave a slight shudder. "Bah! That one I do not like!"

"You're not alone," said Brianna. "But what did he mean by '*we* leave'?" she asked Jesse.

"Aimée," Jesse said, "as long as you're here, would you take Festus and Isaac up to the château for some refreshments and ask Prenshaw to make some sleeping arrangements for them?

Tell him, too, that Brianna and I will be up shortly and that we'll dine at eight.''

"But of course," Aimée answered. Then she grabbed Festus by the arm, smiled at Isaac and said, "Gentlemen, you are about to meet a genuine English butler. Perfection in every flawless detail, you know." Aimée mimicked Prenshaw's haughty stance and did a passable job at imitating his crisp British syllables, despite her French accent.

But as they began their way up the path, Isaac was heard to say, "We'll see about that!"

When they had gone, Brianna turned to Jesse. "Well?"

"Well, what?"

"You obviously wished to speak with me, or you wouldn't have sent them on. It's about Honoré, isn't it?"

"Astute, aren't you, Green Eyes?" At Brianna's frown of annoyance he added, "Yes, I'm afraid it is about Honoré."

"You don't like him, either." It was a statement, not a question.

"*Very* astute," Jesse responded. "There's something about the man . . ." He shrugged. "Well, perhaps it's just his dour nature. Such people rarely make friends easily."

"Honoré," spat Brianna, "is a swine! And I have good reason to call him such—and worse! Believe me, he earns his dislike!"

"I was afraid that might be the case," said Jesse. "Nevertheless, I am forced to include him on the trip."

Brianna's winged eyebrows flew up toward her hairline. "You *what*?"

"I had meant to tell you earlier, but it somehow escaped mention. For business reasons I cannot go into with you, Honoré Dumaine is to accompany us to Jefferson's home."

Across Brianna's face flitted a series of looks that ranged from stunned incredulity, to anger, to complete dismay. She had been viewing the upcoming trip with some measure of anticipation, even eagerness, for she welcomed the chance to change her surroundings for a while, to get away from Le Beau Château which, though much beloved as her childhood home, had been the scene of recent sorrow. Above all, the visit to Monticello was to have afforded her the chance to think, to ponder all that had been happening in her life of late. Now, however, all such anticipations were shattered with this unwelcome news.

"You couldn't know," she said dully, "but once, when my sister and I were little, she discovered a robin's nest in a tree near the barn and told me of it, and each day we would quietly go to check on it, waiting for the hatching. But Honoré had overheard her tell me of it, and he was waiting, too." She raised sad green eyes to look at Jesse. "One day we went there, expecting that surely this would be the day. When we arrived, the entire nest lay on the ground, its bloody blue shells smashed horribly between bits of—oh, God, it was *awful!*" She shook her head slowly, tears trickling down her cheeks.

Jesse took two quick strides and closed the gap that separated them, wrapping big, comforting arms about her. "Honoré? You're sure?" he asked softly.

Brianna nodded, her face against his shirt. "He—he even boasted about it to us later," she said, choking on a sob. "He was with us for a rare fortnight's stay—someone in the family had died, someone in his household, and Mother had offered the invitation for him to visit with us. She—she said she hoped it would help us get to know him better, and—and—" Brianna suddenly pulled back out of Jesse's arms, and looked up at him. The green eyes narrowed. "Well, we got to know him, all right. Right now, I know enough of Honoré Dumaine to last me a *lifetime!*"

Jesse looked at her and sighed. "I'm sorry, Brianna. And I'll admit, even before you said anything, I had a host of negative feelings about the man. Enough so that I did all I could to dissuade the Governor—it's Governor Pinckney whose business I am about—from using Dumaine in this business, but I was not successful."

Jesse stepped forward, lay an arm gently about her shoulders and began to walk with her toward the château. "Suffice it to say," he continued, "that now that I know for sure how well founded my fears about the man are, I'll be doing everything in my power to keep him apart from you during the visit. Festus, Isaac and Father Edouard will be told, too—"

"Oh, Father Edouard knows all about Honoré," interrupted Brianna. "He's the one we told after discovering the—the nest."

"Not Etienne?" queried Jesse softly.

"No, not Papa. Deirdre was all for telling him, but I—I thought he might be too—too saddened by such news. So I persuaded her that we should tell Father Edouard instead."

Jesse was silent for a moment. "I see," he said finally. "Brianna, how old were you then?" He had stopped for a moment on the path and was looking down at her, a curious expression on his face.

"Oh, about six, I think, why?"

Again there was silence as Jesse seemed to be digesting her reply. "Oh, no reason," he answered at length. "Are you feeling any better now?"

"Yes, thank you," Brianna replied softly, a shy half-smile on her lips.

"Good," Jesse answered firmly, "because I'm getting hungry, and it's less than an hour until dinnertime. We'll have to hurry if we don't want the dining hall to smell of the stables instead of a roast of the wild geese I saw hanging in the kitchens this morning. Come, the last one down to dinner owes the other a small gift."

"Giver's choice, or winner's choice?" she queried.

Jesse looked down at her as she stood next to him in the lazy September sunshine and smiled. There were times, as now, when, for all her vexing ways, she reminded him of a delightful child, eager, inquisitive, intellectually open. And the account of her sensitivity to her father at the age of six had not been lost on him. It was also in the spirit of answering a child's need that he had just comforted her in his arms, everything about her calling upon the protective instincts in him. Yet he was never completely unaware, as well, of the delicious perfection of the woman's body that housed all that childlike innocence, the compelling quality of those huge green eyes in a face that was beautiful beyond—Jesse gave his head a brief shake in what was becoming of late a habit of trying to dispel certain thoughts he preferred not to deal with. Broadening his smile into a grin, he answered her question with one of his own. "If you win, what would you have?"

It was Brianna's turn to grin, for she had no intention of losing. "An afternoon—no, make that a morning, prearranged with you, in an area you've approved of, for I shall expect you to stand guard and protect my virtue—in which I shall be allowed to ride astride with impunity." She finished with a look of delighted satisfaction as she gazed up at him with delicately cocked eyebrows, waiting for his reply.

Jesse couldn't help chuckling as, with a helpless shake of his head, he said, "You aren't one to yield easily, are you, Green Eyes?"

His use of the epithet tempted Brianna to a sharp retort, for she was inexplicably bothered by it, but she bit back the words and merely smiled up at him, waiting.

"Very well," Jesse chuckled at last, "but, as you said, I'm to escort you to the starting point, and I must approve of time and place, not to mention," he added, "a properly concealing cloak of some sort, which you must don and wear until we get there, and afterward, on the ride back." He finished with an admonishing finger brandished in her direction.

Eagerly Brianna nodded, then asked, "And if I lose—which I have no intention of doing—what would you have of me, Sir Guardian?"

"Ah!" exclaimed Jesse softly. "Now, this requires a moment of consideration." He began to rub his chin thoughtfully with his fingers as he gazed pensively at Brianna, and she resisted the urge to squirm and fidget under his perusal; as he looked at her, the blue eyes intense in the handsome face as they focused on hers, she had the distinct sense of a moment of intimacy between them, an intimacy she couldn't explain, for they were standing several feet apart and nowhere near touching. But she willed herself to hold his gaze, feeling it was important, for some unknown reason, to do so. Later she was to wonder at her feelings of this moment and call herself silly and foolish over them, but for now, her gaze did not falter.

At length Jesse smiled, saying, "Ah, I have it!" He looked at her silently for a moment and his smile grew. "If I win—and I, too, do not intend to lose—you must let me call you Green Eyes whenever I wish, without objection—even silent ones," he added knowingly. "You do really have the most incredible eyes, you know." He focused directly—intently—on the objects under discussion.

More than a little nonplussed, Brianna at last turned away, saying nervously, "Have you never seen green eyes before?"

"On the contrary," Jesse answered lightly. "My brother, Garrett, wears a pair of emeralds in his face, but I assure you, lovely ward, they do not compare in color, or light, or form, to what I see when I look at yours. Now," he added, "the hour grows even later. Are the terms agreeable, and will *Mademoiselle* race?"

Brianna turned back to look at him then, and as green eyes met blue, she gave a short, delighted laugh. "She will!" she said with a shout, and proceeded to dash for the château.

"And may the most deserving win!" called Jesse as he sprinted after the slender figure already a couple of yards ahead on the path.

Chapter Fourteen

"Wake up, *chérie*, wake up!" Aimée's cheerful voice pushed, unwanted, through the haze of sleep as Brianna turned away and pulled a soft feather pillow over her head.

"Go away, you gypsy tyrant!" groaned Brianna as she sought to burrow deeper under the feathery softness. "It cannot be morning yet!"

"Ah, but it is," came the response, "although a bit earlier than even you are used to rising." With a single swoosh, Aimée opened the green velvet drapes at the east window near the bed, sending a wash of early September dawn into the chamber. "It is nearly five o'clock, *mon ami*, and you know Monsieur Jesse said we leave promptly at six!"

With a soft moan, Brianna reluctantly pushed the pillow away from her head and dragged herself into a sitting position. She hadn't slept well at all last night, the most memorable of the intrusions on her sleep having been a recurrence of the dream that had plagued her for over a week. In it she was sitting in a dark cave, on the ground, near the entrance. Outside, it was black as pitch; suddenly the night sky was broken by a tiny pinpoint of light, like a single star, but as she gazed at it, the light began to grow and come nearer. Frozen, unable to move, she stared at it as it advanced, her mind terrorized. Brighter and brighter, it grew, until at last it filled the entire opening to the cave and revealed its shape. It was a huge, glowing silver eagle, and with this revelation, Brianna always awoke, her body bathed in perspiration. Even now, as she recalled it, she felt a renewal of moisture along her limbs.

"Oh, damn!" she swore in unladylike annoyance, but the oath helped restore her confidence, her mood lifting, as it always had in the face of the glorious Carolina sunshine that had begun to fill the room. Her eyes fell on the silver tray beside her bed; on it, a flaky croissant, a porcelain cup, and a steaming silver pot that gave off the welcome aroma of freshly made chocolate. "Oh, Aimée, you are too good to me! Here I am, fussing about the early hour and you've obviously been up for ages, getting me breakfast and whatever." She reached a slender arm out of the bedclothes and snatched the croissant from its silver salver.

"Ah, but being the early bird has its advantages," grinned Aimée as she extracted several items from Brianna's wardrobe. "I had the pleasure of enjoying *three* of Mathilde's croissants while they were still hot from the oven," she explained with a smack of her small lips. "It is too bad that old woman cannot be accompanying us to Virginia instead of *le bon père*. She is a saint, that one!"

Brianna giggled as she poured herself a cup of the hot chocolate. "But, I thought you liked Père Edouard. You two seem to have been getting on wonderfully."

Aimée paused in her inspection of the russet riding habit they'd decided the evening before, Brianna would wear today. "Oh, I do! In fact, I *adore* him! I think of him as a youngish version of the papa I never had, and I really didn't mean what I just said. It's just that when I think of missing out on all that wonderful baking the good Mathilde is so generous with—and for—how long will we be gone, a month?"

"More or less," laughed Brianna, her spirits completely restored now.

Aimée advanced toward the bed, the riding habit over one arm. "Of course, what I should have wished for, come to think on it, was that Mathilde—or *anyone*—replace your half-brother, *Monsieur* Dumaine, but the very idea of his company on this journey is so distasteful, I've been putting it out of my head. What an odious individual!"

At the mention of Honoré, Brianna felt the threatened return of the darker humor she'd just succeeded in banishing. "Yes, isn't he?" she said softly, half to Aimée, half to herself.

"You know," said Aimée, "it is a shame, for he is not half bad looking, and he fancies himself quite the ladies' man, I can tell you!"

"Oh? I hadn't really noticed," said Brianna as she set aside the croissant she had bitten into, somehow no longer hungry. "But what makes you say so?"

Aimée stopped on her way to one of Brianna's partly filled trunks and threw her friend a disgusted look over one shoulder. "When he was here the other afternoon to deliver his message, his manner toward me when he gave it was *grossly*— flirtatious."

"Aimée!" Brianna gasped. "What did he say or—or do? If he in any way insulted, or—"

"Bah! Do not worry about me, *mon amie*," said Aimée with a small snort and wave of the hand. "I can assure you, I let him know, in no unsure terms, just what I thought of such behavior! He will think twice, that one, before he attempts any forwardness with Aimée Gitane again!"

Intrigued, Brianna sat forward as she prepared to slide out of bed. "What did you say to him?"

"Oh, it is not so much what I said as what I implied," answered Aimée with a mischievous grin. She turned to face Brianna. "As you recall, I had spent the afternoon berrypicking with Père Edouard, *oui*?" At Brianna's nod she continued. "Well, *chérie*, I had just returned when I encountered *Monsieur* Dumaine in the entry hall where he surprised me by coming into the château unannounced—without even knocking, as if he *owned* the place! Well, that is neither here nor there, but I mention it just to underscore his ill-mannered arrogance. At any rate, to make a long tale short, the lecherous wretch was wearing an ensemble of the palest pastel colors, those effeminate hues that are the rage with all the dandies, and I had sticky, deeply stained, berry-tinted hands, as I had not yet had time to wash, so when *Monsieur* Dandy left, his waistcoat and sleeve were newly—*accidentally*, of course"—she gave a delighted smirk—"decorated with an *unfashionable purple*!"

Brianna's eyes widened for an instant and she burst out laughing. "Oh, Aimée! *You didn't!*"

"But I *did!*" exclaimed Aimée triumphantly; then she added with a look of mock regret, "All done with the most profuse of apologies, *naturelment*! I even followed him—for by this time he was backing toward the door—and offered to try to clean his poor, offended garments for him, enthusiastically reaching out to better examine the nature of the damage, and therefore—alas!—creating even more purple decorations!" A look of pure joy graced her features before she finally exploded with laughter, matching that of a Brianna fairly doubled over with mirth.

"Of course," Aimée chuckled after the laughter had subsided, "if looks could kill, the priest would have had to be summoned back for my last rites that day. But enough of your nasty sibling, I say! We have better things to do and talk about on such a morning as this, eh?" She peered at Brianna with a look that bespoke satisfaction; she had successfully helped restore her friend's normal high spirits.

The two of them chatted amiably together as they went about completing Brianna's *toilette* and the last-minute packing, their enthusiasm for the long-anticipated trip coloring their conversation and mood. At last all stood ready, and Aimée prepared to summon the footmen to come and take Brianna's baggage to the awaiting carriage in the courtyard; at that moment Brianna stopped where she had been standing before her mirror for a final consulting glance and made a sudden dash toward the bed, saying, "Wait! I almost forgot!" Carefully, so as not to do damage to her new riding skirt, she knelt beside the bed and extracted a small, compact bundle from beneath it, near the foot. Rising quickly, she moved toward the smaller of her two trunks, saying, "We mustn't forget these."

Aimée threw her a look of surprise. "Your male attire? But you cannot say you won that wager with *Monsieur* Jesse, Brianna! After all, you both arrived at the door to the dining hall at exactly the same time. I know, for I watched as you almost collided with his back when he was about to enter. *Sacré bleu*, but I have never seen you dress so quickly—seen anyone do it so fast in all my life! And you are just lucky you did not catch an ague from bathing in ice cold water!" She brandished a wagging finger with this last remark as she finished in rapid French.

Brianna smiled, recalling the moment. It was true; she had never moved with more haste, but she had been determined to win that wager, not only for the prize she had been promised, she now realized, but because, somehow, it had been important—critical, even—that she show Jesse Randall she was not to be bested, or ruled by him in every respect; that he was not to have complete power over her simply because of a legality, or the fact that she was female, or the fact that he was older and stronger, or... whatever.

Her smile faded, however, as she recalled his reaction that moment when, as Aimée had said, she had almost, in her haste, careened into his broad frame as he stood before the dining hall's double doors. He had turned about slowly and looked down at her upturned, surprised face with an expression of indolent amusement. Then, the mockery in those blue eyes clearly evident, he had taken a step aside and rendered an elaborate, ironic bow, all the while raking his eyes over her still form from head to toe and back again.

Even now, as she remembered that blue-eyed appraisal, Brianna felt the heat rushing to her cheeks as it had then. Finally, as he straightened, he had reached out with strong, tanned fingers and tucked a wayward auburn curl back in place behind her ear, drawling, "*Voilà, Mademoiselle! Enchanté.* Now your *toilette* is complete. We wouldn't want the others to have the impression you were accustomed to dining *en déshabille* due to untoward haste, would we?" And as she had stood, uncustomarily tongue-tied in the face of his immaculately groomed, arrogant composure, he had calmly offered her his arm, his handsome features sporting a cocked eyebrow and a maddening grin as he queried, "Allow me?"

"Whatever are you pondering?" Aimée now asked, breaking her reverie. "Or *whomever*? By the saints, I shouldn't like to be the recipient of such looks, I can assure you," she added with a pointed look of her own.

"Never mind, Aimée," Brianna answered breezily. "As I see it, we both won the wager. It was a tie, as they say."

"As *who* says?" questioned Aimée warningly. "Have you checked with your guardian to see if *he* sees it that way?"

"Jesse?" said Brianna innocently. "Well, no, not in so many words, I haven't. I've wanted to wait until the moment for discussing it was just right."

"*And* we were already underway," Aimée added slyly. "Oh, Brianna, I hope you know what you are doing. You know he threatened—"

"Aimée! I *must* be allowed to ride freely again—I must, that's all." With a quick movement she opened the trunk lid and thrust the small bundle inside, rapidly closing the lid as she pushed unwelcome memories of the wine cellar aside. "Now," she added, straightening, "please don't worry. Just you leave the handling of my dear guardian to me!" And with a flourish of confidence she didn't completely feel, she opened the door and headed for the stairs.

But as she neared the top of the stairway at the end of the long hall, she froze, for there, quietly standing before the portrait of Deirdre, was Jesse. Obviously deep in thought—or memory, she guessed—he hadn't heard her approach, and Brianna waited silently, hardly daring to breathe as she observed him. Even in the dim light of the hallway, his handsome profile was sharply evident as he gazed at her sister's likeness. She took in the perfect wide brow overhung with a casual fall of dark curls, the straight, chiseled nose, the firm, sensual mouth and strong, square jaw, amazed at herself at how, every time she beheld these features, she should again be so transfixed by them. No one, she thought, and not for the first time, had the right to be that handsome! No wonder she felt half intimidated by him in their every encounter.

She allowed her eyes to traverse his tall frame, emboldened by the knowledge he wasn't aware of her presence. He was dressed for travel, his broad shoulders covered by a carefully tailored dark-green riding jacket, his lean hips and long, muscular thighs encased in buff-colored riding breeches. She noted his high black riding boots were polished to the shine that is only given off by the patina of the finest leather.

Again her eyes found his profile. There was a flicker in the light given off by the wall sconce near the portrait, and for a moment Brianna thought she saw a look of pain cross his eyes, but at the same instant he was turning his head in her direction and, seeing her, his face became an unreadable mask, and he moved a step away from the painting.

To cover her awkwardness at having been caught watching him, Brianna walked quickly forward until she too stood in view of the portrait, saying, "Father commissioned it on her sixteenth birthday, as his gift to her, although it wasn't completed until some seven months later. I know, because Deirdre wrote me all about it in more than one letter. She was so excited about having her portrait done by Mister Peale! She told me she and Mother made several trips to Philadelphia for sittings, although, for the final one, Mister Peale traveled here and was a guest at Le Beau Château for a fortnight."

Brianna edged closer to the painting and gazed upward at the charming young woman who smiled serenely down at them with warm, sherry-brown eyes. "He captured her likeness, I think," she said tentatively. "Of course, I can't be completely sure, for I'd never seen her at that age, but I am certain of the smile and—and the gentleness—the—the inner softness that you see in the face, that was so much a part of my sister's personality." Her eyes fell on the soft rose-colored gown in the portrait. "It seems odd, in a way, to see her standing here, looking so alive, in a gown I never even knew she owned. She—she was very beautiful, wasn't she?" Brianna added at last, pulling her gaze away from the painting to look at him.

There was a half-moment of silence before Jesse answered her. His voice, when he spoke, seemed to her somehow weary—and remote, as if coming at her from some great distance, although she heard him quite distinctly. "Yes," he said, "yes, she was very beautiful."

What Brianna said next, she couldn't explain, not even when she was to question herself about it hours later, and many times thereafter. She only knew that somehow the question rose to the surface and it was there: "Did you love her very much?"

If Jesse's face was masked before, it now became an indecipherable blank. "It's in the past, Brianna. Let's let it rest there, shall we? Now, are you and Aimée ready to travel?" He withdrew a gold pocket watch and flipped open the engraved hunter case. "We're already late, as it's five past the hour." A slight frown of annoyance creased his brow as he uttered the words in crisp, businesslike tones.

"Why, yes, of course we are—that is, I was just going down to—" she broke off with an apologetic look and started down the stairs. "I'll be down below. Aimée's summoned Herbert and Pierre to carry our baggage, I believe."

As she hurried to the appointed place, Brianna grimaced to herself. Damn! He'd done it again. In the space of a few minutes of time alone with her, he'd once more succeeded in making her feel foolish and awkward—and, yes, childish. And what had she done? Nothing. After all, she had loved Deirdre, too. Surely he had to realize that! And Deirdre was seven years dead. What was so wrong in asking . . . *Oh, God!* she said to herself as she entered the courtyard by the stables. *He's probably still in love with her!*

In the courtyard there was a busy hubbub of last-minute activity as final preparations were made to be underway. Footmen scurried here and there, loading and securing heavy trunks in the baggage carrier; Mistress Delaney stood deep in conversation with Aimée and Father Edouard who, it seemed, had volunteered to drive the team of finely matched bays. Festus and Isaac stood nearby, holding the reins of the saddle horses which included Jesse's mare Gypsy and Le Duc, Brianna was glad to note; though she owned no private mount of her own, she had taken to using the stallion as if he were hers and preferred him to any of the other saddle mounts the château had to offer. Off to one side, sitting atop a white gelding and the only one mounted, was Honoré, looking impatient with the delay, his dark looks saying it all as Jesse arrived with a mildly out-of-breath Prenshaw, who carried a large picnic hamper.

But if Prenshaw was a bit breathless, he in no way allowed it to ruffle his very proper demeanor as he somberly marched his incredibly tall, thin frame over to the carriage and ceremoniously set his burden on the ground, preparing to climb upward to the boot behind the driver's seat. But as he placed a shiny, brass-buckled shoe on one of the mounting footholds, Isaac broke off his conversation with Festus and came rushing forward, saying to the surprised butler, "See here, my good man, I shall attend to that!"

Prenshaw dropped his raised foot back to the ground, cast a quick glance at the picnic hamper and then an imperious eye at the dapper little man over whom he towered by some fifteen inches. "I beg your pardon," he intoned, "but I believe you were interrupting my securing of the traveling victuals." Both eyebrows were raised haughtily as he peered down his long, thin nose at Isaac's equally haughty—and indignant—face.

But if this was meant to intimidate Jesse's man, it did not succeed. Drawing himself up to all of his nearly five feet, the little valet gave forth with the coolest of glacial glares as he responded. "It has always been my duty to see to the master's comforts when he travels, as well as at home, and when I speak of comforts, I include the making of proper arrangements for—ah—victuals." The final word was uttered with an expression a hairsbreadth away from a sneer.

Prenshaw was to be commended for his control, for it was clear, anyone else finding himself in a similar situation would have allowed his jaw to gape open in disbelief, or at least, to have sputtered and choked on an answer as his face turned the outraged shade of crimson Prenshaw's did at that moment. But the stiff back of the taller Englishman bent nary a whit as he returned, in clipped syllables His Majesty himself would have favored, "*Your* duties, sir, may commence once this vehicle is in motion. Until that time, it is still an appendage of Le Beau Château, and as such, I am the one whose duty remains clear. Step aside, please."

They stood there, Brianna thought briefly, not exactly nose to nose, but chest to abdomen, as it were, but before she could digest the humor of this comical tableau, the look on Isaac's face told her there might be some trouble if someone didn't break their impasse. She was just about to say something herself when Father Edouard came forward and, bending down to grasp the picnic hamper, by sheer virtue of his huge bulk, forced the two men apart.

"Here, here, now, my good fellows," he smiled. "There is no reason to split hairs over such a small issue! *I* shall place this treasure in the boot and the problem disappears, eh?" He proceeded to climb up to the driver's block, hamper in tow.

As for the two Englishmen, they continued to glare at each other in silence for several seconds, but then Prenshaw did an about-face and, nodding briefly at Brianna and then Jesse, said crisply, "A pleasant journey, ladies and gentlemen. Mistress Delaney, I shall see you in my pantry in fifteen minutes." And with a back that had never faltered in its stiffness, he strode aloofly up the path.

Giggling, Aimée did a pantomime of his walk which endeared her to Isaac forever. Brianna chuckled and headed toward Festus who was holding Le Duc's reins. She was about to take them from him when Jesse's voice rang out behind her. "Brianna! You will join Aimée in the carriage."

Brianna's head shot up from where she'd bent to examine a stirrup, and she whirled about to look at the man who'd just issued that command, in tones, she thought, every bit as imperious as those just used by Prenshaw and Isaac.

Incredulous, she stammered, "But—I—that is, I had naturally assumed—"

"An error on your part, Mistress."

"But—but Le Duc wears a sidesaddle and—" Brianna blushed as she recalled the lie she'd fabricated earlier about Le Duc's lack of training to sidesaddle; obviously Serge or someone on the staff had corrected the misimpression she'd given Jesse, judging by the look he was now bestowing upon her. Frustrated both by having been caught in the untruth and by Jesse's apparent rigidity in this seemingly senseless stance, she thrust out a belligerent lower lip, settled both hands on her hips and asked, "If I am not to be allowed to ride, why, pray tell, did you fail to apprise me of it when I emerged from my chambers dressed in—in—" she made a contemptuous gesture at her skirts "—in this!"

Jesse heaved an exasperated sigh, and assuming a tone much like what one would use in dealing with an obstreperous child, said quietly, "My dear Brianna, I have not said you would not be riding a mount on this journey. Indeed, as you can see, Le Duc as well as the bay mare over there—" he gestured at the horses being held patiently by Festus "—are outfitted with sidesaddles. Two horses equipped for ladies to ride; two... ladies in the traveling company—you, and your companion *Mademoiselle* Aimée. Have I counted correctly?" he asked with dripping sarcasm. "Do the numbers correspond? Ah, I see by your silence that they do, therefore it should signify that with two horses made ready for two women, I must have intended that two women ride eventually... But not at the outset."

He paused for a moment to consider the withering glare Brianna was at that moment sending him. Then, ever so slowly, he strolled toward her until he was standing close enough to take her by the arm, which he did, firmly leading her to a more private place behind the carriage. With a gesture to the rest of the company, who had been watching all of this in apprehensive silence, he indicated they should continue about their business.

As the noisy hum of activity resumed, he addressed her again in low tones of strained impatience. "My dear ward, I appreciate the fact that you chafe at the restrictions imposed on you by my unwanted presence. I can even appreciate the fact that it is not an unwarranted reaction on your part, given what appears to be your...past history of rebellious behavior in the face of impositions of discipline. It may surprise you to learn that I find our present relationship no more pleasant than you."

He regarded her raised eyebrows. "Surely you cannot think that I would embrace the care and supervision of—of someone such as yourself with boundless enthusiasm! So," he continued, still holding her firmly by the arm, "we both find ourselves caught up, most unwillingly, in these . . . unusual circumstances—but with a difference! You, my dear, seem for all the world bent upon thwarting the demands of the situation while I, in case you haven't noticed, have endeavored to assume, *without complaint*, the duties imposed on me by a man for whom I held the utmost regard and feelings of friendship. Surely, as his surviving daughter, you can do no less?"

The look he gave her was powerful and riveting, and Brianna felt herself shrinking in embarrassment at the import of it and his last statement. Shamefully, she lowered her eyes.

"Ah, I see I've begun, perhaps, to reach you," Jesse continued, a bit more softly. He reached out and grasped her other arm, turning her to face him squarely, and then, with the knuckles of his right hand, lifted her chin until she was forced to look at him. The anguished look of adolescent uncertainty and painful confusion he saw in the huge, luminous green eyes nearly made him gasp. God! She was so *young*! And so exquisitely beautiful, and yet not even aware that she was. And so very proud...and vulnerable. It was this last that finally caused him to smile down at her without any trace of mockery. "Lady, have done with it. Cease this cavilling. It hardly makes things any easier—for either of us, and—"

"Cavilling!" The green fire was back in her eyes. "You regard my objections as—as trivial or unnecessary when all I'm trying to do is make sense out of *your* actions!" Twisting her shoulders to break his hold on her, Brianna took a step backward and looked up at him, defiance blazing in her eyes now. "How am I to—to cooperate with you when you make what seem to be arbitrary decisions regarding my movements—or *lack* of them, I should say—and when you won't even give me the reasons for those decisions?" She again thrust her hands on her hips, warming to her subject. "I'll tell you why, too! Because you *haven't* any reasons for them! It's all spite and—and meanness, that's what!"

"Brianna, *enough*!" Jesse checked the urge to step forward and shake her, seizing on his softer thoughts of moments before to summon control over his own simmering temper. He heaved a sigh while delivering her a look of tight-lipped exasperation. "It was my intent," he began softly, "to have Festus, you, Aimée and the baggage in the carriage—its heaviest possible load—at the outset, and only for a couple of hours at most—so that we might gauge time and distance for the expedition, hence allowing me to set a reasonable pace, not to mention an estimate of our time of arrival. That done, I had every intention of allowing—nay, encouraging your companion and you to ride if that was your preference. I'd already spoken to Aimée about riding, and when she assured me she not only knew how to ride, but that horses were 'in her blood,' whatever that means, I immediately went about selecting an appropriate mount for her—and Le Duc, of course, for you. I was right on that score, wasn't I? You do prefer your father's steed in the absence of one of your own?" Jesse's voice had remained soft, but the blue eyes fixed on hers meaningfully, and once again Brianna felt herself squirm and was uncomfortable under their keen regard.

Softly, in tones so low Jesse had to strain to hear them, she murmured, "Yes...I—that is...I see you have had your reasons for—" She gestured around her almost helplessly, the wind quite gone from her sails. "—for everything. I—I stand corrected," she added, swallowing in mid-sentence. She took a deep breath. "Well, I shall excuse myself now, if you don't mind...sir. I'll be joining Festus and Aimée...in the carriage." With her head held high, despite the misery of embarrassed tears stinging her eyes, Brianna turned and headed for the carriage door.

When she had gone, Jesse stood for a moment and silently shook his head. *So young! So very proud. And with so much to learn! How in hell do I find ways to gentle her without breaking that incredible spirit? How do I ready her to become a wife to some poor, damned fool in a few months?* With a final shake of his head, he moved from behind the carriage and addressed the traveling party. "Very well, everyone, five minutes, and we're underway."

YVONNE AHEARN   197

Please. With her head still bent, despite the misery of acquiescent Jesse sniffing her ears. Brianna turned and took
the carrot and then...

When she had gone, Jesse stood for a moment and silently
and the indecisiveness of her patience, already with the
of ladies, knew it as if it as a child, and by gently for which
had caught the smile as she turned. Her patience, by a second
and when even more thinner, and a hesitation. With the
soul after a child. But by even of the breaths, maybe, already
followed the far of shoulders on the thinner. Be soon
little, any way to summary.

Chapter Fifteen

The journey commenced smoothly, and they found at the
outset they could make good time, owing to the dry, sunny
weather that had continued since the week prior to their departure; the road surfaces were hard and relatively smooth for
carriage wheels, and the pleasant sunshine of September lent an
air of holiday to the first few days of the trip. True to his word,
once Jesse had gauged speed and time to set an acceptable pace,
he allowed the ladies to ride their mounts, and despite the sidesaddle, it was then that Brianna truly began to enjoy herself.

She spent most of her time riding beside Aimée who was
thrilled to be atop a horse again, and the two were reminded of
their days at the Abbaye when they had been equestrian companions; they spent long hours in amiable conversation or,
sometimes, companionable silence, as they took in the beauty
of the Carolina Upcountry at summer's end. Giant camellias,
sweet olives and mimosa trees perfumed the air as they made
their way along roads carved out of what was essentially virgin
forest.

Brianna overheard Father Edouard tell Jesse and Festus that
the year before, on his state visit to Columbia, President
Washington had termed the capital "an uncleared wood with
very few houses in it." But if it was uncleared, Brianna was glad
of it, for she had spent the happiest years of her life here,
roaming freely among the oaks, elms, hackberries and countless other wooded friends of her dearly missed early childhood.

They spent the days in the saddle, but each night, Brianna
was surprised to learn, there were prearranged accommoda-

tions, at various farmhouses and other scattered residences, that had been made by Governor Pinckney's office well in advance. Sometimes these homes at which they were overnight guests were large enough to accommodate all of the party, but more often than not, there was interior sleeping space for only the ladies, the men making do with shelter in haylofts and stables. And if Brianna voiced guilt on the occasions that she realized she and Aimée were displacing the occupants of a modest farmhouse's single bedroom, the gracious counter-protests of the farmer and his wife notwithstanding, she was usually too tired to maintain her protestations for very long and gratefully fell into bed along with Aimée, both asleep the moment their heads found the pillows.

On the fifth day they awoke to a sky dark with threatening clouds, and by mid-morning they were treated to the steady downpour of a Piedmont rainfall. At not only Jesse's insistence, but Father Edouard's as well, Brianna and Aimée took to the carriage which they shared, by one-hour turns, with each of the men, with the exception of Jesse who maintained his place on horseback at the front of the procession. Progress was slow, and when the dark afternoon gave way to an even darker evening, Jesse halted the retinue, drawing alongside the carriage on Gypsy to confer with Honoré, whose turn it was to rest inside.

This occurred none too soon for Brianna who had endured with silent unease, each of the stints with her half-brother as carriage companion; though she felt no specific threat from him with Aimée in attendance and the other men so close at hand, she was acutely aware of his dark-eyed, sardonic looks when in her company, the silent message in them somehow accusing and also anticipatory; Honoré—watching and waiting, although she knew not for what.

"Honoré," called Jesse, for they were all on a first-name basis by now, "we stand little chance of reaching the Cherokee trading camp by nightfall, as I see it, and even with the brief hour we have before sunset, I'm afraid we can expect to cover little distance. The road is a virtual quagmire, and it's already so dark I fear for the horses' footing. Do your briefings include information on anything closer in the environs?"

Honoré uttered a muffled oath as he pushed at the carriage door and made to join the men outside. A gust of wet wind caught the open door and tore it back against the side of the carriage as he stepped down, and Brianna and Aimée felt the sharp sting of wind-driven raindrops assaulting the carriage's interior. But Jesse immediately closed the door, raising his voice above the pelting deluge to inquire of them, "How goes it in there, *mademoiselles*? Have you managed to stay dry amid the comings and goings of your half-drowned carriage companions?"

A chuckle broke from Aimée's throat as she answered, *"Oui, Monsieur!"* Then, in English, "Nevertheless, we are grateful that, at his last turn in the carriage, Father Edouard recounted the promise made by *le bon Dieu* at the end of the Flood, that He would never again destroy the world by water!"

There was an answering chuckle before they heard Jesse's voice fall to a confering murmur as he discussed with Honoré the possibilities of gaining shelter by nightfall. At length the door reopened and Father Edouard's great bulk squeezed through, water teeming from his broad-brimmed black priest's hat before he removed it and set it quickly on the carriage floor. Then, as he began to remove as carefully as possible, so as not to soak the ladies, the oil-soaked animal skins he wore over his priest's robes, the carriage began to move again.

"Father," said Brianna, handing him a thick towel from a coffer under the seat, "what is happening now? Are we to be caught short of our overnight destination? Will we have to camp out in the open in all this downpour? How will—"

"Hold! Peace!" laughed the priest. "Am I to be allowed no time to take a breath in dry air?" He inhaled deeply and, perceiving the musty closeness of the carriage's humid interior, amended, "Well, relatively dry, that is." With the towel he rubbed briskly at his red beard, quite wet despite the clothes he'd worn, and handed the cloth back with a smile of thanks.

"Now," he said, settling his large torso as comfortably as he could into the carriage's cushioned seat, "here's what's afoot. We are indeed too far from the Cherokee trading cabin to take shelter there, although Honoré argued hotly for attempting to reach it in the dark." His voice dropped lower, and he muttered, "He thinks nothing about guarding the horses' safety, that one.'' Then, with a brightening smile, "But good sense and a bit of luck prevailed, for when I was shown Honoré's map, I discovered we were less than a half-hour's distance from an abbey I'm familiar with, although it was not marked on the map. It's near the Catawba River we've been following, but on high ground, so there's no danger from flooding. I know the abbot there, but even if I didn't, there would be little problem in their taking us in.''

"An abbey, in this wilderness!" marveled Aimée. "What do they do there during Matin and Compline, sing their chants for the deer and the trees?" Suddenly she gasped and clamped both hands over her mouth, aghast that she could have forgotten herself and been so flippant with a man of the cloth.

Father Edouard reached out and gave one of Aimée's black corkscrew curls a tweak. "No, they still sing of the wonders of God's love and heavenly mercy," he smiled, "but they also minister to those Cherokee in the area who need help. There are some who have even taken the faith, you know, although these brothers do not actively seek converts. Most of them have taken the vow of silence, and they keep pretty much to themselves. With your convent background, the two of you should have little trouble feeling comfortable there, but do not expect anything as elaborate as the Abbaye de Panthémont. This is a simple outpost of the Church.''

Father Edouard's words proved true in all respects, for less than thirty minutes later they found themselves filing through the narrow gates of a stonewalled courtyard that housed a modest, single-storied building constructed of stone and rough-hewn timber. The monk who answered their call at the gate quickly summoned others who saw to the horses and carriage while he quietly and efficiently led the seven weary travelers into the abbey. There they were shown to clean, if simple, sleeping cells and told that after they had changed to dry clothes, the abbot would see them and they might dine.

The meal served in the abbey's candlelit dining chamber was simple, yet well prepared, the roast of venison and braised roots and vegetables augmented by a subtle, yet ingenious use, Brianna thought, of various herbs and wild onions the brothers cultivated or gathered from the forest floor. The abbot, Father Paul, was, like Brianna's father and Père Edouard, a

French *émigré* who proved to be a gentle and gracious host, his vow of silence notwithstanding, for it did not extend to circumstances involving guests or other outsiders when the necessity for speech arose.

When the meal had been consumed, the travelers were once again shown to their quarters by silent monks bearing thick, white candles, and as Brianna and Aimée reached the cell they were to share, the monk named Brother Theodore nodded and left them, but not before using his candle to light a similar one in a sconce on the wall outside their door and handing Aimée a folded note.

"A message for me? From whom?" questioned Aimée, but Brother Theodore's silent form had already padded down the dark hallway and out of sight.

"Well, just open it and see, silly." As Brianna entered their small chamber, her hands were already busily removing the fichu at her neckline.

Aimée grabbed the candle Brother Theodore had left them and brought it into the cell, using its light to scan quickly the piece of white parchment she held in her other hand. "It is from Père Edouard," she said in a whisper. There was something about the quiet solitude of the abbey that caused them to speak in hushed tones, that, and the lateness of the hour. "He wishes me to come to the stables where our horses are being kept, says he has something for us he almost forgot about—a 'parting favor from Mathilde'! Brianna! That dear old woman remembers our palates even when we are far away! Oh, I hope it is not something that can have grown too stale in all this time! Trust a man to overlook such important details!" She reached for the cloak she had hung on a peg near the room's tiny fireplace, then used the candle she carried to light a similar one in a simple candlestick that stood on a small table between the cell's two narrow cots.

"Aimée!" Brianna scolded. "How can you rush so eagerly for food when we've just eaten a delicious dinner?"

Aimée's face lit up with gamin delight. "Ah, but you will recall, it was a dinner without dessert! And, if I know Mathilde, this promises to be just such a morsel or two! *Donc*, I hurry off to claim our 'favor'!" She fairly skipped toward the door.

"Aimée, wait!" called Brianna, laughing. "Please, before you go, help me with my fastenings, would you? You know it's nearly impossible for me to manage them by myself."

"Ah, of course, *ma chére*. I'm sorry I forgot," Aimée added, not looking a bit contrite. "But I hope you do not fall asleep before I return. It would be a shame if I were left the only one awake to enjoy this treat, would it not?" With a grin that hadn't faltered since she'd read the note, she quickly helped Brianna out of her gown before grabbing her candle again and making a beeline for the door.

When she had gone, Brianna heaved an amused sigh and moved toward the door which, in her haste, Aimée had not shut completely. But just as she reached it, it swung wide to reveal the dark-cloaked figure of Honoré Dumaine.

"Honoré!" gasped Brianna, her hands instinctively going to her chest and crossing over her semi-clad breasts. "What are you—"

Honoré's hand shot out and snaked around her waist, yanking her against him while, with the other, he covered her mouth. Frightened and confused, Brianna brought both hands up in an attempt to dislodge his upper hold, but to no avail. For all his leanness, her half-brother had incredible strength.

Shutting the door with a backward kick, Honoré began to manipulate her toward one of the beds. "Do not struggle so, my lovely little *sister*," he hissed. "I'm afraid there is no help for it. You are about to be compromised tonight, and in a most incestuous fashion!"

His words stirred a deep and chilling terror in the pit of Brianna's stomach, and she felt it heave when the full extent of their import hit. My God! He intended to *rape her*! With a strength she didn't know she had, she tore her mouth away from his grasp, but as she would have screamed, the dull gleam of metal in his other hand, the one around her middle, caught her eye and she froze.

"You dare to threaten me—*here*—with a *knife*!" she whispered, but her voice came out a hoarse croak.

Honoré's smile was more of a leer as he took in the heaving breasts beneath her semi-transparent shift. "But of course, here," he replied smoothly. "Whose word should be doubted less than the good brothers'? And when the word gets out, and get out it will, there will not be a gentleman alive who would offer for you—not only soiled goods, but incestuously soiled!" His free hand moved to cover one of her breasts, and at its touch, Brianna felt the bile rise in her throat.

"Honoré, do not do this! Think, I beg you!" Brianna cast about wildly in her mind for reasons. "Surely you cannot do it with impunity! Everyone here will feel compelled to deal with you, you will face prison, you—"

Honoré's chilling laughter cut her off as his long, thin fingers tore at the thin material of her shift, the knife still held firmly in the hand of the arm that clutched her to him from behind. "Think again, my sweet. When they discover what has occurred, they will want to do everything in their power to keep news of it from escaping. Punishing me would only serve to draw unthinkable attention to the deed. As for me, I shall be long gone, calmly awaiting, in an apartment in Paris, the news of my inheritance, the inheritance you will forego when there is no one to wed you!" With a savage jerk, he pulled her down with him to the bed.

Brianna's brain whirled, seizing on anything it could, to stall for time. She thought that Aimée couldn't be gone too long before—*Aimée!* "You—" she choked. "*You* sent that note!"

Low, ugly laughter greeted her ears, all the more ominous for its softness, when all of a sudden, the door to the cell tore open, and with a primitive sound, the tall form of Jesse Randall filled the entrance.

Startled, Honoré jumped off the bed, away from his captive, the knife thrust out in front of him. But Jesse left him no time to consider its use. With a snarl, he lunged for the knife hand, his huge, agile form a blur in the candlelight. Honoré sought to feint, but Jesse's speed and reflexes were too much for him; in seconds the knife clattered, useless, to the stone floor.

"Scum!" swore Jesse savagely as his huge fist collided with Honoré's jaw.

Brianna watched in numb awe as her half-brother's tall form crumpled to the floor near the bed.

Then Jesse was reaching for her, helping her up and enfolding her in his big, soothing embrace while at last the floodgates broke and Brianna found herself weeping wildly in his arms.

"He—he meant to r-rape me!" she choked out. "He—he—he d-didn't even care if—if he g-got caught!" she stammered between sobs. "He s-said—"

"Sh-h, I know, little one, I know," Jesse soothed, stroking her hair. "But it's all right now. No one is going to hurt you, I swear."

And when she had calmed somewhat, he took a step away from her. Surveying the damage to her chemise with tight, angry lips, he removed his jacket and wrapped it around her, at length, taking her in his arms again until the sobbing had dwindled to a soft hiccoughing.

Finally, when he felt she had calmed sufficiently, Jesse made her lie down on the bed, covering her with a blanket before saying gently, "I need to remove this—" he glanced downward at Honoré's inert form "—this piece of garbage and think on what's to be done with him. Will you be all right until—"

At that instant a breathless Aimée and Father Edouard appeared at the door.

"Brianna!" gasped Aimée. "*Mon Dieu*, what has happened here? I came with Père Edouard as soon as I—we realized—" She stopped, dead still, as her eyes found Honoré's body.

The priest's black-robed figure quickly knelt down beside it. With deft fingers he felt his neck for a pulse. "He still lives," he said, rising. "Jesse, what—"

"I'll fill you in on what happened while you help me carry him to his cell, Father," said Jesse. "Aimée, see to Brianna. Perhaps you can find someone in the kitchen who would be willing to help you brew some herb tea for a mistress who is having 'trouble sleeping'—just 'trouble sleeping,' understand? Above all, I want no one besides us to learn of what has happened here tonight. Even an unsuccessful rape attempt could be enough to blacken Brianna's reputation." He bent to lift Honoré's still form.

"*Rape* attempt!" breathed Aimée, sitting on the bed beside Brianna and placing her arms around her friend's shoulders. "That *swine!*" she spat. Then, "Oh, *ma petite!* How dreadful!"

When Jesse and the priest had left with their burden, Brianna slowly sat up in the bed and gazed for a long moment at the spot on the floor where Honoré had lain. "Do you know," she at last, whispered in shaken tones, "I was never without the feeling that he would try something? Not since the reading of the will. But I guess I just never realized to what lengths he might go, Aimée."

"Or what a desperate man your half-brother might be. I only regret, *mon amie*, that I was unable to see it more clearly. Ah, what use is this gift if it fails me at times—"

"No! Do not blame yourself! I, for one, won't have it! It is as you once said. This gift is not to be examined too closely. And, after all, we ultimately had no real need of it tonight. Jesse handled things well enough, thank heaven."

But when she slept later that night, Brianna dreamt of the eagle, and Aimée didn't sleep at all.

"No! Father, you cannot mean it!" Brianna's face looked ashen as she faced the priest. They were standing outside the abbey's stables, having just taken a hasty breakfast with the brothers; the rain having stopped shortly before dawn, preparations were underway for an early start. Brianna shook her head in disbelief as she continued. "How can we possibly keep him in our company? It's madness, now that we know what he's capable of!"

With a weary sigh, Father Edouard gently took Brianna's hands in his huge ones. "*Enfant*, do you doubt for one moment we haven't examined all the alternatives? My dear, if this were merely a social visit, of course we would rid ourselves of Dumaine, but it isn't, as you already know. Jesse has important state business with Secretary Jefferson, and your half-brother figures strongly in it. He is the Governor's special aide in the matter!" He paused for a moment, taking in Brianna's doubtful expression. "But, more importantly, I can assure you that your guardian has taken some precautions, shall I say, against anything like last night's terrible ordeal ever happening again. He—"

Just then Jesse appeared from behind the side of the stable, wearing a grim expression. Behind him followed a greatly subdued Honoré; he was followed closely by Festus, whose expression was menacing. But what startled Brianna greatly was the physical appearance of her half-brother. Several purple bruises marked his face, and he walked with a decided limp while one arm was carried in a sling. He looked neither right nor left, but directly at the ground in front of his feet as Jesse and Festus escorted him to the carriage. This he slowly entered and was joined by Festus before Jesse slammed the door shut.

"Father!" exclaimed Brianna. "What—what has happened to him? I mean, I'm aware that my guardian dealt him a blow that sent him unconscious to the floor last night, but—but that was all! Just a single blow to—to his jaw. This—"

"This," interrupted Jesse as he joined them, "is the result of a—um—discussion *Monsieur* Dumaine and I had earlier this morning. It was the reason you missed seeing the two of us at breakfast."

"You—you *beat* him?" queried Brianna incredulously.

Jesse's harsh rasp of laughter was as deadly as the expression he wore. "Not without giving him every opportunity of doing the same to me. You see, your relative wasn't willing to see things the way I wanted him to see them. You could say we had a slight difference of opinion. Had we been in Charleston, we might have used dueling pistols, but, of course, here, in this religious house, I couldn't allow that. Fists were more than adequate."

Brianna stared up at him, listening, and she only now became aware of two small cuts on Jesse's face, one over his right eye and another on his chin. "I see," she said, nodding her head slowly. "May I ask what it was you were able to—to convince him of?"

A ghost of a smile broke over Jesse's face. "He is to accompany us to Monticello, but will remain in the carriage with Festus for the duration of the trip, unless I say otherwise. Once there, he is to avoid your presence at all times, to the point of not even remaining in the same room with you. When this proves impossible, say, when we all dine at Jefferson's table, he is to be sandwiched between me and Father Edouard—with no exceptions." Jesse's smile widened. "Does that give you some reassurance, little one?"

Brianna nodded. "But what if he should decide, once there and under Jefferson's roof, to change his mind and—"

"*That*," said Jesse, his voice suddenly hard as flint, "would prove very unfortunate for *Monsieur* Dumaine, as I've already informed him. You see, I've spent long periods living with the Cherokee in my time, and I'm afraid it's Indian justice I would mete out then.''

Father Edouard looked curious. "Do they have a specific punishment for those who go back on their word?"

"Oh, yes," said Jesse softly, "but I was referring more specifically to their punishment for sexual offenders."

"What do they do?" asked the priest.

Jesse gave the carriage a sidelong glance of disgust. "They castrate them," he said grimly, and then proceeded to walk to the waiting horses.

Chapter Sixteen

The mountain on which Thomas Jefferson's home stood was surrounded by heavy forest, and as the party followed the road that threaded its way through the trees, Jesse entertained the riders closest to him with details he'd come to know about Monticello through his briefings from Pinckney's office. Brianna and Aimée, riding on either side of him, just ahead of Father Edouard, listened intently as he rambled informatively in his familiar drawl.

"The plantation stands five thousand acres square, with the Big House itself situated at the top of this mountain on a clearing. Pretty soon we ought to be able to see some of the fields where wheat, tobacco and cotton are raised. Of course, across the river Jefferson owns several thousand additional acres in the form of seven other, separately named, plantations."

"*Monsieur* Jefferson is a very wealthy man, then," commented Aimée.

"Oh, I suppose he does all right, as would any planter among the Virginia gentry," answered Jesse, "although I should mention that there are those among his class whose wealth easily dwarfs Jefferson's." He arched an eyebrow at Brianna. "Le Beau Château, for example, is many times larger than the sum of all of Jefferson's lands."

Aimée grinned at her friend. "Brianna, you hear? I suppose you are very rich, eh?"

Brianna gave her a thoughtful look and darted a brief glance at Jesse before answering. "Don't count my goslings before they are hatched, *mon amie*. My male counselors will be the first to remind you that there are a few—ah—legalities before I become mistress of all those acres. Is that not so, *mon gardien*?'' She threw Jesse the most dimpled, sugary smile she could muster.

Jesse was quick to return a similar smile, saying, ''*Oui, ma pupille*, but none too insurmountable, I think, for a lady who can keep a cool head upon her young shoulders.''

''Perhaps,'' retorted Brianna, struggling to keep her annoyance from showing. Would he forever be reminding her of her youth? ''But then,'' she added, ''even presuming all the legal difficulties are met, the question arises as to whether, even then, my inheritance would be truly mine.'' She paused for a second to assess whether Jesse's attention was fully on her and, finding it was, continued. ''I mean, sir, that if I succeed in hurdling the primary obstacle, that is finding a husband by year's end, how do I then account myself rich when, by law, all that I own accrues to *him*?'' The same smile again.

Riding behind them as he had been, Father Edouard had missed none of this conversation and now, seeing the turn it was taking, drew his horse up alongside Le Duc and addressed Brianna in gentle tones. ''*Ma petite*, come, come, what cynical pessimism is this? Surely you cannot fail to realize that in the joys of marriage you will share *with* your husband in all your *mutual* bounty? Such is the nature of holy matrimony, my dear. In it a woman gladly cedes all her earthly possessions to the man who has promised to love and care for her, and in return she is cherished and protected by him—for life! There is much giving and taking on *both* parts, you see.''

Brianna's laugh was brief and mirthless. ''Ah, yes, *mon père*, I see, but I also see that all of *her* giving in cases such as the one we are speaking of, entails the transfer of tangible goods, denoted in black and white—utterly measurable in terms of its wealth; all of *his* giving is in the nature of promises and the kinds of things manufactured out of what the English poet, Mister Shakespeare, called 'airy nothing'! I do not hold the exchange as necessarily equal, Father.'' And with as much control as she could summon at that moment, Brianna urged Le Duc forward and rode a good distance ahead, leaving them in her dust.

Watching her go, Father Edouard sadly shook his head. "My poor little dove. So frightened and so *angry*!"

Jesse gave him a thoughtful sidelong glance before commenting, "Hardly a dove, *mon ami*." He glanced briefly at the ring on his hand. "Rather more, I think, like a young female eagle." At the priest's look he clarified, "Oh, a bit young, perhaps, and still unfledged, but when this one flies, she will soar with the strongest, even the males, I think."

He moved to urge Gypsy forward to follow his ward, but before he did, out of the corner of his eye he caught sight of Aimée looking at him with the strangest expression on her face.

It was late afternoon when the visitors reached the crest upon which Monticello was built and at last had the Big House in view. To Brianna, used as she was to the size and proportions of Le Beau Château and various French buildings she'd known, it seemed rather small and unprepossessing, but she was nevertheless struck by the symmetry and elegance of its design. Saying as much to Aimée, she was dumbfounded when Jesse, whom she hadn't intended to overhear her remark, informed her that the architect for Monticello had been none other than Thomas Jefferson himself!

"But—but—" she stammered, "he is such a vastly busy and important man: Secretary of State, former Minister to France, author of our Declaration of Independence, and God knows what else! How could he possibly find the time to steep himself in enough knowledge to design and plan the likes of this?" Her arm made a sweeping gesture to denote the gracious home they were approaching as they rode their mounts up the entry drive.

Her words made Jesse smile as he reflected on a similar tirelessness and energy that had been fired by a personal passion. He, too, had been thus driven during the past couple of years when he had designed and completed his own private residence, or, more importantly, the place he was to call home for the rest of his life. He could well understand Jefferson's reputedly passionate involvement with Monticello, for it was a kind of passion he was only too familiar with, and this similarity between them had, he knew, been one of the primary motivating factors in his accepting Pinckney's offer.

He gazed appreciatively at the handsome brick structure with its four white columns supporting a classical portico in front. The columns were broken by a roof that ran the width of the front porch and separated the ground floor from the second. Low-walled steps running the width of the porch were gracefully proportioned to the overall size of the structure; Jesse could readily see that. His gaze shifted upward. Resting atop the columns and stretching over the second story was a triangular roof that ran the entire width of the porch and, to the rear, the length of the building, just barely visible from the angle at which they were approaching. This was classical elegance at its best.

Jesse smiled. There was a great deal he was viewing here that was shared by the Big House at Riverview. It had to be Palladio's influence! It had to! As he took in the two wings that flanked the central section and were themselves flanked by a pair of octagonal projections, Jesse made a mental note to ask his host about his acquaintance with Palladio. He himself had come across the four volumes of Leoni's *Architecture of A. Palladio* in the archives of a library in Florence while on his Grand Tour of Europe years ago and had been so impressed by their Renaissance interpretation of classical styles that he had labored there for hours, making drawings and taking copious notes. Could it be possible that Jefferson also had access to those volumes? He would soon find out.

They were nearing the front lawn now when all of a sudden, from around the far side of the house, a small crowd of people appeared. Eight or nine individuals of varying ages, male and female, were accompanying a tall man on a bay horse who seemed to be issuing orders; as the rider addressed each one, accompanying his remarks with a series of pointings and gestures, the crowd began to disperse, scurrying in different directions, some back around the side of the building, a pair of women into the house, still others going off toward a group of buildings across the lawn. At last there remained two young men and the man on the horse who, having now seen Jesse's group approaching, gestured toward the visitors while speaking something briefly to the young men; these two then began to run toward the oncoming guests, greeting them in the most enthusiastic manner, hands waving, smiles creasing their eager faces.

"Ya'll mus' be the guests from Carolina," called the nearer of the two. He looked to be about sixteen years old, Brianna was thinking, tall, lanky and quite handsome, with dark hair and hazel eyes.

"The Master says we're to see to your horses and, um, welcome to Monticello!" cried the second, a lad of no more than twelve or thirteen. Like the first youngster, he was dressed in the working clothes of a servant and was hatless and barefooted. But what confused Brianna was his use of the term "Master." Wasn't that the term a slave might use? Even though Le Beau Château used no slave labor, she'd seen enough of her homeland in childhood as well as a glimpse here and there since she'd returned from France to recognize certain customs and practices, and those relating to the institution of slavery had drawn her particular notice; she suspected this was largely because of its alien, repugnant, and yet curiosity-provoking, nature. She peered closely at the youth who had referred to the "Master." There was not a hint of dark skin about him. Indeed, although his eyes were brown, the rest of his coloring was quite fair. Brianna shrugged. Perhaps she was mistaken. Maybe it was the custom in Virginia for servants as well as slaves to use that term of address. And yet she'd heard that Jefferson did keep slaves.

Just then her reverie was broken as the man on horseback rode up to meet them, and as he drew nearer, Brianna had no doubt that they were being met by the owner of Monticello himself.

Thomas Jefferson sat easily in the saddle for all his sinewy, lean, six-foot frame, and his face seemed to have been ruggedly cut, feature by feature, by the same hand that had carved the body. It was a long face, accented by a long, well-formed nose, a thin, wide, sensitively molded mouth, and a long, square-cut jaw that denoted both stubbornness and strength of purpose. His coloring was high and vivid, with shoulder-length, light red hair queued with a blue ribbon, and skin whose rosy hue was well sprinkled with freckles, but it was his eyes that held one's attention. They were a bright, vivid blue, heavy-lidded and intense as they gazed at the onlooker with a forthrightness that bespoke an honest and keen intelligence. It was those eyes that now rested on them, quickly taking in their party while at the same time the wide mouth broke into an open, boyish grin.

"Mister Randall, I take it?" said Jefferson, and at Jesse's courteous nod and answering smile he added, "Welcome to Monticello."

Gypsy and the large bay gelding with two rear white feet stood parallel to each other, nose to tail, while the two men shook hands. Following this, Jesse turned in his saddle to make introductions.

"This is the young woman we wrote you about, my ward, Mistress Brianna Devereaux, sir."

"Ah, yes, the young lady who was educated at the Abbaye de Panthémont with my daughters." Jefferson's blue eyes fixed on Brianna in quick, assessing appreciation, causing Jesse to make the first of many mental notes appraising the character of his host. Jefferson had an eye for a beautiful woman!

"And may I present Father Edouard-Gérard . . ."

Introductions passed quickly and the visitors soon found themselves being led inside and shown to the rooms they were to occupy during their stay.

While Aimée remained behind to direct the unloading of Brianna's trunks, Brianna found herself being shown to her chamber by a young woman with the same dark hair, hazel eyes and fair skin as the one youth who had hailed them outside, and, recalling the lad, she was suddenly struck by the resemblance between him and this woman who was hardly more than her own age.

"Excuse me," said Brianna, "but I fear I didn't catch your name, Mistress. Mine's Brianna Devereaux."

The woman turned and nodded slightly as she continued to lead the way down the hall. "I am Sally Hemings," she replied in a soft, melodious voice.

"I'm pleased to meet you, Mistress Hemings," said Brianna. Then, for want of anything better to say and because she found herself curious about something she couldn't quite put her finger on, Brianna asked, "Are—are you on the staff here?"

The quiet, somber face of Sally Hemings broke into the barest ghost of a smile as she paused in the hallway and looked at Brianna. "Yes'm, you might say that. But it wouldn't be entirely accurate unless additional information were forthcoming.''

What a curious thing to say! ''What information, Mistress Hemings?'' They were standing at a point about three-quarters down the length of the hallway, and as Brianna waited for Sally's response, she took a moment to contemplate the woman. She was diminutive in size, but her tiny, almost fragile looking body nevertheless gave the impression of considerable strength and good health. The small, heart-shaped face that so resembled that of the youth outside was finely formed and, indeed, she was quite pretty. She wore her dark, straight hair severely drawn back into a low chignon which drew attention to the lovely shape of her face and long, slender neck, and her almond-shaped, hazel eyes were thus also shown off to their best advantage: they dominated a face whose every feature was delicate and well proportioned. But as those eyes now beheld hers, Brianna thought she detected a hint of sadness about them, suggesting things deeply felt and carefully hidden.

''I should explain,'' Sally was saying, ''that although I am in service here at Monticello, there is more to it than that. You, see,'' she explained, continuing down the hallway at last, ''I *belong* to the place, or, more specifically, to the Master.'' Sally paused again when they had reached the end of the hallway. ''I am a slave here, Mistress Devereaux.''

The sharp intake of breath that betrayed Brianna's shock was something she was to damn herself for many times afterward, for she was simultaneously conscious of how rude it must appear, and quickly hastened to soften her offense by saying, ''Oh, please, I never meant—''

But at that moment they were interrupted by a high-pitched voice that cried, ''Mama, Mama!''

Turning to find its source, Brianna saw a small boy, a toddler of about two years, racing down the hallway toward them on chubby little legs. He was blue-eyed and fair, with strawberry-blond hair and freckles, and as he reached Sally Hemings's skirts, she whisked him up and held him, saying, ''Thomas! What are you doing up here? Why aren't you out in the kitchen with Lucy? Don't you know you're not supposed to be running about the Big House like this? Oh, where *is* that Lucy, anyway?''

But the child, having found what he'd been looking for, merely inserted a small white thumb in his mouth contentedly and proceeded to stare at Brianna from the comfort of Sally's arms.

Sally sighed and looked at Brianna. "My son, Mistress Devereaux," she said softly, "Thomas Jefferson Hemings."

This time Brianna managed to forestall any audible evidence of shock at the revelation Sally's words imparted, but her face must have said enough, for in the ensuing silence the young mother merely nodded as if to say she understood; she'd seen similar reactions before.

"I haven't meant to shock you, Mistress," said Sally at last. "I'm afraid you would have found out sooner or later, anyway. Almost anyone who stays to visit Monticello for very long, does."

Taking a deep breath as she struggled to regain some composure, Brianna reached out a gentle hand and ruffled young Thomas Hemings's silky hair. "How do you do, Thomas?" she smiled. She reached down into the pocket of her riding skirt and extracted a piece of sugar cane she had left over from several she'd brought along for Le Duc. "Would you like to have this to chew on?" She saw, by the look in the toddler's eyes, that he knew what it was she held out to him, but instead of taking the proffered gift, he looked questioningly at his mother.

Sally smiled at her son. "Yes, it's all right. You may have it," she encouraged. And as a chubby little fist came quickly forward and eagerly seized the sweet, both women laughed.

Just then, a tall, thin woman with skin the color of creamed coffee came down the hall at a fast clip, calling breathlessly, "Thomas! Thom— Ah, theah you is, you devil!" As she reached the trio at the head of the stairs, she paused, gave Brianna an apologetic look and reached to take Thomas into her arms, saying, "Oh, Sally, please don' scold. 'Lizabeth done got us busier 'n bees makin' honey, whut wid de pie bakin' an' de pig she got roastin' on de spit fo' dis comp'ny dinnah, an' de hahvest jes comin' up, an' dis chile, well, he jes plumb got hisself away 'fo ah kid kitch 'im, dass all." She looked sternly at the youngster in her arms. "Yo' is a *rascal*, yo' is!" she scolded. "Lahk t' skeert me half t' deaf, runnin' off lahk dat!"

But young Thomas Jefferson Hemings merely shoved the stick of sugar cane more firmly into his mouth; at the same time he managed a wide smile as he looked directly at Brianna with eyes of the same vivid blue as Jefferson's.

"You've made a friend," said Sally to Brianna with a smile. To the tall woman who held her son she also smiled, saying, "It's all right, Lucy. I know how quickly he can move these days. He almost got away from me yesterday when I was searching for the right color thread to mend that tear in the Master's new riding coat." She peered at her son. "You be a good boy and go out to the summer kitchen with Lucy, now, hear?"

With a contented gurgle, Thomas allowed himself to be carried efficiently back down the hall and out of sight, leaving Brianna and Sally alone again.

Brianna looked silently at Sally for a moment. "You—you are his mistress, then?" she queried softly.

Sally Hemings nodded. "Yes, that . . . and his slave."

"But you're white!" exclaimed Brianna as the import of all she'd just witnessed sent renewed shock waves through her brain. "Slaves are—are supposed to be—"

"Black?" interrupted Sally softly, and the sadness that now emanated from those hazel eyes said much, much more. "Not always. Many of us look white. You recall the young men who came to take your horses? My brothers. One—like me—sired by Mister Quales, the father of the Master's wife who died, the other, by a white itinerant carpenter who decided to take what he wanted from my mother . . . and left her something to remember the incident by. You see, in Virginia the law holds that any child born of a slave mother is a slave as well, no matter what the racial factors in his heritage. And my mother was—is—a slave."

Brianna's eyes went wide as she digested this information. "Then—then that means that little Thomas—"

"Is a slave," said Sally flatly. She began walking down the hallway where Lucy and Thomas had just gone, her fingers on a ring of keys at her belt.

Brianna moved silently behind her, her mind ablaze with confusion, shock and outrage. "But—but Thomas is his *son!*"

Sally nodded, her expression again immensely sad. "Yes'm, that he is." Then, as if to forestall any further comment from Brianna, she continued in a brisk, efficient tone of voice. "Your room is the last one down here on the right. It has a lovely view of the Ravenna and there's a small dressing chamber next to it where your maid can sleep. I've had a cot made up for her there." She inserted one of the keys into the lock of the door she'd just indicated and turned it.

"Oh, Aimée's not really my maid," said Brianna as they entered the small, neat chamber. "She's more of a companion, really."

Sally looked at her quietly for a moment. "Is she a slave?" she asked directly.

"Why, no!" said Brianna, shocked by the query. "She's my friend, and I—I've never owned a slave—and never shall," she added meaningfully.

Sally nodded. "Then, if she's not a slave, it doesn't matter what else she is . . . maid . . . companion, whatever. She's free, and that's the whole of it." She gestured to indicate the room they were standing in. "Well, here you are. I hope you'll be comfortable here, Mistress. I'll be going now, and I'll send someone with some fresh towels and orders to fix you a bath if you want one. Just pull on that cord over there if you need anything else. And enjoy your visit here at Monticello." Then, amid a soft whisper of skirts, she turned and disappeared down the hall.

Chapter Seventeen

"**B**ut she's his *slave*! Aimée! There she stood, I tell you, with skin as fair as mine and—and perfectly articulated English—"

"Her French is excellent also," interrupted Aimée, "although she accents it with just a touch of that lazy drawl your Southern countrymen are so prone to using when they speak the English."

"You've met her then?" asked Brianna at Aimée's reflection in the looking glass before her.

Aimée inserted a hairpin into the braided coronet she had just fashioned at the crown of the auburn head, then nodded. "We spoke briefly regarding the meal hours and other aspects of the household routine here. Oh, by the way, she told me Martha is coming from some place called Edgehill with her husband. Did you know she's sometimes called Patsy? We'll see her at dinner."

Brianna nodded. "It will be pleasant seeing her again. Yes, I remember her once saying we might use that name. Lord, now that I've met her father, I can see where she gets those looks and all that height! And she—did you say Sally Hemings spoke French, Aimée?"

"Beautifully. She traveled to Paris and stayed with Monsieur Jefferson when he was Minister there, although I'm told it was as the younger daughter's maid that she officially went—what was her name, the younger one?"

"Maria, I think." Brianna watched Aimée brush the lower section of her hair as it fell from beneath the coronet, down her back. "Aimée, I just cannot stand it! She's white-skinned, beautiful, the mother of his child; she has all the grace and polish of any of us who went to that fancy convent school, and, yet, she's *his* slave! He *inherited* her from his dead father-in-law! I cannot actually believe it. It—it's *shameful*, that's what. And now, in just a few minutes, we're to go to dinner and sit at the table of the man who wrote the most famous treatise on human liberty of all time, our Declaration of Independence, while all the while he lives here with this poor woman whom he *owns*—like property!—and, moreover, keeps as—as his *concubine*! Oh, I can't bear it. I won't go, I just won't, that's all.''

Aimée paused for a moment and stared into Brianna's face in the mirror. ''Brianna, calm yourself. If you don't appear at dinner, *Monsieur* Jesse will be furious and, what's more, he'll never let you get away with it. Oh, and by the way, we must hurry, speaking of your *gardien*—ah, guard*ian*. He told me he wishes to see you briefly in the music room before dinner, and since it is almost a quarter before the hour now—''

''My guardian! My *guardian*! I tell you, Aimée, that man—''

''Yes, yes, I know, he is an impossible, overbearing—'' Aimée's eyes rolled upward as she searched for the exact and deliciously suitable English words to match her friend's feelings about the man. ''—insufferable tyrant,'' she finished at last with a grin. She took a step backward and admired her handiwork. ''*Voilà*! Your *coiffure, Mademoiselle*!''

Brianna couldn't help responding to Aimée's infectiously happy nature and grinned back at her in the mirror before looking at her own reflection. The shiny copper of the braided coronet bespoke a sophistication she was beginning to feel; complementing it, however, as well as adding a demure note to her looks, was the mass of long, curling locks that Aimée had brought from behind and draped over one shoulder. It was just enough to offset the severity of having the forward hair pulled back and sleekly upward, away from her face. Rising, she removed the large white cloth Aimée had draped over her shoulders to preserve her gown from stray falling hairs. Had she been one to powder her hair, it would have been used to prevent the powder from falling where it wasn't wanted, but Brianna had never used powder and was glad the fashion was passing from mode. And she was equally happy about the change away from panniers and tortuous stays and corsets.

Her gown tonight was again designed in the fashion Republican France had imported from England, the *robe en chemise*. Made of the softest deep violet muslin, it had long, close-fitting sleeves, a softly gathered, scooped neckline, and was belted at the midriff by a wide satin sash of bright leaf green. From there it fell softly to her feet which were clad in satin slippers of the same green. No voluminous petticoats marred the straight, soft, natural line of her skirt, and the effect on Brianna's appearance was to make any onlooker aware that she had long, lissome legs and slender, sylphlike hips.

Nodding, Aimée grinned once more. "The new style, it suits you, eh? But, wait. We forgot this." She came forward from the highboy where she'd been standing with a long, green double plume of ostrich feathers.

Brianna shook her head. "No, Aimée, I think not. I know plumes in the hair are all the rage now, but somehow, I don't think it's right for a simple country dinner party. If I were dressing for a ball, perhaps, but—"

Just then, a knock sounded at the door, followed by Father Edouard's voice. "Brianna, are you in there? What keeps you? Jesse sent me to see and to escort you to the music room. Please, my dear, can you hurry?"

Brianna took one look at Aimée's *I-told-you-so* expression and headed for the door, muttering, "Jesse this, Jesse that, Jesse, Jesse, Jesse," but she quickened her step as she moved.

Minutes later she and her escort entered the music room, but as she came through the door, Brianna halted. Across the room, near a window, stood Jesse, tall and elegant in formal clothes, but near him, in a maroon velvet wingchair, sat Honoré.

"What is *he* doing here?" asked Brianna as she glared at her half-brother. It was her first face-to-face encounter with Honoré since the incident about which everyone had seemed too incensed or horrified to speak, or at least it had seemed so to Brianna during the remainder of the journey, but she recalled having wondered what they would do with him once they arrived at Monticello, and now, it seemed, she was about to find out.

Seeing her, Honoré rose from his seat and came forward, his expression guarded. He was also dressed formally, in a bright blue evening coat, pale yellow waistcoat, deep gray breeches and snow-white hose and cravat. In contrast to the high boots Jesse seemed to favor and almost always wore, even with formal dress, as he did this evening, Honoré's feet were clad in shiny red high-heeled shoes, such as those recently worn by the aristocracy of the ill-fated *ancien régime*. He also carried a slender cane ornamented with a silver animal's head of some sort; this he wielded with a gracefully practiced turn of the wrist as he came toward her.

"Ahem—ah, Brianna," said Father Edouard as Honoré approached, "your brother has a few words he requested he be allowed to speak to you, and your guardian and I have agreed he might, in our presence."

Brianna had only a moment to glance at the priest after he had said this before Honoré rushed forward to close the gap of the remaining few feet of floor space between them, grasped her hand in imploring fashion, and began to speak in urgent tones.

"Brianna, can you ever find it in your heart to forgive me? I must have been *insane*! There is no other explanation for it, for I have racked my brain and prayed to heaven itself for answers to account for my despicable behavior toward you that night, and no other answers appear. But if you will just listen to me, *ma soeur*, I think, perhaps, I can offer some rationale." He was looking intently at her with those dark, brooding eyes, and his fingers pressed fervently into her palm as he continued.

"You see, I loved our father, Brianna, and I always knew he had difficulty in returning that love. Even as a small boy I knew—knew he was trying to be kind, but it was not out of love, but out of guilt—no, let me go on, for these things are the truth as I see them, and nothing anyone can say now is going to erase the events and circumstances of years...

"Nevertheless, I loved him, and I mourned for him—for him, and for us both—the father and son we could not be. Then, when that—when the will was read, something inside me snapped, and my grief became commingled with a greater sense of loss. Oh, I know, he had never promised me Le Beau Château—not outright, but he never told me I wouldn't receive it, either, and when, last Christmas Eve he lay ill abed and sent for me and bestowed upon me that generous gift—a hundred thousand! A small fortune!—Well, I began to hope. You see, my mother died close to penniless, cut off in disgrace by her family, and as I had no legitimacy, her family ties held even less for me.

"So that brings us to my treatment of you." He took a step backward, simultaneously releasing his grip on her hand, but his eyes remained riveted on her face.

"It is so simple, really, my dear," he said quietly. "I have ever been deeply jealous of you—you and your poor dead sister. You were both so well loved, there in the bosom of your family... my father's family, the family I yearned to be a part of and knew I never would."

Honoré took a deep breath and ran his fingers through his hair before glancing for a moment at Father Edouard and then continuing. "All I could think of, after the funeral and that terrible session in the library, was that, once again, as when we had been children, you were getting it all and I—" Honoré's breath was deep and ragged "—I once again, was left with naught."

This time when he looked at her there were tears in his eyes, and Brianna was moved to murmur, "But, Honoré, *we* always felt it was *you* shutting *us* out! You would never allow us to get close to you, never—"

"Alas, it is true, all too true," he returned. "I was already, even in those years, too stopped up with bitterness to respond differently."

"And now?" questionned Brianna. "What makes you suddenly—"

"Wish to make amends?" Honoré's expression suddenly registered astonishment. "Why, my bestial behavior toward you several nights ago! It—it brought me to my senses!" He looked around and stole a quick glance at Jesse and then rested his eyes on Father Edouard who remained patiently quiet at Brianna's side. "That is why I went at my first opportunity to our mutual confessor here and unburdened myself of everything. And when he suggested I talk to you, I knew it was the only way—to gain complete forgiveness." Suddenly Honoré dropped to his knees before her, saying, "Please, *ma soeur*, I beg of you, in the name of the father we both loved, forgive my hideous behavior that was born of so much grief and pain. Forgive it, and forget it, if you can. It will not—*cannot* happen again! I am prostrate with shame over it." At last Honoré hung his head, sobbing softly at her feet.

Brianna stood awkwardly above him in the otherwise silent chamber, not knowing quite what to say. She looked briefly at Father Edouard who seemed, by the look on his face, to be trying to read her reaction to all this. Then she looked at Jesse. He remained where she'd seen him when she entered the room, tall and silent as he leaned against the wall near the window, his expression closed, but at her questioning look, he glanced briefly at the huddled figure at her feet with what appeared to be a fleeting expression of disgust. Finally he gave her a brief nod and then looked off into the distance out the window.

"I—Honoré," stammered Brianna, "please, I...forgive you. Now, please, get up. You mustn't—oh, I feel so awkward. Father?" She looked imploringly at the priest.

"Yes, yes, Honoré," said Father Edouard briskly as he bent to help the kneeling man to his feet. "It is finished now—behind us, eh? We will say no more about it."

Honoré rose, and as Brianna studied his suddenly tearless face, he bent forward and embraced her in brotherly fashion. "My dearest little sister," he smiled. "So compassionate, as well as beautiful." He held out his arm for her then, adding, "Allow me to escort you to the drawing room where our host awaits us in preparation for adjourning to the dining chamber." With a flourish of his cane, which Brianna now saw bore a silver wolf's head, he led her out of the room.

Behind them, as Father Edouard waited for Jesse to join him, the priest queried, "Well?"

Jesse remained where he'd been standing for a moment, his eyes on the empty doorway. Then he looked at the priest. "The Indians have an expression I've found it useful to recall from time to time, my friend: 'The coat of the wolf never wears the spots of the fawn.'" At last he came forward to join the cleric, his expression grave. "One can do a lot worse than follow Indian wisdom," he said as they walked toward the drawing room. "A lot worse."

Thomas Jefferson was resplendent in a tastefully embroidered evening jacket of peacock blue as he greeted Jesse and Father Edouard at the door to the drawing room. Like the others present, he too wore his hair unpowdered, but he held to the older fashion of wearing it long and tied, again with a bright blue ribbon at the back of his neck. A waistcoat of pale blue with silver embroidery, white cravat and hose, and low-heeled, silver-buckled shoes completed the picture of the prosperous country gentleman. At least, to Jesse's way of thinking, it was this image he seemed to be affecting more than that of his official position, that of Washington's Secretary of State, and Jesse made careful note of this, for its relevance to his mission.

"Come in, gentlemen, come in," smiled Jefferson. "I'm anxious for you to meet my other guests." He gestured then toward the group assembled in the center of the room, a group consisting of eight people. There were five Jesse didn't recognize, in addition to Brianna, Honoré and Aimée, who, he was pleased to see, had been included as a dinner guest, owing to her status as a companion, rather than maid; this was something he had taken pains to point out in the letter he'd forwarded. As introductions were made, he learned that the tall young woman near the sofa was Martha Jefferson Randolph, his host's older daughter, now married to the cross-looking gentleman who stood beside her, Thomas Mann Randolph. Then there was a neighbor of Jefferson's, a planter named Walker and his houseguest, *Monsieur* Fauble, a French *émigré*. Finally, there was a short man with dark, curly hair, high forehead, large brown eyes and arched, quizzical eyebrows.

"My charming, sometime noble, opponent in public and official business," Jefferson was saying, "Aaron Burr."

So this was the notorious Aaron Burr, thought Jesse. He hadn't expected him to show up at Jefferson's table. They could hardly be friends and were, at best, as Jefferson had implied, cautious adversaries, though their differences were hardly on the scale of the schism that divided Jefferson and Hamilton. It would be interesting to see what fruit their social coupling would bear.

While Jesse and Burr nodded politely to each other, *Monsieur* Fauble came forward, saying, "Do you gentlemen perchance play any musical instruments?" He looked at his host. "We are always eager to put together some music for after the dinner at *Monsieur* Jefferson's home, you see, and any guest who can contribute—'' He made an open-armed gesture and shrugged, smiling.

"*Monsieur* Fauble, I am happy to boast, is an extremely talented musician who kindly tunes my fortepiano for me," said Jefferson. "Forgive us, but it's true. We're always looking for after-dinner additions to our little orchestra here at Monticello. Do you play?" he asked Jesse.

Jesse smiled an apology. "When I was a boy my mother taught me how to play a harp we were fortunate enough to own, but when I was nine it was destroyed in a fire which also destroyed our home, and I'm afraid I've never touched a musical instrument since then. I can still read music, though, and I don't mind singing if a baritone's called for."

"Excellent!" exclaimed Jefferson. "I love to sing myself." He turned to Brianna. "Do you play, my dear?"

Brianna smiled shyly. "Oh, I can make a passable stab at the harpsichord, sir, but it is Aimée here who has the true talent. You should hear her with—do you, by any chance, own a hautboy?"

"Why, yes, we do!" enthused her host. He looked delightedly at Aimée who had been in the process of battering Brianna's instep with her toe, an activity she instantly ceased to engage in, once she found their host's gaze on her; she grinned at Jefferson in mock innocence.

"Will you favor us with your talent, *Mademoiselle*?"

Aimée smoothed an imaginary wrinkle from the front of her new raspberry pink gown with both hands before answering with an audible gulp, "*Oui*, if *Monsieur* wish—wishes it."

"Splendid, splendid!" replied Jefferson. "And once I gather a few of the members of my household staff to fill in, we should be able to lend a bit of grace and beauty to the evening."

"Your servants have musical training?" questioned Father Edouard.

"Some of them," Jefferson replied. "You see, after my stay in Europe, with all of its cultural riches, I couldn't bear to return home and leave all that behind. Think, sir, what would we be without architecture, art, drama and music? Uncivilized savages, that's what, and I hardly think those of us who were instrumental in achieving our land's separation from the powers across the sea ever intended that the separation be cultural.

So, when I came back, I made it my business to import as much as my purse would allow of all that's fine and beautiful from that older culture.'' Briefly Jefferson gestured about the room they were in, indicating various *objets d'art* scattered here and there; fine French porcelains, a landscape by Turner, a pair of exquisitely wrought silver candelabra, beautifully crafted furniture in Chippendale's unmistakable style and plush Oriental rugs bore testament to his words.

''And music,'' continued Jefferson, ''has ever been among the first of the arts with me. When we retire to the music room after dining, I'll be pleased to show you the harpsichord Mistress Devereaux has so kindly indicated she might play. I had it built to my specifications in London in '86 after consulting there with the wonderful Dr. Burney.''

''The *famous* Dr. Burney!'' interjected Father Edouard. ''And, then, I assume, sir, once you had taken the time and trouble to import this and other musical instruments, you found you needed to have someone to play them, so—''

''He sifted out those among his slaves with talent and trained them,'' interrupted Walker. ''No small undertaking, I can assure you. I've had considerably less luck with my own house Nigras.''

Brianna stiffened at these words, her discomfort with this face-to-face confrontation with a slave-owning society increasing minute by minute, it seemed, since she had arrived here. As Jefferson advanced toward her now, with daughter Martha beside him, she had a brief moment to ponder the whereabouts of Sally Hemings. Obviously she had not been included in the dinner party, although Brianna had no doubt that they would later be hearing some of her musical talents if she had any, or those of her poor, unfortunate kin!

''I thought it was about time you young ladies became reacquainted,'' Jefferson was saying, ''so I have taken the liberty of seating you next to each other at dinner. Patsy,'' said Jefferson, using the family's nickname for his daughter, ''you remember Brianna Devereaux?''

''But, of course,'' said the nearly-six-feet-tall redhead at his side. ''How delighted I am to see you again, Brianna. And Aimée! I have no trouble remembering you!''

Aimée made a brief curtsey; she was well aware that Martha would not have forgotten, from their days at the Abbaye, that she had definitely been of an inferior social rank, but her smile for the tall woman was genuine and returned in kind; Martha "Patsy" Jefferson, owing to her plain looks and gigantic size, had on occasion also fallen prey to taunting barbs and other cruelties from their more vicious schoolmates and, as such, had more than once been the recipient of sympathy and support from Aimée and Brianna.

The young women had time for only a few pleasantries before Jefferson's butler announced dinner was about to be served and the entire group, led by Jefferson, filed into the dining room.

The dining room at Monticello was another example of Jefferson's passionate flirtation with European things cultural. It was a room ablaze with light as appropriately placed, gilt-edged mirrors reflected the flames of dozens of beeswax candles in graceful wall sconces and a magnificent rococo chandelier. The shine of hand-polished mahogany and softly gleaming fruitwoods echoed this radiance, as did the sparkle of finely cut crystal and hand-painted Sèvres china as everyone sat down to dine.

As the dinner proceeded, a number of things became clear to Brianna as she savored the tastes of a wide range of excellently prepared foods. With the freshly shucked Maryland oysters, newly arrived that afternoon, by boat, where they had been carefully preserved in ice, according to Jefferson, she learned that Martha was aware of Sally Hemings' presence in the household and hated it. (It had merely been her father's passing reference to "my housekeeper" which had inadvertently told Brianna of this, for at the remark she had seen Martha stiffen with anger and grow tight-lipped and silent for several moments afterward.)

When the squab stuffed with wild rice and herbs arrived, Brianna learned that Burr and Jefferson were indeed at odds with each other, the former not above baiting his host with sly innuendoes regarding Hamilton's success in currying favor with the President at the moment; these remarks would cause Jefferson's eyes to grow dark and brooding or else flash dangerously as his face reddened with anger. (Then Brianna also learned that Jefferson had a temper he might not be above losing when provoked.) Volatile currents of tension and hostility simmered and seethed beneath the surface between these two, the air, at times, fairly crackling around them.

The arrival of the roast of suckling pig brought another revelation Brianna's way. Honoré seemed highly taken with Aaron Burr, and Burr, with him. She watched in fascination as Honoré seemed to second every one of the remarks Burr made to taunt Jefferson, but always with a subtlety that left him room to escape if pressed. And escape he did, especially when Jesse did the pressing, for it was now becoming obvious that Jesse's anger was also brewing mightily beneath the surface, an anger fed by Honoré's imprudent remarks, if not Aaron Burr's.

Why, Honoré's not supposed to be doing any of this! Brianna suddenly realized. *Whatever this important mission from Governor Pinckney's office is all about, it certainly doesn't involve antagonizing Thomas Jefferson! What can Honoré be thinking of?*

"Sir," Jefferson was saying to Burr over the flummery (or *blancmange*, as Aimée referred to it), "the financial system devised and now being implemented by Alexander Hamilton has only two objects. First it is meant as a puzzle—"

"A *puzzle?*" queried Burr, his eyebrows arching even higher than usual, his tone derisive. "Really, sir, I—"

"A *puzzle*," Jefferson emphasized, "to exclude popular understanding and inquiry." His face pinkened with each emphasized word.

"But surely," Honoré broke in, "it would only be *puzzling* to those lacking adequate intelligence and education to comprehend." He smiled thinly at his host.

"Honoré," said Jesse, his eyes like blue flint, "are you implying that those citizens of the United States who are unfortunate enough, by virtue of their humbler backgrounds and origins, not to be able to understand our Secretary of Treasury's complicated financial system, do not *deserve* to understand it?" His look pinned Honoré to his seat; Honoré squirmed uncomfortably.

A quick glance at Jefferson told Brianna her host was angrily awaiting Honoré's answer. Honoré glanced quickly at

Burr and then at Jefferson before stammering, "Why—ah—
that is, why, no—"

"Because if that's what you intend," continued Jesse, "I
would next ask that you be prepared to reconcile that point of
view with the words, '...that all Men are created equal, that
they are endowed by their Creator with certain unalienable
Rights, that among these are Life, Liberty and the Pursuit of
Happiness...' or these words: '...that whenever any Form of
Government becomes destructive of these Ends, it is the Right
of the People to alter or abolish it...'"

Jesse paused and continued to impale Honoré with his eyes,
which were fiercely angry, but a glowing Jefferson placed his
hand on Jesse's shoulder, saying, "Well put, Mister Randall,"
and then in a softer voice which Brianna could barely hear,
"You and I will have to talk more...privately."

But Honoré was saying, "Now, Jesse, I was only implying
that it is for the legislature, more than the populace it represents, to attempt to comprehend and deal with Hamilton's financial mechanism."

"Aye," retorted Jefferson, "it is a mechanism, all right, a
machine for the *corruption* of the legislature!" Again the
freckled face grew pink.

"Well," drawled Burr, "there are those in Philadelphia who
would swear that illustrious body would not then be changed
much from what it already is." He smiled sardonically at his
host.

Brianna thought Thomas Jefferson was going to explode, but
evidently Father Edouard recognized the danger, too; quickly
glancing at Jesse, he conspicuously cleared his throat in the silence left by Burr's remark, saying, "Ahem, gentlemen, forgive me for interrupting, but I find I cannot put this off a
moment longer." His hand went to the crystal brandy snifter
near his plate of pudding, holding it aloft, toward the light.
"Mister Secretary, sir, this is a most splendid brandy! May I
inquire of its origins? Such spirits deserve special recognition."

"Why, I managed to rescue a couple of cases of it from the
wine cellars of my friend, the Comte de Tesse, whose house
succumbed to the mob in the aftermath of the storming of the

Bastille. In his gratitude, he gave me a case." Jefferson was once again the genial host.

"Superb," pronounced Father Edouard. "But that leads me to what I have been most anxious to bring up this evening, sir. You see, I happen to indulge in a little pastime every now and then, when my clerical duties permit me the time. I myself have learned to ferment and brew a few simple homemade brandies and liqueurs, and—"

"Simple!" chuckled Jesse. "Mister Secretary, I assure you, this man is far too modest. I've sampled some of his 'simple' nectars, and they are—your excellent French brandy notwith- standing, sir—without rival!"

"Really?" smiled Jefferson, pleasantly intrigued.

"And I was just wondering whether, before we adjourn to the music room," Father Edouard continued, "I might not present you with a few bottles I brought with me?"

"What a marvelous idea," Martha chimed in. "Father, why don't I take the ladies on ahead while you gentlemen enjoy your spirits?" She nodded toward Brianna and Aimée as she spoke, and at Jefferson's nod, the three women rose to depart.

The men rose from their seats as the women rose, Jesse coming quickly around to help Brianna with her chair as Fa- ther Edouard and Thomas Randolph did the same for Aimée and Martha. As he did this, Jesse bent forward and with a grin, whispered in Brianna's ear, "You cannot believe, little ward, how relieved I am, not to have had to chaperone *your* tongue as well this evening. Perhaps," he added as he walked her as far as the door, "your time with the nuns served us well after all." Then, not allowing Brianna a moment to reply, he propelled her lightly through the door behind Martha and Aimée, made a courtly bow, and closed the door in Brianna's outraged face.

Brianna stood where he'd left her, consumed with fury. How *dare* he imply she was a child to be monitored in sophisticated company! Oh, she'd had about all she could take from that man! Clenching her fists for control, she suddenly found she had to escape somewhere. Jefferson could find someone else to play his old harpsichord! Quickly she hurried forward toward Martha, saying, "Oh Patsy, I hope you and your father won't be too upset if I excuse myself? I find I am suddenly very weary from all that traveling. Surely you can make do with Aimée's

talents in the music room while I retire early to my chamber?''
She caught a warning look from Aimée but ignored it, saying,
''It's been an awfully long and tiring day.''

"Why, of course, my dear Brianna," Martha replied. She
clapped her hands twice, loudly, and suddenly Sally Hemings
appeared, so silently she seemed to Brianna to come like a
wraith, from nowhere.

- "Sally, show Mistress Devereaux to her room," said Martha. Her tone left no doubt as to who was mistress and who was
slave.

"Yes'm," said Sally softly, and to Brianna, "Follow me,
please, Mistress."

And in the face of a suspiciously frowning Aimée and the
suddenly authoritative Martha, Brianna followed Sally down
the hall.

Chapter Eighteen

As she followed the soft footsteps and lighted taper of Sally Hemings, Brianna's sudden urge to escape the events around her increased. All she could think of was to remove herself from her surroundings, from an awful feeling of being caught, trapped—hemmed in. She was vaguely mindful of the things that contributed to that feeling—the tense undertones of the dinner conversation, where she had, indeed, been hard put to mind her tongue; the face-to-face confrontation with slavery, underscored even now by the quiet movements of the woman who was lighting her way to her chamber; the real and constant presence of a guardian whose overbearing attitude was beginning to prey on her nerves. She began to feel she was suffocating under it all, and so, when the two women had reached the dimly lit hallway outside her door, she had all she could do to thank Sally before slipping inside the chamber and closing the door with a hasty "good night."

Once inside, she leaned her back against the closed door and took a deep breath. No help. The choking feeling was still there. What could she do? Wildly, she looked around the still room where a lone candle burned in the stand beside the tester bed. Another deep breath. Still no relief. Her thoughts darted about for a way out of her strange panic. If only she dared to don those breeches! Then she'd be able to leave, for it was that kind of physical escape she was now craving. If only she could get away from nere, get out of the house for a while… Her eyes fell on a small open trunk near the entrance to the dressing room where Aimée was to sleep. It was her little gypsy's trunk, the last to be unpacked and somehow never completely emptied—there had been too little time before dinner.

Suddenly Brianna started, seizing on an idea. Yes, there *was* a way to fashion an escape, and it wouldn't involve the pitfall of masquerading in boy's clothing, either. Quickly she went to the trunk; rummaging through it, in a moment she had what she needed: the gray servant's dress she had borrowed at the inn! She almost fell over the trunk in her excitement. *Brianna Devereaux* might not go wandering about outside in the dark with impunity, but a serving wench—let's see, what was her name? Ah—Brielle!—*Brielle Gitane might!*

Some twenty minutes later, pushing a stray auburn curl beneath the concealing mobcap, "Brielle" emerged from the rear of the house into the moonlit gardens of Monticello. Exultantly, she took a deep breath of air, and it worked. She was feeling free again (if only for a while, her poorer self reminded her). But she made a pirouette on the path and felt even better. Calmly, she surveyed her surroundings. In the balmy air she could smell the heady scents of honeysuckle and primrose. Ahead of her, their small, dark green leaves edged with silver by the moonlight, she could make out the shapes of boxwood hedges and yew. Crickets and cicadas sounded their steady staccato from unseen corners and thickets. Ah, but the beauty of Virginia's late September evening was magic and Brianna made up her mind to love every piece of it.

She wandered up and down the paths of Jefferson's gardens for some time, not really stopping to think about how long she'd been there. She was enjoying a wonderful game, and the passage of time had no relevance now. Whatever the cares and pressures she'd eventually have to return to, this was not the time nor place to consider them. They'd be all too real when she had to.

Suddenly, just as she was noticing how high the moon had ridden in the sky, and how absolutely golden it looked, Brianna heard a noise somewhere nearby. Ducking behind a small clump of laurel, her foot pressed on a twig and it snapped.

"Who's there?" demanded an all-too-familiar voice.

Jesse!

Brianna crouched down lower, cursing her lack of care in watching where she stepped.

"Why, it's a white-capped miss, hiding in the moonlight," said Jesse. "You can reveal yourself, girl. No one's going to harm you." His voice came closer as he spoke.

Deciding she had no alternative but to brazen it out, Brianna muttered a silent imprecation to the spirits of successful disguises and slowly stood up. Jesse was less than four feet away, and the look on his face when she saw it was incredulous.

"Well, I'll be damned! It's the little French serving wench from Charleston," he marveled. "What brings you here, *chérie*, of all places?"

Thinking quickly, Brianna stammered, "I—I am now—een ze employ of *Monsieur* Fauble, a guest 'ere, *Monsieur*. 'E—'e bring me 'ere to 'elp weez ze dinnair, as—as a favor to *Monsieur* Jefferson. I make ze best *blancmange,* you see," she fabricated, but as she did so, Brianna was aware she was beginning to really sink into the business of her masquerade and she began to relax with it.

"Ah, Fauble, yes," murmured Jesse as he took a step to narrow the distance between them. A grin. "Brielle, isn't it?" he questioned, peering intently at her face as if trying to get a better look at it beneath the cap.

"*Oui, Monsieur* . . . Jesse," answered Brianna, who suddenly felt very brave. The disguise held! With this added incentive and an abundant residue of the sheer joy she'd been taking in her freedom, she added, "You see I 'ave not forgotten *you, Monsieur.*"

"Nor I, you, it seems," smiled Jesse; he took the remaining step that separated them and drew her boldly to him in a single movement.

His embrace, as it began, was sure and demanding, as if refusal could not be considered. As his arms engulfed her, Jesse took a moment to tilt her head back as his eyes sought her face, and, more specifically, her mouth.

"Yes," he murmured, "how well I now remember that mouth."

Suddenly his own mouth came down on hers in a demanding kiss that seared and enflamed Brianna from the moment it started. Gone was the garden, Monticello, the night itself. All she could focus on was the sudden heat emanating from her core, the immediate sense of pleasure gathering in that secret place between her thighs, and the heady warmth of the big, masculine arms that drew her to him. The kiss deepened.

But a moment later he withdrew his lips and gently held her a few inches away from him, his blue eyes intense as they searched her face. Bewildered, she stared mutely up at him, her lips parted and burning.

Jesse gazed at the alluring creature before him. "So lovely," he murmured, and again he gathered her, softly this time, into his arms and lowered his mouth until his lips found hers. And this time he began the kiss in earnest.

Brianna closed her eyes as she felt his lips' touch, and without even thinking about it, she moved her arms upward to encircle his neck. Somewhere, in the recesses of her other mind, she thought she had a sense of standing on tiptoe to reach him. But in her nearer brain, all she could focus on was the soft, warm sensation of that wonderful mouth possessing hers, of his tongue silkily gliding along her lips, causing them to open, and then the touch of tongue on her teeth, moving, gently moving....

Brianna's head swam. Her whole world became sensation. There was the feeling of his tongue as it touched and played with the tip of hers; there was the steely hardness of his body as it molded hers to him; there was the scent of him, pleasingly masculine and faintly redolent of tobacco and the sandalwood soap she knew he used; there was, finally, the deliciously shocking sensation of his heated palm sliding around her waist and up between them to cup her breast....

Suddenly Brianna froze, the feeling of his fingers as they coaxed her breast free from its confines sending a quick alert to her brain. Feebly, she struggled to remind herself that danger lurked in these intoxicating waters, even as she shivered when his thumb began to brush across her hardened nipple. Again, wave after wave of pleasure assaulted her senses. Now she became aware of a certain hardness pressing against her belly, and when Jesse released her lips and breathed raggedly in her ear, she knew she had to summon her strength.

Somehow she found it, suddenly pulling away with a gasp. "*Mon Dieu!*" she breathed.

Startled by her change in behavior, Jesse allowed her to wrench free, and this was all Brianna needed, the sudden coolness of the night air on her naked breast reminding her all too clearly of how close she'd come to disaster. What was the matter with her? she had an instant to ask herself. And then, as she whirled about and caught a glimpse of Jesse's perplexed expression, she chided herself: *Fool!* He's your guardian, Jesse—the *jailer* you *hate!* And she began to run.

"What—? Brielle, *wait!*" Jesse called, but the wench was already several yards away from him, and with a stab of regret, he was about to leave her to her flight when he had a moment's recall of a similar moment at the Black Swan. But then he remembered that at that time he'd had to let her go in the face of pressing business. Tonight there was no such claim on his time, and with a sudden grin, he set off on the path after her. *This* time he would have her!

Brianna was nearly out of breath when she reached the stable block, the nearest group of buildings she could find, for she had had the ill luck to set her flight in a direction that took her away from the house. Breathing heavily, she chanced to look down; she blushed as she spotted her naked breast and hurriedly tucked it back inside her dress. Then she realized it had begun to thunder and she knew she now needed shelter as well as a place to hide. Glancing about, she saw no one, and so quickly pushed open the stable door. But as she did, she glanced furtively over her shoulder and froze. There, several dozen yards away, came Jesse, running at an easy pace, but definitely toward the stables. Cursing both her foolishness and her bad luck, she slipped inside the darkened stables while outside she heard the first heavy drops of rain hit the ground.

Near panic now, Brianna cast about for a hiding place, grateful someone had left a high-hanging lantern burning above the inner entryway. Equine sounds of stomping hooves and a heavy snort of breath or two met her ears as she fixed her sights on the ladder to the loft. Too obvious? But as another peal of thunder set her already clenched teeth on edge, she decided she had to gamble on it; there was nowhere else.

She had just reached the hay-strewn reaches of the loft's floor when she heard the stable door's hinges creak loudly, above the sound of the rain which was now pelting the roof overhead with a steady rhythm. Dropping to her knees, she held her breath and waited.

Down below she heard a couple of booted footsteps on the brick floor before Jesse's easy chuckle broke the sounds of the rainy night.

"Give it up, *ma petite*. We are beyond games," he called, his voice coming from a place that sounded all too near. "Or if we aren't," said Jesse a few seconds later as his head appeared at the top of the ladder, "this time the game—" He drew himself up to stand at full height above her. "—is mine!"

And with a quick movement he was beside her as she knelt before him, vulnerable, in the hay.

"Please, *Monsieur*," she pleaded in a shaky voice, "I—I *must* not!"

But Jesse was far beyond listening to any refusals. He had made up his mind; his lust was heated, and there was no room for anything else.

Roughly he drew her to him, whispering hoarsely, "No, *ma petite*, not this time, for I have tasted enough of you to know what lies beneath, and escape is no longer possible." He pressed her forcefully into the hay, at the same time covering her body with his own, and before she knew what was happening, Brianna felt his hot mouth on hers. But this time she was too frightened to do anything but struggle. In a clutch of raw panic, she tried to twist herself away from him, but to no avail. His huge, muscular body was heavy on hers and she found it impossible to move, much less maneuver. But then Jesse released her lips as his mouth moved to the delicate skin beneath her ear, and she had time to gasp another "Please" before the touch of his fingers fondling a nipple sent a jolt of pleasure through her. Jesse felt it too, and his next move was to yank sharply at her immodestly low *décolletage*, sending both pink-peaked breasts spilling free. At her sharp intake of breath he nuzzled her neck, murmuring, "Just the beginning, little one, for I mean to give you pleasure." He shifted his weight and began working his magic on her aching, yearning breasts, their pink crests telling him all too clearly they wanted more.

And more he gave her as she felt his lips descend and close over one hardened peak. Moaning, she momentarily forgot to struggle.

"You are made for pleasure, *chérie*," Jesse whispered hoarsely as he felt her give a weak push at his heaving chest. "Give it up, *ma chérie*. It is time."

And as his hand slipped deftly under her skirts, and still further, beneath her chemise, the dam of Brianna's resistance broke and she moaned deeply in her throat, her thighs parting for his knowing fingers. Expertly, he stroked in the place where no one had ever touched her as a woman, and Brianna felt her belly twist and coil into a heated knot of longing. Again Jesse's fingers moved, finding the tiny bud he sought, and with all the expertise at his command, caused her to cry out with a whimper, "Please!" But this time it was with hunger, not fear.

His own desire at a fever pitch, and sensing she was ready, Jesse pulled aside for a moment to begin removing his clothes. He made himself concentrate on this to avoid tearing off the mobcap she wore, this concealing object something he'd already forced himself to ignore at least a dozen times during their intimacies. He would wait. He knew the moment he would remove it; they were almost there.

But the time that passed while Jesse undressed had a sobering effect on Brianna. Averting her eyes to avoid seeing his male nakedness, she shook her head to ward off the passion-numbed state that had stolen over her, and then made a great and final effort to throw off this strange lassitude; drawing on a deep reserve of strength she hadn't known she possessed, she began to struggle to her feet.

But Jesse caught the movement as he was casting off his second boot; totally naked now, he threw his huge form against her and instantly pushed her to the loft floor.

"No!" shrieked Brianna. "No, you *cannot*! I am not—"

But her words were cut off by his mouth as it sliced against hers, this time in almost brutal fashion, for Jesse was by now growing angry with what he took to be her teasing manner.

"Enough!" he rasped against her trembling mouth, while with one knee he forced her thighs apart. Brianna's eyes grew wide with fear as she realized the import of this action. She had a dim awareness that somehow she must stop him, even at the cost of revealing her identity; with a sudden clarity of thought advanced by fear pumping extra oxygen to her brain, she reached to remove her mobcap.

But she was a split second too late; at the moment she was able to wrench it from her head, she thought she heard Jesse's sharp "Don't!" just as there came a deep and painful thrust between her thighs.

She felt herself scream with the pain as it tore through her body, but the sound was lost as a great, ear-splitting peal of thunder tore open the heavens. Lightning flashed, turning the night into day for several suspended seconds, and it was then she heard Jesse's disbelieving *"No!"*

But, his disbelief notwithstanding, it was too late for Jesse to stop now; his overheated lust took total charge, and driven by the age-old movements dictated by this mindless state, he thrust and thrust again. Then, with a mighty groan, he drove the final thrust home and knew it was done.

As Jesse's whirling senses returned, however, he knew it was far from over; the reality of his actions was just beginning. Looking down into the tear-washed, trembling face of Brianna Devereaux, he swore an oath and tore himself off her. There was another lighting of the skies and yet more thunder as he ran his hand roughly through his damply curling hair and forced himself to gather his wits together. Then the anger hit.

"You damned little fool!" he swore at her between clenched teeth, but a moment later, over his rage, he caught the anguished sobs that racked her body and saw the terror, still undiminished, in her wide eyes; with a ragged sigh, he drew her shaking body to him and held her, saying, "No, little one, no, it's all right. It's over, and it was a terrible mistake, but it's going to be all right. *You're* going to be all right." And as the long minutes passed and the thunder gave way to silence and the rain stopped, he held the sobbing girl in his arms until finally the sobbing also ceased.

At last, when they had lain this way for neither knew how long, Jesse loosed his hold on her, putting her far enough away from him to observe her face. Through a small window high in the eaves the moon appeared from behind a cloud, and Jesse saw its ethereal wash of light bathe Brianna's sculpted features and turn them to alabaster, her unloosed hair into swirls of silver silk.

My God, she's beautiful, he thought, even as his head spun with seized and discarded notions of what to do about the unthinkable actions that had just occurred. He glanced down at the rumpled mass of petticoats about her thighs and knew a sickening feeling of disgust at the telltale sight of dark smears he knew were blood. With a teeth-grinding oath of self-reprimand, he gently drew her skirts down over her legs. *Damn! Of course, she had to be a virgin! And she's a child, playing grown-ups' games, and you were too damned lust-driven to see through it!* But as he covered her naked breasts with his discarded shirt, Jesse amended to himself, *No, not entirely a child, and in at least one major way, a woman now*. To her he said, "Brianna, look at me," for her eyes were closed, yet he knew she was awake.

With a hesitating blink, two huge green eyes, their thick lashes spiky with tears, gazed at him from a desolate looking face.

"Are you in pain?" Jesse asked as he reached for the rest of his clothes and began to dress.

Brianna shook her head negatively as she continued to gaze dumbly up at him.

"Are you ready to talk—about this, then?" Jesse pursued softly.

"I—don't—that is, I d-don't kn—kn—" Suddenly a blur of tears reappeared in her emerald eyes as Brianna choked on a sob.

"Sh-h," whispered Jesse as he knelt to take her gently by the shoulders and offer a comforting smile. "*Don't*, little one! Don't, if it's going to make you—"

"B-But I *want* to!" choked Brianna, struggling to control her sobs. "I—I've *got* to!" She stopped and swallowed hard. "I—I mean, I've *got* to talk about this to *some*body, and since you're the only one who— Oh, *God*! What a mess I've made of everything!"

"Don't punish yourself too severely, sweetheart," Jesse said as he drew on his remaining boot. "At least, not yourself alone." He smiled ruefully. "From what you now know, you should remember it takes two people to engage in what we—what just transpired. I'm just as much to blame—maybe more so. I'm your guardian and as the one in charge, ought to have—"

"All I ever wanted was a breath of freedom!" cried Brianna as she sat up with a sudden movement. But as she did this, Jesse's shirt fell away and she stared down, aghast, at her exposed breasts. Quickly, she took both hands and yanked her bodice upward, the heat rising to her face, her embarrassed remembrance rendering speech impossible.

The motion was enough to stimulate Jesse's recollection, too, and with a violently muttered oath, he grabbed his shirt and turned away from her to don it.

"What the hell were you doing wearing this—this *outfit* in Charleston?" he questioned, his anger rising easily to the surface again.

"I *told* you—"

"Yes! I know—a 'breath of freedom,'" he mimicked savagely, "but didn't anyone ever explain to you that the world out there—or out *here*—is a dangerous place where little girls—"

"I am *not* a little girl!" cried Brianna. "I—"

"*Spare* me!" Jesse retorted sharply as he turned to face her after finishing with his shirt. "You may, indeed, no longer be a girl—now—in one respect especially, but the fact is—dammit, look at me, Brianna!"

Brianna had shamefully lowered her head at his stinging reminder of the loss of her virginity, once again mortified by the hot blush that suffused her cheeks, but at his sharp command, she forced herself to raise her head and look at him. It was a difficult thing to do, for as she took in the masculine presence of him standing there in front of her, his full-sleeved white shirt open to reveal the muscular chest covered with dark, curly hair, his handsome face chiseled and strong in the moonlight, with a lock of boyishly curling hair falling over his forehead, the overpowering height of him making her feel weak and vulnerable, Brianna had the urge to run away and never return, so frightened was she suddenly of the power she recalled he could summon over her. Swallowing hard to push her fears away, she willed herself instead to say to him, "Yes. The world *is* a dangerous place."

"That's something you should have learned in Charleston," said Jesse crossly. "Tonight might never have happened. Didn't that little scene outside your chamber at the inn tell you enough of what might go on when you pursued such avenues of adventure?''

"O-h-h,'' moaned Brianna in utter embarrassment at his reminder of those other intimacies. She shot him a damning look. "I cannot believe you would rub salt in my wounds this way by bringing up—oh-h! Jesse Randall, whatever you are, you are no gentleman and I've had enough of you to last me till *doomsday*!'' She scrambled to her feet.

"Brianna, now you—''

"Stop!'' she spat, pushing past him and moving toward the ladder. "Now it is *my* turn to cry 'Spare me!'—Spare me the *lecture*, and spare me your *presence*!'' And in a huff of skirts and petticoats, she pivoted and began to back down the ladder.

Jesse rushed forward to stop her, but at the sight of her drawn face with its renewed wash of bitter tears, he halted and let her go. He listened to her final movements below and then, outside; then he stood in the silent stable and breathed a deep and ragged sigh. At last he whispered to the empty loft, his voice strained and tight, "Where the hell do we go from here?''

Out of breath and panting, Brianna somehow reached the haven of her bedchamber without benefit of guide or candle. She took a moment to check the dressing room and found Aimée sleeping soundlessly; careful not to awaken her, she quietly closed their adjoining door and with quick, soft footsteps, made her way to a Windsor slipper chair near the bed and sat down.

Wordlessly, but in rich, sensual images, as if in a dream, the events of the past few hours came to her: the heady scents and silver shapes of the garden as she'd walked its moonlit paths; the strong, masculine presence of Jesse as he'd responded to her fateful masquerade; the warmth of Jesse's hands on her and the impossible delights he'd initiated on her body; the storm with flashes of light and sound and its frightening parallel in the devastating moments that had brought a painful conclusion to their union . . . yes, the pain . . . She couldn't forget that. Even now she could feel a dull ache between her thighs, an ache that reminded her all too surely that what had happened had been real and no dream.

Dully, she looked about her in the quiet chamber, still faintly lit by the guttering bedside candle. Seeking some remedy for the hollowness that seemed to pervade her spirit, she tried her favorite trick of breathing deeply; she felt somewhat restored. Now... what to do...

She knew she felt one thing strongly above all else; she was, by the events of this night forever changed, and not in just the obvious way... in having lost her chastity, although she knew she would have to deal with that, too...

No, it was the other things that had *led* to that loss—the incredible, mindless responses she'd found her body capable of, her reactions to Jesse's very nearness. With certain clarity of hindsight she now knew Jesse had been right in what he'd said about the fact that she should have been warned by Charleston... Why hadn't she? And what had there been about Jesse that had caused her to ignore her wiser self and plunge, headlong, into...?

But she knew the answer to that, didn't she? After all, Jesse Randall was an unbelievably handsome and virile man, and—*but*, that wiser self now coaxed, is that *all* there was to it? Why had she never responded to any other man in the same way?

But you've led a totally sheltered existence, she argued. *How were you to realize a man's mere physical closeness could set off such yearning, such—*

Yes, but if it was purely physical, why had Honoré's touch been so repulsive?

But he is your half-brother! It would have been incestuous!

Yes, I know, but— Here she felt herself stymied. She couldn't logically argue her case using the incest factor because then she would have to admit there were factors involved other than just the physical; to admit this was to destroy her logic.

She took another deep breath and plunged onward, anxious now to ascribe some sense and reason to what had happened. *Very well,* she told herself, *the incident with Honoré is not comparable because you had never liked or felt comfortable with him from the beginning... but what of your prior feelings about Jesse? You hated him! How, then, can you account for that total capitulation to his—*

"Oh, Sweet Mary!" Brianna suddenly cried aloud. "What am I to make of all of it? Holy Mother of God—someone, please help me! I'm so confused and I feel so *lost*! I cannot seem to find *me* anymore!'' With great, choking sobs, she bent her head over her lap and covered her face with her hands; then she began to weep brokenly.

"Saints! What is *this*!" It was Aimée's voice. "Brianna, what is it?" She rushed from the dressing room with a lighted taper, for Brianna's room was by now in total darkness. Frantic at hearing her companion's sounds of distress, her long night braid flying behind her, the little gypsy advanced like an avenging angel, ready to do battle with anything or anyone who was harming her friend.

Setting her candlestick down on the table, Aimée quickly ascertained Brianna was alone and then moved to comfort her, pulling her friend's hands from her face and, kneeling, wrapping her small arms tightly around the taller girl.

"*Chérie*, please, you must not weep so! Whatever it is, it cannot be so terrible that we cannot overcome it, no? Oh, please, *mon amie*, can you tell me what is wrong?"

"Oh, Aimée," sobbed Brianna, "it's all so *awful*!"

"Not so awful that you cannot tell me of it!" chided Aimée gently. "Come," she said, leading Brianna to sit on the bed. "We shall talk it out and you will see—two heads and two hearts, better than one, to banish ill, eh?"

Brianna calmed a bit then, hiccoughing on a few half-sobs before at last quieting down to a sniffle. At last she stopped and looked at her friend who, standing before her while she sat on the high tester bed, met her at eye level. "Tonight I am no longer a virgin," she stated flatly.

"No longer a—*Brianna*! That beast, Dumaine—do you—"

"No, Aimée, not Honoré," said Brianna with a rueful half-smile. And then she began at the beginning and told her what had happened—all of it.

" . . . and, so, you see, I am not quite myself anymore, Aimée. I suddenly have all these unfamiliar feelings inside me and—"

"Bah! I will never believe that of you, Brianna! You are who you are, a very strong person—yes, strong! Look at all the pain and loss you've endured in your life already. Were they able to beat you—break your spirit? No! And I will tell you why. Because you have *courage* and a belief in yourself, not to mention a much better passing acquaintance with *le bon Dieu* than I seem to have! What is one little loss of a maidenhead?"

"One little loss?!" Brianna was incredulous.

"It was bound to happen sooner or later," retorted Aimée with a shrug, but as Brianna fixed her with a suspicious look, she quickly continued. "You are just upset because it did not happen in the romantic way we girls used to dream and whisper about, back at the Abbaye. If this were your wedding night—"

"Yes, but it was *not* my wedding night, Aimée, and—oh, dear heaven! What about my real wedding night, when it comes? What am I going to tell my husband when—"

"Brianna! First things first. We are straying away from the subject!"

"Which is . . . ?"

"Your reactions to your guardian."

"Ah, yes," said Brianna with a bitter laugh. "My guardian. *Some* guardian!"

"Do you know what I think?" said Aimée with a thoughtful look on her face.

"What?" asked Brianna, suspicious again.

"I think it is *because Monsieur* Jesse is your guardian that you are so confused."

"Go on," said Brianna, attentive now.

"Well, as your guardian, he is supposed to engender feelings of daughterly respect—you know, the kinds of feelings you might have for . . . Père Edouard, let us say. Aren't guardians usually somewhat older men . . . more—more paternal? After all, who ever expects a guardian to look like a god, eh? But yours does, does he not? So you see, *he* is the source of your confusion—not *you*! *Monsieur* Jesse does not come off the way he is supposed to, and you, poor *chérie*, wind up paying for it with this confusion, *oui*?"

Brianna was silent for a moment. "We-l-l, I suppose that *could* account for it," she mused.

"Of *course* it accounts for it! *Voilà!* You see? It is entirely *Monsieur* Jesse's fault!" Her head gave an assertive nod.

Brianna considered her friend's reasoning for several more moments. Finally, as she stifled a yawn, she nodded back to Aimée; by the softening of the light out the window, she could tell it was nearly dawn, and she now realized she was exhausted. "Very good, Aimée," she smiled drowsily, climbing under the coverlet. "It sounds logical, and you have ever had a clear head on your shoulders, so I accept your explanation. Yes, I like that very much," she murmured as her eyes closed " . . . all Jesse's fault . . ."

Aimée watched her sleeping friend for several moments while the pale dawn continued to seep into the room. *Ah*, chérie, she thought. *It is well that you accept this notion of mine...at least for now... It will put you off from what I suspect are the deeper emotions you are not yet ready to deal with,* mon amie. *Love...the kind of love I have long known awaits you, always has a difficult time getting the heart to accept...and trust! But some day,* chérie, *some day very soon, you will know... May I be a good enough friend to help you through the pain before you reach the joy.*

And with a gentle smile, the little gypsy tucked the covers tenderly around her friend's shoulders and tiptoed out of the room.

Chapter Nineteen

Thomas Jefferson's long, raw-boned frame appeared out-sized and uncomfortable, folded, as it was, into the small confines of a Queen Anne armchair in his library, but Jefferson didn't seem to notice as he observed the golden color of the liquid he swirled in a snifter with his right hand. "The cleric brews a fine brandy," he said to his guest.

Jesse smiled. "I wasn't exaggerating about his talents, sir. As a matter of fact," he added as he raised his own glass and lightly inhaled its aromatic contents, "I'm not given to exaggeration. It's not my style."

"No, I don't imagine it is," retorted Jefferson.

"Then, if you believe that, sir, you shouldn't have trouble believing the messages I convey," Jesse told him. "There are a lot of powerful people sitting down there in our legislature who are desperate to keep you in the job, Mister Jefferson."

Jefferson continued to play with the rich amber liquid in his snifter before fixing Jesse with a steady look. "And their motives, in your opinion, Mister Randall?"

Jesse smiled at Jefferson's directness. He seemed to be hitting a mother lode of forthright politicians these days! "Mister Jefferson, I'd be dishonest with you if I purported to know all their reasons. I don't. But I can tell you what my own are—my own and mayhap those of a few others I've met and spoken to personally."

Jefferson raised a quizzical eyebrow and nodded, waiting for Jesse to elucidate.

"Republicanism, sir," said Jesse simply. "Or, to paraphrase the words of a friend of mine, you're the only hope this nation has against the—ah—extreme Federalist position of Alexander Hamilton and his band of aristocratic bankers and moneyhandlers. I repeat, sir, for me and him and, I suspect, a good many others, it's to save Republicanism and the democratic viewpoint."

Jefferson nodded briefly when Jesse had finished and was then thoughtfully silent for several moments. At last he fixed his bright blue eyes directly on his guest, saying, "My antipathy toward the machinations of the Secretary of the Treasury are well enough known to be almost common knowledge, for I have opposed him both publicly and privately for years. And if it were merely that kind of two-faceted battle I were now facing, Mister Randall, I would gladly continue with as much energy as I could muster.

"But the fact is, you see, that the scales are no longer so evenly balanced." Jefferson paused for a moment to lean forward in his seat, his brandy snifter held in two hands as his forearms rested on his knees. "You heard Aaron Burr at my table last night. The President himself is showing increasing signs of favoring the Federalist position. In short, sir, he is choosing Hamilton!"

Jesse almost recoiled from the intensity he saw in Jefferson's face at that moment, so blatant was its pain. Immediately he became aware of the great passion there resided in this man, of his deep personal involvement in the struggle they discussed, and he became instantly saddened by the discovery. The games of high politics were best played by those who had thick hides and could afford to lose battles now and then. This man would never lose lightly or successfully. Thomas Jefferson had too much pride.

At length Jesse nodded toward his host, his own face reflecting understanding and compassion. "You're sure that's the way of it, then?"

Jefferson nodded sadly. "In addition to the rumors, the President and I have had correspondence. Oh, no," he added hastily, seeing Jesse's unformed question, "he's never said outright that my views are to be subordinated to Hamilton's, but he consistently hammers on the merits of the man's viewpoint."

"Yes," Jesse agreed, "I can see where that might cause you to reach your conclusion, but, sir, if I may suggest it, there is another possibility here, I think."

Jefferson's eyebrows raised in questioning fashion, but his look remained doubtful. "Go on," he said.

"Well," said Jesse, choosing his words carefully, "suppose yours isn't the only such correspondence Washington is having. Suppose he and Hamilton are involved in a similar exchange, with the President doing all he can on that end to set forth and argue the merits of *your* views to the Secretary. Sir, I had the good fortune to meet with George Washington during his tour of the South last year, and—" Here Jesse threw Jefferson an embarrassed grin. "—owing to a personal acquaintance on the part of Washington and my father, I was lucky enough to be able to meet personally with the President and speak privately with him on a number of occasions. Forgive me, sir, but at those times George Washington did not strike me as a man who would be partisan in these matters. On the contrary, Mister Jefferson, I felt he was a man operating under a heavy burden—that burden being the difficult task of steering his Ship of State without veering too sharply to starboard *or* to port, but to do the perhaps impossible task of balancing the conflicting extremes and steering a safe course in the center."

Jefferson smiled. "You have, I take it, some nautical experience in your background, Mister Randall?"

It was Jesse's turn to smile. "My brother and I have some shipping interests, yes, and as youngsters we were required by our father to hire out as cabin boys on the vessels of sea captain friends of his. The required stint was for two years."

Jefferson's smile turned into a grin. "I'll wager you didn't remain at cabin boy status by the time your stint at sea was over, Mister Randall. Am I right?"

"You are," grinned Jesse, "though that's because I returned to the sea for a couple more years following my parents' deaths. It was my brother Garrett's idea, and my nautical education was completed on our own packet, *The Marianne*." A flicker of a frown crossed Jesse's brow as he added, "We named her after our mother."

"You are enamored of the sea, then?" questioned Jefferson.

"Yes and no. I was, when I was young, but after I attended William and Mary, my interests broadened, and there was a new fascination, one I carry to this day." He looked pointedly at his host. "Architectural design, Mister Jefferson," he added simply.

Jefferson's eyes lit brightly at the revelation. "I *knew* I saw a kindred spirit when I met you! And, for heaven's sake, stop calling me Mister Jefferson. It's Thomas."

Jesse gave a nod. "Thomas. And I'm Jesse."

"Well, Jesse, you and I shall have to take some time to indulge ourselves and discuss our mutual fascination. Yes, I recall Father Edouard mentioning you've been busy working on a new residence for yourself. Yes, after dinner this evening, perhaps, we can pursue our shared interest and I'd be pleased to show you some exciting new plans I have for expanding Monticello, but for the present, I'd like to get back to our original topic. So you think Washington's playing the fence?"

"Well, I wouldn't exactly put it—"

"Oh, I know! I meant that only in the very best sense, which is how you originally presented it, of course." Jefferson looked pensive for a moment. "Well, of course, if you're right, then that would explain it," he said cryptically.

"Sir?"

"Thomas! Well, you see, Jesse, the one thing they haven't told you—because *I* haven't told anyone—is that in May of this year I already *did* what you and all those well-meaning Carolinians are so bent on preventing. I sent Washington my letter of resignation."

"You *what*?"

"Hold on, now, Jesse. I said I sent it. I *didn't* say the President accepted it. As a matter of fact, his refusal to do so has been the subject of much additional correspondence between us. You know, that was the one perplexing element I couldn't quite piece out. If he was so inclined to favor the other side, he should have been relieved to see me resign. But he wasn't. Now, perhaps, you've given me reason to understand why." Jefferson smiled. "And hope!" he said enthusiastically.

"You see, Washington's far too wise to have picked for his Cabinet, men he knew nothing about—I mean, in terms of their personal convictions and character. Washington—indeed, anyone who knows me—realizes soon enough that I am not primarily a politician. Look around you, man.'' Jefferson's arm made a sweeping gesture. ''Do you know what you see? You see the things that reside foremost in my heart. My home...my Monticello with its graceful columns, its fields and streams, and its books and music, too. This is where I would prefer to spend my time.

''But, do you know what's curious? Washington himself feels the same way! Mount Vernon is where *he's* happy—not Philadelphia—or New York, or wherever the public men meet.

''And Washington is perceptive enough about me—and honest enough—to know he could never ask me to do what he is loathe to do himself!''

''You mean,'' interjected Jesse, ''that being honest—and fair—he could not call upon you to give up your personal happiness for affairs of state when he himself knows how painful that would be, so he's had to select other avenues of persuasion—he's refused to use the call of one's duty and all that!''

''Exactly,'' said Jefferson, ''so it's entirely likely, if your guess is correct—and I do say '*if*'—that he's decided to involve me instead in the philosophical persuasions that perhaps he has used on himself to—er—steer his course. He's appealed to my *reason*!'' Jefferson gave a laugh and raised his still untouched brandy in the air. ''Well, by Jove, it's a brilliant ploy, and, I don't mind admitting, it just might work! To the President, sir! I drink his health!'' And with a grin and a sparkle in his blue eyes, Jefferson drained the glass.

Sipping his own brandy after joining the toast, Jesse sat back and felt himself relax. He had been feeling the tensions of trying to succeed in his mission all day, and he hadn't felt too sanguine about the possibilities, either, given some tendencies toward irresolute behavior he'd observed in his host. Now, suddenly, it all seemed possible, and he made a mental note not to underestimate Jefferson again. The man might have his stubborn side, but he was, more importantly, an example of the foremost type his century had to offer: a man of reason.

The two men talked for a time more on a number of topics, many of them touching on ideas contained in books they had both read, though when the subject of architecture again arose, Jefferson begged off, saying he was savoring that for later when they would have more time. Then the meeting ended, with Jefferson excusing himself to oversee the grain threshing that was in progress on the plantation, and with Jesse heading for his chamber to make some perfunctory notes on their meeting, this in accordance with a promise he'd given Pinckney.

He was just leaving the library after Jefferson's departure when he heard feminine chatter coming from the end of the long hallway. Slowing his steps, he took in Brianna's and Aimée's excited voices as they discussed "Patsy" Jefferson's new baby.

"He *looks* like a Jefferson too!" chuckled Aimée.

"All that fuzzy red down on his head!" exclaimed Brianna, "and I do believe his eyes will be blue."

"She certainly looks the proud *maman*," said Aimée.

"Yes," Brianna agreed, "and to think, there she was at dinner last night, and we never even guessed she was just out of childbed!"

Knowing they hadn't yet seen him, Jesse watched the two young women walk down the hallway, taking particular observance of his ward. She appeared more beautiful than ever, dressed as she was in some ultra-feminine concoction of sorts— a day gown, he supposed it was—white with tiny green embroidered flowers and a wide green sash at her small waist. He was surprised and, he supposed, glad to see her looking cheerful and none the worse for what had happened last night. Indeed, she looked so fresh and buoyant, she seemed to him to have enjoyed a far better night's sleep than *he* had had! In her hand she swung a bonnet that matched her gown, and Jesse was just thinking he was glad to be enjoying the sight of those magnificent auburn tresses before she covered them up, when he saw her clutch the bonnet to her with a sudden jerk; she had spotted him.

Then he saw her stiffen and throw Aimée a private look before nodding coolly in his direction and passing beyond him into the extreme end of the hallway. As Jesse turned to watch the two of them go, Aimée glanced over her retreating shoulder and shot him a quick grin accompanied by a wink.

So the little friend knew. He might have figured that much! Girls just out of the schoolroom together had to share their confidences. He stood for a moment and reflected on an im-

age of Brianna as she'd been just now—before she'd known he
was there and the ice had´appeared. She'd been so lovely—fresh
and young—*vibrant*. He wondered why he hadn't somehow
taken the time until now to notice how vital and full of life she
was. The French had a phrase for it—*joie de vivre*—and she
had it. That, and a highly unusual beauty . . . which was something he *had* taken the time to appreciate, perhaps too *much*
time.

He made a gesture of dismissal, as if to clear away disturbing thoughts. So she was going to play it cool and distant, was
she? Well, so much the better. He was going to have all he could
do to marry the little minx off, and the farther away he could
manage to keep her in the interim. . . .

With a shake of his head, Jesse quickened his steps as he
made for his chamber. He concluded that he had far more important things to occupy his time than the problems that adolescent chit presented; he had work to do. But as he opened the
door and faced the empty guest room, he had a momentary
flash of large green eyes and silvered auburn hair in the moonlight.

Chapter Twenty

Brianna stood on Monticello's verdant lawn and tied the ribbons of her bonnet with shaking hands. Dear Lord, but it had been hard, running into him unexpectedly and facing him so soon after last night! And here she had thought she had it all worked out! What was the matter with her? She had to assume more control over herself if she were going to—

"Are you going to let me help you tie that bonnet, or are you going to stand there working at it all day, *chérie*?" Aimée asked with a sympathetic smile. "And, please, *mon amie*, try not to look so troubled, for, see—here come Isaac and Festus with the baskets for our apple picking." She reached up to assist Brianna with the stubborn bonnet ribbons, but not before hailing the two men with an enthusiastic wave.

"Aimée, you're a godsend!" smiled Brianna as she began to relax. "What would I do without you?"

"Oh, play the ravished maiden, I suppose," Aimée grinned, her manner so infectious that Brianna responded with a laugh. "But, there—you see? I have the old Brianna back instead! I tell—*told* you you had the courage, *ma chére*!"

"Courage? What courage is it you speak of *Mademoiselle*? The apple trees are not all that tall, and, besides, it is Festus and I who shall do the climbing and shaking!" Isaac's usually serious face broke into a toothy grin as he approached the women.

"Isaac, Festus! How are you?" Brianna smiled. She glanced at the small, dark shadow that seemed to be dogging Festus' footsteps. "And how is Lil Bits?"

"How do, ladies?" grinned Festus. "Oh, dis cat be mos' lahk a trained pup, Miz Brianna. He done larnt t' folla me step fo' step, jes lahk Ah follas Isaac o' whoevah—we *bof* uses ouah *eahs*!"

Brianna bent to address the fast-growing kitten whose health and good care were attested to by the fact that he'd easily doubled in size since the day Festus had claimed him. "Good day to you there, Lil Bits! Are you going to help us pick apples for Father Edouard, too?"

"Mo' lahkly t' worry dem birds whut he kin flush up!" chuckled Festus.

"Well he certainly shan't be encouraged to catch any!" Brianna warned, fixing the kitten with a threatening look.

With Festus avowing that this was one cat that would never be a successful hunter, the four trod off in the direction of Jefferson's orchards, their conversation gay and easy as they walked. Once amid the heavily laden apple trees, they fell to their task, happily filling their baskets as they talked, joked and companionably passed the time together.

They were an hour or so into their work when Brianna found herself separated from the others, having spied a stand of trees with apples of a different type from those they had been harvesting. Humming to herself as she gathered the plumpest specimens from the lower branches, she was absorbed in her task and unprepared for the male voice that intruded into her tune.

"It is good to see you so content, *ma soeur*."

Brianna's head jerked up with a start as the apple she'd been holding tumbled wide of its mark and fell to the ground beside her basket. "Honoré!" she exclaimed in alarm.

"Brianna, you wound me with such looks and tones," her half-brother said easily, his fingers moving to the area of his heart. "Surely I do not frighten you any longer?" He stood against a low stone wall near the edge of the orchard, a tall, darkly clad figure in the bright sunlight, and the sight of him made Brianna shiver despite the warmth of the day.

"You wished to speak with me?" Brianna made an effort to appear casual, despite the fearful hammering of her heart. What was it about him that immediately put her off so? It had little to do with their recent *contretemps*. Honoré had always, even when they were children, inspired distrust and dislike. She made an effort to dispel these feelings, however, in the light of their recent reconciliation, and with a willed smile added, "I am frightfully busy, brother. We gather apples for Father Edouard's nectars, you see." She glanced about her when she said "We," hoping to emphasize she was not alone in the orchard.

"Ah, the good cleric and his avocation!" smiled Honoré as he took a few steps toward her. "Aaron says he's rarely tasted better brandies made from homely craft, and I tend to agree with him."

A momentary recollection of the dinner conversation of the previous evening struck Brianna, and she found herself frowning as she replied with irritation, "It seems that is not the only arena in which you tend to echo Burr. Whatever have you been thinking of, Honoré, to be seconding that man's ideas so readily, even when they risk angering Jefferson?"

Honoré took a couple more steps in Brianna's direction, which brought him within touching distance of her. "Do not trouble yourself about it, *ma petite*. Women need not worry their pretty heads with such matters." He reached out and touched a lock of her hair as if to punctuate his meaning.

Bristling, Brianna took a recoiling step. "Our 'empty heads' is what you really mean, isn't it?" she retorted hotly. "Well, I assure you, sir, *this* pretty head is far from such barrenness! Now, I repeat, why did you join Aaron Burr in baiting Jefferson last evening? Isn't it your job to somehow create a smooth liaison between Jefferson and my guardian, on behalf of your employer—the Governor?"

Dumaine's eyebrows raised in appreciation of her apparent understanding, but he answered her smoothly. "Well, what if it is? We were merely lending some . . . ah . . . spice to the dinner conversation, *ma chére*, nothing more serious. And, at any rate, your guardian seemed to have matters well in hand, didn't he? There was no harm done, you see." He closed the gap between them again with a single step.

"If Jesse did manage well, it was no thanks to you," retorted Brianna, "and that still doesn't explain your sudden handholding with Burr. What are you planning?" she added suspiciously.

"Brianna, enough of this talk," said Honoré with easy evasion. "The day is much too beautiful and so is my enchanting sister." He ran the tip of his finger down the side of Brianna's face, and once again she found herself succumbing to an involuntary shiver before a thick, deep voice interrupted their parlance.

"Dat be fah 'nuff, Mistah Dumaine. De lady got apple pickin' t' do!" Festus' face looked grim and purposeful as he appeared, as if out of nowhere, to stand beside Brianna.

Honoré's expression grew sullen as he glanced upward at the black man's irresolute mask. But as his lips drew into a thin, hostile smile and he would have responded, Brianna cut him off.

"*Monsieur* Dumaine was just leaving, Festus. Good day to you, brother," she said to Honoré in a dismissing tone. "As my friend rightly put it, I have apple picking to do."

"Your 'friend,' is it?" sneered Honoré. "My dear sister, I would warn you, in brotherly concern, of course, of your easy use of that term. You should remember, you are no longer in France, but in the Southern American States now, and there are those who would do worse than look askance at your bestowing that term upon one of an inferior race." He bowed briefly in courtly fashion to Brianna before turning and walking quickly away, but not before Brianna was able to call after him with a heated rejoinder.

"Inferior men will ever attempt to raise their status by seeking out those whom they can pretend are lower!" Then Brianna turned to Festus and placed a comforting hand on his huge forearm. "Inferior, indeed!"

"Now, Miz Brianna, don' go knottin' yo'se'f all up wid de angries. Dat man ain' wuth de trouble." Festus smiled down at her.

"Very well, Festus," said Brianna as she returned his smile, "but only if you agree—this very minute—" she added with mock severity, "to drop the 'Miz' when addressing me and call me Brianna. Will you?"

Festus gave a faint grimace and swallowed hard. "Well, Ah specs Ah kin *try*, Miz—er—Brianna, but it ain' gonna be easy. Ya'll gotta reelize whut it's lahk t' be brung up black 'n' slaved in dis lan'. Ah ain' *nevah* called no white lady nothin' but Miz 'n' Ma'am.''

"Yes, but you're free now, Festus, and I am—that is, I hope I can be your friend.''

Sorrowfully, Festus shook his head. "Dis freedom still pow'rful new t' me . . . Brianna. It's so't o' lahk a new fit o' clothes. Ah ain' got used t' it yet." He shook his dark head again. "Sometahms Ah wondahs if Ah'll *evah* git used t' it." He fixed her with a serious look. "Freedom's a heavy coat t' weah."

Brianna nodded with understanding. "Sometime you and I shall have a talk about this at greater length, Festus . . . Freedom . . . yes, it is a garment that may not be worn lightly."

Festus gave her a tender smile. "But Ah considahs it a priv'lege t' call ya'll mah friend, Brianna—an' a . . . *honah* t' have ya'll call me yoah's. Now, Ah specs Ah better see ya'll t' de Big House. Isaac 'n' de lil lady done gone up wid dere baskets stuffed. Ya'll ready, cat?" he called over his shoulder.

A ready "meow" came in reply.

"Well, let's git, den!" And hoisting Brianna's heavily laden basket plus two of his own with complete ease, he escorted Brianna back to the house.

Back in her chamber, Brianna stretched wearily out on her bed while she waited for Aimée to return from downstairs where she'd gone to order her bath. She rubbed at the muscles of her right arm. Apple picking was hard work! *Not half as much fun as pilfering cherries!* she chuckled to herself as she recalled those madcap moments at the Abbaye with a surprising stab of nostalgia. Her smile grew wistful as she thought of the many kindnesses of Madame Mézières during her tenure there, and especially during those parting moments before she and Aimée had left.

"Try to curb that fiery nature and walk a milder path toward maturity," Madame had importuned softly as Brianna had prepared to board the coach that took her and Aimée to Le Havre that last morning.

Suddenly hot tears stung Brianna's eyes as she reflected on the kind Abbess and her wise counsel. *And what am I now, in the face of all those tender admonitions?* Silently the tears fell.

Caught up and tied like a trussed Christmas goose, bereft of family, freedom and virginity, that's what! Oh, but I wanted so much to be able to prove to Papa and Madame and all the others that I could make them proud of me! And what has happened? Why, I am not even able to be proud of myself!

Darkly, her thoughts turned toward the fateful encounter with Jesse. She felt her cheeks burn hotly beneath the tears as they dried, unable to stave off thoughts of Jesse's hands on her and her body's responses. *Am I a total wanton, then?*

No, another inner voice reminded. *Honoré, just now—he evoked nothing but disgust, remember? It is Jesse's touch, and his, alone, that made you burn. Wherefore, then, wanton?*

Very well, then, what if it is only Jesse? What are you going to do about the man and, worse, your reactions to him? As she heard Aimée's returning footsteps in the outer hallway, Brianna sat up in bed and hastily dashed away her tears with the back of her hand. Summoning the courage Aimée had avowed she had, her thoughts turning to their conversation before she'd fallen asleep in the early dawn, Brianna took a deep breath and said aloud to herself, "I don't have to do a damned thing but expect my guardian to *act* like a guardian and that, dear Jesse, will be *your* problem—not mine!" And with a determined grin on her face, she greeted her friend as she came through the door.

Chapter Twenty-One

During the remaining days of their stay at Monticello, Jesse and Brianna managed to avoid each other's company completely, he spending the time with Jefferson while they discussed politics and architecture, she and Aimée visiting with Martha and her children or helping Father Edouard compile his ingredients for the spirits he was making to leave as a gift for their host when they departed. Even their meals were taken apart from each other, Jesse always joining Jefferson and the other men at table, the two women dining with Martha in the nursery or pleading fatigue in order to have trays sent to their rooms. It was a happy arrangement for each, and if their host or anyone else questioned this carefully engineered separation, no one mentioned it.

But now it was the final evening at Monticello for the Carolina guests, prior to their departure in the morning, and as Jefferson had planned a farewell banquet and musicale for them, the end of this physical estrangement could no longer be avoided.

Brianna stood before a large Chippendale mirror in her chamber and nervously assessed her appearance while Aimée bent behind her and fussed with a last-minute adjustment of her hem. For at least the dozenth time in the several days since her disastrous encounter with Jesse, she worriedly scrutinized her face, fruitlessly searching for some tell-tale clue that might reveal her fall from maidenly grace. There was none. With a sigh, she studied the whole reflection. What she saw was a tall, slender young woman wearing yet another *robe en chemise*, this time tinted a pale robin's egg blue, with deep mauve sash and matching satin slippers. The gown's material was of whisper-soft gauze that clung to her willowy figure and molded it into a vision of gossamer enchantment. Her shiny auburn curls had been piled high on the crown of her head by Aimée in an intricate arrangement of tiny braided loops and contrasting swirls of thicker locks of hair. At her ears and on a gold chain around her elegant neck she wore three deep amethyst stones set in delicate filigreed gold—maternal family heirlooms passed on to her by her father after her mother died. Her rose-petal-soft skin had taken on a slight apricot tint from the sun, despite the frequent donning of bonnets while she was out of doors, but the light dusting of freckles which had always graced the bridge of her nose and cheekbones during the summers of childhood had not materialized this year, and Brianna gave a brief shrug at the sudden realization. Briefly she wondered if her coloring was beginning to favor Papa's. Mother and Deirdre had always been the true redheads in the family, she recalled, freckles ever a part of their summer complexions, no matter how hard they tried to cover up, while she, who had happily romped in the sun with the barest minimum of clothing, had never accrued more than the scant dusting, and her hair had always remained a darker shade as well.

Tentatively and with reverence, Brianna's fingers went to the pendant at her neckline, the thoughts of the woman who had once worn them causing her a moment's sadness. *How different things might be if Mother were still here! Ah, but she is not, and it is time for you to get on with the business of living,* her maturer self answered. *Courage is all it takes . . . courage.*

With this word her mind switched immediately to the problem at hand: how to go into that drawing room in just a few moments and face her guardian. Well, she'd known it would have to be endured sometime. Courage, that's all it took. She breathed deeply. "Very well, Aimée," she announced, "I think I am ready."

"Thank God!" Aimée blurted out in English as she rose from her position near the floor. "The cramps I was getting in my knees down there while you were collecting yourself were worse than in the old days in chapel. *Maintenant*—you are ready, but what about *me*?" Aimée spun about, making a quick, if not too graceful, pirouette. "How do I look?"

"Charming!" laughed Brianna as she appraised her friend's deep sapphire blue gown. "The bright colors are always for you, *la petite*, but—here—let me adjust a few of these forehead curls for you." Brianna reached to pat some of Aimée's ringlets in place.

"A lost cause," groaned Aimée amiably. "No matter how tightly I braid it for my coronet—" she patted the heavy circular braid at the top of her head "—I cannot wring an ounce of respect from these curls that stubbornly pop out around my face." She joined Brianna in trying to smooth back some of the errant tendrils she spoke of. "*Voilà!* You see? No respect whatsoever," she grumbled as yet another ringlet sprang into view. "Bah! It is useless! Let us go."

And with a whisper of gauze and silk, the two young women left for dinner.

Jesse leaned against the mantle of the unlit fireplace in Jefferson's drawing room and conversed easily with Father Edouard, but his carefully hooded eyes reflected none of his thoughts as they marked Brianna's entrance into the room. *Damn, but she's exquisite,* he thought as he watched her move through the door. *Dressed in those soft colors she reminds me of some fairy creature from another world. She puts all other women out of my mind with her beauty, all save one.* Jesse nodded politely to some comment made by Father Edouard while his mind tried to fasten on a picture of Deirdre, but, somehow, her image eluded him. Abruptly he changed the focus, trying to imagine her in a different setting. Nothing. Then the drift of a softly feminine voice floated over to him from across the room where Brianna was standing in conversation with the Randolphs and the focus shifted again, and clarified. Brianna was whom he saw in his mind's eye, even as his physical gaze remained steadfastly on the priest beside him. Brianna, with her hair cascading about her shoulders, wearing a sunny yellow dress and holding a kitten, Brianna, grinning as she raced him to the château, Brianna, sobbing in his arms because he'd made love to her under the worst possible circumstances and taught her more of pain than of pleasure.

"Damn!" Jesse swore out loud. Then, seeing Father Edouard's startled expression, he amended, "Sorry, my friend. I just remembered something I forgot to include in my instructions to Isaac when he was packing. Ah, but I see our host signalling for us to adjourn to the dining chamber, and I find I am somewhat hungry. Are you?''

Father Edouard patted his portly girth with a smile. "Not a moment too soon, Jesse. It is not that I am hungry. I am *ravenous*! *Alors!* Let us dine!''

Brianna allowed Thomas Jefferson to take her arm, and together they led the company into the dining room. As she savored the honor bestowed upon her, Brianna took a last glimpse of what was already one of the most famous residences of the South, if not the country. Carefully, she observed the elegant lighting devices, handcrafted moldings, carpets, and vast array of *objets d'art* that graced Monticello's halls, committing them to memory, for one day, she was sure, she would tell her children about them and the man at her side. She glanced sideways at the profile of her host as he walked with her, noting the straight, long nose, the sensitive mouth and strong chin.

But as they turned a corner and prepared to enter the room where they would dine, she caught a glimpse of a retreating figure with dark hair and fragile form—Sally Hemings. And it was this bare glimpse that quickly set Brianna's teeth on edge and would set the troubled course of the remainder of the evening.

The dinner began pleasantly enough, with a first course of delicate fillets of pheasant that were rolled around pitted prunes, skewered, broiled and served with a piquant sauce over wild rice. In addition to the guests who had been present on their first evening at Monticello, Brianna and the others were introduced to several newcomers, three of whom were eligible bachelors from the vicinity, and Brianna had occasion to wonder whether her plight—the need to marry soon—had been divulged to Jefferson or Martha and these gentlemen served up for her inspection as last-minute fare in the husband-seeking game. She had had her suspicions in the drawing room, but when the seating arrangements at dinner put one on either side of her and the third directly across table, she began to smell a plot along such lines for sure.

The gentlemen, all neighbors, seemed, at first glance, agreeable enough sorts. The one on her left, a Mister Jonathan Chillingham, was dark-haired with unremarkable blue eyes in a pleasant-looking face. He spent the time during the first course telling her about his plantation which was some five miles down the Ravenna and where he lived in apparently boring bliss with an unmarried sister who had been unable to attend the banquet "because of the toothache."

To her right sat Mister David Whiteside, a recent widower of about forty who took no trouble to disguise the fact that he was looking for a wife to mother his eight children, ages two to fourteen. He seemed somewhat discomfited to learn she was of the "Popish persuasion," however, for Brianna had informed him of her convent schooling and related matters in answer to his many eager questions about her background. Seeing this attitude on his part, Brianna lost no time in letting him know she regarded herself as a "most devout daughter of Rome," for she had no intention of encouraging the red-faced, overweight and balding widower.

When the creamed pumpkin soup arrived, Colonel Jeremy Grenfield drew her attention across table. This happened largely because, as Brianna turned slightly to allow a footman to serve her, she caught the handsome, blond officer staring at her *décolletage*, and when she let out a small gasp of outrage at his indiscreet ogling, he pushed the limits of courteous behavior still further by raising his heavy-lidded brown eyes and fixing her with a definite leer.

Making a deliberate show of turning her attention elsewhere, Brianna gazed up and across the table at her host who was in the midst of telling a rapt Aimée the story of his penning of the Declaration of Independence.

"I can assure you, *Mademoiselle* Gitane, that, especially in those difficult days, it was not unusual to lose a night's sleep working on some matter or another. Yes, I sat up all night to finish it, but as I worked, I must tell you, the exhilaration I felt at the importance of the task before me and the weight it would carry drove all thoughts of fatigue from my mind." Here Jefferson took a moment to smile at his daughter. "As the members of my family will attest, it is a habit of mine to burn the midnight oil when working on some project dear to my heart, and in this case, it wasn't merely my heart which was at stake—it was the country's."

At the mention of the members of his family, Brianna saw her chance. It was an opportunity she suddenly realized she had been seeking all week, ever since her encounter with Sally Hemings, and having that brief glimpse of Jefferson's mistress again this evening had further spurred her resolve.

"Tell me, Mister Jefferson," she said sweetly, "when you penned our nation's most famous document, were you aware that the words 'life, liberty and the pursuit of happiness' would become perhaps its most quoted phrase?"

Jefferson had the grace to flush at what seemed to be a compliment, answering her with an indulgent smile. "Actually, no, Mistress Devereaux. I never worked on the Declaration with the intent of creating memorable rhetoric, as such, but I can assure you, my dear, that when I created it, the notions of life, liberty and the pursuit of happiness were foremost in my mind."

"Really?" said Brianna, her smile still at its honeyed best, but with her intonation, she caught a glimpse of Jesse out of the corner of her eye, and the look he gave her was fraught with a cautionary air. Choosing to ignore her guardian entirely, she pushed ahead.

"Well, then, sir, if that is true, can you clarify just one tiny point for me, a simple maid, schooled abroad?"

The indulgent smile never waned from Jefferson's face. "But of course, my dear."

"Was it by any chance a limited selection of the population you were bent on securing those rights for?"

Jefferson's expression grew perplexed. "Limited?"

Brianna leaned forward at her place, the fingertips of both hands gripping the damask covered table on either side of her plate. "Yes, sir—limited. That is—forgive a poor girl's ignorance if I am wrong, but—" Brianna took a deep breath. This was it; it was now or never! Out of her side vision she again chanced to view Jesse. He, too, was leaning forward, and this time there was no mistaking the warning look on his face.

"—but it seems to me, now that our fight for freedom is over, and our country is, indeed, operating under the freedoms your document proposed, that those freedoms, as they apply, are only accorded to a person who is born *male* and *white-skinned*, for the most part."

There was a sudden stir at the table that could not have been more apparent had Brianna announced that they were sitting on a volcano and it was about to explode. Jefferson grew white, his freckles standing out all the more prominently as he hurriedly reached for his wine glass; several of the men murmured objections at once, Honoré spilling his own wine with a sudden jerk of his forearm, Patsy muttering "Oh, dear!" to her husband, Aaron Burr leaning back in his chair with a snide grin, and Jesse, his face livid with fury, his mouth a tight, angry line, beginning to rise from his seat, but being restrained by a worried looking Father Edouard.

Nevertheless, feeling she had entered the breach now and might as well make the most of it, Brianna forged ahead. "So you see, sir, given the inequality of our freedoms for the *whole* population at large, I was wondering whether that was what you, yourself, had in mind or whether there was simply tacit agreement on the part of all the founding fathers—as there has always been, time out of mind—that such freedoms are only deserved by *men* who are already free, white, propertied and—oh, yes—of age?"

Having already drained his wine glass, Jefferson was holding it aloft for his footman—a dark-skinned Negro—to refill. Then he bent his gaze on his green-eyed inquisitor and replied, "Mistress Devereaux, I seriously have my doubts as to whether you are anything near a poor, simple girl, schooled abroad or wherever, but I do think you are a misguided one. There can be no question that the world is operated by men, my dear, and yes, men who are freeborn whites. The education of women does not allow for the governing of cities or the intricacies of commerce, or the professions. Women are primarily educated—as they should be—in the area of household economy, in which the mothers of our country are generally skilled, and generally careful of instructing their daughters. We all know the value of this, and that diligence and dexterity in all of its processes are inestimable treasures. The order and economy of a house are as honorable to the mistress as those of the farm to the master, or the country to those men who sit in the seats of its legislature. Where, then, is further freedom needed?

"And as for my ascribing freedom to the Negro, young lady, it is common knowledge that my original draught of the Declaration included a strong statement against slavery, but the Continental Congress would not tolerate it!'' By this time Jefferson's face had changed from white to a decidedly deep shade of pink, and he glowered as he finished his speech and raised his refilled glass to his mouth.

Brianna was silent as she digested his words, still uncomfortable with his handling of women's rights and freedoms, and before she could collect herself to speak, Aaron Burr cut into the conversation.

''Well, sir, if what you say is true—and I have no reason to doubt it (the irony in Burr's tone was unmistakable)—how, then, do you account for your personal ownership of several hundred slaves?''

Again there was tumult at table, this time forestalled quickly by Father Edouard. Pushing himself up and out of his seat, the red-bearded priest rose to his full height and looked around at all who were seated with a kindly smile. ''Come, come, ladies and gentlemen, let us not upset ourselves unduly over an innocent's''—here he cast a benign smile at Brianna—''curiosity. We are all here this evening to enjoy ourselves under the auspices of our host's magnificent hospitality, are we not? And to show our appreciation for this wonderful largesse, I have taken the liberty of ordering from the kitchens, where several of my fellow guests and I have been laboring all week, a serving of some of my latest efforts at spirit-making. The brews are, of course, quite young, and some of them can only improve with age—but I shall leave those as a parting gift for our host to enjoy as he sees fit. At any rate, may I suggest that Mistress Randolph take the ladies and retire to the drawing room to sample the gentle concoction I rendered palatable for their tender tastes while we gentlemen remain here at table for a time to enjoy our—er—somewhat headier brew?''

''Thank you, sir,'' said Jefferson, and in a lowered voice meant only for the cleric's ears, ''for the diplomacy as well as the spirits.''

''Sounds like an excellent idea, Father,'' said Jesse, but his look as he voiced this was bent only on Brianna, and it said a great deal more—none of it kindly.

Not at all pleased that she was being herded out of the way to a safe place for docile ladies, but unable to do anything about it, especially now, in the face of Jefferson's ready assent, Brianna sighed and allowed herself to be escorted to the door by Father Edouard. As she and the other women entered the hallway, however, and before the door was completely shut behind them, she heard the sneering voice of Aaron Burr once again.

"But, Mister Secretary, you never did respond to my question, and then there was also that query I had on the Central Bank—"

The door shut and the women were alone in the hallway, except for a footman who appeared, ready to light their way to the drawing room. But Brianna was remembering Jesse's face as she'd just seen it, before the door closed. As Burr's voice had risen behind her, she had whirled about and come eye to eye with a mute mask of blue-eyed fury. Shivering from the force of it and a bit terrified of what might happen when she had to face him later, she suddenly knew she couldn't continue on with the other women.

"Aimée," she whispered, "make my excuses for me. I've got to get a breath of air!" And without waiting for an answer, she hurried along the now-familiar route to the gardens.

She had just stepped onto the path she remembered so well by moonlight when a whisper of skirts and a soft "Mistress Devereaux?" halted her stride and she turned to see Sally Hemings approaching from the house.

"Mistress Hemings! I—that is, I was just—"

"Yes, I know. I saw everything. That is why I wished to speak with you." Sally fell in step beside her on the brick path.

"You . . . *saw*—?"

"Oh, forgive me, Mistress, but there has never been a dinner party at Monticello where I haven't spied on what was going on. Oh, it's all right. The Master knows all about it. I have this little peephole, you see—"

"So you saw—you *know* what just happened back in there."

"Yes'm, and, well, I was hoping, if you don't mind, that is, that we might walk a bit together and just talk some."

"All right," said Brianna with a thoughtful nod, and the two women continued to walk, side by side, in the quiet garden.

"You see," said Sally after a moment, "I felt I had to tell you, I admire your courage in saying what you did in there."

Sally's use of the word "courage" made Brianna catch her breath slightly, but her next thought was of the various looks of incredulity and anger she'd witnessed on the reacting faces around the table, and she shrugged, saying, "Some would call it foolishness or worse, I fear."

"Ah, but that is just the point, Mistress! It takes great courage to voice opinions that others might consider foolish—or worse—and even greater courage to question those who hold and operate on opinions one considers wrongly held, especially if those people happen to be in positions of power. You did both of these things tonight. They were neither foolish nor worse. *You* did not think your remarks foolish when you spoke them, did you?"

"Well, no," said Brianna as she stopped by a splashing fountain in the center of the carefully tended greenery. She turned to face Sally, pausing for a moment to gaze intently into her dark hazel eyes. "You see, I'm afraid I'm a bit different from most of my native countrymen in these parts. My education took place in France, whence I've only recently returned, and, although sequestered—a convent, you know—the fomenting revolution was all around us and I couldn't help being exposed to some of pre-revolutionary France's egalitarian ideas. That, and some very liberal-thinking parents have, I think, shaped me into a very radical person where human liberty is concerned. I *hate* slavery, Mistress Hemings, now that I've finally been exposed to it in the flesh, and since I've always been a person to speak my mind—" Brianna stopped short and made a helpless gesture "—of course, I can also tell you it's never failed to get me into a heap of trouble." She sat down on the low stone wall that surrounded the fountain and bestowed on her companion a look that was sheer bewildered misery.

Smiling softly, Sally sat down beside her and took her hand and patted it comfortingly. "Please, Mistress, don't be so hard on yourself, and never discount the courage of your actions simply because the world takes you to task for it. It *is* courage, you know. *I know*, for you see before you one who had the opportunity to show courage also—and *failed* to take it."

"You?"

"Yes, Mistress. You see, I too returned from France not too long ago. I was there with my Master and the young mistresses, his daughters, serving them as ladies' maid when they were not at your school."

"I'd heard," said Brianna, nodding.

"Yes, but did you also hear that I could have had my freedom and lacked the courage to follow through on it when I was there?"

Brianna's eyes grew wide at the revelation, *"How?"* she whispered.

"My slave's status held no legality in the France of recent years. It is abolished there. All I would have had to do was to refuse to return home." Sally's voice took on an anguished quality.

Brianna looked incredulous. "Then *why?*"

Sally's eyes searched for her face for understanding. Then in a voice so soft, Brianna almost thought she hadn't heard it, "I would have had to leave *him* as well."

A deep flood of comprehension washed over Brianna then, and more from the look of pain in her companion's eyes than from her words. Sally Hemings was deeply in love with Thomas Jefferson, so much so, that *she gave up her very freedom because of it*! Nodding sadly with this realization, Brianna gripped Sally's hand and held it fast. "How very hard it must have been for you, my dear," she said slowly groping for the right words, "and I'm not so sure it didn't take some kind of extraordinary courage to—to make such a decision. I—"

"Oh, but, Mistress—"

"*Please!* We must be Brianna and Sally to each other, now, I think." Brianna felt the urgent need to say this because she suddenly felt a kinship with the young woman sitting beside her near the softly splashing fountain, a kinship she couldn't even explain. In a wordless whirl, her head reeled with a number of impressions all at once: Sally Hemings had chosen love over freedom, returned willingly to bondage for a man she apparently could not—did not want to—live without. Could she, Brianna Devereaux, ever make such a decision? Her whole body reverberated with a silently resounding *No!* She would never become so attached to a man that she would give up her own freedom! But at the same time, a niggling, mocking voice in the back of her head told her that, as a woman, she had precious little freedom as it was, passing from the hands of father, to guardian, to husband.

"But if I should see you again in private," Sally was saying, "then I should be happy to call you Brianna and I would be glad to have you name me Sally. And now, Brianna, I fear I have stolen away for as long as I dare and must return to the Big House."

"I'll walk back with you," said Brianna as she rose from her seat on the wall, but before she could take a step, Sally embraced her, saying, "Never let them intimidate you, Brianna. Hold fast and keep your courage, and—thank you for sharing these moments with me!"

"And you, for sharing your heart with me," Brianna replied warmly, and the two women returned to the house, Sally to the kitchens and Brianna to her room.

Once there, she began to undress herself, having learned from Sally that Aimée would be spending the night in the nursery, where Martha had asked for her help to replace the nursemaid who was ill. On Martha's instructions, Sally had offered to help Brianna get ready for bed in Aimée's absence, but Brianna had refused, wanting time to be alone to try to sort out her feelings.

Pensively, trying to piece together the various unrelated—and yet somehow related—events of the evening, she moved about the room, discarding her clothing and stripping down to her shift, for the night was warm, the air, sultry. Unbidden, as she felt the concealing clothes leave her body, thoughts of the interlude with Jesse again stole into her thoughts. Angrily, she pushed them away, a nameless terror lurking somewhere in the depths of her imagination, ready to seize her, she somehow felt, if she allowed herself to make an association between the events of that night and—

Suddenly there was a sharp and insistent rapping at her door. "Brianna!" *It was Jesse's voice!* "Brianna, open the door, for I've words I'll have with you, by God!"

The anger in his tone alone was enough to alarm her, but beyond that was his sudden presence at the very moment when she'd been wrestling with— "Go away!" she spat without thinking of the consequences. "I need my sleep!"

"The hell I will!" Jesse stormed, and with a mighty crash, the door flew open, its lock splintered from the wood. He stood there, angry and terrible in his fury, the big, muscular frame of him filling the doorway. Then he was in the room, advancing toward her after shutting the door with the heel of his boot.

Brianna had been sitting on the low sill of the window where she'd been trying to catch a breeze to sooth her heated body as her mind had spun with equally heated and unwanted thoughts. As Jesse moved toward her, she instinctively crossed her hands over her breasts, for the scant, lacy bodice of her chemise left them half exposed; she felt herself recoiling from Jesse's advance, but a split-second later, she caught herself, stiffened her spine and said with out-thrust chin, "How *dare* you break into my chamber!"

The quick change in attitude did not escape Jesse's attention, and in a more rational moment it might even have elicited his admiration, but such was his mood at the moment, that it only brought him to a short stop immediately before the window where he loomed dangerously above her seated figure.

"How do I dare?" he ground between tightly clenched teeth, "I'll *tell* you how I dare! I dare because you are my ward—a ward who has almost single-handedly destroyed, by her brazen and unthinking behavior, an entire mission's worth of diplomatic work and energy, not to mention causing impossible *ramifications* that could come once the mission *failed*!"

He bent forward, thrusting his chin within inches of her face. "I dare because that selfsame ward has, with her unpardonable rudeness, insulted one of the most powerful and important men in the land, a man at whose home she has been an invited *guest* for a *week*! And, finally, I dare because, unless she can talk herself out of this one—which I *doubt*—that ward is about to receive—"

Suddenly Brianna stood up with a near-violent reaction of her own, both hands pushing against Jesse's shoulders, and because of his bending position, she succeeded in forcing him back apace while she herself was able to stand straight and face him boldly.

"Don't you dare threaten me, Jesse Randall! You may not like what I did or said tonight, but the fact is that I did say it, and what's more, I said it because it was *right*! That very important man whose roof we're under was talking about how he would have criticized the institution of slavery in a major document while, along with us under this very roof, he houses dozens of human beings who are *his slaves*, some of them white as we are, and among those, a young woman who has borne him slave children who are also white like us! How can you stand there and berate me for questioning, if not his hypocrisy, then at least, the abomination that is slavery itself!''

Jesse halted and his thoughts spun in the face of her words. How could he in all honesty disagree with her? He was in a devilishly ticklish situation, with his private views on slavery perfectly aligned with hers on one hand, his bond-as-his-word commitment to Pinckney's mission on the other. There was no question as to where he stood morally here, yet this fire-spitting hellion had threatened an entire diplomatic mission of national importance! He *had* to take her to task for that! No matter that, in the waning hours of the evening, he had been able to set things to rights with Jefferson through his own persuasive skills—or his luck!

''Brianna,'' he said, his tone softening only slightly as he towered over her, ''I mean to go on record with you here and now, that I do not condone or operate within the slave system personally. You must know, as I have learned through Festus, what my views are, for you are aware of how he came to be in my employ—is that correct?'' The blue eyes were intense as they focused on hers.

''Yes,'' she said, nodding, ''but—''

''But—nothing!'' he thundered. ''Young lady, don't you realize there is a great deal at stake here?'' Jesse stepped back a pace and gestured toward the door. ''Do you know what went on down there after you women left the dining room?'' As he remembered some of the worst moments of the evening, Jesse's temper returned with full force. ''Aaron Burr, one of this country's most dangerous men, in many people's opinion, had a *field day*! He *acidly* questioned Jefferson on everything from his *possible* contradictory views on certain politics to his part-black mistress—yes, the very one you just alluded to! And, do you know what else, my *dear* ward? The grilling that he put Thomas Jefferson through is something, I can tell you, Aaron

Burr would never had *dared* put Jefferson through, had he not been given *entré—entré* that was made possible by—*guess who!*"

"That vile man!" spat Brianna. "I never intended—"

"Never intended!" raged Jesse as he reached for her shoulders to give her a shake, but as he did, one of the straps of her chemise fell down, and the action stopped him cold. Suddenly he became aware of her as something more than what she had been up until now—an object of his rage. In the balmy air, the mild scent of gardenia she wore drifted over him, and with a quick movement, he pulled her to him in a punishing embrace.

Brianna's immediate reaction was to deny him, her mind seizing on the resolve she'd made days earlier, to prevent him from acting like anything but the proper guardian, and her efforts were great as she struggled to resist, but her strength was no match for his as Jesse's mouth ground over hers with frightening force. Then it became the force itself which alarmed her, for her next reaction was to connect it with the fear and pain she'd suffered in those final moments in the loft; frantic now, she redoubled her efforts to fight him off, trying to twist her head away, and when that failed, holding herself rigid in his arms.

But as Jesse would have used the raw sexuality between them to subdue and chastise her, there came to him as he held her warm body close, the memory of days of regret—regret for the way in which he'd taken her in the stable—her first time, and most of it fraught with pain. A female ought to know of the pleasure that can exist between a man and a woman, he felt, and *he* had taught *this* female the very *opposite*! There was something very wrong in that, he told himself, and as he felt Brianna's half-clothed, ripe body against his, he knew what he must do.

Jesse's mouth released hers, but Brianna seized the moment to utter in a frantic whisper, "*No!* Please don't hurt me again, Jesse! I promise, I won't ever—"

"Green Eyes," said Jesse softly as he looked at her with eyes suddenly gone soft and quiet, "I'm not going to hurt you." His arms loosened to hold her more gently and he bent to place a tender kiss on her brow. Then, as Brianna's eyes widened with wonder at the change in him, his lips began to move, tracing a warmly sensuous path along her face; softly, they found the tender, perfumed skin at her temple, then moved, ever so lightly, to her ear, where they hovered and nibbled, his teeth finally pulling at the lobe before he moved lower, to the sensitive skin below her ear and at the base of her neck. All the while his muscular arms held her carefully, his big hands caressing her bare shoulders and thinly clad back, soothing her fears, warming her.

"Brianna," he murmured huskily, his mouth returning to her ear, "sweet Brianna—so very... very... lovely."

Slowly she began to feel herself relax, and the feeling was so good, so wonderful, Brianna forgot all about her resolve to keep him acting like a guardian. In fact, as she languidly submitted to the warm sensations that were stealing over her, she forgot to think about anything at all where Jesse Randall was concerned. All she knew was that she was here, in his arms, and he was no longer angry with her, or treating her like a child, or any of the hundred and one distasteful things she'd been wont to associate with him. This was a Jesse who knew he had *her*, Brianna Devereaux—not some French serving wench—and was still holding her, kissing her, making her feel as if she never wanted this to end. *Was this what it felt like to be treated as a woman?* she asked herself somewhere in the back of her mind. But before any definite answers could form, she felt Jesse's hand cup her breast and she shuddered with pleasure.

"Do you like this, little one?" Jesse asked as he looked deeply into her eyes. Deftly, he slipped the remaining strap of her chemise from her shoulder, and with another quick movement, had the bodice about her waist. His blue eyes never left hers as he did this, nor when he took both hands and lightly touched her nipples, causing them to stiffen into small pink buds. Then, the blue gaze still intently holding hers, he whispered, "Do I give you pleasure this way, Brianna? Tell me." His thumbs brushed both nipples once, twice... yet again, and Brianna could contain herself no longer.

"Oh, yes!" she breathed, her whole body aflame now, with a curling feeling in the pit of her stomach threatening to descend lower until it made her knees give way. Wildly, she threw her arms around Jesse's neck, and as she felt him gather her close, felt the rough fabric of his coat press into her bared and tingling breasts, she cried, "Yes, Jesse—oh, please, I want more!"

Brianna felt her face go crimson with her admission, and she heard Jesse chuckle lightly as he swung his arm beneath her and lifted her easily into his arms. Then, while he gazed warmly into her flushed face, her murmured, "This is going to be my pleasure, Green Eyes," and he carried her to the bed.

Once he had laid her tenderly on the coverlet, he quickly drew off his coat and tossed it aside. With rapid movements, he undid his cravat, and his shirt soon followed.

As Brianna saw his hands move to his belt, her eyes grew wide, but Jesse caught their reaction and immediately bent to soothe her, bringing his lips down gently on hers, and there followed a kiss that took Brianna's very breath away. Warmly, softly, and with utmost care, his lips moved over hers, his tongue slipping tentatively between her teeth, only to withdraw and slide to the corner of her mouth and back again. His mouth never left hers as his teeth pulled gently at her lower lip, and lightly grazed the tip of her own tongue which had begun, hesitantly, to seek and meet his. Meanwhile, his hands had resumed their magic on her body, sliding smoothly over shoulders, arms and waist; he seemed to avoid the breasts he had played with moments ago, and the omission caused Brianna to twist and turn toward him with expectation. Then he was with her on the bed, laughing lightly at her movements, saying, "Easy, little one. We don't want to rush this. This time, I promise, you're going to know only pleasure—every inch of you."

And Jesse proceeded to make his promise good, taking his time as he played with her body, teaching it to respond in a hundred different ways, but all the while watching her carefully, attuning himself to her growing passion, never allowing things out of his control as he took special care to keep all thoughts of fear and pain from Brianna's mind.

Her head swimming, Brianna succumbed completely to his attentions as she became caught up in a whirlpool of her own desires. Mindlessly, her body a mass of sensations, she moved under his fingers' touch; still, he refused to touch her aching breasts, choosing instead to focus on her waist, the smooth line of her hips through the chemise, and, then, on her long, lithe legs. Finally, when she thought she could bear it no longer, his mouth came down and closed over one nipple, its contours puckered and peaked with longing, and Brianna moaned with pleasure. Expertly, his tongue and lips played with the pink bud, while with his hands he began to slide her shift down over her hips. Then, when she was completely naked to him, he raised his head and looked at her, his eyes traveling slowly, from her head to her toes and back again, until they met her own eyes—heavy-lidded and deep green, their pupils dilated with passion.

"I've never seen anything as beautiful as you, Brianna," he breathed. "You are perfection, sweet."

Brianna had a dim awareness that he had at last resumed shedding his clothing, but, as he worked, he continued to talk to her in lazy, hushed tones so that she could only focus on his voice and the blue eyes which never left her face, while all the while her body tingled and yearned for more of the exquisite ecstasy he could bring it.

"I'm going to make love to you for a long, long time, sweet," Jesse was whispering. "I'm going to teach you deep and delicious pleasures that are your right to know and enjoy, as a woman."

There was a dull thud on the floor, quickly followed by another, and Brianna realized these were his boots and he was now completely unclothed beside her, but as she glanced in the direction of these sounds, Jesse's mouth again closed over hers, pulling her back to him—only him, and the pleasures he spoke of. The kiss was honey-sweet, tantalizing for its languid slowness, drowning her in a pool of pure sensation, and this soon grew into a white-hot heat, for his fingers were now tracing a course between her thighs, stroking, lightly stroking.

Soon Brianna heard a moan, and as she realized a moment later that it was coming from deep within her own throat, her legs parted for his now more insistent fingers, and she gave herself up to him completely.

"Ah, sweet virgin—for you are still a virgin, little one," Jesse murmured. "There are things you haven't known yet, lovely Green Eyes, things like . . . this."

Jesse's knowing fingers entered her wet warmth, while with his thumb he stroked the tiny bud above, and Brianna arched upward with a soft cry, her entire being now centered on the pleasure emanating from her core. Again, the expert strokes caressed, and suddenly Brianna became a wild thing, reaching to pull him to her, her hips thrusting toward the source of this incredible pleasure.

Now she heard Jesse's breathing echoing her own, felt his chest heave as he rose above her, and as she looked up, she saw his face, grand and urgent, the blue eyes fierce with passion.

"Stay open to me, sweet," she heard him rasp hoarsely, "and we'll know perfect pleasure *now*!"

And just as Brianna thought she could wait no longer, he pushed into her waiting warmth, his bigness filling her with such exquisite sensation that she could only cry out again, this time sharply, and with complete abandon.

Now she felt his rhythmic movements deep within her, and with each stroke, her pleasure built until it was almost pain. Still, she yearned, longing to be taken—

Then it happened, a high, sweet, perfect sensation that shut out all else. All feeling met and exploded at the center where they were joined; wave after wave of it, spiraling outward from her core, taking her with it, higher...higher...

Brianna's lips opened in a scream, but Jesse's mouth forestalled it as it covered hers, and then she felt him, too, shuddering mightily above her and within, as he joined her on the heights.

For a long time, then, there was silence, except for the rapidly diminishing sound of their breathing, until at last it was completely still.

When she could open her eyes, Brianna saw Jesse looking at her, the white teeth flashing in his tanned face when her eyes met his.

"Hello, Green Eyes," he grinned.

"Oh, I—hello," said Brianna in the barest whisper. She was hard put to speak at all, for she suddenly felt very drowsy and—she had to admit it—her body had never felt so wonderful in her entire life.

"You'll probably want to sleep now, kitten," said Jesse as he pressed his lips into the hair above her ear.

Then Brianna felt him slip out of her, and at the sensation, she gave a small gasp and snuggled closer to him, somehow wanting him to stay near. "Don't," she whispered shyly. "Don't go yet."

She heard Jesse's sharp intake of breath at the request before he answered her huskily, "No, sweet, I won't go yet if you don't want me to." He gave a throaty chuckle as he held her close and nuzzled her ear. "And I thought you'd be ready for sleep! You're full of surprises, Green Eyes." He leaned over her and kissed her lips softly. "But I do think you ought to let me leave soon. This was, in many ways, the first time for you, and I won't have you hating me in the morning because you're sore. Now try to sleep, pet. You're going to need some rest for the traveling we're doing tomorrow."

"Umm," murmured Brianna, snuggling closer.

For a long while Jesse held her, neither saying anything to the other. Then, when Brianna had finally drifted off into a contented slumber, Jesse stole quietly from her bed, and with a parting kiss on her forehead, slipped silently from the room.

Chapter Twenty-Two

Aimée gazed thoughtfully at the broad back of Jesse Randall as he sat easily in his saddle a few yards ahead of her, on the road that wound down the side of Jefferson's mountain. Aside from the brisk instructions he'd issued during the time of their departure an hour earlier, the man had been conspicuously silent this morning. And he hadn't been the only one of their party to remain unusually taciturn, she mused; she turned slightly in her sidesaddle to catch a glimpse of the solitary figure of Brianna riding several yards behind her. Something had happened between those two last night, she was sure, but as to its exact nature, she could only guess. Contrary to what generally passed between her and her friend, this time there had been no sharing of intimacy; for some reason, Brianna had elected not to confide in her, and yet Aimée knew with a certainty that Brianna was troubled—or, at the very least, had something weighty on her mind.

And Jesse. He, too, carried disturbing thoughts, thoughts that had to do with Brianna. As they'd all begun to mount their horses this morning, Aimée had chanced to see him looking at her friend when Brianna had been unaware of it, and the look had been complex and fraught with import—Aimée knew that much.

From a good distance behind Brianna, where they were bringing up the rear and escorting the carriage that held Honoré, Father Edouard and Festus shared a joke with Isaac as he sat in the driver's seat, and Aimée smiled as she heard their laughter. She counted herself more than fortunate of late, actually, ever since she'd embarked on the journey that had led to these American shores. She felt she'd made real friends among these people she'd met through her ties with Brianna. Through all her former life at the Abbaye, she'd never felt as at home—as if she were accepted and truly belonged—as she did here, in this wild, new land.

A momentary frown creased her brow as she wondered if she didn't, indeed, feel more comfortable here than Brianna herself, whose native country this was. But then she smiled, reminding herself that Brianna Devereaux was a far more complicated person than she—a person who had much to unravel before she found herself—but, the unraveling done, the rewards would be great. Suddenly, Aimée's smile became a grin as she watched a shaft of sunlight catch the glint of silver from the eagle on Jesse Randall's ring finger when he moved in his saddle. Ah, yes, she sighed to herself, *the rewards will be great.*

Brianna's thoughts were not too far removed from Aimée's as she stared at Le Duc's bobbing head in the bright sunlight. Ever since they had left Monticello amid a chorus of the usual goodbyes, thank-yous and good wishes, she had been thinking of home. Home. Yes, Le Beau Château was truly her home at last, but what could she expect when they returned? Peace? A feeling of belonging? Security? She wasn't so sure. At one time, indeed, during all those yearning years in France, she had felt she had only to regain the home she had left, return to the place of her birth, and all would be well.

But I was a different person then, she thought soberly. *In many ways, life was so much simpler. Now, with all that's happened, what am I about? Where do I begin?*

Slowly, reluctantly, she made herself focus on the most insistent among the many vexing notions she'd been plagued with of late—the feeling that she had passed—what was it, one of the officers aboard the *Liberté* had called it?—the point of no return. It was that place, the point in a journey which, before it was reached, always allowed one to change one's mind and go back, but, once passed, allowed only the forward course, for the return would then be longer, the store of supplies inadequate.

Somehow, she knew beyond a doubt, she had passed her own point of no return. But a return to what? Surely, not childhood? Or, if so, then why was she so uneasy about the cross-over? Hadn't she been bent upon, indeed, *driven* to, proving herself a mature woman in the eyes of people like Jesse?

The intrusion of his name, the first she'd allowed into her private thoughts since awakening this morning to that empty bed, opened a floodgate to immediate confusion. She remembered as keenly as if it were occurring now, the conflicting emotions that had assaulted her as she'd rubbed the veil of sleep from her eyes—that first, incredible sense of pleasure and joy that had filled her, met at once by a bewildering sense of loss and desolation as she'd stared at the indentation left on the pillow where his head had rested. Had she perhaps dreamt it, that unbelievable pleasure and fulfillment? But an aching tenderness between her thighs and elsewhere told her otherwise; with a gasp, she drew one arm roughly across her suddenly tingling breasts, trying to appear casual as she sought to dispel the returning sensations her remembrances brought.

Then, behind her, the jovial boom of Father Edouard's laughter cut into her thoughts, and Brianna's immediate reaction was a sudden wash of guilt. *Bless me, Father, for I have sinned. I have had impure thoughts—no, strike that—I have had carnal knowledge—no—not that, either—I enjoyed what this man did to—* Again, her thoughts shifted. *I actually did enjoy it, didn't I? And, before, because it had hurt and frightened me, I had thought it to be a terrible thing, the intimacy a man and woman share. Not that there hadn't been pleasure at first, but to have it all lead to pain in the end! But last night— oh, last night...*

With a sudden need to look at him, she sought out Jesse on the trail up ahead. Bareheaded, handsome past describing and tall in the saddle, he rode with the easy grace that characterized all his movements; he appeared to her now, larger than life; once again, only after last night, even more so, he seemed godlike—beautifully male, compelling and somehow—for her—dangerous.

Dear Lord! How, after what's happened between us, am I to behave in his company? It was easier, the day after he'd taken her virginity, to deal with Jesse, she now knew, because of the very fact that that experience had been so negative for her; she'd been wrapped up in enough anger afterward to be able to manage the necessary distance between them and feel comfortable with it. But *this*! All at once she had to struggle to dispel a pair of urges that warred within her: one sought to seek him out and somehow tell him of the exquisite joy he'd brought her, the pleasure beyond imagining; the other, just as insistent, told her to run from here, out of his presence, and never return. Unbidden, an image of Sally Hemings, as she'd seen her during their talk beside the fountain, appeared in her mind's eye, and she trembled under its impact. Summoning all her energy, she wiped away the vision and forced Le Duc to slow his gait, preparing to fall in beside the men at the rear of the entourage and make a conscious effort at taking part in the camaraderie she heard them sharing. What had Sally Hemings' plight to do with *her*? she reasoned, and with a shrug of dismissal, she reined Le Duc in beside a merrily chuckling Father Edouard.

"So, our dear *enfant* has decided to join us!" smiled the cleric. "We must take care now, Festus, and fashion our talk at a level more—ah—suitable for a lady's ears."

"Dass fine, suh. Ah wuz jes doin' some pow'rful jugglin' wid mah own notions o' whut's fitt'n fo' a *man o' God's* eahs!"

The priest's broad chest quivered with mirth. "Never think that the taking of holy vows enjoined me to forswear *all* of the pleasures of this life, Festus. Before I assumed the cloth, I'd lived a hearty life, growing up under the roof of an earthy French peasant woman who liked a good joke or bawdy tale as well as my Irish seaman father, not to mention my twelve older brothers."

"*Twelve!*" marveled Isaac from his seat on the carriage. "What a pair your parents must have been! And all sons, were they?"

"Not a daughter in sight," grinned the cleric. "Although I must confess, *Maman* was not with child quite so often as the number implies, for there were two sets of twins in the batch, but, suffice it to say that in the intervals between my father's long voyages at sea, my parents lost little time in making up for his absences."

"Are all twelve of your brothers still alive?" questioned Isaac, still impressed by the figure.

"All but one," said the priest, his tone suddenly serious. "My twin, Jean-Pierre, was taken from us by a fever the year we turned sixteen." There was silence for a moment, except for the sounds of horses' hooves and carriage wheels. "Six months later I was in Rouen, studying for—" Father Edouard gestured at his priest's robes which he wore awkwardly hiked up, over black boots and riding breeches, when mounted "—my vocation," he smiled.

"Father! You never told me any of this," exclaimed Brianna. "Do you mean that the loss of your brother caused you to—"

"Oh, no, nothing so simple and direct as all that," said the priest. He swatted at a fly that buzzed over his horse's ears. "You see, before *le bon Dieu* took Jean-Pierre, we had both been thinking about the priesthood, he, perhaps, a bit more seriously than I. But with his death, my flirtation with the idea, begun in the days when we were altarboys, grew into a deep, steadfast desire. No, becoming a priest was not a withdrawal from grief for me, as I have witnessed among some men and women who have taken the cloth. But in the days before my brother's death I was—how shall I put it?—too young—in doubt—confused and unfocused, perhaps, or caught up in the bewilderment that accompanies the passage to manhood, to make any kind of decisions involving the future. With the loss of Jean-Pierre I think I reached a point of no return. Childhood disappeared with my lost brother and I suddenly—well, within a few months, I mean—knew what it was I wanted. And, what's more important, I knew who I was."

As she vaguely heard Festus adding comments on his closeness to his own twin and his expression of compassion at Father Edouard's loss, Brianna found her thoughts turning inward again. That Father Edouard should have used that *very phrase*, "the point of no return"! Was there a message here for her somewhere? Father Edouard had, at a similar age, experienced just what *she* was going through—the bewilderment, the confusion—he'd felt them, too! Did everyone feel these things in the process of growing up? Was everything she was undergoing only normal, after all, and not the product of her intimacy with a man who was not her husband? After all, Father Edouard's experiences came to him under the most respectable—even holy—of circumstances.

Suddenly Brianna felt lighter and more relaxed than she had all morning, as if some great weight had been lifted from her shoulders. There was nothing, she decided, so dangerous and terrible about what had happened to her last night in Jesse Randall's arms. And Jesse himself was not a god, either, she reasoned. *What's been plaguing me is just a normal reaction to—to becoming a woman—an adult, and Jesse Randall be damned. I can dismiss him entirely if I choose.*

But as she looked up to see Jesse advancing toward them on his mare, Gypsy, Brianna wondered why her palms suddenly grew damp and an area near the pit of her stomach gave a lurch that was not from the trail's bumpy course.

After Jesse gave the signal to halt and take time out to rest and water the horses, he avoided any prolonged contact with Brianna. Somehow, for the first time in his life, he felt awkward the morning after intimate contact with a woman. Heretofore, he'd handled them all, from those foolish enough to think bedding would lead to marriage, to the few he'd later learned were guilt-ridden because they'd had husbands or lovers they'd betrayed. Always finding just the right words to send them away courteously, yet firmly, he was at a loss now at how to deal with Brianna Devereaux.

Covertly, from beneath lowered lids, he studied her at a distance while sitting casually on the ground with his back against a tree. She was sharing a cup of water with Aimée, the two of them perched on a large, flat rock that flanked the stream they'd stopped beside. A soft breeze ruffled some tendrils of hair that had escaped confinement about her face, and he suddenly found himself fighting an urge to see it tumbling about her, massive and free, as it had last night.

"Damn!" he swore softly to himself as he tore his eyes away and rose to check on the horses.

Some minutes later, as he made ready to give the signal to move out, he noticed Brianna standing off to herself beside the carriage, but as he debated going over to her, perhaps to indulge in a casual bit of talk to prove things were proceeding normally enough—and unchanged in any important way—he saw her approached by Honoré who had left the carriage to stretch his legs. Seeing the frown on her face as Honoré began to address her, Jesse had all he could do to keep from running and assaulting the man; in seconds he'd moved quietly, but swiftly, to her side.

"But you look somewhat weary, *cherie,*" Honoré was saying. "A turn in the carriage might give you some much needed rest."

"*Mademoiselle* Devereaux is managing her saddle quite well, I think," Jesse interrupted. "But you, Honoré, isn't it time you were back in the carriage? We are about to resume traveling."

A flicker of resentment flashed in Honoré's dark eyes before he gave a polite bow and withdrew, leaving Brianna alone with Jesse.

But where Honoré's emotions had been controlled, Brianna's fairly exploded in the warm air.

"There was really no need, you know," she fired at Jesse. "I can take care of *myself*!" She whirled to search out Le Duc and, spying him among the other saddle mounts, began to head in that direction, but as she left, she heard Jesse's low, easy laughter behind her.

"Can you, now?" came his softly mocking query. "Can you, really, Green Eyes?"

The journey back to Le Beau Château progressed uneventfully enough, much in the manner of their trip out; the weather proved dry and sunny, with just enough lessening of the humidity and an occasional nip in the air at night as they crossed points of higher elevation, to signal the approach of autumn. Often, on the trail, Jesse would stop to point out various ripened berries and nuts they might pick and eat safely, his knowledge in this area being rather thorough, owing to his time spent in Indian company.

Brianna and Aimée whiled away the long hours in the saddle by conversing with each other and, frequently, with Father Edouard; the cleric, a sometime hunter and woodsman himself, happily pointed out, often with their Latin names, the various types of flora and fauna they saw; he patiently answered questions about growth habits and nesting patterns, especially from Aimée, whose European rearing found her wide-eyed and curious over the strangeness of the American wilderness.

Jesse kept largely to himself, assuming total responsibility for the safety of the group, now that Honoré was relegated to the confines of the carriage most of the time. Although Dumaine conducted himself courteously—flawlessly so, it seemed—Jesse refused to let him out of his sight during those times when they stopped to rest or took overnight accommodations. During periods when he observed Honoré in Brianna's company, especially, Jesse always made it his business to be present, or near enough to dispel in an instant, anything that might be taken as threatening or upsetting to his ward.

It was just this protective behavior on Jesse's part that caused Father Edouard to remark to Aimée one day, that he'd noticed a major change in the proportions it had assumed, especially since leaving Monticello.

"Do you not think," mused the priest as he handed Aimée a slice of crabapple he'd been paring, "that our gentleman guide from Charleston hovers rather closely at certain times these days, over our dear Brianna?"

They were sitting on a rustic wooden bench under a tree bearing the small, sour fruit they were sharing, not far from the barnyard of a farmer who was to be their host for the night. It was early evening, and as they awaited the call to dinner, they had just observed Jesse emerge from the farmhouse and intrude upon a conversation taking place between Brianna and Honoré near the back door.

"Indeed," nodded Aimée, wincing slightly at the tartness of the morsel she'd bitten into. "*Monsieur* Jesse waxes very protective of late."

"Protective, yes, even possessive, perhaps?" The priest's red beard began to split with a white-toothed grin.

"*Oui, mon père,*" returned Aimée, her grin matching the priest's. "Most possessive."

"And to what, do you suppose, *Mademoiselle* Aimée, might one attribute this notable change in behavior on the gentleman's part?"

Aimée's grin warred with the need to pucker her lips as they closed over another slice of the sour fruit. She rolled her bright black eyes skyward, saying, "*Le bon Dieu* only knows, *mon père*. I, for one, find it most strange, when so often the gentleman in question has vocalized protest over his ward's presence."

"Oh?" questioned the cleric as he handed her another piece of fruit.

"*Oui.* Brianna picks some pears from a tree at the last farm we visit and feeds some to her horse and *Monsieur* Jesse's mare; *Monsieur* protests: he will spoil his *own* horse without any meddling from her! Brianna asks to be present and perhaps help, during our stop at the Cherokee village, at the foaling of the chief's mare; *Monsieur* protests: she will soil her gown! Brianna insists she be allowed to collect her reward for winning a certain wager they once made; *Monsieur* protests: he is not at all sure she *won* the wager and, besides, he has better things to do on the trail than supervise her in an indulgence—she must wait until they return to her home and then—*perhaps*—he will consider it!" Aimée munched her latest slice of apple with a twinkle in her black eyes. "*Oui, mon père.* Protests."

A clanging of the crude iron bell near the back door of the farmhouse told them dinner was ready. As Father Edouard rose from the bench, he extended his hand to help Aimée to her feet. "I think," said the priest as he pulled thoughtfully at his red beard, "we might be seeing an example of what goes on when a man—as someone very wise once put it—'protests too much'!" And with a conspiratorial wink, he led his companion to dinner.

It was early in the afternoon of their last day on the trail. Recognizing the familiar landmarks of the high country outside of Columbia, Jesse knew they would reach Le Beau Château shortly after nightfall. He checked the urge to increase their pace and perhaps outdistance the sunset; they had been moving quite steadily all day, stopping only for one light meal and a couple of times, briefly, for the horses. There was no need to push them unnecessarily, although he was well aware of how eager everyone was, to be done with traveling.

All things considered, he felt the trip to have been a productive one. Jefferson had, he felt, given him a fair ear and, when they had left, was sincerely considering the pleas and persuasions Jesse had presented to him. But what had Jesse even more hopeful of achieving a success in keeping the Secretary from resigning was an idea that had come to him on the trail. Having learned that Jefferson would soon be returning to Philadelphia via a visit to Washington at Mount Vernon, he'd hit upon the idea of buying some insurance for his mission.

He carried in his saddlebag right now a letter he had penned late last night, while staying as the guest of a wealthy Upcountry gentleman. It was a letter to George Washington himself, using the prerogatives of their former acquaintance—and yes, of the association between Washington and his father—to impose a private plea to help the mission succeed. He'd written that the President might use certain measures—Jesse had carefully outlined the persuasions he felt might be most useful, calling on all he had learned of Jefferson on the visit—to keep the Secretary from resigning. Whether his comments would, in themselves, be helpful, he had no idea; it was possible that the President of the United States of America knew far better than a Carolina planter, how to handle his sensitive, high-strung Secretary. But one thing Jesse did know. It was one thing for Jefferson to barge in on Washington unawares, to have the President caught off-guard by a resignation in the flesh; it might be quite another to have Jefferson stop by to see a Commander in Chief fully prepared and ready to do battle in dissuasion!

Jesse smiled ironically to himself as he recognized the success of the very ploy Pinckney had used and Jesse had been cynical about. He'd gotten him to trade on his "family connections" in the mission. Jesse shrugged. Did it really matter? After all, he had become convinced, of his own free will and insight in the matter, that a great deal depended on keeping Thomas Jefferson involved in America's affairs of state. The loss of such a mind would be a tragic waste, and he wasn't at all sure his fledgling nation could sustain it.

As for the other aspects of the journey, he was unprepared to make any definite assessments. He was thinking, of course, of his obligations to Etienne Devereaux, or, more precisely, to his daughter.

He turned for a moment in his saddle and glanced at the retinue that patiently followed behind, taking an extra few seconds as his gaze lingered on the green-clad figure of Brianna, riding two horses behind, with Festus.

Green—that was her color, all right. For all the travel-wearying strain of their long days on route, she appeared to him always as fresh and alive as the favorite color of nature implied. Brianna. Now that they were nearly home, he would have to do some heavy planning on what to do with her. It was October, and good prospective husbands—he wouldn't countenance any fortune hunters—did not just drop from trees!

Suddenly he heard a mirthful peal of laughter, its merry tones at once graceful and melodic, and Jesse gave a start. He looked to see Brianna sharing delightedly in some comment Festus had made, and the big man's chuckles now echoed hers. All at once, Jesse realized he'd never really heard her laugh before. Wondering why he should find this disturbing, he muttered an oath and overrode his own decision; giving Gypsy the signal for a change of gait, he increased their pace toward the château. But if anyone had questioned why he did this, he'd have been at a loss to tell them.

Brianna was feeling the excitement of returning home. When she saw Jesse increase the rate of speed at which they were moving, she urged Le Duc forward with a surge of delight.

"It looks like my guardian wants to make the château by sundown, Festus. Mmm, I can almost taste that crusty, freshly-baked bread Mathilde's sure to have on hand. Just a couple of slices of that with one of our homemade cheeses from the pantry and a glass of wine—that's all I want for supper. What about you?"

Festus grinned as he easily guided his horse to fall in step beside Le Duc. "Soun' good 'nuff t' 'mos eat raht now, Mis—um—Brianna. But Ah's lahkly t' settle fo' anythin' whut'll fill dis big black belly!" He patted the part of his anatomy under discussion as he launched a hearty laugh.

"Oh, Mathilde's French bread is special, Festus. I can remember, when I was a small girl, coming home on my pony, Mignon, after being out riding for hours. I'd be sort of hungry—or so I always thought—and then I'd smell that bread baking in the oven as I came across the meadow. *Then* I'd realize just how hungry I *was*! And dear Mathilde, she'd just ignore all of Mistress Delaney's scoldings about a light repast spoiling a young one's dinner and sit me right down in her kitchen when I came in, plying me with thick slices of that bread, smeared with freshly churned, smooth golden butter from the creamery. Oh, Festus, those were the times!''

Festus smiled at the warm, dreamy tone in her voice. "Ah 'specs ya'll got some real good mem'ries o' doze tahms, den?''

"The *best*!'' Brianna answered. Then she turned in her saddle and looked at him. "Does your brother really look just like you—I mean, *all* of you?—that is—well, it's hard enough to deal with the reality of one man as huge as you—but *two* of you!''

Festus' laughter boomed with delight. "Ya'll maht say dere's mo' dan 'nuff o' us t' go 'roun'. Yes'm, Brothah Vulcan's jes de size o' me.''

At the hint of wistfulness in the deep voice, Brianna gave him a scrutinizing look. "You miss him—your brother—don't you, Festus?''

The giant black man nodded his head. "Y'see, Miz—aw, now lookit me goin' on wid de Miz agin! Brianna, Ah knows ya'll wants me t' drop it, but it's mighty hahd! Kin Ah aks a favah?''

"Certainly!''

"Well, spoze Ah calls ya'll 'Brianna' when Ah kin remembah t' do it, but only when we's alone—in prahvit—an' '*Miz* Brianna' de rest o' de tahm, when othah folks is aroun'. Would dat be all raht?''

Understanding washed over Brianna like a giant wave. It was one thing for Festus to try to accommodate her French-liberal yearnings to put them on an equal footing; it was another to make Festus uncomfortable with her request, especially around others here in the deep South—others who might not only misunderstand, but perhaps even take extreme measures *against* Festus for it! Compassion flooded in her voice as she answered him. "Oh, Festus! How *dense* of me! Here I've been going along, thinking only of my own—*of course* it would be all right!''

Festus smiled at her. "Miz Brianna, don' let *nobody* evah tell ya'll yo' ain' a *real lady*, cuz yo' is, an Ah's proud t' know ya'll!''

Blushing at the compliment, Brianna's eyes momentarily found her guardian up ahead, and she felt a small thrill of triumph, despite herself. Then, remembering what she and Festus had been discussing, her attention swung back to the black man.

"But we were talking about you and your brother, Festus—Vulcan is his name?"

"Uh-huh, an' Ah wuz tellin' ya'll how Ah missess de big fool."

"Fool?!"

"Oh, Brianna, don' min' me—Ah—*we* is always messin' aroun' wid each othah dat way. But he mah brothah, an' *Ah loves him t' death*!"

"Is he all the family you have?" Brianna asked softly, mildly stunned by the impact of the emotion that had colored his last words.

"All Ah got lef'. Ouah folks got sol' away fum us when Vulcan an' me wuz jes tiny pickaninnies." He shook his head sadly, then reached into his shirt, saying, "Ya'll awake, finally, Lil Blackbits?"

Brianna smiled briefly as the black head of the kitten popped into view. "But, Festus," she continued, "don't you remember them or—or *anything*?" She was suddenly devastated by the notion of losing one's loved ones without even a trace, a memory. All at once her own losses seemed trivial by comparison. *She*, at least, had loving remembrances of the family she'd lost.

Festus shook his great head sadly. "Mah mama an' daddy, Ah don' 'collec' at all, but dass cuz dey wuz de fust t' go. 'Bout a yeah o' two latah, dey sol' ouh biggah sistah. Funny, we don' even 'collec' huh name no mo'—but yo' know whut's funny, Brianna? Ah kin still remembah a lil lullabye she done sung us!"

Suddenly his voice broke into a gentle song. "Hush lil baby, don' yo' cry..."

As Festus' sweet baritone filled the air with the sad words and melody of the lullabye, Brianna wanted to weep. How had *she* ever thought *she* had troubles? Here was a man—*two men*—and how many countless others like them?—who had had their parents torn savagely away from the while they were still ... It did not bear *thinking* on!

When Festus had finished, they were both silent for a while, and Brianna noticed that the others in the party, some of whose heads had turned as they'd listened to the song, were markedly quiet too. At last, after they had ridden this way for a while, she turned to the black man saying, "Festus, now that you've gotten your freedom, is there anything special you mean to do with it? I mean, I know you and your brother are committed—happily, I take it—to work for Jesse Randall, but I was wondering, well, if you had any special plans beyond that."

Festus shifted in his saddle as he stroked Lil Bits's head. "Funny ya'll should mention it, Miz Brianna. When we wuz up t' de plantation by Mistah Jefferson's way, Ah got a chance t' see sumpfin'—wid mah fingahs, Ah means—dat done set me t' thinkin'."

"What was it?" Brianna asked eagerly.

"It wuz a—a cup o' some kind—made out o' silvah, wid all kind o' fancy hammah wuk on it. Ah come by it at de silvah-smif's shop wheah one o' de slaves wuz studyin' it—he wuz a—a—'prentice silvahsmif hisself."

"Yes?" Brianna encouraged.

"Well, Brianna, it wuz jes de mos' b'yeautiful piece! Made by some white man up no'th—Paul, Paul Revere—Ah ain't nevah gonna fo'git *dat* name!"

"And . . . ?"

"An', well, Ah done spent a godawful hunk o' time in dat shop wid dat black 'prentice, Brianna, an Ah thinks Ah kin *do it*!"

"Do it? You mean silversmithing?"

"Sho 'nuff!" The grin on Festus's face reached ear to ear.

"But, Festus, are you sure? I mean, I know how you're a blacksmith already, despite your affliction, but there, I hear, you use your brother's eyes. With *this*—"

Festus' laughter caught her up short. "Miz Brianna Devereaux, wheah's yo' *faith*?"

"Faith?" Suddenly Brianna felt like a mildly chastised child. Of course, she had been doubting him—when she *ought* to have been encouraging! "Oh, Festus, there I go again, miles away from putting myself in your shoes! Forgive me, and, please, tell me about the silversmithing. Is it—"

Suddenly Jesse's voice cut into their conversation as he approached, having doubled back on the trail. "Brianna, Aimée says she'd like to talk to you—something about your plans for this evening, once we reach the château." Then he addressed the black man. "Festus, how about keeping me company for a while? I'm getting tired of my own breathing and Gypsy's snorts for diversion."

Soon Brianna was talking quietly with Aimée as the two rode side-by-side behind Father Edouard while Festus and Jesse took the forward position.

"What's this I hear about silversmithing, Festus?"

"Oh, dat! Mistah Jesse, ya'll sho' got eahs all *ovah* de place!"

Joining in Jesse's chuckle, Festus then told him what he'd just mentioned to Brianna.

"Well," said Jesse when he had finished, "if you're so bent on trying this new trade—you are, aren't you?"

"Dat, Ah is. See, Mistah Jesse, fum what Ah heerd up t' Monticello, Ah specs Ah kin learn dis business good 'nuff so's Ah don' need any help, aftah a whahl. Dat'll be a big load off Vulcan's back."

Jesse took a moment's silent admiration of the man riding beside him. The legal papers he and Carlisle had signed had been one step in the freeing of Festus and Vulcan Noslave; Festus had just laid plans for taking the final step.

"Festus," he said, "in one short month I've had the pleasure of meeting two of the greatest men I guess I'll ever know who know the value of human dignity through independence. One of them sits in a big house on a mountain in Virginia and wrote a precious document about such freedom. The other is riding next to me right now. Now, don't say a word, just listen. When we get back to Riverview—no, even before, because I'm going to sit down and write my brother a letter tonight—I'm going to do all I can to procure you some instruction from a master silversmith as soon as possible. Is that acceptable to you?"

Festus was happily agreeing to these plans when they heard a merry ripple of laughter from Brianna as she conversed with Aimée and Father Edouard.

Festus grinned. "Dat Miz Brianna—she a real *fahn* lady, Mistah Jesse—kind o' unusual as white ladies go."

"Oh?" questioned Jesse, curious about the black man's opinion of his ward.

"Yassuh, she a heap mo' full o' spirit an'—an'—oh, Ah don' know...de stuff it take t' do de bes' kind o' livin'—and she *smart*, an' a heap mo' full o' deep feelin' dan mos' white ladies Ah evah met. She pow'rful b'yeautiful on de inside t' me. Mistah Jesse—she be b'yeautiful t' look at, too?"

Jesse was silent for a moment, digesting what Festus had said. Finally, he answered his question.

"Yes, she's beautiful." His eyes were fixed on the rich, green depths of the forest trail up ahead, but in his mind he beheld an image of Brianna as he'd first seen her standing in front of the stables that evening that now seemed so long ago.

"She's tall and incredibly graceful when she moves—lithe as a willow and twice as lovely. She has hair that puts silk to shame and shines in the sunlight like a burnished copper penny. Her face—it could have been formed in heaven to give us poor mortals some idea of how angels look, I think. But it's her eyes that catch you up, above anything. They're green, but a green so full of light and depth at the same time, you wonder if you ever really knew the color at all before you saw them."

Suddenly Jesse stopped, his image of the last time he'd met those eyes filling his head in a different way.

"But there's the worst kind of mischief going on in those eyes sometimes," he countered. "They can conjure up a storm out of nowhere, and for no apparent reason. They're more often accusing, fire-spitting, seething and resentful than any of the milder, gentler qualities one comes to expect from a woman.

"I suppose you know I—knew her older sister years ago." Jesse shook his head in disbelief. "How two women born of the same mother and father could be so unalike! Deirdre was all tender womanhood, soft, pliant—sweetly yielding and eager to please. A natural born lady of soft, subtle charm."

He turned briefly and glanced over his shoulder. Behind them, where Brianna rode between Aimée and the priest, some tale she was regaling them with was sending her two companions into torrents of laughter, Aimée bent over her saddle with mirth, the cleric wiping tears from his eyes as he loudly roared his appreciation. Brianna herself was gesturing broadly as she expanded upon the tale, eyes wide with humor, dimples working merrily.

Jesse turned his attention back to Festus, fighting to keep from his voice any of the annoyance he was feeling. Indeed, he was hard put to know why he was feeling it.

"Brianna Devereaux, as I said, is a beauty, but on the other hand, to anyone who has to deal with her on a more than casual level, I say—'Look to your sensibilities, for she will try a man's patience beyond endurance, and it's that you're left with, long after her beauty has hit you.'"

With this, Jesse murmured something about needing to check the footing on the trail ahead, telling Festus to let his horse pick its own way until he returned; then he rode off.

As he heard him go, Festus shook his head and smiled, saying to himself with a chuckle, "Dat man sho got a heap on his mind 'bout de lady—stuff he ain' *begin* t' be sayin'! It all 'neath him somwheah, bilin' an' bubblin' undah his hide. Mistah Jesse, ya'll comin' due fo' a explodin' one o' dese days, yassah, an' when it do, Ah sho' would love t' see wheah de pieces lan'!"

Chapter Twenty-Three

George Simpson readjusted his spectacles as he gave a final perusal to the document in front of him. He was sitting at Étienne Devereaux' old desk in the library of Le Beau Château where the mantle clock had just finished chiming the hour of eleven.

Across from him, in one of the room's Louis XIII upholstered armchairs, sat a woman who looked to be somewhere in her late twenties, although, physically, she could have passed for younger. It was her knowing, dark eyes that gave her away, not to mention her manner, which was at once sophisticated and confident, filled with an acculturation and poise that could only come with worldly experience.

Laurette Mayfield was a widow, having been left in that state a few years earlier by a husband who was many years her senior. At the time of his death she had thought herself financially secure, the old man's pocketbook—and age—having been chiefest among her reasons for wedding him; however, several bad investments, coupled with lavish spending habits acquired while quite young, had rendered her, if not penniless, then close to it, and in a position where she had to find some means of income. Forced to sell her Richmond estate to satisfy creditors, she had taken the small sum that was left and placed discreet advertisements, through her late husband's solicitors, seeking a position with a family of substance as a companion or female estate manager, if such could be found.

It was through these advertisements that Simpson had come across her as the possible answer to his search for someone to guide and instruct Brianna along the lines stipulated in

Etienne's will. And it was in that capacity that she sat across from him in the library this morning, two days after the Virginia visitors had returned from their trip.

"I take it all the terms of your—ah—employment here at Le Beau Château are acceptable, Mistress Mayfield?" Simpson removed his spectacles as he looked across at the widow. He felt more than pleased with himself at having found someone in the time allotted. She filled all of the qualifications admirably, for she came from a good family, had managed her late husband's household well enough during the time he was alive—she could hardly be blamed for those investments which had been made for her by others and which had gone wrong after his death, he reasoned, and, besides, here at Le Beau Château, her duties would extend only to training Brianna; the estate's purse-strings would be held by him and Jesse until Brianna married.

Finally, as he took a careful look at Laurette Mayfield, he had an embarrassing surge of additional satisfaction, for Laurette was a stunningly attractive woman—not that this had any bearing on her qualifications for the job, he reminded himself. But as he waited for the lovely brunette to finish looking over her copy of the employment agreement, George Simpson couldn't help feeling smug with what he'd managed to pull off.

Laurette at last raised her heavily lashed, dark eyes and gave him a small, curving smile that revealed a row of pearly white, even teeth in a mouth that was otherwise the perfect cupid's bow that fashion favored. "Yes, Mister Simpson," she said in a low, smooth voice, "I think the terms are more than generous, as my solicitors in Richmond said they would be. Allow me one clarification, though?"

"Name it," said Simpson, beginning to flush slightly, for her dark eyes met his in a fashion he would have sworn was bordering on the intimate.

The same, careful smile appeared in the smooth, ivory-complexioned face. "My—um—authority over the child, Brianna—how complete is it? That is, I have been given to understand that the girl is sometimes a bit headstrong, and I should hardly like to fancy coming into any—shall I say, *contretemps*—with her."

"Ah! Well—ah, Mistress Mayfield, I would be dishonest if I indicated the young lady were completely compliant in all respects, but I hardly think there will be any insoluble problems between the two of you. Mistress Devereaux did take the death of her father rather hard, it's true, and there were some—ah—extraordinary terms and conditions left by him in his will—conditions such as the one requiring she marry by year's end, for example. And, yes, she has tried to resist those terms to some degree, but they are not really your concern. Truly, I haven't heard her utter one word where the training in husbandry is concerned. The—ah—husband*ing* may be another matter!" Here Simpson gave a quick explosive guffaw at his own joke before settling back down to the business at hand.

"Suffice it to say, my dear Mistress Mayfield, that the terms of our agreement give you complete authority over the girl *in your specified area of instruction.* If she opposes you in any way, you are to come to me or to Mister Randall, her guardian, but I hardly think it will happen. You see, the terms of the will are quite clear: Either she passes your standards, or she loses the bulk of her inheritance. I hardly think she'd wish to chance that!"

"I see," said the widow. "Very well, Mister Simpson, all appears quite acceptable to me, but now, tell me, when am I to meet my charge?"

"In about five seconds," replied Simpson as he rose to the sound of voices in the hallway.

Just then, Brianna and Father Edouard came through the door, chuckling at some private joke they shared.

Simpson quickly came around the large desk to help Laurette out of her chair while at the same time welcoming the newcomers.

"Brianna, Father Edouard, how good of you to be so punctual! Do come in—ah, can you tell me if Mister Randall—"

"I'm here," said Jesse's voice from the door; all heads turned as he entered, dressed in a deep blue superfine riding jacket, dove gray breeches and the trenchant tall black riding boots polished to a mirror shine. His hair was slightly tousled, as if it had been ruffled by the slight breeze that was now gently blowing through the library's open windows. Nodding casually to Brianna and Father Edouard as he came toward the desk, he extended his hand to Simpson.

"George, good to see you again. Sorry I wasn't available to meet with you earlier. I've been spending most of the time since our return in sessions with Governor Pinckney—but I did read your note on the—" He turned and regarded the standing figure of Laurette Mayfield with a warm smile. "—business I assume we're about to discuss?"

Taking his cue, the solicitor drew near the widow and quickly made introductions all around, finishing with the words, "Mister Randall, Madam, is Brianna's guardian."

As Jesse bowed courteously over Laurette's extended hand, the widow intoned in a voice of liquid butter, "Mister Randall, I do so look forward to the association we shall enjoy in the coming months."

"It will be my pleasure, Mistress Mayfield," Jesse replied with an engaging grin.

Brianna listened with half an ear as Father Edouard made some pleasantries regarding the good weather the Upcountry was enjoying, coupled with polite inquiries about the widow's trip down from Richmond. She was preoccupied with studying her new tutor. Taking in the widow's compact, voluptuous figure which was expensively accoutered in a chic traveling ensemble of lavender velvet, she couldn't help feeling unsophisticated and plain by comparison; she herself was wearing an old gown of faded amber cotton, chosen this morning because she had persuaded Mathilde to show her how to make bread. Now, as she covertly eyed Laurette's fashionably plumed headpiece gracing an intricately arranged coiffure, she was sorry the only preparations she'd made for this meeting were the removal of an apron and the wiping of flour from her hands.

Simpson spent a half-hour acquainting Brianna with the details of her duties under the widow, although Brianna continued to say very little. Nodding occasionally at appropriate moments during this time, she occupied much of it observing the interaction between Laurette and Jesse who, she suddenly realized as the meeting was drawing to a close, had already progressed to a first-name basis.

"I'm sure Brianna will be pleased to give you a tour of the house and grounds, Mistress Mayfield," Simpson was saying.

"Why, that's terribly sweet of you to offer, sir," replied Laurette, "but I've already persuaded Jesse, here, to do me the favor." Linking her arm about Jesse's, she turned for the door. Then, almost as an afterthought, she turned her head and said over one shoulder, "Brianna, my dear child, as it's important for you to learn to manage instructing the servants, run and fetch a couple of footmen to take my bags to my room, won't you? There's a good girl."

And with a graceful sweep of her skirts, Laurette advanced toward the door with Jesse beside her, saying, "Now, Jesse, you were telling me about the château's architectural roots...."

Brianna watched them go before turning to Simpson and the priest; placing her hands on her hips, she said, "You cannot be serious about this!"

"B-but—er—Brianna my—my dear," stammered the solicitor, "whatever do you mean?"

"I *mean* that *woman*!"

"Mistress Mayfield?" Simpson began to retreat behind the desk, sensing a storm brewing; he recognized only too well the green fire blazing in Brianna's eyes.

"The same," came the crack response.

But Father Edouard, by now an old hand at dealing with Brianna's temper, was quick to intervene. "Now, *ma petite*, calm yourself. Since when is it like you to form judgments so quickly, and, certainly, with insufficient evidence?"

"Insufficient?! Father, you saw her with your own eyes! Why, she fairly appropriated Jesse as her own private property!"

The priest stopped short for a moment, seeing, suddenly, the true thrust behind her anger. "Hmm," he murmured, pulling pensively at his beard. "Yes, well, perhaps something will have to be done about that."

"And she called me a *child*!" stormed Brianna; her focus was back on Simpson, who stood behind the desk busily shuffling papers. "If I'm to be instructed in managing a household, with an eye to becoming a *mature woman*, capable of handling the duties of an *adult*, how am I to learn if my..." Here Brianna paused and took a breath before grinding out the next word between tightly clenched teeth. "...*tutor* insists on treating me like a child? Will you *kindly* answer me *that*?"

Just then, a worried-looking Prenshaw tapped urgently at the frame of the library's open door.

"Yes?" inquired Brianna with impatience.

"Pardon the intrusion, Mistress Brianna, but there appears to be a problem with the—ah—Widow Mayfield's baggage."

"What kind of problem?"

"Well, Mistress, it seems that she was anticipating your instructing the footmen to bring it up to the chamber we'd assigned her, but inasmuch as Mistress Delaney had already seen to the task, the lady is now insisting that we *move her* to another chamber so that—oh, permit me to say I hope I haven't misunderstood—so that *you* may have the exercise of directing the *footmen*!" Prenshaw's normally placid, narrow face was screwed into a bewildered mask of incredulity. Somberly, he added, "I await your instructions, Mistress."

Brianna turned back to Father Edouard with an "I-told-you-so" expression on her face, but the priest was busy laying plans of his own and had no intention of allowing things to get off to a worse start than they already had.

"Prenshaw," he said, "your mistress was just telling me that she thought the widow would enjoy the view from the red room better than that from the corner guest chamber. She was just about to call you to effect that change, weren't you, my dear?" He turned to Brianna with a meaningful look.

"What?" Then, catching the expression in the priest's eye, Brianna nodded to the butler. "Oh, yes, Prenshaw. Please inform the footmen, and, also, kindly convey my apologies for the unnecessary confusion they've fallen victim to, won't you?"

"Very good, Mistress."

"Oh, and, Prenshaw—"

"Yes, Mistress?"

"My thanks for your patience."

"Very kind of you, Mistress," the butler replied; there appeared to be a ghost of a smile on his normally rigid features as he bowed and retreated.

"Well, Brianna," said Simpson as he came forward with a weak smile. "I would say you handled the situation quite well—even admirably. You seem to deal quite well with the servants. Given just that bit of aid you received from Father Edouard, here, you were quite in control of the situation."

"And why shouldn't I have been?" asked Brianna with a small stamp of her foot. "I followed my mother about these halls enough as a young girl to glean much from her in the ways of managing a household. I don't care that it was a long time ago. There are certain things that, if learned when one is young, are never forgotten. Training in husbandry, indeed!"

"Yes," smiled Simpson nervously, "but the terms of the will—"

"The will, the will! I'm sick of hearing about that damned will!" Brianna marched toward the door, then whirled and faced both men. "All right. You needn't say it. I'm not handling my temper again. Very well, just to show you I can, I leave you with this: I'll go and do what that woman says, even if it *kills* me! Because Le Beau Château means more to me than suffering under the whims of a *hundred* Laurette Mayfields. And Jesse Randalls, too! You'll see. I'm going to put in my time and pass these ridiculous 'tests' with flying colors, no matter what! But on the day Le Beau Château becomes mine, nobody is going to run roughshod over me, gentlemen. *Nobody!*" And with a fiery gleam in her eyes, Brianna turned and left the room.

Several days later, the late afternoon found Brianna sitting morosely on a bale of hay in front of Le Duc's stall in the stables. Her sitting position at that moment could hardly have been construed as ladylike; she sat hunched forward, her forearms resting on her knees, which were spread, along with her long legs, as far apart as her green and white striped dimity skirt would allow, as she stared in silence at the stable's brick floor.

A quacking noise to her left caused her to raise her head. "Oh, hello, Dependable," she muttered glumly. Then she shifted and reached down into a pocket of the apron she was wearing (donned, according to Laurette Mayfield's instructions, because she was supposed to protect her gowns now, whenever she worked near the animals); she extracted a handful of maize kernels and threw them on the floor in front of the mallard, who avidly began to gobble them up, his colorful, iridescent head making the characteristic forward and back jerking motions of his species as he ingested each piece.

As she absently watched the duck eat his treat, Brianna's thoughts shifted back to the cause of her low humor. As she saw it, the problem was twofold, though each part stemmed from the occurrence of Laurette Mayfield's arrival at Le Beau Château. First, there was the suffocating and insufferable manner with which the widow went about instructing her. In short, the way she treated her, her high and mighty way of fashioning every order to let Brianna know *she* was in charge. *Lording it over me, that's what she's been doing, and because of that idiotic will, here I sit, with no room to say her nay!*

"Ooh, I'd like to be able to tell her a thing or two, Dependable." She saw the mallard raise his head and cock an eye at hearing his name. "Why, she's even worse than Jesse!" If that's possible, she added mentally as she was reminded of the second part of her cause for consternation.

But here she was reluctant to examine too deeply her reasons for being distressed. She only knew she was somehow vexed by the fact that, ever since her arrival, Laurette had been spending an inordinate amount of time with Jesse Randall. *And* he with her, she added to herself, deciding to be honest about it, for she was well aware that it wasn't always the widow who sought him out; sometimes it was the reverse. It had happened this afternoon, when Jesse had interrupted a linen-counting session—Brianna still found it hard to digest that Laurette had wasted her time with *that* exercise!—to invite the widow to go riding with him. And then, what had really set her blood to boiling was Laurette's insistence that Brianna accompany them down to the stables to observe a pair of stableboys mucking out stalls.

"But that's Serge's territory!" Brianna had exclaimed, dreading being dragged along in her apron while the two of them were paired off in their smart riding clothes.

"The mistress of the estate would be wise to be aware of how well her employees are managing the work of their underlings," Laurette had loftily intoned.

"But Serge has been a devoted family retainer for over twenty years!"

"Nevertheless," came the response, "you never know when someday he might have to be replaced, and then where will you be if you lack the experience of keeping abreast of things when his replacement arrives?''

"I suppose, next, you'll want me to go out in the fields and supervise the overseer's 'underlings'!" Brianna snapped.

But then came the last straw, for Laurette had quietly turned to Jesse, a helpless look of appeal in her dark eyes, and Jesse had admonished Brianna, saying, "That will be enough, young lady! You are to do as Laurette says without all this childish protest."

So there it was. Not only was Jesse totally unsympathetic to her plight where her lessons in "husbandry" were concerned, he continued to see and treat her like a child—and right in front of Laurette, too! Oh, it was all too much to bear!

So here she'd been sitting, ever since the stableboys had finished, brooding and feeling a good bit sorry for herself late into the afternoon.

Suddenly, Brianna stopped her musings and jumped up from her seat. She had just gotten an image of herself, of what she'd been doing—feeling sorry for herself—and she didn't like it. *Since when have you been one to indulge in self-pity?* she questioned silently. *Even in France, when the various letters had come, did you ever allow yourself to wallow in self-indulgent despair, ever let the threatening homesickness take charge?*

"No!" came her vehement reply, spoken so loudly that behind her in his stall Le Duc snorted nervously and Dependable embarked upon a series of noisy, scolding quacks.

Making up her mind not to be further distressed or intimidated by the insensitivities of her tutor *or* her guardian, Brianna began to whistle a gay little tune as she headed toward the doorway. She would seek out Aimée, and they would share some amusing conversation before the widow came back and found some new torment for her pupil.

But as Brianna stepped through the stable doors and into the brilliant October sunshine, she looked up to see Jesse and Laurette returning from their ride. Actually, they weren't riding at all, but walking slowly down the drive, leading their horses. Moving together so closely that Brianna could discern no space between them, Jesse was inclining his head to catch some comment of the brunette's and in the next moment smiling down at her while Laurette looked up into his eyes in the most intimate manner.

Intending to escape their notice, Brianna turned and headed for the stable's side entrance which she reached in record time, but as she headed up the path to the château, had anyone been listening, he would have become aware that the tune she'd been whistling had vanished.

Chapter Twenty-Four

The golden Upcountry days of October began to pass rapidly at Le Beau Château, where all those privy to the terms of Etienne's will started to show signs of concern as they realized Brianna had precious little time left in which to find a husband.

Mistress Delaney, with Laurette's help, prevailed upon Simpson to make funds available for a wedding gown and trousseau, and the French seamstress again appeared, hard at work in the château's sewing room, despite the absence of any designated bridegroom. Brianna's reaction to this had been howls of outrage, but in the end, she'd been forced to submit to the will of those in charge.

Laurette, with Jesse's help, began to make forays into the nearby countryside, calling upon neighbors who, in particular, had sons who were of marriageable age, or who, as in the case of two middle-aged widowers, were themselves marriage material. Soon, usually at tea time, Brianna began to have callers, some of them female, but always accompanied by an eligible male relative. On these occasions, Brianna did her best to comply with the admonitions of Jesse, Laurette, Mistress Delaney and even Simpson, that she put her best foot forward, but her attempts at conversation with most of the would-be beaus usually ended in her affecting a most coolly courteous manner, no more, for she failed to shake from her mind the notion that she was being put on display like so many pounds of meat in the marketplace, and this severely constrained her normal abundance of conviviality and social grace.

Even Honoré turned up with Brianna's apparent interests in mind. Insisting that he was still eager to make amends for his unconscionable behavior on the trip that night, he began to appear at almost regular intervals at the château, each time accompanied by a male acquaintance; each of these was an eligible bachelor—often with a favorable position in the legislature—whom Honoré would graciously present to his "beauteous sister." And on these occasions his own behavior was so circumspect and courteous, Brianna was hard put to doubt his sincerity in wanting to help her find an acceptable man to wed, even at the cost of his own inheritance. Unfortunately, her own behavior during these visits fared little better than with Laurette's candidates; the image of the meat market grew entrenched in Brianna's mind.

Only Father Edouard and Aimée, of those seen frequently who were aware of the contents of her father's will, appeared in no hurry to urge Brianna to choose a favorite suitor. Of this Brianna was alternately relieved and delighted, for at times she had begun to feel the entire world was conspiring to marry her off to the first likely fellow to appear on the doorstep. As for the priest and the little gypsy, they were often seen in deep conversation together, though always breaking off and quickly going their separate ways if approached by a third party, especially if this party happened to be Brianna.

Jesse felt himself particularly anxious to see the business done, the tenure of his guardianship over. For one thing, he chafed to return home; his plantation needed him, although he was careful to keep in constant touch with things at Riverview through letters to and from his brother—and one day, to his astonishment, he even received a crudely penned, but entirely readable, missive from Vulcan—his sister-in-law, Christie, had been teaching him to read and write!

Jesse also felt his government service to Pinckney was drawing to a close. He found himself greatly respected now in legislative circles as it quietly became known in Columbia that his letter to Washington had apparently been instrumental in preparing the President sufficiently, so that he was able to dissuade Jefferson from resigning.

Finally, had he been ready to acknowledge them, Jesse might have cited some deep and as yet unadmitted reasons for feeling

restless with the situation at Le Beau Château. But since he was
not, he merely made a point of keeping Brianna at a distance
and readily fell into spending a great deal of his spare time with
Laurette Mayfield. Never one to do without attractive female
company for long, he felt the widow a perfect choice for a safe,
brief liaison. Sophisticated and experienced in the ways of men
and the world, she would provide a pleasant interlude without
making unnecessary demands on him.

As for Brianna, she continued as she had been, dutifully accepting the visits from would-be suitors, some of them quite
attractive and charming, she had to admit; but her attitude remained so cool and aloof during these social meetings that at
one point Mistress Delaney worriedly remarked to Aimée that
she had overheard one of them referring to her as "that beautiful ice maiden." On this Aimée had privately reflected that
Brianna was stubbornly fighting to deny any feeling for Jesse
Randall, and this merely carried over into a general disdain for
emotional involvement with all men.

One day, Aimée and Father Edouard invited Brianna to join
them on one of their berrypicking excursions into the fields
some distance from the château. Relieved at the chance to be
free of afternoon visitors and what she had come to regard as
Laurette's supercilious tyranny, Brianna easily agreed and fell
into the pleasant work they shared with a return of her former
vivacity and high spirits.

"It is a good thing that *Madame* Mayfield decided to take the
afternoon to go riding with *Monsieur* Jesse, eh?" said Aimée
as she handed Brianna a pair of small berry gathering baskets.

"Yes, a good thing," murmured Brianna.

"Poor *enfant*," said Father Edouard sympathetically, "not
much free time under the watchful widow hawk these days,
eh?" He plopped a pair of juicy berries into a basket, and a
third into his mouth.

Just then, a sound from across the field caught Aimée's attention. "Speaking of our lady hawk—" *and Sir Eagle*, she
added mentally "—guess who's riding this way right now."

"Oh, no," groaned Brianna as she wiped at a smear of berry
juice on her hand. In the distance Laurette and Jesse approached at an easy canter.

The priest raised his arm to wave at the oncoming pair while Brianna turned with a deliberate motion and resumed picking berries.

"Watch your feet over there, Brianna," warned Aimée. "The showers we had last night left the ground soggy in places where the drainage is not so good. It looks dry, but is very wet underneath."

Brianna gave a mechanical nod and kept on picking.

Hoofbeats drew near, and then Laurette's voice called out. "Well, I declare, just look at this industrious trio!"

"How are you today, *Madame*?" asked the priest as he helped her dismount. "Jesse, good to see you, as always."

"I see you're laying in stores for another one of your admirable concoctions, Father," said Jesse, also dismounting. "What kind, this time?"

"These berries have no European name as yet, Jesse, though some of the local settlers used them for making a crude, homemade wine and dubbed them 'wineberries.' The local Indians have a use for them in the marriage ceremony where they symbolize the hoped-for fruitfulness, or fertility, in the bride. They are called *ghigau*, or 'beloved woman,' which is also what the bridegroom calls his bride."

"How utterly quaint and droll," cooed Laurette as she swished aside her velvet riding skirt, carefully avoiding a pile of berry baskets lying on the ground. Nodding briefly to Aimée, her gaze fell on Brianna, whose bent back was still toward them as she plucked energetically at some low-hanging branches. "Brianna, child, you haven't even paid us a greeting! Cat got your tongue?"

Brianna straightened and turned, ever so slowly, to face them. "Good day, Laurette, Jesse," she said mechanically as she silently wished them gone. Once again they had come upon her looking at a disadvantage. She wore an old-fashioned, rust-colored gown with a high neckline and long sleeves, a country frock, deliberately chosen for berrypicking where the modest cut would provide good protection against insects and scratches. On her head she'd tied a brown kerchief, securing it at the back of her neck, under her loose hair, which she hadn't bothered to arrange beyond a casual brushing after washing it this morning. Beside Laurette in her wine-colored velvet riding habit and plumed bonnet arranged artfully to dip low over one side of her forehead in coquettish *chic*, she felt like a little brown wren beside a swan. And Jesse, she refused to even look at, although, as she gazed at the ground near his feet, she caught sight of the perfectly polished riding boots he always wore.

"Really, Brianna," Laurette was saying, "you ought to take more care with your clothes and wear an apron on these occasions, although I realize this can't be a particularly *good* or *expensive* frock. And, my dear, you have the most unbecoming and ridiculous looking smudge of berry juice on your nose!"

Brianna's hand went self-consciously to her face as, at the same moment, Jesse stepped forward with a linen handkerchief he extracted from his waistcoat pocket. Reaching out to cup her chin with one hand, he rubbed at the smudge with the cloth.

Brianna started to withdraw with an embarrassed, protesting gesture.

"Hold still," ordered Jesse; he continued to work at removing the smudge.

Brianna chanced to glance up and found his blue eyes dancing with amusement as he looked down at her with a grin that was a slash of white in his deeply tanned face. Together with the startling white of the jabot at his throat, all parts of the formal riding ensemble he wore whenever escorting Laurette, the picture he presented was one of barely leashed masculinity—raw male beauty at war with a civilized façade. Again, Brianna's mind beheld a picture of herself—the little brown wren.

Releasing her at last, he stepped back and perused her face. "There, that ought to take care of it."

"Really," muttered Brianna with a frown, "one can hardly expect to pick berries without getting a bit untidy. There'll be more smudges before we're through, I'll warrant."

Aimée, who'd been watching all this with a careful eye, suddenly sauntered up to Laurette. "These berries are really very tasty, Mistress Mayfield. Allow me to offer you some."

As she extended a hand laden with berries and dripping with juice, aiming directly, it seemed, for Laurette's mouth, Brianna had a flash of an image, remembering her friend's tale of the time Honoré had been similarly honored, and she covered a gasp that rose to her lips with her hand.

Meanwhile, Laurette was shrinking back in horror from the gypsy's offering, taking large backward steps to avoid it.

Suddenly the widow's footing seemed to give way as one riding boot encountered the soggy ground Aimée had spoken of earlier. With a shriek, Laurette landed, bottom first, in the hidden bog. Muddy water went flying in all directions as the widow screeched her dismay and outrage. The four onlookers immediately came forward to help, but not before a number of helpless thrashings on Laurette's part succeeded in thoroughly covering her with mud.

Father Edouard was the first to reach her as he waved Jesse aside, saying, "There is no sense in two of you ruining your clothes." As he hoisted the widow up in a less than graceful fashion, he grinned. "This is my oldest cassock, and completely washable."

"How fortunate for you!" Laurette snapped ungraciously. "But see," she wailed, "my new riding habit—it's ruined!" She held the sodden, muddy skirt away from her with stiff fingertips.

Brianna remained behind Jesse and Aimée, trying her best not to laugh. Oh, but Laurette looked a sight! The fashionable *chapeau* she had envied on Laurette's head a short while ago drooped limply over one ear, its handsome plumage a memory. The brown smears on her face all but obliterated Laurette's ivory complexion, and Brianna thought of justice as she remembered the sting of the barb the widow had tossed at her just moments earlier, when she'd referred to Brianna's smudged nose. Her riding habit was caked with mud from hem to neckline, the sodden weight of it rendering each small step the widow took ungainly and awkward.

Suddenly Aimée came forward, murmuring copious apologies and reaching out with the head kerchief she had worn and now removed to wipe feebly at some of the mud on Laurette's jacket.

"Stay away from me, you clumsy fool!" Laurette raged. "I've had enough of your offers to last me the rest of my days!"

Looking utterly crestfallen, Aimée bent her head to indicate regret at its most sorrowful. "Please, *Madame*, you must allow me to make amends. I shall accompany you back to the château and help you clean your clothes. I know a way to steam velvet—"

"Help me?!" screeched Laurette. "You'll do more than *that*! You'll *do* it for me!"

"*Oui, Madame*—but of course!" The corners of Aimée's mouth quirked, as if at stifling a grin.

"And I'll go with you," said the priest. "I have an invitation to sup at the home of one of my parishioners, and I shall have to hurry back if I am to be on time. Ah—Brianna, *ma petite*, would you mind gathering the unfilled baskets in that sack and returning them to the wine cellars for me? I'll take the filled ones in the dray." He gestured to where a pair of stocky ponies stood, several dozen yards away in the shade at the edge of the forest, patiently awaiting him in front of the cart he often used while berrypicking.

Brianna readily assented while Jesse assisted the widow in mounting her horse, no easy task with the now cumbersome skirt she trailed. Then Father Edouard addressed him. "Jesse, I'm of the opinion that Brianna ought to have a male escort as well. Do you think you—"

"Father!" exclaimed Brianna. "I'm perfectly capable of finishing up here and going home by myself!"

"Of course you are, my dear," answered the priest as he carried baskets of berries toward the dray, "but those storm clouds gathering in the distance might prove a bit of a problem, and I'd be beside myself with worry if—"

"Say no more about it, Father," Jesse cut in. "I'll help Brianna and see her safely home in short order." He glanced at Laurette and then at Aimée, who was also carrying berry-laden baskets to the cart. "Laurette, Aimée, you'd better get started." To the priest he said, "You'd better hurry too. That storm may not reach us for a while, but these things can be tricky. It could come up much sooner."

An unhappy looking Laurette was already riding for the château; Aimée and the priest soon followed, the two of them calling to the widow to stay along the track that had been worn through the field by carts and wagons, and which the priest would need to use with the dray. But Laurette merely gave them a caustic look over one bedraggled shoulder and spurred her mount in the direction in which she'd been moving.

"She might have tried rinsing off in the creek first," said Brianna, watching them go. "That's what I would have done."

"Brianna," said Jesse in a tone one might use to explain to a very young child, "Laurette Mayfield is a lady and does not go about bathing in creeks and streams."

"Oh, *pardon me, Monsieur*," sneered Brianna, stung as much by his implied comparison between her and the widow as by his tone. "I should have realized her *ladyship's* dainty qualities were too much for the likes of *me* to appreciate!" She bent to place the last of the berry baskets in the large sack she held, turned, flung the sack over her shoulder, and stalked off in a huff toward where Le Duc stood in the shade, patiently munching some lush, green grass.

"Brianna!" Jesse came charging after her, determined not to be misunderstood, and just as determined to let her know that it was *she* who was at fault in the misunderstanding. "That's not what I meant, and you know it!"

"Oh, *wasn't* it?" Brianna intoned in her best sarcastic voice. "That's what you'd have me believe, wouldn't you, now that I've seen through you and your *dear* widow!" She swung the sack over the back of Le Duc's saddle with such a violent gesture, the poor animal sidestepped alarmedly several paces.

"Me and my—? Brianna, just what are you talking about? Laurette and I—"

"Oh spare me! If you want to make a fool of yourself running after that—that overpowdered and—and overstuffed creature, that's *your* business. Now, if you'll just step aside, Sir Fool—"

Suddenly Jesse grabbed her by both shoulders and jerked her around to face him. In the near distance a roll of thunder rumbled, but Jesse ignored it as he pinned her where she stood, his blue eyes riveting.

"My dear Brianna," he began, his tone ominously soft, "whatever I am, and I may be many things, some of which you cannot begin to have an inkling of, I am never a fool. Furthermore, though I cannot think why I should have to explain it to you, my relationship with Laurette Mayfield is none of your business!''

At this Brianna fell completely silent. They stood there for a moment, will meeting will, each challenging the other. Then a fierce clap of thunder broke the air. It was sufficient to force each of them to look skyward; what greeted their eyes was a sky grown dark with low-hanging clouds and, a second later, a white lightning streak, quickly followed by an even louder crack of thunder. A strong wind seemed to come up out of nowhere, and suddenly Jesse had to shout to make himself heard.

''Mount up! We're going to have to run for the château, though I hate like hell to cross an open field when there's lightning!''

Quickly obeying, Brianna watched him swing into Gypsy's saddle before raising her own voice to ask, ''What about the forest?''

Jesse shook his head. ''Just as dangerous. The trees—lightning!'' he shouted over another peal of thunder, just as the first huge drops of rain began to pelt the ground.

Suddenly Brianna gave a start, as of an idea hitting, and called out to him, the ever-building wind nearly tearing her words out of her mouth. ''Follow me! I know of a place—shelter!'' And without waiting for a reply, she turned Le Duc's head into the wind, hunched over his withers, and took off at a full gallop.

Unable to question her, Jesse turned Gypsy's head in the same direction and followed, the heavy sheets of rain barely allowing him to see the horse and rider he was forced to pursue.

Brianna led them along the edge of the forest bordering the field, all the time darting swift glances heavenward, trying to gauge where the next arc of lightning might strike. She took them over what had earlier appeared as a low rise on an otherwise flat meadow, and then cut directly into the woods on the other side. When Jesse saw this, he shouted at her to remember the danger he'd already pointed out, but his words never reached her, whipped from his lips by the roaring wind. He had no recourse but to follow.

Then he saw where she was heading. After about a minute of threading their way through the trees, they came upon a small clearing near a stream, and in the center of it stood what appeared to be a small stone cottage and adjacent stable, also of stone, though its wooden doors swung wildly in the wind.

Brianna rode Le Duc directly into the smaller structure and began to dismount as Jesse followed suit.

"What is this place?" he asked in a shout.

"Gamekeeper's cottage—or it used to be," she yelled back.

Then each fell silent as they busied themselves with divesting their horses of saddles and bridles, using their saddle blankets then, to rub both animals down. Surprised to see fresh hay in a miniature loft, Jesse threw a goodly amount into the manger of each of the stable's two stalls, grabbed Brianna's hand, and raced for the cottage's single door.

When they stood safely inside, water puddling around them on the stone floor, they looked about, contemplating the cottage's single room while taking time to catch their breaths.

From what they could make out in the dim light, its source being a lone window on the wall opposite the door, the room was a simple one. It offered a fairly wide hearth, well supplied with firewood which stood in a neat pile nearby, a crude pine table, its stretcher base showing signs of having once been painted barn red, and two old Windsor armchairs, also showing signs of much wear to their bottle-green paint; a double bed stood in one corner, its cannonball-topped posts and carved headboard indicating the hand of a country craftsman; Brianna noticed the lovely blue-green paint covering it had fared much better than the colors on the other pieces.

Eyeing the firewood and the clean looking "log cabin" design quilt and fresh muslin pillow shams on the bed, Jesse asked, "Who lives here now?"

"No one, as far as I know," Brianna replied. "We don't have a gamekeeper any more. The only reason we had one once, was because Papa brought old Jacques with him when he left France. He was a gamekeeper to the old king, but a Protestant and not very comfortable in his homeland in those days. He died when I was a child, though," she added sadly.

"But," said Jesse, looking around for a tinderbox and, finding one, beginning to work it to get a spark, "this place shows signs of recent care. There was even fresh hay and straw in the stable."

"Oh, I think Serge and his sons and Louis Mercier, the overseer, still use it as a hunting cabin. Papa had said they might, after Jacques died." As she watched Jesse throw kindling into the fireplace and succeed in starting a fire, Brianna suddenly realized she was shivering, for she heard her own words uttered through chattering teeth.

Jesse heard, too. Quickly rising from the hearth, he strode to the bed and tore the quilt off it, then approached her.

Brianna saw him stop for a moment and stare at something about her person; looking down at her sodden clothes, she saw her dress plastered against her body, and there, clearly evident and leaving nothing to the imagination, she caught sight of her distended nipples, peaked and hardened from the cold, thrusting blatantly through the thin, wet material of her bodice.

Blushing fiercely, despite the chill, she reached for the quilt that hung suspended from Jesse's raised hands, saying awkwardly, "I—I guess I've t-taken c-cold."

Instantly spurred into motion, Jesse wrapped the quilt about her trembling body. "God, you're icy!" he exclaimed, his voice strangely tight.

"I—I'll b-be all right."

"I'm not so sure. Here, stand over by the fire while I build it up some more."

He ushered her over to the hearth, then threw two more logs and additional kindling on the fire. Outside, the thunder rolled as flashes of lightning illuminated the window.

As she watched him work, Brianna felt herself mesmerized by the display of muscles expanding and contracting under the broad expanse of his back and shoulders, for his shirt, too, was wet and clung to him like another skin. She saw his hair, wet and shiny black, curling at the back of his neck and ears and, unbidden, there came to her the memory of a night she had run her fingers through it, pulling him closer, begging him to—

"There," he said, rising, "that ought to warm you some, now." As he turned to face her Brianna met his eyes and then knew she shouldn't have.

But it was too late. As a particularly loud clap of thunder crashed about their ears, his eyes read hers and she knew she stood naked before him, as naked as if the quilt and the wet gown she wore beneath it, did not exist. And then, in his eyes she caught a look, and it was a mirror of her own. Desire, raw and urgent, arced between them, as potent and stark as the lightning outside.

With a groan, Jesse reached for her, but Brianna was already there. In a split moment, the quilt lay in a heap at their feet as Jesse pulled her into his arms. Fiercely, thinking of nothing but her need, she threw her arms about his neck as she felt his mouth slash across hers, then answered him with lips warm and open.

They stood this way for long minutes, belly to belly, mouth to mouth, feeling nothing beyond a heartbeat between them. Again and again, their mouths met without ever really separating, crisscrossing, moving, tasting each other, knowing only they hungered and must not stop.

Deep in the pit of her belly, Brianna felt a candent fire spreading, its liquid heat moving downward through her trembling thighs, spiraling upward into the vital heart of her. She felt Jesse's need, hard and insistent against her, and her head swam.

At last, Jesse tore his mouth away from hers, only to move it against her ear as his hands came to cradle her head and hold it close. "Brianna," he murmured hoarsely, his voice an urgent whisper, "God, how I *want* you—*have wanted* you! Sweet, lovely Green Eyes." His lips were warm on her ear as he said the words, then moved to trace a trail of fire down her neck while his hands descended to move warmly down her back and, finally, to cup her buttocks and draw that part of her even closer. At this, a jolt of lightning exploded Brianna's being, and she never stopped to sense if it came from the storm outside or the storm within.

"Jesse!" she cried, and then she couldn't stop and repeated his name, again and again, "Jesse, Jesse, Jesse," as the raging thunder drowned out the sound.

Suddenly he stopped and raised his head, his hands going to her shoulders as he gazed into her eyes for a long minute. The noise of the storm seemed to abate somewhat as they looked at each other, eyes drugged and smouldering with passion. In the grate, the fire hissed and crackled, and the sound mingled with those of their ragged breathing.

"Come with me, Brianna," Jesse said thickly as he moved his strong hands down her arms. Then he bent and lifted her into his arms, carrying her toward the bed. As he moved with her, his eyes never left her face. "Beautiful one...Green Eyes...I'm going to make love to you, sweet...teach you, oh, so much more about pleasure...I'm going to love teaching you, pleasing you...."

Then he was laying her trembling body on the bed; his eyes continued to hold hers as he quickly shed his wet clothes, and Brianna thought she had never seen eyes so blue. The dancing firelight caught their color, seemed to magnify it, and she caught her breath at the sight. Then he was with her on the bed, his hands at the buttons of her gown while his lips whispered softly of his need. "I cannot stay away from you, Brianna. I've tried, God knows, I've told myself. But each time I look at you, it seems this is what I want, need. You're lovely, beyond anything made on God's green earth. Do you know that? Do you know how I want you, Green Eyes? Do you feel it, too?"

He was at the last button, now, and with a rapid movement, stripped her gown away, leaving her in her damp shift. This, he left alone for a moment, as his eyes took in the ripeness of her aching breasts, their rosy tips peaking through the sheerness, beckoning for the touch he yet withheld.

Then he took the tips of the fingers of one hand and lightly touched one pink crest. A visible shudder ran through Brianna's body, and he saw it. Again, the finger stroked; those of his other hand came up; they caressed her other waiting bud, and again she felt a tremor rock her.

"Are you sure, though, Brianna?" she heard him ask. "I want you to be sure, Green Eyes, very—" he leaned over and kissed her eyes "—very..."—His lips feathered over her temple—"...sure." His mouth closed over hers in a kiss that plied the honey from her core.

Then he raised his head and looked at her again. Eyes so blue....

"Brianna," he breathed.

Then Brianna could stand it no more. Taking her two hands, she curled her fingers around the shift's delicate neckline and wrenched it downward, splitting the garment in half.

Jesse's breath caught deep in his throat. His eyes flew to the lush charms she revealed to him by this act and then back to her face. What he saw there told him all he needed. With a harsh cry he took her in his arms, and their bodies fused, allowing not even a whisper between them.

Jesse's mouth covered her face in a series of kisses as light as swansdown touching here, grazing there, while with his knowing hands he stroked and petted her body, finding all the right spots to make her tingle and yearn with longing. His thumbs he slid under the heavy crease beneath each of her full, perfect breasts, before coming around to brush across their nipples. Again and again, he played this game, driving Brianna into a frenzy of wanting.

Then, as his lips nibbled at the sensitive spot below her ear, his one hand moved lower, stroking her waist, her abdomen, the downy triangle that glowed red in the firelight. When his fingers parted the curls and touched between, he heard her gasp, but still his fingers moved. Once, twice, again, they stroked the tight, hard little bud that told him she was almost ready.

"You're wet for me, darling," Jesse whispered, his mouth against her ear. "Down here, where I'm going to fill you, you're like liquid velvet. No—don't pull away, sweetling. There's nothing to be ashamed of, I promise. There... beautiful..."

Brianna felt his finger enter her slippery warmth, and she gasped with pleasure. But soon this was not enough. Arching herself against his touch, she ran her fingers through the dark curls of his hair and then down his neck to his shoulders, pulling to bring him closer.

With a small laugh, Jesse withdrew his hand, placing it, along with the other, beside her head on the pillow as he braced himself to enter her.

Brianna was by now a wild thing. Her nails dug into his shoulders as she frantically tried to bring him to her.

"Please!" was her single cry.

And Jesse gave her what she sought. With a sound that only then revealed how much his delay had been costing him, he thrust his hips and filled her.

The immediate pleasure that washed over them both seemed to still them for a moment, but then they needed more. Alive with their need, they began to move, slowly at first, Jesse setting the pace, but Brianna followed with a natural rhythm that matched his, stroke for stroke.

Outside, the storm had spent its fury, but the two in the cabin knew nothing of this as they rode out the storm of their own making. Each taking and giving as much as the other, they were a perfect match in their passion—a union in fire. Then, when Brianna thought her yearning could grow no more, that she would surely die of it, her pleasure broke, sending her high into the stars, the universe at her feet. Spiral after spiral of sheer pleasure washed through her causing her to cry out with it.

Jesse heard her cry as his own release came shuddering through him, catching her up with it, binding her to him with its painful sweetness. For seconds they clung together, spasm after spasm shaking their very souls.

And then at last they lay still with only the diminishing sounds of their breathing breaking the air. And the storm inside was finally quiet, too.

Wordlessly, Brianna and Jesse rode back to the château, their silence a tangible indication of how visibly shaken each was by what had just happened between them.

For Brianna, it was a period of deliberately suspended thinking; she purposefully held her thoughts at bay, willing them out of reach until she could examine things more clearly; for now, it was enough just to bask in the heady flow of her emotions, which were still with her in the aftermath of physical passion. As if drugged by what she had just been through, she carried the imprint of Jesse's lovemaking, lingeringly in her mind, just as surely as its stamp still clung to her body. Sweetly bruised and tender, her arms, breasts, buttocks, thighs and the delicate parts between, spoke to her, telling her to wait—later there would be time.

Not so, with Jesse. Although he tried to push them aside, his head reeled with the implications of what they had just shared. Loudly, as if they would give him no peace, his thoughts assailed him until he found no recourse but to take out each one and look at it closely. Foremost was the knowledge that he had never made love to a woman in the way he had just made love to Brianna. Not only had this been vastly different, it had so far surpassed anything he'd ever experienced, he was at a loss at how to deal with it. First, he had never *wanted* a woman so greatly before. He searched his brain for comparisons and came up empty-handed. Then, there was the behavior of Brianna herself. Never had he encountered such passion! Of course, he told himself, given her otherwise fiery nature, he might have guessed. But, no, he realized, there was nothing he might have dreamed that would have prepared him—nothing. Who could have guessed? Just a few short weeks ago, she had been a frightened virgin! And today—Jesse gave his head a shake and took in a deep breath of the early evening air in an attempt to dispel the sudden tightening in his loins that came now, when he even thought about it.

Which brought him to his next thought. What in hell was he to do with the chit if, whenever he was near her, he had these reactions? He knew the answer before he asked the question. He *couldn't* allow them such nearness again. Brianna Devereaux had to be safely married off—and soon!

But, his questioning self asked him, hadn't he already tried that very avenue? Hadn't he gone out riding with Laurette Mayfield this very afternoon with the idea of bedding her tonight so that he might more safely occupy his lust? And look what had happened! After today and what Brianna had showed him, he seriously doubted if he would ever be willing to settle for the voluptuous widow. Every time he encountered one of her overblown curves, he'd be seeing a graceful, willowy body, its very movements a study in the poetry of form. He. . . .

Suddenly, Jesse closed his mind off and concentrated on the lowering light in the distant sky. Then, when a sound from Gypsy let him know they were nearing the stables, he changed his gaze and allowed it to rest on the profile of the rider beside him. Ethereal as mist and yet perfect in the fading light, her beauty hit him like a sledgehammer blow, and once again, Jesse found his head reeling. As they slowed and let the horses nose their own way through the gate into the stables' courtyard, Jesse was consumed by a flash of angry annoyance. *Tomorrow, old boy, you're going to take some positive steps to see the baggage wed!*

As the two of them entered the courtyard, and then the stables themselves, they saw no one about but thought little of it, it being close to the end of the dinner hour. But a few dozen yards away, returning from his early supper engagement, Father Edouard spied the two of them going through the stable doors; the good priest had a gentle, satisfied smile on his face.

Chapter Twenty-Five

"And then he say—*said*, 'Mistress Delaney, let it be done at once!' and *she* said, 'You mean, today, sir?' and *Monsieur* Jesse bark—I mean, *barked* at her as he left the breakfast room, 'I mean *yesterday*!' leaving the poor woman looking ever so perplexed until at last she fathomed his meaning." Aimée munched casually on a thick slice of warm, buttered bread as she spoke, her bright eyes assessing, curious as to what Brianna's reaction might be.

Brianna nodded as she absentmindedly buttered half of a much thinner slice of the bread she herself had baked that morning.

They were sitting on an apple green, silk-cushioned window seat beneath the double windows in Brianna's bedchamber. A delicate, button-footed Queen Anne tea table rested in front of them holding a silver chocolate service, two Sèvres porcelain chocolate cups and saucers, and half a loaf of warm bread on a silver salver. A pair of snowy linen napkins, a small white crock of butter and a few pieces of silverware completed the gastronomical ensemble.

"So it's to be a richly staged, open marketplace, is it?" Brianna said at last.

Inured by now to her friend's sour references to attempts at steering eligible men her way, to her calling it all a "meat market," Aimée ignored this latest verbal assault, saying only, "Well, the widow is calling it a 'coming out,' such as they usually have during something she called 'the season,' I think, and, at any rate, Brianna, it's to be a grand ball in *your* honor. I, for one—if I were you, that is—would just sit back and *enjoy* it!"

She took another bite of her bread, adding, "Mmm, you've done well in Mathilde's kitchen, *chérie*!"

"So Jesse ordered the invitations to be sent out tod—yesterday!" Here she broke into a small smile, despite herself, as she recognized her guardian's typical high-handedness, and was glad this time it had been directed at someone else. "But if you hadn't overheard, I would still be sitting up here in my chamber, totally in the dark as to these plans!" She buttered the second half of her bread in a suddenly aggressive fashion, nearly tearing its textured surface as she used her knife in a manner worthy of a soldier sharpening his bayonet.

"Oh, I don't doubt he meant you to know about it, Brianna. He's roused the whole staff with his orders. He must have figured it would take little time to reach your ears." Aimée eyed Brianna's uneaten portion of bread, buttered, but now lying on her tray untouched. "Tell me, *mon amie*, if you eat so little of this yourself, why have you industriously applied yourself to learning how to make it?"

"Oh, it's a matter of finding something useful to do with my time—something *I* wish to do, of my own free choosing. But, back to the point, Aimée. Doesn't it occur to you that *mon gardien* might have had the *courtesy* to tell *me* of his plans first?"

Determined not to be led into the trap of helping fuel Brianna's pique, Aimée sidestepped the issue. "Tell me, Brianna, this need you have, to do worthwhile work of your own choice, would it have anything to do with your visits to the forge with Festus, when he met with that silversmith your guardian located in Columbia? Your nails looked a sight when you returned the other day, and—"

"Shh! Aimée, don't *breathe* another *word* about it! The *good widow*, and I don't know who else, would have a blue fit if it was known I was—er—observing such unladylike endeavors! But, you know," Brianna whispered with a grin, "I don't know when I've had such fun!"

Aimée shrugged. "It is nothing to me if you wish to occupy yourself with observations that break your nails." Then she grinned. "Oh, Brianna, it is my fondest wish to see you doing the things that make you happy! There has been far too little to bring the old sparkle to your eyes of late. Of course," she added with a mischievous twinkle in her own eyes, "the best sparkle I've seen in them in a long while came from *'Le Grand Mud-puddle Affaire,' oui?*"

At the reminder of Laurette's comeuppance at Aimée's hands the day before, both burst out laughing and continued until they were bent over in their mirth, tears streaming down their cheeks.

"Oh, Aimée," Brianna said at last, "you really fixed her royally! But hasn't she been awful to you since then?"

Aimée gave a careless shrug. "Not so bad. I rather think she has come to respect me after that—or to *re*spect what she might come to *ex*pect from me in the *future.*"

"Oh, but Aimée! You cannot mean that you might—"

Again a shrug. "We shall see," murmured the little gypsy, noncommittally. "We shall see." But her black eyes were alive with the naughtiest light.

Proving Aimée's descriptions entirely accurate, Le Beau Château began to buzz with activity as Jesse's orders spurred everyone on the premises to prepare for a major ball to present Brianna Devereaux to Carolinian society in a fortnight's time. The word went forth to have the entire place spotlessly perfect, and footmen and maids scurried about washing windows, polishing furniture, waxing floors until they gleamed, airing rugs, cleaning the multi-tiered crystal chandelier in the ballroom until it sparkled; dusting, sweeping, scrubbing, and shining every imaginable nook and cranny of the huge château, the army of servants bent to their task. Laurette and Brianna spent long hours in conference with Prenshaw and Mistress Delaney, and then with Henri and Mathilde, setting up menus, planning flower arrangements, and assigning guest quarters as acceptances to the invitations began to come in. On the grounds, the gardener and his staff pruned, trimmed, snipped and watered to have all in readiness for the big night.

In the sewing room a major upheaval took place as Brianna took it upon herself to order the bridal gown the seamstress had been working on transformed into a ballgown; she and Aimée had foraged in the attic one day and come upon a trunk containing Brianna's mother's wedding gown, and it was this she would wear at her wedding, she had proclaimed, "No matter who the wretch I marry may turn out to be."

And so the night of the ball came. Dusk was just settling over the Upcountry terrain as Brianna stood at one of the windows in her room, dressed in a new lacy chemise and the finest pale ivory silk hose, having just bathed and completed most of her *toilette*. Behind her, Aimée fussed with some of the long curls that hung down her back, suspended from the center, like a horse's tail, of a thickly twisted chignon that rested on the crown of her head.

"There! I can hardly reach the top of your head when you stand, Brianna," said Aimée as she rose on tiptoe to inspect the perfection of the coiffure from behind, "but it appears perfect. Now, if you will turn around, *chérie*, I will help you with your petticoats and gown."

"Never mind, Aimée," Brianna turned and smiled. "I can do the rest myself, remember? It was brilliant of me, if I do say so myself, to help *Madame, la modeste*, design a gown which fastens entirely in the *front*! You run along to your chamber, *mon amie*, and complete your own *toilette*. I can't *wait* to see you in that purple silk!"

Aimée grinned as she made for the door. "Even at the cost of the scene we had to endure when *Madame* Mayfield found out you had given orders that *I* get the purple material when *she* had planned to wear that color tonight?"

"*Especially* because of that!" replied Brianna with a wink. "Now hurry! I'll see you in about a half-hour."

As the door closed behind Aimée, Brianna walked slowly to her bed and looked at the ivory silk ballgown Aimée had carefully laid down across the coverlet. She felt a small thrill of satisfaction as she eyed the hundreds of tiny seed pearls that adorned its square, low-cut, yet traditional neckline, artfully sewn there to disguise the fact that it had been recut to provide a more revealing *décolletage* once she had decided it would no longer be her modest bridal garment. How Laurette had protested that decision, but Jesse, oddly enough, had supported Brianna in the matter, saying he thought it entirely reasonable, since she had located Aileen's wedding clothes and they might be used for the more momentous occasion.

Thoughts of her guardian—*who has also been my lover,* she added to herself as she reached for the petticoats hanging nearby—caused her to seek some activity to occupy her, for she rarely allowed them to intrude these days. Following the afternoon of the storm a fortnight ago, she had briefly attempted to examine her own behavior and been so upset, she'd put such introspection away from her. Deciding her own wanton behavior had been the result of lust and appalled by her conclusion, she had resolved to set it behind her, assuming that it was a contagion of sorts, caught from the extremely lusty nature of Jesse Randall, and that was the long and the short of it. Resigning herself to the fact that she would soon be married and Jesse would thereafter depart, probably going out of her life forever, she need only keep out of his presence as much as possible and bide her time until a match could be made. Then, she felt sure, she might resume living a normal life.

Having assembled and donned the three voluminous silk petticoats, she lifted the gown from the bed and stepped into it, fastening the dozens of tiny hooks cleverly concealed in tiny, pearl-embroidered pleats in the bodice and skirt. Then she walked slowly toward her cheval mirror, stopping briefly to slip her feet into a delicate pair of ivory kid dancing slippers before reaching it and raising her eyes to inspect what she saw.

The image that greeted her eyes was satisfying. While *Madame* Savronièrre, the French seamstress, had been distressed that she had not opted for the new mode, Brianna was glad of it. At the various visits at tea time during the past weeks, she had noted that none of the women in the area were wearing the new styles from Europe; they were too recent to have reached most people in America yet. And Brianna had noticed passing looks of envy on the faces of those she had greeted while wearing a *robe en chemise* on those afternoons. So the aborted wedding gown with its nipped-in waist, tight-fitting sleeves that ended in flounces of lace at the elbows, and wide, panniered skirts had, she felt, been a wise choice for tonight. She needed all the support and approval she could gain from her entrance into South Carolina society; jealous enmity on the part of the women she met hardly accommodated this need.

She gave herself a brief half-turn and back before the mirror, and saw the soft gleam of seed pearls embroidered along the hem of her gown as it swished softly about her feet. Glancing at the scattering of pearls Aimée had placed in the chignon atop her head and the single pearl at each ear, she was satisfied; whoever he might be, that nameless, faceless future bridegroom who perhaps awaited her downstairs tonight, he would not be disappointed by her appearance.

At this notion, her thoughts turned toward the real reason for tonight's ball. Allowing herself, for the moment, to suspend her waspish metaphor of the "meat market," she speculated on the possible outcome of this *fête* in her honor. Perhaps she *would* meet someone handsome and charming tonight who would also—miracle of miracles!—have respect for her need for some freedom within a marriage, someone who would not automatically assume a wife to be a mere possession without a mind of her own.

Suddenly the beautiful face in the mirror frowned. *Not bloody likely!* Brianna said to herself, picking up a phrase she'd overheard Isaac use once or twice. More likely, they'd all be stiff-necked bores, like that Thomas Clendenny, or Marietta Stokes' brother—what was his name?—oh, yes, Percy—or maybe they'd be handsome, but narrowminded and dense about women, like Geoffrey—

A knock at the door roused Brianna from her reverie, and she turned and called *"Entrez!"* thinking it was Aimée.

The door swung ajar to reveal the beaming figure of Father Edouard, dressed in his finest cassock, his huge head of red hair and beard obviously groomed with special attention for tonight's affair. He paused in the doorway when he saw Brianna and just looked at her for a moment.

"Brianna, *ma petite*, what a beautiful young woman you truly are," he smiled, a look of tenderness in his brown eyes. "I only regret your Maman and Papa cannot see you tonight."

Coming forward to greet him, Brianna returned his smile, saying, "Perhaps they can, *mon père*, perhaps they *are* watching." She rose on tiptoe and placed a soft kiss on the priest's cheek.

Clearing his throat with unusual fervor, the cleric took her by the hand and led her back to the cheval glass. Once he had her in place before it, he extracted a black, leather-covered box from somewhere inside his garment and held it out for her in one of his huge hands.

"This is for you, my dear. It belonged to your mother, along with some other pieces Simpson had been hoarding in your father's vault until you are married, but when I learned from Aimée, what you'd be wearing tonight, I persuaded him to pry this loose from the collection. Open it, Brianna."

Brianna looked at the box he offered for a moment. "But, Father, I had no idea. I mean, I've already received the amethyst—"

"Open it, *ma petite*, for the musicians are playing and you are expected downstairs soon."

Brianna took the proffered box and raised its lid, then gasped. There, on a cushion of black velvet, lay a single strand of graduated pearls, their soft luminescence enhanced by the room's generous candlelight.

"Oh, Father!" Brianna exclaimed in a watery voice. "They're so beautiful!" She reached for the necklace with tremulous fingers, adding, "But do you know what's even more special about them? I *remember* Mother *wearing* them!"

As Father Edouard helped her fasten the strand about her neck, Brianna continued. "There was a party here at the château one night, and because Deirdre and I had been especially good and helpful that day—well, for Deirdre it was *de rigueur*, but for me, no simple matter—we were allowed to stay up and watch until all the guests had arrived. It was so thrilling, you see, for us to see all the ladies in their beautiful gowns—and the gentlemen! Dressed like peacocks, they were, much more so in those days. But, most of all, I remember Mother as she stood beside Papa at the door, greeting their guests. She wore a deep brown velvet gown. Beside it, her hair shone like a fiery jewel itself, and at her throat were these pearls. And I remember telling her how lovely they were, almost like her skin, and do you know what? On my next birthday, she and Papa gave me these pearl earrings!"

Brianna gently touched one of the pearls at her ears; then her fingers went to the strand about her neck. At last, she turned to face the priest. "Thank you," she murmured as she wiped a stray tear from her cheek.

"Well," said Father Edouard, his eyes suspiciously moist, "what say you to being escorted downstairs, eh?" He held out his arm to her.

"We should go to collect Aimée," said Brianna, taking his arm.

"Already taken care of," the priest replied. "I persuaded Simpson to escort the little one downstairs tonight and informed her on my way up here. And since Jesse and *Madame* Mayfield are acting as host and hostess at the door, that leaves your poor old confessor to accompany you."

As she allowed the priest to lead her from the room, Brianna had a moment's unease at his last words. Father Edouard was, indeed, her confessor, and, yet, she hadn't been to see him for confession in weeks—not since . . . . She shut her mind like a trap, refusing to contemplate her transgressions tonight. Of course, there had been times in the past when she had confessed her sins and attended Mass elsewhere. There was a private chapel at the home of one of her parents' friends in Columbia, for instance, and she and her family had gone there on occasion when she was a child, attended by that old itinerant priest—what was his name?—Father Andrew, yes . . . but was Father Edouard reminding her in his own, non-scolding way, that she was derelict in her religious duty? Or did he assume she'd been to Columbia to care for her spiritual needs? Well, she told herself as the priest led her down the grand staircase, she couldn't allow herself to ponder all this tonight. Tomorrow, maybe, or the day after.

Brianna laughed breathlessly as she accepted a glass of champagne from Geoffrey Martindale who had stopped a passing footman as they left the dance floor and taken two crystal glasses of the bubbly liquid from his tray. Her green eyes sparkled as she smiled at the handsome young legislator over the rim of her glass. She was having fun tonight! Amazed at what others would have thought a natural occurrence for a young woman whose presentation ball was proving a superb success, she felt like pinching herself to see if she wasn't dreaming.

She watched Geoffrey's hazel eyes as they devoured her every movement under the reflected candlelight of the glittering chandelier. He was being very charming, really, despite his maddening adherence to inane small talk and compliments on her appearance. They all were, the dozens of men, young and not so young, rich and near-rich, that she had been dancing and talking with tonight.

Even the women seemed to admire and like her, although she'd been quick to catch a few envious stares here and there. Invitations had been generously extended by a number of very important matrons, several of them asking her to come down to the Charleston area where tidewater plantation homes would await her visits when her hosts and hostesses were in residence there.

The musicians began a minuet, and Brianna smiled apologetically at Geoffrey's chagrined look as Honoré Dumaine stepped between them, handed Brianna's champagne glass to Martindale, and ushered her back to the ballroom floor. As they picked their way through the carefully measured steps, Honoré gave her a disarming smile. *Why,* Brianna thought, *when he smiles like that, he's positively charming!*

"Enjoying your success, *ma soeur*?" Honoré queried as the pattern of the dance brought them near each other.

"Naturelment," Brianna nodded. Then, as she turned away from her partner, she caught sight of another ivory gown, its owner's dark head inclining coquettishly toward the man beside her. Laurette. And Jesse. Fighting to subdue the one wrong note that threatened the lovely melody of her evening, Brianna looked away. No, she would not allow those two to spoil things for her tonight!

Catching her movements, Honoré inquired, "Is everything well with you, Brianna?" His dark eyes traveled to where Brianna could see Laurette and Jesse dancing out of the corner of her own eye. "You are not upset, are you, that *Madame* Mayfield chose to wear a gown whose color duplicates yours?" He fell silent as the steps of the dance separated them again. Then, when they were once more close, he continued. "Although she must have known you would be in ivory tonight, *n'est-ce pas?* Of course, you have little to worry about with her for competition," he added. "She spends all of her time with *Monsieur* Randall, your guardian. She has little interest in your beaus."

Suddenly, Brianna no longer felt like dancing, though she didn't stop to ask herself why. She only knew her throat had all at once grown parched, her lips, dry.

"Excuse me, Honoré," she implored, "but would you mind if we rested and I had a glass of—of water?"

Honoré's eyebrows arched with a show of mild surprise. "Perhaps the champagne has gone to your head, *chérie*? But, of course, you shall rest." He took her arm and led her to a quiet corner of the ballroom, the only people nearby, a group of elderly gentlemen exchanging war stories. Looking about for a footman and seeing none, Honoré muttered something about how he would better train his own help and excused himself to find the requested glass of water.

Brianna looked out at the dance floor as she waited. She saw many couples whose acquaintance she had made previously, others, she had only met tonight. Far to her left she spied a vivid movement of purple silk and smiled. She knew Aimée was having a good time, and it pleased her. Suddenly, she saw Honoré moving across the floor. *He* was dancing with Laurette Mayfield! *Well,* she sniffed to herself, *so much for a loyal brother and my glass of water!*

She was about to find a footman herself when a male voice she recognized at once softly murmured from behind her, "You're stunning, you know, even when you stand there all by yourself, looking lonely, with a frown on your face."

She turned to face Jesse, who stood next to her with a glass of water in his outstretched hand.

"Your erstwhile sibling said you were in need of this," he offered, an enigmatic half-smile on the handsome mouth.

"Thank you," Brianna returned as she accepted the glass. "I appreciate it."

"Then why are you still frowning, sweet?"

"I'm not *frowning*!" she snapped with a frown. "And I'm *not* lonely!"

"But you *are* stunning," Jesse pronounced, the familiar mockery making his blue eyes dance with amusement.

"If you say so, *Monsieur*." Brianna raised her chin a haughty notch, refusing to acknowledge his teasing. Let him try his games on the widow!

"I do, and so, apparently, does every man here who isn't blind or in his dotage. Cheer up, my sweet, your evening is a huge success."

"Yes," sneered Brianna, "it shouldn't be long, now, before you're able to marry me off and rid yourself of that tiresome Devereaux brat. A huge success, indeed! Yours, most of all, I'll warrant!" She took a large gulp of water, larger than she'd intended, and instantly began to cough and choke on it.

"Now see where that fire-spitting temper's gotten you?" Jesse took the glass from her hand, placed it on a passing tray and resisted the urge to pat her on the back. When the choking and sputtering had subsided, he gently took her arm.

"Where are we going?" Brianna asked, feeling foolish, for they were obviously heading for the dance floor.

"I think it's about time we danced together, don't you?"

"Oh, I don't know. I hadn't thought you'd considered it, seeing how *engrossed* you've been all evening."

"I simply wanted to give you all the room you needed to meet the people you were supposed to meet tonight," Jesse answered.

Brianna wanted to reply with some barb related to the meat business, but the musicians had summoned up a lively reel, and there was suddenly no chance for conversation. Soon, as she followed Jesse's lead about the floor, however, Brianna found herself falling into the gaiety of the dance and several minutes later, when it was over, she was even laughing as Jesse led her to the side of the floor.

She chanced to look up at him then, and the look she thought she caught in his eyes was one she'd never seen before, but before she could puzzle out its meaning, his eyes shuttered and he was once again the Jesse she could easily recognize.

"This next tune seems a bit more sedate," he said. "Care to dance another, *Mademoiselle*, or is your temper going to vie with your feet again? Never mind," he added, "I think I've discovered the way to still that rapier tongue." He took her arm and led her out to the floor once more.

As Jesse and Brianna remained on the floor for a series of dances, two pairs of watchful eyes observed them.

"My dear Laurette," said Honoré to the widow as they stood at one end of the ballroom, "if looks were swords, the poor girl would be dead right now."

"What?" Laurette raised startled eyes to his.

"My sister," smiled Honoré knowingly, "you would have her removed, if you could, to clear the way for your—ah—affections toward her guardian."

Laurette gave him a coolly appraising look. "I'd assumed I was not *that* obvious, Mister Dumaine."

"Please, as I've asked you before, call me Honoré. And regarding your assumption, you are *not* obvious. It is merely that it has been, shall we say, in my own interest to observe a few things closely."

Intrigued, Laurette tore her eyes away from the striking couple she'd been following about the floor for the past twenty minutes and looked at him. "Meaning . . . ?" she inquired, removing an imaginary speck of lint from the skirt of her gown.

"Meaning," said Honoré as he took her arm and led her to an empty corner of the ballroom while looking casually about to determine they would not be overheard, "that I conclude I would not be wrong if told you of a plan I have that would serve both of us equally in a certain matter and enlisted your cooperation to put it into effect."

"Go on," said Laurette, her attention fully on him now.

"Fact number one:" said Honoré. "You desire a clear avenue for pursuing the wealthy planter from the Charleston area. Fact number two: I desire a clear avenue to an inheritance that should, by all rights, have been my patrimony in the first place. Fact number three: Brianna Devereaux stands in the way of both."

Honoré watched the widow's dark eyes and saw her nod of agreement, then continued. "Proposition: We see to it that the purpose of tonight's *fête* is thwarted, that my dear sister finds it suddenly impossible to find anyone who will marry her, and do it in such a way that, not only all the eligible men here will wish to avoid her—at least in terms of any honorable liaison—but, in passing, arrange it so that *Monsieur* Randall himself will have to stay away from her."

"But how?"

"Listen carefully, my dear Laurette. Already, the two people in question are spending, shall we say, an imprudent amount of time together?" Honoré gestured toward the ballroom floor where Brianna and Jesse could be seen enjoying yet another dance together. Laurette followed his glance and saw Jesse bend forward to whisper something in his ward's ear, saw Brianna dimple at the remark and then join him in a moment of shared laughter as they matched each other's steps in the dance. Frowning, she turned her attention back to Honoré.

"Suppose it should enter the minds of all the good, decent folk here, these pillars of Carolina society, that those two are something more to each other than guardian and ward," Honoré continued. "Suppose, once such suspicions are in place, the two should be seen disappearing from sight—simultaneously, and for a substantial amount of time, substantial enough to—ah—lend credence to certain rumors?"

"Do continue," said Laurette carefully, her eagerness betrayed only by a sudden light in her eyes.

"Well, my dear, you can guess the rest. Brianna will become a pariah whom no decent man will offer for. And once her reputation is compromised by her name being linked in such a nasty way with that of her guardian, the two will be forced to separate to try to preserve any of the shreds of her reputation that might remain—not that there will be any, once we have done our work!"

"Which is?"

"First, the rumors. You will circulate among the ladies; I, the gentlemen. Then, you will invent some excuse to call my sister away from here for a goodly amount of time. At the same precise moment, I shall contrive to have Randall summoned to another part of the house. By the time they return, more or less together, Brianna's reputation will be in shambles, Randall implicated in the process. Well? How do you like it?"

A slow smile spread itself across Laurette's carefully arranged features. "My dear Honoré," she said at last, "it is a plan worthy of genius." She raised an ivory and gold fan to her lips. "And now, if you will excuse me, I believe I have some important *news* to convey to some of the ladies." Nodding briefly to Honoré's courtly bow, Laurette turned and made her way to where some matrons representing the *crème de la crème* of Carolina society were gathered.

It all happened in less than an hour. In the ballroom, gentlemen previously engaged in discussions involving hunting or politics suddenly found themselves privy to the latest gossip. "Did you know," went the whisper, "that the beautiful heiress and her guardian are often observed spending a great deal of time *alone* together?" This, attended by lewd looks and suggestive intonations, was repeated in differently locuted wordings, from group to group. And among the various gatherings of ladies, the talk changed from the usual complaints over servant problems and the rising cost of French lace since the Revolution, to snide innuendo regarding the recent behavior of the beautiful daughter of the late Etienne and Aileen Devereaux. "If those poor, dear parents only knew what their offspring had become! Yes, she was convent reared, but, after all, when a young, inexperienced woman is placed in the hands of a handsome, unscrupulous guardian! Oh, yes didn't you know? His brother had a scandalous reputation for being quite the rake! And now— Well, blood will tell, will it not?"

While the rumors flew, no one noticed Mistress Mayfield slip away to the kitchens where she quietly instigated a quarrel between two scullery maids. But when Laurette returned to summon Brianna "as part of your training" to put a stop to the quarrel, a couple of whispers in the right ears saw to it that many noticed the Devereaux heiress disappear from the ballroom. Nor did anyone miss the simultaneous disappearance of Jesse Randall who withdrew to the library, to meet a friend of Aaron Burr's who, Honoré was careful to point out, was interested in forming an alliance with Jefferson supporters to thwart Hamilton and the Federalists.

When Jesse and Brianna returned to the ballroom, they were shocked to see many of the guests departing, some of them even changing plans that would have had them remain as overnight guests.

"Why is everyone suddenly leaving, and the hour not even near midnight?" questioned Brianna of Father Edouard. "And most of them have not even bid me good evening!"

The priest wore a perplexed frown as he heard her query, for he, too had—as who hadn't?—noticed the strangely emptying château.

Just then, Mistress Delaney approached, looking worried, a grim-faced Jesse Randall at her side.

"Father Edouard, Mistress Delaney and I would like to see you privately for a moment." He glanced at his ward. "Brianna, Aimée's been looking for you, and Simpson sent her to your chamber when you couldn't be found earlier. Would you see what she wants? The message was that it was urgent."

"But I—"

"This isn't just to send you out of the way, sweetheart," Jesse smiled. "When Mistress Delaney and I are through conferring with Father Edouard, one of us will come up and tell you about it, I promise. Now, will you go to Aimée?"

Although she'd been about to protest against the very thing Jesse had just denied, that she was being shooed away like a child who shouldn't be allowed to overhear, Jesse's unusual handling of his request, as if he were being sensitive to *her* feelings for once, had the effect he'd hoped for. Smiling at his gentle tone as much as at his words, she gave an acquiescent nod of her head and went to find Aimée.

When she had gone, Jesse turned to the housekeeper and said, "Now, Mistress Delaney, tell Father Edouard, if you will, of the smattering of rumors you've picked up from some of the servants tonight."

Chapter Twenty-Six

"I tried to find her and tell her of the rumors that were spreading last night, but when I did, she was nowhere to be found." Aimée stood beside Father Edouard in the library where the priest and Jesse had called a conference of those who might be able to shed some light on the disaster that had befallen the household during the ball the previous evening. As they awaited the arrival of Jesse, Simpson, Mistress Delaney, Brianna and Laurette, the two pieced together what they had learned so far.

"Mistress Delaney found out, early this morning, that Laurette Mayfield summoned Brianna away to the kitchens to handle a quarrel between Suzanne and Annette," said the priest, "but she says the two maids swear Laurette *arranged* their quarrel!"

"Arranged their—" Aimée's black eyes met Father Edouard's. "I begin to—how do they say it *à la anglaise?*—smell a rat!"

"Perhaps a *pair* of rats, Aimée," said the priest. "Jesse spoke last night of being drawn away from the ballroom at the critical time by what *he* swears was a ruse staged by Honoré Dumaine!"

"Ah! *Oui*, two rats!" Aimée agreed. "And fine company they are for each other, those two. And now what, *mon père?*"

"*Ma petite*, I have an idea whereby we may yet wring from the evening's disaster a fortuitous turn of events. Listen carefully, before the others arrive, so you may know what I intend and perhaps help me when the time comes."

The two bent their heads together and conversed in whispers for several minutes, before they were at last interrupted by the arrival of Jesse and Mistress Delaney with Brianna and Simpson a few feet behind.

Brianna was mildly apprehensive as she entered the library on George Simpson's arm. The solicitor had himself appeared on edge as he called for her at her chamber this morning, saying little beside the fact that a meeting was being held to "discuss matters pertaining to recent events." She had slept poorly last night, having gone to bed after a conversation with Aimée that had led to only one conclusion: the night of her grand ball had ended in disaster. Aimée's revelations, corroborated by a short visit from Mistress Delaney following *her* meeting with Jesse and Father Edouard, had made it clear that by now half the countryside suspected Brianna of having a compromising relationship with her guardian, and before long, the other half would likely believe it as well.

What was most unsettling to Brianna, however, was the *irony* contained within the concocted scandal. She *was*—*had been*—on compromising terms with Jesse Randall! Not that anyone other than Aimée, Jesse and herself was aware of this, she was sure. But to have someone instigate rumors based on lies which, in fact, weren't lies at all, was almost too much to contemplate calmly, and Brianna had to school herself to avoid an urge toward hysterical laughter that threatened to take over if she thought about it too much.

"I take it we are all here?" Simpson was saying as he helped Brianna to a chair.

"Mistress Mayfield was asked to join us," Father Edouard replied.

"Laurette sends her regrets that she will not be able to attend," said Jesse. "Her note said she has taken ill and cannot leave her chamber."

Father Edouard's eyes met and held Aimée's for a split second before he commented. "Ah, just so. It was to be expected, I suppose."

Jesse lifted an eyebrow at the priest's comment and came forward from where he'd been standing, near the door, and addressed the cleric in careful tones. "Not an idle remark, by my guess, Father Edouard. What prompted it?"

"I'll answer that in a moment, Jesse, but first, let me ask a question. Do you, or does anyone here—" The priest looked around at the room's other occupants. "—know the present whereabouts of Honoré Dumaine?"

"I learned, after riding into Columbia early this morning, that Dumaine has left for Philadelphia on a mission for Governor Pinckney," Jesse replied with a look of disgust. "It seems the coward appeared late last night at the Governor's door, anxious to be away on a trip that wasn't scheduled until several days from now. Perhaps it's just as well. In my current mood, I'd have dealt less than rationally with the blackguard."

Father Edouard nodded. "That news, too, comes as no surprise."

Brianna rose from her chair and approached the priest. "Father Edouard, I don't understand. Why—"

"All in good time, my dear," said the cleric as he motioned her back to her seat. "Now, to answer Jesse's earlier inquiry." He turned to the housekeeper who stood, nervously fingering her apron, near the door. "Mistress Delaney, would you be so good as to tell everyone here what you told me earlier this morning?"

The old Irishwoman smiled hesitantly and then embarked upon a reiteration of the tale about the quarrel between the scullery maids. When she finished, she was gently dismissed by the priest who then turned to the others in the room as they sat looking at him with varying degrees of shocked surprise, anger, or both, on their faces.

Brianna was the first to react. "That—that despicable woman arranged the whole thing!"

"Not quite," said Jesse with quiet disgust. "She had a little help, I'm afraid." And in a few short sentences, he explained his suspicions about Honoré, finishing with, "The man Dumaine introduced me to last night, may or may not have come from Aaron Burr, but it quickly became clear to me that he had nothing of substance to offer on the politics I've been involved in. It was obviously a ploy to get me away from public view and make it appear I was somewhere being indiscreet with my ward."

Only Brianna caught the fleeting glance he threw her, but in that brief second she knew he'd been thinking the same things she had. Again the urge to laugh at the bitter irony of their situation welled up in her, but she kept a tight control on her emotions and pushed it aside.

"But, I'm not sure I completely comprehend all the motives here," Simpson was saying. "I mean, Dumaine's actions, underhanded as they were, are understandable enough, but why would Mistress Mayfield jeopardize a rewarding position with us by instigating this terrible scandal?"

"Perhaps she was clearing her way toward what she felt was a much *more* rewarding position," Brianna remarked. She looked coolly over at Jesse as she spoke.

"Well," said Simpson, "motives aside for a moment, the fact remains, we have a problem on our hands, and what are we going to do about it?"

"Honoré's won," said Brianna flatly. "Only this morning, Prenshaw handed me a fistful of hand-delivered letters, each of them containing a barely polite excuse for declining a social engagement arranged with me this week. No one will want to marry me now. Honoré will get it all."

"I think not," said Father Edouard, who had been conferring privately, in whispers, with Simpson for a moment. "There is one possibility, the only one, as I see it, that may save the day—and your inheritance," he added, looking intently at Brianna.

"What is it, then, Father?" Brianna's voice took on a note of eagerness, a wide swing from the note of dull resignation that had characterized it moments before.

Father Edouard's eyes held hers for a long moment, then came briefly to rest on Jesse who now stood apart from the others, across the room, near a window; finally, they found Brianna's face again. "You will marry Jesse Randall—at once."

The silence that followed the priest's quiet statement seemed to scream in Brianna's ears. Incredulous, she stared at Father Edouard, then wildly cast about the room, seeking the faces of the others, as if asking them to confirm that she hadn't heard right. But Simpson and Aimée returned her look with silent nods, Aimée even smiling in a strange, enigmatic fashion. And Jesse! Jesse stood with his back to them, staring out the window, it seemed. Hadn't he *heard*?! Finally, Brianna's eyes returned to the priest. "You jest, surely," she said in a half-strangled whisper.

"Oh, no, my dear," said Simpson as he moved to stand beside the priest. "It's a very sound idea, really. A marriage between the two of you—the very *objects* of the scandal—would have the effect of all but stilling the wagging tongues. And it wouldn't have to be a *real* marriage, Brianna. Much as I deplore using the letter of the law, but not its spirit, I see this highly unusual situation calls for—er—highly unusual tactics. You would marry immediately, wait several months—until the talk dies down—then arrange, through Father Edouard and me, to have the marriage annulled. It's all quite simple, you see. A marriage in name only, to preserve a reputation unjustly besmirched. Brilliant, Father Edouard, simply brilliant."

At this, Father Edouard suddenly looked uncomfortable. "Yes," he said awkwardly, "well, I'm not sure the Church sees the arrangement in exactly the way Simpson has explained it, but, well, we won't quibble on the fine points right now. What about it? Brianna, Jesse, will you agree to the solution?"

"No!"

"Yes."

The conflicting responses, uttered simultaneously, came from separate parts of the room. As Brianna voiced hers in the negative, she turned to look at Jesse, then gaped with astonishment as she realized what he'd answered.

Jesse still stood at the window, but had turned toward them; his expression remained hidden, however, for the sunlight that streamed through the window hit his back, throwing his face into shadow.

Before Brianna could question him, however, Aimée rushed forth and took her by both hands, saying, "Oh, Brianna, you must agree! Don't you see?" she added in a whisper meant for her friend's ears alone, "Marrying your guardian will free you from the restraints of the will! You will no longer be forced to choose a husband you don't want, and Le Beau Château will be yours."

Aimée's reasoning, as she presented it, appealed so clearly to Brianna's sense of logic that she was forced to take a moment to consider her argument. Silently, she began to weigh her risks against what she might gain, but at that moment Jesse came forward and, stopping beside Brianna's chair, spoke to all of them.

"I think the proposal makes sense. It certainly would take the wind out of the gossips' sails to discover they were whispering about a liaison between a *husband* and *wife*. But, more than that, I'm agreeing to the idea because it was partly my fault the scandal came about."

As each person in the room suddenly focused more intently on what Jesse was about to say, Brianna knew a moment's panic.

Good God! Don't tell me he's going to confess our true liaison!

"If I hadn't heedlessly danced a number of dances in succession with Brianna," Jesse continued, "there would have been little to fuel the fires Honoré and Laurette started."

Brianna let out the breath she'd been holding.

"The least I can do," Jesse was saying, "is to give Brianna the protection of my name to make amends. I should have been the one to remind both of us that our society frowns on the sharing of more than one dance by couples who are anything less than engaged to wed each other, but since I was remiss. . . ." Jesse turned to look down at Brianna as she sat beside him. "I will require one thing, however, Brianna. I must insist that we remove to my home, Riverview, as soon as possible after the ceremony. I've been absent from my plantation far too long already, and I cannot delay my return any further."

"But—but who will run Le Beau Château while I am away?" asked Brianna as she weakly seized upon the first excuse she could think of to forestall the momentous event that she feared was quickly becoming a reality. They were discussing her *wedding* Jesse Randall!

"Why, those of us who ran it during your father's illness," Simpson replied easily. "And quite smoothly, too," he added, "if I do say so myself."

"And your removal to Jesse's home will aid in letting the talk die down," Father Edouard put in. "Out of sight, out of mind, eh?"

"What do you say, Brianna?" Aimée asked hopefully.

Brianna sat perfectly still for a moment and had a faint sense of impending disaster. It was all happening so fast! At length, she took a deep breath and fixed a steady gaze on Father Edouard. "Father, could you clarify the conditions placed upon the process of annulment by the Church, please?"

The priest returned her gaze with an uncomfortable look before clearing his throat rather audibly and then answering. "Well, my dear, I'm afraid you have me in quite a bind with your question. You see, as a representative of the Holy Church, I'm supposed to be acting in good faith when I perform a marriage ceremony. So, for me to prepare the prospective bride with instructions on annulment—well, my dear—you see my difficulty."

"Perhaps I can be of some assistance here," Simpson offered. "I've been party—on the legal end, that is—to a couple of annulments in my day, so if I do the explaining, Father Edouard will be freed of his—er—dilemma."

Brianna nodded to indicate he should continue, but not before glancing at Father Edouard, who had bent to catch a whispered message from Aimée.

"Well," said Simpson, "firstly, it might be adequately demonstrated that either one, or both, of the wedded parties entered into the marriage under false pretenses." Seeing the curious looks on his listeners' faces, the solicitor rushed to clarify his statement. "By way of example, let me cite the last case I was privy to. In that instance, it was discovered by the bride's family, only hours after the ceremony, thank heaven, that the groom's first wife was not dead, as had been supposed, but merely incarcerated in an asylum for the insane."

"Mon Dieu!" Brianna breathed.

"Of course, there were legal niceties involved which included the fact that the marriage would have been illegal anyway—bigamy, you know—but, nevertheless, the priest at the time felt the sanction of Rome was required because holy vows had been spoken."

"I see," said Brianna. "What else?"

"Well, barring such bizarre occurrences, there is the possibility that either the bride or groom was not of sufficient mental awareness when taking the vows. This could mean that the bride, perhaps, was too young to be considered sufficiently able to make such a decision for herself. I remember the case in which the parents of a twelve-year-old girl were able to—"

"Yes, yes, I see," Brianna interrupted. "Is there more?"

Suddenly George Simpson grew somewhat red in the face as he considered her inquiry. "Ahem—ah—well, yes there is. Ah—" He looked nervously at Jesse, then at the priest and Aimée before turning his attention back to Brianna, whom he at last addressed—as awkwardly as she could ever remember the man appearing in all the years she had known him. "The— the marriage must not have been consummated," said Simpson in rapid-fire fashion. Then, having said his piece, he reached in his waistcoat for a linen handkerchief with which he proceeded to carefully mop his brow.

"Consumma—*oh!*" Now it was Brianna's turn to redden. Embarrassed, and at the same time, furious with herself for causing the situation, she quickly rose from her chair in an attempt to cover her discomfort. "I see. Thank you, Mister Simpson."

Seeing her distress, Aimée came forward and laid a hand on her arm, saying, "Well, *mon amie*, have you decided?"

"Ah—just one more thing before you do, my dear," said Father Edouard as he came to join them. "For the reasons I've already cited, I think I must make one thing perfectly clear." Here the cleric looked first at Jesse, then at Brianna, with great solemnity. "If you should both agree, and I perform the ceremony, I shall be doing so in true fashion, following all the tenets of our faith and my calling. In my eyes, and therefore in the eyes of God, you will be truly wed. I can do no less."

As Brianna digested his words, Jesse, who had been quietly listening with little expression on his features to indicate what he felt during all of this, came forward and addressed Father Edouard. "I understand your position, Father, and I agree to the marriage."

Then the room went silent as all eyes fell on Brianna.

A dozen thoughts assailed Brianna's mind at once as she groped for an answer: Marriage—annulment—consummation—lust—love—freedom—Le Beau Château—gossip—holy vows—faith—they swam in her head until she thought it might burst. At last, she could stand it no more, and, looking around at the waiting faces, she gave them the answer she'd somehow

known she would—because she could summon no reasons for
an alternative. "Very well," she said quietly, "I agree."

Brianna wandered aimlessly about the area behind the stables, feeling herself in the throes of an indifferent, strange kind
of brooding. She knew she should feel relieved, now that the
situation had been resolved, but as she spent the time that
ticked steadily toward tomorrow's ceremony, she wondered at
the emotions that held her. There was a time, she realized, when
the idea that she should wed a man under such conditions
would have had her crying out to the heavens in protest, fighting with all available energies to resist the trap it represented,
for any marriage she had not chosen to enter into of her own
free will would have been seen by her as such.

Now, however, no such cries came. Only a dull, uncertain
sense of foreboding, that she was being carried along by currents whose origins she could not begin to fathom. Jesse Randall, of all men! Had it been any other, she felt she might be
able to take some kind of a practical position about the whole
thing, but how was she to position the presence of the man in
her mind when she wasn't even sure of her own reactions to
him? When he was the one person who continued to confound
her, rendering her unsure, so often, of who she was herself?

"How do, there, Brianna?" said a deep male voice she instantly recognized.

"Why, Festus! How did you know who it was?" she asked.
The big man came slowly down the path beside Serge's carrot
garden, a large hickory limb tapping the ground in front of him
as he walked.

"Ain' no gahdenias 'roun' heah fah's Ah knows, but yo'
puhfume always smell lahk 'em!" Festus grinned.

"You could smell my perfume from way over there?"

"Mo' dan dat, Ah 'specs. De good Lawd done gimme extra
smellin' t' make up fo' mah not seein'," he laughed. "An' Ah's
keen in de hearin' depahtment, too! Now, tell me, Brianna,
whut's 'mos a new bride doin' out heah muckin' 'round 'hin'
de stables?"

"How did you know I was 'muckin'?" Brianna asked with
a smile.

"Specs Ah *sees* some stuff othahs don' see, too," Festus grinned.

"Oh. Well, you're right of course. You see, it—it's a big step, the one I'll be taking tomorrow and—you've heard how it all came about?"

"Yes'm, guess Ah did," Festus replied, sounding slightly embarrassed. Then he brightened. "But, cheeah up, lil lady, ya'll be marryin' one of de bes' men ya'll kin fin'."

"Jesse is pretty special to you, isn't he?" Brianna asked softly.

"Special! He somethin' *mo'* dan special, Brianna. Why, Ah nevah met no white man—no, fo'git dat—Ah nevah met no man, 'cept mah brothah, Vulcan, dat could measuh up t' him! Brianna, he got strong an' sof' qualities all tied up t'gethah wheah it count, know whut Ah means?"

"Strong and soft?"

"Yes'm. He strong, all raht, lahk mos' men's 'spected t' be, but he don' min' usin' his heart when it count. Take him helpin' me wid dis silvahsmiffin'. Ah didn' even haf t' *aks* him t' unnerstan'. He *knowed*. Knowed all 'bout how Ah needed t' git me mo' freedom t' be mah own man." Festus shook his head in wonder. "Even mah brothah nevah seed thin's dat cleahly. Used t' jest laugh when Ah worried him 'bout wantin' t' do wuk whut didn' need his eyes, said Ah could always count on 'im. Whut wuz brothahs fo'? But see, Brianna, he couldn' see into de *heart* o' de mattah! Mistah Jesse—he *did*!"

Brianna continued to listen as Festus went on about Jesse, fascinated to hear about him from this unusual viewpoint—a point far removed from her own. He told her of his enormous respect for the man—and even love. This he found a remarkable thing—to love a white man—and wondered if he might not have trouble explaining it to his sighted twin when he returned to Riverview, though in the end, he felt, Vulcan would probably grow close to Jesse too. He saw Jesse as cut from a unique mold among men, white or black; he characterized him as having that rarest of combinations: male gentleness and sensitivity within a framework of strong inner resources. "He got de strenf t' be vulner'ble, Brianna," he told her, "but don' nobody go 'round mixin' dat up wid weakness!" Festus had laughed. Then he told her of how, since he'd known Jesse and traveled with him into Columbia and thereabouts a few times, he'd seen a few men make the mistake of confusing his sensitivity with weakness, and how they'd tried to take advantage of him for it, and each had come up decidedly short!

Finally Festus spoke at length about his new dream, silversmithing, and the freedom and independence it would bring. Then they talked together for a while about freedom and about love, too. Brianna told him about Sally Hemings, and Festus grew wisely philosophical when he'd heard her story, speaking of how freedom is always precious, but love has its own bonds, and of the difficulty of choices.

At last, Festus left her, saying he had to help Isaac prepare for the trip home, but not before wishing her happiness in her future after the big day tomorrow, "no mattah whut yo' choices is."

Left by herself, Brianna pondered the things they'd discussed, especially Festus' comments on Jesse. She realized she, too, had seen some of the things he'd cited in the man who was about to become her husband. She thought of the note she'd received from Jesse just a few hours ago, saying he was putting it in writing that, when they were married, he would lay no claim to any of Le Beau Château or her other holdings, that they were hers, and hers alone. It was a sensitive thing for him to do, to say the least, and by the act she'd begun to glimpse the man Festus had just described. And she'd seen evidence of the respect Jesse commanded in others, too. Thomas Jefferson had accorded him a great deal of respect, and must not her own father, a very exacting and demanding man, have been greatly drawn to Jesse, to have made him her guardian?

Then her thoughts took a different turn. Would she, too, fall under Jesse's spell? Had she, perhaps, already? Each time she had responded to him physically, when they had been— Suddenly, Brianna bristled. *No!* She must not let Jesse Randall get any closer—or even *that* close again! To surrender, would be to surrender her very *self*! She would lose her last hope for freedom and independence.

And, she argued, love did not enter into it. He could never love her anyway. He was surely still in love with Deirdre, so what would come of loving him? Only pain.

"No!" she whispered aloud. "I won't be fool enough to love you, Jesse Randall. I'd be lost, forever and hopelessly lost. If I must take you as husband to rid me of my present chains, I'll do it, but this, I promise: Wife or no, I'll wear no shackles!"

Laurette Mayfield tapped the well-manicured ovals of two fingernails on the desktop in agitated fashion as she leveled a cool gaze on the men across from her. "As I see it, gentlemen," she said in carefully controlled syllables that didn't quite match the dulcet tones she usually used, "there is no possible way you can dismiss me from this position before my year's tenure is up. This contract speaks for itself."

"But Mistress Mayfield," George Simpson protested. He threw a nervous glance at Father Edouard, who stood beside him near the desk, and then at Jesse, who leaned casually against the mantelpiece of the library's fireplace. "In view of the circumstances surrounding the ball last evening, and considering the evidence we have—"

"Evidence? Circumstantial clap-trap, you mean!" snapped Laurette. "No matter what you think, there is nothing you cite that proves anything at all. Those two sculleries are lying through their teeth because they resent me for the way I've forced Brianna to make them toe the line in their work. They—"

"Laurette." Jesse's voice carried clearly across the room's length as three heads turned toward the fireplace where he stood. Then he began to walk toward the desk, his gaze on the widow. "You were to receive ten thousand for your services, weren't you?"

Laurette's eyes flew briefly to the document on the desk in front of her, then to Jesse's face. "I was," she answered carefully, keeping her eyes on his face.

Jesse reached the desk and withdrew an envelope from his waistcoat pocket. He placed it on the desk in front of her. "This is a letter to my solicitor in Charleston, instructing him to place ten thousand on deposit in your name at the bank of your choice. It is yours if you agree to leave Le Beau Château in the morning, and not return."

"*You're* paying me? The—the full amount?" A thread of emotions flitted across Laurette's face. There was incredulity, then doubt, finally, anger. "You're paying me off! But *why*? I thought we—you and I—"

"Gentlemen," interrupted Jesse as he turned to the other two men, "would you be kind enough to leave us alone for a moment? There are some things I need to discuss with Mistress Mayfield in private."

"Yes, yes, of course," murmured Simpson, as astonished by Jesse's offer as Laurette. Father Edouard, who had had the benefit of knowing ahead of time what Jesse planned because they had discussed it on their way up to the library, merely nodded and accompanied the solicitor to the door.

"Meet us in the drawing room when you're through," said the priest as he closed the door behind them.

When they were alone, Laurette came from behind the desk where she'd been standing and angrily confronted Jesse. "Why are you doing this?"

"I might ask you a similar question, Laurette."

"But I should think it would be very apparent," she answered as she smoothly swept her gold velvet skirt to one side and half-seated herself on the edge of the desk. "At least I thought it was apparent," she continued, her voice grown suddenly low and soft. "I was under the impression that you wanted to spend more time with me, and I've arranged it." She slowly raised her dark eyes from under artfully lowered lashes and gave him a heavy-lidded appraisal.

Jesse studied her for a moment and then sighed. "It was a mis-impression, Laurette," he said tiredly.

"*Mis*-impression!" The heavy-lidded look gave way to wide-eyed astonishment. "After the way we—what we *were* to each other?"

Jesse shook his head slowly as he regarded her. "We were never anything more than a moment's flirtation, Laurette. No more."

"A moment's—! Why, you—!" Suddenly, Laurette stopped herself, visibly struggling to assume better control of her responses. At last she continued, this time, her voice sultry, smooth. "You bedded me willingly enough," she said, rising to place two hands against his broad chest. "Can you forget the time we spent in each other's embrace?"

"No," said Jesse quietly. "I'd be lying if I said so, but when it happened, there were no promises between us, though I'd also be dishonest if I didn't say it was not for lack of your trying." He took the hands she was slowly moving upward to his shoulders and removed them, adding, "Laurette, it was never my intention to go beyond a casual friendship. Even that night we spent in my room was your doing. *You* came to *me*, remember? You appeared at my door well after midnight, wearing only your dressing gown."

"And you accepted what I offered—freely!"

Again, the tired sigh. "Yes, I did, and it was a lovely interlude, Laurette. You are a beautiful woman and I—as you said, I accepted your offer of yourself freely. But now that's changed."

"Changed? How? The only thing—"

"I'm no longer free."

"In what way?" Laurette challenged.

"In the way that a man engaged to be married does not involve himself with other women. Laurette," he said quietly as he placed both hands on her shoulders and fixed his blue eyes intently on hers. "I wed Brianna Devereaux in the morning."

The gasp that came from her open mouth preceded a look of pure venom as Laurette took in the full import of his words. "That insolent bitch! You're marrying *her*!? I don't believe it! Why, she's nothing more than a skinny brat! She's no kind of a match for you! Why, that convent probably taught her to hate what she has between her—"

"That's enough!" said Jesse curtly. "I'll remind you that you're speaking of the woman I'm to marry."

"Woman! Childish twit, hardly out of the schoolroom, you mean!" Laurette hissed. "Well, my good sir bridegroom, you will not be rid of me that easily. What if I were to be with child as a result of the 'moment's flirtation' you spoke of so casually? Can you tell me that?"

Jesse allowed himself a brief half-smile. "As you might well remember, being the experienced woman you are, Laurette, I took careful precautions that night to ensure there wouldn't be any repercussions, but just so you won't take me for the blackguard you seem bent on making me out to be, I assure you, here and now, that if there should be a child, I will see that it has all it could need in financial care."

"But not your name!" Laurette cried.

"No, my name goes to Brianna. She has the greater need of it. You helped see to that."

Laurette raised her head and glared at him with all the ire of a woman scorned. "You will regret trifling with me, Jesse Randall. I suggest you take care, for I do not intend leaving your company until my year is up. And, as for your *wife*! She had better look to her lessons if she wishes her—"

"Have done!" Jesse approached the widow, and angry blue eyes pinned her where she stood. Softly, but with menace underscoring every word, he addressed her. "Hear me, Laurette. Brianna is to be my *wife*, and as such, she enjoys my *complete protection*. If you so much as allow a *whisper* of discomfort to touch her, you'll answer to me for it, do you understand?" And without waiting for her answer, he strode angrily to the door, opened it and left.

As Laurette watched him go, she began to seethe. "So you think to put me aside for that inconsequential tart, do you? Well, you've soon to learn I'll not be so trifled with, my handsome friend. You'll rue the day you ever spurned Laurette Mayfield, I promise you. And so will that green-eyed bitch!" Snatching her contract from the desk, her dark eyes spewing fury, Laurette slid noiselessly from the room.

Chapter Twenty-Seven

The wedding took place at ten o'clock the following morning in the family chapel at Le Beau Château. The bride wore her mother's wedding gown of faintly yellowed silk and Irish lace and was attended only by Aimée and a softly weeping Bridget Delaney as Father Edouard officiated. George Simpson gave the bride away, and Isaac and Festus shared the honor of standing by the groom.

It was a strange sort of celebration, with the groom notably silent, except for the necessary recitation of vows, and the bride behaving much as if it were something to be matter-of-factly gotten over with. Indeed, the only people at the ceremony who behaved as if it were a real wedding at all, were the housekeeper, the priest and the maid of honor, whose black gypsy eyes glowed as if with some deeply mysterious satisfaction, when anyone chanced to look at them.

After the rite was completed, all adjourned to the château's drawing room where Father Edouard produced one of his excellent brandies for a wedding toast. At one point, following the toast, Jesse asked the priest why, though the brandy was a fine one, it didn't compare in quality to the one they had shared on other important occasions, but the cleric merely smiled enigmatically and said something about their having to wait a while before there would be another uncorking of *that* remarkable nectar.

Then, following a tearful farewell between Brianna and Father Edouard, and Aimée and Father Edouard, and then another between Brianna and Mistress Delaney, they were off for Jesse's home near Charleston.

Included in the party, but opting to travel in the carriage by herself, was Laurette Mayfield. She had succeeded in staying on, though the relationship between her and Brianna had deteriorated to the barest of monosyllabic exchanges. Brianna braced herself for worse, however, realizing that, once they reached Riverview, she might well again find herself under the domestic thumb of the widow, the terms of the hated contract being viable after all.

The journey to Riverview proceeded without mishap, although there was one incident that served to relieve the tedium of long hours in the saddle. It was midafternoon of their second day out, and because the weather was fair, the travelers had elected to dine on the trail in picnic fashion, on some bread, cheese and fruit they had procured that morning from the host of the inn where they had spent the night.

They were just finishing their meal, with Jesse, Festus and Isaac standing near the horses and talking casually on one side of the carriage, Brianna and Aimée bundling up the remains of their repast on the other, and Laurette making ready to reenter the carriage. All of a sudden, there was a loud shriek as Laurette drew sharply back from the carriage's open door, whirled about and began to run in the opposite direction at a less than ladylike speed.

"Get it out of there!" she screeched at what had to be the top of her lungs. "Oh, I can't *bear* it! My clothes—the carriage— it will all be *ruined*!" Wildly, she looked about her, then back at the carriage. "Oh, there it *is*! *Shoot* it—*do* something I tell you!" This last was directed at the three men who, by now, had come round the carriage to see what was wrong.

Suddenly, Aimée, who, along with Brianna, had been following Laurette's behavior with alarmed interest, jumped up from the ground where she'd been kneeling and ran toward the carriage.

"Bon-Bon! Oh, what are you doing up and awake? Those herbs were to keep you sound asleep until we got there!" Reaching the open door, she bent to pick something up from the carriage floor.

"Are you *insane*?" Laurette cried at her from a position of some twenty feet away. By now the widow had stopped running and was holding a white linen handkerchief to her nose.

"You French *idiot!*" she continued, screaming at Aimée. "Don't they have *skunks* where you come from? Put it down before it—E-e-e!"

The source of Laurette's latest shriek was indeed a skunk—the very skunk Aimée had been holding, but which had now somehow escaped her embrace and was on the ground, heading pell-mell, straight for the widow.

"Bon-Bon, no!" shouted Aimée, and she took off after the small black and white animal as she called out to the three men to her left, "Don't shoot, gentlemen! He is harmless!"

What Aimée didn't realize in her excitement was that she had spoken this last communication in French, and Isaac, who had in fact come around the carriage wielding the musket that was always stored under the driver's seat for protection, was holding the weapon in a businesslike fashion. But Jesse had understood, and, signaling to Isaac to desist, began moving quickly toward Aimée just as the little gypsy proceeded to take a flying leap in the direction of the wayward animal.

"Bon-Bon!" she cried. "Ah! I have you!" Then, rolling over on the ground into a sitting position, legs outstretched, under her disheveled skirts, in a V, with a triumphant grin on her face and "Bon-Bon" safely clutched, Aimée called out to them, "Gentlemen—Brianna, I have him!" And this time it was in English.

Laurette, who, by now had maneuvered herself to a small stand of trees, thrust her head out from behind a young oak, waved her handkerchief at Aimée and shouted, "Who *cares* if you have him, you ninnyhammer! The *point* is, *not* to have him!"

Jesse had stopped in mid-stride when he saw Aimée's flying tackle, and now the spectacle on the ground, coupled with Laurette's ravings, became too much for him. He found himself bent over with helpless laughter. Brianna, who had also been in the process of pursuing Aimée, held her sides in mirth as she witnessed the debacle. Isaac, perceiving their reactions, caught the fever and followed suit, whereas Festus, who had seen nothing, but heard enough, stood beside him chuckling at the humor in the air, and besides, he had smelled not a whiff of skunk.

At last the laughter subsided and Jesse went to Aimée and helped her up from the ground where she too had enjoyed the joke. Then Brianna came toward them and peered at the small creature in Aimée's embrace.

"*How* are you *sure* he is *harmless*?" she queried. "I thought—"

"Aimée, what in hell is going on here?" Jesse interjected, but as he tried to assume his most severe tone, a damning grin forced its way to his lips and he threw up his hands in a gesture of mock disgust, adding, "It's been descented somehow, hasn't it?"

"*Oui, Monsieur,*" chirped Aimée, nodding her head avidly. "Bon-Bon is as harmless as a kitten!"

"And where does Bon-Bon come from?" Jesse inquired, again doing his best to look authoritative as he waved Laurette out from the trees. "It's all right, Laurette. This skunk has had its odor-producing abilities removed. You can come back, now!"

Aimée was reaching into her pocket as if searching for something important, but she answered Jesse's question. "Père Edouard had him from an Indian family he knows. He said he was carefully drugged and put to sleep and a—a surgery performed." She stopped, having apparently located what she searched for, and withdrew the object from her pocket. Tilting the skunk in her arm until its head was back, she slipped this into its eager mouth. "Bon-bons," she said matter-of-factly as she raised her head to look at Brianna and Jesse. "He love—*loves*—to eat them!"

"So the good priest has given us a parting gift?" Jesse asked.

"*Oui, Monsieur.*" Aimée produced another of the sweets and offered it to Jesse. At his negative headshake, and Brianna's too, she popped it into her own mouth with unabashed delight.

By now Laurette had emerged from the trees and, giving them a wide berth, headed cautiously for the carriage. But as she passed, she scowled at Aimée, saying, "Scent or no scent, that beast is not riding in this carriage with me!" Then she gave an elaborate wave of her handkerchief, lifted her skirts, and stepped haughtily into the vehicle.

As the carriage door thudded shut, Brianna's mouth broke into a wide grin. It matched the one Aimée was already sporting. "Not for all the tea the patriots dumped in Boston Harbor, would I have traded that spectacle, Aimée! Bon-Bon," she added, gently patting the inquisitive head that peeped out of her friend's arms, "you were perfection itself!"

"Perfection?" chuckled Jesse as he led them back toward their mounts.

"Of course. He could have chosen to follow anyone, but he chose Laurette! It was *perfect*!"

A pondering look that changed to one of pure inspiration crossed Aimée's features as she stooped to place Bon-Bon in the all-but-forgotten picnic basket, but no one saw it. Then, grinning deliciously from ear to ear, the little gypsy ran to catch up with the others.

They reached Riverview by late afternoon of the following day where they were greeted warmly at the stables by Vulcan Noslave. The sighted twin was then taken aside by his brother for several minutes, ostensibly for a private reunion, but Festus hurriedly took the moment to inform him of the unusual wedding that had taken place, this by prearranged planning between Festus and Jesse while they were on route. Then Festus returned with his brother, and Jesse made formal introductions between him and the ladies.

As Brianna heard the words, "my wife, Brianna Devereaux Randall," she gave a start before quickly extending her hand to the big black man. It was the first time she had heard herself called by her married name, and the words, coming as they did from Jesse's lips, had a disconcerting effect on her. In the brief moment she had to examine her feelings as she returned Vulcan's smiling greeting, she was assailed by an ambivalence that she was at a loss to identify completely. Commingled with an urge to deny the permanence of the appellation was a fleeting prick of pleasure at the sound of it, and it was this latter reaction she couldn't explain. But the moment passed, for Vulcan was busy informing them of the state of things with regard to accommodations at the Big House, something Jesse was anxious to know; he had told them earlier that if the furnishings weren't further along than when he'd left, he'd be taking them on to his brother's home instead.

"Mistah Jesse," Vulcan was saying, "dat Miz Christie done got a whole heap o' stuff in place while y'all wuz gone. De beds an' a mess o' chairs an' tables an' whutnot came all de way fum up No'th 'bout a fo'tnaht ago, an' she come ovah wid a mess o' womenfolk and dey bin sweepin' an' fussin' lahk t' beat de ban'!" The big black shook his head with wonder. "She sumfin', dat lady!"

Jesse smiled and nodded agreement, then turned to Brianna. "We'll have to take a look at the house to see if there's enough in place to make you all comfortable, and if it meets with your approval, you can move yourselves in, but, in any case, I think I'll be riding over to Riverlea to see Garrett and Christie and borrow a small staff of house servants from them until we can hire our own. Perhaps you and Laurette will want to handle that."

Laurette stepped forth and informed him that there was no "perhaps" about it; Brianna's training demanded the ability to hire and dismiss servants. Then she complained of how weary she was and insisted he accompany them to the house at once.

They took their leave of Vulcan who had followed the widow's statements with an expression of growing dislike, and as the group left, the big overseer was startled to see Aimée turn and throw him a grin and a wink over one shoulder. When she followed this by proceeding to walk behind Laurette and blatantly mimic her haughty stride, the huge man was forced to muffle his laughter in his sleeve.

A brief tour of the Big House confirmed Vulcan's estimation of the industriousness of Jesse's sister-in-law. As they walked through the spacious rooms, Brianna marveled at the beauty of the place, noting that, even though it was far from being completely furnished, the quality and design of its construction had been carried out with faultless taste, and knowing it was Jesse alone who had been responsible for this, she began to add some positive assessments of his abilities to what was becoming, she suddenly realized, an ever-growing list.

Aimée bubbled over with enthusiasm for the loveliness she saw, and even Laurette could not suppress murmurs of awed appreciation at the beautifully carved moldings, richly appointed wainscoting or varied examples of handsome paneling. Everywhere they looked, an architectural feast fed their eyes: Balusters ever-so-finely turned on an elegant sweeping staircase to the upper story; windows that were a testament to grace and light; floors that shone with the polished grains of only the finest hardwoods.

Jesse let them look their fill, himself pleased with the final results of his years of hard work, and he nodded with satisfaction at the various examples of exquisitely constructed furniture that had arrived in his absence from the shops of master cabinetmakers. Made in places like Newport, Boston, Philadelphia and New York, bonnet-topped highboys, delicate Hepplewhite pembroke tables and an assortment of fine cupboards, secretaries, beds and chairs met their eyes. They were made by men with names like Townsend, Frothingham, Seymour and Appleton, and their fine workmanship softly complemented the various corners and rooms where Christie Randall had placed them.

Satisfied that the women were pleased with the accommodations, Jesse left brief instructions with Isaac as to the installation of their luggage in specified bedchambers and, saying to Brianna he would leave them to their own devices for a temporary settling-in, left for Garrett and Christie's home at Riverlea, promising to return in time for dinner, which would probably accompany him.

True to his word, Jesse returned a few hours later, followed by a retinue of servants bearing covered dishes of food and the like as well as a landau carrying Christie with his young niece and nephew, and finally, his brother, Garrett, bringing up the rear on horseback.

As the small infantry of Randalls and their retainers invaded the kitchen and dining area, an excited Aimée burst into the large bedchamber where Brianna had refreshed her *toilette* and then tried to rest as she'd somewhat apprehensively awaited Jesse's return.

"Brianna! You must come downstairs at once! Nevair 'ave I seen such 'ospitality! Zere ees food—*everywhere*!"

Brianna sat bolt upright on the huge tester bed where she'd vainly been trying to nap for the past hour or so. She became instantly curious over what it was that could cause Aimée's stark relapse into such heavily accented English, for the little gypsy had proved to have an amazing ear for learning her new language, owing to a naturally inborn talent for mimicry. Smiling briefly at the appearance of Bon-Bon from behind Aimée's skirts, Brianna was further reminded that in the excitement of the little fellow's appearance on the trail, Aimée's relapse then had been into pure French.

"Well, tell me all about what's—and *who's*—down there, Aimée, while I straighten my gown a bit and fix my hair, and then, don't you think you'd better see that Bon-Bon stays out of sight for a while? I mean, if some of these new servants were to see him, it—"

"Oh, *oui, chérie*, Bon-Bon weel 'ave to go back to 'eez basket," Aimée answered as she bent to scoop up her new pet. "But, Brianna, eet eez not only servants zat 'ave arrived. Ze most beautiful woman—"

"Woman!?" Brianna interrupted with a frown.

"*Oui*, and—"

"Now, Aimée, calm down and speak more slowly. Your English is suffering! Now, what's this about some woman?" Brianna bent to peer into the looking glass above an intricately inlaid dressing table and hastily began to fuss with her hair.

Only then realizing how her English accent had been deteriorating, Aimée borrowed a trick she had learned from Brianna and took a deep breath to calm herself. Then she began to speak, slowly. "It—it is your husband's sister-in-law—and, I guess, yours too—who has arrived, *chérie*, but that is not all! The most beautiful man with her, *Monsieur* Jesse's brother, is here, too. Who would have believed there could be *two* of them so handsome!? And their little ones! Oh, you must come down and see them! Such adorable—"

Just then, a delicate knocking sounded at the door, and both women turned with surprise at the sound.

"Yes, who is it?" Brianna inquired as she quickly drew a brush through her hair and motioned Aimée to the door.

"It's Christie Randall. I hope I'm not disturbing you, but Jesse sent me up to see if you needed anything." Christie didn't add that if Jesse hadn't sent her, she'd have gone up anyway, dying as she was of curiosity, and anxious beyond words to meet the new bride whose strange marriage and attending circumstances her brother-in-law had carefully explained on the way over, although making her and Garrett promise not to let on to Brianna that they knew.

Brianna took one last anxious glance at the looking glass and signalled to Aimée to open the door. When she did, Brianna saw an incredibly beautiful, tall, slender woman standing in the doorway, a warm smile on her lips.

"Come in, please," said Brianna softly as she stared at the exquisite blond, although she was already privately noting that "blond" didn't adequately describe the magnificent hair that ranged from the color of winter wheat to shades of the palest flaxen, where it had been stunningly streaked by the summer sun. Wide aquamarine eyes met hers in a look that was open and direct, and Brianna knew that instant, that she would like this woman.

"I'm Christie," her sister-in-law said simply, and then added, "Why, you're *beautiful*!" A pair of dimples appeared in the heart-shaped face as Christie flushed lightly and reached for Brianna's hands. Taking them both in hers, she murmured, "Forgive my directness if it embarrasses you, and—oh, welcome to the family!" She pulled Brianna into a sisterly embrace.

Brianna returned this greeting with unthinking warmth, feeling a welcome and unexpected release from the tension she'd been fighting off all afternoon. Then, suddenly she realized that whatever befell her here in these unknown surroundings, she would have a friend, perhaps even an ally she could count on to help her through the difficulties of being an outsider, not to mention the problems that might attend her relationship with Jesse. Christie Randall was a woman close to her own age, and she had to *know* Jesse well! With a soft smile, she stepped back and met Christie's eyes. "I'm Brianna, and thank you."

"I've already met Aimée, here," Christie told her. "How wonderful for you that your friend could come with you all the way from France!" Suddenly, Christie gave a start. "Um—is that animal what I think it is?" She peered warily at the black and white bundle of fur wriggling impatiently in Aimée's embrace.

"Well, yes and no," Brianna answered hastily with an apologetic smile. "That is, yes, Bon-Bon is a skunk, and no, he isn't a skunk who can do what skunks do best."

Seeing Christie's perplexed look, Brianna, with Aimée's help, quickly explained the way things were with Bon-Bon and his installation into the household.

"I see," laughed Christie, "but, tell me, why does he seem so eager to meet me?"

"That, I don't know," said Aimée, eyeing the skunk who was, indeed, thrusting his nose inquisitively in Christie's direction and sniffing enthusiastically.

Just then, the sound of rapidly moving feet filled the hallway, and the door, left partially ajar by Christie when she'd entered, swung open to reveal a small, dark-haired toddler, about a year and a half old, who promptly ran to Christie with quickly moving, chubby legs and buried his curly head in her skirts.

"Adam, you little mischief!" Christie exclaimed. "What are you doing here without Millie?"

"I'm right behind 'im, Miz Christie," said a carrot-topped girl who approached the doorway. She was wearing servant's dress and in her arms she carried a peacefully sleeping infant in a soft pink satin blanket. "I'm sorry, ma'am," added the girl, who looked to be no older than fifteen or sixteen and had a bright, cheerful face decorated with endless freckles, "but he's been carryin' on like somethin' fierce, lookin' fer ye, and he just plumb outdistanced me after I got Marijen t' sleep." She moved toward the small boy who had taken his head out of the deep turquoise folds of Christie's skirts to peer impudently at her while she was speaking, but now reburied his face.

"That's all right, Millie," Christie said softly, "I wanted to have the children meet their new aunt anyway. Oh, and, Millie, this is Mister Jesse's new wife, Mistress *Brianna* Randall."

The carrot-top bobbed a quick curtsey in Brianna's direction. "Pleased t' meet ye, ma'am."

"Millie," Brianna smiled, but she was quickly diverted by a small voice.

"Mama, Adam eat good din!" chirped the toddler as he turned a beaming face up toward his mother.

"Oh, you did? You ate *all* of your vegetables *and* your fish, did you?" Christie asked him with a grin.

The small head nodded vigorously.

"Well, then, I suppose you've earned your treat," said his mother, "but, first, I want you to say hello to your new Aunt Brianna." Christie took one small hand and led him over to where Brianna had been standing, watching with a charmed smile on her face.

The tiny figure raised his head and appraised her with a pair of deep emerald eyes. Then he smiled, revealing a set of dimples, just like his mother's, in a heart-shaped face, and bent his short body into a perfect little bow. "Aunt B'ianna," he beamed at the lovely lady he saw before him.

"My son, Adam Jeremy Randall," Christie said with a soft, proud smile.

"How do you do, Adam?" Brianna smiled at the enchanting youngster. "I see you have green eyes, too, though they're a different shade from mine. And we both have dimples as well, just like your Mama."

Hearing his mother mentioned, young Adam turned to her and pronounced in very serious fashion, "Adam eat *all* his *fish.*" Then he held out his palm and gave Christie a hopeful look.

Laughing, his mother reached into a pocket that was so artfully sewn into the folds of her skirt, it had seemed invisible, and withdrew a small, plump bon-bon and placed it in her son's waiting palm.

Suddenly, Aimée squealed, "Bon-Bon, so *that's* what you were after!" She struggled to keep her grasp of the squirming black and white creature in her arms.

"Apparently he wasn't the only one who was after it," chuckled Brianna who then hastened to explain the source of the pet's eagerness to a bewildered-looking Christie.

Meanwhile, young Adam, greatly intrigued by the sniffing creature he saw the dark-haired lady holding, took a few curious steps toward Aimée. "Kitty," he gurgled around a mouthful of his partially consumed confection.

"No, this is no kitty," smiled Aimée. "This is Bon-Bon. Would you like to see him and help me feed him? He like— *likes*—bon-bons, too!" She looked at Christie. "May I take him back to my chamber with me, *Madame*? I was just about to feed Bon-Bon and put him—ah—out of sight for a while.'' She cast an appraising glance at Christie's expression. "Not to worry. Bon-Bon is harmless. He is just a baby himself.''

"Adam,'' said Christie to her son, "this is Mistress Aimée. Would you like to help her feed her pet?''

"Kitty,'' nodded the toddler with a cherubic smile; he promptly reached for Aimée's outstretched hand, and, together with Bon-Bon, they left the chamber.

When they had gone, noting Brianna's glance at the bundle the redhead held, Christie took the sleeping infant from the nursemaid, whom she dismissed with a smiling nod, saying, "And this is our daughter, Marijen.''

Brianna peeked at the sweetly sleeping face topped by a faint down of flaxen hair. "Oh, she's beautiful!'' she whispered. "And what a lovely and unusual name!''

"She's named after Garrett's mother and mine—Marianne Randall and Jennifer Trevellyan, as Adam Jeremy was named after Garrett's father.'' Christie looked up at Brianna from where she'd been gazing at the sleeping babe she held. "And Jesse's, too, of course,'' she added quickly.

Brianna's eyes met Christie's. "And *your* father . . . ?''

"Still with us, thank God,'' Christie answered. "Hale and hearty, and every inch the doting grandfather. We'll name the next one after him. Father's plantation is in Virginia, which is where I grew up, but he's so attached to all of us, he spends fully half the year on visits to Riverlea.'' Suddenly Christie grew somber. "I was deeply sorry to learn you lost your own father so recently,'' she said gently.

"Thank you,'' Brianna whispered, feeling a sudden rush of tears. Turning her head quickly to avoid embarrassing her new sister-in-law, she wondered why this mention of Etienne's death should suddenly move her so, after all these weeks. She had thought to be done with crying after the funeral, and now, here she was, helplessly moved by the briefest mention of his passing.

"It's all right,'' said Christie in a low voice full of compassion. "I found myself crying at the most unexpected times for months after Uncle Barnaby died.'' Seeing Brianna's query in the moist green eyes that now turned to her, she added, "He was Father's partner, but, oh, ever so much more to us than that. He was like a second father to me—my godfather, as well, and when he passed quietly away in his sleep about a year ago, it was truly like losing a parent.'' Christie shook her head sorrowfully. ''I was newly pregnant, and, oh, if it hadn't been for Garrett—''

At that moment, an enraged feminine voice cut sharply through the still open doorway. ''Brianna, I want you to come with me at once! That *beast* is still at large in this house, and for some perverse reason, it's taken to following me about whenever—well, well, well,'' purred Laurette in suddenly altered tones, ''if it isn't the Virginia Belle, herself!''

Both Christie and Brianna had whirled to look toward the door at the onset of the widow's verbal barrage, but now, while Brianna looked at Laurette with mere distaste, Christie's face held unmistakable anger as she gazed in astonishment at the widow.

''Laurette Mayfield,'' said Christie at last, through tightly clenched jaws. ''What brings you on the prowl in these parts?''

''You two know each other?'' Brianna's voice held open amazement.

''Not through any fault of my own,'' her sister-in-law replied with barely concealed contempt. ''Brianna,'' she said, blatantly ignoring the widow, ''what is *she* doing *here*?''

When Brianna had explained, in a few succinct sentences, the circumstances arising out of the now detestable clause in Etienne's will, Christie became furious.

''How dare they hold you to something like that, even now, after you're married!''

''They dare because *I* dare,'' Laurette told her. Then she turned back to Brianna. ''My dear child, I have already waited long enough idling words with you and Miss Trevellyan here—oh, dear, it's Madame Randall now, isn't it? Well, small matter. Suffice it to say, I am retiring to the drawing room right now to join the gentlemen for a glass of pre-dinner sherry, but if I do not hear that you have gone to do your duty by admonishing that miserable little companion of yours about the creature she's turned on the loose—by the time we sit down for dinner—I shall take immediate notice of it and put it into writing for your solicitor, Mister Simpson, to ponder.'' Then, in a whirl of crimson silk, Laurette turned and went back into the hallway, but before she disappeared, she threw a glance over her shoulder and said, "Look to your lessons, Mistress. Look to your lessons—or be sorry!"

"Of all the—" Christie fumed. "I'd hoped to have seen the last of that *witch*! Of all the wretched luck for you to wind up with *her* for a tutor!"

"How do you happen to know her, Christie?"

"That—that creature," said Christie, modulating her tone as she noticed her daughter begin to stir in her arms, "had a snare set for Garrett once upon a time. Oh, it was before we were wed, I'll admit, but that doesn't stop it from rankling. Besides it being under my very nose, in my own home, it was coupled with that same supercilious attitude toward me that I just saw her use with you. 'My dear child,' indeed! And did you hear her slip in that '*Miss* Trevellyan' just now?!"

Brianna nodded in disgust, recognizing the implied insult in the "Miss," if not the use of Christie's maiden name, for young women of marriageable age in the society of their time were addressed only as "Mistress," the term, "Miss," being reserved for very young female children or women of questionable repute.

"Brianna, if I were you, I wouldn't trust Laurette Mayfield farther than I could throw her, and, judging from the added half-stone or so she's put on since I last saw her, that would be an impossible feat altogether." Christie looked down at the now wide-open green eyes of the babe in her arms and watched the infant begin to root in the direction of her breast. "Oh, Lord, if looks as if she didn't get enough earlier. May I . . . ?" She gestured with her head at a blue-and-cream-striped upholstered armchair at one side of the marble mantelpiece across from them.

"What?" Brianna asked, perplexed, and then, hearing the soft sucking sounds coming from the blanket as Christie thrust her knuckle into its folds, she understood. "Oh, yes, of course. I didn't realize you nursed your own babe. In Paris I heard that ladies of quality—"

"Oh, in this country, too," interrupted her sister-in-law as she took the infant to the chair, "but I wouldn't have missed the intimacy of nursing our children for the whole world." She eased herself into the chair and began opening her gown which Brianna only now noticed had cleverly concealed ribbons tied under its fichu, which was also doffed. "And don't believe that nonsense about it causing a woman to lose her figure," she added as Marijen's tiny rosebud of a mouth closed over her nipple. "Garret said, after I'd weaned Adam, my breasts were firmer and prettier than ever." Suddenly aware of Brianna's blush, she hastily added, "Oh, dear! I'm sorry, Brianna. I just forgot that you were a new bride. I didn't mean to embarrass you."

"That's all right, Christie." Brianna fought to control the flush she felt spreading across her face. Then, glad to change the subject away from her newly acquired status, she asked, "What did you mean about not trusting Laurette?"

"Hmph!" Christie answered, the mention of the widow's name causing a return of her former annoyance. "I meant that she's a maneater, Brianna. She's on the prowl for a rich husband. I know, because after she had to give up on Garrett, she even pursued my father for a while! And I wouldn't put it past her to go chasing after a married man, either. Why, look, right now she's downstairs with our husbands!"

A startled look crossed Brianna's face. *But mine's not a husband, in earnest.* Glancing at the lovely blue and cream porcelain clock on the mantel to see how much time she had before dinner, she made up her mind to something she'd been considering doing almost since the first moment she and Christie had begun to become acquainted.

"Christie," she said tentatively, as if feeling for the right words, "I think there's something you should know about me before things go any further, something about me and Jesse." And in a few carefully worded sentences, she told her about her temporary marriage of convenience. "So you see," she finished, almost apologetically, "I really shouldn't need to worry about Laurette's being a husband snatcher at all. I mean . . ." She gave a small shrug. "I mean, it's not as if Jesse and I were really married, you see."

Christie looked at her with eyes that spoke of admiration and respect. She was glad Brianna had chosen to be open with her about the circumstances she already knew, but, of course, wasn't about to say she knew. She realized how much it must have cost her to reveal her secret to someone she'd barely met. To Brianna she said, "I admire your courage in being frank with me. It cannot have been easy for you. As for your situation, never think that it will alter how I feel toward you. I liked you the instant I entered through that door, Brianna, and I have every hope that we may become fast friends—because of who *we* are, and for no other, far less important, reasons!"

Brianna let out the breath she hadn't realized she'd been holding ever since she'd finished her explanation. She smiled at the woman nursing the contented infant in her arms. "I liked *you* the moment I met you, Christie Randall, and I'd be pleased to become your friend." She glanced again at the clock. "Oh-oh! Please excuse me, now, would you? I've got to go to find Aimée and pretend to scold her. I'll see you at dinner in about ten minutes!" A smile of warmth passed between the two women. Then Brianna picked up her skirts and sailed through the door, her heart somehow lighter than it had been in days.

The warm glow of candlelight bathed Christie's face in softness as she turned contentedly in her husband's arms, while outside their bedroom window, crickets chirped their insistent farewells to the warm season. Garrett smiled lazily as he traced soft little circling patterns over his wife's lush breasts.

"Penny for your thoughts, love," he drawled as he pressed warm lips to her temple.

Christie sighed. "You always know when my mind's far away, don't you?" She smiled tenderly up at him.

"Let's say I just make it my pleasant business to know my wife," he returned warmly.

"In more ways than one."

Grinning, Garrett gave her a playful pat on her beautifully rounded, bare little *derrière*. "Naughty puss!" Then his look became serious. "But, seriously, sweet, what's amiss?"

Again, a soft sigh. "Oh, it's nothing too serious, darling. It's just that, after these wonderful hours together this evening, I couldn't help wondering about another husband and wife, and what's going on in *their* bed tonight—or *isn't* going on, I'll warrant."

"You mean Jesse and Brianna."

"Yes. Oh, Garrett, they're both such fine people! They deserve something better than this—this marriage that isn't a marriage!"

"Yes, I know what you mean." Garrett sat up in the bed and looked carefully at his wife. "You're already quite fond of Brianna, aren't you?" Watching her nod, Garrett continued. "Well, after meeting her, I have to say I'm impressed, too. Not only is she quite a beauty—though not nearly as beautiful as my wife," he added, tapping the tip of her nose with his forefinger, "—but the girl has substance—and a hell of a lot of spirit, too, I'd wager. I saw it in those eyes of hers, not to mention some of the things she talked about at dinner."

Christie chuckled, "Can you imagine the uproar that would have ensued at any other than a Randall dinner table when she spoke of blacks and women getting the vote someday?" She focused wide turquoise eyes innocently on her husband. "Not that I found it such a wild idea myself, you know."

Garret grinned, refusing to rise to her bait. "Leave it to the Randalls to wed a pair of radically liberal females!"

Christie frowned. "But that's just it. Jesse isn't really wed to Brianna."

"Oh, don't be too sure of that, love," Garrett said to her as he bent to take her hand and nibble at its fingertips.

Christie rose up on one elbow and carefully scanned his face. "What do you mean?"

"I mean that Jesse's in love with the wench."

"He *told* you that?!"

"Oh, no—not Brother Jess—not in so many words, he didn't, but Christie, he's my brother, remember? I know him better than he knows himself in some ways, and right now I'd say that my brother has fallen—and fallen hard."

"What makes you say so?"

"Oh, all the noises he's been making about what a nuisance the chit is. When we were alone together, he couldn't rant on and on about her enough. Now, I *know* him. If Jesse didn't care about her, he'd hardly have mentioned her between us. He's that way. No, take my word for it, sweetheart, he *cares*!"

Christie considered his words for a moment as she absentmindedly played with a whorl of hair on Garrett's chest. "Well, if you're right," she said at last, "then what worries me is how

Brianna feels about *him*. You wouldn't care to offer any conjectures on *her* heart's involvement, would you?''

Garrett's right eyebrow rose at a jaunty angle as he gave her a questioning look. ''You expect me to read the thoughts of *that* free spirit?'' He shook his head. ''That's one little keg of gunpowder I'd just as soon stay away from. The wench is young, Christie, far younger than you at the same age, if you take my meaning. She's got a bit of growing up to do yet, love, and, the way I figure it, she won't know herself how she feels until she does.'' He chuckled softly and shook his head a second time. ''Poor Brother Jess! I wouldn't want to be in his shoes right now for anything.''

''Oh? And where would you want to be?'' asked Christie as she ran a slender forefinger lightly across his hard, well-muscled abdomen.

''Just where you have me!'' growled her husband as he reached and drew her boldly to him.

As Christie watched his green eyes begin to grow dark with passion, she whispered throatily, ''Which is where you'll always have me!'' And as they came together, all thoughts of other husbands and wives fled their chamber for the night.

Chapter Twenty-Eight

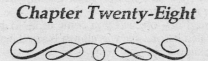

Brianna paced the expansive length of the bedchamber for the fourth time in as many minutes before catching herself and stopping to scowl at the clock on the mantle. Five to nine, and still Jesse hadn't come. Peevishly, she glanced at the thin ribbon of light under the door she had learned earlier led to an adjoining bedchamber. She'd opened it to discover a chambermaid preparing the room, as for someone's imminent occupation, but when she'd asked the girl who was to occupy it, she had only shrugged, saying she was from Riverlea and knew nothing of the inhabitants of Riverview.

Whirling about in a fit of exasperation, Brianna went over the possibilities for the umpteenth time in the last hour or so. It wasn't for Aimée, for she'd already visited the comfortable chamber across the hall where her friend had been happily ensconced; and Laurette's room was down the hallway some distance.

Pacing the length of the chamber yet a fifth time, Brianna turned her mind to the real source of her consternation: her discovery after dinner, when Garrett's family had left for home—Jesse had walked them out to the stables, and she had come up here to retire—that this was the Big House's *master suite*!

Silently, she fumed as she reexamined this discovery. *He's installed me in here just as if I were a real wife! And now, more than two hours after I sent that chambermaid to tell him I wished to see him about it, he bides his insufferable time somewhere and—*

A knock on her outer door broke her reverie. "Brianna, are you still awake?"

Brianna whirled from the window where her pacing had led her. "Jesse Randall, of course I'm awake, as who shouldn't be, after sending for someone to come and see her?"

"Well, may I come in then?" came the impatient response. "I mean, are you decent?"

"Of course, I'm—oh, *will* you come in?!" If Brianna had been exasperated before, she was almost beyond her limits now, and her tone showed it.

The door opened to reveal her husband—*husband in name only,* she reminded herself for, it seemed, the hundredth time that day alone—wearing the same clothes he'd worn to dinner, minus his jacket and cravat. Tall and handsome as ever, he wore a dazzling white dress shirt open at the throat, creating a marked contrast with the deep bronze color the sun had given his face and neck; tight formal breeches of a dark blue hue hugged his narrow hips and muscular thighs, and the ever-present high black riding boots were in place. The utterly masculine picture he presented nearly took Brianna off-guard with its impact; with difficulty she suppressed a gasp, then turned away to cover her reaction.

"I've been waiting for you for over two—"

"I'm sorry about that," Jesse cut in as he closed the door quietly behind him, "but Isaac and Vulcan noticed a problem with the axle of your carriage and asked me to take a look at it when I was seeing Christie and Garrett off. When I received your message, I was on my back, under the rear wheels, and in the midst of solving the problem. Again, I apologize, but you have my complete attention now."

Noting his shutting of the door with a wary eye, Brianna turned to face him; she saw, upon closer inspection, he, indeed, had smears of axle grease and bits of straw on his clothes and hands, and she started to soften her tone when the remembrance of why she'd asked him here fired her anew.

"I just learned this evening, from one of the Riverlea staff, that this is the master suite," she said, indicating the handsome room and dressing alcove decorated in cream and varying shades of blue. "Is that correct?"

"It is," said Jesse quietly.

"But why have you installed *me* in it?"

Jesse's expression revealed nothing as he answered her. "Because you are the mistress of the house."

Brianna's eyes widened at the inadequacy of his response. "But not in the usual sense! I mean, and I'd hoped I'd never have to remind you, that I am only temporarily—"

"Temporarily my wife. Yes, madam, I more than recall the arrangement, but the fact remains that we shall be living under this roof together for some time, and there will be others about—servants and whoever—and I thought wagging tongues were what we wished to *avoid*."

"But—"

"*Where* would you have had me put you?" queried Jesse, his ire beginning to rise, "in the servants' wing? Woman, what is your *problem*?"

Thinking at that moment of exactly what her problem was, Brianna felt herself begin to blush, but she answered him anyway, with steadfast green eyes. "The problem is the sleeping arrangements! I won't—"

She was interrupted by a bark of laughter, before Jesse queried, "Is *that* what you were worried about?"

Now it was Brianna's turn for rising ire. Stamping her foot, she hurled at him, "And why shouldn't I be? I have no intention of sharing a bedchamber with you like a true wife, and—"

"Cease your worrying, then." Jesse's tone had grown suddenly calm. "My dear Brianna, I have no intention of joining you here." Seeing her astonishment, he continued. "My room is there." He gestured at the interior door with the faint sliver of light coming from beneath it. "I regret the shared door, but it was the only room, after Laurette and Aimée were given theirs—and you, yours—that had adequate furnishings at this point. It adjoins this one because I had it designed with the idea that it would one day become a lying-in nursery where a 'true wife' of mine would wish easy access to a babe that was new-born and needed frequent nursing. And, frankly, it simply didn't occur to me that you would assume the *sleeping arrangements* were otherwise, or I'd have told you sooner." This last was uttered with a decidedly derisive tone, its irony clear.

Brianna found herself blushing even further under his regard and started to stammer an apology, but Jesse cut her off.

"Now, was there anything else you wished to see me about?" Seeing her silent headshake, Jesse reached into a pocket and withdrew something which he then held out to her. "The key to that door there, madam," he said as he put the object in her hand, "to protect your virtue." And with a bow as mocking as his tone, he turned and left the chamber.

The shape of things at Riverview began to take some definition for Brianna as the days passed and she and her party settled in. As she had expected, Laurette continued to be a thorn in her side, for, with her supercilious manner and the weight of Etienne's will and her contract behind her, the widow lost no opportunity to burden the Devereaux heiress with countless orders regarding domestic tasks to be seen to. Her haughty ways were curtailed sharply, however, Brianna quickly noticed, whenever Jesse was present.

One of the chief surprises of Brianna's new lifestyle came about through Jesse as well. On her second day in residence, he met her at breakfast and presented her with complete authority to finish decorating Riverview's Big House. This he accompanied with a more than generous amount of funds, put at her disposal to "complete the work in proper fashion," adding that she need consult Laurette only when she felt she needed to, and that, if she had any questions or problems, she should "feel free to see me about them." Brianna accepted the task warily, quick to note he was entrusting her with a major responsibility.

On the other hand, once she began to become involved in the selection of fabrics, wallpapers, china patterns and carpet styles, from the parade of merchants and importers that started to appear in a seemingly unending stream, straight from Charleston, Brianna soon felt the excitement of a challenge and fell into the activity with energetic enthusiasm.

As for her contact with her husband, Jesse was true to his word; the door between their chambers remained locked, with nary an exchange spoken between the two of them at bedtime, although Brianna often found herself staring at the narrow strip of light coming from under their adjoining door as she tossed and turned in the big pencilpost bed in her chamber, sometimes far into the night. At these times she would wonder where he was that kept him so late, but she never asked him about it. She was, moreover, troubled more than once by that strange dream about the eagle, fears of its recurrence being the main source of her restlessness at night.

During the days she noticed Jesse's work on the plantation kept him out of doors almost all of the time, intermittent appearances at meals being the only exceptions. Also true to his word, he made arrangements with his solicitor in the city to send a swarm of candidates for the staff positions at Riverview, and, one by one, the interim servants from Riverlea were sent home, replaced by people Brianna herself had chosen, although her satisfaction in assuming this responsibility was frequently marred by the almost constant surveillance of Laurette Mayfield.

But Jesse was always courteous to her when they spoke, his manner considerate and even solicitous as he sometimes asked her how she was faring and whether he could be of any assistance in helping her run things inside the Big House. And when he occasionally even complimented her on the decor of a particular room he knew she had worked on, Brianna began to wonder if she hadn't misjudged him somewhat in the past. Perhaps, she told herself, when he had been away from home, operating under the double strain of the directives of Etienne's will, just as she had, and the vagaries of pressure from his government business, he had not been entirely himself. Of course, she hastily added at these times, she was not going to make the mistake of entirely dropping her guard around the man who was now her legal husband. Too much water had passed under their mutual bridge for that!

One day Brianna was finishing her breakfast chocolate alone; Aimée had excused herself earlier, saying, somewhat mysteriously, she had business down at the stables, and Jesse had disappeared even earlier, sending word through Isaac that he would not be breakfasting with them. Just then, Jesse appeared in the doorway with a smile on his face.

"I see you've eaten, Brianna, and I was wondering if you'd have some time this morning to accompany me. There's something I'd like to show you."

Noting the unexpected warmth in his bluer-than-blue eyes, Brianna assented readily, but as she allowed him to lead her out, stopping briefly to place about her shoulders her light-weight cloak he'd already sent one of the servants to fetch (the fall days had begun to grow considerably cooler, although there was still an abundance of sunshine), no amount of question-ing on her part could pry from him the nature of their excur-sion out of doors.

When Brianna at last saw that he was leading her to the sta-bles, she began to grow even more curious, wondering if he had a journey in mind. But Jesse continued taciturn as he escorted her through the stable's main wing, and there remained about his mouth the suggestion of a smile.

At last he led her through a rear door, into a small court-yard that abutted a fenced-in area where they stopped; Brianna looked out at the paddock and gazed upon the most beautiful horse she'd ever seen. He was a lovely light shade of dappled gray, with much deeper gray coloring on his nose, ears and lower legs, though his mane and tail were white. He had the delicately chiseled head that signaled Arabian ancestry, al-though his size—over seventeen hands, she guessed—indi-cated other lineage as well, and the length of his legs told her this might include thoroughbred breeding. The colt arched his graceful neck and pranced excitedly, then nickered softly and trotted over to the fence when he saw Jesse.

Brianna looked to see her husband smiling down at her. "Meet Lightning," he said to her.

"Oh, Jesse, he's magnificent!" she breathed as she took a few careful steps toward the fence. As she started to reach her hand out slowly to touch the velvety nose that was now thrust inquisitively in her direction, she turned to Jesse over her shoulder and asked, "May I? I mean, is it safe? Is he gen-tled?"

"Go ahead," answered Jesse as he came to stand behind her. "He wasn't completely broken to saddle and bridle before I left for Columbia, but he's always had the best of dispositions, and now he's well-schooled as well. He learns unbelievably fast, but, I'll admit, I've spent almost all my waking hours training him these past weeks since we arrived."

Brianna reached out and stroked Lightning's soft nose, then laughed softly when he began to nuzzle her palm as if searching for something.

"Oh, Jesse, look! I'll bet he'd like a piece of that sugar cone I saw in the kitchen. If only you'd told me, I could have—" She peered intently at him for a moment. "Why *did* you maintain all that secrecy about showing him to me?"

Nodding to two grooms who suddenly appeared with a side-saddle and other tack, Jesse gave her an even broader smile. "That would have spoiled the surprise of my gift."

Brianna's jaw dropped as she stared at him, wondering if she'd heard right. "Did you say *gift*?" she finally whispered.

"Lightning is yours, Brianna." The smile continued, deepening the two grooved, dimples in his handsome face. "That is, if you want him."

"*Want* him? Oh, Jesse," she exclaimed as she turned and exuberantly threw her arms about his neck in an unthinking gesture of appreciation, "he's the most *wonderful* present I could ever *think* of! Thank you, thank you so *much*!"

Jesse's laughter was soft as he hesitated a split second, then caught her to him in a reciprocal hug. "I'm glad you like him, sweetheart," he murmured before releasing her and looking down into her upturned face. What he saw there made him catch his breath for a silent second. Her eyes, wide with joy, and suffused with a light that rendered their color an almost indefinable shade of green, were sparkling as they met his, making her whole face a study in childlike delight. Never had he seen her meet his regard so openly, and he had, for the first time, a sense that here he was seeing a Brianna he had only from time to time glimpsed before.

Brianna continued to meet his gaze with open wonder, a wellspring of sheer happiness bubbling up inside her and flooding her whole being, and they stood there like that for several seconds, as if they dared not speak and break the spell.

But the moment was suddenly shattered as one of the grooms who had been saddling Lightning called out, "He's ready, Mister Jesse."

Turning in the direction of the paddock, Jesse murmured his thanks to the man, then took Brianna's hand, saying, "Well, come on. Let's get you mounted." He began to lead her back into the stables.

"But-but, I've no proper attire for—" Brianna began to protest.

"You will in a moment," said Aimée's voice, and Brianna looked up to see her friend advancing toward them with Brianna's russet velvet riding habit draped over her arm. Aimée grinned as she added, "This was even worth wolfing down my breakfast for, *chérie*. You can change in the tackroom."

"It was a conspiracy!" grinned Brianna, as she happily followed Aimée. "And it's not even my birthday!"

"Speaking of which," called Jesse, "just when *will* you turn eighteen, Brianna?"

There was just enough time for Brianna to throw him a dazzling smile and answer, "Why, the second of April, of course! My mother had just five minutes' leeway to ensure her offspring would be no April fool!" Then Aimée whisked her through the tackroom door, leaving Jesse standing alone outside.

"Of course," he murmured to himself with a smile, savoring, without thinking on it, the smile she had just bestowed on him.

Minutes later, Brianna emerged from the tackroom fully outfitted for riding, and a short time after that, Jesse helped her mount her new colt and joined her, on Gypsy, for a ride.

Soon after they had started out, Brianna noticed a stronger-than-usual companionship that seemed to exist between the two horses and mentioned it to Jesse.

"Yes, they are close," Jesse told her, "and there's an unusual story behind it."

"I'm all ears," said Brianna, feeling curiously at ease as she rode beside him, and, indeed, as she had since he'd come for her after breakfast. Of course, she told herself, her own mood was excellent, as whose wouldn't be, having received such a splendid gift. As soon as they had left the paddock, she had gone about putting Lightning through all his gaits, and the butter-smooth perfection of his responses had told her not only of the superior quality of the gray colt, but of the excellence of his training.

"Well," Jesse was saying, "Lightning is what one might call Gypsy's adopted son."

"Adopted?"

"Yes, you see, a little over a year ago, we bred Gypsy to that magnificent stallion you've seen my sister-in-law riding."

"The gray—Thunder?"

Jesse nodded. "The breeding was successful, but there were complications during the delivery, and I'm afraid the foal didn't survive." Jesse stopped as he noted the look of compassion that flooded Brianna's face at this news, her eyes, a soft green now, resting tenderly on the mare at her side.

"At the same time that Gypsy went into labor," Jesse continued, "Charles Trevellyan, Christie's father, arrived from Virginia with a problem on his hands, a yearling colt who had arrived from some Arabian sheikdom, along with the dam who foaled him; but the mare died two days after leaving their ship, and since the colt had never been separated from its mother during the long voyage to these shores, he went into an extraordinary bout of mourning."

"The colt was Lightning?" Brianna asked.

"Yes, and when Charles brought him to Riverlea in desperation, hoping to consult with me and my brother on what to do, the colt was just a bag of bones from refusing to eat. We were just about to try force-feeding him—not a pleasant prospect— when Gypsy here, who was also grieving, somehow took to the youngster, even though he'd been weaned, and began to mother him. After half a day in the same paddock together, both of them began to recover—fast, and while they're no longer inseparable, as they were for the first few weeks, Trevellyan thought they ought to remain near each other and offered Lightning to me—no, that's not exactly right—he refused to take him back, actually, said his only payment was seeing the colt restored to health."

"He sounds like a lovely person," Brianna commented.

"To be sure. I hope you'll have the chance to meet him one of these days. I'll be writing to tell him whose horse Lightning is now, and that might please him, too."

"Oh?" Brianna smiled. "Why is that?"

"Because, from what I've heard, his daughter, Christie, has grown wonderfully fond of you, and she's sure to have told

Charles about you in her letters. And Lightning is a full brother to her stallion, Thunder."

"Oh," said Brianna, who had just been about to ask him about the source of the gray colt's name. "So Lightning followed Thunder. But, Jesse, in nature, isn't it the other way around? I mean, during a thunderstorm...."

Jesse smiled as he heard her questions and attempts at reasoning in fathoming out natural science. It was unusual to see such intellectual curiosity in one so young, let alone a female, and, although he knew many men who would feel threatened—or worse, *amused*—by it in a woman, he found himself strangely pleased. Indeed, he began to realize as the day wore on, there was a whole host of surprising discoveries emerging where Brianna was concerned, facets of her character and individuality that crept into his awareness and provoked a growing admiration he couldn't fail to acknowledge.

It was odd, he thought, that they should have spent the whole time, prior to coming to Riverview, engaged in a kind of undeclared warfare—or, at best, a contest of wills—never taking the time to get to know each other in terms of the positive qualities each had to offer, and that only now, through a situation made possible by this strange marriage, were they perhaps really able to take each other's true measure. He was tempted to speculate on whether it would all end with the annulment he knew never to be far from Brianna's thoughts, but he put this temptation aside, refusing to let it mar what was turning out to be a wonderful day. For now, Jesse was enjoying himself more than he had in years, and it was a condition of his basically optimistic nature to accept this without examining it too closely and perhaps destroying it in the process.

As for Brianna, she, too, was having an unexpectedly delightful time. It was the first she could recall, since she'd met Jesse, in which he seemed to treat her as an adult equal, sharing intelligent conversation with her, answering her questions with no hint of condescension or derision, giving and taking in a spirit of easy companionship and mutual respect. Not that she took overly long to reflect on this; she was too busy having fun!

They wound up spending the whole day riding together, stopping briefly in the early afternoon to assuage their hunger with some wild plums and a few handfuls of nuts Jesse was able to locate in a wooded section of his property. During the hours that seemed to pass with unaccountable speed, they talked about a host of things, ranging from their childhoods and the people they were fond of, to the places they had been and the things they had learned there. Sometimes they laughed together, each glad to discover a well-developed sense of humor in the other, but most of the time they just talked. And when there were stretches of silence, these were never strained or self-conscious; instead, they seemed to punctuate the substance of the communications they shared, coming naturally out of their give and take as each blended with the other in a kind of harmony neither had once thought possible.

When at last they returned to the Big House, more than an hour after dark—they had been taken by surprise by the sunset a good distance from the house, and it had taken them that long to make their way back—they were both happily exhausted, and Jesse gave Isaac—now officially his butler—instructions to have dinner trays sent up to their rooms, as well as baths prepared there, saying they would be making it an early night.

When Jesse escorted Brianna upstairs, they stood in front of the door to her chamber, pleasantly weary, but somehow not sure they were ready to say good-night. As Jesse turned to her in the softly diffused candlelight of the hallway's brass sconces, he looked down into her upturned face and smiled wryly, his sense of the ironic never more acute.

Here she was, the woman who had given him more pleasure in bed than any he'd ever known, standing here, beautiful and desirable, and legally his wedded wife; yet he was committed not to touch her. And he wanted to touch her very much. Every fiber of his mind and body cried out with wanting her, and yet, he knew he must not, especially tonight, which rode so tenuously on the fragile fabric of the magical day they had spent together. Whatever it cost him, he knew he must not jeopardize the new relationship that had begun to grow, perhaps turning her into a hell-bent spitfire again, and so he armored himself against his inclinations.

"You should sleep well tonight," he said softly as he gazed into the wide green eyes that met his own.

"Yes," Brianna murmured, "and so should you." He was standing very close to her now, and as she looked up into those blue, blue eyes, beheld the tanned face with its perfectly chiseled masculinity, she was suddenly caught up in a longing so fierce, it robbed her of a moment's breath. This, she quickly covered by saying, "Oh, Jesse, I thank you for everything! I mean, not only for Lightning, who's a perfect gift, but for such a lovely day. I can't remember when I've had better!"

"Nor I, little one, nor I," Jesse murmured, his blue eyes on hers.

They stood there in silence, then, but this was not one of those easy silences; it was fraught with yearnings and denials that each would have wished away but could not. Finally, Jesse took his hands and gently placed them on her shoulders; then he bent his dark head and lowered his mouth.

Years afterward, he would recall the soul-drugging moment of the kiss; there was the memory of the day they'd shared and the warm, soft silk of her lips under his own, though, most of all, there was the tender pain it carried, of longing denied.

Brianna, too, was caught somewhere between pleasure and pain as she opened her lips under his. Yearning, like a flower opening its petals to the sun, budded within her, flooding her body with an aching sweetness.

But when it seemed it had hardly begun, it was over as Jesse raised his head and looked at her.

"Good night, Green Eyes," he breathed, and then he turned and went to his own door. There he stood for a moment and looked at her again, with an expression she couldn't read, before opening it and going within.

As Brianna saw his door close, she caught her tingling lower lip between her teeth before releasing it and whispering, "Good night, my husband."

Suddenly she sucked in her breath, aghast at what she'd uttered, and her mood suddenly switched to one of unnameable terror. An image of Sally Hemings flashed in her mind, and she whirled and stepped toward Aimée's door across the hall and knocked urgently.

"Aimée! Can you come to help me with my bath?"

As the little gypsy opened the door and saw her friend's face, she exclaimed, "Oh-oh, certainly a bath, *chérie*, but I have a feeling we ought to make it a cold one!"

Chapter Twenty-Nine

The tidewater weather grew cooler and wetter as November spun out its dreary course and gave way to December, and life at Riverview, for Brianna, settled into a waiting game. Letters from George Simpson, which had initially told of a wave of speculative gossip over her hasty marriage, began to speak of the talk dying down in the Upcountry, though, for reasons George was too much of a gentleman to spell out, the solicitor advised "a good eight or nine month wait" until she returned and sought her annulment.

Brianna spent her time decorating the Big House, acceding to the demands of Laurette as best she could, and riding Lightning, usually in the company of Aimée, to whom she had given Le Duc. Sometimes they were accompanied by Festus or Vulcan, whenever one of the twins could spare time away from his work, and when this happened, there was often much mirth and high spirits, for Aimée and the Noslave brothers had developed a habit of indulging in witty repartee when they got together; jokes and hijinks were ever a part of their antics during these rides, which often ended with the participants coming back to the stables with aches in their sides, having spent so much time convulsed in laughter.

In fact, it was on one of these rides that Vulcan spilled the beans about something that was a source of their humor that day and which had been puzzling Brianna for some time. She had just been giggling with Aimée over the fact that Bon-Bon seemed to be growing in his mysterious ardor for Laurette Mayfield, of all people, escaping from his basket on all manner of occasions and padding happily after the widow, the woman's outraged protests notwithstanding.

"And this morning," Brianna was laughing, "Bon-Bon made it all the way to her skirts before she shrieked in horror and bolted from the room."

Chuckling happily, Vulcan pointed at Aimée and said, "Gal, y'all bettah nevah run out o' dem bon-bons. An' Ah sweahs, it be a wondah dat de widda don' smell 'em on huh!"

Suddenly Brianna stopped giggling and gave him a puzzled look. "On *her*?"

"Uh-huh," answered the black man. "Yo' know, in dem lil 'net sacks dis chile bin sewin' undah huh petticoats." He gestured, with a grin, at Aimée.

Looking suddenly very sheepish, the little gypsy threw Brianna an abashed grin of her own.

"You've been sewing bags of *bon-bons* onto Laurette's petticoats?!" Brianna's mouth hung open for a brief second; then she let out a howl of delight. "But Aimée, why wasn't I privy to this?" she demanded when the merriment had subsided.

Wiping mirthful tears from her eyes, Aimée sobered and gave a small snort. "Bah! That one—she always have—*has*—it out for you anyway, Brianna, so we just thought it would be in your favor to be truly innocent of the deed if the cursed creature ever found out."

"Oh," said her friend. "Well, I thank you for your protection, *mon amie*, but I'd rather be a party to the fun, and—did you say 'we'?"

It was Vulcan's turn to give her a sheepish look. "Yes'm. Ah bin de one whut got de bon-bons fum Chahleston." His look gave way to a wide grin.

Brianna's surprise turned to more laughter as she discarded the notion of even pretending to scold them. They were, she realized, two of her best friends, a number that had been growing since she had come to Riverview. Not only had the twins become people she cared about and could count on for all kinds of support and genuine caring, but there was now Christie Randall and her family as well. When she had first met Garrett, she had been taken aback by his close resemblance to Jesse and had, as a result, been awkward and shy with him, but the handsome older brother had quickly put her at ease, send-

ing her unspoken assurances, early on, that he not only liked
her, but respected her as a person in her own right, a status that
he clearly seemed to indicate had nothing to do with her relationship to his brother.

And then, of course, there was Jesse himself. As the days
wore on and he continued to respect the limits that had been
drawn around their liaison, she often thought of him as a
friend, strange as this might seem. With the disappearance of
worry over succumbing to the lust she had once feared and decided to put out of temptation's reach, she found she could begin to enjoy his company, and, apparently, he, hers whenever
they chanced to find time together. But, then, this was not very
often. For some reason, Jesse always seemed to have business
on the plantation—or at his brother's—that took him out of the
house early in the morning and kept him away until long after
dusk.

And if, on such nights, Brianna lay awake on her big double
bed and stared at their adjoining door and the seam of light
given off under it by the candle a servant had left burning, she
chalked it off to a casual curiosity over his whereabouts and
nothing more. She could think of him as a friend, she told herself, but she must be cautious and never allow him to become
more. That way lurked disaster.

It was this caution that punctured her awareness at the
strangest times during her stay at Jesse's home, often raising its
head at unexpected moments. One day, when the December
weather waxed unusually warm and they were graced with a
pleasant dry spell, Brianna decided to take Lightning out for
some exercise by herself. Festus was deep into his silversmithing apprenticeship by now, Vulcan, busy at the forge, and Aimée, deeply engrossed in gathering pine cones and such for
decorating the house for the forthcoming Yuletide season.

She rode the colt out past some of the fields leading down to
the river, fields that were barren now, but would, come spring,
she had learned, be flooded and soon covered with the little
green shoots that were rice plants, one of Riverview's most important crops. Since the path she rode was one she hadn't traveled before, she kept Lightning to a moderate pace that took
little equestrian effort, and soon she found herself ruminat-
ing.

But the avenue her thoughts took suddenly seized a nearer part of her consciousness, and she froze for a moment in alarm. The action was quickly translated to the gray colt, who sensed her mood and tossed his head as if to ask what was amiss.

What was amiss was that Brianna had all of a sudden realized she had been out *looking for Jesse*—not just wondering casually where he might be, but actually, actively seeking him out on the Riverview acreage! It was, she now admitted to herself, the reason she had chosen a path previously unknown to her, but she hadn't realized it until now, when, after rounding a bend in the bridle trail, she had been filled with, first, a mental picture of him on his horse and, then, a moment later, an acute sense of disappointment when the path ahead of her turned out to be empty of any rider.

Fool! she chastised. *Have you let him get that far under your skin that you would seek him out like a puppy his master? Do you care so little for your near-won freedom?*

She continued on this way for several minutes, berating herself for her emotional weakness as she guided Lightning around another bend in the trail.

Then, suddenly, she heard hoofbeats, and, looking up ahead, she spied a group of riders approaching. There were six of them, and it took her only a moment to recognize Jesse and Garrett at the fore; they were followed closely by Christie and three riders she'd never seen before. As the group came closer, it was these last three who held her attention. One was a bronze-complected man who rode bareback and wore woodsman's clothing of the most unusual design. This was tan in color, made of some kind of leather, with brightly colored beading here and there, and feathers—an Indian! The woman beside him, sitting as tall and proud in the saddle as he, wore similar dress, but she was dark and had Negroid features, as did the boy of twelve or thirteen who brought up the rear. But what finally caught Brianna's eye was not the garb of the strangers, but what her sister-in-law was wearing. Christie Randall was dressed in a boy's shirt and breeches, and she was riding her stallion *astride*!

Brianna had just a moment to glance down with disgust at her own green velvet riding skirt and the sidesaddle under it when she heard Christie's voice call out.

"Brianna, hello! How good to run into you out here! And on Lightning! Isn't he superb?"

"A pleasant surprise, to be sure," added Garrett as he flashed her a warm smile.

Jesse had paused through this, for he was busy trying to make some sense out of the mutinous look Brianna was sending him. Now, however, deciding to ignore it until he had a private moment with her to ascertain its cause, he gave her a polite smile and said, "Brianna, let me introduce you to some good friends."

He gestured to the three figures on horseback who waited behind him. "Meet Laughing Bear and his wife, Lula, and her son, Jasper—ah Jasper-Dark Arrow, it is now—and, oh, yes—Lula's and Laughing Bear's young son, Night Cryer."

It was only then Brianna noticed, as the black woman gave a half-turn on her mount, that she carried an infant carefully strapped to her back in a leather sling of sorts.

"We call him Night Cryer *for now*—and for *obvious* reasons," snorted the diminutive black woman. She looked to Brianna to be about thirty years old and was truly striking in appearance. In her tiny, shell-like ears she wore bright gold hoops while her close-cut hair covered a finely molded head. It framed perfectly her beautiful, chocolate-brown face with its high, wide brow and perfectly-proportioned African nose, the nostrils delicate and flaring; full, proud lips complemented a small, pointed chin, and all this rested gracefully above a lovely long neck and delicate, feminine shoulders. But it was her eyes that said the most about her. Deep set and coal black, they looked to have the ability to penetrate whatever they saw, missing nothing, and right now they were resting on Brianna. "But Ah don't expect you would know all that much about babes and their lung power yet. Pleased to meet you, Miz Randall. Ah've been hearing a great deal about you," she said in perfectly articulated English that was softly laced with a Southern drawl.

"Call me Brianna, please," replied Brianna, again feeling uncomfortable being addressed by her married title.

The Indian man Jesse had introduced as Laughing Bear inched his horse forward a bit and held out his hand. When Brianna thrust hers forward to meet it, he took her fingers and drew them to his lips in perfect, courtly European fashion. "We are truly delighted to meet you, Brianna. You are every bit as beautiful as we had heard." His English, too, was perfect.

The youngster called Jasper-Dark Arrow gave Brianna a gentle, shy smile as he dipped his head briefly. "Ma'am."

Brianna returned the friendly smiles all of them were now wearing and was about to ask them where they were going when Garrett answered her unspoken question for her.

"Christie and I are on our way to the Cherokee village where we'll be involved in a naming ceremony for young Night Cryer, here. We're already his Christian godparents, but we're about to become what you might call the Indian equivalent as well."

"You and your husband are welcome to join us," added Laughing Bear.

"Yes, why don't you?" Christie piped in enthusiastically. "You won't be able to participate in any part of the ceremony, for you're not an adopted member of the tribe as Jesse and we are, Brianna, but guest observers are always welcome."

Brianna's head began to swim. Jesse, an adopted member of the Cherokee? And Garrett and Christie, too? She recalled Jesse having spoken of spending a lot of his younger years in Indian company, but she hadn't actually realized. . . .

Seeing her hesitation and the look of surprise, if not shock, in her eyes, Jesse decided to answer for her. "Many thanks, Laughing Bear, but I believe Brianna's tutor told me this morning she must be at Riverview for the next few days. She wants us to arrange holiday festivities and, especially, a New Year's ball this month so that Brianna will have further domestic training in planning and carrying out such activities. I'm afraid it's something I've already committed us to, but I know Brianna joins me in wishing you and your family much happiness and good fortune on this important occasion."

"We understand," said Lula. "Perhaps you can both visit us another time."

"Yes," said Brianna, feeling not a little annoyance at Jesse's preempting her decision. A New Year's ball, indeed! This was the first she'd even heard of it! But she gave the black woman a small half-smile as she added, "I'd like that. I'd like it very much."

Then Garrett and the others made their goodbyes, with Lula and Laughing Bear adding brief comments again on how glad they were to have met Jesse's new bride, and the group departed, leaving her alone with Jesse.

Jesse watched Brianna's eyes follow the departing figures; again, he sensed a smoldering anger in her look. "All right—out with it. What's troubling you this time?"

Brianna jerked her head around to meet his regard. Her eyes were, indeed, blazing. "*Both* those women were wearing *breeches* and riding *astride*!"she fumed accusingly.

Jesse chuckled. "Oh, so that's all."

"That's *all*? No, that is *not* all, Jesse Randall! After what you put me through, and here's your own brother's wife—"

"You *ought* to have noticed Brianna, that both those women were on their way to an *Indian village* and *accompanied* by their *husbands*!" Jesse's tone began to match hers.

"And where does that leave me? It's been months now, since the wager, weeks, since I've been—officially—a married woman, and yet I still trail about wearing—wearing—" Frustrated tears began to well up in the green eyes, and seeing them, Jesse softened.

"Wearing beautiful clothes that make you look every inch the lady you are." At her startled reaction Jesse continued. "But, I tell you what, lady wife. Why don't we turn back to the Big House right now and fetch you some breeches and a shirt? I'll wait while you change and we'll slip out for an hour or two before Laurette finds out what we're about and tries to get you under her claw again." He finished by gazing into her eyes with a warm smile.

A heartstopping smile for Brianna as she took in what he said. Suddenly she felt her anger evaporate, though she could hardly believe her ears. Here was Jesse, actually being understanding and—and *kind* to her! And when he smiled at her that way, her stomach did little flip-flops, and she could barely find her tongue.

At last she was able to react, however, and it was with a dazzling smile of her own. "Oh, Jesse, do you really *mean* it? Oh, I can't *wait* to see how it feels on Lightning! Oh—"

"Take it easy, little one," laughed Jesse. "We don't want to miss your ride because we haven't spared the horses." He, too, had been having a reaction to a smile—hers, which, when she looked at him with all the open warmth he saw now, gave him a gut-wrenching lurch in his middle somewhere, and it was all he could do not to throw caution to the wind and head for a secluded spot somewhere, take her in his arms, and make sweet, passionate love to her for endless hours. But, though he knew how badly he wanted her, he also knew the possible from the impossible right now. One wrong move could send his "lady wife" running back to Columbia for an early annulment, and, he now realized, that would not fit in with his plans.

They rode back to the Big House at an easy pace, talking comfortably about many things, including the strange little family Brianna had just met. She learned that Lula was Christie's closest friend, although once she'd been her ladies' maid and had traveled from Virginia with her even before Christie became Garrett's wife. Laughing Bear was the son of a major Cherokee chief and a powerful woman of the tribe, for the Cherokee were a people who recognized separate ownership of property and other major rights among their women. Jasper-Dark Arrow was Lula's son from her first marriage—his father had died years ago—and he had been adopted into the tribe, as had Lula, not to mention Garrett, Christie and Jesse.

Jesse answered all of Brianna's questions about life in a Cherokee village, and she had many. He smiled with delight as he watched her listen to his answers, her large green eyes growing wide with wonder and interest as he gave her what details he could think of.

At length they arrived at the Big House where Jesse had some words with Isaac while Brianna dashed upstairs to change. She was just opening the bottom drawer to her tall chest when Aimée joined her, having heard her come upstairs from her room across the hall.

"Brianna, I was just looking for you. Isaac said I was to get the key to your interior door because we have a new piece of furniture for your other room that must be brought in this way. It is a mite too large for that room's outside door, but will just fit—what *are* you looking for?" she asked, interrupting herself as she noticed Brianna's frantic rummaging. "If it's your flow you've finally gotten, the cloths you need are in the next to the last drawer. You've gone right past them!"

Hearing her words, Brianna stood up with a start. Her flow—it was a topic she'd been putting out of her mind for days, now, ever since Aimée had asked her last week whether she needed more of the folded, clean cotton cloths a woman used for such hygienic purposes and she had then briefly realized she couldn't remember her last monthly, although she knew it had been well before coming to Riverview.

"Um—no, Aimée, it's my breeches and shirt I seek," she said awkwardly. "Jesse's making good on—on our wager."

"Ah," said Aimée, looking at her peculiarly. "We moved them to the lowboy, remember? And, *chérie*, the key to that door. May I have it?"

"Oh, oh, yes," said Brianna absentmindedly as she wandered in the direction of the lowboy that stood between two tall windows on the far side of the bed. "It—it's in that little Chelsea dish on my dressing table—the one with the blue acanthus leaves on it. Just put it back when you're done with it."

After Aimée had helped her out of her gown and gone, Brianna managed to finish changing her apparel, but her mind was no longer on riding astride. *Dear God, I cannot be with child! I must not! Holy Mother of God, let it not be so!* she prayed silently as she made her way back downstairs. *No, it just isn't so—it is not! I've just skipped a time from all the turmoil coming from that damned wedding, that's all. Just as I did when I learned Mother had died. It will all straighten itself out shortly and I'll be fine.*

"Ah, there you are, Brianna." Jesse's voice reached her from the end of the entrance hall. "I was just about to come looking for you." The blue eyes roamed appreciatively over her lithe form, its alluring curves well revealed by the clinging attire she wore. "But I hope you haven't forgotten I'd like you to wear this until we leave the stables." He draped her dark green woolen cloak over her shoulders.

Brought back to the moment at hand by his words, Brianna took a deep breath and thrust her worrying thoughts from her with a great spurt of resolve. The *last* person she wished to read the trouble on her mind was Jesse Randall! Summoning the best smile she could muster, she took his arm and let him lead her to the stables.

They rode together for a couple of hours, and in the excitement over the exhilarating feeling of freedom that came with letting Lightning have his head as she moved beside Jesse on the flats, Brianna was able to forget her worries. Just the sensation of the wind flowing through her long hair, which she'd left loose, and the sound of the gray colt's hooves on the ground were enough to dispel all gloom from her mind. She hadn't felt so free in years, and it showed in every bend of her body as it crouched low over Lightning's neck, every shake of her head as it met the breeze, every laughing syllable that bubbled in her throat as they sailed over the ground.

Jesse saw it all, and found himself grinning with pleasure at *her* pleasure. Keeping Gypsy carefully under control, he let Brianna have the lead most of the time, content just to watch her from the distance of a length or two, careful not to intrude on her exuberance. And he mentally kicked himself a dozen times for not allowing her this sooner. Here was another Brianna he'd not seen before—a free spirit, triumphant in her capacity for loving that freedom, and totally, joyously happy. And Jesse pondered for the second time that day, a plan that had been forming in his mind that he hoped to bring to fruition in the future.

At last it grew dark, and they returned to the stables. A pair of grooms came to take Gypsy and Lightning, and Brianna and Jesse were left standing together under the high lantern that hung over the entrance. Jesse noticed she had grown unusually quiet as they'd neared home, but he attributed it to tiredness, for they'd done a goodly amount of hard riding. What he couldn't know was that Brianna had begun to worry over her delayed menses again, once the exhilarating thrill of the ride had passed, and she was now bent on only one thing—making haste to her chamber to think on her problem, without the obstruction his presence presented. Still, she stifled the urge to retreat too quickly, lest she give him reason to guess something was wrong.

"Thank you for fulfilling your part in the wager," she said as she turned to him, "although, to be fair, you have your prize coming to you, too. That race did finish in a draw." A shy, half-smile.

Jesse returned this with a grin. "I'll do that, Green Eyes." He was looking directly into those eyes right now, and then his glance became bolder as it took in her entire form, almost as if he were memorizing it prior to wrapping her in the green cloak he now held draped over one arm. He saw the saucy outward thrust of her full breasts as they pushed against the thin muslin of her shirt, the tiny waist that gave way to those slender, yet curving hips, the long, long, shapely legs in the tight-fitting breeches and riding boots. But then his gaze returned to her face and the heavily cascading mane of auburn hair that framed it, swirling wildly about her delicate shoulders and arms. Seeing the silken tresses, made coppery by the lantern's glow, he again had to fight off urges he knew could not be met tonight. Instead, he took a lock of the fiery mass of curls and, fingering it softly, said, "You know, your sister had hair of a similar color, but I never saw her wear it loose, as you are wont to do, to let the light gleam and play upon it, so I was never quite so struck by its beauty as I now am by yours, Green Eyes."

It was the wrong thing to say. Growing increasingly nervous by the minute, over being alone with Jesse in what had become a far too intimate moment—especially in the light of the fears that were running through her brain—Brianna decided his comparison could mean only one thing—that he was sorry she was not Deirdre. Of course, given the logic she was so often fond of using, it should then have made no sense for him to be wanting her instead of Deirdre right now, but logic had no place in her thoughts at this moment.

"Of course, *she* wouldn't wear her precious locks in this wild and wanton fashion!" she snapped. "Deirdre always *was* the *proper* young lady! And maybe you'd better stop calling me Green Eyes! I'm sure you have enough reminders of how I differ from her!" Then, pulling the lock of her hair from between his fingers, she grabbed the cloak from him, whirled about and headed for the Big House at a run.

"Brianna, wait! I didn't—" But Jesse decided to let her go for now. Somewhat bewildered and chagrined by her reaction, he wondered at its cause. He hadn't *meant* to compare her to Deirdre—*un*favourably, at any rate. Why had she taken his words thusly? Perhaps they hadn't been entirely well chosen, but she'd taken them in the worst possible light when he had only intended—and they had been getting on so well together! The afternoon had practically soared by, with nary a wayward word or glance between them, and now.... He heaved a weary sigh. His wife still had some growing up to do, but if he had been at fault.... Well, he would find out later, at a quiet moment, and make amends.

Chapter Thirty

Later that night Brianna sat in the blue and white enameled brass tub that Jesse had imported from France with much trouble, owing to the revolutionary turmoil over there, while Aimée bent to pour a final pitcher of scented water into the fragrant and already steaming liquid that surrounded her friend's weary muscles.

"That should do it, Aimée. I'll just lie here a while and soak, and I can towel dry and get into my nightrail by myself. You run along and relax. I know we both need to after that gruelling session with Laurette."

"*Oui, mon amie*, not to mention our concerns over the other matter we discussed. But, as for that, I beg you to consider everything carefully, Brianna. You would not wish to do anything rash, *n'est-ce pas?*" With a pointed look in her friend's direction, Aimée left the chamber.

What she had alluded to was Brianna's taking her into her confidence on the matter of her tardy flow. The two of them had retreated to Brianna's chamber after dinner (and an ensuing lengthy conference with the widow over the planned ball for the New Year celebration), and Brianna had then confessed her fears to the little gypsy. Not that there had been any shock or surprise on Aimée's part; she had for some time suspected Brianna's dilemma, but had been biding her time until Brianna herself decided to confront the problem and share it with her.

Aimée's worst fears now, however, were not about the child that might be on the way, but for the course of action Brianna had outlined and asked her to help with, "should the worst come to be true." She had told Aimée she would never remain at Riverview if she carried Jesse's child, for she had the certain feeling that Jesse, if he found out, would keep her with him, *within the marriage*! "That must never happen, Aimée," she had said. "We'd both be trapped in an unwanted marriage, he, because of some damned sense of honor I know he has—I can sense it about him—and I, because I would have no choice once he made such a decision. You must, if there is a babe, help me to run away, back to Le Beau Château—you *must*!"

As Aimée heard her words, she had been gripped by an icy fear. Somewhere, at some future time, something terrible threatened Brianna on the trail that led away from Riverview into the high country. Of this, Aimée was certain, and though her prescient abilities failed to tell her the specifics of how or when, she feared it might be at the time of this very escape she was planning.

Moreover, Aimée knew she didn't want Brianna to leave Jesse. She was almost sure her friend was on the verge of falling in love with her handsome husband, if she hadn't already, and now was not the time to see it thwarted. It was to be the fruition of everything she and Father Edouard had discussed prior to Brianna's coming here. Brianna Devereaux and Jesse Randall were so *right* for each other—*meant* for each other in ways only Aimée understood and which went beyond even the priest's promise to Etienne Devereaux, that he would try to bring them together. Here was a pair that would, indeed, soar together with the wings of eagles, once they could be brought to shed the scales of blindness that covered their eyes, and she, Aimée, would do all she could to ensure they had a chance at their mutual destiny, despite the obstacles her headstrong friend threw in that path. Her friendship with Brianna required it!

And so it was that, when Jesse heard voices and the sound of Aimée leaving the room next to his, he glanced at the shared interior door and saw it was not only unlocked, but ever so slightly ajar, for Aimée had "forgotten" to relock it after borrowing the key that afternoon. And since he had been feeling concerned over the way he and Brianna had parted at the stables, and meaning to set things aright, he decided as long as she was still awake, to talk to her in her chamber.

Brianna was still sitting in her bath, her eyes closed as she leaned her head against its high back and thought about her day. The ride with Jesse had been so wonderful! Why did it have to be spoiled by— Her mind shifted to the scene at dinner where she had avoided Jesse's eyes, her own still burning over the remark about her hair, and Deirdre's, but Jesse himself had been polite, sounding at ease. Still, she couldn't be sure of much that had taken place at the table, what with the turmoil that had been raging inside her.

"Brianna, may I come in? This door is ajar, so I assume—"

But Jesse quickly saw his assumption was incorrect. That is, she wasn't "decent," as he would have put it, but sitting there, bare to her waist, her face rosy and flushed from the bath, under the mass of auburn ringlets Aimée had piled high on her head. And her green eyes were now wide with alarm. He saw her quickly grab a large bath sponge and draw it to her chest, blocking his view of the pink-crested ripeness of her high, lush breasts.

"It—it would seem you are already in, sir!" The green eyes flashed a warning.

Jesse made a helpless gesture, but stood, rooted to the spot. "Someone unlocked the door." He continued to gaze at her, the picture she presented, of sweet, seductive innocence, something he found impossible to ignore. Aside from the perfect breasts he had just glimpsed and so well remembered, there were her long, lissome legs, one of them thrust forward, with foot propped on the tub's rim, rendering its gracefully alluring shape totally visible to him. He felt his mouth go dry as desire stirred in his loins.

"Well, it wasn't *I* who left it unlocked!" Brianna was saying as she sank down lower in the water. "What is it you had to say to me? Is it so important that it could not wait?"

She had intended to order him out. Why hadn't she? As she gazed at him, standing there in the open doorway, she only knew the inclination had somehow left her. He was wearing one of the full-sleeved white cotton shirts he seemed to favor, and it was open nearly to his lean waist above a close-fitting pair of soft gray breeches and, of course, his tall, black boots. His hair was slightly tousled, with a single curl falling rakishly over his forehead, and with those blue eyes which seemed to pierce right through her soul, he was oh, so handsome, and she wondered if her heart hadn't stopped beating at the sight of him.

"No," he said softly, "I didn't think this could wait." He took a few steps and quickly closed the distance that separated them, arriving to tower above her beside the tub. Brianna felt her breathing go shallow but said not a word.

"Brianna." Jesse's voice came out low and hoarse, and he quickly cleared his throat, propping one booted foot upon the tub's rim and leaning his elbow across his knee as he did so. Then he began again. "Brianna, I came to apologize for saying what I did out by the stables. I never meant to compare you with Deirdre. It's just that, when I saw you standing there with your hair down and . . . believe me, little one, I meant no affront."

His gaze was bent intently on her now, and Brianna knew she would be lost unless she distracted herself from its power, so she said the first thing to come into her head. "No, you meant no affront to me, but that doesn't change your feelings for *her*! Jesse Randall, you—you're just hopelessly tied to—to Deirdre's *ghost*!"

The frown that crossed Jesse's brow gave testimony to the fact that he took in what she said and was examining it for the possibility that it might be true. But in a few seconds he discarded the possibility, saying quietly, "That's not true, Brianna. I swear it."

"Oh, really?"

"Yes, really," said Jesse tartly, his anger beginning to mount. "But, I'll tell you what you might do to prove it to yourself, Brianna." He leaned forward, taking his finger and making little jabs with it in the air at her as he spoke. "Why don't you try being more of a *real* woman yourself? A real woman might easily dispel the presence of any *spirit*!"

Brianna answered him with a fiery look as she half-rose in the tub, the bath sponge forgotten and falling into the water. "I need to prove nothing! Why don't you—"

But she never finished her sentence. In the moment before he'd crossed the room, Jesse had made a quickly calculated judgment as to how much temptation he could resist and decided he might chance talking to her as she was—the subject warranted the risk, and he felt he had the strength. But now, as she rose out of the water just in front of him, displaying all those enticing charms he'd spent weeks trying to put from his

mind, his resistance crumbled like a mountain before an earth-
quake.

With a groan, he pulled her to him; then he drew back from
the tub, and wrapped her in his arms. Brianna felt the hard,
muscular planes of his huge body against hers, the well remembered strength of his arms pressing her close, and she was
lost. She threw her arms about his neck and clung to him with
desperate need. Fiercely, they embraced this way for several
long moments, Jesse's face buried in the fragrant mass of her
hair as it tumbled loose from its pins, his mouth murmuring his
need for her. "Brianna—sweet, lovely creature—I can't get you
out of my mind—come to me—stay with me—ah, sweet lady
wife, how I want you—only you...."

And Brianna's head was swimming, her body filled with one
giant ache of longing for him. "Jesse ..." she breathed, "Oh,
Jesse, you make me want you as soon as you *touch* me, make
me ... make me want to tell you—never to stop—never...."

Then Jesse lifted his head and looked down into her eyes,
those twin pools of liquid green that gazed at him now under
lids heavy with passion. "Green Eyes, little one, though it cost
me everything right now, I still must ask—do you really want
this now? The choice is yours, sweet wife. I would not have you
hate me for it later." As he spoke, his blue eyes blazed, meeting hers, while his arms continued to hold her about the waist
and hips. Brianna could feel the heat emanating from him, the
proof of his desire hard and firm against her naked thighs while
he waited for her response, but she was beyond words now.
With a small cry, she raised her mouth to his, and he took it for
the answer he craved. Lowering his head, he met it with his own
in a violent kiss of unthinking passion.

Then he was sweeping one strong arm under her thighs and
carrying her toward the bed as if she weighed nothing at all. In
the fireplace on the far wall, the fire burned brightly, but neither had need of its warmth. They fell together on the bed in a
blaze of desire too long denied, limbs entwined, breathless,
yearning.

Then Jesse pulled away from her for a moment, both in an
attempt to slow their passion, to savor it, and because of a
gnawing inkling he'd had when he first stumbled upon her nakedness. There was something about her—her breasts seemed

somehow fuller, even more ripe than he'd remembered. He took a finger and traced a course down the side of her neck and then downward again, touching a swelling mound of flesh. "So beautiful," he whispered. But when his other hand came to join the first, to cup and hold the twin orbs and both thumbs brushed the rosy peaks of her nipples, Brianna moaned and held out trembling arms to him, wiping all questions from his mind.

Pulling her to him, he pressed his mouth against her ear, saying, "Softly, love. It will be better if we don't give in to our need too soon, but, faith, you make it hard to wait!"

Then he took his hands and tenderly held her head on either side, lacing his fingers through her hair while he looked deeply into her eyes. "You're beautiful, Brianna. More than my poor words can tell you." He let his fingers run through the tangled, silken mass that was made copper by the fire's glow. "This hair—how oft I've ached to touch it like this while we would meet and talk of daily, mundane things and I dared not!" He drew a lock of auburn fire to his mouth and pressed his lips against it.

But, from somewhere, out of what perverse and fearful depths she didn't know, couldn't begin to fathom, even later when she questioned herself on it, Brianna froze as she heard his words about her hair. Bitter bile, like a monster that looms where one would least suspect it, rose in her throat as she recalled what he'd said earlier in the evening, his mention of Deirdre and her hair, and suddenly all kinds of doubts assailed her mind. Fearfully, tentatively, her question formed on trembling lips.

"Did...had you—had you ever been intimate—this way with Deirdre?" she whispered.

Jesse looked at her in stunned silence for a moment before he answered with a firm and resounding "No!" But the moment was broken, and she knew it as she saw him roll away from her and leap off the bed, his body stiff with anger. Turning to her, his eyes blue ice, he gritted out between clenched jaws, "Brianna, there is someone here who *is* busy chasing ghosts, and it is not I!" He strode toward the adjoining door they shared before turning back to look at her. "I can tell you this. I have never wanted a woman as I have wanted you, but it

seems you are bent on denying such feelings yourself. Therefore, madam, I leave you to yourself—and your ghosts!" And
with an angry gesture, he left the room, slamming the door in
his wake.

It was still an hour before day would break as two figures on
horseback rode stealthily along the trail that led along the
western acreage of Riverview into the high country. They kept
abreast of each other, one on a big gray colt, the other on a
chestnut stallion, and from time to time, one or the other rider
turned to glance over a cloaked shoulder.

"No one could possibly be following us yet, *mon amie*," said
Aimée as she joined Brianna in yet another furtive glance. "We
got away from the stables without anyone seeing us, and you
know Jesse is in Charleston until this evening."

"Yes, but what if Laurette doesn't believe that note about
our going off to return Bon-Bon to the woods? What if she de-
cides to send Isaac or Vulcan out looking for us?"

"Bah!" Aimée made a dismissive gesture. "She will be only
too glad to be rid of her little nemesis here." Aimée patted a
leather saddlebag where a small, pointed face with inquisitive
black eyes peered up at her. "And, besides, Vulcan is also in
Charleston."

"Oh?"

"He rode with Jesse yesterday to purchase, among other
necessities, some more bon-bons." The little gypsy flashed
Brianna a grin in the near-darkness, its whiteness made visible
by the faint glimmer of the waning moon.

Brianna tried to smile, but a myriad of dark musings that had
been accosting her mind for the past few days prevented it. The
worst had begun on Sunday when she was climbing out of bed
with the idea of attending church (a two-hour trip to the family chapel of a plantation downriver; Jesse had told her the only
nearby church—his family's—was Anglican, but had quickly
arranged with a Roman Catholic planter friend of his to have
her and Aimée attend Mass with the man's family who heard
it said at home by an itinerant priest). As her feet had met the
pile of the lovely blue and cream colored Aubusson carpet beside the bed, she had been overwhelmed by a wave of nausea.
It had persisted, causing her to miss breakfast—and the Mass—

and then disappeared—only to return again for a similar length of time each morning since then: the morning sickness, with her for six days now.

Then had come the difficult discussions with Aimée. It was the only time in the history of their friendship she and the little gypsy had ever been so at odds with each other. At first Aimée had simply refused to help her leave, much less accompany her. "It would be dangerous enough for two women traveling alone," she had said, "but with one of them pregnant, such a trip would be sheer folly!" Much cajoling and pleading on Brianna's part had had no effect, but when, yesterday morning, she had at last threatened to go alone, Aimée had grudgingly given in. "You 'ave ze obstinacy to try ze saints, Brianna," she had said, reverting back to the heavily accented English that said the most about the stress and irritation she was feeling. But, of course, Aimée's poorer moods never lasted long, so by mid-day the two young women had embraced and were happily friends again as they withdrew to Brianna's chamber to plot their escape.

The trickiest part had been to secure a copy of a reliable map that showed the route between Riverview and Le Beau Château. They knew Isaac had once had one, for Festus had told of Isaac's using it when Jesse had sent for them in September. But how to get it from him—if he still had it—without raising suspicions! Finally, they had hit upon an idea. They simply told Isaac that Father Edouard had written he was considering a visit to Riverview, but that the priest had been supplied with a *faulty* map—sent in his letter, for their approval, of course—by *Prenshaw*! That did it. All Isaac had to hear was the Le Beau Château butler's name and he was off to his chambers to find them "the only proper map to use!"

Now, as she and Aimée made their steady way toward the Oconee Mountains ("Cherokee country" according to the labeling on the map that Aimée had been quick to point out to her), Brianna was filled with a strange mixture of emotions that ran the gamut from vague regret to trepidation. Relentlessly, a parade of unanswerable questions invaded her brain. Would she find true sanctuary at Le Beau Château? Would Father Edouard, Simpson and the others allow her to remain there without facing or returning to Jesse when he came for her, which, she had no doubt, he was sure to do, once he realized where she'd gone? Would there be a way of dissolving the marriage, now that a child was on the way? Would she be capable of raising a child without a husband? Would the contract with Laurette cause a problem? Would there, would she, would it—the list was seemingly endless. Yet, even with the burden these bedeviling queries put on her, Brianna was, in a way, grateful for them. As long as they preyed on her mind, she could push away some deeper images that menaced, not the least of which was a pair of blue, blue eyes that haunted her dreams at night and threatened to touch her soul by day.

They were able to cover a goodly amount of distance that day, the only real interruption to their progress being yet another bout with the morning sickness Brianna experienced after nibbling on a cold croissant a couple of hours after dawn. But, after spilling the contents of her stomach on the side of the trail and gratefully accepting a cold compress from Aimée (a handkerchief she had soaked in water from a nearby stream), the two had remounted and were again on their way an hour later.

Dusk found them approaching the foothills of the Oconees, and they were elated to find, exactly where the map said it would be, the deserted log cabin where Isaac and Festus had spent their first night away from Riverview on their journey in the early fall.

"You unroll these feather ticks and spread them on the bed, there," said Aimée as she indicated the one-room dwelling's single piece of furniture. "I'll build a fire while you rest, and then we can do some more serious eating!"

Brianna smiled wearily at Aimée's not unexpected reference to food. Then she moved to cover the woven rope supports of the simple bed with the ticks they had each carried, rolled and tied to the backs of their saddles, and gratefully stretched her slender frame upon them, too tired to protest more than once, weakly, that Aimée shouldn't be doing all the hard work.

"You must think of the little one and rest when you can," Aimée had scolded, "and, besides, to me, preparing food is not work—it is one of life's greatest pleasures!"

And so the two had successfully reached the end of the first leg of their journey. By the time it had grown completely dark, smoke was rising cozily from the cabin's chimney, and the two women were warm and enjoying a tasty meal of delicate mushroom omelettes and flaky biscuits. All seemed secure for the night. What they couldn't know was that, several hundred yards away, from the crest of a little ridge, four pairs of greedy eyes watched and waited.

Chapter Thirty-One

"Where the hell would they go with the damned animal that would keep them until after dark?" Jesse thundered. "It's my guess they got lost. Vulcan, I know you're tired after just riding in with me, but—"

"Sho' don' hafta say nothin' mo', Mistah Jesse. Ah's ready t' saddle up agin," the big overseer told him. He walked toward the door they had just entered moments before.

"We'd better take fresh horses," Jesse said with a worried look in his eyes. "Laurette, are you sure no one saw them leave? Or that they didn't mention their direction or destination?"

"As I said, it was only a brief note I received, slipped under my door at some ungodly hour. 'To the woods' was all it mentioned. I'd show it to you now, but I disposed of it in my fireplace soon after I read it," the widow replied. Then she yawned, and in a laconic drawl added, "Oh, Jesse, I wouldn't worry myself about them too much if I were you. Those girls have never had a good sense of time—always late for this or that chore or whatever. You'll see. They probably lost track of the hour and didn't head back in time. I'm sure we'll see them coming in that door any moment now. Why not join me in the drawing room for a bit of sherry while we wait and see, hmm?" Laurette finished this last by taking a step closer to Jesse and running a finger slowly up his arm.

Jesse's reply was clipped and terse as he brushed her hand away. "You'll drink alone, Laurette. I'm going to find my wife!"

He was almost through the door, with Vulcan close behind, when Isaac came rapidly down the grand staircase, calling for him to wait.

"What is it, Isaac? You know we should be on our way. Hurry up, man! They could be vainly trying to locate the way home right now, and—"

"But that's just it, sir! They may not be *trying* to go home!" Isaac's thin face looked pale and distraught.

"What say you, Isaac?" The little butler had Jesse's full attention now.

"Bessie, the chambermaid assigned to Mistress Randall's room, says all of your wife's—ah—more personal things are gone—toiletries, combs, undergarments, as well as a few of her gowns, and then we checked Aimée's chamber. It was the same there."

Jesse froze when he heard this, alarm written on his face. "You're sure?"

Isaac nodded, a pained expression on his narrow features. "And I fear *I* gave them the tool to make it possible."

"Make what possible?" demanded Laurette. "And if they duped us into thinking they'd be returning when they had less innocent intentions, why? And where could they be traveling?"

"To Le Beau Château, madam," said the little Englishman. "I myself unwittingly gave them a map that showed the way."

"But that's impossible!" exclaimed Laurette. "Two girls, alone, in all that wilderness! You must not have—"

"Vulcan!" Jesse's voice cracked the air like a whip. "Ride hard for my brother's place. Tell him what's happened and that I'm already on my way to Columbia. He'll know the route. The two of you will probably catch up with me in a few hours since I'll be going more slowly, looking for signs that they didn't stray from the trail or—God forbid—have a mishap." He was following the black man out the door now. "Oh, and, Vulcan, if my brother's houseguest is still there, expect him to join you. Laughing Bear knows those hills better than any of us, and I only hope you do find him at Riverlea."

As Jesse's words trailed off into the night, Laurette gave Isaac an exasperated look. Then, stifling another yawn, she turned toward the staircase, saying, "I really am very sleepy this

evening. You may send someone up with my sherry. I'll have it
in my room.'' She walked upstairs.

As Jesse guided his horse carefully along the darkened trail,
his mind was a tangle of questions, much as Brianna's had been
many hours earlier. But his had mostly to do with finding his
wife and bringing her safely back, though of course he did
puzzle more than anything else over *why* she had chosen to
flee—and so secretively.

Something must have happened, and recently, he told himself, but what? He tried to think back to the last time he'd seen
her. It hadn't been for several days, because she'd been absent
at breakfast, and he'd been too busy to dine at home since…the
night of her bath! That's when they'd last had words—and
what words! Still, when he examined their encounter in her
chamber, he could find nothing to account for her disappearance, he thought.

He decided to take another tack. When young women run off
from home, what are their most prevalent reasons? To seek
fortune, adventure? No, he thought, even given Brianna's
freedom-loving nature, it was unlikely. A fortune was already
hers, and she appeared more inclined to carve out her adventure within the lifestyle she already knew. (His mind flew to a
picture of her wearing a servant's disguise, but he summarily
banished it, for there were discomfiting images attached to that,
images he wasn't sure he wished to ponder now.) So he dismissed the adventure and fortune-seeking motive as one more
likely to appeal to a young man.

But, what then? Suddenly he remembered a conversation
he'd had only last week when visiting his friend Jonathan upriver. He'd encountered Kathie, the lass from the Black Swan,
swollen with child now, and, among her profuse thanks to him
for the position he'd obtained for her on Jonathan's plantation, Kathie had told him that if he hadn't helped her, she'd
have been forced to run away to some other city to—

All of a sudden, Jesse focused on an image of Kathie at the
Black Swan, of her breasts that had grown fuller than before,
with darkened nipples. The image changed, and he now saw
Brianna in her bath. *Her* breasts had— Of course! The most
likely reason of all to send a young woman running from

home—an unwanted pregnancy! Brianna was carrying a child—*his* child!

All at once, a surge of emotions gripped Jesse. At first, there was an immediate flood of elation, but in the next instant he was seized by an overwhelming fear. She was out there somewhere in the dark, her only companion a young woman even smaller and slighter than she—

He turned in the saddle and made a quick gesture to the first of the four men who rode behind him. When the Indian had reached his horse's side, he spoke urgently to him in a low tone of voice. "Laughing Bear, where were those renegades last seen?"

"Not five leagues from here, I fear," the Indian replied.

"And you're sure Blood Man was their leader?"

The Cherokee nodded. When he, Garrett, and the twins had caught up with Jesse an hour or so earlier, he had warned of the presence of a small band of renegade Indians that had been making trouble in the area, reluctantly describing the nature of the Seminole outcast who had led the raids that had been witnessed. Blood Man was a bad one, making his living, if it could be called that, from the misery of others. His chief means of securing wealth involved kidnapping women and children and selling them into slavery. It made little difference whether they were red, white or black, rich or poor; the only motive that guided where he would strike was his victims' availability. Now, as Laughing Bear read the concern in his white brother's eyes, he could only add, as a small comfort, "But remember, Jesse, his band is small—only four of them when last seen."

Jesse nodded. There were five in their own party, although he wondered how much help Festus could be. The main reason the blind twin had come along was that none of the other three were able to dissuade him once he'd heard about their purpose.

Jesse turned in his saddle again and this time signalled to his brother. When Garrett rode alongside him, he asked, "Garrett, how far do you reckon, at our present pace, until we reach that deserted cabin we used when we hunted together last year?"

"Less than an hour, I'd say. We should reach it about the same time the dawn begins to break. What say you, we push the horses just a bit more? If they're there, they might decide to leave at daybreak, and I, for one, would rather we found them at the cabin, because the trail forks after that, and we don't know how clearly that map indicates it, or how well the women are able to read maps.''

Jesse gave him an assenting nod. His map had been drawn for Isaac, who'd had enough familiarity with this part of the country not to need very explicit instructions on the early part of his trip. Garrett's words made good sense.

As he urged his mount to a greater speed, the others following suit, Jesse concentrated on the task ahead, refusing to allow any more negative thoughts or fears to enter his mind. He *must* find her—he would. And *safe*! And when he did, he would have it out with her about running away. He—

Suddenly, his thoughts turned to an image of Brianna beside the paddock the day he'd given her the colt—eyes so open, greener than green, suffused with light and ebullient joy. Jesse shook his head to clear it. *You've got to be gentle with her, old man—that is, if she'll let you. And first, you've got to find her!* With that thought firmly in his mind, Jesse changed the pressure of his knees on his horse's flanks and rode harder.

Brianna sat bolt upright in the bed, a scream caught in her throat. Perspiration beaded her upper lip and trickled down her neck and back. The dream again, but this time, it had seemed even more real, closer somehow. As she made an attempt to slow her rapid breathing, she groped in the dark until she felt Aimée's reassuring form. The little gypsy stirred as Brianna tried to survey the almost pitch-black of the one-room cabin. For some reason, though she was awake now, she had the strangest feeling that something menacing still lurked.

''Aimée, please wake up. I—''

Brianna's words were cut off as a rough palm clamped over her mouth. At the same moment she felt herself seized by an iron grip that bound her arms to her sides as she was yanked off the bed. In abject terror she watched by the faint light of the fire's dying embers as a tall shadow hovered over Aimée. She heard her friend give a short yelp of fright before her voice, too, was silenced.

The one who held her was far larger than she, and though she twisted and kicked furiously to free herself, he easily dragged her toward the door. From behind her she could hear faintly thrashing sounds that told her Aimée was also putting up a struggle.

Suddenly the door opened, and she found herself propelled through it into the cold night air. The hand that held her mouth released it, but her arms remained in a viselike grip, twisted behind her back now.

There was enough of the moon to light the clearing, and ahead of her she saw several horses and two more strangely garbed figures. *Indians!* She screamed as they loomed up ahead of her and received a cuff on the side of her head for it from one of them.

"*Bâtard!*" she heard Aimée shriek through the ringing in her ears. But this was followed by the sight of the little gypsy violently thrown to the ground while her captor delivered a brutal kick to her ribs. Aimée whimpered with pain.

"Tell your friend I, Blood Man, *parle français!*" the man who held Brianna ordered. "I have fought with the French against the English!" He was leaning forward, his head above her left shoulder as he spoke, and Brianna shuddered fearfully when she saw his face. Numerous wedges of scar tissue formed a decorative pattern across his angular cheekbones, and there was another, more ghastly kind of scar that ran from his right eyebrow downward to his temple, dragging his eye with it. His hair was drawn back in a high knot of sorts, secured at the crown of his head with feathers. Piercing slits of ebony formed his eyes while a leering grin split his face as he waited. It was an evil face, and Brianna had to take a great gulp of air before she could bring herself to respond to his demand.

"Aimée," she called, the sight of her friend shivering on the cold ground bringing tears to her eyes. "Ai—Aimée, he—he says—"

Just then, the sound of an exploding musket broke the air, and the brief whine of its ball ceased when it met with the wall of the cabin behind them. Brianna found herself mercifully released as Blood Man dove toward the ground near the Indians' horses. There was a babble of strange sounding tongues as his three companions followed him. Two of them reached their horses.

Then another voice broke the night air with alien sounding syllables. As she crouched over Aimée's prone form, Brianna thought it appeared to be issuing orders. Then she heard Blood Man, also on his horse now, give an ugly laugh before hurling back some sort of guttural reply.

Another musket shot intervened, but, again, its ball lodged in the cabin wall, a good distance from any of them. Then the voice of the unseen Indian, or so Brianna guessed, as he was speaking their language, barked sharply what sounded, from its tone, very much like a threat.

There was a brief discussion among the men who had captured them, with much gesturing toward Brianna and Aimée as they remained where they were, on the ground. Then Blood Man uttered a violent sounding word—an oath, perhaps—and, giving a furious glance in the direction from which the musket had been fired, he signalled with his arm, and the four would-be captors turned their horses' heads and rode off.

When their horses' hooves could no longer be heard and the air was again still—except for Brianna's quiet sobbing—several figures emerged from the trees on the other side of the clearing. Running footsteps sounded, and then strong arms were pulling her up, enfolding her.

"Brianna, are you all right?" Jesse inquired anxiously. His voice sounded taut and strained.

Then the dam broke, and Brianna began to sob violently in his arms.

"Kitten, if they've hurt you, I'll—"

"N-no, not me, but—but Aimée—" She raised her head to see Aimée being held tenderly aloft, in Vulcan's huge arms.

"Oh, Jesse, it was *awful*! H-He *kicked* Aimée!" She broke into more sobs, her whole body shaking with them.

"Vulcan, how is she?" Jesse asked as Garrett, Festus and Laughing Bear joined them in a close circle. Laughing Bear was holding a musket and warily scanning the edges of the clearing with alert eyes.

"Ah done checked huh ribs, suh. 'Pears dey coulda cracked one o' two."

"But I am 'ardly dead yet, *mes amies*," Aimée said in a shaky voice as she tried to lift her head from Vulcan's shoulder.

"Put yo' head back down, woman!" the black man ordered. "Ain' yo' got no sense at all?"

Jesse looked down at his wife's face and found her grinning through her tears. "She's not dead yet," she told him in a quavery voice.

"No, but you both could have been—or worse," Jesse said to her softly as he took his fingers and gently wiped the moisture from her cheeks. He saw her wince when he stroked the side of her face where she'd received the cuffing. "You *are* hurt!" Brianna saw his blue eyes narrow with fury in the gray light of the coming dawn.

"Jesse, who were they?" she asked him. "I mean, I know they were Indians, but—"

"A band of renegades—outcasts from various tribes," Laughing Bear told her as he drew near. "Their trade is in kidnapping and slavery."

"Slavery!" There was shocked terror in Brianna's voice, and she shuddered violently, feeling Jesse's arms tighten about her as he murmured into her hair, "Shh, it's all right now. You're safe."

"Do you feel well enough to travel for a few hours?" This was Garrett's voice. "Your friend's ribs need some looking after, and it isn't that far to Laughing Bear's village. His mother is a knowledgeable medicine woman, and I think she ought to tend her."

Brianna looked to see Aimée, still carefully held by Vulcan, as she sat sideways in front of him on his horse. "If Aimée can make it, then I certainly can," Brianna told them.

"Dass de spirit!" smiled Festus as he laid a gentle hand on her shoulder.

"Well, let's ride then!" said Garrett as he led Lightning and Le Duc from around the side of the cabin. Brianna saw they'd already been saddled and outfitted for travel with the various packs they'd originally carried.

Then Laughing Bear came forward with the women's cloaks (it had grown suddenly far colder than the day before), and they were off.

Jesse insisted she ride double with him on Lightning until he could be sure she was completely well. (The gray colt's saddle accommodated them, for it was not a sidesaddle; Brianna had ridden astride, in her breeches.)

As they rode, he explained the logistics involved in their rescue. Through stealthy spying, Laughing Bear had ascertained the renegades carried no guns. He'd also determined that their knives—the only weapons they did have—had been casually left with their horses during the actual abduction; they were that confident they wouldn't require them to overpower two slight women, he supposed. This information made possible the ploy of firing the musket—wide of any human mark—to surprise and scatter them. Then it was just a matter of Laughing Bear's assuring the renegades, in his own tongue, which he knew even the Seminole, Blood Man, would understand, that they were surrounded. After a few threats and negotiations, an agreement was reached: the renegades would be allowed to leave with impunity if the women were left safely behind.

"But, Jesse," Brianna asked him when he had finished, "What did that—that awful leader of theirs—Blood Man, I mean—what was he saying at the end there, just before he took his men and rode off?"

Jesse looked down at her with raised eyebrows. "You don't miss much, do you, little one?" Then his jaws clenched and the skin across his cheekbones grew taut as he gazed at the trail up ahead. When he answered her, his voice was tight and drawn. "He said one key word: 'Revenge.'"

Brianna's green eyes grew wide with apprehension. "You weren't going to tell me that part, were you?"

Jesse looked down at her again, and his expression was grim. "No, I wasn't, Brianna. Because, before that bastard even begins to think about going near you or any one of us again, he's going to find himself on the receiving end of Indian justice. Seeing Aimée tended to isn't the only reason we're going to Laughing Bear's village. Laughing Bear intends to go to Long Arrow, the chief—his father—and request a party of warriors to track Blood Man and his filthy crew, hunt them down."

"All because of—"

"Because they dared to lay hands on the wife of a blood brother, yes. The only reason they were allowed to ride off safely back there was because we didn't want the lives of you and Aimée endangered. No promises were made for the future. Blood Man is going to pay!"

Chapter Thirty-Two

It was snowing as they entered the Cherokee village. Great white flakes fell softly, for there was almost no wind, but Brianna nevertheless huddled snugly within Jesse's embrace, glad of his gift of imparted warmth. As she peered through the falling whiteness from the loose hood of her cloak, she could make out several long, low wooden structures and, here and there, a leather-draped figure, scurrying through the snow. Up ahead of them she saw another structure made of rough-hewn logs, but this one was wider than the others, though in height, no different.

"That would be Long Arrow's dwelling, up ahead there," said Jesse, "where Laughing Bear's leading us."

The small procession advanced toward the chief's lodge, Laughing Bear at the fore, followed by Festus, Vulcan with Aimée, Jesse with Brianna, and, at the rear, Garrett, leading Le Duc and the horse Jesse had first used. As they neared the entrance, the boy Jasper-Dark Arrow emerged from the lodge's low portal and, after a brief exchange of low-voiced words with Laughing Bear, retreated back into the structure.

Laughing Bear dismounted and gave the signal for the others to do the same. As Brianna felt Jesse's strong arms carefully lower her to the ground, she saw Garrett rush forward to take Aimée from Vulcan's arms while at the same moment two figures emerged from the lodge. The first was the small black woman, Lula; the other was a large Indian woman of proud and regal bearing. They both wore heavy fur wraps of some sort, though their heads were bare. Then, as they stepped to either side of the entrance, a tall male Indian appeared. His head was partly shaved in front with the rest drawn back into a feathered top-knot at the crown of his head. He wore no furs, but was dressed like Laughing Bear, in leather breeches, beaded leather shirt and moccasins; but for the iron gray of his top-knotted hair, he greatly resembled Laughing Bear, right down to the hawklike nose and cleft in his chin.

Brianna heard him exchange a few words with Laughing Bear in the Indian tongue before the brave turned to face them.

"My father, Long Arrow, bids you all welcome and invites you to enter his lodge until the guest lodges can be made ready," said the brave, then added, "My mother—" he gestured at the big Indian woman on his left "—White Fire Woman, wishes to see the little one who is injured." He indicated that Vulcan, who was again holding Aimée, should bring her forward.

When Vulcan did so, White Fire Woman gave a nod, peered briefly at the wide-eyed figure of Aimée in his arms, and pointed to the lodge's entrance. Vulcan bent, still cradling the little gypsy to him with apparent effortlessness, and passed through the opening; White Fire Woman followed them in.

Then Lula stepped forward, saying, "Come on, all of you. We can't have you freezing to death out here."

When they were all inside, Brianna found herself being led by Jesse to a low bench along one wall. She noted several European-style lanterns hanging from the rough-hewn rafters; they gave off a goodly amount of light in the windowless building. She saw clusters of furniture such as one might find in any simple farmhouse owned by a white family placed in various groupings here and there, for the lodge was larger than she had guessed from the outside.

"The Cherokee have an eclectic culture in some respects," Jesse said quietly, bending his head toward hers as he spoke. "When they saw the utilitarian qualities of certain of the white man's furnishings, they adapted them to their own needs." He indicated a long harvest table that graced the center of the dwelling, the only thing marking it as different from similar ones Brianna had seen elsewhere being its legs, which were sawed off to a length of perhaps two feet. All around the table, covering the rough wooden floor, were piles of furred animal skins.

"Because these dwellings are purposely designed with low roofs—the better to hold in heat—taller pieces of furniture are either not used or modified, like that table there," Jesse continued.

"It is surprisingly warm in here," Brianna remarked as her glance fell on a lone cast iron stove that stood not too far from the harvest table.

Jesse chuckled. "Don't underestimate the heating ability of that little piece of apparatus. Garrett and I sailed our ship, *The Marianne*, all the way to Philadelphia to acquire it and several others for Long Arrow's village. And we got to meet the inventor before he died, too." At Brianna's inquiring look he added, "Benjamin Franklin himself. Remind me to tell you all about it sometime." He looked, a bit anxiously Brianna thought, into her eyes. "How are you feeling, little one?"

She gave him a soft smile. "Much better, thank you, though a bit tired." She glanced down at one end of the lodge where Lula appeared busy with some clay pots from which a delicious smelling aroma was emanating. "And hungry, now that I think about it."

"So's Aimée," said Vulcan as he came to join them on the bench from where he'd been watching White Fire Woman's ministrations to the little gypsy along the opposite wall of the lodge. "Dass all dat l'il squirt bin fussin' 'bout since Ah laid huh on dat cot. She sho *love* t' eat! Ah sweahs Ah cain' tell wheah she *put* de food once it git *inside* huh!"

"How is she, Vulcan?" Brianna asked.

"Bettah dan Ah figgahed. Don' 'pear t' be no ribs cracked aftah all. Jes some bruisin'."

"She made o' strong stuff!" added Festus as he came to stand near them, accompanied by Garrett.

At that moment Lula came forward and held out a heavy iron pot to Festus. "Here, man, make yourself useful. Ah need a strong arm to—" She stopped and did a double take, glancing from Festus over to Vulcan and back again. "Twins?" she whispered with an incredulous look on her face.

"Yes," Brianna told her, "and the reason Festus hasn't taken that pot is that he hasn't seen it. He's blind."

Suddenly the pot in question crashed to the floor, its contents of crayfish shells spilling at Lula's feet. *"Blind?"* she questioned in a shaking voice. "Oh, my God!" She turned to Vulcan. "You—what's your name? Vulcan? Do-y-you have a scar...?" She bent toward him and pushed his leather shirt collar aside to uncover his collarbone. Her small hands were shaking.

"Lady, whut dis all 'bout?" Festus inquired, frowning.

A sound like a strangled sob tore from Lula's throat as she exposed a scar about two inches long on Vulcan's shoulder near his collarbone.

By now everyone in the lodge had gathered near, with the exception of Aimée who was peering at them from a sitting position on her cot across the room. They watched the small black woman stand up from where she'd been bending over Vulcan. Tears were streaming down her cheeks. She had one of Vulcan's huge hands in her grasp and took her other hand and reached for Festus's. Then she started to croon in a watery soprano.

"Hush lil baby don' you cry..."

But she got no further. Festus gave out with a loud cry whose origins sounded somewhere between joy and pain, and he pulled the tiny woman into a crushing embrace. Vulcan jumped up and joined them, his huge arms enveloping both his brother and the weeping Lula.

"Sistah!" Vulcan cried. "Sistah, it be a miracle!" And the tears rolled freely down his ebony cheeks.

Festus by now was alternately laughing and crying, his face, too, unabashedly wet as the three of them rocked and trembled with their miracle.

During all of this the others in the room had stood in amazed silence, and now they began to look at one another with expressions ranging from sheer perplexity to astonished gladness.

Brianna turned excitedly to Jesse and Garrett. "They found their *sister*! *Lula's* their *sister*! She was sold away from them when they were only wee mites! Festus told me about her. He—"

"Hold on, hold on, Green Eyes," Jesse laughed as he watched the green sparkle. "Why, I believe you're as excited as they are!"

"Oh, I am, I am!" cried Brianna as she threw her arms around his waist and gave him a fierce hug. "Oh, Jesse! Isn't life wonderful sometimes?"

"It surely is," Jesse murmured into her hair as he held her close. "Wonderful."

Garrett had just finished translating Brianna's explanation to the chief and White Fire Woman, and the two stood before the still embracing trio with beaming looks on their otherwise stern features. Laughing Bear and Jasper-Dark Arrow were behind them grinning.

When at last the twins and Lula broke apart (though they continued to hold hands, a twin on either side, Lula in the middle), Long Arrow addressed them in his Indian tongue.

When he had finished, Lula looked up at one, then the other twin, saying, "My father-in-law, Chief Long Arrow, says this is a strange wonder, a gift of the good spirits, and his village is fortunate, indeed, to be the sight of this wondrous reunion." She wiped a stray tear or two from her cheeks as she spoke, then continued. "He and my mother-in-law wish us continued happiness in our lives which the favoring spirits have worked to join together again."

All three of them turned to Long Arrow and White Fire Woman then, as Lula voiced their thanks, first in English, then in Cherokee. This accomplished, the three fell to hugging all over again, and the lodge filled with the sounds of laughter and celebration.

And a celebration it truly was, for Long Arrow and White Fire Woman sent Jasper-Dark Arrow to the other lodges in the village to spread the news. A village gathering was called, even in the softly falling snow, but then they all withdrew to a large building Brianna hadn't noticed before. It was called the town council house and sat apart from the other buildings on a high mound of earth. Here songs were sung and even a dance performed by the young men of the tribe before each family returned to its lodge for an impromptu feast.

In the lodge of the chief, food was piled high on the center table, for, in addition to the meal Lula had prepared, there were numerous dishes from the other lodges; following the outside celebration, women from each of those other dwellings had appeared at the chief's door bearing gifts ranging from plucked pheasants to pots of venison stew.

The feasting lasted far into the evening, until all of the participants were sated and tired; they remained continuously happy through it all and broke apart only when White Fire Woman announced the guest lodges had been prepared and the guests were to accompany her to them.

Soon Brianna found herself out in the snow again as she, Jesse, Garrett and the twins followed the lantern-bearing Indian woman to two dwellings at the far end of the village. (Aimée had remained behind to be looked after during the night by the chief's wife; White Fire Woman had insisted.)

The houses they approached were considerably smaller than the others in the village, for, as Garrett explained to Brianna and the twins, they were designed only to provide sleeping quarters; guests always ate in the chief's lodge.

Brianna walked beside Jesse as they followed the others, and there was a light and relaxed mood about her, owing to the events of the past few hours. It was only when she saw Garrett and the twins directed to the lodge on the left while she and Jesse were ushered into the other that she began to feel her spirits sag.

It was here, the moment she'd refused to let herself think about on the way to the village, and had had no time to ponder afterward. She would now be left alone with Jesse, and he would surely demand they discuss her running away. She bit her bottom lip to keep it from trembling and waited.

Silently she watched White Fire Woman gesture at a huge pile of furs—obviously bedding—in a corner of the room not far from the Franklin stove. The chief's wife had a broad smile on her face. Then she pointed to a huge brass tub on the other side of the stove. European in fashion, it was half filled with water and had steam coming from it. To the side were several large urns that also contained steaming water, and near those, Brianna's saddle packs that had been on Lightning.

Brianna heard White Fire Woman exchange a few Cherokee words with Jesse, and then she exited, leaving Jesse and Brianna alone.

Jesse came up behind her as she stood near the door and removed the green woolen cloak from her shoulders. Noting the stiffness of her posture, the rigidly held carriage of her neck and shoulders, he guessed what was going through her mind and decided to do what he could to make this difficult time easier for her.

"You'll probably want to take advantage of that bathwater, Brianna. Why don't you relax in the tub while I go down to the creek to bathe?" Jesse picked up one of several large cotton blankets that seemed to have been provided as toweling, for they were stacked on a low stool near the tub.

"The *creek*? In this weather?" Brianna's voice cracked with her question, advertising the tension she felt.

Jesse laughed as he reached for a bar of soap that had been left near the tub. Breaking it cleanly in half with a snap of his wrists, he kept one half after putting the other back. "I've used the Cherokee village's bathing facilities more than a few times over the years, and in colder weather than this. See you later." He ducked his head and was out the door.

Brianna stared at the heavy flap of deerhide that fell back into place over the portal when he left.

Safe for now! What do I say to him when he returns, though? She looked askance and eyed the bundle of furs near the stove. *And what happens when—*

Her thoughts were interrupted by the sound of soft feminine laughter as the flap to the portal swung open and a young Cherokee woman entered the lodge. She was followed in quick succession by two others who lined up beside her inside the entryway and looked at her with smiles on their faces. They doffed the fur-lined animal skins they were wearing, revealing garb that was similar to what Lula and White Fire Woman had worn inside the chief's lodge: beaded leather tunics, reaching to the knees, over leather leggings of some kind, with leather moccasins on their feet. All three were quite young—no older than fifteen or sixteen, Brianna guessed—and quite pretty, with smooth coppery skin and long, ink-black braids down their backs.

The one who had entered first now took a step forward and tapped her chest.

"*Kawi*," she pronounced. Then she pointed to Brianna. "*Ghigau*," she said, grinning now.

Brianna's eyes went wide with recognition. The girl had obviously identified herself and then ascribed to Brianna the Cherokee word for—what was it Father Edouard had said? She pushed her recall back to the day of the berrypicking, when the priest had described a term used in the Cherokee marriage ceremony. She had it! *Ghigau* translated to "beloved woman," meaning the bride! Kawi was calling her a bride!

But Brianna had no more time to contemplate the ramifications of this at the moment, for the three young women were coming toward her, their actions full of rapid movement.

One dipped her hand into the bathwater as if to test its temperature; another shyly approached and began to unbutton her shirt; the third went through the saddle baggage until she found what she wanted: Brianna's soft, sheer white cotton batiste nightrail with green embroidery at its neckline and hem.

Soon she found herself stripped naked, amidst numerous giggles and soft, blushing sighs of admiration over her physical attributes. Then she was gently coaxed into the brass tub, after which an additional urn of water was poured over her long hair.

Kawi produced what looked like a handful of fine soap shavings from a tiny clay jar and began to work these through her hair, all the while making further exclamations of appreciation over her tresses. There was a wonderful light, floral scent given off by the lather.

The other two were meanwhile rubbing the half bar of soap over her shoulders and limbs and gently massaging them with their fingers. The effect was heavenly; a feeling of total lassitude stole over Brianna's body, enveloping her with a sense of luxurious well-being. She leaned back and closed her eyes, her fears of moments before out of mind.

At length they rinsed her hair with the remaining urns of water, sweetly urged her to stand and climb out of the tub with gentle miming gestures, and proceeded to towel dry her hair and body.

As they were doing this, she felt a draught of cool air and turned to see Jesse standing inside the doorway. He was now dressed in clothing that much resembled the apparel Laughing Bear had worn, except that the leather of the shirt and breeches was almost white in color. His dark hair was damp and softly curling over his forehead and around his ears and neck, and as he stood there staring at her, his blue eyes vivid and intense, the corners of his mouth tipped up in a lazy smile.

All at once, the relaxed feeling of serenity and peacefulness she'd been enjoying fled. Under his keen regard she felt herself flush from head to toe; noticing it, the young Indian women began to giggle anew. But they proceeded with their ministrations, pulling her gently to a low stool they'd placed near the stove and combing and brushing her hair with her own grooming implements, produced from her saddlebags.

Finally, they formed a human wall to shield her from Jesse's view, removed the toweling that had been wrapped about her, and settled her nightrail over her shoulders, at last completing the change of attire. Then, in a flurry of further giggles and a softly spoken but unintelligible phrase from Kawi, they left. And she was alone with Jesse again.

"Are you warm enough?" he asked, his eyes never straying from her form as he walked slowly toward her.

Brianna wanted to laugh and would have if it hadn't been for the lump that seemed to have formed in her throat. Warm! She was on fire from her blushing! Swallowing, she answered, "Quite warm enough, thank you."

"Good, but perhaps you'll join me in this drink anyway. I, for one, can use it. The creek was fairly icy."

It was only then Brianna noticed a pair of woodenware goblets that had been left on a low table near the pile of furs. They were filled with a steaming brew of some kind.

"Wh—What is it?" she asked as he took her by the hand and led her toward the table. She nearly jumped as the touch of his hand sent a sudden wave of shock through her.

"Oh, a berry and herb concoction the Cherokee reserve for certain occasions." With his free hand Jesse took one of the goblets and placed it in hers. Then he took the other for himself.

"For certain occa— What *kinds* of occasions? And what was all that *'ghigau'* business? Jesse, if—"

"Shh, love. In a moment," Jesse said quietly as he raised his cup in a soft salute. "For now, drink with me. It won't hurt you. I swear it."

Wondering as much at his mood as at what he was up to, Brianna heaved a sigh, raised her goblet, and drank. Finding the brew deliciously sweet and pungent, she nearly drained its contents, then set the goblet down on the table.

In seconds she felt a warm, heady sensation stealing over her: she glanced up to see Jesse's eyes focused on her face, and there appeared to be a knowing smile on his.

"We've drunk the *ghigau* wine," he told her.

A small frown creased Brianna's brow. "Those women, they—Jesse Randall, I *know* what that *word* means! Father Edouard once mentioned it in connection with a—a marriage ceremony of some kind, and I demand to know—"

"Of course," Jesse interrupted as he pulled her by the hand to indicate they should sit among the comfortable pile of furs. "Here, sit and we'll discuss it."

Knowing in her mind the last thing she wished to do was join him on those furs, Brianna gave a weak tug of resistance but somehow found herself unable to do more and followed him to the bed. She vaguely realized the drink had made her more relaxed than she was supposed to be in this situation, but she was unable to do anything beyond giving it this passing thought.

When they were both comfortably seated beside each other, she looked at him. "Well?"

Jesse smiled. "It seems Lula and Laughing Bear put out the word to the village that we've recently married, so I'm afraid Long Arrow and White Fire Woman arranged for us to enjoy some of the trappings of the wedding ceremony, if not the ceremony itself." He reached out and fingered a curling lock of her hair which had fallen over one shoulder. "Your hair puts silk to shame, Brianna."

Swallowing nervously, Brianna looked away, saying, "You should have explained and saved them the trouble. Why didn't you?"

Ignoring her question, Jesse took his fingers and gently turned her chin so that she faced him again, asking, "Brianna, why did you leave Riverview?"

Here it was, the moment she'd been dreading. Brianna ran her tongue over her lips and replied, "I needed to go home."

"Yes, and why was that?" Jesse asked as he let his fingers trail slowly down her arm. "You knew it was too early for those at Le Beau Château to have summoned you."

Brianna watched his hand descend to cover her own hand which she had unwittingly brought to rest over the place below her abdomen where she carried his child. "I—I just had to," she stammered.

Suddenly Jesse moved her hand slightly and placed his own where hers had been. "Was it because of the babe, Brianna?" he queried softly, his blue eyes holding hers.

Feeling as if he were looking directly into her soul, Brianna knew she couldn't keep the truth from him. Mutely, she nodded as tears threatened her eyes.

"Ah, little one," Jesse sighed as he drew her to him, "don't you know there was nothing to run away from? A child is a blessing, not a shame."

Brianna drew back from him and some of the old fury blazed in her eyes. "Not a child of unwed parents!"

"But we *are* wed," Jesse assured her.

"No!" The denial was almost a shout. "We are *not* truly wed!"

"Oh?" countered Jesse. "That's odd. I was there and I surely—"

"It matters not," she returned hotly. "You know as well as I, the marriage has not been consummated!"

Lantern light danced in the blue eyes. "Well, my *ghigau*," Jesse replied softly, "we'll soon amend that!"

And with the sleek swiftness of the giant cat he often reminded her of, he reached for her and pushed her down into the furs; then he claimed her lips and branded her with a searing, possessive kiss.

Brianna's first, instinctive reaction was panic, and she sought his chest with her hands, intending to push him away, but as the sensual warmth of his mobile mouth met hers, as she felt his body's strength against her own, smelled the clean, masculine scent of him, she suddenly could think of nothing except how long it had been since they had tasted each other fully, of the nights she had lain awake and—yes, she had to admit it now—ached for him.

Hungrily, she reached for him in return, her body already succumbing to the dizzying sensations only he had ever aroused.

Jesse acknowledged the change in her actions with a low, husky laugh against her ear. "That's better, that's much better," he murmured hoarsely.

But Brianna was past caring about this implied acceptance of her surrender. She opened her lips under the silky probing of his tongue and touched it with the tip of her own.

At this Jesse groaned and drew her even closer, entwining limb with limb. And as his tongue played with hers and traced lightly across her teeth and the soft inner recesses of her mouth, Brianna's senses became located in a hot, molten core somewhere in the lower center of her body. Then she felt his manhood pressing, hard and rigid, against the place where her nightrail had ridden up above her thighs.

"Green Eyes," Jesse murmured as his lips traveled over her face, kissing her lightly on cheek, brow, eyelid and temple, "lovely Brianna, God, how I want you . . . always you . . ." His hands were roving over her neck and shoulders, but when they found her breasts and lightly cupped their fullness, Brianna moaned and dug her fingers into his shoulders. Then he was caressing the rigid peaks of her nipples that thrust outward to meet his knowing touch through the sheer fabric of her nightrail, and Brianna went mindless with the pleasure it brought her.

"Jesse, oh, Jesse!" she cried as she arched her body upward against his hardness.

Jesse breathed a shaky laugh before bringing his mouth down to close over one nipple, right through the thin batiste of her gown. And with his hand he sought the silken flesh of her thighs, stroked, then found the sweet, moist place between.

At this touch Brianna became a wild thing. Arching again and twisting against him, she ran her fingers through his hair, pulling his dark head closer. She opened her trembling thighs and felt his fingers find the delicate bud of her longing, and when they stroked it, she let out an unintelligible sound that rent the night air with a piercing sweetness.

Then Jesse was loosing his clothes, half tearing his shirt from his body, swiftly sliding off his breeches while he spoke to her in hoarse, breathless tones. "Hush, sweet love. I know you're ready, but patience will bear you greater pleasure, I promise... sweetheart...mother of my child. You're the woman who's haunted my empty nights, but now you're here, and you were meant for this."

With a quick movement, he removed her nightrail. Then he leaned over her, bracing his arms with a hand on either side of her as he stared deeply into her eyes. "Tell me this is what you want, Brianna," he whispered. "Say it, sweet *ghigau*."

With eyes dark with passion, Brianna looked into his. Her need for him was so great it was a sweet, aching pain and she could not refuse him. "I want you inside of me, Jesse," she whispered. "Take me now."

"Now," rasped Jesse as he plunged and filled her aching void.

Brianna gasped at the sensation of him inside her, then moaned with the pleasure it brought. But quickly she found her longing building again under his slow, rhythmical stroking, and she yearned for more.

And then it came, a great spiraling whorl of pleasure that built and built until....

It broke within her in a shower of stars that sent her mindless, out into the universe, shattering her being as it joined with his.

Jesse felt her convulse beneath him as he spilled his seed where only his had been spilled before, and he triumphed in what they shared. She was truly his now, and he reveled in their oneness as they reached the heights together.

It was many long minutes later before either of them could think or feel in any meaningful way. They lay together wrapped in each other's arms as they felt their breathing return to normal, Jesse with his head buried in her fragrant hair, Brianna with her lips pressed against his neck.

But then she felt him nuzzling her, planting tender kisses against her hair and then her ear. At last he raised his head and looked into her eyes.

"Sweet wife," he whispered with a soft, gentle smile, "you belong to me now, and I can't think of ever letting you go." He lowered his head and softly kissed her love-bruised lips. "Stay with me, lady, for I belong to you as well. Will you stay?"

Brianna met his look with a realization that shook her very being. *She loved him!* Deeply and passionately, wholly and without question, she *knew* she loved him! And now she truly was his wife, and he'd asked her to stay with him. But what of him? She hadn't heard him speak of love. Vaguely, she recalled from the heated moments of their passion, his speaking of the child she carried. Was that it? Was that the reason he had bound her to him?

But she knew she wouldn't leave him now. The ties were too great. So she answered him as best she could, hoping he couldn't read too much in her eyes. "Yes, my husband, I'll stay."

And as Jesse pulled her against him in a glad embrace, she bit back the bitter gall that comes of feeling unrequited love and said no more.

In the early hours before dawn, Jesse lay awake and watched his sleeping wife as he held her in his arms. Happily he let his mind wander back over the events of their night together, savoring each little detail of the hours they'd shared. Tonight it had been different somehow—*she* had been different—and *splendid*! Wistfully, he shook his head. There were so many evanescent moods to this lovely creature who was now truly his wife, and he felt he had yet only begun to know them, to know *her*.

Brianna stirred in her sleep for a moment before settling down to snuggle closely against him, and he smiled, then planted a tender kiss on her brow.

She'd been totally without reserve in her passion tonight, that he knew—more open somehow, although he also sensed there were things on her mind—discernible when the heat of passion passed—that she held from him. What might they be? Did they have to do with the child?

Gently, Jesse took his hand and placed it over her still flat abdomen. A *child*. Sometime next summer he would be a father! And here, beside him, this enchanting, sylphlike sprite who had alternately vexed and fascinated him for all these many weeks—months!—was his and would bear him that child. His head swam with the implications.

Then, thunderstruck, he faced the truth that had lain lodged, unnamed, in his mind and heart for some time now. *He loved her!*

When had he fallen in love with her? He couldn't rightly say. And, more importantly, when did he dare tell her of that love without frightening her away like the wild creatures of the forest she often reminded him of?

He turned and gazed at the sleeping face with its perfect contours and exquisite lips, softly parted now in slumber.

Dearest Brianna, beloved woman, take the love I bear you and know that it cannot harm you, take it and hold it in your heart and let it bear the fruit of loving in return, as you have taken my seed to bear within your body. For my part, I will hold my tongue and bide my time until I know the moment is ripe to tell you of my love. And in the meanwhile, my beautiful darling, I will do all I can to show you without words, and mayhap lead you to trust and—God, I pray it may be so!— learn to love me in return.

Jesse smiled as he finished this silent paean to his wife. From now on he would woo her, pleasure her, delight her, do everything he could to make her happy. Then, maybe, if he was lucky and the fates were kind—but they *had* to be! He would not give up until it happened, until his wife and he could love each other, openly and freely, he swore it!

At last feeling a great matter had been settled in his mind, Jesse pressed his head into the furs beside his wife and slept.

Chapter Thirty-Three

Brianna sat before the mirror of her dressing table in the master bedroom at Riverview—the chamber she now shared with Jesse while the adjoining room he'd once occupied was being readied as a lying-in nursery. She casually examined her reflection while thoughts that were tangled and disjointed ran through her head.

Soon Lula and Aimée would be calling her downstairs to help them make garlands and wreaths for the Yuletide celebrations. Christmas was a week away.

She saw herself smile as she thought of Lula. The small black woman had accompanied her brothers back from Long Arrow's village and had remained as Riverview's guest so she could get to know them better—or as Lula herself had put it, "to see they stay out of trouble!" More than that, she had taken to ordering her huge "baby brothers" about on a regular basis, doing everything from scolding Vulcan for taking too much of Festus' time away from his silversmithing (of which she heartily approved—"a man needs his independence") to insisting they eat more vegetables and grains ("The Indians know how to eat right—why can't you?"). Half their size, she ran them ragged with orders, and they loved every minute of it. There was real love there.

Love—Brianna's eyes suddenly grew moist with tears as her mind tripped on the word. Slowly, her hand strayed to the spot below her abdomen as she thought of the babe she carried. Such a tiny thing, and yet she loved it fiercely already. She closed her eyes and tried to stem the flow of tears. If only—

With an angry swipe of her hand, she dashed a tear from her cheek, but the pain remained.

Unbidden, her thoughts crept back to the hours before dawn when Jesse had held her in his arms, making sweet, passionate love to her helplessly yielding body and touching her very soul as he did so, though she prayed to God he didn't see it.

What torture! To love a man as deeply as she did and yet dare not let him know. To know the love was unreturned and still hope against hope this might change; this was especially so during those moments when he claimed her body, which, since their return from the Cherokee village, was often—frequently again and again, during the night.

Brianna smiled in spite of herself. There was even the morning he'd returned for his gloves and surprised her in her bath. They'd gotten water all over the floor with their sport, finishing by making sweet, wild love on the carpet beside their bed.

But always, later, as he held her tenderly in the aftermath of their lovemaking, there was the anguish. And there were also those moments when they ran into each other during the day; these, too, offered her little respite from her plight. She'd be busy arranging holly in a vase or some such casual task, and Jesse would walk through the door, surprising her; just seeing him, then—his blue eyes meeting hers as that wonderful mouth formed a heartstopping smile, as those devastating male dimples turned her knees to jelly, as the sheer maleness of him overpowered her senses—was enough to so unsettle her mind, she couldn't think clearly; and when the moment passed—often not before he had touched her in some way, kissing her softly on the ear or fingering her hair as he passed through the room—she would remain more shaken than ever, with thoughts of Sally Hemings crowding her mind.

A sharp rapping at her door broke Brianna's reverie. "Who is it?"

"It's Laurette," came the widow's sharp response. "Milady may not be aware of it, I realize, but the hour is past ten," she added sarcastically. "I require your presence in the library immediately, Brianna. Or did you forget that we have a ball to organize in a fortnight's time?"

"No, I've not forgotten," Brianna replied wearily. "I'll join you there in about ten minutes, Laurette."

"See that it's no more. Really, Brianna, since you've taken to lying about in your chamber in the mornings, I've begun to hold some doubts about your progress in your training. Try to be more punctual in the future! I'll see you in ten minutes—no more!"

As she heard Laurette's footsteps retreat down the hallway, Brianna slammed her brush down on the dressing table. "Be more punctual," indeed! And what about the widow's punctuality, or the hours *she* kept? For some time now, during the last few weeks, Laurette had taken to riding out on the mare Jesse had provided for her use at Riverview and disappearing for hours at a stretch. She told no one where she went, and since Laurette had never been known to be overly fond of pleasure riding—unless accompanied by a man—Jesse, in particular—Brianna and Aimée had begun speculating on the nature of her excursions into the countryside. Why, once Lula had even encountered her going out after dark! And the tiny black woman had at that time commented to Brianna and Aimée that "she looked for all the world like a woman on her way to an assignation!"

Well, Brianna thought as she hurriedly removed her dressing gown and searched through her armoire for something to wear, if Laurette had a lover, so much the better for the rest of them, for perhaps it would blunt the edges of the nasty temper she had displayed ever since coming there, that is, unless the lover were—

Brianna's mind closed like a steel trap to shut out his name. She had enough problems handling her current relationship with her husband, and she couldn't bear to think—

With a furious yank, she tore a moss green and cream striped day gown from the armoire and began to dress.

Laurette marched through the door to the library with a luffing of skirts, only to slow herself to a graceful glide when she noticed Jesse seated at the large kneehole desk there. Seeing him intent upon some sort of ledger in front of him, she let out her best version of a ladylike sigh in hopes of catching his attention as she approached.

"Oh, Laurette," said Jesse as he looked up from his work, "good morning."

"It is *now*," replied the widow as she lifted one generously rounded hip and perched on the edge of the desk before him. "Honestly, Jesse, I hardly ever see you anymore. You're always running off somewhere on this old plantation of yours." She threw him a practiced pout.

"Well, Laurette," Jesse told her, annoyance showing in his voice as he snapped the ledger shut and rose from his seat, "as one who advertises herself as a specialist in managing the interior workings of a large estate, you shouldn't be too surprised to find its exterior workings require time and energy as well." He came around the desk and began unrolling his sleeves as he started in the direction of the door.

Seeing his movement, Laurette rose and placed herself in his path. "Are you leaving already? Come, come, sir! And no time to stay a moment and converse with a lady?" She reached a heavily beringed ivory hand up and smoothed an imaginary wrinkle from his shirtfront.

"I'm expected at the granary shortly, Laurette, so if you've something important to tell me, I pray you, please be quick about it. I've no time for idle conversation this morning." He turned and reached for his jacket from where it had been draped over the back of a nearby chair.

As she watched the magnificent play of his muscles, visible even under the white cotton shirt he wore as he shrugged into the garment, Laurette's tongue ran slowly over her lower lip. He was such a perfect specimen of masculinity! Why should that childish slut Brianna have him? Quickly seizing on something to force him to bide his time, the widow hastily said, "I'm afraid it's about your wife."

Jesse paused in the act of buttoning his jacket. "Go on," he said quietly.

"Well, Jesse, I fear my report to Simpson this month cannot be favorable. The child had taken to sleeping until far too late an hour these past weeks. Everyone knows the mistress of a great household needs to be up and about at an early hour. How else will her servants—"

"I am well aware of the requirements, madam. And if my memory serves me well, I believe that in the past, Brianna more than fulfilled the one you cite. Suffice it to say, however, that because of her present condition, I myself have told her to—"

"Condition?" The widow's eyebrows shot up suspiciously. "What condition?"

"Why, I'd assumed you knew, Laurette. Brianna carries our child."

"Your *child*?" Laurette appeared to slump visibly at the news. "But I thought—that is, there were rumors even at Le Beau Château that your marriage was not—"

"Disabuse your mind of any such rumors, madam," Jesse replied hotly. "The fact is that my wife is with child and has been suffering with a touch of the morning sickness of late, although she tells me it is on the wane. Nevertheless, I cannot think that she is not in need of extra rest during this time, and I have instructed her to take it when she can, mornings included. You, madam, will therefore make allowances in your schedule and say no more about it, especially to Simpson or any other legal authorities. Is that clear?"

Laurette heard all of this in a state of outraged shock, and as the vehemence of Jesse's tone increased, had begun backing away from him. This caused her to miss seeing the sewing basket she had brought down earlier and placed beside an upholstered chair near a wall of books. Suddenly, her heel collided with the basket, and she whirled in a fury and gave it a vicious kick. The basket tumbled over and lost its lid while at the same moment a furry black and white apparition emerged.

"Ahh!" screeched Laurette. "You miserable beast!" She bent down and lunged for the skunk with hands formed like claws.

Then all at once, Laurette gave out with a piercing scream as she put her hands to her throat and staggered backward. "No-o-o!" she screamed again. "It's *real*! It *sprayed me*! Oh, my gown! Oh-h-h!"

Jesse stood frozen in his tracks as his nose picked up an offensive odor; he watched the furred animal saunter away from the widow, its plume of a tail still high in the air.

By now a bevy of servants were crowding the doorway, including Vulcan who had come to see what was keeping Jesse. Suddenly the big black man went into motion. Removing his leather coat as he moved, he advanced toward the skunk and threw the garment over it. Then, ever so quickly, he bent and scooped up the bundle he'd made—coat and skunk—and headed for the door.

The crowd that had gathered there suddenly dispersed, fingers pinching off noses as they gave Vulcan and his package a wide berth.

During all of this Laurette continued to wail and shriek, carrying on like some refugee from Bedlam, while Jesse shook his head in disbelief.

At that moment, Aimée rushed through the door, followed quickly by Brianna and Lula and, more reluctantly, a pair of chambermaids—prominently holding their noses.

Lula was the first to speak. "Mary, Nancy, take the widow up to her chamber and prepare her a bath." The two chambermaids advanced gingerly toward the hysterical Laurette and ushered her out of the room. When they had gone, the black woman turned to Aimée and Brianna and winked. "Got her good 'n proper!"

As Aimée ran to open a pair of windows, Jesse thundered, "What in hell is going on?"

Suddenly the room echoed with peals of feminine laughter as Aimée and Lula convulsed in mirth.

Brianna stood with a dumbfounded expression on her face as she daintily raised an embroidered handkerchief to her nose. Then her eyes lit up as she glanced from Aimée to Lula and back again. "Oh, no! You two *didn't*—"

"Yes, we did!" howled Lula, still bent over with laughter. "We—We—" more laughter "—We substituted a wild skunk for—for—what's his name, Aimée?"

"B—Bon-Bon!" chortled the little gypsy gleefully as she wiped tears from her eyes.

Brianna looked at Jesse. Jesse looked at Brianna. Suddenly, the two of them found themselves as helpless with laughter as their two companions.

"Ah, ladies," gasped Jesse when he could finally speak, "I ought to be angrier than hell at you for ruining the use of this room for at least a week, but—but—" another hearty laugh boomed from his throat "—I somehow haven't the heart for it!"

"Indeed!" grinned Brianna as she recovered from her mirth in Jesse's arms, having collapsed in helplessness against his chest when her laughter was in full force. "But I assure you, sir, we shall *all* have the *noses* for it!"

A renewal of laughter exploded at her wit before the four of them at last settled down.

"But how did you manage it?" Brianna asked Lula as they left the library and headed for the drawing room where the women had decided to have some tea. They walked at a leisurely pace with Brianna feeling better than she had in hours. She felt Jesse's arm about her waist and had just glanced up to find him smiling down at her with a soft light in his eyes, and she suddenly found herself wishing he didn't have to be off to the granary so soon.

"Ah got this potion from the Cherokee last week when Night Cryer was fussing so badly and not sleeping," Lula told them. "It's perfectly harmless when used carefully, but it sure knocked that skunk out for a while!"

"And where did you come by a real, wild skunk, Aimée?" questioned Brianna.

Aimée gave Jesse a fleeting glance. "Vulcan," she said.

"With a humane trap I got from Laughing Bear," added Lula.

Jesse shook his head and grinned. "I can only say I'd never want to get on the wrong sides of you ladies. Lula, I know Laurette's had it out for Aimée for some time, but how did she get to you?"

"Told me to keep mah 'darky nose' out of the breakfast room until she was finished eating," snapped the black woman. "So Ah decided to stick it in her sewing basket instead!"

There was more laughter before Jesse and the women parted at the entrance to the drawing room. There Jesse hugged his wife to him in a happy embrace, kissed her on the nose and whispered he was glad to see her smiling and would see her at dinner.

Then the three women sent for tea, and spent the rest of the day sitting beside a cozy fire, making Yuletide garlands.

It was Christmas Eve, and the Big House at Riverview was quiet. The servants had been given time off that they might spend it and Christmas Day with their own families or at their leisure; Brianna, Jesse, Aimée, the twins, Lula and Night Cryer

would be joining Garrett's family at Riverlea for Christmas Day
dinner, so Jesse had determined there was no need to keep the
staff on hand, although Brianna and he had distributed gifts to
them that morning, wishing them a joyous Yuletide as well.

Brianna sat before the fire that burned brightly in the master bedchamber and dried her hair, using the new ivory-backed
brush Aimée had given her when they'd exchanged gifts after
dinner. She knew the little gypsy was in her chamber trying on
the wine red satin dressing gown she'd given her, and hoped she
liked it on her as much as she had when it lay in its box.

Her gaze drifted to the small package that lay on her dressing table wrapped in white tissue paper. Her gift to Jesse.
Would he like it? She had had the very devil of a time deciding
what to give him to commemorate the tradition of the Magi and
had finally selected something she herself treasured among the
small collection of valued items she'd brought with her from
France. It was a beautiful leatherbound volume of poetry
written by a man named John Donne who'd lived over a century ago, and she'd purchased it with carefully hoarded funds
last year after hearing Madame Mézières recite one of his po-
ems—in lilting, softly accented English—after Brianna had returned from her brief stay in America following her mother's
death. She could still recall the opening lines . . .

> Death be not proud, though some have
> called thee Mighty and dreadful, for
> thou art not so; For those whom thou
> think'st thou dost overthrow Die not,
> poor death . . .

The fire hissed and crackled as a charred log fell in the grate;
a shower of sparks flew upward, bringing Brianna's attention
back to the present. She shifted her position on the low stool
Aimée had set before the hearth for her following her bath.
"You do not wish to catch the chill with your wet head,
Brianna," she had said. "It would not be good for you or the
bébé." Brianna smiled as she pulled the brush through her
nearly-dry hair. Everyone close to her was so solicitous of her
health these days! But, actually, now that the morning sick-

ss had passed, she knew she'd never felt better. Why, if it eren't for the slight tightness of her gowns—

Suddenly the door flew open, and she looked up to see Jesse anding there wearing his tricorn and coat, which looked ightly wet. He threw her a dazzling smile.

"Bon Noël, madame!" He doffed the tricorn and threw it on e rug in front of the hearth, then began to unbutton his coat. It's a cold and rainy night out there, love," he added, "but I e bounteous warmth in here!" He tore off his coat, hung it tickly over the back of a chair and reached to pull Brianna off e stool and into his arms. "Mmm, all manner of warmth," e murmured as he nuzzled her ear.

As always these days, Brianna felt a delicious spread of the armth he spoke of stealing over her body at his touch. *"Bon oël, Monsieur,"* she whispered shyly as her arms stole around s waist.

"God, but you feel good!" Jesse breathed as he pulled her en closer. Then, nipping her earlobe lightly with his teeth, he id, "But, wait! I've something that will lend this evening easure," and with a quick turn, he reached for his coat and tracted a small flask.

Seeing it, Brianna said, "That has a familiar look to it."

"And well it should, love," Jesse remarked as he went to his est of drawers and, opening the top drawer, took a pair of randy snifters from it. "It's a gift from Father Edouard and me by way of the post coach this afternoon. He also sent this issive," Jesse added as he reached into another pocket and ithdrew a white vellum envelope bearing a red-waxed seal.

While Jesse poured their brandies, Brianna took the letter d read:

My Dears—
The joyous news of your expected child has reached me, and I am delighted for both of you, far beyond what these humble words can relate.

I regret my duties keep me from attending your New Year's celebration, but I look forward to seeing you next summer—perhaps when the babe has arrived.

Until then, joy, peace, love and the blessings of God be with you.

I remain,
Your loving friend,
Fr. Edouard

"Oh, Jesse!" Brianna exclaimed. "He won't be able to mak it to the ball. Oh, I miss him so!"

"I know, sweetheart," said Jesse as he handed her a snifte of the priest's brandy. "But we'll drink a toast to the goo father's health as well as to this blessed eve. Here, love—" Jess touched his glass to hers "—to Father Edouard. Long may h live and in good health, and to this joyous season, may it be th first of many, many we share together, with our offspring b our side."

He looked deeply into the green eyes that met his. "And t us, Brianna," he added softly, "may we share a long and happ marriage."

They raised their glasses and drank, the final words of Jesse' toast filling their hearts, though neither spoke of it. But thei eyes said much that the moment would not allow to form upo their lips.

When they had drunk, Jesse took both glasses and set then down on Brianna's dressing table, then turned to her and hel out his arms. "Come, sweet, for I've a need burning within tha comes from something more than the brandy."

With a gay laugh, Brianna flew into his arms, saying, "Yo have a ravenous appetite, sir!"

Jesse chuckled as he wound his arms about her at the hip and drew her boldly to him. "If I do, it's a hunger matched b my lusty wife's, bite—" he bit her lightly on the neck "—b bite—" his teeth nibbled at her throat "—by bite!" He caugh her lower lip briefly with his teeth, then drew back and looke at her for a moment. Suddenly his expression changed to on of serious mien. "Ah, lady," he breathed, and his mouth close across hers in a hungry claim.

When at last their lips parted, Brianna made a weak effort a stilling her shaky breathing as she murmured, "Lusty!" with a trembling little laugh.

"Aye, lady," whispered Jesse, his own voice strained with passion. "Deliciously, wonderfully—lusty."

But as he spoke, Brianna's eyes strayed beyond his shoulder to the tissue-wrapped package on her dressing table. "Oh, but Jesse," she got out, "I haven't given you my gift. I—"

"Later, love," he breathed. "Later."

And so it was later—a long time later—that Jesse held her tenderly in his arms in the sweet aftermath of their lovemaking and saw her turn to him and say in tones that reminded him of a lazy, sated cat, "Mmm, I'd almost forgotten. *Now* may I give you my gift?"

He looked into the green eyes that were still misty with remembered passion and wondered how he'd ever lived before he met her. *Soon—soon, I'll be able to tell you how loved you are, beloved, when the time is right and you're no longer afraid, and then, watch us soar on eagles' wings to heights we never dreamt were possible.* "You've just given me the rarest of gifts, sweet wife," he said to her as he traced a finger down the side of her neck and shoulder; it followed the swell of her breast and met the crested peak with a touch as light as a butterfly's wing.

Brianna closed her eyes against the onslaught of renewed desire. She wanted to give him that book! With a forced surge of willpower, she disentangled her unclothed body from his and sprang up, then reached for the package on the dressing table. Feeling an overcoming shyness that stemmed as much from standing thus bared under his gaze as from her concern that he would not like her gift, she handed him the package with tentative fingers.

Jesse grasped her free hand and pulled her down on the rug beside him, then planted a soft kiss on her ear before commencing to unwrap the present.

When the book's cover was laid bare and he read the gold-embossed inscription denoting its contents, he flashed her a bold grin. "You've been conferring with Garrett," he pronounced.

"Garrett? Why, no, I—"

"How else, then, would you have known to present me with the works of my favorite poet?"

"Your fa— Oh, Jesse! *Really?* You're not just saying that to—"

"'Busy old fool, unruly Sun/Why dost thou thus,/Through windows, and through curtains call on us?/Must to thy motions lovers' seasons run?'" Jesse quoted. "That's the opening to—"

"'The Sun Rising,' yes, I know," said Brianna. "'Saucy pedantic wretch, go chide/Late school boys, and sour prentices,/Go tell the court-huntsmen that the king will ride,/Call country ants to harvest offices;/Love, all alike, no season knows, nor clime,/Nor hours, days, months, which are the rags of time'." She smiled shyly as she finished the verse he'd begun. "Oh, you do know Donne! Isn't he wonderful?"

"Not half so wonderful as my discovery that my young wife has unsuspected depths and more than wit enough to love and appreciate such. John Donne, my darling, is a very difficult poet!"

"Hmph," sighed Brianna, "and don't I know it! Especially when he seems to be playing on words with perhaps several layers of meaning. Look here—" she said. She turned a few pages of the volume before them and read, "'We die and rise the same, and prove/Mysterious by this love.'" She looked up at Jesse. "Now the word, 'die'—"

Jesse's soft laughter cut her off.

"What's so funny?" she queried, not a little perturbed. "I only cited a word that even the abbess at my convent didn't—"

"Ah, sweetheart," Jesse interrupted as he worked at stifling his amusement for her sake, "if you went to a nun for help with interpretation of that multi-edged meaning, I'm afraid you were bound to be confused!"

"But why? She did suggest Donne's submerged allusion to martyrdom, so—"

"Ah, yes—that she'd be prepared to deal with," Jesse told her, "but as for the other...." Suddenly he took her head with his two hands and looked tenderly at her face. "Little innocent," he said gently, "what you and your abbess couldn't know—or, in her case, perhaps pretended not to know—was that in England in the last century, and even earlier, going back to the age of Elizabeth, in the common language 'to die' referred to the death of..." Jesse took his nose and brushed it lightly across hers and back again. "... physical desire following repletion." He kissed her lightly with his lips.

Brianna's eyes grew wide as she took in his meaning. "No!" she breathed.

"Oh, yes," Jesse replied, grinning. "And not only that," he added as he took his hands and began to stroke the hair that fell riotously about her bare shoulders, "but they also believed that the ultimate lovers' pleasure shortened life."

"Oh-h," said Brianna as she gave him a solemn nod. Then a brief frown crossed her brow. "But of course, none of that's true! I mean, in this enlightened age we know..." Her voice grew softer as her hand dropped to her belly. "... that, if anything, such—such *activity* increases life in a way...."

Jesse's hand covered the one she held over her womb. "Aye, love, it does, in truth."

"Well," said Brianna, flushing under his warm gaze, "I'm certainly glad we live in this time."

"And so am I," Jesse assured her with another grin. "I've no wish to part from this planet so early. But, speaking of time, the hour grows late, and I haven't given you—here," he said, suddenly jumping up and reaching for his discarded waistcoat. He paused for a moment to fish in one of its pockets, then withdrew a small black leather box. Then he knelt down beside her on the carpet and held it out before her in the palm of his hand. "For you, love," he said softly.

When Brianna saw the warmth in his eyes, she found herself almost unable to move. Why, he was almost acting as if—was it *possible*? Could he have begun to care for her in— But then she had a sudden recall of his hand over hers and the babe, and she dismissed her fleeting hopes. It was because she carried his child—no more, and she was foolish to have dared to—

With a quick movement, she seized the box and opened it. There, before her, on a bed of black velvet, lay a pair of the most exquisite earrings she'd ever seen. Two perfectly matched emeralds were each encircled by a double row of brilliant diamonds, and held together by the most delicately wrought gold filigree work. The jewels winked and sparkled at her with light reflected from the fire, and it was a moment before she let out the breath she didn't realize she'd been holding.

"Oh, Jesse," she breathed as she raised her eyes to his, "they're so beautiful! I can't—oh, I haven't the words—"

"Not nearly as beautiful as the woman who will wear them," Jesse told her. "Now, will you put them on? I've an odd wish to see the green of your eyes eclipse that of those emeralds."

Rising with the box in her hand, Brianna went to her dressing table and donned the earrings. As she moved, Jesse watched the play of her auburn tresses as they fell about her back and hips and resisted the urge to pull her back down on the carpet and save the earrings for later.

"Well?" Brianna questioned as she turned from the mirror to face him. "What do you think?"

"I think you take my breath away," he answered as he held out a hand to hers. "And I don't mean because of those tokens you're wearing," he added as he drew her down beside him.

"*Tokens!*" Brianna exclaimed. "You present me with a gift fit for a queen, and you call them *tokens*?"

"Sh-h, softly, love," Jesse whispered as he touched a pair of fingers to her lips. "What brought the word to mind was one of the sonnets in my new book there." He reached for the volume. "Here it is," he said after thumbing over a few pages, "'The Token.'"

"Oh! I remember that one now," said Brianna excitedly.

"'Send me some token, that my hope may live,/'" Jesse read, "'Or that my easeless thoughts may sleep and rest;/Send me some honey to make sweet my hive,/That in my passion I may hope the best./'..."

"Yes," said Brianna, "but then he goes on to cite a whole list of things she should *not* send him—not any 'riband,' or 'ring,' or 'corals,' or 'thy picture,' because—and, here it is, in the final couplet—

> "'Send me nor this, not that, to increase
> my store, But swear thou think'st I love
> thee, and no more.'

"Ah! I see. The token the title speaks of is her belief that she is loved! So the sonnet makes the word itself take on a whole new meaning!"

Jesse watched the excitement sparkle in her eyes and thought of gems rarer than those at her ears. He heard the music in her voice and thought of poetry far sweeter than the words they'd just read. He read the exuberance in her soul and knew his own was touched.

"Sweet wife," he whispered as he drew her down to lie beside him, "I have just begun to discover a whole new meaning to lots of things." And with a heart brimful of love, yet tingled with pain at its containment, he urged her sweetly yielding body to blossom and open under his tutored hands. And it was far into the night before they slept, far into the night.

Chapter Thirty-Four

"But that's impossible!" Brianna exclaimed as she set her cup of breakfast chocolate down on the table with a clatter.

"Nevertheless, it's your duty as a hostess to accept it and render it possible," Laurette replied.

"But why should we accept Honoré into our home when we can no longer abide his company? I don't care if he *is* Governor Pinckney's houseguest! It was the Governor who was out of order to take the liberty of asking him along," Brianna fumed, "not to mention asking us to accept him!"

"Perhaps," Laurette countered, "but if you value your husband's reputation among the people who count for something in this state, you'll go along with Pinckney's social *faux pas* in this matter. You *do* regard Jesse's standing as important, don't you, Brianna?"

Brianna looked at the widow coolly for a moment. She wondered if there wasn't something strange afoot here. Laurette seemed to be pleading Jesse's case well enough, but—she remembered there being something about her and Honoré being linked in the scandal they'd barely avoided over the incidents at the ball at Le Beau Château. What was the widow's interest in Honoré Dumaine?

"Laurette, are you sure I've heard *all* your reasons for seeing Honoré invited here?" Brianna queried.

At that moment the door to the breakfast room swung open and Jesse entered with Isaac a pace behind, causing Brianna to look their way and miss the slight flush of color that infused Laurette's cheeks.

"Hello, love," Jesse smiled as he came toward her. He touched his knuckles under her chin to raise it and brushed her lips with a light kiss. "Everything in order for this evening? You haven't taxed yourself overly or left too many things to be done at the last minute, have you?" he added as he peered into her face with a concerned look.

"Well, no," Brianna replied, "but there has been a last-minute complication."

"Oh? And here I was just trying to head off another that Isaac has encountered, I'm afraid. He says the Pierce Butlers have sent a message ahead to say they've changed their minds and will be staying the night." He turned to Laurette. "Will there be any problem arranging a guest chamber in time?"

"Actually, no," Laurette answered. "John Drayton just sent a servant to say he's coming, but can't stay over, so the two cancel each other out, so to speak. But I think you'd better listen to your wife's—"

"Oh, Jesse!" Brianna cut in. "Pinckney's sent word that he's bringing a houseguest along—Honoré Dumaine!"

"The deuce, you say!" Jesse exclaimed. He looked at the widow. "You knew about this?"

"Ah, only when your wife learned of it—a short while ago," Laurette told him. "But Brianna and I have just been all through it. There's hardly any way we can graciously refuse. The Governor—"

"Yes, yes, I know—*damn* Pinckney anyway!" Jesse turned back to Brianna. "Well, love, it's up to you. If you don't want the man here, there isn't a devil in hell that can make me admit him. I—"

"Pinckney's footman who delivered the message *did* imply there were good *political* reasons for his employer's actions," Laurette hastened to add. She cast Brianna a meaningful look.

"Oh, bother!" Brianna muttered exasperatedly. "I suppose it won't make that much of a difference if he comes. With the great number of guests present, I doubt we'll have to run into him too often anyway."

"Well, if you're sure—" Jesse began.

"Of course, she's sure," Laurette interjected. "Now, Brianna, isn't it time you went up to your chamber and rested? You don't want to be too fatigued for your own ball, do you?"

Speculating again on the widow's motives—she rarely, if ever, showed such solicitousness over her health—Brianna rose from the table. She was feeling a bit tired, for they'd been up rather late the night before, checking last-minute details.

Jesse helped her up from the table, saying, "Laurette is right, sweet. Your health is the most important consideration right now. As for any more last-minute problems, I'm sure Isaac and the others can handle them. Come, now, up to your chamber, madam. I'll not have you looking anything but rested and ravishing tonight."

Brianna allowed herself to be led from the room without any resistance. It was odd, she thought, how the simple occurrence of being with child had mellowed her. She could remember a time when the revelation of Honoré's intrusion would have set her to exploding with angered indignation and worse. But, these days, she realized, she just didn't become as upset about things as she once might have.

Jesse smiled as he looked down and saw Brianna's hand press the spot just below her abdomen. "Do you feel something of him yet?" he queried softly.

Brianna looked up to meet the blue eyes that gazed down at her so warmly. She knew he was thinking of last night when, after a sweetly satisfying session of tender lovemaking, they had lain in bed and taken turns touching her belly to see if they could detect what Doctor Barrett had called a quickening. "You know the doctor said it was probably too soon," she whispered, blushing. "And what makes you so certain it's a *him*? Girl babies do have a way of appearing from time to time, you know."

Jesse bent and kissed her forehead. "Just so long as she appears as the spitting image of her mother, I'll have no objections, madam." He grinned down at her. "Now, off with you! Go and get some rest! I'm for the stables, and I'll see you when it's time to dress for this evening." With an additional kiss to her cheek, he left, and Brianna retired to her chamber.

Guests began arriving throughout the day, but, as she had promised, Christie Randall arrived around mid-day and acted as interim hostess so that Brianna could continue to rest. Most of the Charleston gentry would be there. Middletons, Rutledges, Pinckneys, they'd all accepted invitations. And there would be guests from out of state as well. Thomas Jefferson had regretfully declined (as to why, Jesse thought he understood only too well; there were rumors the Secretary was close to resigning again), but he was sending his daughter Martha and son-in-law Thomas in his place. Garrett's father-in-law, wealthy planter Charles Trevellyan, had already arrived at Riverlea for the holidays and would be attending with his daughter and son-in-law. And then there were the Virginia Lees, known to Jesse and Garrett from business dealings in the past; they were in Carolina visiting relatives and had eagerly accepted, too.

Soon it grew dark over the rainy tidewater countryside, but the Big House at Riverview glowed with warmth and light as the busy folk within prepared to celebrate the New Year. Hundreds of candles shone from chandeliers and candelabra, sconces and candlestands. Everywhere, the house's many rooms glowed with the sheen of the softly polished fine woods of the furniture and beeswaxed floors. Delicious aromas wafted from the kitchens, and flute, harpsichord and oboe broke the air with their individual sounds as musicians tuned their instruments.

In the master bedchamber Brianna waited patiently as Aimée fastened the last of the hooks at the back of her gown.

"*Voilà! Madame*, your gown is secured," Aimée pronounced as the last fastening was completed.

"Yes," giggled Brianna, "but I wonder how secure *I'll* be!" She touched her fingers lightly to the eye-catching swell of her breasts that pushed above the low *décolletage* of her gown. "That *modiste* and I thought we'd allowed for the—ah—developments of pregnancy when she took my measurements at all the sittings, but I fear I've grown some more in the last few days."

"Then our babe won't be lacking of milk," said a familiar voice from the interior doorway.

Brianna turned to see Jesse standing there, a bold grin on his features.

"Ah, well, I shall be running along, *chérie*," Aimée said hastily as she made for the outer door. "Laurette demands help with her *toilette*—from *me*, of all people!" She shrugged. "The maid who usually helps her is busy with the guests. Who knows, maybe I'll get lucky and have an accident, tearing her gown!'' She blew them a kiss and left.

When she had gone, Brianna turned to her husband. She was blushing. ''I—I didn't know you were in there,'' she stammered, indicating the nursery, but thinking of his remark about her milk; she began to tug upward at the neckline of her gown.

''Don't,'' said Jesse as he came toward her. ''They're beautiful. *You're* beautiful.'' He sat on the edge of their bed with his thighs spread as he took her by the hands and drew her between them. Then, holding her gently at the waist, he pulled her closer yet and planted a kiss first at one, and then at the other of her breasts. ''Beautiful,'' he breathed.

''But— But—'' stammered Brianna. ''You won't mind if I go downstairs like this? All the world will see—''

''Of course, I'll mind,'' said Jesse. ''I'm a man, and I'm human, but I'll also remind myself that those gentlemen down there will look, but never dare to touch that which is mine. It will have to do,'' he added with a smile. ''Now, stand back a pace, if you will, madam, and let a poor man gaze in private for a moment on that loveliness he's lucky enough to possess.''

Brianna dimpled and did as he requested. The *dècolletage* in question belonged to a velvet gown of green, a green so deep, it appeared almost black. It was fashioned along the lines of a *robe en chemise*, but Brianna had prevailed upon the seamstress to make a few changes. For one, the sleeves were shorn off into little caps at her shoulders; in their place she wore armlength, black satin gloves that she'd also helped design. The other alteration involved her waistline. Instead of using a sash that was so wide as to encompass all of her midriff, the black band of satin that rested under her breasts was a mere two inches wide. This made for a high-waisted effect that was practical as well as charming, for it perfectly camouflaged Brianna's slightly thickened waistline. From the satin sash, the gown fell in soft velvet folds to the black satin dancing slippers she wore.

Aimée had spent over an hour on her hair, fashioning it into an elaborate cluster of curls atop her head, and curving downward from these on one side were two ostrich plumes, one dyed a deep green, the other, black. Completing the picture were the emerald and diamond earrings, her Christmas gift from Jesse.

"You are incomparable, madam," Jesse breathed when he had looked his fill, "but there is just one more thing." He reached into the pocket of the deep blue evening coat he wore and withdrew a black leather box about the size of his hand. "Here," he said as he stood and held it out to her.

Brianna looked puzzled for a moment. "For me? Oh, but, Jesse, it's not Christmas any longer, or my birthday, or—"

"Open it, love," Jesse said softly.

She took the box and did as he bade her—and then gasped. Inside, resting on a black velvet lining, lay an emerald and diamond necklace that matched exactly the design of her earrings. Six large emeralds surrounded by double rows of diamonds flanked an even larger emerald that hung from the center of the gold filigreed work that held the stones together. The central stone, also enclosed by twin rows of diamonds, was designed to hang lower than the others, almost like a pendant, and the total design spoke of grace and beauty, perfectly balanced.

"Oh-h, Jesse," Brianna whispered, "I've never seen anything so lovely!"

"I have—lovelier—by far," murmured Jesse as he looked into her eyes. "Now, turn around, love, and let me put it on you," he added as he lifted the necklace from the box.

She did as he asked, and Jesse fastened the necklace in place. Then he bent to place a tender kiss on her shoulder while his arms encircled her waist from behind. "You smell good enough to eat," he whispered in her ear.

Closing her eyes and shivering with delight at his touch, Brianna let out a shaky little sigh. "Your appetite grows even greater, sir."

"I can't help it," Jesse pleaded with a grin as he led her over to the cheval mirror. "I'm married to the most beguiling, tempting witch this side of Eden. There—look at yourself, Mistress Randall, and you'll see I speak the truth."

Brianna looked into the glass, but all she could see—cared to see—was Jesse as he stood beside her in the reflection. Towering above her, his wide shoulders and broad chest tapering to a lean waist and hips under the deep midnight blue of his evening coat, he nearly robbed her of breath. The snowy white linen of his jabot played eye-arresting counterpoint to the deep bronze of his face, tanned even in winter from time spent out of doors. And the blue, blue color of his eyes—they were smiling at her in the glass now, as was the handsome mouth; along with those deeply slashed dimples, they sent a jolt of longing through her that wound into a tight knot somewhere below her stomach.

She closed her eyes for a second, then opened them again and tried to focus on the rest of his formal attire—the light blue, silver brocaded waistcoat, the dove-gray, skin-tight breeches, and—for once, in place of his favored riding boots—white formal hose with shiny black, silver buckled shoes. He was oh, so handsome, and she loved him so very, very much, and suddenly her heart fought fiercely with her head as to whether she should tell him, despite everything, and damn the consequences.

"Well?" Jesse asked as he bent to kiss the topmost curl on her head. "What do you think?"

"I think my husband looks very dashing tonight," she said in a subdued voice as she turned and looked up at him with eyes that were soft and vulnerable. The moment had passed, and her fearful head had won.

Having seen the split-second of indecision in her eyes, Jesse almost asked her about it, but then he felt that, somehow, now was not the time. Holding out his arm, he gently placed her gloved hand on it, saying, "So long as I find favor in your eyes, sweet wife, I will count myself fortunate. Now, will you come with me to greet our guests, lady? For, I warn you, if we don't leave right now, Christie and Garrett may find themselves playing host for the entire evening. My appetite is sorely tempted."

With a soft blush and a smile, Brianna let him escort her downstairs.

The large ballroom at Riverview sparkled with light and color; the multiple hues of ladies in jewel-toned gowns and gentlemen in peacock finery caught the eye wherever one looked as the cream of Southern society danced and celebrated beneath the glittering chandeliers.

Brianna and Jesse were the center of attention as they made their way among the more than two hundred guests, many of whom had once attended a certain coming-out ball at Le Beau Château. But if there were any remnants of the rumors and near-scandal that had played havoc with the lives of their beautiful young hostess and her handsome husband, none were willing to let it surface tonight.

More likely, Christie speculated to Brianna once during a quiet moment, everyone who had come (and there had been almost no refusals to their invitations) had decided to let his curiosity over this certain love match override the more stringent dictates of snobbish propriety and attend in the spirit of applauding young love. "Everyone loves a romance," Christie told her, "and when the young lovers are as beautiful and handsome to look at as you and Jesse, and properly married, of course, much can be forgiven even in the eyes of the *crème de la crème*. Of course," she added, her turquoise eyes gleaming wickedly, "it doesn't detract that there *was* just a shade of the *risqué* tucked back in the beginnings of your story!" She finished this by taking Brianna's hand and giving it a quick squeeze. "Remind me to tell you about a similar situation Garrett and I encountered after we made our first real debut as a married couple in society," she said with a wink.

As the evening progressed, Brianna realized she hadn't seen Governor Pinckney (or his houseguest) arrive and was just assuming he'd decided not to come after all, when Aimée touched her lightly on the arm and said, "Do not be overly alarmed at the mask of subdued rage your husband wears when you turn around, *mon amie*. He sent me to warn you that the Governor has just graced us with his presence—*and* that of *two* houseguests he took the liberty of asking along."

"*Two* house—?" Brianna whirled in the direction of Aimée's over-the-shoulder glance and saw Jesse standing at the entrance to the ballroom beside a man whose aristocratic bearing marked him, even at that distance, as the subject of numerous portraits she'd glimpsed here and there, portraits of Carolina's chief of state. Pinckney had been indisposed and thus unable to attend her coming-out ball, so she'd never actually met him, and now, as she perceived the angry look on Jesse's countenance, she wasn't sure she cared if she ever did.

Moreover, standing a little to the rear of her husband and the Governor, Brianna easily recognized the faces of two other men: Honoré Dumaine and *Aaron Burr.*

"*Sacré bleu!*" Brianna exclaimed, switching to French as she spoke into Aimée's ear. "For him to have asked to bring Honoré was bad enough, but then to drag along that *schemer,* unannounced— It is insufferable!"

"*Oui,* I agree, Brianna, but it looks as if your husband has decided to suffer the insufferable as graciously as possible. When he sent me, he told me to assure you he was avoiding a scene and not asking them to leave because he felt *your* reputation would be what would suffer the most under such circumstances. 'Tonight *will* redeem the events of the ball at Le Beau Château,' he said. Oh, and he also told me to tell you the gentlemen in question are going to be 'encouraged' to spend the lion's share of their evening in the gaming room—*not* in here where you are likely to have to deal with them for any length of time!"

"Jesse said all that?" questioned Brianna, smiling. It wasn't that the words surprised her. He had told her he would do what she wished about Pinckney's boldness, spare her any discomfort or whatever, but she still felt a tiny thrill of warmth come over her at news of his actually instigating such protectiveness, so new was her realization that he cared about such things where she was concerned. *Of course,* came the familiarly nagging doubt, *I do carry his child now. If that were not the case—*

But Brianna had no more time to surrender to her latest mental nemesis, for Jesse was approaching with the three newcomers and she found herself mustering all her strength to summon a "gracious hostess" smile.

"Governor Pinckney, allow me to introduce you to my wife, Brianna Randall," said Jesse as he touched her lightly on the shoulder. "My dear, meet Charles Pinckney, the honorable Governor of our state."

Brianna curtseyed in the face of Charles Pinckney's broad smile, then found her gloved fingers taken and kissed as the Governor bowed over them in courtly fashion.

"Governor, we are pleased you were able to come this evening," Brianna lied. "And I trust Mistress Pinckney is on the mend?"

"Mistress Randall, I am delighted to be here. The news of your beauty truly failed to do you justice. Ah, as for my wife, she was more than a little miffed at our physician's insistence that she abide at home tonight. No, it is nothing serious—a slight fever, probably from a chill she took when we went to church on Christmas Day—the rain, you know."

"Ah, yes, the rain," murmured Brianna as she remembered a warm night in front of a cozy fire while the wetness pelted their windows from without. A glance at Jesse nearly sent her blushing, for the blue eyes met hers in that instant and told her he was remembering the same. But she recovered quickly, saying, "Please convey our wishes for her quick return to good health, Governor Pinckney."

"I shall indeed, madam, and now, I must say I hope you and your husband will forgive me for taking the liberty of bringing along my two houseguests—" Pinckney made a gesture at the two figures to his rear who, as he did this, came up to stand on either side of him "—but inasmuch as I was told you are acquainted with them, I thought there would be little harm in my presumption that it would be acceptable to ask them along." All this was spoken with a smile so ingratiating and a tone of voice so charming, Brianna suddenly found herself with little doubt as to the political and social persuasiveness that had seen this man elected governor of a major state in the union.

Honoré and Aaron Burr made appropriate legs as Pinckney finished this speech, and Brianna was forced to nod and smile at them benignly.

"My congratulations have already gone to your husband on your match," Burr told her as his dark, saturnine eyes focused on her face, "but allow me to extend to you my best wishes for your every happiness in the future, Mistress Randall."

"And mine as well," echoed Honoré as he sent her a sly smile. "They're calling yours the match of the season, you know."

"Why, no," Brianna smiled sweetly. "Truth to tell, I did not know. But, come, I forget myself. Allow me, Governor Pinckney, to introduce my dear friend, Mademoiselle Aimée Gitane.''

Further introductions were completed, and, true to his word, Jesse ushered the three men briefly about the ballroom to allow them to greet other guests and then out of the door to the hallway that led to the gaming room. There, Brianna knew, a number of guests, mostly male, had assembled to smoke and drink brandy or other fine spirits while they tried their hands at whist or faro. She made a mental note to check with Isaac to be sure their needs were being attended to and then another to peek in on those there herself a bit later. As hostess, it was her duty, although she admitted to herself with a wry smile that she was also just a mite curious as to how Jesse would be handling their uninvited guests.

At the moment Brianna was wondering about Jesse's capabilities as a defensive host, the object of her curiosity was already engaged in a fast-moving political discussion that included several others in the gaming room.

It began when Thomas Mann Randolph, after confirming Jesse's suspicions that his father-in-law was again near resigning his post, chanced to speculate on who might become President once Washington's tenure came to an end. Hearing this, several men jumped into the conversation and soon were bandying about names like Adams, Madison and Jefferson.

Honoré entered the fray by suggesting Burr as a possible candidate (It was clear the latter was, by now, idolized by Dumaine), and Jesse noticed Burr almost preen with pleasure at his words (prompting Jesse to assess, privately, the huge ego involved here, not to mention the ambition!).

Jesse commented on the probability of Jefferson's shunning any nomination in the near future, causing Honoré to mutter to Burr (but loud enough for Jesse to catch it) that, for his money, he hoped Jefferson would never run. Seeing his anti-Jefferson stance and speculating on the association with Burr and its relationship to this stance, Jesse asked him if he was anti-Republican, then.

"Why, not at all, sir," Honoré replied. "I merely suggest that there are worthier champions of our cause." He turned admiring eyes toward Burr. "Don't you think so, Governor Pinckney?" he added.

With apologies to Burr, Pinckney quickly disagreed with his aide, who had, he added for the benefit of the assembled group, perhaps already consumed a fair amount of their host's excellent brandy, not to mention a libation or two earlier, at the Governor's home.

"I refuse to even consider abandoning Jefferson," Pinckney declared. "Mister Randolph, sir, do you think your father-in-law can be persuaded to come to South Carolina soon to help strengthen and cement the work we Jeffersonian supporters have been doing?"

"Sir, the hospitality here at Riverview has been so delightful, my wife and I have already told our host we shall do all we can to convince her father to make the journey himself in the near future—that is—" Randolph shot his host a questioning look "—if the invitation still stands?"

Jesse smiled. "I have already asked Mistress Randolph to be our pretty delegate in convincing her father to be our guest. But, gentlemen, perhaps we are really being too premature. When the time is ripe and the country is ready for him, I have no doubt Jefferson will be asked, and that he will answer its call. But I feel this is not to occur at any time soon.

"'There is a tide in the affairs of men,' Shakespeare said, 'Which taken at the flood leads on to fortune,' but Thomas Jefferson's tide is not yet at the flood, and we who would follow him must watch and wait until it ceases its ebb and keep the country safe until then." Jesse glanced pointedly at Dumaine and Burr who were conversing quietly in a corner of the room as he spoke.

At that moment Brianna entered the room, followed by Laurette Mayfield.

"Fie, gentlemen, for shame, keeping yourselves tucked away in here, far from the ladies!" Laurette gaily admonished.

"The clock is about to strike twelve, sirs," Brianna added quietly. "Won't you follow us back to the ballroom for a New Year's toast? The champagne awaits." She stepped aside and waited until all except Jesse had filed cheerfully out, then allowed him to clasp her hand and lead her after them.

As she and Jesse entered the ballroom, amid scores of footmen carrying trays of filled champagne glasses, Brianna spied Honoré and Laurette wedged in one corner, having what appeared to be an intimate conversation, for it was punctuated by artful looks on Dumaine's part and coy glances on the widow's.

"Do you see what I see?" she whispered to Jesse behind the jet and green silk fan Christie had given her for Christmas.

Looking in the direction of her gaze, Jesse gave a disgusted sigh.

"Lula and Aimée think Laurette's been meeting a lover," Brianna added pointedly.

"Dumaine?" Jesse's eyebrows raised slightly. "Well, it fits, I suppose. For my part, I would wish them on each other. If it's so, perhaps it will serve to keep Laurette out of my hair, and I know you wouldn't miss her."

Brianna graced him with a warm, appreciative smile as Jesse took a pair of bubbling glasses of champagne from a passing footman's tray and handed one to her. "A new year approaches, love," Jesse said softly enough for only her ears to hear, "and such moments as this are anniversaries of a kind. Do you remember the poem Donne wrote called 'The Anniversary'?"

Brianna smiled. "'All Kings, and all their favorites...'?"

"Yes, but I was thinking more of the final quatrain: 'True and false fears let us refrain,/Let us love nobly, and live, and add again/Years and years unto years...'" He touched his glass lightly to hers. "To us, Brianna, let us drink before I make the common toast for our guests."

Looking deeply into his eyes, Brianna joined her husband and drank, but her head was puzzling over the words he'd quoted from the poet. True and false fears? What did he mean? She would have to ponder.

But then there was no time for pondering, for Jesse had taken the glasses from their private toast, set them aside, and was handing her a new glass as he ushered her further toward the center of the ballroom.

Seeing them, the assembled guests grew quiet. In the near distance, the first chime of the tall case clock in the hallway sounded as Jesse raised his glass high. "Dear friends," he said as he placed his other arm around Brianna's waist, "my wife and I would join you in welcoming in this new year as it approaches." The clock continued to chime as he paused. "May it bring the best life has to offer." More chimes. "Health, sweet liberty, good friends, love and laughter, and the strength to endure with grace." The eleventh chime. "To seventeen ninety-three, and God bless!" And as the twelfth chime sounded, all raised their glasses high, drank, and then joined in a rousing cheer.

The orchestra began a melody Brianna had not heard before, and she watched Jesse grin as he took both their glasses and set them on a passing tray. His grin broadened as he suddenly swept her in his arms and moved her gracefully over the middle of the floor.

Brianna's face was wonderstruck. "What is this?" she asked as he whirled her around to the sound of the music.

"A shocking new dance, my dear," said Jesse, amusement glittering in his blue eyes. "It's begun to take hold on the Continent, but by virtue of a trip Garrett made abroad last summer, we Randalls have begun to introduce it to our friends. Men and women actually get to hold each other. They call it *the waltz!*"

Chapter Thirty-Five

The rainy months of Carolina's winter passed, giving way to an even rainier spring, and the inhabitants of Riverview settled down to await the birth of Jesse's and Brianna's child. As for the parents-to-be, they enjoyed what Brianna thought of as a married truce of sorts. Often her thoughts would wander back to the days when she and Jesse had clashed and fought, causing her to marvel at the newfound state of things between them. They were growing closer during this time, there was no doubting it, though the reasons she partially ascribed to this lay stubbornly entrenched within her mind where, but for the gentle probing of Aimée, no one guessed their nature.

"You can see the man cares for you, Brianna," the little gypsy told her once. "What harm would it do to tell him how you feel? And do not make your pretenses to me!" she'd added with a wagging finger. "I know you love him."

As Brianna had, on that occasion, indeed been about to protest against having any deep feelings of her own, she looked at Aimée with a wondering pair of green eyes for a moment before giving a mirthless little laugh and sadly nodding her head. "Of course, *you* would know, Aimée. I should have realized—you having the Sight, and—"

"Sight! Bah! It doesn't take any deeper perception to see into the heart of a good friend, Brianna! I simply know you that well, *mon amie*. Now, I repeat, what harm would—"

"Oh, Aimée!" cried Brianna. "It would do *every* harm! To let him know I love him in the face of his inability to love me back? I have nightmares of seeing him revert to that mocking, taunting devil he once was—or worse! Of him looking at me with *pity*! Pity for a trapped wife caught up in the throes of unrequited love."

"But that's silly, Brianna! How do you know he would be that way? And what makes you so sure it's unrequited? I've heard him call you by tender, love-like names, you know."

"Yes, but he's never actually come out and said I love you! Never! Not even in the heat of—" Here Brianna's cheeks flamed, but she forced the word out. "—passion."

"But, Brianna, his whole attitude toward you—his behavior—don't actions speak louder than mere words?" Aimée's tone was pleading, her eyes full of compassion as she saw tears fill Brianna's eyes.

"It's the babe, *mon amie*—no more. He cares for me to the extent that I carry his child."

"Ah, *ma chére*," whispered Aimée fervently as she went to put her arms around her sobbing friend, "I feel in my soul you are mistaken in this, but I do not know how to convince you. Do not cry, *mon amie*. We will find a way out of this dilemma for you—I promise." And with arms that barely half-encircled her friend's pregnant girth, she held her for a long time and let her cry out her pain.

Jesse, too, had moments of doubt during this period. At times he wondered if his young wife would ever feel free enough from fear to come to trust him and the way he felt about her. He coddled and pampered her, watched and waited, but he always sensed she held something in reserve. He had to find a way to tell her as well as show her that he loved her, and as the spring ran its rainy course and gave way to the warm season, he made up his mind one night. The following day they were to travel (by carriage, for Brianna was too big with child to ride a horse) to the Cherokee village where Brianna was to be inducted as an honorary sister, or member of the tribe. As they were expected to spend the night, he hoped he might use the guest lodge, the scene where they had consummated their marriage, as an appropriate—he prayed—setting for telling her. It would wait no longer. She had to know.

But then disaster struck, laying all of Jesse's plans to waste. It was the following morning. Brianna was restless as she waited for the hours to pass until they would leave for Long Arrow's village. Jesse had gone to Riverlea to help Garrett and Christie with a difficult new brood mare they'd acquired (Christie shared in her husband's horsebreeding activities as a full and equal partner), and he wasn't expected back for hours.

As Brianna paced the length of the drawing room in restless agitation, she was interrupted by the sight of Laurette Mayfield coming through the door carrying the mail.

"Brianna, the sound of your heels clicking across this floor is beginning to drive me mad," carped the widow. "Here, why don't you peruse the mail while you listen to a suggestion I have." She handed Brianna a packet of envelopes.

"Why don't I have the landau brought around," continued Laurette, "and the two of us go for a ride? It will take your mind off whatever is bothering you so, and by the time we return, you might even feel refreshed."

Since Laurette had never made such an offer before, Brianna might have puzzled over it and found it odd, but she had just opened a letter addressed to Jesse and her, from Thomas Jefferson, and the excitement its message brought caused her to pass this by.

"Jefferson's finally accepted our invitation to visit!" she exclaimed. "He's coming the second week in August!"

"How thrilling for you," commented the widow. "It will be quite a feather in your social cap, although it won't be quite as satisfying as it might have been had he not resigned in January. I mean, he's no longer Secretary of State, you know."

"Oh, fiddle-faddle, Laurette! Jesse and I didn't invite him here for his social importance. We did it because we believe in the man and his politics, and we wanted his company," Brianna returned with some annoyance. She pushed back a sweep of her long hair behind one shoulder as she spoke, revealing one of the earrings Jesse had given her. (She'd taken to wearing them on a regular basis—almost daily—although the matching necklace rested in its leather box, being saved for special formal occasions).

Laurette eyed the sparkling adornment with a split second's gleam of envy before veiling the look and saying, "Yes, of course. Now, about that ride—shall I have the landau brought round?"

"Hmm?" murmured Brianna absently as she thumbed through the remaining letters in her hand.

"The ride I suggested we take!" Laurette caught herself raising her voice and made a visible effort to subdue her inflection. "Shall I tell them to ready the—"

"Oh, well, yes, I suppose you might do that Laurette," Brianna replied as she perused a letter from Mistress Delaney.

"Very well," said the widow. She turned toward the door, and if Brianna hadn't been so preoccupied with a dearly remembered handwriting that spelled out news of events occurring at her beloved Le Beau Château, she might have caught the gleam of triumph in Laurette Mayfield's dark eyes.

An hour later Riverview's shiny black landau was skimming down one of the roads that led west, away from the plantation. Laurette held the reins and had been unusually silent, in Brianna's estimation, ever since they'd left. She was just about to comment on this when Laurette suddenly pulled back on the reins and drew their vehicle to a stop. All at once there was some movement in the underbrush near the trees at the side of the road, and as Brianna turned to discover its source, she let out a fearful gasp.

There, looking every bit as menacing as he had the time she first saw him, stood Blood Man, the renegade Indian who had attempted her abduction that terrible night! And further movement from the foliage behind him revealed he was not alone; slipping from the shadows to stand to his right were four breech-clouted Indians, three of whom she knew, with a sickening lurch of recognition, from that earlier encounter; the fourth was a musket-carrying newcomer whose black eyes scrutinized her with a cold and unerring thoroughness that made her shiver.

"You hid yourselves well," Brianna suddenly heard Laurette say. "For a moment there, I thought you'd failed to keep our appointment."

Brianna's head swung sharply as she looked at the widow and tried to make some sense out of what she'd just heard.

"I do not fail," Blood Man said in reply.

"That is not how the tale of your first attempt goes," Laurette said disdainfully as she made a contemptuous gesture toward Brianna with a black-gloved hand.

Brianna's head began to swim, and she reached to grab onto the side of the open landau as if to steady herself. Here sat Laurette, beside her in the face of certain danger from these men, and she was *talking to them*!—talking to them as if—"Oh, my God!" she whispered as she brought a trembling hand to her mouth. *Laurette was* in *with them!*

The widow caught her words with a contemptuous glare that quickly turned into a cold smile of satisfaction. "So the little fool realizes the nature of our game," she drawled in a tone that resembled a feline purr. "God won't help you where you're going, you sniveling little bitch!" An unmistakable look of malicious triumph crossed her face.

"Which is—?" countered Brianna as she squared her shoulders and raised her chin in a valiant endeavor to appear undaunted.

Laurette shrugged in a manner that suggested she hardly cared. "As to your exact ultimate destination, I really couldn't say, except that it will be in another land, far, far away from here. You see, my dear—" she gestured at Blood Man who was still standing where he'd first emerged from the brush, watching them in stony silence "—Blood Man and his associates are flesh traders. They survive by kidnapping unsuspecting creatures like you and selling them on the various open slave markets which abound up and down this wild country of ours, some of them legal, others, not so legitimate. Unfortunately for you and the child you carry, the latter must be the conduit for your sale into slavery. There isn't much of a market within our borders for aristocratic white flesh, even among the Indians. Besides, your husband's family has certain undesirable ties there which could make such trading difficult, to say the least."

As Laurette's sneering tones droned on, Brianna ceased to hear her words. All she could suddenly focus on was the sharp claw of fear that had seized her consciousness at the widow's mention of the child. Not only were these vicious creatures going to kidnap and sell *her* into bondage—they were going to enslave *her babe* as well! *Sweet Mother of God, no!* Brianna screamed inside her head as she saw Blood Man come forward and grab her wrist to pull her from the carriage.

And then, suddenly, everything began to spin, and somewhere she heard a woman groan. Then there was nothing as blackness descended.

"She's fainted," said Laurette as Blood Man lifted Brianna's swollen form from the landau. "So much the better. It will make our task that much easier. Here, I'll remove her bonnet while your men take the carriage to the riverbank. Make sure the one who plants this bonnet among those rocks downstream doesn't take it in his head to steal the horse. If her husband's to believe it was an accident, the horse must be found with the overturned carriage. And here," she added, handing another man one of her own shoes (hidden under the landau's seat until now) as well as Brianna's bonnet. "Tell him to place this at the water's edge beside the carriage. We wouldn't want them to think *I* survived, would we?" Laurette's low laughter rang out over the sounds of carriage wheels and snorting horses as the renegades set about the business of putting the plan into action. The only one who failed to hear it was Brianna as she slumped, unconscious, in the grasp of Blood Man as he held her before him on his horse and trotted off into the trees.

Jesse stood in exhausted silence, his body rigid with disbelief as he watched his brother and Laughing Bear alight from their horses with worried faces. "You've found naught, then?" he questioned wearily.

"Not a trace so far," Garrett replied in a somber voice. "But Laughing Bear sent Lula and Vulcan to look along the river trail," he added cautiously.

"You mean the river," Jesse corrected with a bitter edge to his voice.

"Now, Jess—"

"Sorry, Garrett, I didn't mean to take my frustration out on you. It's just that—" He ran his hand through his hair in a gesture of weary impatience. They'd been searching for nearly ten hours. First it had been by the extended summer daylight; then, when it had grown dark, they had lit torches and continued to comb the countryside around Riverview. It was a couple of hours past midnight and there was still no sign of the landau's even having passed by the routes they'd surveyed. Where was she?

When Isaac had informed him she'd gone out with Laurette, he'd been annoyed, but when the two of them had failed to return and he'd realized something was wrong, he'd seized upon her being with the widow as good reason to dismiss another runaway attempt as being the cause. Laurette would be the last person Brianna would choose to help her run off!

So that left him with an even more chilling conclusion: something, an accident or other mishap of some kind, had occurred. Jesse clenched his jaws to grind out the sheer, stark band of terror that threatened to seize him. No, please, God, let her be all right. Let her be safe and *alive*—he had to say it, if only to himself, for the frantic fear that had begun to engulf him as hour had followed upon hour, would no longer be pushed aside.

Seeing the look of defeat begin to emerge in his brother's eyes, Garrett stepped forward and lay a hand on his shoulder. "I've never known you to give up this easily, little brother," he said quietly.

Jesse looked up into the emerald green eyes that just missed communicating a taunt and recognized the ploy. It was a silent communication that stretched back over the years to when they were children and Garrett had alternately teased and cajoled his younger brother—his "little brother"—into succeeding in some act of necessity or courage when Jesse would have perhaps resisted plunging ahead or even given up. After their parents' deaths, especially, Garrett had assumed the sole responsibility for rebuilding their young lives, acting as both brother and father to the younger Jesse, often succeeding by childlike taunts, rather than more serious threats or scolding, in getting him to amass a bulwark of strength for survival. It was that strength his brother was asking him to draw on now, and Jesse suddenly knew he possessed it. With a ghost of a half-smile that faintly echoed the boyish grin of earlier days, Jesse said, "Who says I'm giving up?"

Just then, a piercing whistle broke the air, coming from the direction of the river.

"That would be my wife's signal," Laughing Bear announced as the three men sprang from their mounts. He didn't add that the nature of the whistle was the one, from Lula's wide array of well-learned Cherokee signals, which denoted trouble or distress on the part of the sender.

A short while later they stood beside the overturned landau. Garrett helped Laughing Bear and Vulcan extricate the frantic horse from the tangled harness and driving reins while Jesse bent to pick up a gilt-trimmed black slipper from the mud at the water's edge.

"That would be the widow's," Lula told him glumly while her eyes searched the swiftly moving expanse of water before them as it glimmered palely under the light of a gibbous moon.

Jesse allowed his eyes to follow the course of hers as he fought the threat of despair that stalked him. Behind him he heard the soft tones of his brother's voice as he worked at gentling the frightened mare that had pulled the landau. No, he would not give up. Garrett was right. Even as a child, though he'd come close to quitting many times, he'd never actually done so, and he wasn't about to begin now.

"Laughing Bear, Garrett, when the two of you have the horses tended to, scout around here as best you can to see if there are any other signs. I'm taking Lula and Vulcan and searching downstream. Let's use the same signal as before if we find anything. We'll meet back here at dawn if we don't." He glanced at Lula and Vulcan and the three of them moved along the edge of the river with their torches.

Shortly before dawn, Lula's whistle summoned her husband and the older Randall brother. She, Vulcan and Jesse had found Brianna's chip straw bonnet caught among an outcropping of rocks in the river, a few yards from the water's edge. Holding the sodden, misshapen object in his shaking hands, Jesse willed away the pain that assaulted his heart and refused to accept the dismal discovery as a sure sign of anything. He just wouldn't believe her dead. And it went beyond the renewal of determination brought on by Garrett's recent urging. Somehow, whether it was through the soaring surge of love that pounded through his heart and brain as he thought of his wife, or the cry of regret that tore his gut when he remembered he'd never told her of that love, he didn't know—but somehow he sensed that it wasn't meant to end for them like this. Brianna was alive, he told himself. She was a vital, life-embracing force in this world, and he knew he would have felt the loss if she were gone.

Starkly, he gave orders to his companions. "We need to return to the Big House for some rest and the like. Certainly, fresh horses. Later, when it's full daylight, I'm coming back. Those of you who wish, can join me, although I'll understand if you don't."

They all rode by his side when, some five hours later, he returned and renewed his search. And they were beside him again when a week had passed and still they'd turned up nothing. A fortnight passed then, and Long Arrow sent more than a dozen braves to join his blood brother in the search for his *ghigau*, but to no avail, and Jesse became hard pressed to sustain hope, but somehow he did, especially since no bodies ever turned up along the river.

Then one day their first real break came. It was Aimée who provided it, with the help of Vulcan. Vulcan had run into a fellow black freedman who lived in a cabin deep in the woods not too far from Riverview. The man had a hound that he boasted was the best scent tracker in the area, and Vulcan persuaded him to lend them the dog for their search, even though there was some doubt he could pick up a trail so cold. Then the black man sent Aimée to Brianna's and Laurette's chambers for a couple of articles of clothing to use for the hound to establish the scents he was to follow.

Aimée already had one of Brianna's gloves in hand when she opened the armoire in the widow's chamber and caught sight of an object that made her stop short. There, on the bottom of the armoire, lay a gold-trimmed black slipper, identical to the one found by Jesse at the edge of the river! The little gypsy's quick mind spun rapidly as she bent to pick up the slipper. Yes, it was for the left foot—and Jesse's discovery—she was sure of it—had been for the right!

"Vulcan!" she shouted as she bounded out of the chamber and down the stairs to the hallway where the black overseer waited. "Vulcan, come quickly! I've found something!"

She met the black man at the foot of the stairs where she triumphantly handed him Laurette's shoe. "Here—it is the mate to the one that was found, is it not?" Aimée asked breathlessly.

"Sho' look lahk it, Aimée, but whut—"

"Why would that miserable woman have gone for a carriage ride wearing only one shoe?" Aimée demanded.

"No reason at all, fah's Ah kin figger, Aimée," the big man replied, "cuz a lady—" Suddenly his eyes widened with the sudden light of comprehension. "Unless dat so-called lady done wanted t' set up a wild goose chase t' put us off de *real*— Ah's goin' t' fetch Jesse! Gal, yo' stay raht heah wid dat shoe!" he told her excitedly as he headed for the door.

Minutes later, Jesse was striding through the door, Lula and Laughing Bear close at his heels. With a shaking hand, he took the slipper Aimée silently handed him and held it next to the mud-stained one in his other hand. "It's the mate," he announced in a quiet, positive tone. He looked up at his wife's best friend. "Aimée, I could hug you!" he told her with suspiciously bright eyes.

The little gypsy's black eyes were also fighting tears as she answered, "I would have you save the hug—and more, for your dear wife, *monsieur*, but first, we must find her!"

Brought back instantly to the problem at hand, Jesse turned for the door as he began snapping orders. "Laughing Bear, saddle up and ride to fetch Garrett. Tell him about the clue we've come upon. And tell him to bring his musket. There's skulduggery afoot, and we may need it. Vulcan, is that hound ready to go?" At the overseer's affirmative nod, he continued. "Bring him around to the stables. I'll have our horses readied. We ride for the river!"

Brianna awoke to a discomfort greater than that she had been experiencing lately, whenever they'd made camp and she'd been allowed to rest. She suppressed a bitter laugh as she thought of the word, "rest." She hadn't had any real rest in all the days of her captivity. When they hadn't been forcing her to ride relentlessly over primitive trails, across mosquito-infested, swampy bogs or through briar-laden brush, they'd shackled her to a stake, as she was now, in some hastily constructed tent or lean-to, to spend the night trying to find what comfort she could, with her body so clumsy and huge with its maternal burden. Her wrists and ankles were raw from the various bonds she had been tied with, here and there, the worst being the throbbing weal produced by the iron shackle that was currently encircling her left ankle. She was about to reach down to try to ease the chafing as best she could, perhaps by slipping yet another torn strip of gauze from her petticoat under the iron band, when she felt it again. A dull, aching cramp located in the region of her lower back, it held her motionless for a moment before slowly ebbing away.

Oh, dear God, could it be . . . ? She shifted her weight awkwardly, and the aching returned; this time it was more pronounced. *Sweet Mother of God!* her mind cried out. *I'm going to bear my babe in this wretched place!*

Chapter Thirty-Six

Brianna drifted in and out of consciousness as she grappled with the pains that were assaulting her body. She no longer had any idea of the time, of whether it was night or day, only that she had been laboring with her burden for endless hours. In fact, more than twenty hours had passed since she had finally been forced to summon Laurette and plead for some assistance. The widow had been indisposed to do anything at first, but then, realizing that her own plans depended on the safe emergence of the child, as well as the survival of its mother, she had reluctantly agreed. But even then, she had extracted a "payment" for her services, such as they were. Smiling exultantly, she had removed the lovely emerald and diamond earrings from Brianna's ears, slipping them quickly inside her bodice to hide them from the greedy eyes of the renegades outside the tent.

Then, after telling Blood Man what was occurring, she'd sat down with the writhing young woman stretched out on the hard ground in the dark shelter and waited. Her only assistance, since Laurette had had no children of her own and had only heard stories of the delivery of babies second-hand, came in the form of handing Brianna an occasional cup of water to wet her lips and placing an Indian blanket under her when her water broke and Brianna's sodden petticoats had to be removed; even the task of pulling off the wet undergarments had fallen to Brianna herself.

But she stayed by Brianna's side most of the time, and the pain-wracked young woman was grateful for that. Outside the tent she could hear the raucous voices of the renegades as they gambled and drank.

During these hours, Brianna was given to strange and sometimes incoherent ramblings, especially after she tired and her pains grew worse. Laurette heard her rambling about eagles and someone named Sally Something-or-other. Then she caught something she did understand.

"He doesn't love me, Aimée!" Brianna cried out. "It's the babe he wants—oh, the babe—mustn't let them do it—mustn't let them put shackles on my babe. Oh, Mother, what's the Gaelic word for 'free'? *Saor*...my babe...must name it Saor. Oh, Jesse, why couldn't you love me?"

Laurette's face assumed a gloating smile as she took all this in. For the first time in months, she felt the weight of the scorn of Jesse's rejection ease from her breast. So, he'd done it because of the child—and the twit obviously loved him *in vain*! Better and better—not that it made that much difference to her now. No, not now that there was someone else.

With a brief glance at the prone figure who appeared to be unconscious again, Laurette rose to her feet and left the tent. Outside, the moonless darkness of the sky was offset by the light of the campfire the men had built. Sitting around it were several figures, but the widow ignored these as she walked over to the horses where two more stood in whispered conversation.

"What news?" questioned Blood Man of her as he broke away from the other at her approach.

"Nothing new, I fear," replied Laurette, "though I won't pretend I know much of these things."

The renegade gave a growl of impatience. "It must be soon, woman, or we have maybe trouble. Must keep moving... slave trader ship not wait too long. Cherokee hunt for us. *Tlanuwa* hunt for us!" He made an ominous-looking gesture and left to join the others near the fire.

Only then did the shadowed figure of the other man turn to her; the sardonic features of Honoré Dumaine took on a satisfied smile as he faced Laurette. "No matter what he says, my dear, your look says things are well in hand." He reached for her then, and drew her harshly to him. "And now *you* are well in hand as well, my lovely," he added as his fingers closed over one of her ample breasts.

With a breathless laugh, Laurette hungrily threw her arms about his neck and lifted her mouth toward his. "Oh, I have missed you, Honoré," she gasped before meshing her lips with his in a grinding kiss. When at last they separated, she added, "Why must you be away so long? I yearn for you, and this wretched wilderness has begun to get on my nerves!"

"Patience, my dove, patience," Honoré murmured as he slid his arm about her waist; he began to walk with her, away from the sight of the men about the campfire who were eyeing them speculatively. "I must put in my time at Pinckney's office if I'm to be of any help to Burr. It has not been easy in this quagmire of Jeffersonian sympathies."

When they were well within the shadows of the forest, he stopped walking and turned to her.

"Have you made any progress in obtaining those herbs for me?"

Laurette gave him a throaty chuckle. "Those *poisons*, you mean?"

"Damn you, wench, we both know what I mean and what they're for!" Honoré snarled. But then his tone softened almost to a croon. "Ah—forgive me, my dear, but you know how important this business is to my—ah—our future."

"Yes," Laurette nodded, "but I fear they're being terribly stubborn about it. Blood Man—" she gave a shudder "—Ah, the man makes my flesh crawl!" She paused a moment as if to collect herself. "Blood Man says he wishes to see the cargo safely aboard that ship before he'll do any other business."

Dumaine nodded. "Very well. What of our primary business, then? Are you sure about Brianna? Hasn't her labor been overly long? Blood Man may well be right in saying you cannot tarry too long. Word has it the entire Cherokee nation in these parts is aiding her husband in searching, though I assume it's for her body and yours."

Laurette gave a throaty laugh and pressed her body up against his. "Let them look," she told him. "Those Indians covered our tracks well. As to the bitch, your sister, I have a feeling it won't be too much longer now. Soon she and her child will be on board that ship headed for the Indies, and you will inherit when she's declared legally dead. Then, after some time has passed, I shall turn up, my memory at last restored after long ago being fished from the river by friendly Indians, claiming I saw Brianna drown, and then we'll be free to wed!'' She slid one ivory hand down over the front of his breeches and grasped at the growing bulge in their confines. "But I ache for you, Honoré. Say you will come again, soon, *mon amour*!"

Honoré pulled her rounded buttocks toward him and ground the source of her ardor against her as he rasped, "All in good time, my lusty one. I promise you, once our plot is completely hatched—''

A piercing scream rent the evening air, causing them to pause and pull apart.

Laurette gave an exasperated sigh. "Speaking of hatch-ings—I suppose I'd better go and see...." The two clasped each other in another embrace before the silence was again split with an agonized sound, this time so piteous that even they could not ignore it, and Laurette hastened back to the tent.

When she entered, having bade her lover farewell outside, she nearly shrank back at what she saw. There, in a dark pool of blood on the blanket under Brianna's parted thighs, lay a blood-streaked, moving form, its tiny fists knotted and flail-ing in the light shed by the primitive lantern that hung from the tent's supporting pole. From it emanated faint mewling sounds as it drew its tiny knees up to its chest, across which a purplish looking cord lay draped.

A low moan from Brianna caught the widow's attention and she finally moved. Taking a knife she had procured from the Indians at Brianna's earlier insistence, she ran it through the lantern's flame for several seconds before using it to cut the cord. Then, gritting her teeth in revulsion, she tied two knots in the severed pieces of cord and picked the infant up, placing it on a spare petticoat Brianna had begged from among her things. As she wrapped the squalling babe—a boy—in the soft muslin, she bit back the wave of nausea she felt at seeing the afterbirth emerge from between Brianna's thighs.

"Brianna!" she called in a loud whisper as she knelt beside her with the child. "Can you hear? I have your son for you."

At her words Brianna's eyelashes fluttered and then opened with great effort. "My...my son?" she whispered faintly, running her tongue over lips that were dry and cracking.

"Yes, your 'Sare,' as you seem to want to call him. Quaint name. I suppose if it had been a girl, you'd have named her 'Sara.'"

Brianna listened to Laurette's sounding out of the Irish Gaelic word for "free" as she turned and took the tiny bundle that was her son from the widow's hands. Slowly, for she was beyond exhaustion now, she pulled aside the piece of petticoat that partially hid his face. Saor—yes, the name fit, despite the horrendous conditions he'd been born into. He was the living spirit of the freedom she longed for. Slowly she smiled into the tiny, red and wrinkled face as she fumbled at her bodice to free her breast. She watched as her son's head rooted frantically, sensing nourishment was near. At last he found her nipple and began to suck. A faint thrill of pleasure coursed through her fatigued body as she felt the pull and tug of his lips, and then she closed her eyes and slept.

They allowed her barely a day's rest before breaking camp and moving on, and that, Brianna suspected, was only because the renegades had consumed so much whiskey during the night, they needed time to sleep it off. Aching and sore, she wearily assumed her place on the front of Blood Man's saddle where she held her tiny son and spent all her time looking at him and pretending she was not being held by the evil-looking renegade with the horrible scar on his face. Dressed in one of Laurette's old day gowns, for her own soiled one was left behind in a hastily dug pit where they also buried her afterbirth, she managed to endure the relentless pace they forced and never complained. But she prayed a lot, appealing more often than not to the Virgin Mary to intercede, for who would better understand the plight of a terrified mother than the Mother of God? In terms of the earthly world, she fervently hung her hopes on Jesse to somehow realize she and their child might still be alive and search for them. Surely, she thought, his love for the babe would provoke such a search, regardless of what he felt—or didn't feel—for its mother.

Weeks passed, for the time they'd taken to stop for her birthing did indeed cause them to miss their rendezvous with the slave ship Laurette had spoken of, and on the night they arrived too late to make that appointment, Blood Man became so enraged when he discovered their loss, he strode up to Brianna and struck her a blow across the head that sent her reeling and almost caused her to drop the sleeping infant she held. But even at this, Brianna refused to cry out, holding grimly on to whatever courage she could still manage to summon from somewhere deep within her core. This bought her a gleam of respect in the eyes of the renegades, and they pretty much left her alone from then on, though their wandering continued, for there were other ships, she was told, that would be sought out.

After more than a month on the trail—a time that took its brutal toll on the young mother, for she was thinner now than she had been even before Saor's conception, and, it seemed, always tired, not to mention filthy and unkempt—the renegades made camp one night in a place that looked familiar to her. After being allowed to dismount, she was led to a swiftly moving stream by Laurette who grudgingly handed her a cake of finely scented soap.

"Here," said the widow as she gave it to her. "Use this. You smell." She wrinkled her nose in disgust.

Brianna accepted the offer gratefully, and, stopping only to carefully lay her peacefully sleeping son down among some soft grasses, she quickly glanced over her shoulder to make sure they were unobserved and began to remove her clothes.

"Be quick about it," snapped Laurette, "and don't use more than you absolutely must. It's my last cake."

"Your last—? You've had *more*?"

"Well, of course," the widow cut her off. "You didn't think *I* was doing without soap and water all this time, did you? And don't mistake my motives, dear. The only reason you're being allowed to enjoy this now is because, for one thing, you've become offensive to my nostrils, and, for another, we're about to make our connection, and Blood Man wanted your appearance improved so that we might get the best price. Oh, and you'd better clean the brat, too."

"Clean him? Oh, I've been doing as much of that as I could with some of my drinking water," said Brianna as she immersed herself in the icy stream, "but surely you don't expect me to bathe him in this!'' She gave a shudder as she dipped her hair and scalp in the water. ''It's far too cold!''

''Blood Man wants the two of you cleaned up,'' the widow told her. ''You will do it.''

''Yes, but—oh, Laurette, please let me warm some water for him over the cooking fire,'' Brianna pleaded as she began to lather her hair. ''It wouldn't do to present the slave dealers with a sick child, would it?'' She frantically sought a way to protect her son from the immediate danger, pushing to the back of her mind those of the long term.

The widow heaved an exasperated sigh. ''Very well. I'll speak to him about it. Now, hurry out of there and dry off. You're to don another of my gowns, it seems. This rag—'' she held Brianna's recent cast-off between forefinger and thumb ''—is to be buried in that pit where we left your old one.'' She gestured toward a place beyond her right shoulder.

Brianna paused a moment before walking out of the stream and handing the cake of soap back to Laurette. ''I thought I recognized this place,'' she said as she reached for the rough piece of cotton cloth the widow had brought along as a towel. ''This is where I bore my son! We've either been going around in circles or doubling back! All that horrible traveling! And for what? To arrive—''

''Shut up!'' snapped Laurette. ''It's no concern of yours, where we take you. You are merely a piece of chattel now— nothing more!'' She threw a faded blue silk gown on the ground in front of Brianna. ''Put that on, and make haste. It's almost dark.''

But as Brianna slipped the too-large frock over her head— she was to be allowed no undergarments, hadn't worn any since the birthing—she uttered a silent prayer to a diety she hoped hadn't gotten tired of listening to her. *Please God—let me not abandon hope! We're back, nearer to where we started—and nearer to Jesse! Let him not have given up! Let him find us before it's too late!*

Perhaps it happened because, as Father Edouard would have told Brianna, God always listens, or perhaps it was because, as Aimée would have put it, certain things are fated to be, but that night, after Brianna and her son were again shut up and fast asleep in the crude tent that had served as their sleeping quar-

ters for so many weeks, there was a whisper of sound just beyond the circle of campfire light where the renegades sat
talking, and all at once, Jesse Randall appeared. There was a
clamoring of guttural voices as the Indians rose to their feet and
began reaching for their weapons, but Jesse uttered a low-
voiced message in the Cherokee tongue that caused Blood Man
to stop and signal the others to desist. What Jesse had told them
was that he came unarmed (a hand gesture accompanied this)
and that he wished to make a bargain that would increase their
wealth.

At that moment Laurette emerged from her own tent.
"Jesse!" she gasped as she recognized the tall figure beside the
fire.

Jesse nodded grimly. "That's right, Laurette. I've finally
found you. No, don't look for your musket or whatever else
you left over there—" he gestured at a pack of supplies beside
the tent "—I've come to bargain, not to fight."

"What kind of bargain?" asked Blood Man in broken
Cherokee. His Seminole dress marked him as a breed apart
from the others, but in gathering them together as part of his
band, he'd been forced to pick up more knowledge of their
language than he had of English or French, and he preferred
using it to any of the white man's tongues he'd learned.

"First," said Jesse carefully, "I would know whether my
wife and the child are alive and well. Where are they?"

The flicker of several pairs of eyes toward the direction of the
tent next to Laurette's told him what he wished to know, and
Jesse continued. "If they are alive and well, I would like to offer a trade for them." He signaled to the shadows from which
he'd stepped moments before, and suddenly a huge figure
emerged.

"Festus!" exclaimed the widow, recognizing the closed eyes
and stick-cane that always accompanied the blind twin when he
walked about.

"This man is my slave," said Jesse, betting on the fact that,
even if Laurette understood a little Cherokee, she had no understanding of the twins' freedman status because in all the time
she'd been in the vicinity of their whereabouts, she'd dis-
dained any contact with, or discussion of, them. "I propose,"

Jesse continued, "to exchange this powerful slave for my wife and child."

The cold eyes of the renegade leader roamed slowly over the big black man. Then he motioned to Laurette to come over to them, whereupon he engaged the widow in a quick exchange of whispers. Following this, he turned and faced Jesse with a sneer. "The slave is blind!" he spat with an angry gesture. "What do you take us for, fools?"

Jesse impassively shook his head. "No, I had all intentions of telling you of his weakness. But—" Jesse put his hand on the black man's massive shoulder "—he is, as you can see for yourself, remarkably strong. And he is skilled as a blacksmith, despite the handicap. Surely he is still worth more than the sum total of a weak woman and an infant?"

Blood Man cast another glance at the mountain of black flesh before him and then gestured for the watching members of his band to join him as he stepped to the side of the ring of firelight. There was a vehement exchange of words spoken in low, guttural whispers before Blood Man returned to stand in front of Jesse.

"My companions are for taking you both as additional captives," said the renegade with a sly look at his adversary. "What do you say to that?"

Jesse smiled a smile which did not reach his eyes as he concentrated on keeping his eyes from flying to the tent in the shadows. Was she safe? Was the babe alive and unharmed? Why hadn't she appeared or made some sound, for surely she'd heard his voice? Moreover, if he was forced into his alternate plan of action, should the present proposal fail to catch their interest, how would she bear up under it?

Jesse fixed Blood Man with a steady look. "Surely you don't believe I would come here unarmed *and* without some protection?" He gestured toward the woods behind him. "Beyond those trees wait an armed and ready group of men, mostly Cherokees from the village of Long Arrow. Should anything happen to keep me from returning to them within the next hour, they stand ready to attack." He watched the renegades' eyes flicker briefly toward the forest. "You may wonder why, since they are behind me, I haven't simply brought them down on you. The answer is obvious. I don't wish to risk harm com-

ing to my woman or child if I can avoid it. Also, before we ne-
gotiate anything, I wish to see the two of them to ascertain that
you really have them and that they are unharmed. Well, what
is your answer?''

Blood Man returned Jesse's steady, unwavering gaze for
several seconds, then moved again to confer with his band.
Through all of this, Laurette stood quietly by, wishing she'd
picked up more of the Indian's language than she had. At last
the renegade leader returned to the fire.

"My brothers do not trust your offer. They say if we let you
take the woman and the child, there will be nothing to stop you
from sending your allies—if you indeed have them—to attack
us in vengeance."

With an inward sigh of regret, Jesse paused for a moment
over the Indian's words. *The alternate plan. I was afraid we'd
have to use it. God, give her the strength to endure it!* To the
renegade leader he finally said, "Then I have another offer. Let
me at least have the child in exchange for the black. After all,"
he shrugged, "one can always find another woman, but one's
flesh and blood is a different matter. If you keep the woman,
she will be a hostage for you against recriminations. I still do
not wish to see her harmed."

Blood Man was silent for a moment as he digested Jesse's
words. This new proposal sounded advantageous to him and he
could tell from the looks on the faces of his cohorts that they
also liked what they'd heard. But the canny mind of the scarred
renegade searched for pitfalls in the proposal. Would a white
man—an important, rich one, especially—really consider bar-
gaining away his wife to safeguard and secure his child? An
Indian might, he knew, in certain cases, but a white? Yet this
was no ordinary white man. He was also a blood brother to the
Cherokee, an intimate of Long Arrow himself, who sat in his
council house. Perhaps....

Suddenly Blood Man motioned to his companions to join
him as he walked over to where Laurette was waiting. There,
after a conversation in whispered tones of both Cherokee and
English, Blood Man and the others arrived at the answer he
would give the white planter. Telling Laurette of Jesse's latest
offer, the renegade had been delighted to learn of Brianna's
ramblings during childbirth, ramblings that told him even she

felt her husband cared only for the unborn child and nothing for her. After hearing it from the smirking widow, he no longer questioned the white man's motives. The man was simply more Indian—more like *him*—than white. With a final nod of the head to his fellow kidnappers, Blood Man turned and confronted Jesse.

"We accept," he said.

Jesse steeled himself to force back the sigh of relief that threatened to emerge. They were not out of the woods yet. He nodded to the Indian leader. "It is well. But first I wish to see the woman and my child. Show them to me."

Blood Man turned to Laurette and said in English, "Wake the woman and bring her here with the child." A thoughtful look flickered across his face before he added, "Gag her. We do not need the whining and pleading of such a creature to threaten our bargain."

Laurette smiled in snide satisfaction and went into the tent. A few minutes later she emerged, leading a bewildered looking Brianna carrying her son. She was gagged with a strip of the petticoat that had served as swaddling for the infant.

At first Brianna blinked a couple of times as her eyes adjusted to the light thrown by the campfire and the half-moon that had recently emerged from behind the trees. Inside the tent it had been pitch black. Then, when her gaze took in the figures of her husband and the big black man behind him, she froze in her tracks. Eyes wide with apprehension, she stared at the two for a moment, then blinked and glanced quickly at the others before looking back at her husband. *Jesse! He came!* But what was he doing here, looking at her as if he saw right through her? Had they captured him and Festus, too?

But Brianna had no more time to contemplate the nature of what was happening, for a number of things occurred in rapid succession. With a sharp prod at the small of her back, Laurette pushed her closer to the fire. Then the widow wrenched the sleeping babe from her arms and held it while she began to unwrap the petticoat he was swaddled in. This done, while Brianna looked on in bewildered horror, she held the infant out for Jesse to examine.

Jesse worked to control the passive look that masked his features, forcing away a desperate urge to seek Brianna's eyes.

He gazed at his son. *A boy. They had a son!* Fighting down the huge wave of emotion that threatened to engulf him, he raised his head and nodded at Blood Man. Then, keeping his eyes deliberately away from the vicinity where his wife stood, he turned and placed his hand on the arm of the black giant behind him and drew him forward. He watched the black being led by one of the renegades into Brianna's tent, then held out his arms for his son. When Laurette had transferred the child to him, he carefully rewrapped him in the soft muslin petticoat, closing his ears to the low moan of pain he thought he heard coming from behind Brianna's gag or the fretful cries the babe had begun to utter since he'd been taken from his mother. Then Jesse turned and walked away into the trees.

Through all this Brianna had watched like a creature in a nightmare, disbelief and agonized horror warring within her as she stood helplessly by, her arms held cruelly behind her by one of her captors. In the end she might have caught the brief flicker of pain that crossed Jesse's eyes as he turned to leave, but the bitter flow of tears that welled up in her own eyes prevented her from seeing anything. All she could think or feel as she was rudely dragged, her knees buckling beneath her, to the tent, was that she finally had the cruelest proof of how Jesse felt. It had been love for only the babe, all along, just as she'd feared. She had been thrown away.

When she was shoved inside the tent, she saw, by the lantern that had been relit, that Festus was shackled to the stake where they usually bound her. He sat beside it on the ground in a despairing, hunched-over position. *My God!* Brianna exclaimed to herself with bitter realization. *He even sold his friend back into slavery!* She tried to find comfort from the horror this thought brought by telling herself that at least she knew her son was well-loved and safe, but somehow, the notion had a hollow ring to it.

The Indian who escorted her then produced a second leg iron and shackled her as well. With a grunt of satisfaction, he glanced at his handiwork and left.

By now Brianna's gag had been removed and she suddenly fell to uncontrollable sobbing as she huddled on the ground. But in the next instant she felt a pair of huge, muscular arms envelop her as the black twin pulled her to his chest.

"Hush now, Miz Brianna. Stop dat cryin'," he whispered as he held her. "Ain' whut yo'think, heah?"

But Brianna's bitter crying blocked out his words. The big man sighed as he heard great wracking sobs tear through her throat and felt the convulsive shudders that consumed her. "Miz Brianna!" he said at last in a whispered shout as he seized her by the shoulders and gave her a gentle shake. "Look at me. Ah ain' Festus—*Ah's Vulcan!*"

The sobbing stopped, and she raised her head and attempted to focus on what she'd just heard, even as her blurred vision endeavored to focus on his face.

"Dass raht," said the black. "It's Vulcan, only dey—" he made a gesture that encompassed the flap of the tent and the area outside where the sounds of drunken celebration could be heard coming from their captors "—dey don' know dat. An' Ah's heah t' git ya'll *out* o' heah!"

Brianna heard his words in stunned amazement, hardly daring to believe. "But—But, *how*?"

"Ah'll tell y'all 'bout it in a minute," he said with a crafty grin, "but fust Ah gotta give y'all sumfin' fum Jesse." He reached inside the white cambric shirt he wore and withdrew two objects. One was an iron rasp, or file of some kind. He lay this down on the ground beside them and then took her hand and pressed the other item into her palm.

Brianna sucked in her breath when she saw it. There, gleaming softly in the light given off by the lantern overhead, lay the silver ring with an eagle carved on it. Brianna's head began to swim as she seemed to hear, as if coming from a great distance, the words of Aimée spoken so many months ago. "Two pairs of hands reach out to you. One of these pairs of hands is black, but strong and huge; the other pair is also very strong, also a man's hands, but at the last moment, before the image fades, they become the talons of an *eagle*."

But Vulcan was saying something to her, and she shook her head to clear it and concentrated on listening.

"Jesse done tol' me t' tell y' dis be a—" He paused as if searching his memory. "A token!" he finished triumphantly. "An' den he tol' me t' say dis—" Vulcan screwed up his features and recited: "Sen' me no' dis, no' dat, t' increase mah sto', but sweah d-dth—thou th—think'st Ah love d—dthee, an' no mo'.''

The black man's face broke out into a wide grin once he had successfully stumbled through Donne's words. ''Ah ain' much fo' po-tree, Miz Brianna,'' he mumbled self-consciously, ''but Jesse done made me mem'rize dat an' said t' tell yo de minute we wuz alone.''

Brianna heard him as she felt a giant wave of elation sweep her body, and she thought she had never heard anything more beautiful. She felt her heart soar, and the tenuous flame of the thing called hope, the flickering flame she had nursed all these many weeks, grow along with it until it became a bright light that consumed her soul. *He cares! He hasn't abandoned me. Oh, God, can it even be possible? Could he . . . love . . . ?*

But she had no more time to savor her budding joy. Vulcan was busy using his filing tool to attack one of the links of her chains. By now the sounds of drunken revelry outside pretty much masked the noise this made, although the big man had also taken the precaution of removing his shirt and wadding it up over the file to muffle it as he worked.

As Brianna watched the impressive display of Vulcan's giant muscles while he filed away tirelessly at the iron, she heard him tell her how reluctantly Jesse had devised this plan of rescue, explaining with regret how the initial plan to exchange him for both her *and* the babe had been rejected by her captors. Jesse had been beside himself for days with worry over the pain the implementation of the alternative plan would cause her, no matter how short its duration. Then he went on to explain how he hoped to lead her safely out of the camp once their chains were severed and the renegades were asleep or in a drunken stupor. His one concern was that Laurette might desist from the revelry and maintain a light enough sleep in her own tent to awaken and sound an alarm, but soon a high-pitched shriek of inebriated laughter from the widow met their ears from outside, and his concern was put to rest.

Several hours later, under cover of the still darkness that comes just before the dawn, Brianna and Vulcan made their way through the silent encampment. Each still wore a chainless, heavy iron band around one ankle, and they wore no shoes as they picked their way carefully around the slumbering forms of the unconscious renegades, but Brianna felt as if she were weightless, as though her feet didn't even touch the ground as she followed Vulcan into the forest.

Then, suddenly, she was truly being lifted off the ground as her husband's arms pulled her into his in a wordless embrace. Brianna let out a soft little cry as the reality of his presence hit her, and then her arms wound tightly about his neck as she sobbed, "You came, you came!"

But Jesse was murmuring into her hair, her ear, her mouth, "Brianna—thank God. Oh, my darling—forgive me for what I had to do!"

She pulled back slightly within the circle of his arms then, but the emotion coursing through her choked any words she might have uttered to assure him there was nothing to forgive, and she only nodded mutely, tears streaming down her face.

Jesse's eyes, too, were shiny with moisture as he looked deeply into hers. She thought she heard a strangled sound catch in his throat before he gathered her to him in an embrace so fierce, she felt he might never let her go. Then, suddenly, he released her from it, but only to bend and bring his arm under her knees, sweeping her up, off the ground and into his arms as he hoarsely called to Vulcan and gave the signal to move off.

Minutes later, Brianna found herself holding their son in her arms as she sat crosswise in front of Jesse on Gypsy. Behind them, Garrett, Laughing Bear and twenty Cherokee warriors followed on their mounts. Brianna had already seen the restrained fury in their eyes as they mounted to escort them to Long Arrow's village. They were for attacking the renegade camp right away and extracting revenge, but Jesse had prevailed upon them to wait until his wife and son were safely out of harm's way before they acted. But then all thoughts of Indians and vengeance slipped from Brianna's mind as she gave herself over to the blissful peace of Jesse's embrace as it encircled her and tiny Saor. Like the babe in her arms she breathed a sigh and slept.

Chapter Twenty-Seven

"But, I tell you, it was not my fault!" Laurette stood beside the remains of the previous night's campfire and faced her lover of recent months. But it was not a lover's face she beheld. Honoré Dumaine's eyes glared back at her from a visage distorted with rage. Laurette made a quick gesture to indicate the brooding figures of the renegades who stood a dozen or so yards away, near the edge of the clearing. "They all got stinking drunk and never bothered to put anyone on guard. I'm innocent, I tell you!"

Honoré looked her up and down, a malevolent sneer on his face. "You and innocence parted company years ago, madam. That is, if you were ever acquainted at all."

Stung as much by his look and tone as by his words, Laurette took a step backward as if she'd been struck physically, but then she quickly recovered and used a different ploy. Moving closer to him, she reached out until her hands were creeping around his neck, saying, "What's happened between us, *mon coeur*? Can you not fasten on what we've been to each other?"

With a roar of anger, Honoré thrust her from him in a move that sent Laurette reeling backward. *"What's happened?"* he raged. "I've just lost what is likely my last chance at my patrimony, and you ask what's happened? Are you stupid as well as perfidious? I trusted you in this matter. Why do you think I had you remain with these savages all this time? On a whim? It was your duty to see that there were no mistakes, and you failed me, you bitch, you failed us both!"

Laurette gazed at his furious face with horror. "But I told you—"

"Have done!" Dumaine snarled. "I've heard enough of your whining excuses." He turned sharply away from her and strode over to where the renegade band stood watching.

Laurette watched his movements with bitter apprehension. He couldn't be this angry at her for too long, could he? Sooner or later, he had to calm down, she told herself. She had too much invested in this relationship. If Honoré severed it—oh, no, it was unthinkable! What should she do? Where would she go? Nervously, she twisted an onyx ring on her finger as she watched him approach the Indians and begin engaging them in energetic conversation.

They spent many minutes talking this way, and there was much gesturing, some of it toward the widow; then Laurette saw Blood Man break away and go to the pile of supplies near one of the tents. He bent to pick up what looked like a deerskin pouch and something else she couldn't quite see. He opened the pouch, sniffed its contents, and advanced toward Dumaine with a satisfied smile on his face. *The poisonous herbs he's been after them for!* thought Laurette. She wondered how he'd finally managed to get them to hand them over.

But in the next few moments, Laurette was to have her answer—and wish she'd never heard of the lethal herbs—or Honoré Dumaine. Honoré accepted the pouch from the renegade leader with a nod. Then, with only the briefest of glances in her direction—and his eyes were cold—he walked to his horse and mounted.

"Honoré!" she cried. "Where are you going? What about *me*?" But then she saw Blood Man coming toward her. He wore an evil-looking leer on his face, and in one hand he carried an iron shackle with a chain attached.

"What—What are you looking at me like that for?" Laurette asked. And then she knew. A look of horror spread across her features as she began to back away from the advancing renegade leader. Behind him she caught sight of the other members of the band grinning slyly at her. "No!" she screamed. "No, you wouldn't—" She looked off to her left where she saw Honoré riding calmly away on his horse. "Honoré, you could not be so cruel! Come back, *I beg you*!"

Blood Man reached her, and his hand shot out and gripped her wrist. She twisted aside, her face a study in terror, but the leering renegade then grabbed her viciously by the hair and began dragging her to the tent where, only recently, they had incarcerated Brianna Randall and her son.

"*Oh, my God!* You *cannot* have *done* this to me, Honoré!" she screamed. "Honoré—you monster! You *sold* me to them for a pack of herbs!"

It was late morning when the rescue party entered Long Arrow's village. They had ridden slowly so as not to disturb the sleep of the exhausted woman in Jesse's arms, and, even when her husband delivered his wife into the care of Lula and White Fire Woman, Brianna barely stirred from her slumber. As Jesse carried her tenderly into the guest lodge where the two women quickly prepared her a bed, she remained oblivious to the sounds of celebration and rejoicing that had begun to fill the air upon their arrival, nestling peacefully into the cotton-covered feather ticking the Cherokee used for summer bedding, her sleeping infant son by her side.

After a brief conference with the chief and several of the tribal elders, Jesse agreed to let his brother, Garrett, and Laughing Bear represent him in the tracking of the renegades. It was felt it would not take too long to find them and bring them to justice—Cherokee justice—for they had left behind them, back near the renegade camp, a couple of Cherokee scouts to follow their certain attempt to escape, and these braves would be leaving a marked trail to follow. As for Jesse, it was felt by the others—and he readily agreed—that his wife needed him by her side after the ordeal she'd suffered, and, after seeing the tracking party off, he quickly hastened to the lodge where she lay.

Throughout the long, somnolent hours of the summer afternoon and on into early evening, Jesse sat by the side of his wife and son and watched. Twice, the babe awakened, hungry, and each time he saw Brianna stir and rouse herself at his crying, to sleepily undo the doeskin wrapper they had dressed her in and drowsily pull her son to her breast. On each occasion she briefly opened her eyes to meet the tender, blue-eyed gaze of her husband as he hovered watchfully over them; then she would softly smile and murmur his name before closing heavy-lidded green eyes and drift off again in a doze of maternal contentment.

Lula and White Fire Woman came several times, respectfully asking his permission to enter the lodge before they did such things as remove Brianna's shackle, change the infant's swaddling and examine Brianna and the babe for any dangers to their health. (They pronounced both remarkably fit, despite what they'd been through, though the chief's wife prescribed plenty of rest, for Brianna especially, and said she could use some fattening up.)

Just a short while before sundown, with the aromas of the village cooking fires filling the air, Jesse was carrying a wooden board laden with cornmeal cakes and baked, leaf-wrapped trout from the doorway where it had been handed to him by Lula, when he heard his name called in a sleepy tone of voice.

"Jesse?" Brianna called a second time.

Looking in the direction of her voice, he saw his wife sitting up in the bedding as she drowsily rubbed her eyes. Instantly, he set the food he carried down on a nearby bench and hastened to her side. "Yes, love, I'm here," he said softly as he knelt beside her with a concerned smile.

As he spoke he took in her appearance, his eyes roaming carefully over her face and torso, for, despite White Fire Woman's words of assurance, he worried over the effects her ordeal might have had on her. But the exquisitely beautiful face that turned up toward him looked, if anything, more lovely than he had ever seen it. Since the beginning of the time they had begun sharing a bed, he had known his wife was one of those rare women whose beauty remained fresh and pure when she awoke in the mornings, her richly colored auburn hair tumbling enchantingly about her creamy shoulders in sweet disarray, her dewy complexion enhanced by the faint flush it assumed upon rousing from slumber, and the huge eyes incredibly green and clear when they opened. And so she looked now, and as he watched, her entrancing, slightly full and rosy lips parted into a dimpled smile. Then suddenly Jesse gasped as he felt his body rocked by a wave of desire so strong it took his breath away.

Brianna caught the sound and her winged eyebrows rose in concern, the green eyes flying over his face. "What is it?" she asked in alarm.

Jesse gave her a brief chuckle as he struggled to control his passion. "Not a thing, sweetheart," he told her with a warm grin, deciding her knowledge of his reaction to her, following the long weeks of their separation, ought to be postponed, at least until she'd eaten and they'd had a chance to talk. "Not a blessed thing in the whole world, now that I have you back—and safe."

Brianna closed her eyes at his words and took a slow, deep breath. "Safe," she whispered in an echo of what he'd uttered, as if the only way she was to grasp the reality of the concept she had for so long feared would never happen was if she gave it verbal affirmation. Then she opened her eyes and looked into his. "Oh, Jesse, am I really here? It isn't some cruel dream or—" She stopped as she saw her husband's eyes go cloudy with pain at the thought of what had happened to her, and beyond that, to thoughts of what might have happened, had he not come in time. She saw him shut his eyes, then, and slowly shake his head before he reached for her and held her tightly to him.

"No, my darling, it's not a dream," he told her, emotion flooding his voice. "You're here with me, and safe, now, and nothing is ever going to harm you again—I swear it!"

Brianna felt his strong arms enclose her and knew he spoke the truth. She was about to say as much when suddenly the hiccough of an infant's beginning as cry broke the air. Jesse released her, and she turned to the swaddled bundle beside them.

"Oh, Saor," she cried with a watery laugh, "are you all right?" She picked her son up and held him close as she gazed into the tiny face. "Just hungry, I'll bet," she smiled as she pushed the doeskin wrapper off one shoulder.

"*What* do you call him?" Jesse questioned in a wondering voice. "Sare?"

Brianna smiled shyly at him with a light blush as she bared her breast for their son to suckle. "Yes," she said softly, "it's spelled S-A-O-R. It's Gaelic—Irish, for 'free,' a word my mother taught me a long time ago." She frowned slightly with concern, then, as she met Jesse's steady gaze. "You—you don't mind that I took it upon myself to—to name him, do you? I...I felt it so strongly, after he was born, the name, I mean, and—"

She broke off as Jesse's hand closed over the tiny fist of his son as it clutched her breast, and he bent to place a tender kiss on her brow. "No, darling, no," he whispered, his voice shaking with emotion. "Not only is it an apt and beautiful name—it is better than any I could have hoped to have chosen, had I been there." Then Jesse's voice grew hard with anger. "That I was not there when you felt the pain of bringing our son into the world is the only thing that fills me with care. That you should have had to endure—"

"Shh," Brianna whispered, "it's all right. It was terrible when it happened, but, as you said, I'm—we're all safe now, and together. That's all that matters."

They talked for a while as Brianna finished nursing Saor, Jesse gently prying from her the events of her captivity when he saw she was ready to talk about them. But when she mentioned some of the things she'd endured, and he saw she was sparing him the more painful details, his eyes hardened with fury, and he focused on thoughts of Cherokee justice. Laurette Mayfield, as well as the renegades, would pay for what they had done! It mattered not at all to him that the widow was female. She had cost his beloved untold pain, and for that, she would pay.

After Saor had taken his fill, Jesse brought forth the food Lula had prepared, and White Fire Woman came and offered to take the suddenly wide-awake infant to her lodge to bathe and change him while *Tlanuwa* and his *ghigau* ate and had some time alone together.

"Tlanuwa?" Brianna questioned after White Fire Woman had left them.

Jesse smiled as he handed her her second of the leaf-wrapped fish, passing it to her on a small slab of bark. "It's their word for a mythical, eagle-like bird in their lore. Its origins may be Creek, rather than Cherokee, actually. White Fire Woman is Creek by birth. But Long Arrow's people have eclectic tendencies and I've heard them use the term ever since—"

"Ever since they named you and gave you this ring?" Brianna questioned as she brought forth the silver ring he'd sent her from the folds of her wrapper.

Jesse nodded solemnly as he gazed directly into her eyes.

Feeling something stir deep within her under the heat of his gaze, Brianna was suddenly brought to mind of Vulcan's memorized message as he'd handed her Jesse's "token." She swallowed the lump forming in her throat and began to stammer, "Wh—When Vulcan—"

"I love you." Jesse's eyes held hers as he uttered the words he'd waited so long to tell her.

The fish she'd been holding dropped to the floor as Brianna froze, hardly daring to believe what she'd heard. Her eyes searched his face and found the truth in his own. Incredibly blue, they told her what was in his heart, and she saw him nod and smile tenderly. "I love you, Brianna."

The sharp sting of tears flooded her eyes even as a huge wellspring of joy flooded her heart. With a sob, she threw herself into his arms, crying, "Oh, Jesse, I love you! I love you, I love you!"

Jesse held her tightly to him, his voice a blend of joy and tenderness as he murmured into her hair, "Oh, little one, how long I've waited to share this with you! Sweet beloved, wife of my heart." He gave a breathy little laugh in her ear. "Sometimes I thought I couldn't bear waiting— Didn't you guess? Didn't you—ah, no, don't weep, my darling! It's real at last. Truly—"

At this Brianna gave a small cry and began covering his face with kisses, murmuring through her tears, "Oh, Jesse! It was *I* who couldn't bear—couldn't—couldn't—oh, I never *dreamed* you could love me! I thought it was just our child you wanted!"

Suddenly Jesse grew very still. He drew slightly back, placing both hands gently on her shoulders, then moved them to her head and held it tenderly, to gaze into her face. "Of course I wanted our child," he said quietly, "but that was because— perhaps, at first, without even realizing it—I had already fallen so deeply in love with its mother, I could not choose but to love and want it too. But it was you, Brianna, every maddening, capricious, delightful fiber of you—and most of all, your heart, I desired. *You*, my sweet child-become-woman. That's all I waited for. To see you grown into the woman you've become that I might dare to love you equally, man to woman. Can you understand that, love?" he asked as he drew her to him again.

Brianna nodded against his shoulder with a watery sigh. "Oh, Jesse," she murmured, "I was terrible there for a while, wasn't I?"

A low rumble of laughter emanated from Jesse's chest as he squeezed her tighter. "You were a perfect hellion, love—a minx—an impish terror I somehow found myself unable to do without." He turned slightly and tipped her chin up with his finger to look at her. "And so I find it still is with me, love. I cannot do without you. I never will. Do you believe that?"

Brianna beheld his tender, serious look with eyes wide and trusting, and her love shone in their green depths as she answered, "Oh, yes, my darling—oh, it's the same with me!"

Then, suddenly she saw his eyes change as they looked at her, a new emotion coloring their hue; desire, like a tidal wave, flooded over them both as Jesse buried his face in her hair with a groan and drew her closer.

"God, how I've missed you!" he murmured urgently at her temple. "Sweet wife, I'm going to make love to you all night long!"

Brianna felt a heightened thrill of desire ripple along her spine at his words, and when he pressed her back into the bedding, she reached for the buttons at his shirt and feverishly began to undo them.

But when she moved to push apart his opened shirt, Jesse stopped her, saying, "Easy, love. Let's take it slowly. We've all the time in the world now, a lifetime." And he began to make love with his body then, as he already had with his words, baring hers slowly as he removed the wrapper she wore, inch by inch. On each delicious part of her he exposed, he placed reverent kisses, worshiping her beloved flesh as he already did her heart and mind.

"Brianna," he murmured as his lips traced a scorching path down her throat and across her shoulders, "beloved woman, precious *ghigau*. How I love you, want you...."

And when Brianna felt his fingers touch her aching breasts, caress their rounded fullness and then felt him brush their hardened peaks with his thumbs, she moaned a response deep in her throat and tried to pull him closer.

But Jesse only gave a shaky little laugh and held her hands to the bedding on either side of her head as his mouth followed the course his fingers had taken. Slowly, maddeningly, he traced his tongue over her lush fullness, and when a tiny drop of liquid appeared from one throbbing crest, he licked it carefully off with his tongue, raised his head to look at her an instant, then brought his mouth to hers and kissed her, tongue touching tongue.

"Sweet Brianna, taste the honey of the milk your body made for our son. Know its sweetness as we know each other's bodies." He bent to resume his lips' play with her nipples. "As we know each other's hearts, know each other's love."

By now Brianna was mindless with longing. A sweet, almost painful ache was spiraling through her core, flooding the place between her thighs with moisture, causing her to writhe and twist beneath him.

"Jesse!" she cried. "Please! I can't—I need—"

"Yes, love, I know," Jesse whispered. He released her hands and brought his own down to hold her by the waist while his mouth found its way to her navel, and then even lower. The last fold of soft doeskin was swept aside as his lips reached the downy triangle above her parted thighs.

But when Brianna realized the course they would follow, she cried out as if in shame and drew her thighs together, causing Jesse to raise his head a moment and look at her while he held her protesting hands gently in his. "No, love, don't draw back from me now," he said softly. "You're beautiful here as well as elsewhere, like a precious flower with sweet petals opening to the sun, and the sun of my love seeks entrance, my darling. There is no shame in this, only the pleasure I would give you, Brianna."

When she heard his words of love, Brianna felt the fear and shame melt from her mind, and, breathing a soft sigh of release, she opened her thighs to him, eager and willing for his touch.

Seeing the last of her reserve melt, Jesse felt a renewed jolt of longing rip through him, but he bit back the urge to hurry and took his time, bent on her pleasure. Deftly, his fingers stroked the tiny budding swell atop the first pair of lips—the petals he had so fondly spoken of—and Brianna cried out her pleasure and began to arch under his touch. But then his tongue followed his fingers, and she grew wild with this more intimate sensation, thrusting her fingers in the dark curls of his head and moaning with helpless ecstasy.

Then his tongue found its way past the last pair of petals, and ever so gently, it probed and entered.

A piercing cry broke the stillness of the night as Brianna arched once more and sobbed her pleasure. Jesse felt her body convulse beneath his hands as they held her hips, felt her flesh contract under his tongue. Only then did he give vent to his own straining passion. Tasting the honeyed dew of her, the wetness that laced the petals of the flower he'd probed, he raised his head and sought her face. Just for an instant he met her heavy-lidded, sensual gaze, then bent to cover her mouth with his.

"Taste this, too, love," he breathed urgently against her mouth. "Taste your nectar on my tongue, and know how sweet I found you!"

But Brianna was beyond answering him. The first convulsive spiraling of pleasure she'd felt was followed by another, just at his words, and now Jesse worked more quickly.

With rapid, shaking movements, he tore off his clothes, all the while talking to her. "There's more, yet, love. A world of pleasure yet to come. Wait, you'll see."

And then he was bending over her trembling form again, and with a quick gesture, touched her between the thighs. They parted eagerly as Brianna murmured, "Yes, oh, yes!"

And at last he lowered himself and slipped hungrily into her throbbing warmth.

Brianna let out a long sigh of pleasure at the sensation when she felt him fill her, but in seconds this gave way to yet another burst of longing, yet another desire for release from the sweet, almost painful, pleasure building at her center.

Then Jesse withdrew and hesitated, then plunged, and as he did, he rasped, "I love you!" Then he plunged again—and again—"I love you! I love you, Brianna," he cried hoarsely, and then, when he felt her tremble and heave beneath him, her joy a cry in the night, he at last surrendered his love as well, filling her again with his seed as his body shuddered its release.

How long they remained suspended, their bodies joined in sweet oneness, neither could have said. To each it seemed as if time stood still, marking this moment in their lives and branding it within their minds and souls, never to be forgotten. And when at last their world ceased to reel from the rapture of their union, they were silent for an even longer time, holding each other in almost reverent arms, each filled with thoughts of the wondrous gift they had shared.

Finally, Jesse raised his head and looked at her. "There aren't words, Brianna—"

"Only these, my darling," she whispered, "I love you with all my heart and soul."

Jesse closed his eyes and pressed a poignant kiss to her brow.

Wide, clear green eyes met his when he again looked at her. "I loved you in silence for so long, I feel as if I need to make up for lost time and tell you again and again, minute by minute. Do you mind?" she added shyly.

Jesse laughed, a joyous, almost boyish laugh such as she'd not yet heard from him and nuzzled her ear. "Try to make me!" But then he raised himself up on one elbow and looked at her with a more serious mien. "Just know this, Brianna. You are my whole world now. Without you, none of it would have any meaning for me. I love you beyond reason, beyond feeling, beyond life itself, and I know I'll go on loving you, as long as there's breath in my body."

Brianna read the truth in his eyes, and for a passing moment felt overwhelmed by the enormity of what he told her. But then, at last, she felt the final remnant of something hard and brittle melt and give way from where it had been lodged in her heart. It was the thing that she had lived with for so long, the terrible fear of surrendering herself that had caused her to cling to that unthinking yearning for total freedom, no matter what the cost. Now she finally understood what Festus had been trying to tell her that day. Love, indeed, has its own bonds, but they are ties that those who are fortunate enough to find them, know are more precious, and more fulfilling, than all the frantic, mad escapes that men have sought over the ages.

She closed her eyes and sighed deeply, then turned shining eyes up to her husband. She *was* free.

Jesse watched the play of expressions cross her face and finally saw the peace in her eyes. He smiled tenderly down at her then, before whispering, "I'm going to spend our whole lives making you happy. Dear God, how I love you!"

Then, suddenly, he playfully bit her earlobe and said, "As for you telling me you love me, sweetheart, I waited to hear those words from your lips for so long, I wouldn't mind if you began to utter them like a trained parrot, saying nothing else all day long!"

Brianna dimpled. "And I might just grant you that request, sir! Can't you just see me, following my husband about, all day long, not even taking time out to eat or sleep—"

Suddenly, Jesse rose up and gave her a stern look. "Speaking of eating, madam, we're supposed to be fattening you up!" He gestured at the food that lay nearby, cold and forgotten. "We'd better get you something to eat!"

"Well," Brianna murmured, "if you insist. But there are other things I'd much rather do," she told him as she ran a finger sensuously down his chest and abdomen. "I believe you mentioned something about 'all night long'?"

Jesse's eyebrows shot up in mock reproach before he growled and pulled her beneath him. "Madam, you've become a total wanton," he told her with a grin.

"I have only my husband to blame," Brianna answered with a merry giggle. Then the giggle was silenced as Jesse's mouth closed hungrily over hers, and it was a long while before either thought of food again.

Chapter Thirty-Eight

It was late August, and the entire household of Riverview was thrown into a bustling whirl of activity as plans were effected for a grand harvest ball. It was not the usual time for giving balls in the tidewater area, for the gentry usually escaped to their plantations to languorously wait out the stifling heat of the Carolina summer, keeping their entertaining to a more modest level than what was enjoyed when they returned to Charleston after the weather cooled.

But Brianna and Jesse Randall felt they had more than a little to celebrate late in the summer of 1793, and everyone who knew them felt it too. Garrett and Christie Randall were immediately touched by the great blossoming of love they saw between Jesse and Brianna, and they were immediately reminded of their own stormy courtship and its delightful conclusion when they witnessed what had occurred between these two. Aimée was seen to go about the plantation and Big House with a knowing smile on her face as she assumed the privileged task of helping Brianna care for tiny Saor; a person blessed with the Sight is rarely surprised by even life's most radical turn of events. And Festus and Vulcan were frequently seen with proud and happy smiles on their faces as they eagerly recounted to people like Isaac and sister Lula, their own parts in helping to bring the master and mistress of Riverview together. Indeed, it was a happy time for all who were involved in the business of the plantation, truly a time for celebration, now that love had worked its magic.

And so the ball was planned, and when preparations came to a countdown, acceptances had been received from far and wide.

As he'd promised, Thomas Jefferson was to attend, and he was touted as the Randalls' special guest of honor. He would be bringing along his elder daughter, Martha, and his son-in-law. Then, from Columbia came the message that Father Edouard would also come: "Neither wild horses, nor Pharaoh's chariots could stop me," he'd written. And, of course, all the important people of South Carolina itself eagerly accepted invitations, just as they had for Riverview's New Year's ball. Jesse and Brianna Randall were quickly becoming known as *the* glamorous host and hostess of the day, with invitations to their *fêtes* becoming the most sought-after in the entire social whirl that abounded in that place and time.

If there were any sour notes, one was that this time Governor Pinckney asked Jesse and Brianna well in advance if they would extend an invitation to his aide, Honoré Dumaine. But with love lighting their hearts and driving out rancor, the hosting couple quickly forgave the Governor and had the invitation sent.

But there was one added burden that troubled Jesse. Long Arrow's men, along with Garrett and Laughing Bear, had been successful in tracking the renegade band and capturing most of them, but, somehow, Blood Man and Laurette Mayfield had escaped. The others met swift Cherokee justice and no longer lived to terrorize unsuspecting innocents, but the search for the remaining pair continued. Scouts were sent out far and wide, but thus far, the widow and the renegade leader had eluded capture. And though Jesse was careful not to trouble Brianna with his concern, the failure of justice to meet up with those two lay like a nagging thorn in the private chambers of his mind, and he had a deep wish to see the business finished.

But on the day of the ball, as the shadows of early evening approached, such things were far from anyone's thoughts. Upstairs in their suite, Jesse and Brianna were spending a few moments with their son, playing with him on their bed before it was time to put him down for the night.

"His eyes are still blue, darling," Brianna commented to her husband as she watched Saor's tiny fist attempt to close over Jesse's nose.

Jesse laughed. "And my face is going to be *black and blue* if this young man has his way!" He proceeded to push the object of his son's fascination gently into the gurgling babe's fat little belly, sending Saor into a peal of delighted laughter. "In faith," chuckled Jesse, "if the lad grows any more robust, I'm going to have to put him into training with Vulcan and Festus."

Brianna gave him a cryptic look. "One could do worse than having the Noslave brothers as mentors," she said with a rapid, sidewise glance. But then she quickly changed the subject, saying, "Oh, look! It's almost a quarter past the hour. If Aimée and I are to have enough time to finish dressing, I'd better collect our budding blacksmith here and take him to the nursery. He nursed longer than usual tonight." She picked up her son and rose from the bed while Saor's mouth stretched into a tired infant's yawn.

Jesse rose to stand beside her and looked into her eyes with a tender smile. "And I enjoyed watching every miraculous minute of it, love." He didn't add the adjacent thought that crossed his mind—that he indeed found it a daily miracle that she had all the milk their growing babe required after the ordeal she'd been through. Perhaps that was one of the reasons he made it a point in his day-to-day routine to take time out to come by their chamber or wherever she chose to feed their son and watch. He regarded these moments as some of the most sacred and precious in his life, and he missed no opportunity to savor them.

Jesse grinned as he was suddenly reminded of an occasion, just the previous evening, when their son had awakened early and demanded his dinner just as Brianna was emerging from her bath. He himself had been watching his wife's ablutions with an eye toward helping her dry off in preparation for some far more interesting sport between them, and he'd not been overly happy with Saor's interruption.

But Brianna had already read the look in her husband's eyes, had indeed encouraged it by a series of sensuous glances as she'd languidly run her bath sponge over a shapely leg stretched prettily before her, or across the lush breasts that she somehow made it her business to bring into view above the level of the bathwater as she washed.

So when she'd stepped from the tub to the sound of demanding infant cries from the adjoining room, she merely wrapped herself in the sheath of soft, white toweling Jesse handed her, went in to fetch the hungry babe, and nursed him on their bed—again, wearing only a towel. Then, when their son had been properly burped, changed and put back to sleep for the night, she'd reentered their chamber and taken countless, long, sensuous minutes to slowly divest herself of the toweling, while her husband sat back on the bed and watched in disbelieving fascination. By the time she'd slithered sensually across the coverlet to join him, Jesse's head was reeling from the slow, deliberate assault to his senses. And there had followed a heady play of passion between them that had lasted far into the night. Even now, as he thought of it, his loins were gripped by the throes of a desire so fierce, he closed his eyes against the onslaught.

"What is it, darling?" Brianna questioned in a voice tinged with alarm.

Jesse let out a shaky laugh before turning his head toward her and gracing her with a devilish grin. "Not a damned thing, love. But if I'm to help you greet our guests in less than an hour's time, I'd better stop willing the clock back to last night. These evening breeches do little to hide a man's reaction to the inadvertent remembrance of past delights."

Brianna glanced down at the source of the problem he spoke of and blushed.

But Jesse only laughed before he gave her a playful swat on her *derrière*, saying, "Madam, if you do not wish us to completely disgrace ourselves before our son and our guests, kindly take your enticing presence out of here and put the child to bed."

With an impish twinkle in her eyes, Brianna stood on tiptoe to kiss his mouth, then quickly darted the tip of her tongue into one corner of it before withdrawing and sauntering out of the room.

"Minx!" Jesse called after her in good-natured vexation.

But in the next instant there came a knock at their door after which Isaac's voice announced the early arrival of several guests. "Governor Pinckney and Honoré Dumaine are among them, sir," Isaac added, "and I think I hear another carriage approaching outside."

"Thank you, Isaac," said Jesse as he gave a cursory glance to his cravat in the mirror. "Show them into the library, and I'll be right down."

After Isaac went off to accommodate the early arrivals, Jesse called into the nursery to tell Brianna where he was going and then made his way downstairs. As he reached the landing, he heard the front door open and looked down the hallway to see his footman admit a large, red-haired man dressed in black.

"Father Edouard!" Jesse grinned as he hurried to shake the priest's hand.

But then the cleric took him by both shoulders and kissed him on each cheek in the French fashion, saying, "*Mon Dieu*, it has been a long time! I have missed you, my friend—and the little one!" His brown eyes darkened for a brief moment. "She is well, your wife?"

"Yes, thank God!" Jesse told him.

"And the wee one?"

"Thriving!" Jesse replied with a chuckle. "But you'll have to see for yourself. Brianna's just putting him to bed now. Perhaps you can go up and catch him before he falls asleep."

"I'll do that," smiled the priest.

Then, when Jesse had instructed a footman to show Father Edouard to the master suite and told the priest he might afterward join him and the other early guests in the library, Father Edouard paused and withdrew from the folds of his cassock a familiar looking flask.

"Take this into the library with you, Jesse," said the priest. "Then, when I bring Brianna down, we'll all drink a toast I've been meaning to propose for a long time." His brown eyes twinkled as he threw Jesse a merry grin that flashed from the curls of his red beard.

"Good enough, my friend," said Jesse and the two men parted.

When Jesse arrived in the library, he saw Governor Pinckney and his wife talking amiably with Johanna and James Carlisle in one corner while, across the room, Honoré Dumaine seemed to be helping himself to some of Jesse's private stock of liquors from where they were stored in various crystal decanters set on a silver tray above a low, built-in bookcase. Frowning briefly at Dumaine for his presumptuousness (not that Jesse was niggardly about sharing any of his bounty; indeed, he was about to offer his early guests a selection from the tray himself, but where Honoré Dumaine was concerned, all notions of generosity fled from his mind), Jesse made his way over to the foursome in the corner, a smile of welcome on his face.

"Ladies, gentlemen, how good to see you here tonight!" he exclaimed warmly. "Forgive me for not appearing sooner," he added as he bestowed gallant kisses on the outstretched hands of Mistress Pinckney and Johanna Carlisle.

"But there's nothing to forgive," Johanna replied with a quiet smile. "We're the ones who should beg your indulgence for arriving early."

They all continued talking for a while, with most of the conversation revolving around the weather and other such small talk, although Honoré's joining the group moved the discussion to speculation over how soon the guest of honor would appear, and soon there was talk of things political among the men while the two women moved off to one side and discussed with great anticipation all the favorable things they'd heard about the hostess whom each had yet to meet.

A footman appeared, and Jesse signaled for him to offer the ladies some sherry, if they cared to indulge, and to pass a tray holding glasses of Father Edouard's brandy among the gentlemen. (During all of this, Honoré blatantly sipped at his self-indulged snifter of Jesse's own brandy with an air of arrogance Jesse couldn't help observing but chose to ignore; if the man wished to force his unwanted presence on them—and then proceeded to commit further social blunders, that was his problem; in Jesse's present state of mind, what with his private life in such delightful order, he suddenly realized he could afford to be gracious even where Brianna's blackguard of a sibling was concerned.)

Soon Father Edouard appeared, and after Jesse completed introductions, the talk changed to comments on the state of things at Riverview.

"Your son is the picture of health," the priest told Jesse, "and, although he has his mother's hair color, he's the spitting image of you, *mon ami.*"

"O-o-h," cooed Johanna Carlisle, "he sounds adorable. When do we get to see him?"

"At the christening tomorrow, if you can stay on," Father Edouard announced. "I'm to officiate."

"You've agreed to do it, then?" said Jesse, smiling at the priest.

"Do you think you could have stopped me?" the cleric's beard was split by a wide grin.

"In truth, no," chuckled Jesse. "Brianna's been beside herself with eagerness to ask you to perform the rite. She wanted to put the request to you in person which I assume she just did. Ah, speaking of my wife, what's keeping her?"

"Oh," said Father Edouard, "just a little matter of having to change her gown because a certain young man had the bad manners to spit up all over the one she was wearing."

There was a murmur of laughter before Jesse said, "And, now, Father, the moment Brianna arrives, let's have our glasses ready, for I believe you said something about proposing a toast."

Brianna stood before the cheval glass and inspected the image it cast back at her. Fortunately, she'd ordered two formal gowns for this weekend—one for tonight's ball and one for the small dinner party they'd decided to hold for their closest friends, following Saor's christening tomorrow. Having removed the soiled lavender *robe en chemise* and given it to a chambermaid to clean, she now wore a leaf-green silk voile over a darker green taffeta garment cut in the traditional mode. She twisted gracefully to one side and back again, matching her movements to the sounds of the orchestra as they drifted up to her from the ballroom while she eyed the fluid sweep of her full skirts.

"Perhaps this is the better choice for tonight, after all," she told her reflection as she eyed the tiny, nipped-in appearance of a waistline restored to its former size.

"My dear," she told herself with a dimpled grin, "Christie was right. Nursing does enhance the figure if a woman is careful about what she eats, and you look quite marvelous." She made a comic face at her reflection as she pushed her nose up against it. "You're going to love showing off your girlish figure tonight, aren't you, you vain old thing?"

She began to giggle at her own antics while she made a final adjustment of one of the fastenings of the diamond earrings she wore. They had been a gift from Jesse on her birthday last April, and now that she no longer had the emerald and diamond earrings she might have worn with the matching necklace at her throat, she had chosen these to wear this evening. Her green eyes flashed fire into the mirror as she thought of the perfidy of Laurette Mayfield, and she clenched her fists in anger. Oh, if there were any justice....

Just then she heard a loud crash at one of the windows and she spun with alarm in its direction. Then her mouth gaped open at the apparition that met her horrified stare.

There, among a heap of glass shards and splintered window grilles, stood a woman she thought she ought to recognize but, owing to the creature's state of horrendous disarray, somehow failed to identify. Matted and unbelievably filthy black hair hung wildly about a face that was a mass of swollen, purplish bruises and ugly lacerations. It was impossible to see the color of the miserable creature's eyes, for the swellings around them had almost pushed them shut; lips that bore an unnatural, twisted shape were split and caked with dried blood. Her emaciated body was partially covered by what Brianna could only regard as knotted bits and pieces of foul-looking rags. One drooping breast was bared, and across its surface there were various cuts and scars that looked like they'd been put there with a knife; scar tissue that had to be the result of burned flesh was also visible.

Brianna's glance fell upon a huge, long-handled knife that the woman wielded like a club and she realized it was this object the creature had used to smash her way through the window from the balcony outside. Suddenly a wave of nausea swept over Brianna as she saw a familiar looking shackle on the woman's bare ankle, and she now knew who this was.

"Laurette?" she managed to whisper over the sounds of music that came from downstairs.

An inhuman sounding cackle emanated from the apparition's throat before she nodded brokenly and the cackle became a strangled sob.

"Oh, sweet Mary, what has someone done to you?" Brianna managed to ask.

"Not *someone*," the barely recognizable voice of the widow responded. "Two men: Honoré Dumaine and a pig named Blood Man!"

"*Honoré?!*" Brianna whispered incredulously. "*Honoré did this?*"

Laurette glanced at the heavy knife she carried. "Did you know this is my friend?" she questioned in a strange sounding little voice. Then she gave forth with an anguished wail. "He *sold me* to them! Sold me the way we were going to sell *you*— only for me the experience was a thousand times worse! I carried no child to protect me."

She took a step toward Brianna and half stumbled into the bedpost, then leaned against it wearily as she continued. "Do you have any idea what it's like to be passed around and used by a pack of barbaric savages? No, of course you don't. But I'll tell you, Brianna, because if I don't tell someone, I swear, I shall go mad!

"First that scarred animal took me, but not in any of your more usual forms of rape, ah no, not that one! He dragged me by the hair into the tent and then proceeded to use me in—" Laurette gave a shudder of revulsion "—in the way a certain type of man would take a boy." She paused to watch a look of confusion pass over Brianna's face and then uttered a mirthless laugh. "Ah, well, you are an innocent, after all, aren't you? He *sodomized* me, Brianna! There, in the dirt, in the darkness of that stinking tent!

"But that wasn't the end of it. Oh, no! Then he brought me, naked, out before the others, and they drew lots for the order in which they might have me! And, one by one, while the others watched, they raped me, again, and again, and again, and again!"

"Dear God!" Brianna breathed.

"And, still, that wasn't all," the widow continued. "When they had ridden themselves dry, they tied me to a tree and—"

"Oh, dear God!" Brianna cried, "don't go on, Laurette, please, I beg of you. Here," she added, pulling the coverlet off the bed, "let me help you." She draped it over the widow's half-naked form like a cape. "I—I can call some of the servants, and you look like you could use medical attention."

Laurette shook her head in weary disbelief. "You would help me after all I did to you?"

Ignoring her question, Brianna went to her washstand and dipped a small hand towel in the pitcher there. "How did you escape?" she asked to change the subject.

Laurette allowed her to use the wet cloth to gently blot away some of the caked blood around her lips, then answered, "You remember those earrings I took from you? One night, after a couple of days had passed, I managed to extricate them from where they were hidden among my things. First, I buried one under the ground beneath the tent. Then I showed the other to them and bartered with it and a promise of its mate, for my freedom. God knows why, though I suspect it was because they were tired of me, they accepted the bargain."

"But, Laurette, if that happened only two days later," Brianna questioned as she wrung out the towel in her basin on the washstand, "why has it taken you all this time to—"

"Because that grotesque parody of a man, Blood Man, reneged on the bargain! In the middle of the night, leaving the others behind, he followed me! I had the poorest of the horses—they gave me that—but, more than that, I was lost and had no idea where I was going, so I thought I'd be wise to follow the river. But the mud along its banks left easy tracks to follow, and he found me soon enough."

"Then you became his prisoner again?" Brianna asked as she moved toward the door to call a servant. She wondered why no one had appeared already to see about the noise of breaking glass, but then she assumed the music playing downstairs could have covered the sound to any who were not standing in the very chamber where the crash had occurred.

Just then they heard the sound of a coach pulling up in the drive, and Laurette called, "Wait!" and ran to look out the window. Peering down at the drive for a moment, she then whirled about to face Brianna.

"It's Jefferson's coach. We must hurry!"

"Hurry?" Brianna asked with a puzzled frown.

"I've little time to explain," Laurette said rapidly. "Listen carefully. Jefferson and your husband, and perhaps the others down there, are in grave danger."

Brianna froze and became fearfully attentive when she heard Jesse mentioned.

"The day he sold me to them," Laurette continued, "Honoré Dumaine procured a pack of subtly poisonous herbs from the renegades, and he means to use them tonight. His plan is to kill Jefferson by poisoning the liquor he drinks, the liquor Jesse serves to him. He somehow found out that Jefferson prefers only a particular type of liquor—a brandy, I think—when dining out or being entertained. He has it all planned so it will appear Jesse's fault. He is a madman, I think, Brianna, filled with some insane idea that he can advance the political fortunes of his idol, Aaron Burr. He's taken great pains to forge letters and documents which suggest Jesse is a double agent, secretly committed to Hamilton and the Federalist cause, and he plans to leave them somewhere in this house tonight—where they can be easily found, once Jefferson dies and—"

"Laurette, you wait here!" Brianna suddenly told her as she quickly moved into action. "I'll send someone up to you," she added as she opened the door, "but first I've got to go down to the library and warn them!"

Brianna rushed down the hallway and bounded down the grand staircase, two steps at a time, the skirts of her green ball gown flying. She passed a startled looking Isaac in the lower hallway, saying, "Isaac, come with me! Hurry! I've no time to explain." And the two of them ran toward the library, the tall young woman in the green ball gown with the diminutive butler right behind.

Jesse had just poured some of his best brandy into a snifter and was handing it to Thomas Jefferson when he saw a vision in green sail through the door.

"Brianna, what—"

"Don't drink that brandy, please, Mister Jefferson!" Brianna cried as she searched the room for Honoré. But as her bad luck would have it, her brother had been examining some books to the right of, and just behind, the opened door where he was hidden from her view.

But when Honoré heard her words, he knew in an instant that his plot had been discovered, and he moved quickly. Once Isaac had followed Brianna through the door, Honoré extracted a pistol he'd been prudent enough to carry concealed inside his coat. Then, in front of the startled, horrified eyes of her husband and everyone else in the room, he lunged for Brianna and caught her to him like a human shield while he held his pistol at her side.

The other women in the room screamed, and Jefferson's brandy snifter crashed to the floor. Then everyone remained motionless as Honoré's voice cracked the silence like a bull-whip. "All of you, remain exactly as you are, and Mistress Randall won't be injured," he announced. "If you do as I say, I'll be taking her with me only as far as Charleston where I'll release her, once I've secured passage on a ship somewhere."

Jesse took an involuntary half-step forward before Dumaine's dark eyes flashed a warning and he raised the pistol to Brianna's head.

"I'm warning you, Randall, don't try anything foolhardy." Then a sly expression crossed Honoré's features as he lowered the gun to Brianna's shoulder. "Actually, since your wife's my passage out of here, perhaps the threat of my maiming her would hold more credence." His eyes focused coldly on Jesse. "*Well?*"

Only a bare twitching in the muscles that clenched his jaws tightly shut showed Jesse felt any overt emotion, but a look of anguished fury burned like burnished steel in the blue eyes as he fell back a step.

"That's much better, Mister Randall," Dumaine crooned in an unctuous tone.

Brianna remained silent through all of this, for her many weeks as a captive had taught her the futility of protest in such a dangerous situation, but her eyes went out to Jesse's in a silent plea for him not to worry. Honoré had promised her release, hadn't he? But in the next instant she heard from her brother's lips what she'd been too shocked to piece together out of Laurette's tale.

"It's too bad my sister has had to become a pawn in my plans for a second time," Honoré was saying as he backed toward the door with her. "But at least, this time, she won't be in the company of savages."

Honoré had been part of the plot to sell her! And suddenly Brianna felt a cold wave of fear wash over her. If he'd been capable of selling her before, what was to stop him from trying it

again? *Oh, sweet Lord, no,* Brianna prayed. Her eyes filled
with terror at the thought of losing all she had recently gained,
Jesse and their newfound love, tiny Saor....

But suddenly she felt Honoré stiffen behind her before she
was pushed forward, away from him. She barely had time to
acknowledge her physical release when she heard the sound of
his pistol clattering to the floor. Then she nearly stumbled,
caught herself and turned back to face her captor, only to see
him bending over before he slumped face forward, to the floor.
The long handle of a large knife protruded from his back.

Then Brianna looked up and saw the distraught figure of
Laurette Mayfield standing over Honoré's body. A bitter smile
barely managed to make itself recognized on her bruised and
swollen lips.

"My friend," she said looking down at the knife and touching its handle. "It killed Blood Man and now it's gotten you,
Honoré." The widow's voice was a near-monotone. "My
friend..."

Then Brianna felt herself caught gently from behind and
turned about as Jesse's arms pulled her into a fervent embrace.

"My God, Brianna," was all he managed to murmur into her
hair as he continued to hold her as if he would never let her go.

There was a maelstrom of noise and activity in the room as
its various occupants reacted to the shock of what had just occurred. From the corner of her eye Brianna saw Mistress
Pinckney swoon into a dead faint in the arms of her husband.
She heard Isaac shouting for some of his staff while James and
Johanna Carlisle came up to her and Jesse to ask whether she
had been harmed.

Suddenly a pistol shot ripped through the din. Jesse dropped
to the floor, pushing Brianna beneath him while several voices
cried out with alarm.

Then Jesse moved aside and reached to pull her close to him,
but as he shifted position, Brianna saw what Jesse had been
bent on keeping from her view.

Laurette Mayfield's body lay slumped over that of Honoré
Dumaine. From his now lifeless hand drooped the smoking
pistol he had briefly reclaimed with his last, dying breath and
with it removed the top of Laurette Mayfield's head.

Chapter Twenty-Nine

"Well, how do you like it?" Jesse asked.

"Like it? *Love it*, you mean," Brianna answered. "It's the most beautiful town home I've ever seen!"

They were sitting in the rear gardens of Le Beau Château, beside a large white marble goldfish pond, taking advantage of the early autumn sunshine. Spread out before them in the grass were architectural drawings and plans for a city dwelling that bore the simple inscription:

Residence to be erected on property
at North Bay Street, Charleston,
South Carolina
Architect: Jesse Leighton Randall

"You're sure?" Jesse questioned as he watched his wife wriggle her bare toes in the soft grass.

"Of course, I'm sure, but, tell me, who's the lucky owner going to be?"

Brianna had already expressed her surprise at finding out Jesse had moved into designing residences other than the one he'd planned for himself at Riverview, and now she began to wonder just who it was he'd found as a client for the magnificent residence detailed in the drawings before them. She supposed it might be someone Thomas Jefferson knew, and to whom he'd proposed his friend in Carolina as a prospective architect, for Jefferson had loved Riverview when he saw it, and she knew he and Jesse had spent several hours discussing their common passion during his visit last month.

"Oh," Jesse was saying, "someone I've recently gotten to know. A very beautiful lady who lives in the Charleston area."

Brianna's eyes flew upward at this news, and a spark of green fire flashed in them. "*Oh?*" she questioned, failing in an effort at sounding nonchalant. "I don't suppose it's someone I know?"

Jesse watched the play of emotions sweeping her lovely features with a serious expression on his own face. "Why, then you'd be supposing wrongly, Brianna. As a matter of fact, you know her very well by now."

The green eyes grew stormy. "Jesse Randall, do you mean to tell me you've been commissioned by some—some brazen female with the audacity to hire you sneakily, under my very nose, without my knowing anything about it? *Who is she?*"

Unable to keep up the game he was playing any longer, Jesse's eyes twinkled with amusement as he grinned at her frowning face. "*You*, my beautiful little idiot!" he laughed as he tapped his forefinger lightly on the tip of her nose. "*You!*"

The irked expression on Brianna's face took a second to disappear before she threw him a smile of sheer delight. "*Me?* Oh, you wretch!" she exclaimed while at the same moment throwing her arms about his neck in an ecstatic hug. "You wonderful wretch, you were *teasing me*!"

Low laughter emanated from Jesse's throat as he hugged her to him; then he replied, "Forgive the teasing love. I was just trying to stretch out my surprise a little while longer. So you really approve of the design?"

Brianna turned within the circle of his arms and glanced again at the drawings. Running her eyes quickly over the details of the graceful classical revival house with its two-tiered columns supporting an upper porch under a front gable, its round-arch windows complemented by a round-arch doorway with a fanlight at the front entrance, its flanking, single-storied wings on either side, she couldn't help but heave a happy sigh. "It's truly lovely, Jesse. And, to think, you designed it all by yourself!"

Jesse chuckled. "I had a little help from an Italian Renaissance architect named Palladio, not to mention a couple of suggestions Tom Jefferson gave me, but I suppose it's basically mine, yes."

"And you're having it built for us someday?" Brianna asked with an eager smile.

"I'm having it built, as I said, for *you*, and, now that I know you approve, construction can start immediately. Next week, if you like."

"Next week!" Brianna chirped excitedly. "Oh, I had no *idea*! So soon!"

"Most of our neighbors have homes in town," Jesse mentioned matter-of-factly, "so I thought perhaps my wife would enjoy one as well. Besides," he added, kissing her lightly on the ear, "I wanted to give you something on this occasion."

Brianna threw him a puzzled look. "Occasion?"

He turned her around to face him fully. "Do you know what today is, love?"

The perplexed look increased. Brianna knew tomorrow was the anniversary of the day of her father's funeral. It was one of the reasons they'd returned to Le Beau Château—other than the need to give themselves a change of scene following the terrible events of the night of their harvest ball. But she quickly shuttered her mind against the horror-filled conclusion to that chapter in their lives, willing away memory of the long hours of working to soothe the sensibilities of their stream of arriving guests, of sitting down with the local authorities to explain what had happened; she thought, instead, of the little ceremony that would be taking place tomorrow in Etienne's library—her library, now—wherein she would officially take her place as the undisputed mistress of Le Beau Château.

Seeing her look, Jesse smiled. "It's the anniversary of the day we really met. I say 'really met,' because, I think you'll agree, we can discount a certain meeting in an inn, in Charleston, between a French maid and a 'confirmed' bachelor." He paused to watch an abashed smile appear on his wife's face. "Or, for that matter, the few seconds we crossed paths that terrible rainy day your father passed out of this life."

They were both silent for a moment as they recalled the moment he spoke of. At the time, Brianna had been so distraught, she didn't even recall seeing Jesse in the room where Etienne had died.

But she also knew her time for grieving had passed. Two days ago, when they'd arrived here at Le Beau Château, she and Jesse had taken little Saor and walked up to the green hillside where the bodies of Etienne, Aileen and Deirdre Devereaux reposed. They'd stayed a while, leaving three bouquets of white roses on the trio of graves that lay under a giant old oak tree, but Brianna had shed no tears; she'd found out on the day of Saor's christening, from Father Edouard, that Etienne's dying wish had been fulfilled when she and Jesse found each other. The beaming priest had uncorked the final bottle of his cache of "the finest brandy I ever made" and offered a toast, not only to the future happiness and spiritual grace of Saor Etienne Randall, but to her and Jesse as well, "now that your marriage is a true one."

"So," Jesse was saying, "that leaves the evening we met outside Le Beau Château's stables. It was a year ago, today." He touched her softly on the cheek. "You remember?"

"Remember!" Brianna exclaimed in mock horror. "How can I forget the night my world was turned upside down by a handsome madman who dared to kiss me breathless when we didn't even know each other minutes before? Um—at least *you* didn't know we'd already met! And, there I was, having a hard enough time dealing with all the emotions you were setting off inside me, and I had the added burden of hiding the fact that I was *Brielle Gitane*!"

Jesse laughed as he suddenly reached to pull her down on her back, beneath him on the grass. "And I was absolutely thunderstruck, I can tell you, to discover emotions I'd thought long since buried, resurrected by a mere slip of a girl straight from the schoolroom!" His eyes roamed carefully over her face before they met and held hers. "Ah, but she had the most incredible green eyes that spit unholy fire when she became angry and later came to rock my very soul when they gazed at me—like now."

The color of Brianna's eyes deepened until they became two limpid, green, midnight pools as she continued to gaze back at her husband. Then they lightly closed as Jesse lowered his head and his mouth took hers in a sweet, delicious play of sensual sharing. Many long seconds passed before Jesse raised his head and he again held her eyes.

"Beloved wife," he breathed, "thank God I found you."

Just then, the sound of a low, male voice intruded, its owner making a noisy show of clearing his throat.

The two lovers sprang quickly apart and looked up to see Vulcan Noslave holding their son. Beside him was a grinning little gypsy.

"Um—*pardonez-moi, s'il vous plaît*," the big man grinned, "but ain'—Ah mean, *don't* you folks have nothin' bettah to do than hug 'n kiss?"

"Anything," Aimée whispered to him.

"Huh?" Vulcan looked puzzled.

"You must say *'anything* better to do,' not 'nothin' bettah to do,'" Aimée smiled.

"Lord, gal, ain'—*isn't* it bad enough you go aroun' makin' me talk French, now you gotta be aftah mah English too?" Vulcan queried in outraged tones. But his eyes, as they looked at Aimée, were soft and gentle.

"So she's teaching you French, is she?" Jesse chuckled.

"Uh-huh," Vulcan grinned good-naturedly. "But it wouldn' be so bad, 'cep'—*except*—it's comin' hot on the heels o' Miz Christie teachin' me to read n' write an' mah sistah fussin' 'bout—*a*bout—mah English! Miz Brianna, you're the only lady Ah know who ain'—*isn't*—tryin' to *re-do* me!"

Brianna and Jesse laughed, and so did Vulcan and Aimée. Then, even little Saor began to chime in, his chubby cheeks dimpled with merriment.

"Well," said Aimée when they had all quieted, "we were just coming to see if it would be all right with you if we took Saor down to Serge's cottage with us. He and Père Edouard have invited us to join them for a little luncheon there."

"Of course," Brianna told her. "Since I just nursed him about a half-hour ago, Saor shouldn't be begging too much of your shares of the food. But, for heaven's sake, keep him away from Mathilde's croissants, if there are any! He gums them to a paste that winds up, like cement, in his hair!"

With chuckles and a promise to do just as she asked, Aimée and Vulcan took their leave with Saor gurgling happily over the black man's shoulder.

Brianna's eyes followed them silently until they were out of sight. She wore a pondering expression on her face. "I don't know about those two," she mused at last.

Jesse gave her a quizzical look. "You mean Aimée and—"

"Uh-hum-m-m," she nodded. "They've been spending an unusual amount of time together, and now that Father Edouard knows the story of the rumors about Aimée's parentage, I think he's begun to enter the picture. And you know what a matchmaker *he* turned out to be!"

Jesse chuckled, then thought about Brianna's speculations. He'd only recently become privy to Aimée's suspicions regarding her origins, especially those about her father. She herself had told him, along with several others in their closely-knit group, among them, the priest, the Noslave brothers and Lula. Was she paving the way for her friends' acceptance of what could be regarded as a highly unusual romance? If so, he hoped the little gypsy had as much fortitude and spunk as she seemed to show. He knew what others might make of such a liaison, especially here in the deep South. Well, he knew Vulcan possessed the courage to withstand the difficulties the two might encounter, and if Aimée's matched it—yes, he thought perhaps it did—it just might work, and he would do all he could to help them. They were good friends and he could do no less.

He looked over at his wife and saw a preoccupied expression on her face while she gazed at the pond where flashes of orange and gold were visible as the carp darted about the dappled sunlight that penetrated the water.

"What are you thinking about in that beautiful head of yours, Mistress Randall?"

Brianna looked up with a start, then smiled softly at him. "Oh, I was just thinking about a sad, lovely lady named Sally Hemings. You know, it's strange, but I used to freeze with fear whenever I thought about her."

"And now?" questioned Jesse, remembering a conversation in which his wife had told him about those fears.

"And now," said Brianna, still smiling, "I only think of her with a feeling of deep compassion and, I think, understanding. Yes, beyond anything else, I think I understand Sally Hemings now. You have to know love to understand the unthinkable risks it's willing to endure." She paused.

"Of course, I know my situation is simply more fortunate, more blessed, than hers, but, darling, tell me, what do you see happening to Jefferson in the future?"

Jesse grinned. "There goes my wife with her unnatural interest in politics again!"

"Unnatural!"

"Sh-h, love, just another bit of teasing. Most men of our day see a woman's interest in politics as unnatural—our friend, Thomas Jefferson, included—but I didn't say—*cannot* say—I'm one of them, not when I've witnessed my wife's keen mind at work in discussions of pertinent topics!" He saw Brianna throw him a dazzling, appreciative smile.

"But, as for Jefferson, Brianna, I simply don't know. My guess is that he'll disappear for a while—out of the public light, that is—to spend some time as a private person, being close to his family, playing—no that's not the right word—*being* the country gentleman.

"He's a proud man, Brianna, and just now, he's too busy licking his wounds over what he regards as Hamilton's victory. But time will pass, and I guarantee, change his focus on things. It's just as well. John Adams is our country's next president, unless I miss my guess. The time is ripe for it. But I do have this unshakable feeling that Jefferson's time is coming. A mind like that will never be satisfied to grow stagnant in the back waters of this country. If he only has the patience to wait it all out—until the country is ready for *him*. Do you follow my meaning, darling, or is this all just so much gibberish?"

Brianna looked at him with an expression of wifely annoyance. "Gibberish? *Gibberish!* Well, if it's gibberish, I must have learned to speak it! Of course, I follow you, you idiot! It all makes perfect sense!"

Jesse winced at her use of the term, "idiot," recalling his own use of the term, earlier, with her. *"Touché*, my love!" he laughed. "So we're both lovable idiots, hmm? But, I was wondering, what is my 'idiot,' darling, adorable wife planning on doing with that keen, incisive intelligence she's loath to hide under a bonnet as so many other women of this day are wont to do?"

Brianna suddenly sat upright and perfectly erect as she caught a look of innuendo in his eye. "What do you mean?" she asked with a wide-eyed look.

Jesse had all he could do to keep from laughing at her deliberate pose of simple innocence. "Oh," he murmured casually, "I was just wondering what it might be that took my lovely wife down to the working quarters of my resident silversmith at home, whenever she seemed to have a free moment."

"Jesse Randall, you've been *spying* on me!" exclaimed Brianna as she rose to her knees and glared at him.

"Never!" affirmed Jesse in a tone of injured innocence. "It's just that I began to wonder what it was that was beginning to cause—" he picked up one of her hands and bent to place a tender kiss on his upturned palm "—these lovely hands to look—on certain occasions—a bit careworn, shall we say? So one day, when I saw you running excitedly down the path to Festus' shop, I decided to follow."

"You *were* spying!" Brianna said with an outraged look.

Jesse merely grinned at her. "Ah, sweetheart, you can call it that if you like, but please don't censure me for it! I was only trying to find out what it was that was obviously giving you so much delight and satisfaction. So *you* made that beautiful cup that Father Edouard used at the christening!"

Suddenly all the ill wind went out of Brianna's sails. "You—you really thought it was beautiful?"

"I said so, didn't I? Brianna, it was more than beautiful! It was a true work of art!"

"But it wasn't as good as some of the pieces Festus has turned out," she countered.

"Nonsense!" Jesse exclaimed. "It was every bit as good or better. Although, I must admit, Festus is doing remarkably well, despite his handicap."

"But," said Brianna in a small voice, "you don't mind if your wife takes up a serious interest in silversmithing?"

Jesse laughed with delight as he reached for her and pulled her to him while he leaned back in the grass. "Sweetheart, I'll be honest with you. I've always been fond of soft, well-manicured fingers on a woman, but if this is your wish—and I think you have the talent, by the way—I'll simply hire someone whose sole business it will be to offer my lady daily hand care. The important thing," he added with a more serious look, "is for you to know I would not have married or fallen in love with a woman who did not master her own life in some way. And so, my beloved wife," he whispered in her ear as he held her, "I dub thee 'Jesse's Lady: Budding Silversmith'!"

Brianna heard his words and closed her eyes in an attempt to deal with the overflowing outpouring of love she felt for this man.

But then she dimpled, saying, "Right now there are some other things I've learned to do with my hands, sir—things you've taught me that I'd be pleased to demonstrate," she added as she ran a finger suggestively along his lower lip.

With a low growl, Jesse twisted until she lay beneath him and her gaze met his. "Green Eyes," he murmured huskily, "that would be my pleasure."

Aimée and Vulcan were nearing the footpath leading to Serge's cottage when the little gypsy noticed Saor's small head tilt backward suddenly as he bent his wide-eyed gaze skyward. Vulcan noticed it too, saying, "Now, lil fella, whut—what's so interesting up there?"

The two adults threw back their heads and looked into the clear blue canopy of sky above them. There, flying high above the earth, soared an eagle, its outspread wings glinting silver in the sunlight.

"It's a lone eagle, ridin' high," said Vulcan.

"Look again, *mon chér*," Aimée told him. She pointed to another bird, somewhat smaller, but almost identical in shape as it swooped upward from a point somewhere beyond Le Beau Château's high roof and began a steady climb skyward in the direction of the first bird. In seconds the second eagle had joined its mate, soaring gracefully until it reached the other's height. Then the two birds began yet another upward glide. Aimée and Vulcan watched until they became a pair of tiny specks in the blue before seeming to melt into the heavens and disappear from sight.

Vulcan returned his gaze to Aimée and shook his head. "Now that was somethin' worth lookin' at!" he marveled. "Fust—first time Ah evah saw a *pair* of eagles flyin' so high together."

Aimée smiled and nodded, her eyes filled with a strange kind of light. *"Oui,"* she acknowledged. "It doesn't happen very often, *mon amour*, but when it does—you are right—it is truly something worth seeing!"

Harlequin® Historical

Another spectacular medieval tale from
popular, award-winning author

SUZANNE BARCLAY

The next book in her ongoing
Sommerville Brothers series:

Knight's Ransom

Watch for this passionate story
of a French knight who captures
the daughter of his enemy for revenge,
but finds love with his captive instead!

**Coming this October
from Harlequin Historicals**

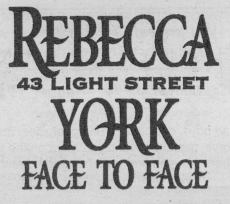

REBECCA
43 LIGHT STREET
YORK
FACE TO FACE

Bestselling author Rebecca York returns to "43 Light Street" for an original story of past secrets, deadly deceptions—and the most intimate betrayal.

She woke in a hospital—with amnesia...and with child. According to her rescuer, whose striking face is the last image she remembers, she's Justine Hollingsworth. But nothing about her life seems to fit, except for the baby inside her and Mike Lancer's arms around her. Consumed by forbidden passion and racked by nameless fear, she must discover if she is Justine...or the victim of some mind game. Her life—and her unborn child's—depends on it....

Don't miss *Face To Face*—Available in October, wherever Harlequin books are sold.

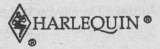

HARLEQUIN ®

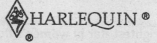